WHEN THE HEAVENS FALL

WHEN THE
HEAVENS FALL

MARC TURNER

TOR®

A Tom Doherty Associates Book
New York

WHEN THE HEAVENS FALL

Copyright © 2015 by Marc Turner

All rights reserved.

Map by Rhys Davies

A Tor Book
Published by Tom Doherty Associates, LLC
175 Fifth Avenue
New York, NY 10010

www.tor-forge.com

Tor® is a registered trademark of Tom Doherty Associates, LLC.

The Library of Congress Cataloging-in-Publication Data
is available upon request.

ISBN 978-0-7653-3712-2 (hardcover)
ISBN 978-1-4668-3120-9 (e-book)

Tor books may be purchased for educational, business, or promotional use. For information on bulk purchases, please contact the Macmillan Corporate and Premium Sales Department at 1-800-221-7945, extension 5442, or write to specialmarkets@macmillan.com.

First Edition: May 2015

Printed in the United States of America

0 9 8 7 6 5 4 3 2 1

FOR SUZANNE

ACKNOWLEDGMENTS

Many thanks to my editors, Marco Palmieri and Ali Nightingale, for having faith in the book, and for helping me to knock it into shape. Thanks also to the folks at Tor and at Titan who variously prepared, published, and publicized the book, and to my illustrator, Rhys Davies, for having the skill and patience to produce a map that fits with the words. I mean, have you seen all the islands on that thing? Rather him than me.

Special thanks to my agent, Andy Zack, for his tireless efforts in finding homes for my books around the world. Thanks also to Rebecca Josephsen for picking my manuscript out from all the others she had to read.

Finally, thank you to my dad for agreeing to read an epic fantasy book when I suspect he'd rather have been doing something else. Or anything else, for that matter. Thanks also to James for disturbing me when I needed to be disturbed, and to my wife, Suzanne, for giving me the support to start out on this writing road. And for carrying me along it a few times, too.

CONTENTS

DRAMATIS PERSONAE

Erin Elalese

Luker Essendar, *a Guardian*

Gill Treller, *First Guardian*

Kanon, *a member of the Guardian Council*

Avallon Delamar, *emperor of Erin Elal*

Merin Gray, *member of the Emperor's Circle, formerly commander of the Seventh Army*

Don Chamery Pelk, *a mage of the Black Tower*

Mayot Mencada, *a mage of the Black Tower*

Sekh Rakaal, *commander of the Breakers*

Jenna Amary, *an assassin*

Gol, *Jenna's minder*

Galitians

Ebon Calidar, *prince of Galitia*

Vale Gorven, *Ebon's bodyguard*

Mottle, *an air-mage*

Isanovir Calidar, *king of Galitia, Ebon's father*

Rosel Calidar, *queen of Galitia, Ebon's mother*

Rendale Calidar, *prince of Galitia, Ebon's brother*

Domen Janir Calidar, *Isanovir's brother*

Tamarin, *chancellor to the King*

General Reynes, *commander of the Pantheon Guard*

Lamella Dewhand, *Ebon's companion*

Captain Hitch, *a soldier of the Pantheon Guard*

Sergeant Grimes, *a soldier of the Pantheon Guard*

Corporal Ellea, *a soldier of the Pantheon Guard*

Bettle, *a soldier of the Pantheon Guard*

Sergeant Seffes, *a former soldier of the Pantheon Guard*

Sartorians

Consel Garat Hallon, *de facto ruler of Sartor*

Ambolina Alavist, *the consel's sorceress*

Falin Hallon, *the consel's brother*

Pellar Hargin, *the consel's first adviser*

Gen Sulin, *commander of the Consel's Guard*

Others

Romany Elivar, *a high priestess of the Spider*

The Spider, *a goddess*

Danel, *servant to Romany*

Parolla Morivan, *a necromancer of unknown origins*

Aliana Morivan, *Parolla's mother*

Tumbal Qerivan, *a Gorlem wanderer*

Shroud, *Lord of the Dead*

Lorigan Teele, *a commander of the Belliskan Order of Knights and a disciple of Shroud*

The Widowmaker, *a disciple of Shroud*

Andara Kell, *a disciple of Shroud*

Kestor ben Kayma, *a disciple of Shroud*

The Lord of the Hunt, *the Antlered God*

Ceriso di Monata, *a novitiate of the Antlered God*

Olakim, *a follower of a dead god*

Mezaqin, *demon lord of the Shades, third of the Nine Hells*

THE LANDS OF THE EXILE

The Red Mountains

To Xavel

Camessil

Mordella

River Sametta

Obenar

Kolamin

Linnar

Silver Hills

Mander

Mercerie

Koronos

KEN'DAH STEPPES

Forest

of

Sighs

Kingswood

River Amber

Majack

Culin

GALITIA

Koronos Hills

Estapharriol

White Road

Montenay

Bethin

Balshazar

THE WAST

White Mountains

Arandas

GOLLOTHIR PLAINS

THE WASTE

Runesong Heights

Talen

Sun Road

Cenan

Arap

Karalat

Kal Kartin

Point Keep

Black Cliffs

KAL

River Kal

Helin

Shield Road

High Fort

Sullen Sea

Kal Giseng

The Shield

River Renner

Javron

Kal Mecath

Renner

Pallane

Wind Straits

Kerin

Mezan

Amenor

Exile

Cortane

Kerin Forest

Bone Road

The Needle

Taradh Fold

ERIN ELAL

Arkarbour

Taradh Dor

Sea of Bones

Port Trinity

Melesse

Dram

Star

Maise

The Necklace

River Maise

Carros

Tresson Mountains

Brena

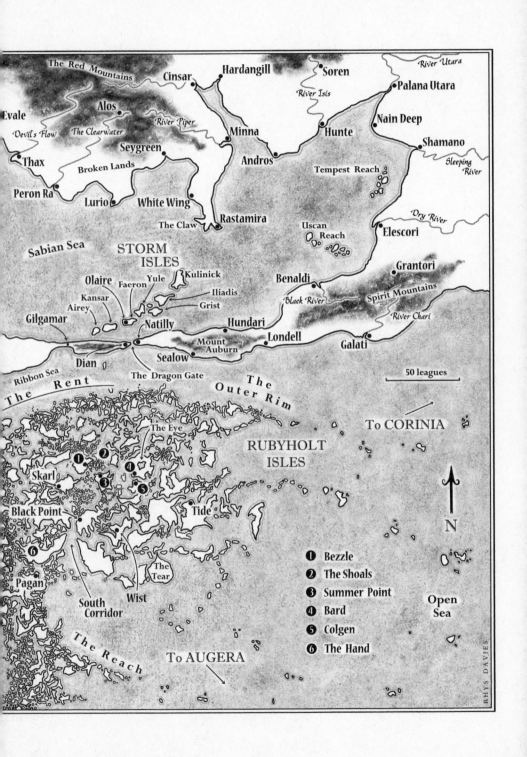

Part I

A Spider's Web

CHAPTER 1

LUKER HAD sworn never to return to this place.

He was not a man who gave his word lightly, yet here he stood, staring at the Sacrosanct through the wrought-iron gates at the entrance to its grounds. His gaze took in the boards across its windows, the tiles missing from the roofs of its turrets, the bleak lines of its walls that rose like black cliffs to seemingly impossible heights. Home sweet home. The place looked deserted, but there was light coming from the windows at the top of the First Guardian's tower—like a beacon guiding him into harbor. He did not need its glow to tell him he had entered dangerous waters.

The scar running from the corner of his right eye to his jawline itched again, and he scratched it absently. He'd expected to feel something on seeing the Sacrosanct again. Had hoped to. But when he searched inside he found only emptiness tinged with disappointment. And he being such a cheerful soul normally. He took a breath. Two years ago he'd closed these gates behind him and walked away without looking back. The place had meant nothing to him then, he was a fool to have believed it would be different now.

I shouldn't have come back.

The gates were unlocked and guarded only by the twin statues of the Patrons, their grim expressions a foretaste of the reception Luker would no doubt receive inside. He pushed open the gates. Before him stretched a path flanked by rows of kalip trees, their branches casting long shadows in the half-light. Luker set off along the trail. To either side, the grounds of the Sacrosanct grew unchecked. Insects swarmed over shadowy shapes partly hidden in the undergrowth.

From tangled grasses protruded the gravestones of the Lost, their epitaphs faded. Some of the graves had been disturbed, and soil lay heaped beside the stones. As an apprentice Luker had spent many evenings wandering the burial yard with his master, Kanon, listening to tales of the fallen Guardians and the sacrifices they had made. There was a time when Luker had known all their names, but not now—the ranks of stones had swelled while he'd been away.

Still, at least he now knew where everyone had got to.

The first drops of rain began to fall. A storm was blowing in from the south, the same storm that had buffeted Luker's ship into port earlier. Through the trees ahead, the Sacrosanct was a darker gray against the gathering gloom. The path ended at a flight of steps that Luker took two at a time. The door at the top was twice his height and made from a wood so dark it looked fire-blackened. It was set in a frame of stone engraved with runes that shone softly green. As Luker brushed his fingertips against them he felt only a faint tingling. The wards were failing. *Like every other damned thing round here.*

Four years ago Luker had watched from one of the windows above as Emperor Avallon Delamar ascended these same steps. The door to the Sacrosanct had been shut then as it was now, but the runes had cast a glow that stained the emperor's face even in bright sunshine. Before entering, Avallon had taken off his coronet and set it on the top step. The gesture had brought a gasp from those watching with Luker, for its message was clear: The emperor left his sovereignty outside the walls of the Sacrosanct. He came to the Guardians to petition, not to command.

And yet the bastard still left with what he came for. The Guardians' decision to side with the emperor that day had opened rifts in their ranks, leaving them vulnerable when Avallon came calling again, this time with poorly concealed demands for allegiance. Luker had known the episode would mark the beginning of the end for the Guardians, but he had never imagined they would be brought to their knees so quickly.

Not that he was about to get all tearful at their fall. It was too late for regrets. He had made his decision two years ago. There was no going back.

So what in the Nine Hells am I doing here?

He drew the sword on his left hip and used the pommel to pound on the door, then resheathed the blade and waited, head bowed in the rain. A while later he heard bolts being thrown back. The door opened inward. In the shadows beyond, Luker saw the weathered face of an old man, his white hair standing disheveled as if he had been disturbed from his sleep. Luker towered over him.

"What do you want?" the doorman asked.

"A little courtesy for starters," Luker muttered. "My name's Luker Essendar. I'm here to see the First Guardian."

The old man looked him up and down like he'd never before seen someone with honey-colored skin. Maybe he hadn't.

Luker reached into the folds of his cloak and pulled out a roll of parchment. The movement caught the doorman by surprise, and he stepped back, arms raised as if to fend off a blow.

"Relax." Luker held up the scroll for the doorman to inspect. The wax seal was broken, but the stamp impressed upon it could still be made out. "Look here—the First Guardian's mark."

The old man bent to peer at the scroll, his nose almost touching the parchment. After a handful of heartbeats he grunted and stepped aside to allow Luker to pass. Once Luker was inside, the doorman set his shoulder to the door, and it closed with a noise like rolling thunder. Luker waited in near blackness as the locks were secured. Water dripped from the hem of his cloak and collected in a puddle at his feet.

"Follow me," the doorman said.

"Save your legs. I know the way."

"Nevertheless. The First Guardian will expect me to announce you." Without waiting for a response the doorman shuffled into the gloom. Luker fell into step behind.

They passed through a series of corridors and entered the Great Hall. A knot of shadows marked the Council table and the wooden thrones surrounding it. Gone were the rich rugs and tapestries, and Luker could hear the room's vastness in the echoes of his footsteps.

The doorman reached the far side of the chamber and entered the maze of passages beyond. Luker could have found his way through with his eyes closed. In his first years at the Sacrosanct he had spent countless nights pacing the corridors, fleeing the memories that sleep would bring. Every time, his footsteps led him to the Matron's shrine—they passed it now—where he'd sit huddled at the feet of her statue, waiting for the goddess to break the silence. And as each day dawned gray and empty he retreated to his room no closer to answers than he'd been the night before. He had lost his childhood somewhere down here in the darkness.

The doorman led him through an archway and up a spiral stairwell. There seemed to be more steps than Luker remembered, but then maybe that was down to the torturous pace his escort was setting. Reaching a door at the top, the old man turned and bid Luker wait, then knocked and went inside. Luker heard muffled voices before the old man reappeared and beckoned him to enter.

The First Guardian's tower was much as Luker remembered it: the open fire; the candles in their holders; the desk with its covering of scrolls. A quill pen lay on a piece of parchment, the last words on the page glistening as the ink dried. The heat felt oppressive after the chill of the Great Hall.

With his back to Luker, First Guardian Gill Treller stood gazing out a window. When he finally turned, Luker saw that the last two years had not been kind to him, for his neatly trimmed beard was shot through with gray and his hairline had retreated a few fingers' widths. He clutched his black robes tightly about him in spite of the heat. But his look still held the same intensity. *And hostility,* Luker realized, frowning. *He's no more pleased to see me than I am to be here.*

The usual warm welcome, then.

"What took you so long?" the First Guardian said.

"Good to see you too, Gill."

"The summons was delivered a week ago. You could have swum from Taradh Dor in that time."

"You're lucky I came at all."

"Indeed? I don't recall giving you a choice in the matter."

Luker shrugged, then crossed to the desk and poured himself a glass of red wine from a decanter.

"Help yourself to wine," Gill said.

Luker took a sip. "Not bad. A bit young maybe."

"If I'd known you would arrive today I'd have ordered something more to your taste. Now perhaps we can begin."

"I've got a question first," Luker said. "How did you find me?"

"I didn't need to *find* you. I knew exactly where to look."

"You've been scouting me all this time?"

"That surprises you? A Guardian does not simply disappear, Luker, however much he might wish to. The emperor would not allow it."

"The emperor?" Luker said, his eyes narrowing. "What's he got to do with this?"

"You thought the summons came from me?" Gill shook his head.

"You walked out on us, Luker. Not for the first time, either. If I'd had my way, you'd have been left to rot on Taradh Dor."

Luker pulled the sheet of parchment from his cloak and tossed it on the floor. "Then why's your seal on the Shroud-cursed scroll? Since when have you been Avallon's errand boy?"

"The emperor judged you would not have come if the summons had been his."

"Damned right. I don't take orders—"

"I suspect Avallon may see things differently," Gill interrupted. Pulling a handkerchief from his sleeve he dabbed at his watery eyes. "You'll find much has changed in the time you've been away. The emperor's power has grown. We are all his servants now, whether we like it or not."

Luker stared at him. Seeing the Sacrosanct's neglect had been surprise enough, but to hear such words from the First Guardian's mouth . . . "We've really fallen that far?"

"Gods below!" Gill said, throwing up his hands. "Look around you, man! The Sacrosanct is falling into ruin. The Council hasn't convened for more than a year. What would be the point? There are barely a score of us left."

"Better the Guardians go the way of your hairline than stain their knees before Avallon."

"You really mean that?"

"Aye."

"Then why did you answer the summons? Why are you here now?"

Luker swirled the wine in his glass. "Maybe I was just curious."

"The Abyss you were. You came back because you're one of us. You always will be."

One of us? This from the man who would have left him to rot on Taradh Dor? "You're way off the mark, Gill, but I'm not going to argue with you. You can't dress this up as some test of my loyalty. The summons came from the emperor, not you."

The lines around Gill's eyes tightened, then he turned his back on Luker and looked out the window once more. The silence dragged out. Luker was beginning to think he was dismissed when the First Guardian spoke again. "Did you see the new citadel on your way up from the docks? The Storm Keep." He pointed. "There, beside the White Lady's temple?"

Luker squinted at him. Just like that, the summons was forgotten?

Had the First Guardian conceded defeat already? *No, not Gill.* A new line of attack, then. Luker joined him at the window and looked down on Arkarbour. He hadn't noticed the Storm Keep on his walk from the lower city, but its towers could be made out easily enough through the rain, silhouetted against the twin fires at the entrance to the harbor. They'd been built just tall enough to eclipse the tower he was standing in. A pissing contest in stone.

"You're looking at the stronghold of the Breakers," Gill said. "You remember them?"

"I know the name. Some squad in some legion. Just one more cog in the emperor's military machine."

"Oh, come now, the Breakers were always more than that. Their commander is a Remnerol shaman—Rakaal—who was spared the noose at Avallon's order. The rank and file are also chosen from men in the emperor's debt. In the fifth Kalanese campaign they gained a reputation for doing the jobs no one else would do. And because of that they became to the emperor what the Guardians could never be."

"You reckon Avallon's grooming them to replace us?"

"I'm sure of it."

"Then he's an idiot. Whatever the Breakers' loyalties, they're still just soldiers."

"Because they don't have the Will, you mean? Oh, but they do, Luker. Amerel and Borkoth are training them. They walked out on the Guardian Council last year."

Luker mastered his surprise. "Borkoth, I get, but Amerel? How did the emperor get his claws into her?"

"Next time she stops by I'll be sure to ask."

Luker sipped his wine. "Even with Amerel on their side, it'll be years before the Breakers master the Will. Just as well, too. It's probably the only reason you're not floating facedown in the harbor already."

"You think I don't know that? The emperor needs the Guardians for now, but each day our position becomes more precarious. We must use the time we have left to counter his plans."

"Right. A score of you left, you said."

A gust of wind set the tower's windows rattling. The First Guardian moved to the fire and held his hands out to the flames. "We are not without allies. The Senate won't stand by and watch us die out. It fears the emperor's growing power, just as we do. For now there are only a few dissenting voices—the senators won't risk open conflict with the emperor while the war with the Kalanese goes badly. But when it ends there will be a reckoning. We just have to make sure we survive long enough to see it."

"The war's turned sour?" Luker said. "I thought Tyrin Malek was holding his own."

"You haven't heard the news? Reports say Malek has suffered a crushing defeat west of Arandas. He was lured into the shadow of the White Mountains by a Kalanese feint and hit with a flank attack by troops hidden in the foothills. The offensive drove a wedge through his forces, then the main Kalanese host fell on them before they could re-form. The Seventh was routed and scattered across the Gollothir Plains. The Fifth—what's left of it—is retreating south to Helin."

"Malek himself?"

"Taken. The Kalanese may try to ransom him, but I doubt the imperial treasury has any coin to spare, even for one of the emperor's brothers."

Not all bad news, then. "What about Arandas?"

"Avallon has ordered a full withdrawal."

Luker grunted. "The Aldermen will love that. Emperor spends years bullying Arandas into joining his Confederacy, then cuts the city loose at the first sign of trouble."

"Avallon had no choice. The Kalanese and their allies are massing in the tens of thousands. Arandas cannot be held."

The fire cracked and popped as wood settled in the grate. Luker finished his wine and set the glass down on the desk. "All of this is fascinating, but it changes nothing. Avallon started this war. If he wants to finish it, he'll have to shovel his own shit for a change."

The First Guardian seemed unperturbed. "I haven't even told you what the emperor wants. Hear me out at least. You may find you're more sympathetic to his cause than you suspect."

Luker eyed him warily, wondering where this was heading. Somewhere with a sharp drop on the other side, most likely. *He thinks he's got me, in spite of all I've said. What's he got hidden up his sleeve?* "I'm listening."

The corners of Gill's mouth turned up. "Let me get you some more wine." He lifted the decanter and topped up Luker's glass, then poured one for himself. "Won't you sit?" he asked, gesturing to a chair. When Luker shook his head, Gill drew his robes about him then said, "You recall the night of the Betrayal? The assault on the Black Tower?"

The change of subject took Luker aback again. Another feint? *He's*

trying to keep me off balance. Disguise the real strike when it comes.
"Aye," he said finally.

"Then you must remember Mayot Mencada. No? He was one of the mages that sided with the emperor. Along with Epistine he pierced the Black Tower's defenses long enough for us to slip through."

"If you say so."

Gill moved back to the window. "After the attack, Avallon installed Mayot and a few others on the Mages' Conclave. Most were quietly removed by the mages when the emperor's attention was focused elsewhere, but Mayot survived."

"You going somewhere with this?"

"If you'll let me. Mayot fled Arkarbour recently. No doubt the mages were delighted to see the back of him—except that he took something from the Black Tower when he left."

"What?"

"The Book of Lost Souls."

Luker scratched his scar. "That supposed to mean anything to me?"

"I'd be surprised if it did. I know little myself, save that the mages consider the Book to be valuable and are anxious to see it returned."

"What's this got to do with me?"

"I would have thought that was obvious. The emperor wants you to hunt down Mayot and get the Book back."

Luker blinked. Then he burst out laughing.

Gill's expression darkened. "I fail to see what is so amusing."

"You're serious? Malek's troops have taken a mauling. Malek himself is probably staked out over a fire somewhere in Kal Kartin. The Confederacy's on the verge of collapse." Luker ticked them off on his fingers. "And the emperor wants me to look for a *book*?"

"Apparently so."

"Why? What's in it for him?"

"I don't know."

"You didn't think to ask?"

Gill waved a hand. "In case it's escaped your attention, the emperor isn't in the habit of confiding in me of late. Perhaps he seeks to win favor with the Black Tower now that the tide of the war has turned." The First Guardian shrugged. "In truth, I don't care. All that matters is that Avallon wants the Book and has come to us for help. This is a chance to earn his gratitude. One we can ill afford to pass up."

"Prove we're still useful, you mean."

"If you like."

Luker picked up his wineglass and raised it to his lips, his gaze still locked to Gill's. "Why me?"

"Why has the emperor chosen you?" The First Guardian shrugged a second time. "As I said, there aren't many of us left. Senar Sol, Jenin Lock, Alar Padre, all gone." He cast Luker a calculating glance. "I can't afford to lose another member of the Council on this mission. And for some reason Avallon seems to hold you in high—"

Luker held up a hand to cut him off. "Wait. You mean I'm not the first to be sent after Mayot?"

"No. There was another, but he vanished some time ago."

Luker's throat was suddenly dry. "You said someone on the Council. Who?"

"Kanon."

Luker set his glass down on the desk with a crack. Wine spattered the sheets of parchment like drops of blood. "Kanon's disappeared? When? Where?"

The First Guardian frowned at the scrolls. "I can't tell you."

"Can't or won't?"

"I'm not in the mood for word games."

Luker ground his teeth together. He should have seen this coming. Gill had remained confident in spite of Luker knocking him back because the First Guardian had always known he had Kanon's disappearance to fall back on if persuasion alone failed to win Luker round. "You think I don't know what you're doing, Gill? You're trying to use Kanon to bring me to heel."

"You leave me little choice."

"And Kanon himself? You going to just—"

"Oh, spare me!" Gill cut in. "This is about more than Kanon. The future of the Guardians is at stake, yours included. You think the emperor will let you walk away if you refuse him? He'll see it as a betrayal."

So now he threatens me. Luker turned for the door. "We're done here."

"Wait!" There was a touch of the Will in Gill's voice.

Luker froze in midstep, then shook his head to clear it of the First Guardian's lingering touch. *He dares use his Will on me?* Luker slammed up his defenses. "Get out of my head!"

The First Guardian studied Luker for a heartbeat, then placed his wineglass on the mantelpiece. Luker felt Gill's power brush his thoughts again, a subtler but more insistent probing. In response,

Luker gathered his own Will and used it to slap the First Guardian's questing aside. As their powers collided, the candles in the room were extinguished. The fire in the grate flickered and died, plunging the room into darkness.

Gill stood silhouetted against the window. "Think carefully before you do something you'll regret. This is not a fight you can win."

Even as he spoke, Luker sensed him drawing on his power again. Gill's next attack struck his wards with a force that made him wince. The pressure in the room increased. A candleholder toppled to the ground with a clang, sending candles rolling across the floor. It felt to Luker as if a great weight pushed against his chest, and he drew in a breath with difficulty. His hands hovered over the hilts of his swords. "I don't like people riding me. And I sure as hell don't like seeing Kanon thrown to the wolves just so you can get cozy with Avallon."

"And this is how you would help him? You want to find Kanon, yes? Tell me, what will you do without my aid? Where will you look?" Gill's voice took on a conciliatory tone. "Track down Mayot and he may lead you to your master."

Luker's head was beginning to throb. The First Guardian's Will hammered against his defenses, driving him back a step. He needed time to think. Gill was right: Luker would need help if he was to find Kanon, but help from where? There was no guarantee anyone else on the Guardian Council knew about Kanon's mission, and even if they did, what reason would they have to share that knowledge? As for the emperor's army of minions, Luker had no way of knowing which of them had the answers he needed. And if he walked out on Gill now, he'd be a hunted man—not in itself a concern, but working out Kanon's last movements would be hard enough without having Avallon on his back. Luker brought his attention back to the First Guardian. *I'm out of options and he knows it.* Biting back on his anger, he let out a shuddering breath. "All right, Gill. I'll play your game." *For now.*

"You'll find the Book before you search for Kanon? I want your word on this."

"You have it. But I warn you, if Kanon dies because of this I'll be calling on you again."

There was a flash of white as Gill showed his teeth. "I look forward to it."

A heartbeat later the First Guardian released his Will. Luker waited for the pressure in the room to ease before following suit.

Gill shuffled to the desk and rummaged through one of the drawers. There was the sound of flint striking steel, and light blossomed as the First Guardian moved round the room, relighting the candles. "To business, then. Kanon's last report came from near Arandas. That was over a month ago. Start your search there."

Luker crossed his arms. "You think Kanon might have got caught up in the Kalanese invasion?"

"I don't know."

"What did his last report say?"

"He was following Mayot. That's all."

That sounded like Kanon. Never one to waste time on words. "Did he say where the trail was heading?"

"If he did, I wasn't told."

"Meaning?"

A look of disgust crossed Gill's features. "Meaning this is Avallon's mission, not mine. Kanon has been reporting to the emperor's men. I know only what they tell me, and that is precious little."

"What about the Guardians' spies? Kanon must have checked in with one of them."

"I'm afraid not. With Borkoth's and Amerel's knowledge, the emperor has moved quickly to dismantle our network of informants. We are now entirely reliant on the scraps Avallon feeds us."

"Then you'll have to speak to him again. I'll need more than 'near Arandas' if I'm to find Mayot."

"That's where your traveling companions come in."

Luker thought he must have misheard. "What?"

The First Guardian drained his wineglass. "Did I forget to mention them? How careless of me. Avallon is sending one of his Circle to keep an eye on you."

Luker shook his head. "I travel alone."

"You're a slow learner, Luker. This isn't a suggestion. It's a command."

Luker's breath hissed out. "Shroud's mercy, does the emperor want me to fail, then? How am I supposed to track Mayot down if I'm playing nursemaid to one of Avallon's lackeys?"

Gill arched an eyebrow. "I hardly think you need worry in this case. We're talking about Tyrin Merin Gray here, formerly commander of the Seventh."

"And now a Breaker, I take it."

"Whatever he is, you'll need his contacts to find Mayot. This is not the time to be sniffing round Arandas for a trail that's likely gone cold."

"If he slows me down I'll strike out alone and take my chances."

"Do what you must."

"I won't take orders from this Merin Gray either. He'll have to do what I tell him."

The First Guardian's lips quirked. "I'll leave you to work out the details yourselves."

"Is there someone else?" Luker asked. "You said 'traveling companions.'"

"Indeed. A necromancer from the Black Tower. The head of his order, no less. Don Chamery Pelk."

Luker's face twisted. "Emperor's got a sense of humor, at least. A Guardian and a mage traveling together? I must remember to sleep with my eyes open."

"No doubt the feeling is mutual." Gill righted the fallen candleholder, then seated himself at the desk. "Now, unless there was something else, I suggest you get some rest. You leave at dawn. Meet the others at the Imperial Stables for a briefing at the tenth bell tonight. Don't be late."

"I'll be there," Luker said.

But in his own time.

He had some personal business to attend to first.

Romany hated it when her goddess dropped by unannounced. Why could the Spider not knock at the door and present herself like other visitors, instead of treating the temple as if she owned it?

Taking a breath to compose herself, the priestess settled back in the pool. Perfumed candles floated among the bubbles on the water, filling the room with the scent of moonblossom and mint. Clouds of steam rose into the air, and the delicious heat of the pool was already easing her aches. She could sense the Spider skulking in the shadows behind, but Romany was not about to acknowledge her until the goddess observed the customary courtesies. Instead the priestess spent some time admiring the fresco of Mercerie's harbor on the opposite wall. Such vibrant colors. Such exquisite detail where the sunlight glinted off the sea . . .

A cough sounded at her back, and she sighed. It was no good. Her equanimity was slipping away. It would be no coincidence, of course, that the Spider had arrived while Romany was bathing, for the goddess never missed an opportunity to ruffle her feathers, particularly during those rare moments when the priestess was taking a well-deserved break from the tedium of her temple duties. And yet, after an absence of more than a year, it seemed unlikely the Spider had come for no other reason than to nettle her.

She sank deeper into the pool. More galling even than the goddess's arrival was the fact Romany had not sensed her coming. The priestess's carefully crafted web of sorcerous wards extended not just throughout the temple but also into every corner of Mercerie: the slave markets, the shrines of the other immortals, the halls of the great and the good. There would be outrage if their denizens ever found out, of course, but Romany had yet to encounter anyone with the wit to detect her illicit and watchful presence. As a result, little went on in the city she did not know about, and absolutely nothing in her sprawling temple. Many of the acolytes soon discovered this to their cost. Only yesterday one of the new girls had seen fit to mock Romany's modest girth to a friend. The priestess had been on the opposite side of the temple at the time, but her web had brought her word of the affront all the same, and the acolyte had swiftly come to regret her impropriety.

For some reason, though, Romany's sorcerous creation had given her no warning of the Spider's approach. She considered checking the integrity of her wards, but resisted the temptation. To do so, after all, would only highlight the fact that Romany's spells had failed her.

A flap of feet, and a red-faced acolyte emerged from the steam to her right. The girl was struggling under the weight of a huge copper kettle. As she wrestled it to the far edge of the pool, metal scraped against the terra-cotta floor tiles. To compound her blunder, the acolyte then tilted the kettle too sharply, sending a gush of water cascading into the pool. The floating candles bobbed precariously, and Romany tutted her displeasure.

Naturally the Spider chose that moment to step into the fuzzy light.

The acolyte squealed and dropped the kettle. It clanged against the tiled floor before falling into the pool. Water splashed into the priestess's eyes and nose, and she half rose, spluttering. The acolyte stood trembling, her gaze moving from Romany to the goddess, then back again, evidently uncertain as to which of them represented the greater cause for alarm. From the girl's expression it was clear she had no idea who the Spider was. The acolyte was new to the temple—the priestess could not remember her name, if indeed she had ever known it—but still, a disciple who did not recognize her own goddess? Absurd!

And yet strangely gratifying.

True, the Spider did not look much like an immortal. Romany had no idea what a goddess was *supposed* to look like, but the Spider was certainly not it. Her ageless, heart-shaped face was memorable only in its plainness. She was short—one of the few people the priestess could look down on—and had long auburn hair. Her gaze never rested for more than an instant in any one place, and her fingers were forever caressing the air as if she strummed the strings of an unseen harp. *What sound would she make,* Romany wondered idly, *if I were to place an instrument before them?*

Rousing herself, she sent the acolyte scuttling away with a look. The girl disappeared into the steam. A few heartbeats later a door opened, then slammed shut.

The Spider approached and made a show of studying Romany's face. "Ah, it is you, Rrromany," she said, putting that little trill on the "r" as she sometimes did. "For a moment I thought I'd taken a wrong turn and stumbled into the Augustine Springs."

"Time has not stood still since you last graced us with your presence, my Lady. You are aware the temple was attacked earlier this year?"

"Someone broke in and built you a bathhouse?"

"Very droll. Alas, the intruder destroyed various parts of the shrine, this chamber included. I took the chance to introduce some much needed trappings of civilization."

"Though only in your personal quarters, I see. So refrrreshing to see a high priestess lead by example."

Romany sniffed. "Perhaps if you had responded at the time to my call for assistance—"

"I'd assumed," the Spider cut in, "that you were capable of keeping your own house in order. Apparently I was mistaken."

"This was no ordinary intruder. A disciple of Shroud."

The goddess's eyes went cold. "Who?"

"I have no idea," Romany said. "Shroud's vermin all look the same to me. Without question, one of the god's elite, though. He cut through the temple's wards as easily as if his master were guiding his hand."

The Spider started pacing along the length of the pool. "You kept the body?"

Romany licked her lips. "Ah. Sadly, no. He escaped. Fortuitously. He left empty-handed, of course, tail between his legs. I remain alive and safe, as you can see. Imagine thinking he could best me in my own temple! Such impertinence!"

"Yes, you really showed him. You're sure it was you he was after?"

"Who else?"

The Spider crouched at the opposite end of the pool and dipped a hand into the water. For an uncomfortable moment Romany thought the goddess intended to join her in the pool, and she was grateful suddenly for the covering of bubbles on the water. "It seems Shroud has become more brazen in my absence," the Spider said. "I have been away too long."

Romany had been trying to tell her as much, but when did the goddess ever listen? "How fare your concerns in the Storm Isles?"

"Adequately. A new empire is about to rise from the ashes of the old, but the battle for its soul continues. It is only a matter of time before the conflict spreads beyond the borders of the kingdom."

"And the Emira?"

"Is no more than a minor player, though she knows it not. When the game begins in earnest she will soon be swept aside."

"And which faction do you favor?"

The Spider laughed. "Oh, Romany. You should know by now that I am never on just *one* side. Only a fool would risk everything on a single roll of the dice."

"Who, then, are the other players?"

"That does not concern you."

Romany sighed. "How is a high priestess meant to further her goddess's cause when she is kept ignorant of such matters?"

"I tell you what you need to know," the Spider said mildly. "And besides, I have other plans for you." She stood up. "Perhaps we could continue this somewhere more comfortable."

Romany sighed again, deeper this time. "Very well." She clapped her hands to summon the acolyte before remembering the girl had gone. Romany's robe was folded over the back of a chair a few paces away.

Beyond reach.

She looked at the goddess, but decided against asking her to pass it. The Spider watched her with a hint of a smile.

"If you would turn away, please," the priestess said.

The Spider's grin broadened, but she did as she was bid.

Romany rose and climbed the steps that led from the pool. She toweled herself down hurriedly, then slipped into her robe. The silk clung to her still-damp skin in a most unflattering manner. Her slippers, too, quickly became soaked when she slipped them on. As she crossed to the door to her living quarters, she lifted her chin in an effort to preserve whatever dignity remained to her.

Her footsteps squelched on the floor.

The air in the next room was delightfully cool. Light flooded through the windows to her left, silvering the strands of the huge web that spanned the far wall. There was a flicker of movement as her silverback spider scuttled along the gossamer threads. Romany reached out a hand to it. The creature's legs tickled her arm as it moved down to settle on her shoulder. Her acolytes had not yet lit the candles in the wall niches, and the Spider set them burning with a flick of her hand.

The goddess settled into one of the leather chairs surrounding a low table in the middle of the chamber, then selected a scroll from one of the bookshelves stacked like wine racks along the wall behind her. She unrolled the scroll and raised it to catch the light. Romany sank into one of the other chairs, but the Spider ignored her. Suppressing her irritation, the priestess looked at her desk beneath the windows and saw the acolytes had left one of her astronomical instruments fractionally out of alignment. As if that wasn't frustrating enough, the invisible strands of her magical web—focused in a tangle, here, at the hub of her empire—were quivering softly, indicating that somewhere in Mercerie a scandal was in the offing. Romany's fingers itched, but she would have to wait a while longer to find out what developments the tremors signaled.

She looked back at the Spider. The goddess was gazing at the silverback on Romany's shoulder, her forehead crinkled in distaste. "You realize," she said, "that one bite from that thing will turn your blood to poison."

The priestess snorted. "An absurd notion, my Lady! The silverback makes for a most devoted pet."

"Indeed. Just keep it away from me." The goddess gestured to the parchment she was holding. "What is this?"

Romany squinted to make out the muddle of words and diagrams. "Ah, yes! An exciting discovery at Elipene. A priestess has found a dry well at the center of the village where, at noon on Cartin's Day, the rays of sunlight shine right to the very bottom, meaning—"

"The sun is directly overhead. What of it?"

"I have had a post erected in one of the courtyards here and measured the angle of its shadow at the exact same time and date. Thus, knowing the distance between Mercerie and Elipene, I am able to calculate the approximate circumference of the globe."

"And?"

"I estimate it to be fourteen thousand four hundred and twenty leagues."

"You misunderstand. I meant, of what rrrelevance is this?"

Romany rolled her eyes. "The writings of Isabeya, if they are to be believed, put the distance from Mercerie to the Alkazadh Sea at eleven hundred and forty leagues. This continent, therefore, is but a small part of the world's vastness."

The goddess tossed the parchment onto the table. "My congratulations on proving something I have known for millennia."

"Ah, but I have ascertained the truth through empirical evidence."

"Meaning you do not trust my word?"

"Of course I do. I would simply observe that at times you can be less than generous in sharing your knowledge."

The goddess regarded her with raised eyebrows for a while, then said, "Game of hafters? It has been so long since I had a worrrthy opponent."

Romany's eyes narrowed. It would be just like the Spider to try to use the game to distract her from some more important matter. On the other hand, she had come so close to beating the goddess last time . . . "As you wish." She rose to fetch the playing board.

"No need," the goddess said. With another flutter of her fingers, a checkered battlefield appeared, floating in the air between them. Romany could not help but notice the Spider had given herself the queen's pieces. The figures had been animated in breathtaking detail. A harpy's wings beat the air as the goddess advanced it three spaces.

They exchanged a few moves in silence.

It was the Spider who finally spoke. "An unexpected opportunity has arisen to gain revenge for Shroud's raid on your temple. A powerful artifact has surfaced in an empire to the south. You have heard of Erin Elal, of course."

Romany succumbed to her curiosity. "What sort of artifact?"

"A book containing forgotten lore from the Time of the Ancients. It was an era of great upheaval for the pantheon. Many elder gods perished. Some fell to the titans, some to . . . pretenders. The knowledge of the fallen died with them."

"Or not, in this case."

The Spider nodded. "Somehow the Book of Lost Souls, as it is known, found its way into the possession of a fellowship of mages. They must have recognized its potential, for they wisely decided to keep it concealed beneath formidable wards. By pure chance, word of its existence came to me along the threads of my web."

"And you want this book . . . *stolen?*" Romany could hardly bring herself to say the word.

"No, that task has already been accomplished. At my instigation, of course, though the thief and his emperor are unaware of that fact." The Spider moved one of her witches to a position where Romany could capture it. "And besides, I have no interest in acquiring the Book for myself. Its use would draw attention to me, and as you know I prefer to remain hidden behind the veil."

Romany hesitated, then took the Spider's unprotected piece. The witch gave a piercing cry as she vanished from the board. "So instead you will arrange for the Book to fall into the hands of someone sympathetic to your cause?"

"Not quite. The thief himself, a mage by the name of Mayot Mencada, should be a suitable tool for what I have in mind."

"And how does Shroud fit into this?"

"In the hands of the right person, the Book could do him untold harm, for the secrets contained within it are inherently linked to the source of his power."

"Death-magic, then."

"Yes."

Romany advanced her wyvern one space, ignoring the goddess's amused look. "If the threat is as great as you claim, will Shroud not intervene personally to quash the danger?"

"And risk setting foot on unsanctified ground? I think not. No, he will send his disciples to do his grunt work."

As immortals are wont to do. "And you intend for them to walk into a trap?"

"Very good. The elimination of a few of Shroud's most capable followers would prove highly damaging to him. There is, however, a problem."

As the goddess spoke, she advanced another of her harpies in an apparently sacrificial move. Romany frowned. A ruse, perhaps, to draw Romany's pieces out of position? She tore her gaze from the board. "Problem?"

"Until now the thief's attempts to unlock the Book's mysteries have proved ineffective. He will be easy pickings when Shroud's disciples arrive."

"You mean to help him?"

"I mean for *you* to help him, yes—not just in penetrating the Book's defenses, but also in opposing whichever disciples Shroud sends to claim the artifact once it is activated. Ultimately the forces arrayed against Mayot will prove irresistible, but before then you should get a chance to exterminate some of Shroud's rrrabble."

Romany moved her king's champion to the center of the board. "And when Shroud finally gets his hands on the Book? Could he not use it as a weapon against you?"

"I suspect the Book contains few secrets that are not already known to him. He owned it once himself, after all."

"Owned it once . . . and lost it?"

The Spider shrugged. "As I said, it was a time of great upheaval."

"All the same, you are taking quite a risk."

"I do not see it so. After all, how can one lose a game if one has staked nothing on it? If there is a price to pay, Mayot Mencada will pay it for me."

Not that you have ever hesitated to sacrifice your own followers in the past.

The goddess considered the battlefield for a moment longer before waving a hand. The board faded. Romany had been holding a piece, and she watched openmouthed as it too melted away. *Looks like I was winning, then.*

"We don't have much time," the Spider continued. "No doubt you will want to leave instructions before we leave."

Romany stiffened. "Leave? I had assumed . . ."

The goddess wagged a finger. "Tut-tut. You should know better than that."

"Where are we going?"

"The Forest of Sighs."

Romany's hope rekindled. The forest was scores of leagues to the west. "A voyage of many weeks, my Lady. By the time I arrive the contest may be over."

The Spider looked to the heavens. "Romany, Romany. Have you never wondered how I'm able to travel so quickly between my various concerns?"

The priestess *had,* actually, but there were more important things on her mind just now. She adopted what she hoped was a suitably rue-ful expression. "Alas, it has been a long time since I left the temple."

"Too long, one might say."

"Nevertheless, my appetite for adventure is not what it was. I have a number of capable deputies. The vigor of youth . . ."

The goddess shook her head. "I cannot afford any mistakes. Shroud is unlikely to be forgiving if he discovers my involvement in this mat-ter. I need someone I can trust. Someone who can walk the trail with-out leaving footprints behind."

"But my responsibilities at the temple—"

"I'm sure your 'capable deputies' can cope without you for a while." The Spider's voice hardened. "No one is irreplaceable, after all."

A threat? No, surely the goddess would never stoop to anything so vulgar. And yet her expression did have a distinctly uncompromis-ing cast to it. "But a *forest*," Romany said, aware of the desperation in her tone. "Perhaps the thief could be persuaded to relocate to more congenial surroundings."

"As it happens, Mayot Mencada's choice of destination is inspired. It should be, since I chose it for him. Why else do you think he would travel so far from his homeland?" She rose. "You are familiar, of course, with the history of the Forest of Sighs?"

"Most distasteful," Romany said. "Though I fail to see what rel-evance it has to the Book."

The Spider's slow smile cut through her like an arctic wind.

CHAPTER 2

HIS PREY was close. Prince Ebon Calidar could smell it.

The stench of decay rode the breeze as if some vast burial pit lay out of sight beyond the crest of the hill. His gelding must have caught the scent too, for it snorted and tossed its head, pulling away to the north. Ebon slowed the animal to a walk, then ran a hand over his shaved head and stood up in the stirrups to gauge the wind's bearing. *From the west.* It had changed direction. And since the stink of the Kinevar remained strong in his nostrils . . . *So too has our quarry.*

The Forest of Sighs must be close.

A trickle of sweat ran down Ebon's back. He'd hoped to catch the Kinevar before they came within sight of the woods, for if the creatures reached the trees there would be no following them in. And yet, he couldn't pretend his growing unease was due solely to the thought of losing his prey. For the last quarter-bell he'd felt like a condemned man rushing to the headsman's block—because the sight of the forest might tug free more than just a memory of the last time he'd ventured into Kinevar territory. But that was all in the past, wasn't it? He'd already fought that battle and won. "I'm free of you, spirits," he said aloud.

As if saying it made it so.

The prince signaled to Vale farther down the valley—the Endorian acknowledged his gesture with a wave—then wheeled his horse into the breeze and dug his heels into the animal's flanks. The gelding sprang forward, and Ebon thundered at a gallop up the hillside, the wind tearing at his face. He bent low over the saddle until his cheek almost touched the horse's neck. The ground passed below in a blur of mud and sun-bleached grasses. When he eventually reached the hill's summit he tugged on the reins, and the gelding came to a stumbling halt, covered with sweat.

Ebon looked out over the plains. In the distance the Forest of Sighs rose like a wall. The prince raised a hand to shade his eyes from the sun. Sour memories were already crowding in on him, but he pushed them away. The Kinevar raiding party was less than halfway to the safety of the woods, strung out over a hundred paces. Ebon did a head count. Roughly five score. Some of the group would be Galitians seized in the raid on the village to the east, but even taking account of their presence, the prince's party was outnumbered four to one.

A whispering sound reached him, but he paid it no mind. Just the wind, most likely. Then it came again, like voices. One of the guardsmen, perhaps? But when Ebon looked over his shoulder he saw Vale and the soldiers who'd survived the attack on the village still urging their horses up the slope through the dust churned up in Ebon's wake. The hilltop itself was deserted.

The whispers returned, too faint for the prince to make out words. With a growing sense of foreboding he pressed his hands over his ears.

The voices became louder.

Ebon let his hands fall to his sides, his breath coming quickly.

It had started with the voices four years ago. Four years ago, when the roles had been reversed, and it was the *Kinevar* hunting *him*. Another raid, another village attacked, and Ebon had responded by leading a mounted troop into the Forest of Sighs north of the White Road. He shook his head. Barely two score Pantheon Guardsmen against a limitless foe, but what did numbers matter when the soldiers had their prince's pride to sustain them? Fortune had been with them at first, and they had destroyed an enemy war band and burned two villages. Then, as night fell, they retreated to the edge of the forest.

Into an ambush.

A Kinevar force had silenced the Galitian scouts and now came in a howling rush against Ebon's tired riders. The prince himself led a charge in an attempt to carve a path free, but a wave of sorcery from a Kinevar earth-mage had blunted the thrust, and within the space of a few heartbeats the battle became a rout. Ebon should have died with his men. There'd been times over the years when he wished he had.

Instead he alone of the Galitians had broken through the enemy ranks. Or been allowed to, as he later realized. The Kinevar must have marked him as the leader for they had toyed with him in their pursuit, killing his horse under him before driving him south in the direction of the White Road and the horrors that lay in wait there. As Ebon neared the road, spirits had come shrieking from the shadows, clawing at his mind's defenses. His swordsman's training had been the only thing to offer any protection from their attacks: the iron control that came from emptying his mind of exhaustion and fear, doubt and hope. Even then, when Ebon had stumbled from the trees at first light, half his memories had been erased and replaced with recollections not his own. And while he had thwarted the spirits' attempts to possess him, the voices of his tormentors had remained in his mind, mocking his efforts to sift his own thoughts from the scores of alien whispers. It was two years before those voices began to fade, another three seasons before they vanished for good.

Or so he had believed.

Why had they reawakened *now*, though? This was hardly the first time he'd seen the forest since that day. Could they sense the presence of their kin to the south? Did they taunt him with the recollection of his suffering at their hands? Ebon shifted in his saddle. So many things were taken from him by the spirits, yet the memories of his ordeal remained. His hands trembled. He clasped the pommel of his saddle to steady them, but the shaking only became stronger. The voices were growing louder, and Ebon imagined he heard a note of scorn in them. His anger slipped its leash. *Shroud take you, spirits! Maybe I was a fool to think you were gone. Maybe I will never truly be rid of you. But for as long as you remain, our fates are tied. When the end comes, I'll drag you down with me!*

Vale drew up his horse alongside. The Endorian's face was streaked with grime, and his thinning gray hair was plastered to his skull. Taking in the size of the Kinevar raiding party, he hawked and spat. "There's too many of them."

Ebon did not respond. Unstrapping his shield from his back, he transferred it to his left arm.

Vale looked at him. "You still mean to go through with this." It was not a question.

"What choice do we have? We cannot let the Kinevars' attack go unanswered."

"Figures. You've always got to have the last word."

Ebon gave a half smile. "Can you see any of the prisoners?"

"Not from here. Probably dead by now anyhow."

In other words you think we are wasting our time. "Enough, Vale. My mind is made up."

The Endorian grunted. "Do we circle round and cut them off from the forest?"

Ebon shook his head. "We do not know what is hiding in there. We could be attacked from the trees."

"You'll leave the Kinevar an easy way out."

"That's the idea. If we hit them hard they may abandon the captives and make a run for it."

"If our side don't break first."

Ebon stared at him for a moment, then looked over his shoulder. The village's guardsmen had formed up behind and were now watching him with tight expressions, their horses prancing nervously as if sensing their riders' tension. Ebon scanned the squad until he found its commander, a sallow-faced man loading a crossbow. The figure of a scorpion was etched into the left cheek-piece of the helmet perched at an angle atop his head. As his gaze met Ebon's, he nodded.

The prince turned back to Vale. "They will do their duty."

"You know their sergeant?"

"Seffes, he is called. He used to be a Pantheon Guardsman."

"Used to be."

Ignoring the comment, Ebon dropped back to give instructions to the soldiers, then rejoined Vale at the head of the squad.

The Endorian unsheathed his sword. "Let me take point. I'll draw their fire. No need for you to risk yourself."

"I will race you for the honor," the prince replied, digging his heels into his horse's flanks.

The gelding leapt forward gamely. Ebon held it back during the descent from the hilltop, then gave it its head as the land leveled out. The plains had been baked hard by the summer sun to leave the mud riddled with potholes, any one of which could snag a hoof and bring the gelding down. Ebon, though, did not slow its flight. As he closed the distance on the Kinevar back markers, the smell of rot became stronger. The raiders hadn't given any sign they were aware of their pursuers, but it was only a matter of time before they heard the rumble of the horses' hooves. Yet Ebon was still glad for the noise if it meant a respite from the spirits' whispering.

Even as the thought came to him, one of the Kinevar looked back and let out a shrill cry.

The prince could now make out the Galitian captives—a knot of lighter-skinned figures roped together near the middle of the Kinevar column. The enemy nearest the prisoners started milling around, and for a heartbeat Ebon hoped the raiders would abandon the captives and flee for the forest. Then a voice rang out, cutting through the chaos. A score of the raiders separated from their kinsmen and turned to face Ebon. The rest of the party resumed their flight to the woods.

Ebon smiled without humor. That made his job easier. First rule of military engagements: never split your forces. Just because the stationary Kinevar wanted a fight didn't mean he had to oblige them. He raised a hand to signal the troop to ride round and continue the pursuit of the main group.

Then his gaze came to rest on the man who had taken command of the smaller force. A handspan taller than his companions, he carried a staff and was chanting in a deep voice. He thrust his arms into the air as if he were beseeching some immortal for aid. His face was painted with symbols that flashed silver as the sun caught them.

Ebon cursed. *An earth-mage.*

There was no sorcerer in Seffes's troop who might counter the Kinevar's magic, but they still had a chance if they could get to him quickly. The warriors surrounding him had no shields with which to form a shield wall, and there were too few of them to withstand the squad's charge.

Suddenly the mage whirled his staff above his head and brought it down to strike the ground.

The earth trembled.

Ebon's horse stumbled, and he pitched forward in his saddle. He threw his right arm round the gelding's neck and hung on. "Steady!" he shouted as the animal struggled to regain its footing.

The lead elements of Seffes's squad thundered past, throwing up a cloud of dust.

As the earth tremors began to subside, the ground in front of the Kinevar mage bulged and split. A vast head burst from the earth, followed by two arms as thick as tree trunks. Ebon's hands went slack on the reins. The elemental clawed its way out of the ground like a corpse escaping from the grave and gave a gravelly roar. The wind tugged loose dust from its sides, making its form appear hazy round the edges. One of the Galitian riders ahead of Ebon hurled a spear into the creature's chest. The elemental ignored it. It surged to attack the thrower, battering him with an enormous fist. The soldier raised his shield to take the blow, but the metal crumpled like parchment. Man and horse were crushed into the ground with a tortured cry.

"Not the elemental!" Ebon called. "Take out the mage! The mage!"

But his words were drowned beneath another despairing yell as a second man went down.

The prince drew his saber. Somewhere Vale was shouting at him to ride clear, but Ebon ignored him. Wrestling with his horse's reins, he coaxed the gelding into the elemental's shadow. The creature loomed above him, its arm swinging down like Shroud's scythe. Ebon's saber flashed to meet it, intercepting the strike and severing the limb between elbow and fist. It fell to the ground in a spray of dust. Then Ebon was past, the elemental's bellow of rage ringing in his ears.

The Kinevar were waiting a short distance beyond, bonewood swords and spears in their hands. Scalps hung from their belts, and about their necks were necklaces of blackened human ears. They were drawn up in a ring with their commander at its center, and around the mage buzzed a cloud of flies. The ground swarmed with more insects, an endlessly moving mass that rippled like black water.

A spear flashed toward Ebon's head, and he raised his shield. The missile struck with a clatter and fell away. The next spear, though, was onto him before he could react, and it buried itself in his horse's neck. Ebon felt the force of it through his thighs. The gelding screamed, half rearing as it snapped its jaws at the spear shaft. Then its front legs gave way, and the prince flung himself from the saddle.

He took the brunt of the landing on his shield, the impact sending a jolt up his left arm. The ground here was shin-deep in insects, biting and rustling and scuttling. As he rolled to his feet, bugs tumbled from his shirt. No time to put his thrashing horse out of its misery. A glance behind revealed the elemental had stopped the squad's charge and was in among them. Its severed arm had re-formed, and the creature was flailing around in a berserk frenzy, punching riders from their saddles. For a heartbeat Ebon considered going to their aid, then he remembered his own advice.

The mage. The mage was the key.

He could see the man more clearly now. Insects crawled over his bare arms and torso like a second skin, and the power radiating from his staff made the air about him shimmer. A handful of Seffes's squad had fought in close and were hacking down at the fighters circling him. Then the sorcerer opened his mouth and a cloud of wasps spewed out to engulf a Galitian horse and rider. The man shrieked, his horse bolting. For a moment the pressure on the Kinevar warriors eased, but they made no move to advance, seemingly content to defend and watch while the elemental wreaked its havoc.

Time for me to create some of my own.

Insects crunched beneath Ebon's feet as he waded forward. One of the Kinevar moved to intercept him, hissing between black teeth. Its skin looked like tree bark, and its bonewood sword glistened as it swung for Ebon's chest. The prince parried once, twice, then ducked under a head-high cut and kicked his attacker's legs out from under him. The Kinevar went down, tripping another assailant behind. Ebon's saber darted out, quick as a striking wither snake, and both raiders died.

Their bodies sank beneath the heaving swell of insects.

A Kinevar female jabbed at Ebon's face with her spear. He raised his shield at the last instant but could only deflect the weapon's point, and it traced a line of fire across his left temple. Blocking another thrust with his shield, he hacked his attacker's spear shaft in two with his saber. As the Kinevar reached for a knife at her hip, Ebon stepped in close and ran her through, then spun in time to parry a lunge from a second assailant. The saber danced in his hand, feinting high before striking low as another enemy fell.

Seffes's squad was now pressing in all about in a melee of dust and blood. The thunderous steps of the elemental were close behind Ebon, but he dared not look round. Vale was to his right, also on foot, attacking in a blur of motion too fast for the eye to follow. Ebon was damned if he'd let his friend have the kill. As the Kinevar mage turned toward the Endorian, the prince saw his chance. He thrust his shield into the chest of a defender, sending him staggering backward. A gap opened in the Kinevar ranks, and Ebon burst through.

A swarm of flies enveloped him, so thick the world disappeared behind a buzzing black curtain. Better flies than wasps, though. A wave of Ebon's shield scattered the swarm enough for him to make out the mage beyond. The Kinevar was facing away from him, chanting as he unleashed a shaft of crackling sorcery at an unseen target. *Not Vale. Please, not Vale.*

Ebon shouted a challenge.

The mage swung to confront him.

Ebon's saber flashed out, and the Kinevar lifted his staff to block.

The blade should have cut a good chunk out of the wood, but instead when the weapons clashed there was a shower of sparks and the prince's saber shattered midway along its length.

A heartbeat passed as he stared disbelieving at the broken blade.

The mage counterattacked. Ebon tried to angle his shield so the Kinevar's weapon would glance off it, but the crunching contact still drove him to his knees. The staff punched a hole through wood and steel, only to trap itself in the mangled slivers of metal. A sharp twist of the prince's wrist wrenched the weapon from the mage's hand. Ebon surged to his feet. The Kinevar tried to back away but found his retreat checked by the ring of his defenders. Trapped by the very warriors meant to protect him.

A backhand cut with the stub of Ebon's saber opened his throat in a spray of blood.

There was a roar of frustration behind, and the prince turned to see the elemental a dozen paces away, a snarl frozen on its face. As it advanced a final faltering step, its left leg crumbled to dust. Then its entire body collapsed, raining dirt down on the combatants.

The fight went out of the remaining Kinevar, and they were quickly dispatched.

Breathing heavily, Ebon shuffled through the mass of insects until he reached clear ground. He shook loose the bugs in his hair and clothing, but he could feel more moving beneath his shirt, and he tore it off and flung it away. His skin was swollen with bites, and burned as if flames played across it. A tic-beetle had burrowed into his right wrist. Swearing, he used his broken saber to dig the insect out.

The body of his gelding lay a pace away. Flies had settled around the horse's eyes, and the prince bent down to close them. Blood was running down his cheek. Raising a hand to the cut at his temple, he found a flap of skin hanging loose. He pushed it back into place and held it there. His fingers came back sticky red. He saw again the Kinevar's spear coming at his face, his shield rising to intercept it. A moment later with his block and the thrust would have taken him through the eye. The years of seclusion that followed his spirit-possession had left him weak and slow. *It is time I put that right.*

Ebon searched the distant line of trees to see the main Kinevar party disappear into the forest. There was movement both north and south of the point where the group entered, and the prince kept his gaze on the shadows between the trunks in case the creatures returned. Screams started up as the Kinevar began avenging their mage on the Galitian prisoners. In Ebon's mind, the sound was echoed by the spirits. *The sound of my failure.*

Vale moved alongside. The Endorian had emerged from the battle with no more than insect bites and a shallow cut to his neck. "Tell me we ain't going in after them."

Ebon shook his head. "We have done all we can."

"Sense at last," the Endorian said, turning to leave. When Ebon made no move to follow he added, "You done admiring the view?"

A single Kinevar warrior stepped from the forest. He hopped from one foot to another, gesturing at Ebon with his spear. "It seems daylight no longer holds any fear for these creatures," the prince said. "The villages bordering the forest will have to be evacuated."

Vale eyed him skeptically. "Because of one raid?"

"The Kinevar would not leave the forest unless they had to. They must have known they would be hunted down."

"Fancied a change from chewing on roots, I expect."

"The forest is full of easier prey."

Vale bent to tear up a handful of grass and used it to clean his sword. "You reckon this marks the start of something? We got another Jirali's Bane on our hands?"

"Perhaps."

"Then why this raid to warn us it's coming?"

Three survivors from Seffes's squad were moving among the fallen Kinevar, cutting the throats of any that still breathed. The remaining soldiers were tending to the wounds of their injured companions. "Reynes tells me scouts have spotted the Kinevar as far north as Linnar," Ebon said. "Not just hunting parties, either. Whole tribes. Maybe they are on the move."

"You reckon they're fleeing something?"

Like birds taking flight. "Why not?"

The Endorian considered this before shaking his head. "I don't buy it. Ain't no army this side of Shroud's Gate that could drive them out of the forest."

"We will find out soon enough."

Vale must have heard something in his voice, for he looked at him sharply. "There's something else, ain't there? Something you're not telling me." He studied Ebon. "It's the voices. They're back."

Ebon hesitated, then nodded. "They returned when we came within sight of the forest. The spirits are close."

The Endorian drew a breath, then blew it out. "Do you think they're caught up in this somehow? With the Kinevar?"

The voices in Ebon's mind grew louder as if to confirm the Endorian's suspicions. There was something in their tone that troubled the prince, some new note that hadn't been there when they had last afflicted him. *They're afraid,* he realized with a start. *And what do spirits of the dead have to fear?*

Footfalls sounded behind, and the prince turned to see one of Seffes's soldiers approaching. There were flecks of vomit on the woman's chin and down the front of her uniform. She gave a tired salute.

Ebon glanced at the stripes on her shoulder. "Corporal," he said. "What are our losses?"

"Nine dead, your Highness. Two more about to join them."

"Sergeant Seffes?"

The corporal shook her head.

A dark day, indeed. "Is there a healer among your squad?"

The soldier looked back to where the bodies were being laid out. "Not anymore."

"Then round up the horses. Strap the dead in their saddles . . ."

Just then the air ahead of Ebon crackled, and a ghostly figure materialized a few paces away, hovering a handspan above the ground. The corporal's sword was halfway out of its scabbard, but Ebon put a hand on her arm to restrain her. The newcomer was a gaunt old man, standing barefoot and wearing a grubby white robe. The top of his head barely reached Ebon's shoulder. He grinned, showing yellow teeth. "Ah, there you are, my boy!"

"Mottle," the prince said. "As ever your timing leaves much to be desired. A quarter-bell sooner and you could have made yourself useful."

The mage's nose was in the air, sniffing like a tracker dog. "Earthmagic. An elemental, yes? Its spirit lingers still . . ." His voice faded away, and a thoughtful look crossed his face. "And something else." He spun toward the forest.

Ebon was suddenly conscious of the soldier at his shoulder. "That will be all, Corporal," he said. The woman flinched as if she had been roused from some reverie, then saluted and backed away. When she was gone, the prince turned to Mottle. "What is it? What do you sense?"

For a while the mage gave no indication he had heard. Finally he said, "The burgeoning of fell powers, my boy. Chaos, and its partner in devilry, Ruin. A storm is coming. The Currents have long warned Mottle of its approach."

"I have no time for your riddles. Why are you here?"

The old man turned back to him. "Did Mottle not say? Sincerest apologies. A genius such as Mottle's is invariably prone—"

"Mage," Ebon warned.

"Ah, yes. To the point, indeed. Your humble servant brings a message from the king. Your father summons you to the palace with all speed."

A chill ran through Ebon. He thought he had prepared himself for this news, but still it felt like he had taken a punch to the gut. "Is it time, then? Has his health deteriorated?"

"No, no. He keeps Shroud waiting still, though the hunt is nearing its end and death's Lord is ever patient."

"Then what is so urgent that my father has dragged himself from his sickbed?"

The mage spread his hands. "Would that Mottle could tell you. A meeting of the King's Council, yes? But as to why? Shrouded in mystery."

"Meaning you do not know."

The old man's voice dropped to a whisper. "Mottle has his suspicions, of course . . ." Then, as Ebon leaned in closer to hear his words, he went on, "But your humble servant has never been one to deal in rumor, as you know. The answer to your questions must await your return. Make haste to Majack! Mottle will beseech the Furies to speed your passage." He cast a final look at the forest. "We have much to discuss."

Before Ebon could respond the old man's ghostly image began to fade, dispersing on the breeze like smoke.

The prince snorted in disgust. "I am going to wring his scrawny neck when I next see him," he said to Vale. "Let's get out of here."

"We're leaving now?" the Endorian asked.

Ebon nodded. "The corporal can finish tidying this mess. Find us some horses and saddle up. We ride for Majack."

"They are coming for you, my Lady," a voice said.

Parolla looked across. To her left a young man leaned against one of Xavel's slums, striking a pose as if he were having his portrait painted. He was no one she recognized—hardly surprising since she'd only arrived in the city yesterday—and so she shifted her gaze back to Shroud's temple on the opposite side of the Round.

Six weeks it had taken her to reach this place. Ordinarily she'd have traveled six weeks to avoid one of the Lord of the Dead's shrines, but this particular temple had a notoriety she couldn't afford to ignore. The dark, hulking structure was windowless but for two round, high-set openings, gaping like the sockets of a skull. Doubtless the building's maker had intended it to look foreboding. Parolla wasn't so easily intimidated, though. One day she would rip this shrine down, along with all the others. The power bleeding from the place had an alien undercurrent, faint as a dying man's breath. She'd encountered nothing like it at any of the scores of similar temples she had visited over the years, but different was good . . .

The youth stepped into her line of sight and cleared his throat.

Parolla shot him a look. She'd assumed when he'd spoken earlier that his words were meant for someone else, yet now when she glanced about she saw she was the only person within earshot. The youth's cheeks were colored with some crimson blush, and he wore a blue silk shirt and matching pantaloons tucked into calf-high leather boots. A dueling sword hung from a scabbard at his waist, its hilt too shiny to have ever seen use. He returned her gaze with unashamed interest.

"Do I know you, *sirrah*?" she said.

"If we had met before, you would not have forgotten me. I am Ceriso di Monata"—he performed an extravagant bow—"second son of the Compte di Monata." The youth spoke the name as if he expected her to know it. He waited for Parolla to reply, then added, "And whom do I have the pleasure of addressing?"

She ignored the question. "You must excuse me, *sirrah*. I need to be alone."

"Perhaps you did not hear me when I first spoke. They are coming for you."

"They?"

"The Hunt. You are marked by the Antlered God—even a mere novitiate such as I can detect his sign upon you."

Parolla's skin prickled, but she kept her expression even.

Ceriso said, "You seem strangely indifferent to my tidings. Are you ignorant, perhaps, of the seriousness of your plight?"

"This is not the first time I have crossed paths with the Hunt."

"Whatever dealings you may have had with the Antlered God's followers in the past will not prepare you for what you face now." The youth spoke with a solemnity ill-suited to his piping voice. "The high priest of Xavel himself leads the Hunt, and with him are the Riders of Dorn. My Lady, now might be a good time to make peace with whatever gods you favor."

Movement to Parolla's right caught her eye. A three-legged dog was nosing through the refuse at the edge of the Round. It entered the temple's shadow, then shrank away, growling.

Parolla looked back at Ceriso. The youth lingered like a courier wanting a tip for his news. She'd wasted enough time on him already, but perhaps she should take this opportunity to find out more about his masters—and how he had managed to track her down with such apparent ease. "Who sent you, *sirrah*?"

"The high priest of the Antlered God, of course."

"Why? Why would he warn me he was coming?"

"Why would he not? He is, after all, a servant of the Lord of the Hunt. The thrill is in the chase."

"And if I choose not to run?"

Ceriso winced. "That would be ill-advised. The high priest would be most aggrieved."

And we wouldn't want that, would we.

A gray-robed acolyte, hooded and stooped, emerged from the temple's arched doorway, flinching as he passed from shadow into daylight. The three-legged dog took flight.

"My Lady," the youth continued, "your accent betrays you as a stranger to this city, yet its provenance, I confess, eludes me. Never before have I seen eyes such as yours, like pools of deepest night, or skin so pale and lustrous." He put on a smile Parolla assumed she was supposed to find alluring. "Where is your homeland?"

"I have none."

Ceriso blinked. "Well, whatever place you hail from, you must surely recognize the temple before you. The patron god is Shroud, Lord of the Dead. If you are looking for a place of refuge, you will find no welcome here."

You speak more truth than you know. "Would the Hunt dare to storm the temple, then?"

"It would not have to. Should you enter, you will find the air inside somewhat"—he groped for the right word—"unpalatable. No one of sound mind can breathe it for long. Better to die outside with the wind on your face."

"Your concern for me is misplaced. Warn your *mekra*. For his own sake, tell him to stay away from me."

Ceriso waved a hand at the feathermoths floating round him on the scorched afternoon breeze. "I will, of course, report your words, but I fear they will be greeted with a degree of skepticism. The high priest will not believe that you speak out of concern for the Hunt's well-being."

"I have never borne the Antlered God any ill will. This *bakatta* is of his making, not mine." She hadn't asked, all those years ago, to be held against her will. She'd made it clear to the god's servants there would be consequences if they tried to stop her leaving the temple that had once been her home.

Ceriso must have misconstrued her meaning for he said, "Ah, I understand now. You wish to end your feud with the god. To plead for clemency, perhaps." He shook his head. "Alas, I am but a humble messenger, and thus have no authority to adjudicate your cause. You may petition the high priest, of course, but I would counsel against it. Once unleashed, the Hunt cannot be recalled."

"Tell your *mekra* anyway. If he ignores my warning, the blood spilled will be on his hands, not mine." The gods knew, Parolla's hands were stained enough already.

Ceriso made to say one thing before appearing to change his mind. "Forgive my curiosity, my Lady, but who are you?"

"The high priest didn't tell you?"

"He said only that I should approach you with caution. You seem young to have earned the enmity of the Antlered God."

"Appearances can be deceptive." She'd got all she was going to get from the youth, she suspected. "Now, *sirrah*, leave me, please."

"As you wish." Ceriso sketched another bow, hesitated, then seemed to reach a decision. "I admit to being unacquainted with this part of Xavel, my Lady. A man of my standing rarely has cause to visit the more, shall we say, less privileged districts of the city. I am told the streets here are a veritable maze of passages. So easy to lose one's way. It may be some time before I can report back to my master."

Parolla inclined her head. "A gracious gesture."

"Sadly it will serve only to delay the inevitable. It pains me to inform you that no one has ever escaped the Hunt in Xavel. We are truly blessed by the Antlered God."

" 'We,' *sirrah*? Will you be part of the Hunt, then?"

A look of distaste crossed the youth's features. "Certainly not. The

Lord of the Hunt has many aspects. I am not responsible for the unsavory predispositions of others that share the faith. I myself prefer
pursuits of an amorous nature." He tried his smile again. "It is a shame
we did not meet under more auspicious circumstances."

Parolla raised an eyebrow. She had to admire his persistence at
least. "I think you would find I am dangerous company to keep."

"Ah, my Lady," Ceriso said wistfully. "Your words have served only
to stoke the fires of my intrigue. If you should somehow evade the Hunt,
perhaps you would seek me out." He bowed a final time before spinning on his heel and setting off across the Round.

As Parolla watched him retreat she gave a half smile. It quickly
faded. The Hunt again. Everywhere she went, they dogged her heels.
Since arriving in Xavel she'd made a point of giving the Antlered God's
temple a wide berth, but still his followers had found her. And yet
she'd been fortunate, she knew. If the Hunt had come a day sooner,
her carefully laid plans would have been thrown into disarray. As it
was, the presence of the Lord's followers was little more than an irritation. With luck she'd be far away before they had the chance to
interfere.

Nevertheless, she could not linger.

With a last look round to ensure she had no more unwelcome company, she strode toward the temple.

The building cast a shadow black as night, and as Parolla stepped
into it her limbs felt cramped and heavy as if old age had placed a
hand on her shoulder. Closer now, she saw two statues flanking the
arched doorway, worn down over the centuries to amorphous swell-
ings of wind-bitten rock. To the left of the opening, a man was slumped
against the wall, his eyes rolled back in his head. He wore a tattered
kalabi robe, and the soles of his bare feet were crisscrossed with bloody
lacerations. An empty bottle was in his right hand. Parolla wrinkled
her nose as she passed, for the cloying smell of juripa spirits could
not mask the stink of sweat and putrefaction.

She stepped through the doorway and entered a corridor that
opened out into a dark chamber. Smudges of light lined the walls to
either side, the glow of the torches almost entirely smothered by shadows. The noise of the *jadi* crowds outside had dropped to a whisper,
and not a sound reached Parolla from within the gloom ahead. Death-
magic swirled round her on unseen currents. She felt something within
her stir in answer. Digging her fingernails into her palms, she waited
until the sensation diminished.

The light from the wall torches dwindled as she plunged into the blackness. To either side figures knelt on the floor. Some had their foreheads pressed to the stone; others watched her as she passed. Bones were scattered on the ground, as if a handful of worshippers had died in the act of prayer and been left to rot where they fell. Among the bones were scraps of clothing, a rusted belt buckle, an empty scabbard, even the occasional coin.

Amid the gloom, deeper shadows were congealing. When they brushed Parolla's skin, her power rose in answer.

"Curb yourself," a voice said. "Within these walls sorcery is forbidden to all but the anointed."

Parolla halted. Footfalls approached, and an old man wearing gray robes shuffled into view. His eyes were filmed over in blindness, and the skin of his face and hands was covered in liver spots. His straggly white hair had been shaved at the left temple to reveal a tattoo of a snake. As Parolla peered at the serpent, its tongue flickered out.

The priest must have sensed her attention, for he said, "It is a bedra cobra. Do you understand its significance, I wonder?"

"I know something of Terenil customs—that is your tribe, is it not? The year of the snake was, what, thirty years ago?"

"Twenty-eight."

Making the priest just a few years older than Parolla herself. "You display it like some badge of honor."

A cough shook the man's skeletal frame. "And so it is. What better proof could there be of my devotion to the faith?"

"And this is how you are rewarded for that devotion? Your body broken, your days cut short in return for a lifetime spent in your god's service?"

"*My* god? Not yours?"

"A slip of the tongue, *sirrah.*"

The priest grunted. "My reward will come in the next life, as you well know." He raised a palsied hand. "The surrender of this decaying flesh is a small price to pay for an eternity at the Lord's right hand. Death is the one constant in our lives, the one certainty." He turned his empty gaze on her. "Even for you, *jezaba.*"

Parolla tensed. "You know me?"

"I know what you are. How could I not? I am a priest of Shroud."

He was watching her intently, and she forced herself to take a breath. So what if he recognized her? There was no way he could know her true purpose here. "Then why, *sirrah*," she said, adding a note of steel to her voice, "have you not shown me the honor I am due?"

The blind man was still for a few heartbeats before bowing his head a fraction. "Why are you here?"

Parolla looked round. Blurred figures had gathered just beyond the limits of her vision, and she could hear their ragged breathing, sense their cold stares as a tension in the air. Had the priest summoned them as witnesses to their conversation? *Better and better.* She turned to the blind man. "I have heard tales of this temple on my travels. Pilgrims speak of it with awe, yet even their words fail to do justice to its majesty."

The priest started coughing again.

"From the power in this place," Parolla went on, "one would think the temple were newly sanctified. Yet I sense an unfamiliar taint to the death-magic that surrounds us." It felt stronger here than it had outside the temple. And it appeared to be coming from . . . Parolla looked down at the floor. "Is there a crypt here?"

"It has been sealed off," the blind man said. "Access is forbidden, by order of the high priest."

"Forbidden? To me?"

"To all who are not anointed in the faith."

Parolla let the silence draw out. "Would you brand me as an outsider then, *sirrah*?" she said at last, raising her voice to carry to those watching. "Am I no different to you than one of the unhallowed?"

"Of course you are, but—"

"There is something in the crypt you do not wish me to see?" Then, before the priest could respond, "You think the faith holds any secrets from me? Or that I cannot be trusted to keep them, perhaps?"

The blind man shifted his weight from one foot to the other. "That judgment is not mine to make."

"Where is your *mekra*, then? I wish to speak with him."

"Regrettably, the high priest is away from the temple at present."

Of course he is, you fool. Why do you think I am here today of all days? "Where is he?"

"A ceremony at the Tebala Shrine in Kontynan. He will return by nightfall tomorrow."

"By which time I will have left Xavel."

"Perhaps when you next visit the city . . ." The priest's voice trailed off.

Parolla left a pause for uncomfortable thoughts. "How do you suppose your *mekra* will react when he hears what happened here? When he hears that you insulted me, then dismissed me as if I were no more than a thief come to steal from your collection plate? For he *will* be told."

"He will not condemn me for obeying his instructions."

"Would you stake your life on that?"

As if seeking support, the old man shifted his milky gaze to the silent figures clustered round. No one stirred. The swirling darkness closed in on Parolla again, and this time when her power rose she made no effort to hold it back. A shadow settled on her vision.

The priest took a step back.

"My patience is wearing thin, *sirrah*."

He hesitated an instant longer before nodding to Parolla's right. When he spoke his voice was gruff. "The entrance to the crypt is protected by the high priest's wards."

"I can deal with those."

"No doubt. Just be sure to replace them when you have passed through. The defenses were created as much to prevent something getting out as to stop someone getting in."

"Meaning?"

"To enter the crypt you must relinquish the protections afforded by this temple." The priest gave a thin smile. "I fear I cannot guarantee your safety."

Majack steamed in the evening heat. Ebon rode with head bowed as he followed the Merchant's Road through the Low Quarter. Just another traveler arrived from the wastelands. The city rang to the sound of hammers as people boarded up doors and windows in readiness for the Day of Red Tides, less than a week hence, when thousands of stoneback scorpions would sweep in from the east. As the prince passed, a dour-faced merchant paused in his hammering to nudge his wife, and the two of them stared at Ebon, their expressions wary. Probably just noticing the blood and the dust, he told himself. He'd never commanded the same affection as his father, even before the spirits took him, and after his years of isolation the townsfolk were as likely to recognize Vale as they were their future king.

Ebon rubbed a hand across his eyes. During the ride from the forest the babbling of the spirits had been unrelenting, and two bells in the saddle had left him yearning for even a moment's respite. *Like a chorus of the damned.* What was it that tormented them so? Were they trying to communicate with him? At times when he listened he thought he could make out individual words, yet how could that be when he did not know the language? Why did it always seem as if comprehension hovered just a hairbreadth beyond his grasp?

Vale must have sensed his disquiet, for a strained silence had fallen between them. *He fears, as I do, where this will lead—a return to the days of darkness.* Ebon had no words of reassurance to give. When the spirits last possessed him, they had stayed for almost three years, and he didn't know if he had the strength to go through that again. It would be harder this time too, he suspected. The spirits seemed . . . closer . . . somehow, as if whatever barriers existed in Ebon's mind between him and them were already being whittled away. He could *feel* their madness seeping into him. Were they what he was destined to become?

Gods, I must find a way to halt this downward spiral.

Vale had moved ahead, cursing as he tried to clear a path through the crowds, and Ebon kicked his horse forward to join him. Together they skirted the smallest of the city's four marketplaces. In the shadow of one of the countinghouses, the beggars and doom criers were out in force, keeping up a constant wail like a funeral dirge. Music to match Ebon's mood. His gaze was drawn to a woman sitting with her back to a wall. She wore a robe the same color as her sun-blistered skin, and the black tears tattooed on her cheeks marked her as an initiate of the Watcher. Her eyes had been sewn shut, yet still she turned her head to follow Ebon as he rode past.

On the far side of the marketplace, the road leading to Wharf Bridge was choked with people. Ebon's horse was being jostled on all sides, and it snorted its unease. From the prince's elevated position he could see that on the bridge a cart had lost a wheel, spilling melons and sandfruit to the dust. The people nearby fell upon the fruit like a flock of redbeaks, only to scatter again when the driver of the cart—a snowy haired Maru—waded among them brandishing a club. A girl was knocked to the ground, blood streaming from her shattered nose, and the rumble of the crowd swelled in anger. Moments later the Maru was hoisted aloft by a dozen hands and hurled shrieking over the bridge's railing. His cart and the remainder of its contents followed.

"About time," Vale said.

As Ebon crossed the bridge he looked over the railing. There was

no sign of the Maru, but his cart was visible, drifting a stone's throw
away. The prince covered his nose with a sleeve. A sewer must have
burst somewhere upriver because the waters of the Amber ran thick
with scum and stank like a week-old corpse. Floating among the
rushes that clogged the shallows were the bloated bodies of scores of
animals and birds. The air throbbed with flies, and a cloud of the
insects swarmed round Ebon's head wound. He swatted them away
with one hand, but more soon took their place.

Reaching the opposite bank, he squinted east. He could just
make out the crystal towers of Amarixil's Shrine in the Marobi
Quarter, even convinced himself he could see Lamella's house beside it. Another time he might have gone there first, but his father's
cryptic summons demanded his presence. Duty first, always. Spying
a patrol of Pantheon Guardsmen, he requisitioned it as an escort.
The streets became wider as they traveled farther into the city, and
the speed of their progress increased. There were more stares from the
people now, hostility in them. Ebon bore them in silence. Eventually
the palace came into view above the roofs of the buildings ahead:
first its black towers, then its crenellated battlements, like a row of
jagged teeth.

A sixth of a bell later, he rode into the gatehouse and sent a guard
to inform the king of his arrival.

Ebon dismounted. The muscles of his thighs and back were sore
from his time in the saddle. He left Vale to stable the horses and headed
for a nearby fountain. Cupping his hands to hold the water, he drank
until his stomach ached, then washed the dust and dried blood from
his face. The sight of his reflection brought a furrow to his brow. A
day's stubble cast a shadow on his chin and jaw, but a darker shadow
lurked behind his cold blue eyes. *As if the spirits were staring back
at me.* He needed to speak to Mottle before the King's Council convened. What had the mage sensed at the forest? Did he know the voices
were back? If so, Ebon needed to make sure of his silence.

He followed the ramparts round to the east and entered the Dawn
Gate at the foot of Pagan's Tower. A soldier stepped from the guardhouse to challenge him before moving aside with a hasty salute and
a muttered apology. Inside, the coolness of the vaulted stone corridors made Ebon shiver. He kept his gaze on the floor, anxious to avoid
the eye of anyone who might slow him with questions. At the Hall of
Paths he took the arched portal that led to the East Wing. Its architrave had been sculpted to resemble a row of fangs, making it appear

to Ebon that he was stepping into a dragon's maw. Beyond, the passage ran arrow-straight into the gloom.

The sounds of the palace faded behind until the only noise was the tread of the prince's footsteps.

It was years since he had last ventured into this section of the fortress. Running his hand along the wall, he could find no cracks or joints, as if the entire building had been carved from a single piece of rock. Over the years a handful of servants had disappeared in this labyrinthine part of the palace, though whether they had become lost or fallen victim to something prowling the leagues of corridors was not known. Ebon had always smiled at the more lurid tales of their fates, yet today he found himself grateful his destination lay but a short distance ahead.

He passed through a second arch and began counting passages to the side. The way sloped downward. As he descended he felt a draft against his face. It strengthened as the moments passed, rising and falling in a steady rhythm. *Like breathing.* The voices in his head had receded to a murmur. He took the next turn on his right and entered a huge chamber. Dark and featureless, the only light came from long, linear openings in the roof. The wind passing through them carried on it sounds and scents that changed each time the breeze veered: first an icy tingle of mountain air; then a dry rasp of windblown sand; then a moist tang of salt like a memory of the sea.

A crumpled robe lay discarded in the center of the floor. Looking up, Ebon saw Mottle floating naked, high above. The old man's arms were outstretched to form a cross, and his body was slowly spinning round. Ebon cleared his throat.

Mottle continued turning for a few heartbeats before starting to descend. Barefoot, he touched down beside his clothes.

"I hope I am not interrupting anything," Ebon said.

"On the contrary, my boy," the mage replied as he donned his robe. "Mottle is glad you are here. Your coming is like a pebble dropped in a pool of water."

"Meaning?"

The old man straightened. He had put his robe on back to front, but either had not realized or did not care. Spreading his arms to take in the chamber, he said, "Your presence has sent ripples through the Currents. An image was beginning to take shape, but now all is confusion once more. The fragments are scattered anew, the pieces yet to settle."

No arguing with that. No understanding it either. "Speak plain, mage."

"Plain? Why, Mottle is the epitome of clarity and eloquence, though his mind does on occasion wander paths that others cannot follow . . ." His voice trailed off. "Ah, what was Mottle saying?"

Ebon sighed. "Pebbles."

"Of course! The stone that triggers the avalanche, yes? It seems you have a pivotal role to play in what is to come."

"And that is?"

"Unknown, at least for now. Patience is called for. The pattern is still forming, the final picture only hinted at."

This is like trying to catch a fish in my hands. Every time I think I have him, he wriggles free. Ebon looked up into the empty gloom. "What are you talking about? I see no pattern."

"No pattern?" Mottle said, aghast. "Why, it is all around you. Can you not sense it? A tremor in the air, a snatch of sound—they are like threads of a tapestry still in the weaving. Some fragments are as young as the words we speak, others as old as time itself." The old man's voice was bright with excitement. "The fall of civilizations, the machinations of gods, the endless grinding turn of time's inexorable wheel: in the end, word of all things reaches this place. No secret can stay hidden forever from Mottle's perspicacious regard."

Ebon paused to listen but could make out nothing above the mournful whispering of the spirits in his head. *Maybe I'm not the only one who hears voices.* "I will have to take your word for it, mage. Your senses are clearly sharper than mine."

"Perhaps." Mottle tapped his nose with one finger. "Or perhaps your attention is occupied by other matters at present."

The spirits' voices rose in consternation. *He knows.* Ebon found himself battling against the urge to draw his sword.

Mottle went on, "It is not so hard to detect the Currents, my boy, for those who know how. But perceiving is not the same as understanding, yes? So much information to take in, it can overwhelm the senses. One must learn to separate each fragment from the others." His gaze was calculating. "To isolate one voice from the crowd."

"Indeed. And how is this done?"

"By riding the Currents. By surrendering to them—letting them take you where they will. Such is Mottle's fate, like a leaf borne on the breeze—"

"And what if the Currents drag you under? What if there is no coming back?"

Mottle shrugged before turning away. "Come!" he said, setting off for a doorway at the far end of the chamber.

For a few heartbeats Ebon could only stare at the old man's retreating back. Then he followed.

He had to bend low to enter the passage Mottle had disappeared into, edging forward in a shuffle. After a dozen steps he felt a resistance in the air as if he were pushing through cobwebs. The room beyond was even gloomier than the main chamber. Scattered across the floor were rolls of parchment that rustled as Ebon picked his way through. Alcoves were set into the walls, like resting places for the dead. One contained a tattered sheet and a rag scrunched into a pillow; the others were filled with a jumble of scrolls, animal skulls, and piles of roots and dried petals. The prince felt somehow lighter here—as if, were he to jump, he might not come down again. Looking up, he saw scrolls resting against the ceiling.

From the darkness at the far end of the room came a series of irregular click-clacking sounds. Peering into the gloom, Ebon said, "You have something against daylight, mage?"

Mottle glanced across at him. "What? Ah, more light. Of course." He gestured with one hand. The shadows retreated to the corners of the room, forming unnaturally dense pools of blackness and leaving the center of the chamber filled with a pale, indeterminate glow. At the edge of the light, Ebon saw an apparition that made his skin crawl. Suspended from a noose was a skeleton the size of a child. Two stubs protruded like broken horns from the top of its skull. The other bones had evidently been collected from a number of different donors. Some were charred, or discolored with age; others were gnawed, splintered, or carried the marks of weapons. The figure rocked back and forth, its bones striking each other to produce the clicking sounds Ebon had heard earlier.

"Fascinating, is it not," Mottle said, "the unseen powers that act on us."

"What is that thing?" Ebon asked.

"Mottle has not given it a name," the mage replied, frowning as if the oversight troubled him.

"I meant, what does it do?"

"It detects energies. Forces that would otherwise be imperceptible, even to someone with senses as acute as Mottle's." The mage approached the skeleton and began to circle it, moving from shadow into light, then back into shadow again. "Mottle has felt a growing power of late, riding the Currents like an infection. The resistance you experienced as you entered . . . it is a seal about this room to prevent outside interference. Similar barriers exist round the other walls, the ceiling and the floor. The air in here should be still, yet the figure continues to move as if a soul were bound to it."

"And you are using that thing to, what, gauge these forces?"

"Precisely. Mottle seeks a way to manipulate them, perhaps block them entirely."

"Have you been successful?"

"Not yet." The mage gestured to the scrolls resting against the ceiling. "Thus far, your humble servant's changes to the composition of the atmosphere have had little effect on these mysterious forces. Mottle thought to remove all of the air from this chamber, but then how could he be present to observe the result of his experiment? The solution proves elusive, alas, but Mottle will persevere."

The skeleton jerked, and Ebon tore his gaze away. "And the bones? No, don't tell me. I don't want to know where you acquired them."

"Their previous owners no longer had any use for them, Mottle assures you. And he has found bone to be more sensitive to these energies than either wood or stone."

"Indeed. What type of forces are we dealing with, then?"

The mage stopped pacing. "Ah! The same thought has been troubling Mottle. Death-magic, for sure, although as to which denomination, Mottle knows not. Worrying, yes?"

Ebon looked round. Was it just his imagination, or were the shadows closing in? "And where do they come from, these energies?"

"This fortress, in part," Mottle said, placing a hand against a wall. "Centuries of conflict have seeped into the stone, leaving scars that will never truly fade. But these should cause only the slightest of tremors. This"—he gestured to the twitching skeleton—"this *potency* . . . Mottle has never before seen the like."

Ebon held the old man's gaze. "What did you sense at the forest? What do you sense in me?"

The mage's forehead creased. "In truth, Mottle does not know. But there is something different about you, yes? A change since the spirits last took you."

"In what way?"

"Your humble servant is unsure. There is a shadow upon you, but when Mottle tries to concentrate on it, it escapes him."

"You speak as if it were some conscious entity. Something that withdraws when it senses your scrutiny."

"That is Mottle's fear, but then would it not leave some trace of its passing? Mottle can find none, and he is not easily thrown off a scent."

The clicking of the skeleton was beginning to set Ebon's nerves on edge. "All I hear is speculation, mage. Not good enough. I need answers."

Mottle raised an eyebrow. "Then search for them within, my boy. The solutions await you there, if you have but the will to seek them out."

"You don't understand. The spirits . . . If I relaxed my guard, they would drag me down. Theirs is a world of torment, Mottle. I will find no answers there, only madness."

"Certain, are you? Do not be so quick to reject Mottle's sagacious counsel. Centuries ago, the spirits—the Vamilians as they were known—were a powerful race. Civilized, yes, but expansionistic. Their empire was so vast that the sun would rise over one part even as it set in another—"

"You have told me all this before," Ebon interrupted. "What is your point?"

"Mottle's point? Simply this: There may be a way for you to exploit the Vamilians' presence. You have some of their memories, yes? You share their knowledge." Mottle's eyes glittered. "Perhaps there is power, too, that you can use. Power you may need before the end."

"The end of what?"

Mottle smiled innocently. "Why, whatever is upon us, of course."

Ebon regarded the old man sourly. *For a moment there, I thought I had him. I can only hope the mage is as careful with my secrets as he is with his own.* He batted aside a roll of parchment as it floated upward past his face. "Tell me, this presence you sense . . . Has it marked me in some way? Will others be able to detect it?"

"Mottle doubts that," the mage said, puffing out his chest. "There are few as perceptive as your humble—"

"Good. I would have it stay that way."

Mottle was silent for a time, then nodded. "As you wish. Mottle is not unmindful of the complications that would arise if such information were to fall into the wrong hands. His lips are sealed. Discretion is but one of Mottle's many virtues."

"I am grateful for that, my friend."

The old man nudged Ebon in the ribs. "Does this mean you will not be wringing Mottle's scrawny neck?"

My conversation with Vale . . . He heard! Ebon's lips quirked. "Your point is well made. In future I will be sure to speak more carefully when others may be listening."

"A valuable lesson, yes? But fear not, Mottle does not hold such hastily voiced words against you. You are not the first to underestimate Mottle's talents, and he would not have it any other way. So many secrets tumble unbidden into his lap."

"You have an interesting take on eavesdropping."

The mage drew himself up. "Think Mottle a spy, do you? He is not." His tone softened. "Though if he were, there would be none better. A whispered comment spoken even at a distance booms loud in his ears . . ." The old man tilted his head. "And so it is now. The time is upon us, my boy. It seems the King's Council is convening, and Queen Rosel laments our absence."

"Then we had better not keep her waiting." Ebon made for the doorway before pausing and looking back. "I don't suppose you would care to enlighten me now as to the reason for this gathering?"

Mottle gave a secretive smile and strode past.

Ebon sighed. "I didn't think so."

CHAPTER 3

SOMEONE WAS following Luker.

The feeling had been with him since he left the Sacrosanct, and it wasn't the sort of feeling you ignored unless you wanted a crossbow bolt between your shoulders. He looked back, half expecting to spy some fool ducking into an alley, but there was nothing to see except the rain sweeping down in thick gray sheets. He scanned the doorways of the buildings along the street. Deserted. A corner of one of the shop's awnings had torn loose and now shuddered and cracked in the wind. Otherwise, all was still. The sense of being watched would not leave him, though, and he had learned to trust his instincts on such things.

Loosening his swords in their scabbards, he set off again at a measured walk. No point in hurrying. He was already as soaked as if he'd taken a dip in the harbor, and besides, he didn't want his pursuer to know he'd been spotted. For a quarter of a bell Luker followed the twists and turns of Dock Street as it wound toward the port, trying to work out how it felt to be back on home ground. Wet, he decided. He passed the gates to the Gamala Clock Tower on his right, then ducked into a cobbled passage, keeping to the wall where the shadows were deepest. The alley ran like a river, and water seeped into his boots.

He waited.

The tower bells clanged to mark the second hour of eventide, and the wall at the Guardian's back trembled. Above a grumble of thunder he heard chirruping overhead. Looking up, he saw a pair of chitter monkeys watching him from the top of the Clock Tower. A squad of Bratbaks emerged through the gloom along Dock Street, their heads bowed as they labored up the hill. For a heartbeat Luker wondered whether they could be his pursuers. Then he realized they were heading away from the harbor, not toward it.

He swore. His hunter should have passed by now. *Unless the bastard saw me enter the alley.* But then why hadn't he followed Luker in? Had the chitter monkeys given away his presence? *He's good,* Luker thought grudgingly. Another Guardian perhaps, or one of the emperor's men, sent to make sure he did not flee the city? Whoever he was, Luker couldn't allow himself to be followed—one unwelcome guest would be enough for Jenna tonight. Nor did he have time to play hide-and-seek across the whole Shroud-cursed city. *Let's see if he's got the stones to follow me into the Warren.*

Luker retreated down the passage and began threading his way through the streets until he came to the Old City Wall. Following it south, he stopped when he came to a breach leading into blackness. The Wall was an armspan lower than when he'd last been here, the missing stones no doubt pilfered to build more of the hovels that crowded the district beyond. What remained of the Wall was covered with writing in a score of different languages: Kerinec, Fenilar, Remnerol, Maisee, along with others Luker did not recognize.

The black skulls painted to either side of the breach needed no translation, though.

Luker stepped through. He entered an alley so narrow that if he stretched out his arms, his fingers would brush the walls on either side. No light escaped from the shuttered windows. Above, the overhanging eaves almost touched. Luker had gone no more than a dozen paces when he saw a beggar hunched in a doorway. A lookout, maybe. As the Guardian drew level, the man leered at him, then thrust out a hand missing two fingers. Another time Luker might have given him a handspan of steel in his guts. Instead he shook his head and continued on.

Setting a course roughly east, he followed the alleys that led down to the sea. The sound of the wind was muted here, as if the storm prowled the edge of the Warren but dared not enter. A pity the rain hadn't stayed away as well, but at least it seemed to have kept the usual dross at home, for the streets thus far had been uncharacteristically empty.

It couldn't last.

Sure enough, as Luker approached the next corner he heard a noise from round the bend. Halting, he cocked his head to listen, trying to screen out the drumming of the rain on the rooftops. There it was again. A screeching sound. He glanced round the corner. A short distance ahead a wall had collapsed, partly blocking the way. And on an intersection too.

Perfect spot for an ambush.

Luker drew his swords and approached the obstruction. The air was thick with the stench of death. A small body was partly buried beneath the rubble, and dark shapes swarmed over and around it, drifting in and out of the shadows. *Rats*. And it looked like the Guardian had disturbed their feeding. Reaching out with his Will, he explored the streets beyond the debris. As expected, three figures waited in the alley to his left, two to his right, another two ahead, and doubtless more would be coming up behind to box him in. Luker had no intention of retreating, though. Hit hard and fast, and he could turn this ambush before the idiots even knew they'd lost the advantage of surprise.

Now the fun begins.

He clambered over the rubble, expecting the attack to come while the stones were shifting beneath him. Nothing moved in the darkness. Raising a Will-shield in front of him, he stepped down with a splash into ankle-deep water.

Still the ambushers waited.

Luker approached the intersection, looking neither left nor right, his steps unhurried.

His only warning was the swish of parting air. Two crossbow bolts struck his Will-shield and cannoned off. At the same instant a flash of silver sliced the blackness to his left, and he brought up his sword on that side. There was a clang of metal striking metal. The force of the blow jarred his arm, but he still managed to twist his wrist to trap his enemy's weapon, stabbed out with his right blade and felt the tip sink into flesh. There was a groan, followed by the clatter of a sword falling onto stone.

The shadows came alive to either side, flowing toward Luker like wraiths.

The Guardian was already moving. Three strides took him into the opposite passage, his footsteps kicking up spray. Two figures waited in the gloom, but Luker was onto them before they were set.

"What—"

The first could only half lift his sword to meet the Guardian's cut, his mouth making a great "O" of surprise as Luker's weapon tore open his throat. The second—a huge man with a mace—tried to jump back to give himself room to swing, only to trip over his own feet.

"Shit!"

Luker caught the first man as he fell, twisted, and pushed him into the path of a third attacker coming up behind. They went down with a splash and a strangled curse. A fourth assailant threw a dagger, but the Guardian blocked it with his Will. A kick to the face of the mace-man trying to rise, then he was off at a scamper into the darkness, his Will-shield now behind him.

A left turn, a right, checking back every few paces for signs of pursuit.

When he finally drew up to listen he could make out voices behind, but fading quickly beneath the growl of the storm. The Guardian smiled. *Looks like I've stirred up the hornet's nest.* All he could do now was hope whichever of the emperor's lackeys was following him got stung.

Half a bell later he emerged onto the road that fronted the port. In the distance rose the wall that circled the harbor, and Luker heard the boom of waves crashing against stone. Spray was thrown up into the air to hang like mist. He tasted salt on the wind.

The inn he was looking for was set apart from the others on the waterfront. A faded wooden sign hung crookedly from a metal pole outside, squeaking as it rocked back and forth. There were bars over the windows, and a dull red glow came from inside. The front door swung open as Luker approached, and two men emerged with their arms linked, staggering as if they crossed the deck of a pitching ship. Inside, a scattering of people sat at crude wooden tables. Their conversation died away as Luker entered, his footsteps thudding on the floorboards. He scanned their faces, but Jenna was not among them.

A short, black-haired woman stood behind the bar. She was using a sliver of wood to clean dirt from under her fingernails. "What'll it be?"

"Ale," Luker replied, placing a coin on the bar.

The barmaid snatched it up. She filled a tankard and set it down with a thunk. As she turned away, Luker put a hand on her arm.

"I'm looking for Jenna Amary," he said.

The woman glanced at something over the Guardian's shoulder. "Never heard of her."

Following the direction of her gaze, Luker saw three men sitting at a table by the window. On the table lay a pair of dice and several piles of coins. One of the men was making a coin dance across the fingers of his right hand. "'Course you haven't," Luker said to the barmaid. "Just tell her a friend is here to see her."

Without waiting for a reply, he crossed to an empty table from which he could watch the rest of the common room. Shrugging out of his sodden cloak, he drank a mouthful of ale before settling back in the shadows to wait. Within a dozen heartbeats the three dice-players were on their feet. One walked over to speak to the barmaid. The blackened scars of a Kerinec tribesman traced an intricate pattern down his cheeks and neck to disappear beneath the collar of his patchwork cloak. A longknife was sheathed in a scabbard at his hip. His two companions made their way to the front door. The first slipped outside; the second closed the door behind him and stood guard in front of it. When his gaze met Luker's, the Guardian raised his drink to him.

Pressure was building behind his eyes, and he hoped Gill was suffering likewise for his use of the Will. It had been a long time since Luker had last had another Guardian turn his power on him, and never before had he locked horns with someone of Gill's strength. He massaged his temples with his thumbs. For now his headache was mild, but the pain would get worse unless he could find some mesina herbs to blunt its edge . . .

A floorboard creaked.

Luker looked up to see the Kerinec tribesman standing a few paces away. His gaze was fixed on Luker like he was trying to look threatening.

A woman's voice spoke. "Back off, Gol. You're out of your league here."

The speaker came to stand next to the tribesman. Dressed all in black, she might have passed on a brief inspection for the Kerinec's shadow. The tribesman cast her a warning look, but she waved him away. "Leave us."

Gol retreated to his table.

The woman's face was hidden by a hood, but Luker recognized her all the same. "Jenna."

Jenna did not respond. Pulling down her hood, she shook out her long dark hair. Luker's breath caught. Her right eye was half-closed, the skin around it bruised and swollen. There were scratches on her neck, and an angry red cut along her jaw. Her lips were tinged blue, and the sweet tang of juripa spirits hung heavy about her. When she spoke again, Luker could hear smoke in the gravel of her voice. "Making new friends?" she said, looking at Gol.

"Don't think he likes me, but I'll get over it. Since when have you needed a minder?"

Jenna ignored the question. "Why are you here?"

"To see you, of course."

"I know that," she snapped. "The question was why."

"Does there have to be a reason?"

"You didn't stop by to tell me you were leaving. Why bother coming now to tell me you're back?"

Luker sipped his ale, his gaze not leaving Jenna's over the rim of his tankard. "Didn't realize I had to report my movements to you. Matter of fact, I'm surprised you even noticed I was gone."

"For a while I didn't. But when the months became years, I assumed you were dead."

"Sorry to disappoint you. Are you going to sit down?" This was going well. Good to know after so much time they could pick things up right where they left off.

Jenna pulled out the bench across from him, then moved it round to the side of the table so she could see the common room.

"Still don't trust me to watch your back?" Luker said.

"Old habits die hard. Were you followed?"

The Guardian's eyes narrowed. "How did you know?"

"Did you lose him?"

"I reckon so. Took him to see the sights of the Warren. Was he one of yours?"

"Of course not. I didn't even know you were back, remember."

"Then how . . ." Understanding came to Luker. "You reckon someone followed me to find you?" Someone who *did* know he was back.

"It's possible."

"Why? Who's after you?"

"None of your damned business." Jenna beckoned to the barmaid, and the woman arrived moments later with an empty glass and a half-full bottle of spirits. Jenna pulled out the cork with her teeth and poured herself a drink. The vapors made Luker's eyes water. "So how long's it been?" Jenna said. "Three years? Four?"

"Two."

"From the sight of you, I'd have thought it was longer."

Luker eyed her cuts and bruises. "We can't all have your pride in our appearance. What happened to your face?"

"I slipped putting on my makeup. What do you bloody well think happened?"

"One of your targets fought back, did he? How rude of him."

Jenna's eyes flashed. "Her, actually. And I made sure she wished she'd gone quietly."

"Not like you to get up close and personal on a job."

The assassin knocked back her drink and refilled her glass. "I had no choice. My employer wanted a *trophy*." She spat out the word. "My crossbow bolt took the bitch in the shoulder. She fell badly from her horse. Lay so still I thought she was dead."

"She didn't offer you the chance of a second shot?"

"I'm glad you find it amusing."

Luker's headache was getting worse, and he rolled his shoulders to relieve the tension in them. "Seems she put up quite a fight. Who was she? Another pro?"

"You don't want to know."

"Try me."

Jenna shook her head. "Even you wouldn't want to get mixed up with these people."

"Then why did you?"

The dice-player guarding the front door had returned to sit with the Kerinec tribesman, Gol. An argument started up over the size of one of the piles of coins. In answer to Luker's question the assassin said, "My agent cut corners—didn't ask as many questions as he should have. Too bad for him. He soon regretted—"

"Spare me the details. I know how this story ends."

Jenna shrugged. "He had it coming. I couldn't risk the woman's friends tracing me through him. No loose ends." She seemed anxious to change the subject. "You still haven't told me where you disappeared to."

"Taradh Dor."

The assassin waited for him to continue. Then, when Luker remained silent, she gulped down another glass of spirits and said, "That's it? Two years explained away in as many words?"

"There isn't much to tell."

"I thought Arandas is where it's all happening. Strange for you to be so far from the action." She smiled the crooked smile he remembered so well. "What's the matter, Luker? Getting a bit old for this, are you?"

He screwed up his face. "I'm thirty-six, not sixty-six."

"If you say so."

At that moment the door to the street burst open. Gol stood up so quickly his chair toppled over behind him. Jenna was also on her feet, a dagger appearing in her right hand. A gust of wind blew rain through the doorway and set the torches flickering. Outside, all was darkness.

A few heartbeats passed, but no one entered.

Then the spell broke, and Gol strode over to the door and slammed it shut. Jenna released her breath and sat down again.

"Bit edgy, aren't we?" Luker said. "You've spent so long in the shadows, you've started jumping at them."

The assassin stabbed her blade into the tabletop and looked at him askance like she thought he might have been the one who opened that door—with his Will. "Why have you come back, Luker? You still haven't told me."

He shrugged. "Didn't find what I was looking for on Taradh Dor."

"Which was?"

"Never worked that out. Hoped I'd know it when I found it."

"I could have saved you the trouble of looking. The place is a shithole."

"No arguments there. Whole Shroud-cursed island smells of fish. As for the islanders themselves . . . miserable bastards, the lot of them. Use the same word for 'stranger' as they do for 'blood enemy.' "

Jenna threw back another glass of spirits. Her cheeks were becoming rosy. "So what happens now? Are you going back to the Guardians?"

Luker told her of his meeting with Gill. The assassin listened without interrupting, her face expressionless. When he finished she said, "You're going to look for this Book?"

There was something in her voice he could not place, but the way his skull was pounding he was in no fit state to think on it. "I'm going to look for Kanon," he corrected her. "If his trail leads me to the Book, so be it. If it doesn't . . ."

"And if it leads to Kanon's grave?"

The argument between Gol and his companion was growing more heated. Luker had to raise his voice to speak over them. "Not a chance. Kanon's too sharp to get caught up in the war with the Kalanese."

"What about this mage he's chasing?"

"You mean, could Mayot Mencada have done for him?" Luker shook his head. "Kanon survived everything the Black Tower threw at him on the night of the Betrayal. Never met a mage yet who could match him."

Jenna pursed her lips. "When do you leave?"

"Tomorrow."

"So soon?"

"Is that allowed?" Luker regretted the words even as he spoke them. The assassin scowled, and for an instant the Guardian thought she would get up and walk away. Instead she reached for the bottle of spirits and poured herself another drink. The silence dragged out. Jenna took a hairband from a pocket and tied her hair in a ponytail. Her expression was contemplative. When she finally looked back at Luker he could see she had made a decision. "I'm coming with you."

It took a few heartbeats for her words to sink in. *Just when I thought I was done with surprises for today.* "Why?" Luker said. "You don't even know Kanon."

"This isn't about Kanon. I've been thinking of leaving Arkarbour for a while. Now seems like a good time."

"Not to visit Arandas, it isn't."

"That's not where I'm heading."

"Then where?"

Jenna looked away. "Why don't you let me worry about that."

She doesn't even know, Luker realized. *She's running, and she doesn't care where to.* Clearly the assassin was more concerned about staying put in Arkarbour than she was about bumping into a Kalanese soulcaster on the Gollothir Plains. *What in Shroud's name has she got herself caught up in?* Luker opened his mouth to speak then shut it again. He knew better than to ask questions when Jenna was in this mood. *Always did like her secrets.* "You should know I'm not traveling alone," he said. "There'll be two others coming."

"Are you afraid to be seen with me?"

"Should I be?"

"They don't need to know who I am."

"And if they recognize you?"

"I don't leave witnesses," Jenna snapped. "I also don't take 'no' for an answer."

Luker searched her eyes for a moment before leaning back against the wall. *Guess that's settled.* Now he thought about it, it might not be such a bad thing having Jenna along. It was three years since they'd made that fateful voyage south from Mercerie. Luker had been sent there to eliminate Keebar Lana, an Erin Elalese senator who'd turned traitor. The Guardian had tracked him down to a mansion in Mercerie's Temple Quarter, but when he climbed to the roof of the Sender's shrine opposite he found Jenna already perched in the one place that gave a clear view of the house's entranceway. It was probably only the sudden appearance of Lana at his front door that had stopped the two of them coming to blows.

Jenna had insisted on taking the killing shot at Lana. After, as the night erupted with the shouts of his guards, Luker and Jenna had parted without a word. By pure chance they'd met again on the road to Koronos, though the assassin had needed convincing that Luker wasn't following her. Later he found out she'd been spotted fleeing the shrine, and was forced to leave Mercerie when Lana's sorcerer, Peledin Kan, began slaughtering every female assassin in the city. The demons he'd sent to pursue her had caught up to her just as she and Luker were renewing their acquaintance outside some nameless village—just as she was training her crossbow on him, in fact. Three years on, she still hadn't thanked him for stepping in to help against her hunters, and even after the demons were dispatched, the journey to Arkarbour had been something of a bumpy ride.

But then anything beat traveling with just a Breaker and a mage for company.

"We leave at dawn," Luker said at last. "Doesn't give you much time to get ready."

"I'm ready now," Jenna replied. This time, her crooked smile was forced. "Can't stand tearful good-byes."

Meaning you've got about as many friends in this Shroud-cursed city as I have. Luker drained his tankard and stood up awkwardly, the backs of his knees pressing against the bench. "We're meeting tonight at the tenth bell. Imperial Stables by the North Gate. I'm going to get some rest." He glanced at the near-empty bottle of spirits on the table. "You should do the same."

"Yes, Father," Jenna muttered. She looked at the door. "And if anyone out there is still following you . . ."

"I'll deal with him. If he trailed me here, though, he may have seen you arrive. Watch your back."

"Always."

Romany despised forests: the roots and brambles that tripped her; the mud that sucked at her sandals; the needleflies that seemed attracted to her skin as if she were smeared in blood honey. It was remarkable, she mused, that so many trees could exist in such a hot climate, but then, as she knew from her studies as an acolyte, the ketar and wolsatta trees that made up the Forest of Sighs were uniquely adapted to the heat and dryness with their deep root systems and waxy leaves. The priestess sighed. It was strange to think she had been so intrigued by the physiology of the trees when she'd first read about them in the temple library, but nature was always more interesting when considered from the comfort of an easy chair.

She was still feeling disorientated after her journey to the forest along the threads of the Spider's sorcerous web, a voyage of scores of leagues completed in as many heartbeats. It was not an experience she wished to repeat—as if her body had been pulled apart and whisked away on a gale born of the Furies themselves. Arriving battered and shaken in the forest, she had been thrown back together by the goddess with unseemly haste. It felt to Romany as if her heart had rematerialized in her mouth. More disturbing still, her waistline appeared to have filled out noticeably from how she remembered it. *The Spider's idea of a joke, no doubt.*

To ensure Romany's arrival was not witnessed, the goddess had deposited her a considerable distance from her destination. The trek had been uphill, naturally, and the priestess's legs were aching from the climb. Forced to hitch up her robe to avoid it dragging in the dirt, her ankles and shins were being scratched bloody by knots of nettleclaw. After what seemed an eternity she arrived, breathing heavily, at the outskirts of the dead city where Mayot Mencada was holed up. The Spider had called this place Estapharriol, which meant "refuge" in the language of the people who once lived here—an unfortunate choice of name, considering the city's history. All that remained of the buildings were crumbling walls and mounds of rubble, interspersed with trees. A few trunks even sprouted from the middle of roads, leaving the flagstones round them cracked and buckled.

The layout of the ruins indicated the buildings here had been clustered tightly together. They were small too, smaller than the quarters of Romany's servants—acolytes, she corrected herself—at the temple. No sign of marble either, just some coarsely veined white stone that reflected the sunlight with a dazzling glare. Sweat trickled into the priestess's eyes, and she wondered if there was a bathhouse in this godforsaken place. Hardly likely, she conceded, for she had yet to see even a single building with its roof intact.

The trees thinned out as she approached the center of the city, and she found herself longing for some shade. The air ahead was filled with the sound of rushing water. Romany came to the first of dozens of stone channels snaking between the ruins, each half filled with water and narrow enough for her to step over. It was a while before she worked out what she was looking at: the River Amber, split into scores of tiny watercourses and redirected through the city. One of the streams had overflowed its channel, flooding the ground to either side. Rather than wade through the muck, Romany decided to circle round. Looking back from a short distance upriver, she saw the watercourse was blocked by the corpse of a dusken deer. Behind it had collected the bodies of scores of coral birds and ruskits.

So it has started, then.

Romany could now sense the invisible strands of death-magic all about. Where they brushed her skin she felt a chill that cut through the stifling heat. The air stank of rot, and she shook out a perfumed handkerchief and held it to her nose. She saw her destination then, rising above the treetops: a vast domed structure beside a densely forested hill, an eighth of a league away. To have survived the millennia, the building must once have been a place of powerful magic, though what significance it had held to the people who used to live here she could not say—the Spider had proved typically frugal when it came to sharing her knowledge of the city.

A quarter of a bell later, Romany stood before the dome. The base of the building had been sculpted to resemble a rocky shore pummeled by waves. Snaking through those foaming waters were the curls of some huge, barbed sea serpent, while higher up the priestess saw a carving of a three-masted ship in full sail. The image stirred an uncomfortable recollection of the one time, five years ago, when she had been reckless enough to surrender the sanctity of dry land . . .

Grimacing, she pushed the memory aside.

The reason for the dome's longevity was readily apparent in the whiff of decaying sorcery that bled from its walls. Not death-magic this time, but . . . something else. The power appeared to have seeped out into the rest of Estapharriol, for the buildings surrounding the dome were more intact than the ones on the outskirts of the city. Romany followed the wall of the dome east until she came to an arched entranceway. Stepping through, she found herself in a corridor. A breeze blew into her face. To either side, the walls were pockmarked with an apparently haphazard arrangement of holes. As the wind entered and exited the openings, it made a rhythmic hissing sound like the lapping of waves. Romany's stomach heaved.

After a dozen paces the passage opened out onto an immense, gloomy chamber. Light filtered through star-shaped openings in a roof so high the priestess half expected to see clouds passing beneath. Around the sides of the dome were the remains of tiered stone seating, while in the center was a square dais with steps leading up to it on all sides. At each corner of the base was a ketar tree, apparently growing from stone. *A false floor then,* Romany surmised, for she could see no roots aboveground. Over the dais, the trees' bare branches intertwined to form a tangled canopy. The floor of the dome was covered in leaves that rippled in the wind.

On a rusty throne near the middle of the dais sat a shrunken, white-haired old man dressed in black robes. His gaze followed Romany as she crossed to stand at the foot of the steps. He might have been expecting her arrival for all the reaction that showed in his bloodshot eyes. She could tell from the stench of sweat that bathing was a lost art to him. He also needed a new tailor, judging by the way his robes swallowed his gaunt frame. With his left hand he stroked a leather-bound book that rested on his lap. Death-magic oozed from its pages.

Romany forced a smile and said in the common tongue, "Ah, Lord Mayot, I believe." She doubted he merited the honorific, but—as with all men—he would be easily swayed by flattery. "I am delighted to make your acquaintance."

Mayot was so long in answering, the priestess had begun to look round for a chair. "Who are you, woman?"

"A worthy question. Alas, modesty forbids me from revealing my identity. Think of me only as . . . a friend."

"A *friend*," Mayot repeated, speaking the word as if it were new to him. "It appears you have me at a disadvantage then, friend. For while you seem to know who I am, I know nothing of you."

"A grievous blow to my pride."

"I take it our meeting here is no coincidence," Mayot went on. "A strange place indeed for a chance encounter, wouldn't you agree?"

"Irrefutable logic, my Lord. My congratulations—"

Mayot's right arm snapped out, and a wave of grainy black sorcery shot from his hand toward Romany.

She stiffened, no time to react . . .

As it was, her magical wards were not unduly troubled, channeling the mage's power away to leave her standing unscathed. She heard an explosion behind, followed by the sound of grinding stone. The leaves on the floor had been thrown up in the wake of the sorcery, and they now started floating down again, scorched black by Mayot's death-magic.

Romany sniffed. "Such deplorable manners," she scolded the old man. "And such foolishness, too, to strike at me before I have even stated my cause."

Mayot's expression showed neither surprise nor remorse. "I think an explanation is called for if you wish to continue this conversation in a more civil fashion. Now, who sent you? Avallon? The Black Tower?"

Romany recalled the names from her discussions with the Spider. "Does my accent sound to you like that of someone from Erin Elal?"

"I'll ask the questions. How did you find me?"

"Why, through that, of course," the priestess said, gesturing to the book in his lap.

"Explain."

"You cannot be blind to the magic radiating from that thing, nor the effect it is having on the forest outside. Did you think your meddling would go undetected?"

"Meddling?" Mayot said softly.

"Well, if I may be blunt, your clumsy attempts to unlock the Book's secrets have proved less than successful to date, am I right?"

The mage's left eyelid began to flutter. "Careful, woman."

Romany had to admire his self-control in the face of her provocation, yet at the same time it made her curious to see how far she could goad him before his composure cracked. "You are finding that the passages are blurred or unintelligible, yes? That the language defies comprehension? That you read some sentences only to discover you have forgotten the words before you reach the end?"

"And you are offering to help, I take it?"

The priestess smiled her most endearing smile, only to see it fall on stony ground. "Precisely. To read the Book of Lost Souls is to traverse a great maze. You might wander for years and still not find what you are seeking. To decipher even the simplest section will take more time than you have."

"Time?" Mayot said. "I have all the time I need."

"Would that were so. Alas, I am not the only person to have been alerted by the Book's . . . reawakening. Your next visitor may not prove as genial as I am."

"Then he will die at my hands."

Romany rolled her eyes. The arrogance of men! "And if Shroud himself has taken an interest? Sent his servants against you?"

Mayot took the bait. "Now why would he do that?"

"Perhaps because he felt threatened."

The mage's eyes glittered. "The Book would give me such power?"

Romany made no response. Instead she put on an exaggerated frown. Let the old man think he had deduced something she would rather have kept secret.

Mayot studied her for a long moment, then continued, "And you expect me to believe that you would just surrender this power to me? Why? What do you stand to gain?"

"Perhaps in promoting your interests, I further my own."

"Which are?"

"Not your concern, my Lord."

Mayot considered. "You say it would take centuries to learn the Book's secrets. How is it, then, that you claim to know them?"

A fair point, but Romany was ready for it. "Not *know* them, merely how to *unlock* them."

"Nevertheless, the question stands. I sense an immortal's hand in this."

Not a muscle twitched in the priestess's face. "You flatter me."

"That's not what I meant, as you well know."

Romany unleashed the voice she reserved for her most troublesome acolytes. "Do not presume to tell me what I do and do not know." An evasion, of course, but all part of the game. Her caginess would do nothing to allay Mayot's suspicions, but doubtless she'd already done enough to catch this particular fish on her hook. All she had to do now was wait for the old man's ambition to reel him in.

Sure enough, it was the mage who at last broke the silence. "I assume this help of yours involves me handing over the Book to you."

"Not at all. You need only lower the wards you have placed round the dais. A few moments—"

Mayot's chuckle cut her off. "Ah. Now I understand."

"No, you do not!" Romany said, stamping her foot. "If I wanted the Book for myself, would I not take it *before* I delivered its power to you?"

"I see no reason to put that to the test."

"And if I should decide to dismantle your defenses myself?"

The mage clasped the Book to his chest. "If you could, you would have done so already."

Not true, but battering down the old man's shields would serve only to advertise her presence here as clearly as Mayot had heralded his. "That would hardly be a good way to build trust between us, my Lord. Trust we will need if we are to work together in this."

The mage snorted. "You expect me to trust you?"

"I don't see that you have any choice. Without my aid you will still be wearing your eyes out on page one of that thing"—she nodded at the Book—"when Shroud taps you on the shoulder."

"So you say."

The priestess tutted her frustration. *Spider give me strength!* Could the old man not see the Book was useless to him without her aid? Did his stubbornness eclipse even his avarice? *Too arrogant to know he is outmatched, too proud to accept help when it is offered.* But these were only the opening exchanges in the game, and Romany had countless other moves to confound him with.

The first of which was indifference.

"It would seem," she said, "that you have yet to grasp the true gravity of your predicament. I will leave you to reflect on my offer. Perhaps by the time I return—"

"You cannot leave, woman. Not now. Not knowing what you do."

An empty threat, but all the more irritating for that. "I said I was coming back, did I not? In the meantime, I think I will take a bath." The priestess looked round. "Where are your servants?"

"Servants?" Mayot squinted at her. "I have no servants."

Romany stared at him.

Holding a hand out to the wall for support, Parolla followed the spiral staircase down into blackness. It had taken her longer than expected to dispel the sorceries that barred the entrance to the crypt. The high priest's defenses demonstrated a level of sophistication that spoke of days of careful crafting, an almost feverish zeal. Parolla's hands had trembled as she undid his work, her excitement building as each layer of wards peeled away. What could the high priest be so anxious to keep hidden from prying eyes? After years of searching, could Parolla dare to hope her quest was nearing its end?

Her breathing sounded harsh in the confines of the stairwell. She had taken one of the wall torches from the temple, but its light was beginning to dwindle, as if the flames were being smothered by the weight of darkness below. The stairs became increasingly cracked and worn, and she was forced to slow her pace. A short time later the steps came to an end, and she drew up.

The closeness of the stairwell was replaced by yawning emptiness, and Parolla stood at the brink of it. The light from her torch penetrated no more than a dozen paces beyond a narrow precipice. To her right, a forest of pillars rose from the gloom below and disappeared into blackness above. The nearest pillar, less than a score of armspans away, was covered in carved images. Parolla held out her torch and peered at them, only for the flames to gutter and die.

Shadows rushed in from all sides.

Muttering an oath, Parolla tossed the torch over the precipice and started counting. She reached five before it hit something—the floor of the crypt, no doubt—with a muted clatter. Drawing her cloak about her, she waited for her eyes to grow accustomed to the dark. A faint glow came from far below and to her right, its source obscured by the pillars. Parolla paused, considering. There were no obvious ways down to whatever lay beneath, but the high priest would not have gone to the effort of sealing this place off if it was inaccessible. And since she hadn't seen any passages leading off the stairwell during her descent . . .

Lowering herself to her hands and knees, she groped blindly along the vertical rock face below her until she discovered a gash hacked into it. Twisting around, she swung her legs out over the ledge. Her left boot scuffed stone until she found the first precarious foothold. The second was farther down than she would have liked, and little more than a scratch in the rock.

Whispering a silent prayer to the ether, she began to descend.

By the time her feet touched solid ground again, both her fingers and her nerves were scraped raw. She turned and put her back to the wall. The glow she had noticed earlier was now in front of her: a rectangular doorway of pale light, fifty paces away. To either side, rows of pillars, each as wide as Parolla was tall, faded into darkness. A sound came from her right, and she looked across, but saw nothing. She tilted her head and listened. All was quiet, save for the pounding of blood in her ears . . .

No, there it was again—a noise like the flap of leathery wings. *Bats?* Parolla let out a breath, silently berating herself for her skittishness.

She edged forward, fragments of stone and shattered floor tiles cracking underfoot. There was a dusty dryness to the air that soon coated the inside of her mouth, and she raised a hand to her lips to deaden the sound of a cough. Shapes took form in the shadows ahead—two huge statues flanking an altar of similar scale. From the altar pulsed echoes of death-magic. Its stone sides were covered with carvings. She walked round to the other side where the light was brightest, then moved closer to inspect them. An orgy of bloodlust was being acted out by a throng of animal-headed figures wearing enraptured expressions. The light playing across the carvings gave the impression of movement, as if the souls of the figures were trapped within the stone.

This is no crypt, Parolla realized. She was standing on sanctified ground. It had to be another temple, but to which god? And why had Shroud built his own shrine over it? She turned to examine the statues that flanked the altar. Both were unmistakably male. Standing on a mound of skulls, the figure on the left was so tall that its shoulders and head were lost in the darkness above. Its right hand clutched air where a spear must once have been. Nothing remained of the second statue save for the figure's lower torso and legs around which were curled tongues of stone flame. Its upper body had been hewn away from left shoulder to right hip. What hand could have inflicted such a blow? More importantly, who would dare deface a god's image in his own temple?

Parolla turned to the rectangular doorway from which the light came.

There was an explosion of noise from the darkness round her. Something brushed her face.

She threw herself to the left, rolled, then rose on one knee and flung out her right hand toward the source of the sound. Death-magic erupted from her fingers. The sorcery split the air between the two statues before rumbling on into the heart of the temple.

To be swallowed by darkness.

Ahead of Parolla, nothing, no one.

She let her sorcery die out. Moments later there was a crack of stone, followed by a thunderous boom as one of the pillars came crashing down, then a series of smaller concussions. Parolla's eyes darted as she searched the darkness overhead, fearing the roof of the temple would cave in. A cloud of dust rolled over her, and she turned her head to one side, narrowing her eyes to slits. She breathed in a mouthful of powdered stone, and she coughed until her eyes streamed. Silence descended again.

Then, faintly from above, Parolla heard the flutter of tiny wings. Shaking her head, she rose to her feet. *Coolly done.*

There was little point now in trying to move stealthily—if anything lay in wait ahead, her theatrics were sure to have alerted it to her presence. Releasing her power, Parolla raised her left hand. A glow enveloped it, driving the darkness back.

Approaching the doorway again, she paused to scan the chamber beyond. No more than a score of paces across, it was empty save for the remains of a pulpit in its center. Blocks of smashed stone and shards of pottery covered the floor. Along each of the room's other three walls was a doorway. From the one to Parolla's right, rubble spilled into the chamber; from the one to her left came a drip, drip of water. The light she had been following emanated from the doorway ahead.

She crossed to it before stopping at the threshold and looking inside. The room was of a similar size to the one she had just passed through. Dominating the wall opposite was an oval-shaped portal enclosed by a frame of metal. The surface of the portal shimmered like oil on water. Her pulse quickening, Parolla took a step forward. Then halted. There was a ripple in the air in front of her, a smell of dank fur.

She was not alone.

"Show yourself," she said.

The echoes of her voice had almost died away when light began to coalesce to form a tall, spectral figure. Clad in blood-spattered hides, he held a spear in his right hand. His long black hair, braided with fetishes, hung in a tangle to his shoulders. Filed teeth protruded from a prominent lower jaw to overlap his top lip. When he spoke his voice was rusty from lack of use. "You go no farther."

Parolla's brows knitted. The language used by the newcomer was a variation on an ancient Mirillian dialect—a dialect she had never heard spoken before. A knowledge of archaic languages was, though, just one of the . . . gifts . . . carried in her blood. "What is this place, *sirrah?*" she asked, matching his tongue.

"Turn back now," the stranger said. "On sanctified ground."

"Sanctified to which god?"

"Name mean nothing to you."

"Because he is dead?" Parolla took the man's silence for confirmation. "When was he killed?"

"In Second Age."

Her eyes widened. "The Time of the Ancients? That was two score thousand years ago. You have been here all that time?" *Alone?*

The spearman shrugged. "Commanded to guard portal."

Parolla scowled. *As if that were answer enough.* Such was the tyranny of the gods, twisting devotion until sacrifice was made to feel like a privilege, until allegiance became no more than slavery by another name. And what did the immortals offer in return? "Your *mekra* is gone, *sirrah.* I'd say your loyalty is misplaced."

"You not understand. Force of master's command remains."

"Nevertheless, do you really think you could stop me if I chose to pass?"

The warrior's form glowed suddenly bright. He grasped his spear in both hands and lowered its tip until it was level with her chest. "We find out."

Parolla blinked against the light. "And if I were to release you from you bonds?"

The spearman went still. "Your power rival that of gods?"

"No," she conceded. "But sorcery fades. Whatever magical chains your *mekra* forged about you will have weakened over the millennia. Perhaps I can break them."

The stranger's spear remained pointed at her chest.

"Is your prison so appealing, *sirrah,* that you would refuse the chance to escape it? Shall I leave you, then, to eternity?"

The man regarded her impassively. He adjusted his grip on his spear, first sliding his hands apart before bringing them close together again, and all the while shifting on the balls of his feet as if he meant to attack at any moment. A score of heartbeats passed before he finally relaxed his stance and raised his weapon to the vertical. "What you want?"

Better. "What is your name?"

"Olakim."

Parolla's gaze strayed to the portal on the wall behind him. "Well, Olakim, you can start by telling me where this portal leads."

"Free first. Then answer."

"You are in no position to make demands."

Olakim considered this, then said, "Leads to dead lands."

Parolla's heart missed a beat. "You're sure? The realm of the dead?"

"One of them."

"You mock me. There is only one underworld."

"No," Olakim said firmly, his voice betraying emotion for the first time. "Old underworld—kingdom of master—destroyed by usurper."

"Usurper? His name?"

"Shroud."

Parolla's mind was racing. "You are saying Shroud deposed your *mekra*? Took his place as Lord of the Dead?"

Olakim nodded. "In Second Age, pantheon riven by war. Shroud betrayed master. Took Book of Lost Souls for his own. Dead lands laid waste in clash that followed."

"And the portal here . . . it leads to that broken world?"

He nodded again.

Parolla began to turn away in disgust. It seemed this was not, after all, the gateway she was looking for . . . Then she stopped. Assuming that Olakim was telling the truth, of course. She glanced back at the spearman, studying his face for any hint of duplicity. Could she afford to trust his word? What if he were actually one of Shroud's servants? What if he knew that he could not prevent her passing, and so instead sought to trick her into turning back? "Stand aside, *sirrah*," she said. "I wish to see for myself."

The tip of Olakim's spear came down again, and he dropped into a fighting crouch. "Cannot let pass. Said would release me."

"So I did." Parolla reached out with her senses. The sorcery holding the warrior bore the same signature as that which seeped from the altar in the main chamber. The invisible bonds had grown frayed and brittle, and Parolla severed them with a flick of her mind. "It's done."

With the sundering of Olakim's shackles he had become once more a creature of flesh and blood, and the glow round the spearman faded. His image darkened and solidified. A ruddy hue returned to his cheeks. He took a deep breath, his chest swelling with a sound like creaking leather. Then he looked about as if seeing the world with new eyes.

Parolla tensed herself for his attack.

Instead the warrior grinned at her. "Great gratitude."

She returned his smile. "Now, stand aside."

He did so.

Parolla approached the portal. The device seemed straightforward enough—no choice of destinations to select from, no magical traps woven into the glyphs that decorated the frame. All she had to do was . . . awaken it. Parolla lifted a hand, and the surface of the portal rippled as her power brushed against it. Colors swirled to form patterns that drew back toward the frame. The darkness left in their wake paled like a dawn sky, blurred shadows sharpening to form swirls of cloud.

There was a roar like a storm-swept sea, and a chaotic swell of sorcery burst outward. With a despairing cry, Parolla raised wards to shield herself. Just in time. Even then when the magic struck her defenses she was hurled a score of paces back to slam into the wall behind. Her head cracked against stone, and she slumped to the floor, lights flashing before her eyes. She tried to lever herself into a sitting position, only to fall back. *Fool!* she rebuked herself. Most likely this had been Olakim's plan all along: let her open the portal, then strike when she was incapacitated. She thought she heard a footfall now, and she rolled to one side, expecting to hear his spear tip graze the stone where she'd been lying.

Nothing.

Her vision was clearing, and when she looked up she saw the warrior still standing beside the portal, his face expressionless.

But no doubt laughing inside.

Wincing, Parolla heaved herself to her feet. A wave of nausea swept over her, and she bent double, retching. The surge of energies continued to crash against her defenses, but her blood had risen in answer to her need, and her power now ran like acid through her veins. Pushing back against the sorcerous maelstrom, she drove it through the portal and caged it behind a barrier of invisible wards.

The sudden silence left her ears ringing.

She spat vomit to the floor. The back of her head tingled, and when she raised a hand to it she felt a swelling the size of a mitrebird's egg. The wound was already starting to heal, though, the lump shrinking beneath her fingers until all that remained was the blood matting her hair. Letting her hand fall, she glared at Olakim. "Thanks for the warning."

The spearman's look was unapologetic. "Did warn. Said world destroyed by sorceries. You not listen."

Grumbling, Parolla staggered back to the portal. Through it she saw a featureless wilderness of blasted rock and sorcerous clouds. Not a single tree broke the uniformity of the landscape. Olakim had been telling the truth, then. A barren world, long dead.

And for now, at least, an end to her hopes. Shroud's realm remained out of reach.

Parolla sighed. "Is it all like this?"

Olakim did not respond, but then he did not need to. If the storms had been caused by Shroud's clash with his predecessor they must have raged for millennia. Nothing could have survived out there.

A thought came to her. "Do you know where your *mekra* fell, *sirrah*? Was it near this portal?"

Olakim shrugged. "You still go through?"

"Maybe."

"Why?"

Parolla hesitated. She had no reason to trust the man, but perhaps he could still be of use to her. "I seek a way into Shroud's realm."

"Think find one in dead lands?"

"Where vast magics are released, they can burn a way through to the place from which the sorcerer's power originates. I have seen the phenomenon before, in the gateways leading to the demon worlds. Maybe the same has happened here. Maybe a portal to the underworld was created by Shroud's magic."

"You search entire world to find?"

He had a point. If Parolla passed through the portal, how long would she be able to withstand the barrage of sorceries? A day or two? Enough time to seek out what she was looking for? The storm obscured everything beyond a few score paces in each direction. If a way through to Shroud's realm existed, she might pass within a stone's throw of it without knowing. And if she needed to return here, what chance would she have of retracing her steps? Parolla hissed in frustration. Could she even trust Olakim not to close the way behind her? And if *he* did not, might one of Shroud's priests?

She began to turn away, then froze.

There was movement beyond the portal. On a rocky ridge a short distance away, a crowd of wraithlike figures was gathering. They started drifting toward Parolla like a bank of mist.

Olakim moved up to stand alongside her.

"Who are they, *sirrah*?" she asked.

"Spirits of dead."

"Then why are they here, and not in Shroud's realm?"

"Not know. Perhaps left behind when world destroyed. Perhaps sent to this place as punishment."

"They are trapped here? For eternity?"

Olakim shook his head. "Souls will die in time. Some survive longer than others."

The unlucky ones. Parolla watched the ghosts for a heartbeat longer before looking back at the spearman. "They sense the portal."

"Of course. Chance of escape. Will you open way to them?"

"Why should I?"

Olakim made no response.

The spirits had now come to within touching distance of the portal, but they could not pass through the wards Parolla had fashioned. Her gaze was drawn to a man in the front rank—a Jekdal with the scarred cheeks of a warrior just passed through the rites of adulthood. Shoulders hunched, he stood with his arms hanging by his sides, his dead eyes focused on nothing. The edges of his form were blurred, as if his soul were unraveling.

Parolla scanned the dozens of spirits behind him. She had no idea what these people had done to warrant their imprisonment here, nor what she might unleash on the citizens of Xavel if she freed them. Then again, she mused, if these souls were released, Shroud would surely come to hear of their escape. With luck, their loss would irritate him greatly. Parolla smiled faintly. If she could not confront the god in person, she could at least send him a message. *One he won't be able to ignore for a change.*

"I will not lower my shield," she said finally to Olakim, "but the sorcerous storm will gradually weaken it. In time it will fail completely." *By which point I should be long gone.*

"And if others come to close portal?"

"You will just have to stand guard over it a while longer, *sirrah*."

Was the spearman's look one of disapproval? Resignation? It was so difficult to read anything in his expression. Would he risk staying here until her sorcery faded? If the priests in Shroud's temple came to investigate the opening of the portal, Olakim might find himself enslaved again, or worse. Shrugging, Parolla turned away. She had done her part. The rest was in Olakim's hands now.

Then the realization struck her. Since the portal was of no use to her, she would have to leave this place by the same way she had come.

Another thought followed close behind.

The Hunt.

Parolla closed her eyes.

She could only pray now that Ceriso di Monata had been able to buy her the time he had promised.

CHAPTER 4

MOTTLE'S DESTINATION served only to pique Ebon's curiosity—not the throne room as he had expected, but an antechamber to the Royal Quarters. This was to be a private gathering then, not a meeting of the full King's Council as Mottle had implied. Ebon's gaze fixed on the mage's back. A deliberate deceit on the old man's part? He could never be sure of anything where Mottle was concerned. The mage was clearly enjoying himself, though, judging by the spring in his step and the discordant tune he was whistling.

Mottle threw open the door to the Royal Quarters before stepping back to allow Ebon to enter first. The chamber was filled with smoke from a fire in a grate along the left-hand wall. A tall wooden chair had been drawn close to the flames, and in it sat the king, a blanket draped over his shoulders. Isanovir was staring into the fire, the Serrate Crown lying forgotten in his lap. The flesh had melted from his face, and he appeared to have aged a year for every week Ebon had been gone. The prince felt a weight settle on him. *A mercy I was not here to witness his decline.*

Also present in the chamber were Prince Rendale, General Reynes, and Queen Rosel. Ebon's mother sat in a chair as far away from the king as decorum would permit. She wore a long blue gown buttoned up to the neck, and her hair had been scraped back to give her face a severe cast. In her right hand she held a nail file that darted across the nails of her left. *Sharpening her claws again.* Rosel, evidently sensing his scrutiny, looked up. She frowned when she saw the wound at his temple, but no more than she did at the dust on his clothes.

General Reynes stood to Ebon's right. His ever-present cinderhound was curled between his legs, and the soldier crouched to scratch it behind the ears. His face fell as Mottle scuttled over to speak to him.

There was no sign of either Domen Janir or the chancellor.

Ebon's gaze finally settled on his brother. Rendale was pretending an interest in one of the tapestries on the walls. His shirt and trousers were spotted with food stains, and his unkempt, wavy black hair hung down over his eyes. Seeing Ebon, he sauntered over.

"Ebon," Rendale said. "Words cannot express how relieved I am to see you."

"Just as I am surprised to see you. Are the taverns not open yet?"

"They had to drag me out kicking and screaming, it's true. Thank the Watcher you weren't there to witness my humiliation."

Ebon could feel blood trickling down his cheek, and he pulled out a handkerchief and lifted it to his temple. "Do you know what this is about?"

"Our beloved mother would say only that my attendance was required. Perhaps she needs someone to straighten chairs when we're done." He raised an inquiring eyebrow at Ebon's wound.

"I had a brush with the Kinevar near the forest," Ebon explained.

"I thought you were in the borderlands, putting the world to rights."

"A fragile truce was the best I could manage. I have ordered Yemar and Cenil to send their firstborn to Majack to ensure their cooperation."

Rendale's eyes twinkled. "As I recall, Domen Yemar has sired only daughters. His eldest, Maria, is said to be a vision."

"I do not recall."

"Ah, but then Lamella has blinded you to all else. My eyes, on the other hand, are always open to beauty."

Before Ebon could respond, the door to the chamber opened and Chancellor Tamarin strode in. *Fashionably late, as usual.* Ebon was beginning to suspect the man enjoyed making others wait—a measure, perhaps, of his growing confidence now the king's health was failing. Ignoring the others present, Tamarin crossed to stand behind Isanovir's chair. Firelight reflected off his bald pate as he bent to speak in the king's ear. Isanovir seemed oblivious.

After a few heartbeats the chancellor straightened. "My Lords and Lady. Thank you for coming."

Ebon pursed his lips. It seemed they were going to start without Domen Janir, which could only mean his uncle had not been invited. *This should be interesting.*

"A messenger arrived this morning," Tamarin went on, "bringing news from the north. It seems Consel Garat Hallon of Sartor is set on paying us a visit. He is due to arrive on Black Saint's Day, two weeks hence."

The nail file paused in Rosel's fingers. "Did he say *why* he is coming?"

General Reynes did not look up from stroking his cinderhound. "I think we can guess—war."

"Well if he's looking for an excuse to start one, it won't take him long to find it. There's the small matter of our forces massing near the Sartorian border."

Reynes shrugged. "The consel won't learn anything by coming here that his spies haven't told him already."

"Nevertheless, he'll view the deployment as a provocation."

"Better he sees we're ready for war than open to an attack."

"And if we give him the justification he seeks to strike first?"

Ebon held up his hands. "Enough. We have been through this before. If the Sartorians want a war, they will start one no matter what we say or do. The question is whether we need to step up our preparations. General, what is the precise disposition of our armies?"

Reynes gathered his thoughts. "The Bronze Guard has moved north to reinforce Kolamin. General Ton has begun fortifying the strongholds along the Sametta River. The Blue Shields and the Plains Guard already have contingents stationed there. More will follow before the year is out."

"And the Sartorians?"

It was the chancellor who answered. "There are reports that Consel Garat Hallon has won a decisive victory in his war against the Almarian League. The city of Villandry has fallen, and the League is suing for peace. Sartorian troops are returning in large numbers from the west."

General Reynes said, "I think we can assume they won't sit on their hands for long. The offensive will come in the spring."

Ebon saw his unease mirrored in the faces round him. The escalation in hostilities between Sartor and the Almarian League on its western border had brought Galitia a welcome respite from the threat of invasion by its northern neighbor. Now it seemed the years of peace were coming to an end. "Will we be ready?"

"We'll have to be. Sartorian troops are converging on Camessil. They won't risk provoking the Merceriens by crossing the Sametta River west of Kolamin, so the attack will come from the north. We can't match the Sartorians' numbers, meaning we'll have to fight smart. Caches of food and weapons have been concealed throughout the wildlands and the forests north of Linnar, enough to support scores of small fighting units. When the Sartorians come, we'll burn the land ahead of them, disrupt their supply lines behind, and hope they flounder when they reach the Sametta."

"And the bridges?"

"Pulled down or rigged to fall." Reynes's cinderhound rolled onto its back, and the general scratched its belly. "Come spring, the river will be flooded with snowmelt from the White Mountains. We'll have a few surprises ready for the Sartorians when they try to cross."

And no doubt the Sartorians will have some for us.

The chancellor cleared his throat. "What of the lands north of the Sametta? Are you suggesting we surrender them without a fight?"

"With or without a fight," Reynes replied, "we lose them."

"And Linnar?" Ebon said. "The city will be cut off."

The general shrugged. "The defenses are being strengthened. Janir thinks he can hold."

And, as ever, my uncle's mind is not for turning. "The Sartorians will not leave an enemy city holding out behind their front line. The consel will throw everything he has at it."

"Then Janir will stand alone," Rosel said. "We cannot sacrifice troops just to indulge his pigheadedness."

A maid entered, and the room fell silent. Seeing she was the center of attention, the girl scampered to the hearth and scattered a handful of powders on the fire before retreating. The heady scent of ganda spices filled the chamber.

Ebon looked at the chancellor. "Where does the balance of power lie in Sartor? The rise of this Garat Hallon has been remarkable."

"Strictly speaking, the Patrician remains in command, but there can be no question the consel is pulling the strings. Presumably he intends to retain the Patrician as a figurehead until he is ready to make the transition of power official. Meanwhile he tightens his hold on Sartor by installing his supporters in positions of influence."

"Has there been no opposition to his maneuverings?"

"None worth mentioning. The war with the Almarian League has seen Garat's star rise far. He is now commander of the Sartorian armies, and every success on the battlefield strengthens his hand." Tamarin glanced at Mottle. "There are also reports of a powerful sorceress in his employ. A woman called Ambolina."

Mottle nodded gravely. "Her name has been making ripples on the Currents—"

Ebon held up a hand to interrupt. "Later." Then, to the chancellor, "The title 'consel,' what does it mean?"

"It is an ancient honorific that Garat Hallon resurrected when he first came to prominence. I suspect it means whatever he wants it to mean."

"What do we know about him?"

"First son of a minor noble who died a few years ago under suspicious circumstances. He is said to be ambitious, intelligent, educated . . ." The chancellor paused. "He is also, lest we forget, the liege lord of the Sartorian village that Domen Janir . . . eradicated."

Ebon let out a slow breath. "That was five years ago."

"I think it unlikely the consel has forgotten the affair."

"If he comes seeking reparation he will be wasting his time. With Irrella's death . . . My uncle will not so much as offer an apology."

"No doubt the consel is counting on it."

Ebon looked across at Isanovir to see if he was paying attention. The king's gaze, though, remained on the fire. Ebon could have done with his father's advice on what had been said, but it seemed Isanovir's illness had broken his spirit as well as his body.

Mottle strode into the center of the room, smoothing his robe as if he were conscious of his disheveled appearance. "Much though he is loath to be the bearer of yet more ill tidings, your humble servant is honor bound to raise a further matter of consternation. Upheaval in the Forest of Sighs! Disturbances of the direst portent! Prince Ebon's wounds bear testimony to the veracity of Mottle's words if ever you were to doubt them, which of course you would not—"

"On my ride north from the borderlands," Ebon cut in, "I encountered a Kinevar raiding party, more than fivescore strong." He turned to Reynes. "They attacked a village in daylight, just a couple of bells from here."

The general rose from his crouch. "It's been coming, your Highness. I've sent three patrols into the forest this past fourday. Not one man has returned."

"Patrols? Why?"

"The River Amber has been poisoned. You must have seen it on your ride through the city."

The chancellor spoke. "Disease is spreading through the poorer quarters. Not in itself a concern, admittedly, but with the outbreak of Yellow Plague last year . . ."

Ebon considered this, his gaze still on Reynes. "To blight a river like the Amber would take a sizable force."

"I know what you're thinking, and you can forget it. Missing scouts or not, we'd have had word if an army was close."

"Then what's behind the poisoning?"

All eyes turned to Mottle. The mage sighed. "Alas, the sordid taint of the forest's earth-magic makes it impossible for Mottle's arts to penetrate its borders—earth is dominant over air, yes, just as air rules water, water fire, and fire earth. But the Currents bear warning of a convergence to the south and west."

"Convergence?" Reynes said. "Of what?"

"Power. Something is drawing energies to it like a lodestone."

"Is it a threat?"

"Unknown as yet. The pattern is still forming."

Reynes snorted. "That's it? That's all you've got?" He crouched again to stroke his cinderhound. "As ever, the mage talks much but says little. By the time he's got anything useful to tell us, the war will be over."

Mottle scratched at an armpit. "The general believes, perhaps, that the future is an open book to peruse at one's leisure? A grave misapprehension! The Currents carry only fragments of what is and what has been, not of what is to come."

Rosel pointed a finger at him. "Mage, could this convergence have anything to do with Consel Garat Hallon?"

"Certainly not! He does not control such power. Indeed, such power is beyond control."

"Is it directed against us?"

"Unknown."

"Then what do you suggest we do about it?"

Mottle looked puzzled. "Do? Why, nothing, my Queen. What can one do when a storm bears down, save bar the shutters and hope the brunt of its fury falls elsewhere?"

Reynes grunted. "For once we are in agreement."

"Nevertheless," Ebon said, "we should increase patrols along the borders of the forest, bolster the village garrisons. If a strike comes, we must not be unprepared."

The general grimaced, but made no response. It did not need saying that, if they were attacked from both west and north at the same time, no amount of preparation would save them.

The chancellor raised his hands. "I suggest any further deliberations should await the convening of the full King's Council. We have two weeks to make ready for the consel's arrival. I will use the time to invite delegations from Mercerie and Koronos to the reception. Perhaps Garat Hallon will be less inclined to aggression if there are witnesses present. The king will receive the consel in—"

"No."

Ebon started. The voice had been his father's.

Tamarin turned to the king. "Your Majesty?"

"I will not host Garat Hallon," Isanovir said. "Ebon will."

Ebon exchanged a look with the chancellor. "Is that wise, Father? The consel will not be slow to take insult. He will expect the king."

"And he shall have him." Isanovir lifted the crown in a trembling hand and tossed it to Ebon, who caught it awkwardly. "It's yours, take it." His father slumped back in his chair.

A heavy silence had fallen on the room, the only sound the crack and pop of wood on the fire. The crown felt cold and heavy in Ebon's hand. "Why?" he asked. "Why now?"

When Isanovir spoke there was bitterness in his voice. "Would you have our enemy see me like this? Look at me! A kingdom is only as strong as its king. The consel will see in me a nation ripe for the picking."

"The physicians—"

"No! My time is almost up, Ebon. You know it as well as I do. I can see it in your eyes." He raised his voice. "I can see it in all your eyes."

Ebon's response was forestalled by a commotion in the next room. The door to the chamber was thrown open with such force that it crashed against the wall and rebounded, shuddering. Reynes's cinderhound was on its feet, growling.

Domen Janir filled the doorway, but Ebon could still make out a maid on the floor behind him, a bruise forming on her cheek. Janir's face was flushed, and veins throbbed at his temples. "What is the *meaning* of this? Why was I not told about this meeting?" His gaze settled on Ebon and the crown in his hands. The color drained from his face. "Isanovir," he said, "what have you done?"

"What I should have done a long time ago."

Janir pointed at Ebon. "You would leave the kingdom in the hands of this . . . this *boy*?"

For a moment Isanovir's eyes flashed with their old strength. "This 'boy,' as you call him, is twenty-four—"

"He is possessed!"

Ebon kept his expression even. Janir could not know the spirits had returned, but then his uncle had never believed they'd left him the first time. *For once he was right to doubt.*

Isanovir tried to stand, but fell back in his chair. His breathing was ragged. "You go too far, Janir. He is my son."

Queen Rosel spoke. "The spirits are gone, Domen, as you well know."

"Gone?" Janir said. "How can you be certain?"

"Because Ebon tells me so. Can you prove otherwise?"

The domen looked round the room. His voice took on a more reasonable tone. "We have *all* seen people taken by the spirits. How many have *you* known to recover? Not one!" He waved a hand in Ebon's direction. "Why should *he* be different?"

"I've heard enough," Rosel said.

Janir rounded on her. "I'm not finished! So what if the boy seems himself *now*? How do we *know* his mind is his own? Maybe the spirits have been waiting for a moment such as this to take control."

"You have a suggestion, Domen?" the chancellor asked.

"Perhaps a steward should assume command until we can be sure of the boy's reason."

"And you are volunteering yourself, I take it?"

"Who else has a better claim?"

"And how long," the queen said, "before you are satisfied the risk has passed? Five years? Ten? You're a fool if you expect us to believe you would ever relinquish power."

"You question my honor? Isanovir, hear me. The boy is untried."

The chancellor spoke. "And is there not experience enough in this room to guide him, Domen?"

Ebon's eyebrows lifted. He had not expected support from that particular quarter, but the chancellor's motives would be colored, as ever, by self-interest. Not that Ebon needed Tamarin's backing. The kingship was his right, his burden, and no one was going to take it from him. "I am tired of people talking about me as if I were not here," he said, meeting Janir's gaze. "Tell me, Uncle, you have heard the news about Consel Garat Hallon's visit?"

Janir was stunned silent for a few heartbeats. "He's coming here? The snake would deliver himself into my hands?"

"He comes to talk."

"And you would treat with him? Then you are more of a fool than he is. He comes to start a war!"

"And if you are wrong?" Ebon looked about him. "What if we are all wrong? What if the consel comes to petition for peace?" He swung back to Janir. "Would you refuse him? I was there when Irrella died, remember. You swore—"

"I know what I said!"

"Then explain to us, Uncle, how the consel is to speak with his head on the end of your spear. If Garat Hallon wants peace, can you put aside your enmity and parley with him?"

A slow smile crept over Janir's face. "Save your pretty words for that wench of yours." He looked round. "Let the King's Council select Isanovir's successor."

"The Council has no standing on matters—"

"Then perhaps it is time that it *did*!"

Ebon eyed him skeptically. Not even his uncle was deluded enough to believe he would command the support of the domens, but there was more at stake here than who had the larger following. A king did not rule by council. "Enough. Centuries of convention cannot be disregarded simply because it serves your—"

"Nor sheltered behind because it serves *yours*!"

"Interrupt me again, and I will have you put in irons."

Janir gave a strangled choke. "You threaten *me*!"

"I am your king," Ebon said. "Whether you approve or not means nothing to me. Now, I am done talking with you. I want your oath. Here, before these witnesses. Kneel and swear allegiance."

His uncle barked a laugh, then spun round and took a step toward the door.

"Mottle," Ebon said. "If you please."

The door slammed shut.

Janir stumbled to a halt, before turning to face Ebon again, his hands clenched into fists.

Transferring the Serrate Crown to his left hand, Ebon drew his saber in his right. "What is to be, Uncle? I trust I do not have to spell out the options for you. Choose, or I will choose for you."

"You wouldn't dare—"

"Choose!"

His uncle's chest was heaving, and his shirt showed sweat patches beneath his arms. Again, he looked round the chamber for support, his expression darkening all the while.

Ebon's gaze flickered to his father. In all likelihood Isanovir had arranged this gathering of key players not just to discuss Garat Hallon, but also to firm up support for Ebon's claim to the throne. And while Janir had unquestionably complicated matters with his unscheduled appearance, in this company his uncle remained isolated from those who might have backed him. Isolated, and now trapped. Janir knew it too. His frustration showed in his look, and for a heartbeat his right hand strayed to the hilt of his sword. *Do it,* Ebon silently urged him. At least then this would be finished now. For even if Janir *did* pledge his support here, his backing would last only as long as it took him to return to Linnar.

Instead, Janir gave a wordless growl and dropped to one knee. He would not look at Ebon, but he spoke his oath clearly enough to carry to those present.

From the corner of his eye, Ebon saw movement. Glancing across, he watched Mottle kneel as well, a hint of a smile on the old man's face. After a pause, Rendale, General Reynes, Rosel, and finally the chancellor followed suit.

Isanovir remained seated in his chair, staring at the fire.

With a grunt, Janir pushed himself to his feet and stalked from the room.

From the shadows of an alley, Luker kept watch on the gates to the Imperial Stables. His mood was as black as the storm clouds overhead. After leaving Jenna he had returned to the Sacrosanct to find his old room filled with dust and memories that were better left undisturbed. Sitting on the floor, he'd closed his eyes and spirit-walked in an attempt to locate Kanon, but the distance to Arandas was too great, as he had known it would be. Hadn't stopped him trying, though, had it? What had he expected to find, Kanon sitting next to a Shroud-cursed bonfire, just waiting to guide him in? Instead, Luker had stumbled across some alien presence abroad in the dark emptiness, and he'd been forced to flee back to his body. The experience had left him on edge, and he'd paced the Sacrosanct's cold corridors until the tenth bell roused him.

Where the hell are you, Kanon?

There was a creak as a window opened behind him, then a splash as something was emptied onto the cobbles. Ahead a cart rumbled by, a pack of skeletal dogs trailing in its wake. Luker rubbed his gritty eyes. To his right the North Gate and the battlements of the city walls were just visible through the curtain of rain. A handful of figures huddled in the shadows of the gatehouse. Luker wondered if Gill had assigned any Guardians to watch the exits from the city, and whether they would be foolish enough to stand in his way if he tried to leave. *Wish I could.* First, though, he needed to find out what this Merin Gray knew about Kanon.

There was no sign of Jenna yet, but that didn't mean she wasn't here—he would only see her if she wanted to be seen. No one had entered or left the stables in the time he'd been watching. Two Bratbaks carrying spears stood by the gates, their hooded heads bowed. One of the figures carried a lantern that the other was using to light a blackweed stick.

This meeting with Merin was supposed to have started at the tenth bell, but it was closer to the eleventh now. Late enough, he reckoned.

Let's get this over with.

Striding from the alley, he approached the soldiers. The smoker saw him first. He tossed his blackweed stick on the ground and nudged his companion. They came to attention, crossing their spears to block Luker's path. The smoker was the shorter of the two, the top half of his face all but hidden by a mop of hair. The other soldier—a Kerinec tribeswoman wearing the same patchwork cloak as Jenna's minder, Gol—wore a battered helmet that was missing its feathered crest.

Luker halted in front of them. "I'm here to see Merin Gray."

The woman's eyes narrowed. "Guardian, yes? You're late."

"And you're in my way."

The Kerinec muttered something, then gestured over her shoulder. "Tyrin's waiting for you in the main building."

The Bratbaks raised their spears to let Luker pass, and he walked between them. The smoker was already crouching to search for the discarded blackweed stick.

Gravel crunched beneath Luker's boots as he followed the path to the stables. He came to a semicircular forecourt, in the center of which was a statue of a rearing horse. Beyond was a squat, black-stoned structure. The only light came from the main door, which stood ajar. The Guardian ignored it and walked round the side of the building. He entered a yard with stalls on three sides that stank of manure and wet straw. A balding, one-armed man stood beside one of the stable doors, bathed in the light of a lantern that hung from the eaves. He was feeding a horse from his hand. The animal must have been eighteen hands tall, and its coat was the color of bone.

"Impressive," Luker said. "A palimar, right?"

One-Arm inclined his head. "You're the first who's ever known her."

"Seen herds of them on the steppes north of the White Mountains. Never been this close to one, though."

"You wouldn't be standing here if you had." He showed Luker the remains of the bloody carcass he was feeding to the horse. "They're specially fond of human flesh."

"Best watch your hand, then. She might confuse it for her next meal."

One-Arm gave no response.

"You the stableman?"

"Yeah. And you're with Merin Gray."

Luker blinked. "Word gets round quickly."

"I was told to expect visitors. He's inside."

"Let him wait."

One-Arm spat on the ground. "The tyrin won't like that. Keen on his discipline, is Merin Gray."

"You know him?"

"Served under him at Helin, fifth Kalanese campaign. Many years ago now, before I lost the arm. Tyrin's a hard man, but fair. Popular with the lads. Has a knack of keeping them that's serving under him alive. Don't like to lose."

One thing, at least, we've got in common. "I'll remember that."

One-Arm tossed the remains of the carcass to the palimar and crouched to wash his hand in a bucket of water. "You looking for a ride?"

"Aye."

"Seen anything you like?"

"Was hoping you might be able to help me there."

"What do you want? Speed or stamina?"

"Both."

The stableman chuckled. "Figures."

"And a good temperament too." *The thing will need it to get along with me.*

"I'll see what I can do. You got your own tack?"

Luker spread his hands. "I am as you see me."

"I'll get you kitted out."

"Appreciate it." The Guardian made to leave, then remembered Jenna. "Oh, and I've got a friend coming along for the ride. Think you can sort her out too?"

One-Arm straightened. "Merin Gray didn't mention nothing to me."

"That's because he doesn't know yet."

The stableman chuckled again. "I can see you two are gonna get on real well."

"We'll get on fine as long as he does what he's told."

One-Arm grinned.

Luker retraced his steps to the front of the building and passed through the main doorway. In the entrance hall a uniformed clerk sat hunched over a desk writing in a leather-bound book. Without looking up, he jabbed his quill pen toward a door across from him. Luker heard voices on the other side and entered without knocking. The conversation died away. He found himself in an office. Light came from lanterns set on stands in each corner, and an assortment of battered armchairs surrounded a desk across which a map had been rolled out.

A young man was curled up in one of the armchairs, a wooden staff resting on his lap. He wore black robes, and his chin was covered by a wispy beard.

An older man—in his early fifties, perhaps—sat on the edge of the desk. The sleeves of his shirt were rolled up to the elbows. His face and forearms were tanned leather, and his short-cropped hair was the color of steel. The top of his left ear was missing. He held Luker's gaze for a moment, then stepped across to shake hands. His grip was iron. "Luker Essendar, I presume. I'm Merin Gray." He gestured to the seated figure. "This is Don Chamery Pelk of the Black Tower. Good of you to join us."

Luker couldn't decide whether that was meant as a rebuke for his tardiness. "I thought so," he said, sitting down in the chair closest to the door.

Merin exchanged a glance with Chamery. "We were discussing the siege at Cenan," he said to Luker. "It seems Chamery and I have met before, though I confess I have no memory of it."

The Guardian stared at the mage. Cenan was ten years ago, yet the boy looked barely old enough for the beard he was sporting.

Chamery must have guessed his thoughts for he said, "I was only an apprentice at the time." His voice was a soft lisp. "My master was called Laon Kaltin. Perhaps you've heard of him."

"Can't say I have."

"Well, you should have," the mage snapped. "He was one of the Conclave killed by the Guardians on the night of the Betrayal."

"That supposed to narrow it down for me?"

Merin cleared his throat. "You were at Cenan too, I hear," he said to Luker.

Someone's done their homework. "Not the siege itself. I drew the short straw and ended up hunting down the sacristens who fled the city when it fell."

"And you found them?"

"Aye, at a watering hole to the north. Three days it would've taken them to reach the oasis. Bastards came stumbling out of the desert like younglings to the slaughter. Must've thought they'd made it to safety. Instead they found me there waiting for them."

Merin looked out a window, arms behind his back. "I remember the place. I was a day behind the sacristens, with a troop thrown together from what remained of the Second. When we got there we found nothing but bones, picked clean."

"You tracked them across the Waste? How?"

"We had an air-mage with us. One of the emperor's Circle. Tough woman—one of the few to survive. Even with her, though, we struggled to follow their trail." He looked at Luker again. "And yet somehow you knew exactly where they'd be." The tyrin made it sound like an accusation.

"I grew up near Talen," the Guardian said. "Know the ground. There's only one oasis near Cenan they had any chance of making. Surprised they even got that far." He nodded at Merin. "You too. Avallon sent you to your death."

The tyrin shrugged. "Given time, the sacristens would have stirred up a rebellion. The emperor wanted them dead at any cost."

Luker grunted. *Aye, I saw what price was paid.* He had witnessed the aftermath of the siege of Cenan when he'd arrived to deliver the heads of the sacristens. The sandstone walls of the ancient citadel had been stained red with the blood of the dead. The Second was butchered almost to a man; the Fourth suffered crippling losses. The bodies of the dead, friend and foe alike, were stripped and piled outside the city walls for the creatures of the Waste to feast on. For nine days the desert sands boiled with sandclaws and roths, and carrion birds had formed a cloud that could be seen from leagues away. And all so the emperor could stick a pin in a map and pretend the city was his.

There was a knock at the door. At Merin's call, the shaggy-haired Bratbak from the front gate entered. He crossed to the tyrin and whispered something in his ear before departing.

Frowning, Merin turned to Luker. "There's a woman outside asking for you. Were you followed?"

"No. I told her to meet me here."

"Why?"

"Because she's coming with us."

Merin eyed him coolly. "I wasn't told about this."

"I'm telling you now."

"That's not what I meant. You're here at the emperor's command. It's not for you to say who travels with us."

It seemed the tyrin needed setting straight on a few things. "It is if you want me to come with you on this Shroud-cursed fool's errand."

Merin set his fists down on the desk. "Have you told her about the mission?"

There was something in the tyrin's voice that gave Luker pause. "No," he lied.

"So why's she coming?"

"She has her reasons. None of which have anything to do with you, or the Book. Anyhow," the Guardian added, "she'll only be with us part of the way."

Merin stroked his jaw. "Who is she?"

"A friend."

"Does this friend have a name?"

"Jenna." Luker watched for the tyrin's reaction, but there was no flicker of recognition.

"Can she be trusted?"

"Aye."

The silence stretched out.

Luker's gaze held steady on Merin's dark, unblinking eyes. Doubtless the tyrin was used to his subordinates shrinking beneath the weight of his stare, but Luker wasn't going to back down just because of a bit of eyeballing. *Bastard will want me "sirring" him next.*

"If she steps out of line," Merin said finally, "I'll hold you to account."

The Guardian's sense of foreboding returned. That was too easy, but he'd have to worry about what the tyrin was up to later. "Wouldn't let her come if I thought she'd slow us down."

Merin was already turning to the map on the desk. He beckoned the others to join him, and Luker stood. Chamery remained slouched in his chair.

The map was the largest Luker had ever seen, showing the lands stretching from Brena in the south to Majack in the distant north. It was also the most detailed, charting the route of the White Road where it passed through the Forest of Sighs north of Arandas, and even the spice routes that snaked across the deadlands of Kal. As the Guardian studied the territories that separated Arkarbour from Arandas, his chest tightened. If Kanon's silence since his last message spelled trouble, Luker was too far away to help his master.

Merin said, "I've been giving some thought to the route we'll take to Arandas. We're a couple of months behind Mayot Mencada, meaning we've got no time for sightseeing. We'll follow the Bone Road north to High Fort, then cross the Shield to Point Keep and descend—"

"Aye, just like that," Luker cut in. "The Kalanese'll be watching the road down from Cloud Pass."

Merin ignored him. "From Point Keep, we head east toward the Black Cliffs before turning north again. We've no idea how much of the Gollothir Plains are under Kalanese control, but by skirting the Waste we should be able to stay clear of their scouting parties."

"We'll also put the desert at our backs. If we hit trouble, we'll have nowhere to run."

"You got a better idea?"

"Helin," Luker said, tapping the map. "Should still be a few ships willing to risk the Wind Straits this time of year."

"The Kalanese have blockaded the port."

"A small boat could slip through—"

"I'm not done," Merin interrupted. A corner of the map had curled up, and he unrolled it again. "Getting to Helin would be the easy part. Scouts report the Kalanese are on the move toward Arandas. Their army would lie between us and the city."

Chamery spoke from his chair. "Then we go round. Head east from Helin to Point Keep and approach Arandas from the south."

Merin shook his head. "The Kalanese will expect Avallon to hit back after Malek's defeat. Most likely place to strike from is Helin. Kalanese will be watching the city like crakehawks. There's no way we'd get out unseen."

Luker rolled his shoulders and heard them crack. In truth he didn't care which route they took. Either way, the Kalanese would be lying in wait. "Have you heard any more from Kanon?" he asked Merin.

The tyrin's mouth was a thin line. "No. There should be news when we reach Arandas."

Chamery was rolling his staff along the armrests of his chair. "And if the city has fallen by the time we get there?"

"Won't happen," Merin said. "The emperor tried to take Arandas before it joined the Confederacy. Ended up getting his nose bloodied. The place is a nest of vipers. The Kalanese won't take it without a fight."

"The city will be under siege, though," Luker said. "What happens then?"

"Then we make contact with one of the emperor's agents in the surrounding towns."

"Did Kanon's last report say where Mayot was heading?"

The tyrin crossed his arms. "I've told you all I can."

"Why?"

"Because those are my orders."

And you always do what you're told. Luker focused his Will on the tyrin, discreetly enough to ensure his target did not sense his questing, but found Merin's mind as unyielding as his handshake had been. Given time, Luker might be able to wrest some information from him, but not without doing permanent damage. *Let's hope for his sake it doesn't come to that.*

The Guardian looked at Chamery. "Where will Mayot take this book?"

Chamery waved a languid hand. "As far from here as possible."

"He knows he'll be tailed, then?"

"Hah! Into the Abyss itself."

Merin spoke. "Why? What can the Book do?"

Chamery sneered. "In Mayot's hands? Nothing. He doesn't have the wit to use it."

"And if you're wrong? I need to know what I'm dealing with."

"No, you don't. Your job is to find Mayot, that's all. I'll deal with him from there."

The silence that followed was broken by a knock at the door.

Just as things were getting interesting . . .

Merin frowned at Chamery for a moment before shouting, "Come!"

The shaggy-haired Bratbak was back with another whispered message, pausing to jerk his thumb toward the door through which he had entered. The tyrin listened in silence, his expression masked. When the guard finished speaking, Merin rose. "Gentlemen," he said, looking from Chamery to Luker. "We'll have to finish this later. My clerk has booked us rooms at the Gate Inn. I'll join you there shortly."

He strode from the room.

Beyond the door, Luker caught a glimpse of a short, dark-robed figure—a woman, judging by the white gloss on her fingernails. Her skin was olive-colored, and the fifth finger on each hand was missing. *A Remnerol.* The woman's face remained hidden by the shadows of her cowl, but Luker could feel her gaze on him nevertheless.

Then Merin closed the door between them.

Luker glanced across at Chamery. The mage had straightened in his chair, a calculating look on his face. *Aye, even the boy senses it.*

Something was afoot.

CHAPTER 5

EBON'S THOUGHTS were dark as he approached Lamella's house. The memory of his father's frailty would not leave him. Isanovir had always hated weakness in others, and he would not spare himself the same disdain. Already he had lapsed into brooding and introspection. The end, when it came, would be a relief to him, Ebon suspected, and that end could not be far off. A matter of weeks, if the Royal Physicians were to be believed, but at least that left time for Ebon to make his peace with the king. *No, king no longer.* Just a father, perhaps for the first time in Ebon's life. Had there ever been a time, he wondered, when he had been anything but a prince to Isanovir?

He felt a twist of guilt for his deception at the gathering earlier, for while he had not spoken out to deny Janir's accusations of spirit-possession, he hadn't volunteered the truth of what had happened at the forest either. Would he be able to hide the fact the voices had returned? He had to try, that much at least was clear, for if Ebon was forced to abdicate, civil war would likely follow. His brother did not command the respect of the King's Council any more than Janir did. Of the other domens, Hebral Pallane or Dorala Feriman might stake a claim. The chancellor, too, had made no secret of his ambitions. None of them would bow the knee to the others, even if popular opinion turned against them. For years now, the only thing keeping the disparate factions in line had been Isanovir. Now that responsibility would fall on Ebon.

The jostling for places had already started. Following the showdown in the Royal Quarters, Ebon had attended a series of meetings with various domens, the King's Companions, the heads of the Guilds—all hastily convened by the queen in order to shore up Ebon's position, and consequently her own. For more than two bells he had cajoled and coerced, received promises of allegiance and given assurances of friendship in return. After a time, the discussions had begun to blur into a confused murmur, indistinguishable from the whispering of the spirits in his head. When Ebon had finally called a halt to the proceedings, Rosel's disapproving look had made it clear she knew where he was going.

Reaching Lamella's house, the king heard the strumming of a harp inside. He opened the gate and stepped onto the path beyond. Candles had been placed along its borders, their light reflecting off the front of the building. Standing a short distance away was a Pantheon Guardsman. Her full-face helmet covered all but her eyes, yet Ebon still recognized her from the image of a dove etched into the left cheek-piece.

"All quiet, Corporal Balia?"

The soldier's voice was muffled. "As Jirali's grave, sir," she said, moving aside.

Ebon could feel the day's stored heat radiating from the house. Dozens of yellowfoot lizards clung to the façade, but they scattered as the king drew near. The front door was unlocked, and he entered and closed it behind him. Crossing the shadowy hallway, he drew aside the heavy curtain on the opposite wall. The room beyond was lit by yet more candles that crowded the tables between the divans and piled cushions. The shutters on the windows had been thrown open against the heat, and gauze curtains fluttered in the gentlest of breezes.

The music died away.

Lamella sat in a chair beside her harp, her hands motionless over the strings. Her long strawberry-blond hair was swept back and held in place with bone combs. She wore a white susha robe, tied at the waist with a belt. A threadbare tasseled shawl covered her shoulders. She looked up as he entered.

Her eyes were red again.

Rising awkwardly, she shuffled over to him, her twisted right leg dragging behind her. The scars round her knee appeared unusually lurid in the candlelight. Ebon folded her in his arms and breathed in the scent of her hair before lifting her from her feet and spinning her about. She laughed breathlessly, then told him to set her down. He did so, drawing back to look into her eyes.

"I knew you'd come," she said. Then her gaze fixed on the wound at his temple. Taking his chin in one hand, she turned his head to catch the light. "Why haven't you had that seen to?"

"I wanted to see you first."

Her expression softened. "Come." She led him to one of the divans. Before he could sit, she placed a hand on his chest. "Take off your shirt."

He gave a half smile. "You do know it's my head that was cut."

Lamella blushed. "Fine. *You* can wash the blood off the chair when we're done."

Ebon's smile broadened. Unbuttoning his shirt, he peeled it from his back and tossed it onto the floor. Lamella's eyes widened when she saw the insect bites across his arms and torso. She made her way to a bureau near the harp and returned with a small bag and a wooden bowl filled with water. Setting the bowl down on a table, she sprinkled some powders into it from the bag, then lowered herself onto the divan and gestured for Ebon to join her. The acrid fumes from the water made him gag. Lamella dipped a cloth into the water, wrung it out, and touched it to his wound.

Ebon gritted his teeth against the sting.

"What happened?" she asked.

He told her about the Kinevar raid, leaving out all mention of the spirits. By the time he was done, Lamella had finished cleaning the wound. She crossed again to the bureau and returned with a clay pot and a needle and thread. After threading the needle, she placed its point in the flame of one of the candles until the metal glowed red. Her hand was trembling as she raised it to his temple.

Ebon hissed at the first stab of fire. He glanced at the harp. "I heard you playing when I arrived. You're getting better."

"I've had lots of time to practice."

He tried to turn his head to look at her, but she held him still. "I missed you too."

The needle paused a moment. "I know. One day, though, you won't come back to me."

"Meaning?"

"Balia tells me stories of things wandering the plains. About the Watcher's Light fading in the temples. They've started shutting the city gates at night, had you heard? Now Balia says I can't go riding in the Forest of Sighs."

"What of the Kingswood?" Even as he spoke the words, Ebon

wished he could take them back. His gaze flickered to her leg. "I am sorry, I did not mean to reopen old wounds."

Lamella did not respond. Tying off the thread, she set the needle to one side. Then she uncapped the clay pot and dipped three fingers inside, scooping out a pungent gray paste. "I heard about the kingship," she said. "Were you going to tell me?"

"Why would I not?"

Lamella applied some of the ointment to the insect bites on his arms and shoulders. Immediately the flaming itch of the stings subsided. "I'm sorry. About your father, I mean."

Ebon frowned. There was a strange formality to Lamella's words tonight, a self-consciousness in her speech. "My father has always gloried in his power. Now the sickness has taken hold . . . I fear his spirit is broken."

"It isn't easy living with weakness when all you've known is strength."

"He does not have your courage."

Lamella was a long time in answering. "My courage, yes." She resealed the pot of ointment, then wiped her hands on a cloth. Levering herself to her feet, she hobbled over to sit on the divan across from Ebon, her hands folded in her lap. She would not look at him. Ebon found he was holding his breath. "Is it over between us?" she asked suddenly. "I have to know."

"Why would you say that?"

"Rosel has put up with me—"

"My mother?" Ebon cut in. "What does she have to do with this? Has she been here?"

"A king needs a queen, Ebon. And we both know I can never be that."

"That is my mother speaking, not you."

"Is it? What happens when Mercerie or Koronos comes calling, offering an alliance in return for the hand of some padishah's daughter? What will your answer be?"

Ebon shifted in his seat. "My mother wants only to deny me what she could never have herself."

Lamella's expression was resigned, but there was something else in her eyes, something she was trying to keep from him. "You always do your duty."

His eyes narrowed. Is that all she thought she was to him? A duty? A way to assuage his guilt for what had happened in the Kingswood two years ago? Before he could voice the question, though, Lamella continued, "I knew today would come. We both did. I have no regrets."

Ebon's breath was tight in his chest. He moved to sit beside her.

"You have to let me go," Lamella said.

"I cannot."

"The longer we leave it, the harder it will get. If it has to end, let it be at a time of our choosing."

"No!"

Lamella stiffened, then shied away.

"What is it?" Ebon said, his anger fading as quickly as it had come. "Lamella?"

She searched his gaze. "I don't know. For a moment something stirred behind your eyes. As if your face was just a mask."

Exhaustion swept over Ebon, and he bowed his head. He had been a fool to think he could hide the spirits from her. Lamella was the one who'd got him through it last time, but could he lean on her again? He drew a breath. "It is the voices. They are back." He watched a host of emotions play across her features: pity, confusion, hurt—because he had tried to hold back the truth from her, he realized. The hurt stung him most.

After a while she drew him into her embrace, his head on her chest. He could hear her heart beating rapidly. "Who else knows?" she said.

"Vale, Mottle, that is all. It must stay that way."

Lamella made as if to say something, then seemed to change her mind. "Why, Ebon? Why are they back?"

"I suspect they never truly left. Just faded and . . . slept."

"Then what woke them?"

"I do not know." He told her about his conversation with Mottle. "It is not just voices this time. I see fragments of blurred images, shadows that should not be there, as if I were looking out through another's eyes."

The footfalls of Corporal Balia could be heard outside as she paced the grounds. When Lamella pulled away, some of the ointment from Ebon's skin had transferred to her susha robe. "You overcame the spirits before," she said. "You can do so again."

Ebon didn't have the strength to disagree. "Sometimes I wonder . . . The voices, the visions . . . Are they even real, or just delusions? What if my mind—"

"Hush," Lamella said, putting a finger to his lips. "Doubts can wait for tomorrow. You need to rest."

Ebon rubbed a hand across his eyes. "Rest, yes. Until now I have been afraid to close my eyes for fear the spirits would overwhelm me. But here, with you, the voices are stilled. I feel at peace."

"Then stay with me."

"I will. Until dawn."

A shadow fell across Lamella's face. "For as long as you wish."

Parolla paused at the doorway of the temple to look out. The shrine's unnatural shadow now extended all the way across the Round. The walls of the tenement blocks on the far side were covered with cracks, and one of the buildings listed so acutely it seemed it might topple at any moment. Its occupants would be suffering from the touch of death-magic too, Parolla knew, but she would waste no pity on anyone stupid enough to live within spitting distance of a shrine to the Lord of the Dead.

She scanned the alleys leading off the Round, but nothing stirred, and so she moved outside and followed the wall of the temple to the right, stepping over the corpse of the beggar. As she left the shrine's shadow she was enveloped by breathless heat. Sweat broke out on her forehead. The sun had dipped to the level of the roofs of the buildings across the Round, and light now reflected off the tiles as if the skyline were aflame. Far away, a blacksmith's hammer kept up an even clang like the tolling of a bell.

How long had it been since she'd entered the temple? Two bells, maybe? If she had thought she'd be returning this way she would never have spent so long talking to Olakim. Ceriso di Monata would have delivered his message to the high priest of the Antlered God by now, and the Hunt would be under way. But then where were the Huntsmen? Parolla scowled. Closing in at this very moment, no doubt, while she stood waiting for them to arrive.

Keeping to the shadows cast by the tenement blocks, she set off for the Inner Wall.

By the time she reached the Fire Gate, a quarter of a bell later, her nerves were aflutter. She hadn't seen a soul. On her way to the temple, the din of the crowds had set her ears thrumming, but now Xavel was like a plague city, hushed and empty. Ahead the roof of the Fire Gate's archway had long since fallen, and the dirt road that bisected the surviving pillars was lined with blocks of stone, each one taller than Parolla. The front of the Gate was pockmarked with holes housing nesting blackcraws, and more of the squabbling birds crowded the tops of the pillars.

All at once they took flight in a raucous cloud, and Parolla ducked into a side street. Her heart pounded in her ears. Was it her approach that had caused the birds to scatter? That must be it, she decided, because when she risked another glance round the corner at the Gate, she saw the road passing through it was deserted.

But then why weren't the birds returning?

An ululating cry pierced the dusk, followed heartbeats later by an answering call, shrill but distant. Parolla swore. She knew that sound better than she would have liked. *A dactil.* Pressing her back to the wall, she looked up. There was a flap of wings like the crack of a whip, then a huge form sailed over the rooftops, its barbed tail snaking behind. The dactil's long, sinuous neck twisted from side to side as it scanned the ground beneath it, but the creature could not have seen her, for it banked south and flew out of sight.

A scout.

Parolla had encountered the Hunt enough times to know how the Antlered God's followers operated. While mounted riders quartered the city in small bands, dactils would range far and wide in search of their quarry. Once Parolla was flushed out into the open, the other hunters would converge. The fact the high priest was using trackers suggested he did not know where Parolla was, but then doubtless he would have expected her to flee Shroud's temple as soon as she received Ceriso's message. If that were the case, this part of Xavel— still close to the shrine—might be the last place he thought to look for her. That gave her time to consider her options.

So what now?

Hide? No, when she'd tried that in Axatal the Hunt had sniffed out her bolt-hole soon enough. Fight? It might come to a clash, but she would not go looking for one. The high priest himself led the Hunt, Ceriso had said, and with him would be a host of priests, *magi,* warriors and other hangers-on, all keen to win their god's favor by spilling her blood. And yet, hadn't the high priest himself warned Ceriso she was dangerous? Was he oblivious to the scores of innocents that would be caught up in a confrontation? Or had he chosen the setting for the Hunt for that very reason, hoping Parolla would hold back part of her power when she attacked?

That left flight. The problem was, Parolla had arrived in Xavel only yesterday. If she tried to run, she might wander the streets blindly until she stumbled into a party of Huntsmen. And even if she *could* navigate the maze of alleys, where would she go? The Serpentine Bazaar, perhaps? Speaker's Mount? The whole city could not be deserted, and if she found a crowd she might slip away unseen. But would the high priest stay his hand if he caught up to her when there were others present? Parolla could not afford to take the risk.

There was always the Xavellian Barracks by the palace complex, somewhere to the north. The city's padishah must be less than thrilled to have Huntsmen running amok in his city, but would he risk the wrath of the Antlered God by intervening? Parolla doubted it. If she went to the barracks seeking refuge, she might find herself detained and ransomed to the Hunt. Her best plan was to escape the city. But how?

She remembered suddenly the route she had taken when she entered Xavel from the north and west: through the Guild Quarter, past the Temple of Ral, over the river . . .

The river.

The Water Gate was no more than a quarter-league to the east round the Inner Wall. From there, a northerly course would bring her to the Xintha River. But then what if north also delivered her into the lap of the Hunt?

She would have to chance it. She would wait until the light faded further, though, before—

A triumphant cry sounded above, and Parolla looked up to see a dactil plummeting toward her, its taloned feet outstretched, its near-translucent wings tucked in to avoid the eaves of the buildings to either side. Her right arm snapped out, and she unleashed her power. Waves of sorcery struck the creature, and its jubilant screech rose to an agonized shriek. For an instant it flapped its blazing wings in a vain attempt to reverse its descent. Then its outline dissolved in a flash of white.

A handful of smoldering feathers fell about Parolla.

Brushing herself down, she muttered an oath. A hollow victory, for even if no one had seen the dactil fall, the Hunt's *magi* would have detected her sorcery and would now be directing their companions in this direction. Already she could hear distant hoofbeats to the south.

Time to leave.

Releasing her power in a trickle, she cloaked herself in shadow and set off east for the Water Gate in a half crouch, half scamper, not knowing whether speed or stealth was her main concern and no doubt failing to achieve either. Reaching a crossroads, she checked it was deserted, then darted across into the street opposite. Her heart was doing a quickstep, and in response to her fear the darkness within her began to rise. She took the next left, then right, then left again, always choosing the narrowest, darkest alleys where her shadow-spell would hide her from any watching eyes.

But the hoofbeats were getting closer. Parolla could now hear voices as well, no more than a couple of streets behind. She broke into a run. A bend to the right, a left turn, past a fountain swarming with needle-flies, over another crossroads. Parolla hadn't heard any barking, but in case the Huntsmen were using dogs to follow her scent she splashed through the effluent running down a channel in one of the alleys.

Still the hoofbeats drew nearer.

Breathing heavily, Parolla halted and looked up. There were no dactils overhead, but the Huntsmen had to be tracking her somehow. Odds were they had a *magus* in their party—someone powerful enough to detect her spell of concealment—but if she let the spell fall she'd only make it easier for the other Huntsmen to spot her. What choice, though? The hoofbeats had reached the corner behind her.

Cursing, she surrendered her power and ducked into a doorway.

From her left, a dozen horsemen came riding along the street carrying spears, crossbows, and nets. Their breastplates were adorned with the emblem of a stag, and antlers protruded from the conical helmets on their heads. At the sight of them, a shadow fell across Parolla's vision. It would be easy to cut them down as they approached, but instead she shrank back farther into the gloom, and the Huntsmen cantered past to the noise of jingling harnesses, leaving in their wake the smell of waxed leather.

Twoscore heartbeats later, shouts of confusion sounded to the east. It wouldn't be long before the *magus* doubled back and found Parolla's hiding place. She had to think of something quickly. If she raised her shadow-spell again, the sorcerer would hone in on it, but how far could she get without it before someone saw her?

Think!

Parolla looked up at the eaves of the building across from her. She might be able to scramble up onto one of the rooftops, but what then? She could hardly leap from roof to roof, and if she were fool enough to try, the dactils would surely see her.

From along the alley to her right came a faint snuffling sound, and she froze. A three-legged dog was limping toward her—the same animal she'd observed outside Shroud's temple? It stopped a few steps from the doorway where she hid and looked at her. Baring its teeth, it growled.

Parolla smiled. *The White Lady's own luck.*

She had to act swiftly, though, if she was to take advantage of its arrival. Summoning her power, she weaved a shadow-spell about the dog and watched its form blur. Almost invisible in the gloom of the passage. The Huntsmen would soon discover the deception, of course, but not before she was far away.

A kick sent the dog shuffling off with a yelp.

More shouts came from somewhere to her right, shrill with excitement, and a horn emitted a braying note. Apparently the *magus* had sensed his new target. Parolla's priority now was to put as much distance as possible between herself and the dog, and for once she did not have to think long over which direction to take. The Inner Wall was visible over the roofs of the buildings to the north—follow it east, and it would soon bring her to the Water Gate.

Simple.

She dashed off in the opposite direction to that which the dog had taken, ducking into the first passage she came to.

Keeping the Inner Wall to her left, she zigzagged through the alleys. The clamor of the Hunt fell farther and farther behind.

An uneventful half-bell later she passed through the Water Gate and entered the Mount. The dirt roads gave way to paved, tree-lined avenues, the squat slums to mansions set in immaculately groomed gardens. From behind the safety of gates, private guardsmen watched her stride by. They were, she realized, the first people—barring the Huntsmen—she had seen since leaving Shroud's temple.

There were sounds of life ahead now: the lowing of temlocks from the cattle markets; the cries of a *jadi* seer screaming his promise of apocalypse. No horns. No hoofbeats. Parolla could not afford to relax just yet, though, for the Antlered God had many followers, and not all of them wore antlered helms. Ceriso di Monata had recognized her as being marked by his Lord, but he had not said *how*. Would all of the immortal's servants be able to identify her?

She raised the hood of her cloak.

A scattering of people were still abroad: slaves mostly, judging by the tattoos on the backs of their hands. Eyes downcast, they scurried through the lengthening shadows. If Parolla set a bearing north she would stumble on the river eventually, but perhaps she could risk asking someone the quickest route. A young girl, barefoot and wearing an ill-fitting yellow robe, was coming along the pavement toward her. As the girl walked, she brushed the fingers of her left hand against the trunks of the trees that lined the avenue. On seeing Parolla approach, she made to cross to the opposite side of the road.

Parolla raised a hand. "Please, *mestessa*," she said in the common tongue. "I will not detain you long. I seek directions to the river."

The girl's gaze was fixed on the ground. She was no more than ten years old, Parolla judged, but someone had tried to make her look older by painting her lips red. When she did not respond, Parolla repeated her question in Xavellian. The girl hesitated before pointing to a side road. On the back of her hand was a tattoo of an antlered deer.

Even as the significance of that detail sank in, Parolla saw the girl's gaze flicker to her face. Her golden eyes widened, and she turned to run.

Wait! Instinctively, Parolla snatched out and grabbed her sleeve. She felt a jolt as sorcery passed like a shock between them, crackling up the girl's arm. Light flashed behind the slave's eyes. She opened her mouth to scream, but all that came out was a moan. For a moment she remained upright on watery legs. Then she collapsed, her sleeve slipping from Parolla's grasp.

Her head bounced off the pavement with a crack.

Parolla stomach knotted as she crouched beside her. *No, mestessa! I didn't mean . . .* Blood trickled from the girl's nostrils, and her eyes gazed sightlessly up at the sky. Parolla shook her shoulders, but her body was limp. A urine stain spread across her robe round the thighs and knees. Seizing one of her hands, Parolla released her power in a flood through the contact. A flicker of a heartbeat was all she needed, the smallest flame to fan to life. *Breathe, mestessa, breathe!*

The girl's body jerked as if she were having convulsions. Parolla could *see* her heart beating, rippling the cloth of her robe as it thundered in her chest. At her neck, her skin twitched with an irregular pulse. But Parolla knew it was only her sorcery that sustained the illusion of life. The girl's soul had already fled to Shroud's keeping. After a time the girl's skin grew warm to the touch, then uncomfortably hot. Parolla saw her beautiful golden eyes start to melt, her hair to curl at the roots. The air filled with the sickly sweet smell of burned flesh.

Letting go of her power, Parolla lifted the girl's body and hugged it to her. Her eyes misted.

Why, damn you?

A servant of the Antlered God.

A girl!

Parolla had only wanted to prevent her from escaping. Instead her tainted blood had come surging up, and she had been unable to hold it in check. How many more would die before she learned control? Why did Shroud's Gate always seem to remain so far out of reach for her, yet so close for those she came into contact with?

She rocked the slave in her embrace.

Forgive me, mestessa.

Parolla did not know how long she knelt with the girl in her arms. Finally a noise made her look up. A man was watching her from along the street, half hidden behind a tree. Another servant of the Antlered God? Parolla no longer cared. As their gazes met, the stranger turned and bolted.

A needlefly alighted on the dead girl's cheek, and Parolla waved a hand at it. The *magi* of the Hunt would have sensed her sorcery, gained an insight into what she was capable of. Would they now see sense and keep their distance? She suspected not. Once unleashed the Hunt could not be recalled. Worse still, the high priest would now know where Parolla was. Perhaps he would even deduce her destination from the direction she was heading in. Her thoughts turned again to the river. The promise of escape, and an end to the killing.

She had lingered here too long.

Blinking back tears, Parolla lowered the girl to the road, then rose and set off again.

Luker was beginning to suspect it hadn't been mere luck that he'd found this table empty when he arrived at the Gate Inn. The sawdust on the floor below looked like it'd been brushed recently, but spatters of blood and other fluids remained, and the air stank of excrement. To Luker's left, Jenna sat staring at him like she thought he'd made the smell. In her fingers she rolled a blackweed stick, which she lit from one of the wall torches. Chamery sat across from them, stroking the fluff on his chin that passed for a beard.

Luker used a nudge of the Will to catch the innkeeper's attention, and the man heaved his bulk toward them through the press of people in the common room. He took their order, then snatched up the coin Luker put on the table and bit down on it. Evidently satisfied, he dropped it into a pocket.

"Keep the change," Luker said. The emperor was paying, he could afford to be generous.

His gaze swept the room. He had never set foot in this place before, but he was already starting to understand the reason for its colorful reputation. Along the wall to his right, a young man with bloodred tattoos on his scalp was fluttering his fingers over one of the wall torches. His lips moved soundlessly as shapes began to twist in the flames. Over by the door, meanwhile, a squad of Bratbaks was drinking away their pay. A serving-girl had just arrived with the next round, but when one of the soldiers ran his hand up her skirt, she started and dropped the tray of drinks. It fell to the floor with a crash, spilling ale to the sawdust. The men jeered.

The Bratbaks weren't the only soldiers present, Luker knew. The others might not have been wearing uniforms, but he'd crossed swords with enough scarred veterans in his time to pick them out in a crowd. A number of sets of hooded eyes studied him from the shadows at the edges of the room. Some of the watchers stared at him blankly; others returned his gaze with unspoken challenge. Not so long ago, no one would have dared hold the eye of a Guardian. Or maybe it was just Luker. *Good times.*

Chamery's lisp interrupted his thoughts. "Fascinating place the tyrin has chosen for us, wouldn't you say?"

"Seems Merin Gray wants an eye kept on us."

"Hah! It is *we* who should be watching *him*! Something's going on, you know it as well as I do. We're not even clear of the city and already the scheming has begun."

Jenna blew out a mouthful of blackweed smoke. "A mage accusing someone else of double-dealing? Did I just imagine the Betrayal when it happened?"

Chamery sneered. "And what would you know about it?" He looked back at Luker. "History is always written by the victors. The real treachery that night was committed *against* the Black Tower. Do you deny this, Guardian?"

"No," Luker said. He had long since come to realize that the emperor's quarrel with the mages' Conclave two years ago had been engineered by Avallon to give him an excuse to approach the Guardians for help. It had been a clever ruse, all things considered. An informer among the mages' ranks had alleged the Black Tower was seeking to make contact with the empire's ancient nemesis, the Augerans—like the Conclave was some fatted calf gone searching for the butcher's ax. And while the emperor had been careful to appear skeptical about the claims, his demand that the High Mage surrender himself for questioning was delivered just provocatively enough to raise the mages' hackles.

Looking back now, it was hard to believe there had been so many Guardians prepared to throw their weight behind Avallon, but the seriousness of the accusations, together with the intransigence of the Conclave, had left most of the order feeling they had no option but to give the emperor their support. The night of the Betrayal had weakened both the Black Tower and the Sacrosanct. Indeed, the only winner had been Avallon himself, for with one fell stroke he had succeeded in decimating the ranks of two of the factions that might have put a check on his power. And, conveniently, the subsequent disappearance of the informer had left the emperor's detractors with no way of proving he'd masterminded the affair.

For a few heartbeats Chamery was taken aback by Luker's admission. Then the sneer returned. "And yet the Guardians sided with Avallon."

"Not all of them."

"You think your opposition absolves you from blame? You were part of the attack on the Black Tower, weren't you? The blood of the Conclave is as much on your hands as it is your colleagues'."

Luker shot him a look. "Aye, I was there. Kanon was there too. You think I should have hung my master out to dry like you did yours?"

Chamery's face went white. "You dare accuse me . . . I was in Trote on a shadow-sending."

"Of all the days, eh?"

"Fortunately for you."

"You think the result would've been any different if you'd been there? You'd have bled as easy as the others."

"But I did not! And I will make sure the emperor comes to regret that I survived!"

Luker leaned in until his face was a few handspans from Chamery's. "Careful," he said, looking meaningfully over the mage's shoulder at the common room. "Someone else here might be stupid enough to take your threats seriously."

"You think I care?" Chamery replied. But he had lowered his voice all the same.

The innkeeper returned with a bottle of juripa spirits, two chipped goblets, and a glass of red wine for the mage. Jenna snatched up the bottle, filled a goblet to the brim and passed it to Luker. Already regretting his decision to let the assassin order for him, he took a sip and winced as the fiery liquid seared the back of his throat. "Tell me," he said to Chamery. "Did anyone from the Black Tower go north with Kanon?"

The mage paused before answering. "No."

Figured. Kanon enjoyed company about as much as Luker did. The mage's hesitation made him curious, though. "Why not?"

"Because we knew nothing of his quest at that time. And I suspect we never would have done, had your master been successful."

"You're saying Avallon wants the Book for himself?"

"You tell me. You're the one taking his orders."

A scuffle had broken out between a Bratbak and one of the inn's other patrons. As the soldier's companions stood by cheering, the Bratbak took an upper cut from his opponent that sent him tumbling over a table. The innkeeper waded in brandishing a cudgel.

Luker said, "For the emperor to have wanted the Book he had to have known about it first. So who told him?"

Chamery's voice betrayed his uncertainty. "Mayot Mencada. It must have been."

"Mayot tells Avallon about the Book, then snatches it for himself? That makes sense."

"It was Mayot! No one outside the Black Tower could have known the Book was there."

"You wanted it kept secret? Why?"

The mage sipped at his wine, but said nothing.

"Meaning you don't know."

"Of course I know! The Book of Lost Souls has been hidden at the Black Tower since before the Exile. After the death of my master, it was I who spun the wards to keep the Book quiescent."

It was proving all too easy to stir the boy up and get him talking. "Explains how Mayot was able to get his hands on it."

Chamery glared at him.

"What happens now this thing's in the open? If it's as powerful as you say, won't others be drawn to it?"

"Why do you think *I* am here? The emperor needs the Black Tower's help to recover the Book."

"And you're just going to hand it over to him when you get it?"

Chamery smiled.

Jenna's nudge alerted Luker to Merin Gray's approach. The tyrin weaved through the crowd, acknowledging a look from a hidden watcher. The table of Bratbaks had fallen silent. Merin came to stand beside Chamery but made no move to sit. He glanced at Jenna, then shook his head as she pushed the bottle of juripa spirits across the table toward him.

"Trouble?" Luker said.

"Word's come in that survivors from the Seventh are still trickling into High Fort from across the Shield. Last arrivals were less than a week ago."

"Coordinated withdrawal?"

"No, scattered groups only."

"Meaning the Kalanese now control the Gollothir Plains."

"Meaning the majority of the survivors have retreated to Helin."

"Even so, I reckon a change of plan—"

"The plan stands," Merin cut in. "We leave at dawn, back of the Royal Stables." With a final look at the common room, he spun on his heel and headed for the stairs.

Luker watched him go. In his mind's eye he saw again the Remnerol woman who had interrupted them at the stables. Somehow he doubted she had come to tell Merin about troop movements across the Shield. He scratched his scar. Merin was holding his cards close to his chest, but there was no reason to think they had anything to do with Luker.

Then again, there was no reason not to think that. Like Jenna, the Guardian would be glad when Arkarbour was behind them.

Moments later Chamery drained his wineglass and followed the tyrin upstairs.

Luker leaned back against the wall. Sensing Jenna did not want to talk, he cupped his hands round his goblet and listened to the ebb and flow of voices in the common room. After a while music struck up, and he squinted through the haze of smoke to see a woman seated beside the bar, her face turned away from him. She was tuning a lyre cradled in her left arm. A hush settled on the room. She began to sing the "Song of the Exile," tentatively at first, then with increasing assurance. Her voice was soothing, and Luker's eyelids started to feel heavy.

Before the performance ended, Jenna excused herself and made for the stairs, the half-full bottle of spirits in one hand.

Luker hesitated, then set off after her.

He caught up to her as she opened the door to her room. "A word with you," he said.

Jenna raised an eyebrow, but nodded her assent.

Her room was chill and bare. The noise from the common room was a hum below, barely audible above the rain pattering against the large, solitary window. Jenna slipped out of her cloak and slung it over a chair. Sitting on the edge of the bed, she removed her hairband and shook out her hair. "Interesting company you keep."

Luker reversed a second chair and straddled it. "Not out of choice."

"Who is this Merin Gray?"

"Emperor's man. Breaker probably."

The lines around Jenna's eyes tightened. "He doesn't trust me, nor does the mage—I have seen their looks. But they trust you even less."

"There's something to be said for keeping your enemies close."

Jenna uncorked the bottle of spirits and took a swallow. "We'll just have to disagree on that."

"You think your admirers will come after you when we leave Arkarbour?"

"If they know where I've gone."

Luker took the bottle from her. "Won't be the first time we've had friends of yours on our trail. That time in Mercerie—"

"I was wondering when you'd get round to that," Jenna cut in.

"I warned you Peledin Kan wouldn't play by the rules when it came to tracking you down."

"I didn't need your help."

"'Course you didn't." Luker took a swig from the bottle. "Hadn't realized the whole thing still bugged you so much."

"No more than it bugs you that *I* was the one who brought Keebar Lana down."

"I could've made that shot."

"Talk is cheap."

"Maybe I was happy for you to take the blame for it. Maybe I wanted you to be the one hunted."

Jenna snatched the bottle back from him. "And happier still to take the credit for my kill, no doubt. You still owe me for that."

"I thought me stepping in against those demons made us even."

"You thought wrong. Like I said, I didn't need your help."

Luker caught her gaze and held it. "It'll catch up with you one day, you know. Too many powerful enemies."

"I know."

"So why go on? Not for the coin, surely."

Jenna looked away. "It's not what I do. It's who I am."

The musician's performance must have finished at that moment, for there was an eruption of applause and foot-stamping from the common room below. As the noise died away Luker said, "We're not so different, you know. Kanon always believed in what the Guardians did. He had a cause. Not me, though. Makes me just another killer."

"Then why did you come back? To Arkarbour, I mean."

"For Kanon."

"You didn't know he was in trouble until you got here." She paused, then went on. "Perhaps, like me, you have nothing else."

Frowning, Luker gestured at the bottle in Jenna's hand, but she shook her head and raised it to her lips. The blackweed and spirits were starting to take effect, for her eyes were glazed. Luker regarded her thoughtfully. "Wasn't always like this," he said. "When I traveled with Kanon, he had belief enough for both of us. I fought for him, not for the Guardians, not for the emperor. But when we went our separate ways, that's when the doubts came. The Will's a fickle thing. My power was beginning to fail near the end—no conviction in what I did. On its own, the will to survive can keep you going for only so long, and when that too starts to fade . . ."

"At least you still have Kanon."

"Aye, there is that, I guess. But it's only half the truth. Because like it or not, when I walked out on the Guardians, I walked out on Kanon too."

Into the silence that followed came another burst of applause from below.

Then the window exploded inward.

Two black-clad men holding ropes swung into the room, and the storm came howling in behind them. As they touched down they released their ropes and drew throwing knives from the baldrics across their chests.

Jenna reacted first, flinging her bottle of spirits at one of the newcomers. It glanced off his chin, and his head snapped round. Luker made to rise, only for his feet to tangle in the legs of his chair.

He toppled backward. *Shit, shit, shit.* A throwing knife sped toward him, and he seized the fallen chair by its back and raised it as a shield.

The dagger thudded into the bottom of the seat.

The man who'd been struck by the bottle drew a knife and sprang to engage Jenna.

Still holding the chair, Luker surged upright and charged the second stranger. The man drew a sword and swung it wildly. The blade shattered one of the legs, but Luker used the other three to pin his foe and drive him back. The stranger tried to set his feet, but Luker's rush had caught him off balance, and a shove from the Guardian sent him screaming through the window. The chair followed.

Luker spun round.

Jenna had drawn a knife and now fought the first stranger. Luker considered going to her aid, but it quickly became clear his help wasn't needed. Jenna's thrown bottle had left a gash on her opponent's chin, and with each passing heartbeat more cuts blossomed across his shoulders and chest as Jenna picked holes in his defenses. Luker had expected the juripa spirits to slow her reactions, but her movements were precise and unhurried. In desperation her opponent lunged with his knife.

Jenna turned her body to evade the attack, then continued the motion, stepping round to take her behind her enemy. Luker didn't see her land the killing blow, but suddenly her assailant was clutching his throat. Blood bubbled out between his fingers, and he dropped his blade and pitched forward.

Luker exchanged a look with Jenna. No way that was all of them.

Over the growl of the storm he heard footsteps in the corridor outside.

He drew his swords just as the door burst open and a man threw himself through the doorway. Rolling expertly, the newcomer came up on one knee. In each hand he carried a small crossbow. Twin bolts of darkness flashed toward Luker.

He batted them aside with his blades.

A second figure entered the room: a Remnerol woman with olive skin and shoulder-length, flame-red hair. *The one from the stables.* She stood no taller than the Guardian's shoulder, yet still managed to adopt a manner of looking down on him. Her hands came up, and streaks of fire flew from her fingers.

Not interested in small talk, it seemed.

Luker used his Will to fashion a shield and grunted as the sorcery struck it. The air about him ignited, the bed and chairs bursting into flames. Behind him, Jenna cried out, and there was a thud as she hit the floor. For a dozen heartbeats the magic continued to rage, lapping round the edges of Luker's Will-shield. He grimaced at the touch of fire against his skin.

But his defenses held.

The Remnerol's sorcery died away, and she lowered her hands. The flames eating at the furniture fizzled out as rain blew into the room through the smashed window. Luker hawked and spat. The sorceress looked surprised he was still standing, but as yet her mask of arrogance wasn't showing any cracks. When she spoke, she had to raise her voice to make herself heard above the wind. "This is not your fight, Guardian. Step aside and you may live."

Luker did not respond. Not taking his gaze from the two strangers, he crouched and felt behind him for Jenna's motionless form. Her head was partway under the bed. His fingers probed her neck for a pulse.

The Remnerol spoke again. "Last chance. Step aside."

Luker took a breath to quell the rage swelling inside him, for anger would only weaken his grip on the Will. He swayed as he pushed himself upright. Maybe he had drunk more spirits than he should have, but he was still too much for these Shroud-cursed fools to handle. Odds were they'd been expecting to find Jenna alone and were now regretting the timing of their attack, but it was too late to back out.

The sorceress's hands came up. "You leave me no choice."

Spears of fire battered Luker's defenses, casting a wild glare all about and spraying flames like sparks off a grindstone. Sweat sprung to the Guardian's brow. An overturned chair flickered to light again, and he kicked it across the room toward the sorceress. For the first time, a flicker of doubt showed in her eyes. Already Luker could feel the force of her assault waning. The bitch was a fire-mage. Without the sun's energy to draw on, her power would soon fade.

My turn.

Gathering his strength, Luker pushed back with his pent-up Will. His counterattack carved through the sorceress's waves of fire and slammed into the woman herself, making her stagger back against the wall. Before she could recover, Luker pulled back his right arm and flung one of his swords at her end-over-end. It took her in the neck, the point driving through flesh to clank against stone behind. She gave a gurgled choke and slid down the wall, leaving a smear of red.

Luker swung to face her companion. The man was clean-shaven and bald, and his left eye was half-closed in a permanent squint. For an instant he stared slack-jawed at the body of the dead Remnerol. Then his expression hardened as he turned on Luker. In one hand he held a scimitar, in the other a serrated dagger. The metal of both blades was blackened, and their tips wove an intricate pattern as he whirled them through the air.

Luker extended his right arm and reached out with the Will. The sword skewering the sorceress's neck worked itself free and flew back to his hand.

His opponent advanced. "Let's see what you've got."

Luker attacked.

Their blades clashed. The stranger was fast, his weapons a blur, his footwork sure.

Luker had faced much better.

When the intruder's scimitar next darted out, the Guardian caught it and allowed it to slide along his left blade, drawing his assailant closer. It was the opening Luker had been waiting for, but before he could take advantage, his foe made a clumsy attempt with the Will to drive him back. For the blink of an eye the Guardian was caught off guard, yet there was no more force in the attack than a breath of wind, and he pushed through it to launch a series of lightning strokes that had the stranger parrying frantically. Luker feinted with his left sword. As his opponent moved to block a strike that never came, the Guardian's right blade flicked out and stabbed him through the heart.

Or where his heart would have been had the man not stumbled in attempting to evade the thrust. Instead of delivering a fatal blow, Luker's sword took him below the left shoulder, and he staggered backward, his dagger slipping from twitching fingers even as his legs buckled. Luker let him fall, then kicked the scimitar from his hand.

"Wait!" the man said. "I have information."

The Guardian slashed open his throat. "Nothing I don't already know."

Returning his swords to their scabbards, he crouched beside Jenna again. The sight of the assassin brought his breath hissing out. The skin of her face had been split by the sorceress's magic, masking her features in blood. Curls of black smoke rose from her scorched clothing.

But her chest still lifted and fell, her heartbeat an irregular flutter.

Luker breathed a silent prayer of thanks to the Matron, then turned at a creak and saw Chamery in the doorway. The mage's look was guarded. "I sensed sorcery—"

Luker rose. "Heal her," he cut in, gesturing at Jenna as he strode from the room. "If she dies, so do you."

CHAPTER 6

THE DARK of the night was almost total, the moon and stars hidden behind a veil of cloud. Romany raised her hood against the drizzle that misted the air. Earlier she had spent two bells combing the city for a building with its roof intact before settling for the remains of a house that was sheltered by the drooping branches of a wolsatta tree. With nowhere to sit, she was forced to clear rubble from the ground—her! A high priestess! Then, sitting cross-legged on the newly exposed tiled floor, she had found it impossible to get comfortable. Her back ached abysmally, and every few moments some unseen piece of debris would clamor for attention beneath her posterior.

Her stomach grumbled. The Spider had warned her there would be no food or drink in this place, even suggesting she should be grateful for the chance to shed some of the excess weight she was carrying! True, the goddess's sorcery meant Romany would not need provisions during her time here, but didn't the Spider understand there was more to eating and drinking than mere sustenance? The priestess's mind wandered. Sweetmeats from Balshazar, a glass of chilled Koronos white wine . . . Then again, even if such delicacies had been available, the prospect of having to serve herself was too offensive to contemplate. No servants! What other unpleasant truths had the Spider kept from her?

More than enough time had now passed for greed to weave its spell on Mayot, but Romany was minded to let him fret a little longer before returning to the dome. Let him think she had flown, and with her any chance of him gaining mastery of the Book. The more anxious he became, the more likely he would be to seize a second chance when it was offered. Such an odious man! A part of Romany hoped he declined her assistance, for he would soon come to rue his stubbornness when he stood alone against Shroud's disciples. Of course, even if Mayot accepted her aid, the Book's power would serve only to delay the inevitable, for against the Lord of the Dead there could be no victory. Romany gave a contented sigh. *A downward spiral to oblivion.* All she had to do was ensure Mayot took the first step on that precipitous road. Ultimately her victory over Shroud in this game would be no less a victory over Mayot himself.

The priestess put such thoughts aside for now. She had begun the task of weaving a web of sorcerous threads across Estapharriol and the forest beyond. It was proving to be a frustrating exercise, for the tendrils of death-magic emanating from the Book warped whichever parts of her web they touched. To the north she had observed scores of Kinevar settlements, some abandoned, others being evacuated. The Book's death-magic had infiltrated the creatures' sacred glades, blighting the trees and poisoning the river. Romany stroked her chin. Strange that they had chosen to flee instead of striking at Mayot, but then no doubt the Kinevar were too witless to determine the cause of their plight.

A handful of leagues to the south and east of Estapharriol, the forest was thronged with spirits—all that remained of the people who had once inhabited Estapharriol and the settlements round it. *The Vamilians.* Dead for millennia, yet seemingly cursed to wander the land for eternity. They must have been able to detect her ethereal presence, for their hollow gazes followed her as she passed among them on the threads of her web.

And in the midst of the spirits, cutting through the forest in a gentle arc . . . *The White Road.* Clear of leaves and roots, it glowed white even when the moon was hidden behind clouds. There was magic here, Romany sensed, buried deep beneath the ground as if the road had been constructed along some ancient axis of power. The sorcery had a primeval flavor to it, unquestionably older than the Vamilian civilization, perhaps even than the Forest of Sighs itself. Whatever its origin, the spirits must have been drawn to it—why else did they not dwell in the cities where they had once lived?—and yet it appeared none of them were able to set foot on the road itself. *Intriguing.* She would have to remember to ask the Spider about it when they next spoke.

Not that I'll get an answer.

From the north and west came a twitch along the priestess's web. Not so much a twitch, in fact, as a tremor. Frowning, she followed the threads to the source of the disturbance.

And stiffened. A rider beset on all sides by a howling tangle of spirits. The stranger's horse was black as Shroud's soul, and its hooves were shod in a metal that burned with white fire. Eyes rolling, it snapped its teeth at the Vamilians all about. When it reared, its flashing hooves cut a swath of destruction through the spirits in front of it.

Its rider was covered from head to foot in the most battered suit of armor Romany had ever seen. He—for it was surely a man—wore a plumed helmet with a horizontal slit for the eyes. Through it the priestess saw crackling blue light, as if a lightning storm raged behind the faceplate. The same infernal glow played across the man's sword, and where the weapon fell the spirits seemed to dissipate. The spectral forms were throwing themselves not at the man but at his blade, Romany realized. *They seek oblivion.* A fate that the rider appeared only too happy to dispense. The priestess could feel him drawing on the tendrils of death-magic in the air to fuel his slaughter. She pursed her lips. Only one of Shroud's minions would have the power to deliver such finality to the dead.

Retreating from the apparition, she fled back to her body along the strands of her web and opened her eyes. The knight was only a few leagues from Estapharriol, and the spirits would not detain him for long. Maybe his coming was a blessing, she told herself, for Mayot would surely have to see sense now and accept her offer of assistance. And yet even if she were to unlock the secrets of the Book, would the old man be able to harness its sorcery before the knight arrived?

So little time!

Romany clambered upright and set off for the dome.

It took her half a bell to retrace her steps to Mayot's lair, stumbling and cursing in the gloom. Inside, the building was silent but for the susurrant whisper of waves, softer now that the wind had dropped. Nothing stirred on the dais. Had Mayot fled? No, as her eyes grew accustomed to the blackness she saw the mage's outline on his throne. She'd half expected to find him pacing up and down, anxiously awaiting her return, but instead he just sat there, still as a corpse. Halting at the foot of the steps to the dais, she called out, "I have come for your decision, my Lord. It is time."

"Your time perhaps, woman," Mayot said. "Not mine."

The priestess ground her teeth together. *If he calls me "woman" one more time . . .* "A servant of Shroud is coming. Surely you have sensed his approach."

"And you assume I need the power of the Book to defeat him? You forget, I am a necromancer. The death of the forest releases energy I can draw on. I am in my element here."

"As is your adversary."

"Then, if it is a confrontation he seeks, we should be well matched."

Romany shook her head in disbelief. Was the old man really such a fool? She could not make out his expression in the gloom, but his voice revealed no quaver of fear. *He truly thinks he can win.* "And if you are victorious?" she said. "What of the next disciple Shroud sends, and the next, and the next?"

"What of them?"

Along the strands of her web, the priestess could sense the knight nearing the outskirts of the city. There was no time to play out the rest of this game as she would have liked. She would have to try a different tack. "Enough of this," she said to Mayot, her tone hardening. "Even if you *are* capable of single-handedly defeating Shroud's army of servants, this is your last chance to accept my offer of aid. Or had you forgotten the Book of Lost Souls? Decline now, and I walk away. The Book's secrets will forever remain out of your reach."

"Indeed? It occurs to me, woman, that you need my help in this as much as I need yours. If I refuse you, whatever scheme you have dreamt up will fail."

Romany was grateful for the darkness that covered her frown. "The difference is in the stakes we have wagered. *My* life does not hang in the balance."

"It also occurs to me," Mayot continued as if he had not heard her, "that I stand to lose whichever course I choose. If I destroy this disciple, I make the Lord of the Dead my enemy."

"Then give up the Book, old man," Romany said, her voice dripping scorn. "Grovel at the feet of Shroud's servant, if you must. Just stop wasting my time."

The mage did not respond.

The priestess spun on her heel and headed for the exit.

Mayot's voice drew her up as she reached the mouth of the passage leading out. "Wait. What price your help if I accept it?"

"We have no time—"

"What price, damn you!"

Romany bridled at his tone. "No price, my Lord. As I have already said, my aid is freely given."

"There is always a price."

The priestess kept her silence. Mayot's last comment had been spoken so softly she suspected it was not meant for her ears. She held her breath, sensing the old man's decision wavered on a knife edge. A wrong word from her now and the game would be over before it even started. Imagine the indignity.

As she waited, she shifted her attention to the threads of her web. Shroud's knight had entered the city and was riding along one of its main thoroughfares. The strands of death-magic would serve as a beacon, guiding him to the dome. He was but heartbeats away from taking Mayot's decision out of the old man's hands.

"Very well," the mage said at last. "I will lower the wards round the dais. But I warn you, woman, any hint of trickery and I will kill you."

Romany released her breath. "A wise choice, my Lord." There was no time to savor her triumph. With the knight closing in, the moment had come for the Spider to take up the baton.

She sent a thought inward. *My Lady.*

Nothing.

Were those hoofbeats she could hear outside the dome?

My Lady, she tried again.

Still no answer.

Romany muttered a most unladylike obscenity. Her mind worked furiously. Had the Spider already grown bored of this game and moved on to another? Or had Shroud found out about the goddess's involvement and taken steps to deny her interference? The Spider would not think twice about abandoning Romany to her fate . . .

Suddenly the goddess was in her mind, a vast suffocating presence. The pain was excruciating, like Romany's worst migraine multiplied tenfold, and she raised her hands to her temples. Lights flashed before her eyes, and she felt consciousness slipping away.

The Spider's mental nudge was like a slap in the face. Abruptly the pain eased, and the goddess's voice filled her head. "You took your time."

I could say the same of you. For once, though, Romany could not muster the will to retort. The Spider had entered her mind before, of course, but never so intimately. The goddess masked her thoughts with wards of steel, yet Romany could still detect whispers of her emotions:

determination, assurance, but also . . . anticipation. It occurred to her then that she should be shielding her thoughts in the same way the Spider did. She sensed the goddess's amusement at the idea.

"What secrrrets does a high priestess need to keep from her patron?"

"If I told you that, they would no longer be secrets."

The Spider's attention had already moved on, though. She stretched out her senses toward the Book of Lost Souls, and Romany watched with grudging admiration as the goddess set to work, peeling away layer upon layer of the Book's wards. Whoever had last owned the thing had spared no effort in safeguarding its secrets, for the Book was protected by traps within traps, each deadlier and more devious than the last. As one was disarmed, another would be triggered; one neutralized, another activated. And so it went on. Feints and illusions, strikes and counterstrikes, like two blade masters dueling. Indeed, the Spider showed a deftness of mind that, Romany had to acknowledge, almost matched her own.

As each set of defenses fell away, the magic of the Book grew stronger. The priestess's migraine returned, a throb of pain accompanying each new ward undone. The power that remained locked within the Book was now pushing against the shields that held it back. An idea occurred to Romany. Dare she risk breaking the goddess's concentration?

No choice.

"Perhaps you should hold something back, my Lady. We may need it to bargain with later."

"Yes, thank you, High Priestess," the Spider said. "The thought had already occurred to me. There are some secrets here that I will not deliver into Mayot's hands, however pressing the need. Shroud may be my enemy, but at least he has learned the rrresponsibilities of power."

A dozen heartbeats later, the goddess disengaged herself from the Book's defensive onslaught. Then, without so much as a word of farewell, she was gone, withdrawing with a wrench that left Romany's mind reeling. The priestess waited for the inside of the dome to stop spinning.

All in all, it had not been a good day.

It stood to get much worse, though, if Shroud's disciple were to find her here. She sensed another vibration along the threads of her web. The knight was but a street away. Romany took one final glance at

Mayot. The mage had reestablished his wards about the dais and was now clutching the Book to his chest, mumbling something over and over in the darkness as if he had been robbed of his wits. Not an encouraging sign, admittedly, but Romany had done all she could for the old man now. He would have to face Shroud's knight alone.

There was always the possibility, she supposed, that they might destroy each other in the struggle.

Her mood brightened.

From the darkness of an alley, Parolla looked left and right along the waterfront. Her breath caught. As she had feared, the Hunt had guessed her destination and made it to the river ahead of her, for the street was dotted with antlered horsemen. If her bearings were correct the docks lay upriver, and judging by the number of dactils wheeling in the distant gloom that was where the high priest was focusing his search. Downriver four riders guarded the approach to a bridge, a gentle curve in white stone supported by three evenly spaced pillars— and from what Parolla could make out, the last bridge east of her position within the city borders.

That gave her an idea.

For her plan to work she'd need to find a better vantage point within striking distance of the bridge, and she retreated along the alley into deeper shadow. Then hesitated. Something had set her teeth on edge. Something nearby. She stilled her breathing and listened. Nothing. *Just my imagination.* If the Hunt knew she was here they would have come charging in with all fanfare. At the very least Parolla would be able to hear approaching hoofbeats or the creak of a dactil's wings, but instead all she could make out was the low rush of the river behind her.

Raising her hood, she strode along the alley and turned left at the first intersection. The passage she entered smelled like a latrine, and the cobbles were greasy underfoot. She would have to circle east to approach the bridge—

A shout from behind.

Parolla spun to see a group of Huntsmen on foot, pounding toward her along the alley. A hundred paces away, but closing quickly. Parolla swore. Hells, where had they come from? The passage had been empty when she turned into it. One of the warriors blew a thunderous blast on a horn that was followed moments later by an answering note from the west. The darkness in Parolla bubbled up, demanding release. Her hands were already pointing at the Huntsmen, but she dragged them to one side, unleashing a wave of sorcery that struck a derelict warehouse between her and the enemy. With a rumble, a section of wall collapsed, spilling debris into the alley.

Parolla didn't wait to see if the way was blocked. Weaving a cloak of shadows about herself—no option now but to hope there was no *magus* nearby—she fled in the opposite direction. Past a turning on her right, shouts fading behind, then she reached a crossroads and drew up. She'd only run a short distance, yet already she was out of breath. From her left came the sound of footsteps, and she pressed herself flat to a wall. Two Huntsmen turned into the alley, so close she could feel the wind of their passage. Shadow-spell or not, it seemed that they *must* see her, but they just continued past her in the direction of the damaged warehouse.

She turned left into the street from which they had come.

Deep breaths, searching for calm. There were shops along this side of the road, and Parolla edged forward, keeping to the gloom cast by their tattered awnings. The bridge was in front of her now, a stone's throw away, together with the four antlered horsemen guarding it. One of them clutched a net and a spear; two held crossbows. The fourth rider was clearly the leader, for the antlers on the man's helm were tipped with silver. There was a glint of armor where his cloak parted at the neck, and he held a sword in one hand, a throwing ax in the other.

And he was looking straight at her.

Parolla froze. Had he spotted her? No, not at this range. Not if the two Huntsmen in the alley hadn't pierced her shadow-spell from an armspan away. Even so she considered retreating into deeper darkness, but what if the rider spied the movement? Better to wait until his attention moved on. His horse was pawing the ground, and he stilled it with a word. From behind Parolla came another horn blast, an exchange of shouts, but the two Huntsmen who'd missed her must have told their friends she hadn't come this way, for the sounds were slowly receding.

The rider's gaze followed them south.

Parolla crept to the corner of the last building. The waterfront was lit by scattered torches, and the oily smoke coming off them had a smell that reminded her of the slave girl's melting eyes. *No,* she thought, pushing the image away. No sense in picking at that scab. There'd be time enough later to wallow in self-recrimination.

Looking west toward the port, she saw distant riders approaching along the waterfront. Scores of them. *By the Nine.* Not since Texiki had the Hunt committed such numbers in pursuing her, and on that occasion she'd only escaped through blind luck when she stumbled across a Merigan portal. This time would be different, she knew. If her plan failed, there was nowhere left to run.

She looked back at the river. *Come on, come on.*

The horsemen were less than thirty paces away. The net-carrier made a comment too low for Parolla to hear. In response, his leader said, "If the Lord favors us, she will. Now be silent." Beyond them, the river was a sweep of muddy black and smeared torchlight. Swarms of feathermoths fluttered above it. A boy was making his way upriver in a boat little bigger than he was, paddling with his hands against the slack current. Parolla's gaze followed his progress through the gloom.

Then she saw it.

Letting her shadow-spell fall, she sprang at the Huntsmen.

The leader gave a warning shout, and two crossbow strings twanged. One of the bolts missed to Parolla's left; the other bounced off her magical defenses. Then the leader hurled his throwing ax. The weapon must have been invested with sorcery, for it cut through Parolla's wards and glanced off her left shoulder, shattering her collarbone in a rush of hot agony. Yet even through the pain she had the presence of mind to aim her answering bolt of sorcery not at her attackers but over their heads, and it exploded with an earth-shaking concussion. The Huntsmen screamed and raised their hands to their ears even as their horses bolted along the waterfront. One of the riders slipped from his saddle. He hit the road and lay unmoving, blood streaming from his eyes and nose.

Parolla hurdled him. As she ran, she cradled her left arm to her body. A warm red stain was spreading across her shirt. Every step jarred her injured shoulder, but she had known worse pain in her time, and would undoubtedly do so again if she did not get clear. She had the bridge now. Feathermoths crowded every finger's width of stone, and they took flight at her approach, fluttering about thick as blizzard snow. Left foot, right foot, willing herself on. It was only as she stumbled to a halt at the center of the bridge that she saw Huntsmen dashing toward her from the opposite bank.

Moving to the stone balustrade, she looked down.

Just as the riverboat—the one she had seen from her hiding place—began to emerge from the arch beneath her.

Parolla sat on the balustrade, facing downriver, and swung her legs over the side. From either end of the bridge the shouts were getting closer, but she did not look across. Below, the prow of the boat slid into view, two men at the rail, followed by the deck. It seemed a long way down suddenly, but there was no changing her mind now.

Parolla pushed off with her good arm, and the deck rushed to meet her. Her legs buckled as she landed, and she fell to her knees. A sharp pain went through her left foot as if she'd stepped on a spike, but that was nothing compared to the agony in her shoulder. Her collarbone had already started knitting back together, but it cracked again with a brittle sound. Her breath snorted in her nose.

"What in Shroud's name?" said a voice.

Parolla glanced up. A balding man—the *casanto* of this boat, she supposed—was watching her from the prow. She could smell his breath even from this distance: ale and blackweed smoke. To his left, a younger man stood knotting a coil of rope. His cheeks were pierced with metal studs, and there was a scar where his right eye had once been.

The *casanto* looked her up and down, his scowl giving way to a leer. "Well, well, what 'ave we 'ere. Takes a dim view of stowaways on board the *Riverbird,* don't we lads."

Parolla heard rough laughter from behind. "Take cover, *sirrah,*" she said.

The man's response was lost in the sound of a crossbow quarrel hitting the deck next to Parolla's foot. A second bolt bounced off her wards. Then the air was alive with missiles, four, five, six of them thudding into the boards. The *casanto* cursed and bounded past Parolla toward the stern, almost colliding with her in his flight. His one-eyed companion took a bolt in the thigh and went down clutching his leg.

Parolla rose and staggered to the mast. The riverboat had floated clear of the bridge and was inching farther away with each heartbeat. A Huntsman climbed to the balustrade and tried to jump across. As he fell, Parolla lost sight of him behind the wheelhouse, but the distance must have been too great, for she heard a splash off the stern. On the bridge, more antlered figures were milling about. One woman gestured upriver, and through an arch Parolla saw a galatine boat drifting on the current, its triangular sail stained red by the dying sun. Another Huntsman clambered onto the balustrade and swung his legs over as Parolla had done, no doubt intending to board the galatine and give chase.

It was time for her to put into action the final part of her plan.

Raising her good arm, she released her power and sent a wave of death-magic rippling toward the bridge's leftmost pillar. The feathermoths in its path burst into flames and fell blazing into the river like drops of fire. As the sorcery struck the pillar, there was a sizzling hiss as if the stone were dissolving. Fissures formed and began to spread. Then a section of the bridge collapsed, pitching a handful of shrieking Huntsmen into the river. The remaining antlered figures ran for the northern bank. They'd done nothing to merit Parolla's restraint, but still she waited until the last of them was clear before destroying the other two pillars. The bridge crumbled into the water, throwing up spray.

A flash of light came from her right, and she saw a flaming arrow fired from the riverbank arc high into the gloom before dropping into the water short of the boat. A second arrow followed, this one overshooting its target to land a dozen armspans beyond the starboard rail. There was as much chance of Parolla being hit by lightning as by the next missile, and so she held her ground and looked at the Huntsmen still flailing in the waters round what remained of the bridge's pillars. A few had climbed onto the stonework and were offering their hands to companions struggling under the weight of their armor.

Parolla watched their struggles until a bend in the river took her out of sight.

It's done.

She rubbed a hand across her eyes. Her plan had worked. There was no prospect of the Huntsmen boarding a boat in pursuit any time soon, and there were no bridges ahead from which they could stage an ambush. She should feel a sense of relief. Of triumph, even. But instead she felt only bone weary, and she leaned against the mast. Shroud's temple was behind her, and what did she have to show for her time in Xavel save an aching shoulder and a few more deaths to blight her dreams? What would she do now? Where would she go? Her months of study among the dusty scrolls of the Great Illicanthian Library three years ago had elicited few ideas, and she'd exhausted them all. The guardians of the Thousand Barrows protected nothing more than the memory of some ancient Fangalar atrocity; the Carin Citadel had long since fallen into ruin; and the Shrine of Ages had proved to be merely the nesting place of some nameless Krakal shade.

There were always other empires, though, other worlds, for Parolla had only just begun to explore the Merigan portals. Perhaps the time had come to risk another journey through them—to leave this continent behind and with it, if luck was with her, the Antlered God and his servants. A path through to Shroud's realm was out there if she could but find the strength to keep searching. No secret could hide from eternity, after all, and Parolla had eternity in which to look. She would go on. She *must* go on, into the Abyss itself, if that's where her path took her.

Her brooding was interrupted by a bloom of sorcery. She tensed, her gaze flickering to the riverbank. But no, the power she sensed was not that of the Antlered God's *magi*. *Death-magic*. It came from the distant east . . .

A net of coruscating sorcery closed round her, sinking into her flesh like a thousand barbed hooks. She screamed and thrashed, tried to grab the net and shake it off, but the links had her tight. Where they touched her skin, her flesh sizzled as if someone were branding her with an iron. Then she was *pulled*, and she stumbled forward. She threw out her arms seeking something to hold on to, but her hands grasped only air, and she sprawled to the boards. The strength of the tug increased, dragging her across the deck to the starboard rail. Parolla locked her legs round one of the supports. She needed to counter the sorcery somehow, but could not shape conscious thought through the pain. Another wrench and her body pivoted about the post, her head and torso now hanging out over the river.

The post groaned, bowed.

Then her tainted blood rose inside her. She tried to fight it down, but her power would not be denied. A shadow stained her vision.

The net of sorcery enveloping her disintegrated.

She smiled. The darkness was like a cool towel pressed to burning flesh, and her pain receded. It made her wonder why she'd resisted its call before. There'd been a reason, she sensed, but it hardly mattered now.

Levering herself back onto the deck, she climbed to her feet.

In time to see a ball of flames come rushing at her across the river, vaporizing the water in clouds of steam. With a cry, Parolla sent a burst of black fire flashing to intercept it. The two sorceries

annihilated each other off the port rail, and the thunder of the detonation set the riverboat rocking. Flames rained down on the deck,
fizzing on Parolla's skin. She barely noticed. A crack sounded, and
the mast came crashing down on the wheelhouse. Sailors scattered.

Parolla laughed.

She turned to the riverbank from which the attack had come. A
hunched figure stood silhouetted against one of the inns along the waterfront, torchlight reflecting off the golden antlers that sprouted from
his helmet. *Ah, the high priest.* Even through the shadows across her
sight, the man's power burned bright as a balefire. Parolla, though,
had taken his measure and found him wanting.

Sorcery coursed through her veins. So the Antlered God wanted
to prolong this *bakatta,* did he? So what if she had destroyed his
temple in Axatal? So what if she had slaughtered a score of his priests?
She'd only done it because the *fekshas* had tried to take her power
for their own. Did their Lord think she should have stood by and let
them? Did he think she would now let herself be hunted, and not fight
back?

But Parolla *would* fight back. She was done with running. Now she
would return to shore and hunt the god's servants as they had hunted
her, and before she was finished she would draw the last wailing breath
from every damned one of them.

Starting with the high priest and his pretty golden horns.

She extended her arms.

"No."

It took Parolla an instant to realize the voice had been hers. She
took a breath, fighting to wrest back control. But the lure of her blood
was strong. She had only to surrender to it, let it carry her doubts away.
The high priest stood alone on the riverbank. He'd thrown his best
at her, and she had kept him at bay. Now it was her turn. Now she
would give answer for the lives she'd been forced to take this day.

And if more should die in the clash? Parolla dug her fingernails
into her palms. The high priest was beaten. She had escaped the Hunt,
and soon she would be clear of Xavel.

It's over.

The darkness receded.

Pain came surging up to fill the void left behind, and Parolla bit
back a scream. Her cloak was smoldering, and the skin of her hands
was a mass of suppurating blisters, but a tingle across her body told

her that her flesh had already started to regenerate, and she waited with gritted teeth for the healing to run its course.

When she looked back at the riverbank, the high priest was gone.

A heartbeat passed, then sailors began scrambling over the deck, beating with scraps of cloth at the flames that had taken hold. The windows of the wheelhouse had shattered, and the sails had burned to ash.

The *casanto* spoke behind Parolla. "Shroud's mercy!"

She prized her burned lips apart. "A moment, *sirrah*," she croaked, "then I will see to your wounded."

"You can piss on 'em for all I care! What about my boat?"

Parolla felt her blood stir once more. She turned to face the man and saw him go pale as he gazed upon her ravaged features. He made a warding gesture.

"You will take me to the coast," she said.

"The Abyss, I will! The mast's shot. I'll 'ave to put in for repairs." Anger rekindled in his eyes. "You owe me big, woman."

She seized him by his shirt and pulled him close enough to see her reflection in his eyes. Tendrils of black sorcery snaked down her arms toward him. "The coast, *sirrah*," she repeated. "You will take me as far as Folar. Unless I find a faster vessel before we get there."

The *casanto* licked his lips. "Three days, it'll take us. We'll be limpin' all the way."

Parolla's blistered skin itched, but she resisted the urge to scratch it. "Then consider yourself lucky I don't make you throw your cargo overboard to speed our passage."

The man's eyes widened. He looked over her shoulder at the riverbank, doubtless wondering whether the Huntsmen meant to continue their pursuit.

"If they do, I will deal with them," Parolla said.

A heartbeat's hesitation, then the *casanto* nodded.

She released him, and he scuttled back to the wheelhouse.

Putting him from her mind, she returned her attention to the east and the mysterious flare-up of death-magic she had sensed before the high priest attacked. The sorcery had grown stronger in the last few moments, and she frowned. By her reckoning, the source of the eruption was hundreds of leagues away. Only the gods wielded power enough to be detected from such a distance, and since the sorcery was death-magic, that must mean Shroud himself . . .

Parolla shook her head. No, the Lord of the Dead would never risk annihilation by setting foot on the mortal plain.

What else could explain the phenomenon, though? The death of an immortal? Perhaps, but wouldn't she have sensed something of the struggle that took place before the fatal blow was landed? The outburst of sorcery had been sudden, like . . . what?

Parolla's pulse quickened.

Like the opening of a portal?

The underworld. Could it be? That would explain why the power was death-aspected. But then why was she still able to detect the sorcery after the initial burst? Wouldn't a portal have been closed now by whoever had opened it? Parolla groped with her mind toward one of the threads of magic . . .

Then stopped herself. Perhaps later, when the darkness within her had fully subsided she would investigate the strands more closely, maybe even travel along one in spirit-form toward its source. For the time being, she was content to wait. Content even to endure the stares of the sailors she felt on her back. A short while ago, she'd despaired of ever finding a way to the underworld. A short while ago she'd wondered what her next step would be in her quest to confront Shroud.

Now she had her answer.

A serving-girl leapt from Luker's path as he strode along the corridor, his Will bunched tightly inside him. His footsteps set the floor shuddering, and the doors to either side rattled in their frames. His thoughts burned. Jenna alive should have cooled some of the fire in his blood, but the juripa spirits were simmering in his veins, and his face was hot like he could still feel the touch of the sorceress's flames. He reached out with his senses, exploring the rooms to either side of the passage until he found what he was looking for. *You should have run when you had the chance.*

Stopping before a door, he unleashed his Will. The door creaked, buckled, exploded inward.

Inside, Merin was sitting at a desk reading a book. He was barechested, his wet gray hair combed back, a towel slung round his shoulders. On the bed behind him, his traveling gear had been neatly laid out. Merin closed his book and rose as Luker entered. There was no surprise in his expression, no fear either, but then doubtless he thought he was safe with his grunts in the common room just a shout away.

Glancing at the door that now hung quivering from a single hinge, he raised an eyebrow. "Come in."

Luker shaped his Will like a noose round the tyrin's neck and lifted him from his feet.

Then *squeezed*.

Suspended an armspan above the floor, Merin clawed at the invisible force holding him. He threw his head left and right, seeking some respite from the force crushing his windpipe, but these were not the hands of some strangler throttling him, and his efforts did nothing to weaken Luker's hold.

The Guardian increased the pressure.

"Any last words?" he asked.

The towel round Merin's shoulders fell to the floor. Gasping for breath, he thrust out a leg toward the chair he had been sitting on, trying to hook it with his foot and drag it closer.

Oh no you don't.

A gesture from Luker, and the chair moved out of range. He watched as the tyrin's face began to flush red. Merin's gaze was fixed on Luker, his expression one of rage. He tried to speak, but the Will was too constricting, and his words came out as a wheeze.

"What's that?" Luker said. "Speak up."

Merin's chest heaved. He made another effort for the chair, but his flailing foot only kicked air. Scanning the room, his gaze fell on his sword propped against the desk, but it too was out of reach. Then his hands moved to his belt-pouch, his fingers fumbling at the ties. Was he going to offer Luker money? Try to buy his miserable life?

Instead of a coin, he drew out a small glass globe and flung it at Luker.

The throw went right. Luker used the Will to catch the missile a handspan above the ground. He left it hanging there and faced Merin again.

The tyrin's struggles were becoming weaker now. Veins stood out across his forehead, and his eyes bulged. But his expression had lost none of its defiance. Luker moved closer until he was an armspan from Merin's twisting form, close enough to hear his breath rattle in his throat, to see the light begin to fade from his eyes.

Only then did the Guardian release his Will.

Be grateful the assassins failed.

The tyrin crumpled to the floor and lay there gulping in air, his limbs twitching. Then he retched, vomiting the remains of his last meal over the floor. It didn't seem like Luker would be getting any sense from him for a while, so he returned his attention to the glass globe and used the Will to call it to his hand. The glass was tinted blue and contained a swirling mist. The Guardian reached out with his senses. *Water-magic.* A deep well of power—the weight of ocean tides, the elemental force of the open seas—bottled up as tightly as Luker's anger was. To cage such energies within a fragile shell of glass was a feat only the most powerful of mages could have accomplished. For the emperor to have entrusted the tyrin with such a weapon was an indication of the importance Avallon attached to this mission.

Luker turned back to Merin. The tyrin had propped himself up on one elbow and was now dragging himself toward the bed. He turned and sat with his back to it. A trail of spittle ran down his chin, and he wiped it away with a shaking hand.

"Interesting trinket you have here," Luker said. "A gift from the emperor's pet mages, right? I'm guessing the fireworks start when the glass is smashed."

Merin did not answer.

"This kind of power," the Guardian went on, "would've destroyed the inn and everyone in it."

"At least I'd have taken you with me."

Luker nodded. He'd have done the same in Merin's position. "You have more of these?"

"Perhaps."

"Stored carefully, I hope."

Again, no response.

"Look after them," the Guardian said, then tossed the globe back to Merin. The tyrin snatched at it, caught it at the second attempt. Scowling, he returned the object to his belt-pouch. Luker could see that the inside of the pouch had been reinforced with some form of steel lining, and the metal was imbued with protective sorcery. "Are we finished?" Merin asked.

"Not quite. The Breakers. You led them to Jenna."

"I didn't need to. They knew she was here."

"With us? Then why—"

"The woman killed one of their commanders," Merin cut in. "That makes her fair game. You think they were just going to stand by and let her leave the city? Would you, if it had been one of yours?"

Before Luker could respond, footfalls sounded in the corridor outside. He sensed a presence in the doorway behind him—one of the tyrin's watchers from the common room, most likely—but he did not turn. Merin looked at the newcomer and shook his head. Heartbeats later the footfalls retreated again.

Luker waited for them to die away, then said, "My problem isn't with the Breakers, it's with you. You should've warned me they were coming."

"Why? She's your bloody friend, not mine."

"You agreed she could travel with us."

"And that's all I agreed to!" The flush had been fading from Merin's face, but now it returned. "Do you know what she is? An assassin. One of the most feared—"

"Save your breath." The tyrin would be needing it again soon the way he was going. "While she's with me, she's under my protection. Warn them."

"I'm not a Breaker."

Luker stepped toward him. "Don't screw with me! You're the emperor's man, they'll listen to you. Or do you want me to tell them myself?"

Merin pulled himself up to sit on the bed, sweeping away his carefully arranged traveling gear with one hand. "It makes no difference what I say. You know how it works. Soldiers look after their own."

"As do I. Any repeat of tonight and I won't wait for them to try again. I'll go looking for them myself." It wouldn't be hard to find the Storm Keep Gill had pointed out. He could check in to see what progress they had made learning the Will.

The tyrin considered this, his expression unreadable. He rubbed a hand across his neck. "I did some asking round about you, Guardian, when I heard you were coming on this mission. Respected, they said, but not trusted. An outsider. Seems the Guardian Council knew nothing about Kanon taking you on as his initiate. And when they found out, they voted to have you executed. Not one of the Fenilar caste, they said. Impure blood."

"What of it?"

"The emperor stepped in to save you. Convinced the Council to think again."

"What Avallon did, he did for himself. Thought he could buy my loyalty."

"He told you that?"

"No, you're right, he's all about the Shroud-cursed charity."

Merin's brows knitted. "If there's one thing I've learned about the emperor, it's that his motives are never predictable."

"To the Nine Hells with his motives! I'm done being another man's tool."

"You owe Avallon your life."

"A debt I've repaid a hundred times."

"That's for the emperor to decide, not you. Now get out of my sight."

"You'll give the Breakers my message?"

"I said get out!"

Luker held his gaze for a few heartbeats, wondering if the tyrin needed another demonstration before he got the Guardian's point. Then he turned to leave.

"Oh, and Luker, if this happens again . . . Next time, you'd better make sure you finish me off."

"If you give me cause, count on it."

At that moment the Guardian sensed a burst of distant power, so faint as to be almost imperceptible. He stiffened. *Death-magic.* Was Chamery in trouble? No, the source of the energies was too far away for it to be the boy. It came from the north. A sorcerous duel perhaps, somewhere beyond the city's limits?

More hurried footsteps in the corridor. Chamery appeared in the doorway, his face bloodless but for spots of color on both cheeks.

Luker's expression darkened. "I told you to watch Jenna."

"I've done what I can for her," the mage said. "Right now we have more important things to worry about. The Book of Lost Souls has been activated."

Merin's rasping voice broke the silence. "How? How do you know?"

"Because I can sense it!" Chamery said. "Guardian, tell him."

Luker's eyes widened. *That surge of sorcery?* According to Gill, Mayot had taken the Book to Arandas, maybe farther north still. To detect its power from such a distance . . . His thoughts shifted to Kanon, and his stomach fluttered. His master would be out there somewhere, sensing this too. What nightmare was he about to walk into? *And not just Kanon either.* Because for all Luker's talk of going after his master and not Mayot, something told him he wouldn't find one without also finding the other.

Chamery's gaze held his. "We must leave. Now!"

Merin said, "We're more than three weeks' ride from Arandas."

"Meaning every moment counts." The mage's look at Luker was imploring. "*Tell* him!"

The Guardian hesitated. Merin was right. It would take them three weeks to get to Arandas, and then only if they didn't encounter trouble in the Remnerol wildlands and the Gollothir Plains north of the Shield. And when was the last time Luker had passed that way without having to blood his swords? He thought back to when Gill's message reached him on Taradh Dor. He'd spent five days reading and rereading the summons. Five days deciding whether to answer it or just throw the damned scroll in a fire. Five days wasted! The need to *do* something was suddenly overwhelming.

"The boy's right," he said to Merin. "We leave now."

Long before Romany saw Shroud's disciple approaching, she heard the clip-clop of his horse's hooves on stone. A glow appeared among the ruins and began weaving its way toward her through the darkness. Moments later the knight arrived at the dome. He did not appear to have suffered any injury at the hands of the spirits in the forest, though the sword in his hand was surrounded by wisps of gray mist as if shreds of the banished Vamilian souls clung to the blade. The pale light radiating from it illuminated the carvings on the dome, and for a heartbeat the image of the three-masted ship seemed to rise and fall on the stony waves. Romany's stomach lurched.

As the knight reined up, he cast a look at her hiding place, and she shrank back behind the cover of a low wall. A trickle of sweat ran down her back—just the heat, she assured herself. There was no cause for alarm because Shroud's disciple could not possibly detect her through her wards. In any case, he had come here not for her, but for Mayot. For the Book. Provided she did not intervene in his struggle with the old man, she was perfectly safe.

She risked a look back at the dome. The knight had loosened a lance from its bindings along his horse's flank and now gripped it in his left hand as he steered his mount toward the dome's arched entranceway. Death-magic flowed from the opening, and the disciple's sword flashed brighter as it fed off the sorcery. The threads of power snaking out into the city had multiplied a hundredfold since the Spider unlocked the Book, but the knight did not hesitate as he plunged into the murk. Did he know that the Book's power had been unleashed? Did he care? He could not, after all, back down from any clash with Mayot, for the Lord of the Dead was not a master who tolerated timidity in his servants. Romany felt a tingle of expectation. How could

Mayot defeat such a man? Wouldn't any sorcery he threw at the knight just serve to make him stronger?

As Shroud's disciple passed along the archway, the light of his sword receded.

Romany let her spirit float free from her body and followed him into the gloom. She chose a vantage point high above the dais from which to observe the confrontation. The glow from the knight's sword was now dazzlingly bright, illuminating the farthest reaches of the dome. It could not, however, penetrate the shadows that hung about the dais. The maelstrom of death-magic radiating from the Book was like a wound in the fabric of creation—a vortex into which all life was being drawn. Romany could feel its tug even in her spiritual form. What toll must it be taking on Mayot himself, sitting at the heart of its power?

The knight's progress across the dome was measured. Deliberately so, the priestess suspected, in order to add to the creeping dread Mayot must surely be experiencing. Clutching the Book to his chest, the mage watched in silence as the rider drew near. He looked small and frail as he blinked against the light, and Romany wondered what was going on behind his dark eyes.

Not a lot, most likely.

Shroud's disciple halted at the foot of the dais and raised his visor. Romany couldn't make out his face from where she hovered, but she did see Mayot flinch. His left eyelid started fluttering, and the priestess smiled. Stupid old man! Did he only now perceive the true measure of the other players in this game? Had he expected them all to have countenances as fair as Romany's? *Impossible!* Would Mayot's nerve hold now he had stared into the whites of his enemy's eyes? Or would he bend the knee to Shroud's disciple as she had taunted him?

Mayot stared down at the rider for a while, his hands turning pale where they gripped the Book. Then he seemed to relax, his expressionless mask slipping back into place.

The knight's voice boomed out. "I am Lorigan Teele, knight commander of the Belliskan Order. Hand over the Book of Lost Souls, sir. I command you in Shroud's name."

When Mayot spoke, his voice sounded shrill in comparison. "The Book is mine. Mine, do you hear! By what right does your master claim it?"

"I did not come here to reason with you—I am the deliverer of Shroud's judgment, not his mediator. My master claims the Book because he can."

Mayot leaned forward in his chair. "He sent you to *steal* it from me, then? Ah, but it is too late for that. The Book's power has already been delivered into my hands."

"Delivered? By whom?"

The corners of Mayot's mouth twitched, and for a moment Romany feared he would betray her presence. Instead he said, "The rules of the game have changed, Lord Knight. Your master is no longer in a position to demand anything of me. If I agree to surrender the Book, what does he offer in exchange?"

Romany stiffened. This was not part of the plan! *Treachery! And after all I've done for him!* In retrospect, perhaps she should have insisted Mayot fight the knight as the price for her unlocking the Book's secrets, but in doing so she would have revealed too much of her hand. Besides, she was not so foolish as to think the old man would hesitate to break such an oath if it suited him.

Lorigan came to her rescue. "Shroud does not deal with mortals," he said to Mayot. "Nor does he look kindly on those who presume to test his patience. Now, hand over the Book, sir, or spend an eternity regretting your insolence."

"You dare threaten me? I hold immortality in my hands! Does your master expect me to give up such a prize for nothing?"

"Immortality?" A chuckle sounded from the knight's helmet. "Shroud is a patient god, mortal. You may cheat him for a time, but one day he will hold your soul in his hands."

"Perhaps it will be *me* holding *his*. The power at my command now rivals that of your Lord."

Lorigan's booming laughter rang out. Romany had to stop herself laughing with him.

Mayot's voice hardened. "It would seem this conversation is at an end."

The knight closed his helmet's visor with a snap. "So be it. Defend yourself—"

Even before he had finished speaking, sorcery roared into life about Mayot. A seething torrent of blackness raced from his hands toward Shroud's disciple, and Romany watched wide-eyed as whatever defensive wards Lorigan had fashioned about himself were ripped apart. The man was knocked backward out of his saddle. His horse screamed as its flesh melted from its bones, then its legs collapsed from under it. By the time it hit the ground it was no more than a skeleton crumbling into ash.

The knight lay sprawled on his back amid a swirling cloud of leaves, still clutching his sword in one hand, his lance in the other. Wave after wave of death-magic hammered into him, pinning him to the floor. Tiny symbols etched into his armor glowed red in the darkness. The sorcery invested in the metal had held Mayot off until now, but Romany could sense it weakening beneath the old man's onslaught.

Somehow Shroud's disciple made it to his feet. He took a heartbeat to steady himself, leaning into the storm of sorcery as if it were a gale-strength wind. Then he pulled his left arm back and hurled his lance at Mayot.

A flash of lightning lit up the blackness.

Mayot raised a hand, and a blast of death-magic intercepted the weapon, smothering the light.

The lance melted into nothing.

Lorigan set one foot on the first step leading up to the dais. The death-magic opposing him intensified, clawing at him with a palpable hunger. A screeching sound reached Romany, like talons drawn along metal. The knight's armor crumpled inward, throwing off sparks. Still he kept his feet. Then, with a roar that transcended the din of the magical conflagration, he took a step toward Mayot.

Another step, and another.

Shroud's disciple was clutching his sword in both hands now. It shone with an impossible radiance, driving Mayot's shadows back to within a few armspans of the old man himself. Romany shielded her eyes. Heavens forbid that the blackness might burn away entirely to leave her looking at the mage again. Lorigan climbed another step, halfway now to the dais.

The swell of Mayot's sorcery escalated once more.

Ripples of death-magic from the battle battered Romany's spectral form, and she retreated higher toward the roof. Below, the glow from Lorigan's sword was rapidly losing its contiguity, bleeding into the darkness on all sides. The air about it shimmered. Then, with a tortured scream of metal, the sword exploded, sending light streaking in all directions like a thousand shooting stars.

The storm of death-magic closed round Shroud's disciple until all that held back the blackness was the red glow radiating from the symbols etched into his armor. Lorigan bellowed his defiance, but for the first time Romany heard pain mixed in with the anger. He raised his right leg to take another step, lowered it inch by agonized inch onto the next stair. A scratch of metal on stone. Then his foot gave way, and he fell to his hands and knees with a clang.

Get up! Romany silently urged him.

She started. Cheering for one of Shroud's disciples? Whatever was she thinking?

Suddenly the blazing symbols on Lorigan's armor were extinguished like blown candles, leaving the priestess squinting into the gloom. Moonlight gleamed on metal, then it was engulfed by the gray rush of Mayot's sorcery.

The knight screamed, a piteous sound that made the hairs on the priestess's arms stand up. On and on it went, a cry of such torment it shivered the air. Romany had left her migraine behind when her spirit floated free from her body, but now the pain was back—a sharp, hot agony as if someone had stabbed a needle through her head. She clawed at her ears, but there was no escaping the noise, and she clamped her teeth together to prevent herself adding her own scream to Lorigan's. Through her spirit-eyes, she saw the small, shining thing that was the knight's soul blacken and shrivel until with a final shriek it was snuffed out by the shadows surging round it.

Mayot's sorceries raged on for a handful of heartbeats. Then the death-magic flickered and died, the tendrils of darkness thinning and dispersing. Romany heaved in a breath. The wind began to fade. The steps the knight had been climbing had melted into molten stone, an orange glow cooling to gray. Leaves whipped up by the maelstrom of power started falling back to the ground. Those that came down on the red-hot rock burst into flames.

There was no sign of Lorigan Teele.

Romany drifted up to the roof of the dome where the light filtering through the star-shaped holes was brighter. For a time she stared up at the stars through a break in the clouds, waiting for the beating of her heart to slow. Her head felt like it might crack open at any moment, and if she concentrated hard enough she could still hear the reverberations of that dreadful scream.

All the same she forced a smile. She wasn't about to let anything detract from the triumph of tonight's proceedings. Yes, there had been surprises along the way, but the knight's death marked the successful completion of the opening moves in the game. Romany had expected Lorigan Teele to give a better account of himself, but then men so often flattered to deceive. Doubtless Shroud was even now wishing he'd sent a woman in his place.

No way, of course, that the Lord of the Dead could have predicted the Spider's interference and thus anticipated the measure of opposition his knight would face. How long before he could summon more of his servants here for another strike at Mayot? A few days? Weeks, even? Shroud, after all, did not have a web such as the Spider's along which to ferry his disciples. And while he was moving his pieces into position, there would be time for the goddess to plan her next move, for Mayot to immerse himself in the power of the Book. When Shroud's followers finally arrived in this godforsaken backwater, they would face a challenge greater even than the one the knight had encountered.

Romany rubbed her hands together. All was going to plan. Her success, she decided, had never truly been in doubt.

Yet still something niggled her. The improbability of what she had witnessed left her feeling strangely apprehensive. Mayot had tried to betray her. Galling, certainly, but not altogether surprising. More unsettling was the ease with which he had brushed aside Lorigan Teele—one of Shroud's elite—particularly since the mage had only just begun to draw on the Book's reserves. How much further might his power grow? What other abilities lay within his grasp? For an instant the priestess wondered whether she and the Spider had created a weapon they could not control.

She snorted. As if such a thing were possible!

The last echoes of sorcery died away and the sound of lapping waves once again filled the dome.

Then, rising above that suddenly, Romany heard the dry rasp of Mayot's exultant laughter.

PART II

SHADES OF BLACK

CHAPTER 7

SHELTERING BEHIND an outcrop of rock, Luker squinted against the grit on the wind. To the north the road that led down from the Shield's foothills disappeared into the cinnamon haze that cloaked the Gollothir Plains, an expanse of scorched earth and rock broken only by isolated stands of rodanda trees. Clouds of red dust hung in the air as if a great host had passed this way recently. And while the plains appeared deserted now, Luker had traveled here often enough to know this land was never as empty as it seemed.

Seven years ago he had stood in this same spot, looking down on the lead elements of the emperor's invading army as it prepared to advance on Arandas. He'd been tasked with scouting ahead of the Ninth, reestablishing contact with the forces guarding food and water drops hidden along the route of the march. Luker shook his head. Sensible military planning, those drops. Straight out of Fuster's manual on logistics. Merin Gray could probably tell him the page number. But you didn't move wagons of supplies through the Gollothir Plains without some tribe or other taking notice, and sure enough when Luker reached the caches he had found them plundered, the soldiers protecting them eviscerated and staked to the ground for the fire ants to feed on.

The revelation had come too late to halt the Ninth's march, for the emperor had never been one to turn back once the die was cast. The tribes of the Gollothir Plains had harried the army day and night as it slogged through the dust and heat. Two weeks later the Ninth had stumbled into the shadow of Arandas's walls, short on rations and bleeding from a thousand cuts. And the fate of the siege was sealed before it had even started.

The dust of the plains was red, Luker had heard the tribesmen say, because of Erin Elalese blood.

Luker liked the place. Sculpted by the sun and the searing wind, the plains were littered with the bones of countless dead civilizations. In his travels he had come across the ruins of cities larger even than Xavel and the other metropolises of the Qaluit Empire to the west; statues of forgotten tyrants each as tall as twenty men; raised circles of sand where bones rose to the surface like bubbles in a lake before sinking out of sight again. The land held secrets, he knew. He could feel it in the charged silences that filled the midnight hours, in the tremors of ancient sorcery that rippled beneath the ground like a heartbeat.

But it wasn't that sense of mystery that drew him to this place. During Luker's mission to find the supply caches he had traveled for days at a time without seeing another soul, and every bell had been a blessed struggle for survival. Blessed because while he was fighting to keep Shroud at bay he couldn't also be thinking about the reasons that had led him to abandon the Guardians that first time nine years ago and go wandering beyond the White Mountains. About how he'd slunk back two years later with nothing more to show for his travels than worn-out boots and the knowledge he was no closer to finding any relief from the sense of restlessness that ever dogged him.

The trail of death-magic from the Book of Lost Souls led north across the plains. To Arandas? Luker was beginning to doubt it. The city was over fifty leagues away, but the source of the power felt more distant still. He rolled his shoulders. After two weeks' travel the Shield was behind him, but Kanon remained out of reach. If there was one consolation, it was that with the Book now activated he could strike out alone if he had to and follow the threads of death-magic to Mayot. He'd wait a while longer, though, before deciding on his next move. There was no guarantee, after all, that when he tracked down Mayot he would find Kanon with him. The tyrin's spies might have information that could help.

Stones clattered behind, and Luker looked round to see Merin climbing the trail, Jenna and Chamery farther down the slope. The tyrin hobbled his horse before scrambling up to join the Guardian. He had refused to let Chamery heal his wounds after Luker's attack at the Gate Inn, and the bruising round his neck was still visible as a yellow cast to his skin. His drawn face and sunken eyes were testament to the punishing pace Luker had set since leaving Arkarbour, but unlike Chamery, Merin had not complained about the hardships of the road. He stared down at the lowlands.

Luker caught his eye. "Time to swallow your pride. We're taking the direct route to Arandas, straight across the plains."

Merin studied him for a moment. "The flow of survivors from the Seventh has dried up since we entered Cloud Pass. Tells me the Kalanese are out there"—he nodded at the plains—"hunting them down."

"Just as the Kalanese themselves are being hunted. They won't get any special treatment from the tribes here."

"You think we can avoid both sides?"

"Going to have to try," Luker said. "It's five days to Arandas if we take the road, maybe double if we go round. We need those days."

Merin had the look of a commander considering the advice of a subordinate. *The tyrin's still playing soldiers.* How long before he woke up to the fact the decision wasn't his to make? "You know the land?" Merin asked.

"Well enough."

"What about water?"

"Well enough, I said!"

"And what happens if we meet any Kalanese out there, or one of the tribes? Odds are we'll be outnumbered."

"We could run into trouble whichever way we go."

Chamery's questioning shout sounded from downslope, but Merin ignored him. "Is there any cover if we need it?"

"Some. Ruins, gorges, gullies."

"Any of which could be used to hide an ambushing force."

The Guardian bit back a retort. The tyrin wasn't telling him anything he didn't already know. The fact was, Luker stood a better chance of crossing the plains unseen if he traveled alone. If Merin wasn't careful, he was going to talk himself out of an escort. "I can scout ahead if need be—spirit-walk our route . . ."

His voice trailed off. A flash of light had pierced the haze ahead. The Guardian placed a hand on Merin's arm and gestured.

"I see it," Merin said. "Sunlight on armor?"

"Bloody careless of them if you're right."

The flicker came again. Luker turned to scan the ridge of hills behind. In the distance he saw the black turrets and crenellated battlements of Point Keep, hewn from the stone of one of the Shield's peaks. Farther west—

There! An answering flash from a shelf of rock overlooking the exit from Cloud Pass.

Luker cursed. "Signals. We've been spotted."

Merin peered at the plains. "I can't see a thing through this dust."

"Whoever they are, they're not ours."

"Behind us too? From Point Keep?"

"No, to the west."

"They'll be circling round to cut off our retreat. We have to move now."

Luker swore again. He hated running, but until they knew what they were up against . . . He nodded.

"We go back to plan A," Merin went on. "Skirt the foothills toward the Waste."

"Once we're down there they won't be able to see us any better than we can see them," the Guardian said. "Maybe we can slip away in the dust."

The tyrin's raised brows mirrored his skepticism.

Arandas felt much farther away suddenly.

Ebon shifted on the Iron Throne. The imperial crest emblazoned across the back of the chair dug into his back, and there was nothing to ease the cold discomfort of the seat. Admittedly the cushion had been removed at Ebon's own bidding, for even now his feet barely touched the ground, tall though he was. A reminder, as if one were needed, that this was his father's throne.

He was used to sitting at Isanovir's right hand in the place now occupied by his brother, Rendale, and while his new vantage point offered only a slight change of perspective, it was telling in its import. A few paces in front, steps led down to the chamber's main floor. At the end of the room, a stone's throw away, were double doors of black steel that stretched up to the ceiling. To Ebon's left and right, Pantheon Guardsmen lined the walls. Above them, in the hanging galleries where the lesser domens and other dignitaries were seated, not a chair remained unfilled, and even the stairs between them were crammed with expectant onlookers. Judging by the babble of their conversation they were looking forward to seeing their new king's mettle tested by the Sartorian consel.

The Serrate Crown felt heavy on Ebon's head.

His gaze was drawn, as ever, to the skeleton near the eastern wall of the chamber. In the shadow of one of the galleries, the skull of some vast creature rose from the floor as if the rock had once turned molten before solidifying to imprison the beast. As a boy, Ebon had climbed into the jaws. Each of the beast's teeth was as long as he had been tall. Not even Mottle knew what manner of creature it was, still less what fate had befallen it. The Currents, it seemed, held no answers—the ripples were too faint to be deciphered.

A khalid esgaril. The name leapt unbidden into Ebon's mind. *Dragon's bane.*

The whispering of the spirits grew loud, and the throne room began to darken. *No! Not here, not now.* Ebon tried to fight the visions, pressed his back into the throne's imperial crest until he thought he must have drawn blood, but it was all slipping away. Flickering images overlapped the chamber, as if he were seeing double. A scene was forming: the same room, yet different. Rugs covered the floor, and a collection of skulls of all sizes, human and animal, were affixed to the walls. Looking up, Ebon saw the tops of trees through the windows above the now-empty galleries. Was this a vision, then, of the throne room from centuries past? Had the Forest of Sighs once extended this far east?

A spectral figure hovered at the edges of his sight—a pale-skinned woman in a coat of chain mail that reached down to her knees. Her image was too blurred for him to see her face, yet still he felt he should know her. Her mouth was opening and closing, but Ebon could not make out her words. He wanted to shake his head to clear it but didn't dare, lest he draw the attention of his kinsmen in the "real" throne room. *Get away from me!* he silently commanded the spirit, but from her lack of reaction it seemed she could no more hear him than he could her. Tearing his gaze away, he found himself looking again at the khalid esgaril. The creature's cavernous mouth appeared to be smiling, and there was movement in its eyes . . .

With a start the king came to, his chest heaving. The images of his second-sight faded to reveal Mottle sitting in one of the skull's eye sockets. He was swinging his legs back and forth. He must have sensed Ebon's regard, for he looked across and winked.

The last vestiges of the king's vision fell away.

To his right a voice was speaking; the chancellor, standing behind the throne, had bent over to whisper in his ear. Ebon concentrated on his words. Tamarin was explaining—slowly and deliberately as if he were talking to a child—that the delegation from Mercerie would not be joining them. It seemed a messenger had been sent ahead to convey the envoy's apologies—something about being struck down by ill health on the road to Majack. The chancellor added, unnecessarily, that he thought this a fabrication. The Merceriens clearly shared Ebon's suspicions as to the reason for the consel's visit and had chosen to stay away for fear of being drawn into a conflict.

As Tamarin's voice droned on, Ebon looked to his left. His mother was perched on the edge of her throne, her hands gripping the chair's armrests. Beside her, General Reynes sat stroking the cinderhound on his lap. Next came Vale, and beyond him a dozen domens, drawn up according to rank. Switching his gaze to his right, Ebon scanned the faces of the Council members on that side, relieved to see Domen Janir had heeded his order to stay away.

There was a booming knock from the end of the chamber, and all conversation died away.

So it begins.

Guardsmen hauled on ropes, and the doors swung open. A score of figures were visible in the gloom beyond, but Ebon resisted the impulse to lean forward for a closer look. The Sartorian party moved through the doors and into the hall. At the front was a man with the rust-colored skin of all Sartorians, who walked with the grace of a swordsman—Consel Garat Hallon, Ebon presumed. Flanking him, two on each side, were four giant warriors, each half as tall again as the consel and covered from head to toe in plate-mail armor. They wore horned helmets and carried double-headed axes in their gauntleted hands. The dull beat of their metallic footsteps kept perfect time as they marched.

From Ebon's left, General Reynes's cinderhound gave a growl. It was followed by a murmur from the galleries as Mottle jumped down from the khalid esgaril and scuttled to intercept the Sartorian party, smoothing his crumpled robe all the while.

"What's the fool doing?" Rosel said.

Ebon did not respond. The consel had halted. He exchanged a few words with Mottle, but Ebon was too far away to hear them. The Sartorian folded his arms, then looked left and right at the ranks of Pantheon Guardsmen.

The tension in the room stretched taut as a bowstring.

"I trust you have good reason for this, Mottle," Ebon whispered, knowing the mage would hear him.

Even as he spoke the words, the consel shrugged and waved a casual hand. The four armored giants detached from the group, swung round, and retreated to the rear of the chamber. Garat cocked his head at Mottle, his lips moving soundlessly, a hint of a smile on his face. In response the mage stepped back, one arm moving in a sweeping gesture.

Ebon could see the consel more clearly now. Tall and heavily built, he looked only a few years older than Ebon himself. His brown hair was oiled back in the style of Sartorian warriors, and there was a scar above his left eye where the eyebrow should have been. A longsword was sheathed at his hip, the pommel and scabbard adorned with the rearing flintcat of Sartor. The chancellor had noticed this too, and he started whispering again in Ebon's ear. *A bold statement indeed of his ambition.*

Garat Hallon halted at the foot of the stairs leading to the throne. He met Ebon's gaze for an instant, then glanced up at the Serrate Crown. His raised eyebrow indicated surprise, but the king was not fooled—on the consel's way here, he would surely have heard about Isanovir's abdication.

"Consel Garat Hallon," Ebon said. "Welcome to Majack."

"My thanks . . . your Majesty," Garat replied. "Forgive my bluntness, but was not your father king when I set out from Camessil?"

"The honor is now mine."

"I see." The consel's tone suggested Ebon had just confessed to something unsavory. Then, raising his voice to carry to the watching galleries, he continued, "I was saddened to hear of Isanovir's decline. To lose a man of his experience at such a difficult time must be a grievous blow."

Difficult time? Was that meant as a warning? Ebon had hoped to avoid the posturing and point-scoring, but if Garat was intent on taking them down that road then Ebon's kinsmen would expect him to give as good as he got. "I'll be sure to pass on your sentiments. Clearly, though, you have not traveled all this way just to inquire after my father's health. I presume you bring tidings from the Patrician."

Garat's smile faltered as Ebon's barb struck home. "I am no one's messenger," he said. His gaze slid away to take in the throne room, lingering on the skeleton of the khalid esgaril. "A remarkable place, you have here. Constructed in the First Age by one of the elder races, I'm told. My scholars have unearthed little else of consequence, though not, I assure you, from any lack of endeavor."

"Indeed. And what is the nature of your interest in the fortress?"

"Purely academic, of course. I consider myself a student of history, yet the building's architecture is unlike anything I have seen before. The sheer scale of it defies comprehension. No doubt the city's entire population could shelter within its walls should the need arise?"

"No doubt."

"Is it true there are levels below ground?"

"We believe so, though as yet we have been unable to access them."

"Because they are shielded by sorcery?"

Ebon nodded.

"And the palace's defenses? Formidable, of course."

"Of course. For them to be tested, though, an enemy would first have to breach the city's outer walls. And that will never happen."

A murmur of approval from the galleries greeted Ebon's words.

Garat laughed again. "Ah, careful, your Majesty. I might take that as an invitation to try." He looked over his shoulder and beckoned to someone at the rear of his retinue. A red-faced man in a servant's livery advanced. He was carrying a sword. "I've brought you a gift," Garat said to Ebon. "A broadsword forged in the fires of Oskirrin itself. The weapon of your father, I believe. Of course, not everyone has his prodigious strength . . ."

The comment was left hanging in the air like a challenge. Ebon felt all eyes on him. He studied the consel for a moment, then rose and descended the steps. Accepting the sword from the servant, the king hefted it in both hands. His weapon of choice was a saber, not this monstrous blade that must have weighed as much as he did. As he examined the jeweled scabbard, he whispered, "Mottle, a little help if you please." Then, placing his right hand on the hilt, he unsheathed the sword in one smooth motion. The weapon was suddenly feather light in his grip, as if it rested on a cushion of air. Ebon took a few practice swings before meeting the consel's gaze. "Nice balance."

Garat Hallon recovered quickly. "I'm delighted you approve."

Ebon resheathed the sword. "I fear I cannot match the distinction of your gift, Consel, but perhaps you would accompany me to our stables later. I know you have long been an admirer of Galitian stock. My stablemaster has chosen a stallion that I trust will not disappoint."

The consel's tone was dismissive. "Later, yes. For now, allow me to introduce my party. This is my brother, Falin." He ruffled the hair of a spotty youth trying to effect a stern expression. "Beside him is my sorceress, Ambolina Alavist." The woman he indicated was dressed in blue robes with a white trim. Her long black hair was tied back in a ponytail, and her fingernails were half as long as the fingers themselves. Her steely gaze stared straight through Ebon. "To my right is First Adviser Pellar Hargin," the consel went on, pointing to a fat, lazy-eyed man whose skin appeared to be melting in the heat. "And next to him, Tarda Gen Sulin, the commander of my Guard . . ."

There followed a list of names that Ebon forgot as soon as Garat spoke them. The king then introduced his court. Only when he came to Vale did the consel show any interest. "Ah yes," Garat said. "The Endorian. I've heard a great deal about you. It's said your people can alter the speed at which they move through time."

Vale did not respond.

"I came across one of your kinsmen outside Villandry," the consel continued. "He was fast." He paused. "But not fast enough."

Vale's voice was gruff. "Then he was weak."

"You believe you would fare better? I look forward to a . . . demonstration."

Ebon spoke before Vale could accept. "Some other time perhaps." He turned away from the consel's party and climbed the steps to the Iron Throne. The chancellor, clutching his scepter of office in one hand, was trying to catch Ebon's eye, but the king ignored him. He handed the broadsword to Rendale before sitting down again on his throne. "I understand congratulations are in order, Consel, for your campaign in the west. I am told the city of Villandry has fallen."

"Villandry?" Garat shook his head, smiling. "Ah, your Majesty, your intelligence is sadly out of date. Villandry fell more than two months ago. Since then, Melandry, Geradry, and Amadry have also been taken."

Ebon mastered his surprise. The enmity between Sartor and the Almarian League went back centuries, yet the consel had crushed his enemy in a single campaign? "Impressive. And yet, after so much bloodshed the Sartorian people will doubtless crave peace."

Garat nodded with exaggerated gravity. "Of course. I know our two nations have had their differences in the past. As it happens, the very purpose of my visit here was to begin addressing them. But what do I discover on my journey south? A kingdom preparing for war." He spread his hands. "You can imagine my distress."

"You are referring, I take it, to the buildup of Galitian forces in the northlands?"

"Unless there is something else you think I should know about."

"I can assure you, Consel, our troop movements are not directed at Sartor. The Kinevar are increasingly a cause for concern. Our scouts report their numbers massing—"

"So I argued with my first adviser," Garat cut in. "Pellar Hargin's geography is much better than mine, however, and he reminded me that the Forest of Sighs extends not just to the north of here but also to the southernmost provinces of your kingdom. Strange, then, that your forces seem to be mustering exclusively between the Sametta and Amber Rivers."

"That is easily explained. We have reason to believe the Kinevar are migrating north."

"Toward Sartor? And you didn't think to warn us?"

"A messenger was dispatched over a week ago. Perhaps you crossed on the road."

Garat did not respond. He was listening intently as his first adviser leaned close to speak in his ear.

"In any event," Ebon went on, "if we wanted a war, surely we would have attacked while you were fighting the Almarian League."

Hargin had now finished talking, and Garat looked at Ebon again. "I'd be inclined to agree, but for one fact. Your father was in command then, now you sit in his place. My people will be asking, 'What are the new king's plans?' There will be those in his entourage—they will say—who seek to exploit his inexperience to further their own ambitions." Garat was looking up and down the ranks of domens to either side of the throne, his gaze settling here and there as if to suggest he knew who the conspirators were. "What if the new king declares war in an attempt to unite a divided court?"

Ebon would not let himself be baited. "It is fortunate, then, that you are here. I will have the opportunity over the next few days to put your mind at rest."

"As you say. I have always been of the view, though, that words should be backed by actions. I must therefore insist on the immediate withdrawal of your forces from all lands north of the Amber River."

There was a rumble of unrest from the galleries. Ebon lifted a hand and waited for the noise to die down. "I see we have much to discuss."

"Indeed we do." Once more Garat raised his voice to carry. "One other matter in particular comes to mind." He made another show of scanning the domens. "I could not help but notice Domen Janir Calidar is absent today."

We come to it at last. "Unfortunately so. He has other business to attend to."

Garat's smile was knowing. "If you say so. Surely Janir must realize, though, that he cannot hide from me forever. It is time he answered for his crimes."

"The events you are referring to took place five years ago. Are we to rake up all the troubles of the past?"

When First Adviser Hargin spoke for the first time, his chins wobbled. "Is an atrocity any less an atrocity, your Majesty, simply because a few years have gone by?"

Garat spread his hands again. "You see the difficulty I face?" he said to Ebon. "Pellar Hargin never ceases to remind me that I am a servant of my people"—there was a snort from someone to Ebon's right, but Garat ignored it—"and the mood of the people is for vengeance. I trust Janir is now ready to offer himself up to justice."

The throne room had fallen perfectly quiet. Were the domens expecting Ebon to throw his uncle to the wolves? Would they even protest if he did? "Justice, yes. I expect Janir would demand the same if he were here."

Garat's eyes glittered. "How so?"

"Must I remind you of the facts, Consel? A handful of brigands attack a heavily guarded company in the forest near Linnar. A single arrow is fired, not at one of the soldiers but at Domen Janir's wife. The only brigand apprehended takes poison rather than submit to questioning. You forget, Consel, I was there."

"And were you also there," Garat asked mildly, "when Janir attacked the Sartorian village and butchered every man, woman, and child in it?"

Ebon's expression tightened. "No, I was not. There are, however, still questions to be answered. Why, for instance, did the bandits' tracks lead to the village Janir attacked? Then there is the arrow that killed Irrella. Its fletching was made of gelin feathers woven together. A technique, I believe, exclusive to the Sartorian military."

"You are suggesting Sartorian troops were involved?"

"I am suggesting we reserve judgment until we obtain all the facts."

"And how do you propose we do that? Janir conveniently slaughtered any witnesses."

Ebon glanced at Mottle. "I will leave that to my mage. Vale, too, has some skill at manipulating time. They would, of course, need your permission to visit the village."

The consel's gaze flickered to his sorceress. The woman was examining her long fingernails. In reply to Garat's unspoken question, she shrugged. The movement set her robes shimmering. "An interesting notion," the consel said. "You will allow Ambolina to witness?"

"You do not trust me, Consel?"

There was a glint of amusement in Garat's eyes. The Sartorian was plainly enjoying playing to his audience, and Ebon suspected he had witnessed only the first act in his performance. "Ah, your Majesty, trust takes time to earn. And in light of recent developments . . ."

Ebon's eyes narrowed. "I have already explained—"

"I was referring," Garat cut in, "to your ambassador in Camessil."

"Domen Fillon Bett? What of him?"

"You had not heard? He has been arrested."

Another angry murmur erupted from the galleries, and this time Ebon did nothing to quell it. "On what charge?"

"Conspiring against the state. We have seized messages passing between Bett and the Chameleon priesthood in Camessil, detailing a plot to overthrow the Patrician. There can be no question as to the ambassador's involvement." An idea seemed to occur to Garat. "He is a friend of Domen Janir, is he not?"

"A friend to us all."

"Yes, yes, such a distressing fall from grace. What could have caused such an honorable man to lose his way, I wonder?" The consel paused, then added, "Perhaps the reasons will become clear during his . . . interrogation."

Ebon felt the blood rise to his face. As if in response to his anger, the whispering of the spirits in his head swelled, and for a heartbeat the ghostly images of his second-sight overlapped the throne room. He fought them down.

His mother was on her feet. "You dare question him without a member of this court present?"

"Sadly that was deemed necessary," Garat said. "You will appreciate the need to root out any treachery before it spreads. It will be interesting to see who the ambassador implicates in his schemes, yes?"

Chancellor Tamarin spoke. "Nevertheless, Consel, this is most irregular. Perhaps one of the King's Council should attend him."

"You are welcome to choose someone to accompany us when we return."

By which time it will all be over. "No," Ebon said. "Now." He looked to his right. "Domen Jeniver, will you go?"

From among the seated domens, Jeniver rose. "Gladly, your Majesty."

"General Reynes," Ebon said. "Arrange a suitable escort. As many as you think necessary."

Garat's eyes twinkled with humor. "Is that wise? The road to Camessil is long and dangerous, and there are—so you now tell me—Kinevar raiders to consider. I would fear for the safety of your party."

Ebon took a breath and let it out slowly. The consel had clearly anticipated his move. Jeniver would be walking into a trap. Yet when the king met Jeniver's astute gaze he saw only determination there. Turning back to face Garat, Ebon said, "Domen Jeniver knows what to expect. You have made that abundantly clear."

The Sartorian's answering smile was cold.

It was the chancellor who eventually broke the silence. "Consel, you must be tired after your journey. Rooms have been prepared—"

Garat cut him short with a raised finger. "That will not be necessary. I have decided to make camp outside the city."

He does not trust us, Ebon thought. *He thinks us as unconscionable as he is.*

"As you wish, Consel," Tamarin said. "I should warn you, however, that the gates to the city are closed at nightfall. The Kinevar—"

"I think we can take care of ourselves," Garat interrupted him again. "Now, if you would excuse me." He inclined his head to Ebon. "Your Majesty. I look forward to continuing our discussions tomorrow."

The hills had been reduced to rubble. Parolla trudged across shattered fragments of stone that slipped and settled beneath her. Some of the rocks glowed softly red, and she could feel heat through the soles of her boots. That heat, though, made a welcome change from the earth-spirits she'd been sensing underfoot for the past few days. Only yesterday the Ken'dah Steppes had been swarming with the souls of the dead shamans who had once served the clans that infested these plains. Those spirits had dogged Parolla's every step through this land, their anger at her presence evident in the keening of the wind, the way the long yellow grasses fouled her stride. Now, though, the spirits were gone—driven off, most likely, by the sorcerous duel Parolla had witnessed from afar last night.

It was a night she would long remember. Huddled in her cloak, she had watched fountains of energies light up the sky to the east, demonic magic warring with interwoven layers of earth and air. Parolla had been leagues away, yet still the ground had bucked more violently than during any earthquake she'd experienced, and the wind had gusted so strongly it threatened to lift her from her feet. When at last dawn broke, the devastation revealed to the lands ahead of Parolla had been a stark reminder of the dangers that lay in wait, for the sorcerous clash had surely taken place at the site of the Merigan portal she was now heading for.

And yet it was too late for her to turn back from her course, even if she'd wanted to. From Xavel, it had taken her three days to reach Folar on the Inland Sea, two more to find a berth on a trader ship bound for Enikalda, another three before the vessel finally docked at its destination. But Parolla's real troubles had begun when she set out across the steppes toward the still-distant source of the threads of death-magic. Every league had been contested by clansmen, no doubt alerted to her presence by the earth-spirits underfoot. Each time Parolla drove the savages off, they returned in greater numbers.

Her horse had been killed in the last encounter, shot in the eye by an arrow she hadn't even seen coming. That was two days ago. Since that time the clansmen had broken off their assaults, content to pursue her at a distance while they waited for her strength to fail. It would not be long now. Parolla hadn't slept the last two nights, knowing her tormentors would attack the instant she closed her eyes. In this wretched land there was no place she could hide, no settlement in which she might take shelter or replenish her supplies. Her eyelids now weighed heavy as headstones, and her pace had slowed to a stumble. Exhaustion stalked her as relentlessly as the clansmen did, and it wore Shroud's baleful grin.

A cawing sound came from overhead, and Parolla looked up to see redbeaks circling. She wet her lips with her tongue. For an instant she had mistaken the birds for dactils. Since leaving Xavel there had been no sign of the Huntsmen, but Parolla doubted their Lord had given up the chase. The high priest, knowing he was outmatched, would have sent assassins to track her. She looked over her shoulder. For now her only pursuers were a dozen clansmen, watching her from a hill half a league away. How soon before the Huntsmen joined them on that skyline? How far behind would the assassins be?

Parolla allowed herself a grim smile. What did it matter? She was about to go where even the Antlered God's servants would not dare to follow.

Reaching the top of a ridge, she stared down into a bowl-shaped depression tenscore paces across. The basin was shrouded in blackness, like a pocket of night the sun could not burn away. *The Shades.* In this place, Parolla knew, the world of the Kerralai demons overlapped the mortal realm. The shadows were deepest at the center, fading to gray at the sides. At the edge of the darkness, the roots of a smoldering tree rose from churned earth. A few paces beyond was a stone archway—the Merigan portal—surrounded by a ring of seven obelisks, only one of which remained upright.

Within the circle of stones, a man wearing yellow robes lay facedown in the dirt, his long blond hair fanned out round his outsized cranium. *A Fangalar.* One of the elder races. To his left were the remains of a horse, its snowy white coat spattered with blood, and crouching over the animal's corpse was a black-skinned Kerralai demon, almost invisible in the gloom. After the fireworks last night, Parolla had been resigned to finding the basin guarded, yet still the demon's presence was a setback—no chance now of her passage going unnoticed. Even as the thought came to her, the Kerralai raised its head to stare at her with its huge red eyes. Its muzzle and fangs were smeared with gore.

Parolla descended the slope, sending stones clattering down into the depression. Her power was drawn about her. She halted at the edge of the shadows, ten paces from the demon. Ten paces? It felt a lot less. Even sitting back on its haunches, the Kerralai towered over her. One of its wings hung uselessly by its side, the skin shredded, the bones broken. The demon's breaths made a wheezing sound.

Parolla inclined her head. "*Glesha,*" she greeted it.

The Kerralai seemed unsurprised that she knew its language. When it spoke, its voice was a throaty growl. "Welcome, *angella.*"

Parolla's skin prickled. *Angella.* Angel of Darkness. "Why do you call me that?"

"Death walks in your shadow. Are you not a harvester of souls?"

"I'm not one of Shroud's disciples, if that's what you mean."

The demon tore another chunk of flesh from the horse's corpse and chewed noisily. "Then why have you come? As you can see, the battle here is done."

Parolla waved a hand at the wall of darkness an armspan away. "When I last traveled these lands, the size of the rent was a fraction of what it is now. The Merigan portal lay beyond the edge of the shadows."

The Kerralai's smile revealed rows of gleaming fangs. "The fabric of your world is torn. The magics unleashed here last night will only hasten its dissolution. Every day the rent grows larger."

Parolla looked at the corpse of the Fangalar. "No doubt this man was unaware of that fact when he chose to use the portal."

"He is ignorant no longer."

"Nevertheless, his trespass in your realm was doubtless unintended. You do know, *sirrah,* that the Fangalar's kinsmen will sense what took place here. They will come seeking vengeance."

The demon's long forked tongue darted out to lick blood from its fangs. "Then perhaps I will destroy the portal. It matters not. There can be but one response to violating the borders of our realm."

"You are fortunate we of this world are not as . . . sensitive . . . as you in such matters." Parolla gestured to the basin. "This ground is, after all, as much a part of our world as it is of yours."

The Kerralai's eyes narrowed with animal cunning. "I see where you are going with this, *angella.* You seek permission to enter the rent so you may use the portal."

Parolla shook her head. "The gateway is of use to me—I know of no other portal close to where I am heading. No, *sirrah,* it is *your* realm I mean to enter."

It was not a decision she had taken lightly. By her estimation, the source of the tendrils of death-magic was still scores of leagues to the east—if she kept to the Ken'dah Steppes. Distances, though, worked differently within the Shades. A journey of weeks across the plains would take Parolla but a handful of bells in the demon world. And there was another rent such as this just a short distance to the west of the Forest of Sighs.

In response to her words, the demon threw back its head and laughed. The sound was like rocks grinding together. Parolla felt an urge to step back. It would take only a heartbeat for that massive head to lunge forward, for the jaws to snap shut . . .

"Has the fate of the Fangalar not touched you at all, *angella*?" the Kerralai said. "True, my wounds prevent me from opposing you, but others of my kind will give answer to your intrusion. No one who enters our realm leaves alive."

"I have done so before."

"You lie."

"No, I do not. At the time, I knew nothing of your people's hostility to intruders. Your *mekra*, Mezaqin, took pity on me. I left your world through this very rent."

The memory was still sharp in her mind. She had entered the rent near the Forest of Sighs, hoping it would lead to Shroud's realm. Instead she'd found herself in the Shades. Oblivious to her danger, she had wandered lost for a bell until she was confronted by the demon lord himself. It was Mezaqin who had informed her of the punishment for trespass, before proceeding to question her at length on her reasons for entering his world. In the end he had spared her life on a whim, she suspected . . . although her parentage might also have played a part in his decision.

The Kerralai had gone still at the mention of Mezaqin's name. "And did my lord give you permission to return?"

"He said he would kill me if I did."

The demon stared at her.

"I was hoping he meant it as a joke."

"Mezaqin is not known for his sense of humor."

"Perhaps I should ask him first, then."

The Kerralai snorted. "And how will you do that? You think you can just summon him to this place to hear your request?"

"No more, I suppose, than I can ask you to carry a message for me."

The demon bared its teeth.

Sighing, Parolla peered through the rent. The darkness in the Shades was deeper than in the basin, and she could see only a few paces into the gloom. Who knew what might be waiting for her if she entered the demon world? Would she even remember the way through to the rent near the Forest of Sighs? She looked over her shoulder. And yet, what choice did she have but to try? For while the clansmen pursuing her were momentarily hidden by the rim of the depression, she knew they would not be far away.

Turning back to the demon, she said, "It seems I will have to take the risk."

CHAPTER 8

ROMANY TOOK a sip of white wine and let it linger on her tongue before swallowing. Pure nectar! Rich, silky, yet bursting with fruit, and wonderfully refreshing against the heat of the day. Yes, it was a little on the pricey side, but the priestess could think of no worthier way to spend temple funds. On reflection, perhaps the fall from grace of her old wine merchant had been a blessing. Imagine thinking he could top up her bottles of Koronos white with cheap Maru dishwater and not get caught! Absurd! She would have to think of a suitably fitting way to get even with the scoundrel beyond the loss of her custom.

Sitting back in her chair, she gave a contented sigh. Her gaze swept the cloister. The gardens round her were an explosion of color, though she noticed with a frown that some of the flowers were wilting in the heat. The air was suffused with the scent of maliranges and cavillas from the trees that surrounded the square. Romany wondered idly if the maliranges were ripe enough to eat yet. She would have to ask one of the gardeners.

Had it really been two weeks since the Spider brought her back from Estapharriol? Romany was only just beginning to recover from the ordeal. On her return to the temple she had spent a whole day in the bath trying to scrub the forest from her skin, and the memory of Mayot's gaze on her flesh still left her looking for the nearest bar of soap. The Spider had not spoken to her since her return, and the priestess was not going to be the one to initiate contact. With each passing day, she told herself, the likelihood of her having to return to the Forest of Sighs receded. Perhaps the Spider's attention had moved on to bigger and better things. Perhaps Mayot had recognized the hopelessness of his cause and surrendered the Book to Shroud. Who knows, perhaps the old man had simply died of his own ego. Whatever the truth of it, Romany wasn't about to let thoughts of the mage spoil her afternoon any further.

She became aware of something intruding upon her tranquility. A noise . . . Faint above the rustle of the trees, and the shouts of the lockkeepers working along Lepers Canal . . . *Crying.* A girl crying. The sound was coming from an open window in the wall to her left. *Ah, that explains it.* The new initiates' quarters.

Romany closed her eyes and tried to rediscover her serenity. The heat in the cloister was growing, and she mopped her brow with her sleeve, then took another sip of wine and spent a moment considering its provenance. The higher, east-facing slopes of the Koronos Hills without question. Two years old, if she had to guess. The more recent vintage was a touch more elegant . . .

It was no use. The girl's crying continued—soft, choked sobs. Not the weeping of someone seeking attention or pity. A private grief. *She is lost.* The child was not an orphan, then, for the urchins in Mercerie had been known to put out their own eyes for the opportunity to be taken in by the temple. The priestess sighed. As the memories of the girl's old life receded, her hurt would fade. Fade, but not disappear completely. *No, never that.*

A scolding voice rang out, and the window to the initiates' quarters slammed shut.

Romany cradled her glass in her hands.

"I'm imprrressed, as ever, by your ascetic zeal, High Priestess," said a familiar voice from behind her.

Romany scowled as the Spider stepped into view. Once again there had been not even a ripple along her web to warn her of the goddess's coming. *She is doing this to spite me.* "I would offer you some wine, my Lady, but sadly I have only one glass."

"No matter." A flutter of the Spider's restless fingers and a glass materialized in her left hand.

Romany paused just long enough to make her annoyance clear. Then she retrieved the wine bottle from the shade beneath her chair and poured for the goddess. Not a full glass of course, just the amount that propriety demanded. The Spider sniffed the wine before taking a cautious sip. "Not bad."

"It *is* an acquired taste. If you wish, I can ask one of the acolytes to bring you something less challenging."

The goddess raised an eyebrow. "*Less* challenging? Ah, you mean water. An excellent idea." Her fingers flickered again, and the golden color faded from the liquid.

It was a moment before Romany could speak. "I had assumed it would be a while before I saw you again," she managed at last.

"Assumed or hoped?"

"Well, since you disappeared last time without explanation . . ."

A casual wave of the goddess's free hand. "Something came up." *Something always does.*

Behind the Spider a priestess emerged from one of the doorways leading off the cloister. On seeing the goddess the woman dropped to her knees and touched her forehead to the ground. Romany looked away in disgust. Such an outrageous show of obsequiousness! Had the woman no shame?

The Spider had not even noticed. "I'm pleased to see you've been putting your time to good use, High Priestess," she said. "I trust you are fully rrrested."

Romany made no effort to cover her groan. "I am to return to the Forest of Sighs, then?"

"Of course. It's taken longer than I expected for Shroud to marshal his forces, but he's now assembled an impressive cast of players to take part in our game. Even as we speak, some are drawing near to the borders of the forest." The Spider smiled. "If I didn't know better, I'd say Shroud's nose has been well and truly put out of joint by the loss of his knight. You will have your work cut out."

Romany sniffed. The goddess was jesting, surely. Was a spider troubled by the flies that became entangled in its web? And yet . . . "I must confess, the thought of assisting Mayot Mencada in his struggles is an unpalatable one."

"Tut-tut. *Mayot* is assisting *us.* The game is ours, not his." The goddess's look hardened. "And I intend to see it through."

"And if the mage profits from our endeavors?"

"What if he does? You forget, the more powerful Mayot becomes, the harder it will be for Shroud to wrest the Book from him." The Spider sipped her water. "For now the mage needs our help."

"For now?" Romany's tone betrayed her disdain. The old man would always need a crutch. Power was nothing without the intelligence to wield it judiciously.

"Don't make the mistake of underestimating him. I have in fact been pleasantly surprised by the mage's creativity. He's made a number of imaginative moves while you've been away."

"Such as?"

The goddess gave a self-satisfied grin. "What, and spoil the surprise? You will see for yourself soon enough."

Romany rolled her eyes. The Spider's reticence was infuriating, if all too familiar. "And if he tries to betray us again?"

"You'll just have to keep one step ahead of him. Of course, if you don't think you can handle him . . ."

"Handling him is the very last thing I would wish."

"Oh, come now, where's your sense of adventure? It might even be fun."

"Fun?" Clearly the goddess was suffering from the heat. "Will you be joining me, then, for the . . . entertainment?"

The Spider shook her head. "I rrrather think it is your turn to be entertained. While you've had your feet up, I've been busy in Arandas running rings round an opponent who might otherwise have proved a thorn in Mayot's side." The goddess drained her glass. "I suspect Shroud will come to regret committing so much of his strength on this venture. In doing so he has stretched himself thin in other places, and I mean to take advantage, starting now." A flutter of one hand and the Spider's glass disappeared. "It's time we were going."

Romany's eyes widened. *Now?* "A few moments, please—"

But the world was already blurring around her. She made a grab for the bottle beneath her chair and smiled as her hand closed about the neck. Her feeling of triumph faded, however, when she noticed how low the level of liquid was.

I should never have offered the Spider that glass.

Luker's spirit drifted through the sky. Far below on the Gollothir Plains the wind blew red dust across the lowlands, smothering in a fiery haze the rocky gullies and spires of wind-blasted stone. He looked round. Nothing to see but the gnarled branches of rodanda trees protruding from the murk like skeletal hands. All in all, this hadn't been one of his better ideas. He could barely make out the Shroud-cursed ground, how was he supposed to locate whoever had spotted his party emerging from Cloud Pass?

As he banked to the left, his spirit was buffeted by swirling energies rising from the land. Not the wind, of course, since it couldn't touch him in his spirit-form, but rather the reverberations of some ancient cataclysm that had scarred the plains. The land's checkered history was written on those dark currents for those who had the skill to read them. Centuries ago a god had fallen here—Luker could sense echoes of its death throes on the updrafts—and the earth still shuddered at the memory. The Guardian's face twisted. Typical. Thousands of years dead, and the immortal still found a way to piss in his eye.

Switching his attention south, he floated toward the foothills of the Shield from which he and his companions had ridden a few bells earlier. Ahead firedrifters swooped and dived into the haze before reappearing with wriggling black shapes in their talons, but when Luker approached for a better look he saw only the corpse of an alamandra beneath a heaving mass of wither snakes. He blew out a breath. The higher he drifted, the less he could make out through the dust, but if he stayed close to the ground it would take him the best part of a day to make a single sweep of the lowlands. *I'm wasting my time here.*

A final glance at the Shield's foothills, rising from the murk . . .

Luker stiffened. There was movement along a ridge to the west.

He covered the ground in a heartbeat. A group of riders was descending a rocky slope. *Kalanese.* They rode bareback on sand-colored mounts and wore gray robes and headscarves. Spears rested across their laps, and wicker shields hung from slings across their backs. The company was drawn up in an arrowhead formation, nineteen horsemen in all.

Nineteen, not eighteen.

That extra rider spelled trouble. Sure enough, at the head of the group rode a man with skin as dark as fellwood. His long blond hair was braided with gold thread, and across his thighs rested not a spear, but a staff of bone. Luker swore. A soulcaster. What in the Nine Hells was one of his kind doing this far east?

As Goldenlocks reached the foot of the slope he raised a fist, and the riders behind him halted. The warriors at the rear of the group moved inward, changing the company's formation from a "V" to a diamond. Spears were readied. The soulcaster didn't look up, but there could be no question he'd sensed Luker. What to do about him, though? Best guess, the Kalanese were ten leagues behind the Guardian's party, so more than half a day's travel. But still too close for comfort. Half a day's lead wouldn't see Luker clear of the plains. *Shroud's own luck the bastard's stumbled across our trail.* He gave a half smile. *His luck, not mine.*

This ends here.

Luker battled down through the gusting updrafts until he was a score of paces above the riders. Goldenlocks barked a command, and all but one of his troops dug their heels into their mounts, scattering outward to form a circle with the soulcaster in the center. The remaining soldier, a woman, dropped her spear in the dust and moved up to flank him. *The sacrificial lamb.* Luker never ceased to be amazed at the lack of ceremony that accompanied what followed. The woman simply nodded to the soulcaster like she was acknowledging her name at a roll call, then slumped across her horse's neck. *Dead.*

One less Kalanese. And Luker hadn't even needed to draw his sword.

Raising a Will-barrier beneath him, he braced himself for Goldenlocks's onslaught. This first round he would give to the Kalanese, for he wasn't going to waste his energy on an attack until he'd had a chance to judge the temper of the other man's steel.

He didn't have long to wait. A burst of energy from the soulcaster hammered into him, and he went spiraling upward, riding Goldenlocks's power like the cataclysmic updrafts. Higher and higher he went until the riders had diminished to blurs in the murk. Moments later they disappeared from sight entirely. Luker's Will-shield began to unravel, and he spun another layer of wards to reinforce it. Then that too started to come undone. A headache prickled behind his eyes. And still his enemy's sorcery continued to batter him.

Not bad, little man.

Finally the waves of Goldenlocks's power subsided, and Luker's ascent slowed. He took a faltering breath. Just as well he didn't mind heights, since he was now level with the lowest of the Shield's peaks. Far below, another of the soulcaster's kinsmen would doubtless be spurring his horse level with his leader's in case the Guardian came back for more, but Luker had no intention of provoking another broadside. He'd learned enough to know Goldenlocks was strong. Too strong to be taken down while Luker was in spirit-form and so far from his body. Tempting, perhaps, to stay a while and let the soulcaster use up more of his followers in keeping Luker at bay, but at what cost to the Guardian himself? No, better to beat a tactical retreat and conserve his strength until such time as he met Goldenlocks in the flesh. For when they did, Luker vowed, the result would be different.

Closing his spirit-eyes, he concentrated on his distant body. After a short while he felt the scorched ground beneath his fingertips, the wind's hot breath against his skin. His spirit sped across the intervening leagues.

When he opened his eyes he found Jenna staring down at him, her face framed by the powder-blue sky. To her left, Chamery watched with hooded eyes, a damp cloth pressed to his face.

Jenna smiled a crooked smile. "Welcome back."

Raising himself on one elbow, Luker hawked and spat. "How long was I gone?"

"Half a bell," Jenna said, passing him a water bottle.

Luker pulled out the stopper and took a swig.

Merin spoke from behind. "Well?"

"Kalanese are on our trail," the Guardian said, looking round. "And they've got a soulcaster."

The tyrin had been rubbing his horse down with a blanket, but now he paused. "You're certain they're following *us*?"

Luker nodded. If they weren't before, they sure as hell would be now. He rose and brushed dirt from his clothes. Taking a final swig from the flask, he handed it back to Jenna.

"What next, Guardian?" Chamery said.

"We keep going. Can't ambush a soulcaster. Too many in his party, anyhow."

"Can we outrun them?"

Luker shrugged. "One way to find out."

The mage's voice was dipped in acid. "Excellent. For a moment there I thought you had things under control."

The Guardian stared at him. *Maybe I should cut the boy loose, see if he copes any better on his own.* Chamery removed the damp cloth from his face, and a drop of water dripped from the end of his nose. For the past few days he'd been using twice as much water as anyone else in the group, but when Luker tried to put a stop to it, Chamery simply started taking from his horse's ration instead. He swung his gaze to Merin. "We should move farther east, closer to the Waste. Less chance of us running into more unwanted company that way."

The tyrin turned toward the desert and frowned at the bruised skyline. "I don't like the look of that dust storm."

"You'll change your mind if we need it for cover."

"How much of a start have we got on the Kalanese?"

"Maybe half a day."

Merin held his gaze.

Aye, not enough. The Kalanese mounts were better suited to the rigors of the Gollothir Plains, and were most likely fresher too. Golden-locks would catch up to them long before they reached the Sun Road.

"There's another option," Luker said. "We split up. Me and Jenna, you and the boy. Soulcaster's bound to come after me. I'll lead him into that storm. Give me a day, I'll have thrown him off our scent."

"How do we find each other afterwards?"

"I'll find you."

The tyrin's look was appraising.

He thinks I'll hang him out to dry. Luker scratched his scar. *It's a thought.*

"No," Merin said at last. "The Kalanese could just separate when we do. And there's still the risk of running into tribesmen. Our chances are better if we stay together."

The Guardian grunted. *Yours are, you mean.*

Parolla kicked a stone as she followed the course of a dry riverbed. She hadn't expected to make it so far through the demon world un-opposed. She had been trudging through the Shades for nearly six bells, she reckoned, and she'd yet to see a single inhabitant of this barren wasteland. But that didn't mean they hadn't seen her. The val-ley slopes to either side were pockmarked with caves from which countless hidden eyes could be looking down, but if she *had* been spot-ted, why hadn't the watchers come for her? Were they waiting in am-bush somewhere ahead?

The charcoal-gray sky hadn't changed tone since Parolla entered the rent, and she was starting to wonder if a sun would ever rise on this cursed land. The Shades made the Ken'dah Steppes feel wel-coming. Such light as there was came from two small moons, one behind and to her left, the other low in the sky to her right. The air felt stale and stagnant as if it had not moved in days, and Parolla's breathing was becoming labored as she climbed higher into the hills. Flakes of rock crunched beneath her feet, and when she looked behind she saw clouds of dust marking the way she had come. She scowled. Like a big arrow pointing any nearby demons after her. It made her wonder why she bothered with her shadow-spell.

Hers were not the only footprints in the dirt. She had encountered two other sets since entering the rent—fellow intruders in this realm, she suspected. The first tracks were small and punctuated by round imprints apparently made by the butt of a staff. The ground between the tracks was scuffed, suggesting their owner moved with a shuffling gait. An old woman, perhaps? The owner of the second prints had huge feet and a stride to match, one for every two of Parolla's.

For a time both sets of tracks had kept her company as she walked. Now, only the old woman's prints continued into the gloom. The giant's had halted half a league back beside a spire of rock. The ground in its shadow had been speckled with blood and scored by dozens of clawed feet. There was no sign of the giant's body, just drag marks in the dust leading up one of the valley sides to a cluster of caves. As Parolla had hastened past, her gaze had been locked on those caves, and her nerves were still raw from twitching at every breath of wind. But nothing had stirred. The one benefit of this desolate landscape, she told herself, was that she'd at least be able to see trouble when it came calling.

And yet, that hadn't helped the giant, had it?

She had come across the prints of both the giant and the old woman at the entrance to the valley she now traveled through. The convergence had puzzled her for a while. It seemed the other intruders were, like Parolla herself, heading for the rent near the Forest of Sighs, but how did they know which route to take? The answer came to her suddenly. *The threads of death-magic.* Even here in the Shades, they were discernible through the distant rent. It would be a simple matter for the giant and the old woman to follow the tendrils, knowing they would lead to a way out of the demon world. And how had they known to track the strands? *Clearly I am not the only one with an interest in following them to their source . . .*

She stumbled to a halt.

It took her a moment to realize what was wrong. The old woman's tracks had disappeared. Parolla retraced her steps until she found them again. Then blinked. They just . . . stopped. There were no claw marks on the ground, no signs of a struggle. It was as if the old woman had simply vanished in midstep. Parolla's hackles rose. *Unless . . .*

She looked up into the yawning gray sky.

It was empty.

Suppressing a shiver, she glanced back at the footprints. There was something lying in the dust to her right—a staff, snapped into three pieces, the wood flame-blackened. Had the old woman been a fire-

magus, then? *A fire-*magus *in a land without a sun.* Little wonder, if so, that she'd been no match for whatever took her.

There was a noise to Parolla's left, farther up the valley. Claws scratched on stone. A small shape flitted across the ground, moving so quickly Parolla could barely follow its course. Anticipating an attack, she gathered her power and waited, her heart thumping, her gaze raking the gloom. The shadow, though, was moving away from her, cutting upslope in front of a group of caves before disappearing over the lip of the incline. Parolla scanned the rest of the valley for movement, but all was still. Eventually the click-clack of settling stones faded, and silence returned.

She released her breath. A coincidence the demon had taken flight just as she was passing through? Hardly. Odds were it had spotted her and judged her too powerful to tackle alone, but her stay of execution would prove short-lived if, as she suspected, it had gone to fetch help.

Her time was running short.

She set off at a run along the dry riverbed, but the Ken'dah Steppes had sapped the strength from her legs, and she soon slowed to a walk again. The gradient increased as the valley began to narrow. Ahead she caught sight of twin columns of stone. Had she seen them last time she was in the Shades? The rent was close now, she thought, but she'd been telling herself the same for the past bell. And while the threads of death-magic told her she was heading in the right direction, they didn't tell her how far she still had to go to reach her destination.

The course of the dry river became choked with rocks, and Parolla abandoned it for a rough track that wound a tortuous path up the slope to her right. By the time she reached the summit her legs were trembling and her shirt was sodden down her back and beneath her arms. The ridge was deserted, and she paused to catch her breath, doubled over with her hands on her knees. The back of her throat felt like someone had stripped the flesh from it. In front of her, the ground fell away into a sea of black. Far in the distance she could make out a range of mountains silhouetted against the smaller of the two moons. She smiled in recognition, for this was the same view that had greeted her when she'd first entered the Shades eight years ago. Towers and turrets rose from among the rocky outcrops, and circling above them . . .

Her smile faded. In the sky, winged demons soared and swooped in their hundreds. *No, thousands.* Most were the size of needleflies at this range; some were as large as spider jays.

Then a cluster of them scattered.

A rumble sounded as a shape rose from the darkness between the spires. Just one of its wings was enough to eclipse the moon entirely. There were horns atop its head, and it had a long, broad snout like a crocodile's. As its ascent leveled out, it beat its wings to maintain its height. It was difficult to judge perspective at such a distance, but it appeared to be heading toward Parolla.

She pushed herself into motion.

On the opposite flank of the ridge to the one she had climbed was a track leading down to a row of caves, and she scrambled down it, her feet skidding on loose gravel. The threads of death-magic guided her to the cave she needed. As she recalled, the portal was just the other side. The entrance was narrower than she remembered, no more than a jagged fissure less than two paces across. Too big, certainly, for that demon to follow her through. As she plunged into the blackness, she held her hands out in front of her face. Her left hip jarred on stone, catching her right on the bone, and she swore. A strong wind blew into her face, reassuringly warm after the chill of the demon world.

After a few heartbeats the passage opened out, the walls to either side dissolving into a starry night sky. In the foreground a dozen stakes had been hammered into the earth in a rough semicircle, a shrunken head on top of each one. Farther away she could make out tall swaying grasses and a grove of trees lit by a flickering fire.

The Ken'dah Steppes.

She released her shadow-spell. *I made it.*

"Welcome," a man's voice said.

Parolla halted.

A figure stepped from the shadows to her right, a glint of silver at his brow that might have been a coronet. He moved to stand between Parolla and the rent. His features were hidden in darkness, except for his eyes, bloodred and unblinking.

"Lord Mezaqin," Parolla said, struggling to keep her voice even. "I was wondering when you'd make an appearance."

"Of course you were, my dear," the demon lord's voice purred. "Would you have me believe, also, that you are pleased to see me?"

"I'm not so foolish as to think I could cross your realm uncontested," she lied.

"And yet you were foolish enough to come back. Perhaps I didn't make myself clear when we last spoke."

Parolla hesitated. Mezaqin's tone was good-humored, almost friendly. Was he as magnanimous as he seemed, or was he just taunting her? She needed more time to judge his mood. "I see you've taken human form to greet me, *sirrah,* as you did when we last met. Should I be honored?"

The demon lord shrugged. "I fear you might find my true form . . . disturbing."

"How considerate. I think you overestimate my sensitivity, though. I am no longer the child I was eight years ago."

"Your powers have grown," Mezaqin conceded. He took a step forward. "But we are in *my* realm, lest you forget. Here, you are still as a child to me."

Parolla swallowed. This was not going as she had hoped. "You misunderstand. My words were not meant as a threat."

The demon lord sighed. "Parolla, Parolla, whatever am I to do with you? The last time you were here I set a dangerous precedent by allowing you to live. Now you take advantage of my restraint by testing it again."

"I had no choice—"

"Your reasons for coming are irrelevant. The penalty for trespass is death, you know that."

"Then why are we still talking?" Parolla retorted, her voice sharper than she intended.

Mezaqin chuckled, and the air within the cave shook. Parolla's blood stirred in response to her growing fear, and her vision darkened. She should strike! Now, before the demon lord raised his guard! Digging her fingernails into her palms, she fought back the rising swell of bloodlust. Mezaqin had yet to call on his power, and Parolla was not going to force his hand while his intentions remained unclear.

The demon lord glanced at the heads on the stakes. "Do you like my collection of trophies? A little crude perhaps, but it seems a reminder was needed of the welcome we give to uninvited guests. You are not, after all, the only one reckless enough to enter my realm of late."

"I saw footprints on my way here," Parolla said cautiously. "A giant and a fire-*magus.*"

"There have been others. People who should have known better. An Everlord. A Beloved of the White Lady. Even one of the Deliverers."

There was a hint of a smile in Mezaqin's voice. "As with you, the Deliverer's intrusion required my personal attention."

"Did you ask him why?"

The demon lord turned his back on her and stared out over the Ken'dah Steppes. Parolla's gaze shifted to the fire in the distant grove of trees. If she could make it through the rent, the balance of power between herself and Mezaqin would shift. But then if the chance to escape truly existed, he would not have left it open to her.

In answer to Parolla's question the demon lord said, "Why the Deliverer risked coming here, you mean? I did not need to ask him. The threads of death-magic . . . I can sense them as well as you." He paused. "Their touch is unsettling, yes?"

His admission left Parolla feeling strangely troubled. "What effect has the sorcery had on your realm, *sirrah*?"

"Little as yet, though the same cannot be said of *your* world. You will see what I mean when day dawns."

Parolla raised an eyebrow. *Am I to live that long, then?* "And you fear the same will happen here?"

"I fear nothing," Mezaqin said. He turned to face her again. "I may, however, be forced to act if the . . . contamination . . . persists. I will not tolerate any violation of my borders, whatever the source."

"And what *is* the source?"

"You mean you don't know? Why, then, are you heading toward it?"

"Because I seek answers," Parolla said. At her first encounter with Mezaqin she had told him of her quest to find a way into Shroud's realm. "The magic is death-aspected, is it not? Perhaps it is a portal to the underworld."

Mezaqin was a long time in responding. "A portal," he said. "You may be right. *Something* has been opened, of that I am sure." His gaze bore into her. "Now it must be closed."

The hordes above the mountains . . . "Is that why your kin are gathering?"

The demon lord's eyes flashed. His form appeared to bulge and lose cohesion, and for an instant the starry sky behind him was blotted out. "Careful, my dear," he said. "Your next shot might hit the mark."

Parolla voice was strained. "My apologies. I did not intend to pry."

"What *do* you intend, then?"

She stared at him blankly for a moment. Then his earlier words about the portal returned to her. *Now it must be closed.* And since the demonkin were apparently occupied on other matters . . . "Perhaps my goals are not irreconcilable with yours. It may be that I can perform a service for you."

Mezaqin nodded. "I think we understand each other. Your feud with Shroud is of no interest to me. If it *is* a portal, pass through first if you wish, but the way must be shut. If it is not a portal, do whatever is necessary to destroy the source of the infection."

"You have my word."

The demon lord nodded again, but did not move out of the way. His gaze held to Parolla's, and she felt herself wilting beneath his scrutiny. Had he heard something in her voice to give him reason to doubt her? Was he reconsidering his decision to let her go? Or questioning her ability to make good on her promise? Perhaps she should say something to reassure him, but she wasn't sure she trusted herself to speak. Her tainted blood stirred again.

Then Mezaqin stepped aside, drawing back into the shadows near the wall to his left.

Parolla needed no second invitation. As she hurried past, she angled her path to give the demon lord a wide berth. His gaze was like a weight on her back. After a handful of paces she drew level with the blood-soaked wooden stakes and their grisly trophies. The face of the head closest to her—a man with a thick, black beard—was turned in her direction, and she saw maggots crawling in his empty eye sockets. Another day, she knew, that head might have been hers.

Conscious that her back was exposed, she did not slacken her pace until the demon world was far behind.

Ebon knew it was a dream, yet still he could not wrest free from its grip.

Ahead the stag was a blink of movement as it flashed between the trees. Steering his horse with his knees, Ebon thundered in pursuit, his breath steaming in the air. In one hand he held a spear; his other hand was raised to shield his face from low branches. As the gelding pounded through a clearing, a swarm of icewing butterflies rose from the ground. Through them Ebon saw the stag disappear into a thicket, and he spurred his horse after it, hurdling a fallen, moss-covered tree before plunging down a steep incline. The gelding snorted as its hooves skated through mud.

Suddenly on one of the forest tracks ahead a figure appeared—a young woman with long strawberry-blond hair. Her eyes were wide, and she stood rooted to the spot as the horse bore down on her. Just a handful of steps away. Ebon dropped his spear and hauled on the reins, knowing already that it was too late. The gelding hammered into the woman, punching her from her feet. Ebon's efforts to slow the horse's descent served only to make the animal rear, and when its hooves came down he heard bones break with a noise like splintering wood. Lamella screamed, and in his dream the scream seemed to stretch to eternity.

Ebon had relived the scene a score of times, and each time it played out he attempted to alter its course. He had tried shouting a warning to Lamella before he reached the incline; tugging the reins left or right instead of hauling back on them; even throwing himself from the saddle as the gelding plunged down the bank. The result, though, was always the same.

Still, I should have found a way.

The dream shifted, and Ebon found himself on his knees in the mud, Lamella's blood staining his hands as he supported her ruined leg. She lay on a carpet of silverspark flowers that glittered like frost. Shattered bone protruded from mangled flesh. Ebon remembered waving a hand at the needleflies that settled on the wound; hearing the questioning calls of his hunting companions as they drew up round him; glancing up to see Vale looking back at him, the timeshifter's expression even grimmer than usual. Yet more than anything, Ebon remembered Lamella's quiet fortitude. Blinking back tears, she had thanked him as he draped his cloak round her shoulders, even managed a small smile as he scooped her into his arms and carried her to his horse. And on the ride back to Majack she had made no sound though her face had twisted in pain with each of the gelding's steps.

The memory was a bittersweet one for Ebon. Were it not for the accident he would never have met Lamella, yet his contentment since that time had been founded on her loss. If he had the chance, would he rewrite the past if it meant giving her up? *I would not hesitate,* he told himself.

The scene changed again, and Ebon was back amid the mud and flowers, Lamella cradled in his arms. Her drawn expression gave way to a ghoulish smile, her image fading like mist. Ebon stiffened, looked round. Darkness was closing in. The silversparks withered and crumbled to dust, and the trunks of the trees blistered and blackened, their leaves falling to the ground in a steady stream. The shadows came

alive with the sound of whispering voices. Figures materialized between the trees, wearing long, flowing robes over pale, almost translucent skin. Ebon had seen these people before, he realized. The spirits
from the White Road. *Vamilians*. His jaw clenched. Was there no part
of his mind they could not access, no memory they would not despoil?

The spirits stood watching him dispassionately as if awaiting some
command. There was nothing to distinguish a leader among them, but
Ebon could sense another presence lurking in the shadows, something
ancient and cold and vast as the empty sky. Not part of the dream, he
decided. A silent spectator. Who, then? The mysterious entity Mottle
had detected in Ebon all those weeks ago? He groped with his
thoughts toward it, only to feel it draw back out of reach.

Suddenly the spirits swept in from all sides, their footsteps leaving the mounds of fallen leaves undisturbed. Cursing, Ebon reached
for his saber, but found his scabbard empty. The hordes came howling over him, their forms blurring together into a ghostly wall. Hands
tore at him, each touch sending a stab of ice through his body. He had
to fight back, but when he lashed out at his attackers he made contact only with air. Amid the murk he saw fragments of faces, hollow
eyes, gaping mouths. There was no escaping them. Four years ago in
the Forest of Sighs he had used a swordsman's detached focus to fashion shields against them, but here in his dream they were already in
his mind. He stumbled forward, half-blind in the spirit-mist, no idea
where he was going or what he hoped to find there. His legs were so
heavy he might have been pushing through water. The shadows deepened. What little daylight remained was fading, and the forest with
it. The spirits tugged at him. Shaking with cold, he felt life flowing
from him as if someone had opened the veins at his wrists. His
struggles became weaker.

Then he heard someone calling to him, so faintly they might have
been on the other side of the world. *Lamella*. He shut his eyes to block
out the spirits, only to find they remained visible through his closed
eyelids. Lamella's voice came again, louder this time, more insistent,
and slowly the Vamilians started to dissolve around him, their cries
fading to whispers. As if sensing their prey's escape, they doubled the
fury of their attacks, but their hands now passed through Ebon without effect. The cold began to thaw, and his shivers subsided.

His dream shattered, the images falling away like broken glass.

Ebon opened his eyes to a new darkness.

He could hear Lamella more clearly now, repeating his name over and over. Her arms were wrapped about him, but the contact made him feel claustrophobic after the suffocation of his dream, and he shrugged her off. He swung his legs round and sat on the edge of the bed. He was shaking, and his body was drenched with sweat. Lowering his head into his hands, he listened for a time to the sound of his breathing.

Lamella spoke, a quaver in her voice. "Can you hear me?"

He nodded.

"I couldn't wake you."

Ebon could only grunt in response. The room was spinning, but he feared to close his eyes in case the spirits were waiting for him. "Where is the ossarium leaf?"

There was a pause. "Ebon, please . . ."

"I will find it myself." The room lurched when he stood up, and he leaned against a wall for support. He waited a dozen heartbeats, then padded to the heavy curtain leading to the living quarters and tugged the cloth aside. The room beyond was dark, a mere trickle of light coming from the windows along the walls to either side. The outline of Lamella's harp and chair was black beyond the divans in the center of the floor. In the corner to his left was the shrine to her forest gods, and beside that a wooden bureau. He shuffled through the shadows toward it, the stone floor cold against his bare feet.

The bureau's compartments contained scores of pungent-smelling bags. Ebon raised them one at a time to his nose until he recognized the herbal scent of ossarium. His fingers fumbled at the drawstrings.

Lamella's hands were suddenly round his. "Let me," she said. Ebon allowed her to take the bag from him. She lifted a goblet from the bureau and poured a little of the bag's contents into it.

"More," Ebon said.

Lamella ignored him, closing the bag and pushing it back into its compartment. Taking up the goblet, she hobbled across to one of the divans and sat down. There was a jug on one of the tables. She tipped some liquid into the goblet, then set it down on the table.

Ebon went to join her.

When Lamella turned to look at him, her face was hidden in shadow. "Let it steep for a while."

They sat in silence.

"Talk to me," Lamella said finally.

Ebon had no wish to remind her of the events in the Kingswood. "Just another nightmare. The spirits—"

"It's more than that," Lamella cut in. "These last few days . . . It feels as if you're drawing back from me."

He watched the gauze curtains ruffle in the breeze. *Drawing back, yes.* Drawing back from everything. "In the throne room today, I saw someone I did not recognize. It turned out to be Domen Geffin. A lifelong companion of my father. I have known him for a score of years."

"We all forget—"

"He is not the only one. Every day, another friend becomes a stranger, or I am reminded of a conversation I do not recall having." Ebon reached for the goblet. "How much have I lost already? How long before I forget . . . all of this."

Lamella's voice was toneless. "Why haven't you told me before?"

Ebon did not meet her gaze. He swirled the goblet once, then lifted it to his lips. The liquid tasted bitter, but he drank it down in one go. "My days are filled with waking dreams—people and places I've never seen before, or the same place but through someone else's eyes. And the nights . . . they are more than just nightmares, Lamella. I fear the spirits will drag me down. That one day I will not wake." He looked across at her. "Or that someone else will wake in my place."

"Ossarium will clear your mind for a while, but when it starts wearing off . . ."

"I know."

"The drug will not drive the spirits away."

"I know!" Ebon said, setting the goblet down on the table. "What would you have me do?"

"The voices came back when you approached the Forest of Sighs. Perhaps if you moved away—"

"While the consel is here? He would see it as a sign of weakness. And who would take my place? Rendale? Janir? Perhaps I should drag my father from his deathbed."

"The consel will not be here for long."

"And if I leave after he does? How do I explain it to the King's Council? They will know the spirits have returned." Ebon shook his head. "I am trapped, Lamella. I have to stay."

"And when the ossarium takes hold of you? I don't want to lose you to it as I did last time."

"You would rather lose me to the spirits?"

Lamella's response was lost beneath the sound of raised voices from the front of the house. A fist pounded on the outer door, then Ebon heard footfalls in the atrium. He rose and looked round for his saber before realizing an assassin would not knock before entering. Light blossomed as someone pulled aside the curtain on the far wall, and the king squinted against the brightness.

Vale strode into the room. He was holding a sword in one hand, a burning torch in the other. He gave Lamella a nod, then swung his gaze to Ebon.

"You'd better come," he said. "The consel's camp is under attack."

CHAPTER 9

A HUNDRED PACES away a fire flickered within a stand of trees, a single point of light in the black emptiness of the Ken'dah Steppes. Mezaqin had warned Parolla the tendrils of death-magic had left their mark on the plains, and even in the darkness she could sense what he meant. For while she was relieved to have left the Shades behind, there was something about the steppes that reminded her of the demon world—a feeling that, in a place that should have been teeming with life, she was alone beneath the stars. The only sound that broke the deathly silence was the hiss of insect wings as gelatas converged on the fire. *Gelatas*. The harbingers of death.

Parolla shivered. The sweat from her exertions in the demon world was now cool against her skin, and she drew her cloak about her. The adrenaline that had sustained her through her confrontation with Mezaqin was fading. How long had it been since she'd last slept? Two nights and three days, she realized. She needed to rest, but where? The earth-spirits of the steppes were already massing in the ground beneath her, and it would not be long before they led one of the clans to her. She could return to the rent—doubtless the earth-spirits would not disturb her there. And yet to risk Mezaqin's wrath by entering the Shades again . . .

Parolla looked at the fire at the center of the grove. She had seen similar stands of trees during her journey from Enikalda to the first demon rent. The grove was encircled by a narrow ditch filled with bones, and yet more bones hung suspended from the branches of the trees by bits of cloth braided into chains. This place was clearly sacred to the clans, yet someone had defiled the grove by entering it, then compounded the affront by lighting a fire. The flames must be visible for leagues in every direction. Anyone so unconcerned about announcing their presence to the tribes was either a fool or too powerful to care. Whichever was the case, Parolla had no wish to share the intruder's company.

Then she saw a small figure, no more than half her height, move in front of the fire and sit down with its back to her. Her breath caught. *A child?* It had to be. But alone, out here on the steppes? The son or daughter of a clansman, perhaps? No, any native of these lands would know better than to violate the sanctity of the grove.

From behind, Parolla heard a noise. Growling. A banewolf, maybe. She paused to listen. There it was again, closer this time. Looking back, she saw movement in the darkness, approaching swiftly. Her pulse quickened. The wolves on the steppes grew to the size of horses and could easily bring down a lone traveler. As yet, Parolla could only see one shadow, but banewolves rarely hunted alone. *But are they stalking me or the child?*

Her mind made up, she strode toward the fire, stepping over the ditch of bones before entering the stand of trees.

By the time she realized her mistake, it was too late.

The small figure, a man, swung round as Parolla approached. She stumbled to a halt. *A Jekdal.* The dwarf was naked but for a loincloth, and thick white hair sprouted from his heavily muscled shoulders and chest. Black paint was daubed across his forehead and cheeks in a series of swirling patterns. Parolla's gaze was drawn to a finger bone hanging from a chain round his neck.

On the opposite side of the fire was the motionless body of a huge four-armed man, his skin scorched black by sorcery. A spear had been driven through his right eye, pinning his skull to the ground. Gelatas crawled over the corpse.

No matter how many wolves were on the plains, Parolla wasn't staying here. She bowed. "My apologies, *sirrah,*" she said in the common tongue. "I did not mean to disturb you." She turned to leave.

"It is too late for that," the Jekdal replied, gesturing with one hand to the ground beside him. "Join me."

It was not a request.

Parolla looked over her shoulder at the steppes and saw a pool of blackness approaching.

The dwarf spoke again. "Calm yourself. For now, they will not trouble you."

They? Parolla scanned the darkness, but she could see no sign of the "others." Nor could she pierce the shadows that shrouded the . . . creature . . . moving just beyond the grove. Standing as tall as the smallest of the trees, it seemed to flow across the ditch of bones as it positioned itself to block her retreat. *And snap go the jaws of the trap.* A trap Parolla had blundered into, green as a youngling. Taking a breath, she stepped past the dwarf and sat down by the fire with her back to a tree.

The Jekdal was no longer looking at her. In one hand he gripped a piece of wood that he was carving with a knife. "Most unexpected, your arrival," he said. "I confess, I sensed nothing of your approach. You came through the rent, yes?"

Parolla kept her silence.

"I must say I am impressed you made it out of the Shades alive. Your triumph, though, will only be temporary," the dwarf went on. Shavings of wood flew from the edge of his knife. "The Kerralai will hunt you down."

Again Parolla did not respond, suspecting it might work to her advantage if the Jekdal thought the demons were coming for her. "You are far from your homeland, *sirrah.* I have visited the realm of your kinsmen. Five, maybe six, years ago, now."

The dwarf set down the piece of wood he had been shaping and picked up another. "Then you have journeyed there more recently than I."

"You are an exile?"

"Of my own choosing. Small-minded are my people. Lacking in ambition." He spat on the ground. "My people no longer." Pushing himself to his feet, he walked to the fire. Using the pieces of carved wood, he constructed a crude frame over the flames. Then he crossed to the corpse of the four-armed man and began cutting strips of flesh from the inside of one of the thighs.

Parolla tore her gaze away.

When the Jekdal returned to the fire his hands were covered in blood. He started threading meat onto wooden skewers that he then suspended over the flames. Behind him, the pool of darkness Parolla had made out earlier had advanced to the edge of the firelight, but she could still see no sign of its companions. Then a branch snapped a short distance behind her. It took a supreme effort of will not to look round.

"Aren't your friends going to join us?" she said.

The dwarf was licking his fingers. "My pets have taken your interest, I see."

"Pets?"

"Conjurings."

Parolla silently cursed. *More demons.* Gods, what an idiot she was! She had walked straight from one hell into another. And why, because she'd thought she could help a child? As she'd helped the *mestessa* in Xavel, perhaps? "You are a summoner?"

"No mere summoner," the dwarf said. "I am a demon lord."

A pity Mezaqin is not around to hear your boast. "And which of the Nine Hells do your servants hail from, may I ask?"

"You may not," he said, turning back to the fire. Fat from the meat was dripping down and sizzling in the flames. The Jekdal grabbed one of the skewers. Pulling off a chunk of flesh, he tore at it with his teeth. He gestured to the remaining wooden spits. "Eat!" he said between mouthfuls.

Parolla was ashamed to hear her stomach growl at the suggestion. "I'm afraid I've lost my appetite."

"What walks on four legs you will eat, but not what walks on two? What difference is there?"

"If I need to explain then I'm wasting my breath."

The dwarf snorted.

"You were unwise to spill blood here, *sirrah,*" Parolla continued. "This grove is sacred ground."

"What of it?"

"Can you not sense the earth-spirits beneath our feet? Their anger?"

The Jekdal shrugged, then tore off another piece of meat. Bloody juices ran down his chin. "Weak, these spirits are. Chained to the land."

"Perhaps, but they will alert the clans."

"And you think this unintended?"

"What do you mean?"

The dwarf cast aside the first skewer and reached for a second. "The land about us is dying, my provisions running low." He grinned. "Now I have no need to go searching for food. *It* will seek *me* out."

Parolla shivered in spite of the fire's heat. The words had been spoken with a chilling confidence. Did the Jekdal really think he could cut a swath through every tribe on the steppes? *Then again, he's made it this far.* She gestured at the mutilated body of the four-armed man. "Who was he?"

"A Gorlem."

"I know *what* he is. I meant, what was the reason for your enmity?"

The dwarf snapped his fingers.

Parolla was only partway to her feet when three pools of darkness swept from the trees and descended on the corpse. Even in the firelight Parolla was unable to pierce the blackness that cloaked the demons. The gelatas swarming over the Gorlem took flight in a hissing cloud, and the body disappeared beneath churning shadows. Bones cracked. Blood misted the air. It was over in a matter of heartbeats, the shadows retreating to leave behind only shreds of clothing. The gelatas returned, settling in their scores on the blood-soaked ground.

As Parolla leaned back against the tree she blinked sweat from her eyes. The speed with which the demons had moved was unnerving. If they had come for her, she would not have been able to react in time.

The Jekdal had now finished his meal, and he was sitting with his hands over his belly. In response to Parolla's earlier question he said, "Our enmity? The Gorlem was traveling toward the source of the threads of death-magic." He paused, then added, "As are you."

"You seem sure of my plans."

"Another reason you have for being here? A convergence is under way. Power draws power."

"And what is your interest in this power?"

The dwarf stared at her for a while. "Resurrection."

"Resurrection?" Parolla repeated. *Through the portal? He intends to bring a soul back through Shroud's Gate.*

"Your ignorance is amusing. Pitiful, also." The Jekdal fingered the object hanging from the chain round his neck. "I seek the rebirth of the owner of this bone."

"A friend?"

"No. We have unfinished business."

Parolla raised an eyebrow. "And what did *he* do to offend you?"

"Not he, *she*. She resisted me. Thought by killing herself she could escape from me. I intend to prove her wrong."

Parolla was on her feet. A surge of darkness flooded her mind, staining her vision so that the light of the fire seemed to dim. The necromantic energies from the Gorlem's death still lingered in the air, seeping into her flesh. One of the shadowy demons moved to flank its master, and Parolla could hear cracking branches behind her again. The gelatas took flight.

The dwarf sat watching her impassively. "Such an ill-advised show of temper," he said. "Much you have revealed to me of yourself, your power. I am tempted to kill you, but why go to the effort when the Kerralai can do the job for me?"

"And if I choose not to let *you* live?"

The Jekdal threw back his head and laughed.

"What will happen," Parolla went on, "if you and your conjurings are here when the demons hunting me arrive?" She glanced at the pool of darkness behind the Jekdal. "Your pets aren't Kerralai, are they? Demons are not known for being tolerant of their kin from other realms. What if even now my hunters are creeping up on us?"

The dwarf's eyes narrowed. "I would sense them."

"As you sensed me? We're only a few hundred paces from the rent. Would you detect the Kerralai in their own world? How long for them to close the distance when they choose to strike?"

"You threaten me? With your own death?"

"I can make sure you share my fate."

"Then perhaps I will kill you after all."

"And rob the Kerralai of their prize? I think not."

For a moment Parolla feared she had overplayed her hand. The dwarf was staring at her with a calculating expression, idly tracing one of the black patterns on his right cheek with the index finger of that hand. *He's wondering why I'm not afraid of the Kerralai,* she realized. *Why I haven't tried to flee.* She returned his look evenly. No doubt the Jekdal suspected all was not as it seemed, but there was no way he could know of her agreement with Mezaqin. When his gaze flickered in the direction of the rent, she knew she had won.

"Be gone, then," the dwarf said.

Parolla stretched and sat down again. "Leave, *sirrah*? But I've only just arrived." She reached her hands out to the fire, noticed they were trembling. "I like it here. I think I'll stay."

"The demons will be coming for you."

"Then why are *you* still here?"

The Jekdal studied her for a long moment before rising to his feet. His lips parted in a snarl. "Your encounter with the Kerralai, I trust you will enjoy."

"Time's passing," Parolla said softly.

Closing her eyes, she listened to the dwarf's footfalls fade into the night.

The guardhouse loomed ahead of Ebon, its twin towers flanking arched wooden gates. With Vale beside him, he passed beneath the first portcullis and entered a broad passage. The ossarium leaf he'd taken earlier made the light streaming through the murder holes above seem dazzlingly bright. As yet the drug had failed to silence the spirits; if anything their whispering had become louder as Ebon approached the guardhouse. The tinge of madness was still present, but he could also detect in their voices a growing sense of agitation as well as . . . something else. *Sorrow?* For some reason the attack on the consel's camp troubled them, but why?

Ebon increased his pace. From beyond the city walls came distant cries, the clash of metal striking metal, the whinnying of horses. A burst of magic—from the consel's sorceress?—shook the guardhouse, and the king stumbled as he entered the guardroom. It was deserted. Red light came from a brazier of coals in the corner to his left. On a table in the center were clay goblets, half-smoked blackweed sticks, and a pile of cards and coins. The room stank of ale and sweat.

Crossing to the far wall, Ebon climbed the stairs that led to the top of the tower. As he stepped onto the battlements a strong wind blew hot and dry into his face. Overhead, the Galitian and Sartorian standards snapped in the breeze. To his left, Reynes stared out over the plains toward the Forest of Sighs. The general's cinderhound was curled up at his feet, and around him stood a cluster of Pantheon Guardsmen. Ebon followed their gazes. The shadows of the consel's encampment were several hundred paces away. With the moon shielded behind clouds, all else was blackness.

Then a flash of magic lit up the sky, and Ebon squinted against the glare. The detonation illuminated the Sartorian camp, and he saw scores of tents arranged in a circle round a pavilion. The ground in front of the pavilion was thronged with combatants. Among them was one of the consel's huge armored warriors, wielding its ax with mighty strokes against the smaller figures swarming round it. More attackers were running for the encampment from the Forest of Sighs.

The light died away, and the night rushed in to smother the camp.

Ebon frowned. It was impossible to identify the assailants at such a distance. Janir's soldiers, perhaps, sent by their domen to gain revenge for Irrella's death? No, his uncle could not have known the consel would camp outside the city walls, and there hadn't been time since this afternoon's audience to plan a raid. That left the Kinevar. But to attack a heavily armed company so close to Majack . . .

Ebon strode along the battlements toward Reynes, the Pantheon Guardsmen in his way parting to let him through. The general's crumpled jacket was unbuttoned, and his short-cropped gray hair was standing up at all angles.

"Reynes," Ebon said.

"Your Majesty."

"What do we know?"

"The show's been going on for a quarter-bell. First warning of trouble we had was when one of those blasts of magic rattled the sky."

"I trust you were not planning on just watching the whole time."

Reynes shook his head. "A troop's on its way down from the Tarqeen Barracks. Grimes has the command."

"Not anymore."

The general's eyebrows lifted. "You're going out there?"

Vale was suddenly at Ebon's shoulder. "A word, your Majesty."

"Later," Ebon said. Then, to Reynes, "Has anyone from the consel's camp tried to reach the city?"

"If they have, they didn't make it far."

No surprises there. Ebon suspected Garat Hallon was not one to retreat readily.

"Been thinking," Reynes went on. "Whoever's out there might be doing us a favor. Maybe we leave it a bit longer before going to lend a hand."

Ebon shot him a look. The general should know better than to voice such thoughts away from the Council chambers. "And if the consel dies? Do you think anyone in Sartor would believe we were not behind the attack?"

Reynes grunted.

Another sorcerous explosion split the air. From the street behind, Ebon heard a house's shutters being thrown open, someone shouting up a question. Ignoring the caller, he looked toward the Tarqeen Barracks. A column of lights was winding its way past the colosseum and over the Amber Bridge. He turned for the staircase. "Vale, with me."

Reynes's voice rang out. "Wait!" Then, "Listen!"

Ebon drew up. He could still make out the sounds of fighting from the consel's camp—a woman's strangled cry, the clang of steel striking armor—but there was another noise too, growing louder with each moment. It came from the west. *Like drums beating.* Ebon's breath came quickly. *No, not drums. Footfalls.* Like an army on the march. He met Reynes's gaze, saw his fears reflected there. *This is no mere raid.*

He looked back at the camp. Two of the Sartorian tents had now been set on fire, the flames fluttering in the wind like ragged banners, but the light given off was not bright enough to reveal whatever approached from the woods.

Reynes barked orders to the soldiers round him. "Andresal, get those Shroud-cursed watchtowers lit. Mertil, find me Captain Hitch. Other officers to assemble in the guardroom in one bell." Two of the Pantheon Guardsmen dashed off. "Jamer, find me that grub, Mottle. I want an Adept at every tower—"

"General!" one of the remaining soldiers cut in. He was pointing over the merlon. "We got company."

Ebon had already seen them. From the direction of the Sartorian camp, figures streamed toward the city. Among them was a horseman surrounded by a knot of defenders. The rider was wrestling with the reins of his panicked mount, trying to turn the animal back to the camp. Then a wave of attackers rolled over him.

Ebon had seen enough. "Vale," he said. As he crossed to the stairwell he tightened one of the straps of his leather armor.

"What in the Watcher's name are you playing at?" the Endorian said in a low voice. "How's Grimes supposed to do his job if he's busy trying to keep you alive?"

"That's what you are here for."

"One stray arrow—"

"Enough! My mind is made up." A commander didn't ask his men to take risks he wasn't prepared to run himself.

As he entered the guardroom, the first peal of bells started up from along the wall. In the time it took him to cross the chamber, the call had been taken up by other watchtowers and rang out across the city. He left the guardhouse and entered the marketplace. Sergeant Grimes's troop had drawn up facing the gates, and the soldiers were making their final preparations with reassuring aplomb. In addition to their lances, a dozen of the horsemen carried torches.

Ebon made for Grimes. The sergeant was settling his full-face helmet into position. The figure of a boar was etched into the left cheekpiece.

"Sergeant," Ebon said. "I need two horses."

The soldier held his gaze for a moment before looking at Vale.

"Save your breath," the Endorian said. "I've already tried."

When Grimes spoke, his voice was deadened by his faceplate. "He's your baby, timeshifter."

"Ain't he always."

Ebon crossed his arms. "Are we finished, gentlemen?"

Grimes looked over his shoulder. "Skip. Turtle. You're on shoveling duty. Give the men your rides."

The king strode to one of the soldiers who dismounted, then accepted the man's offered lance and swung up into the saddle. The destrier snorted and shifted as the Guardsman adjusted the stirrups.

Grimes said, "What're we dealing with, your Majesty? Reynes's runner ain't told us shit."

"The consel is under attack. Maybe the Kinevar, maybe not. The Sartorians have abandoned their camp and are heading this way."

"You want us to cover their retreat?" Grimes's tone held a note of amusement.

Ebon nodded, then raised his voice to carry to the soldiers. "Pick your targets carefully. I want no mistakes out there."

"Aye," someone at the back of the troop said. "Shroud's own luck if we end up spitting the consel."

The soldiers round Ebon chuckled.

"I will pretend I did not hear that," he muttered. Then he shouted, "Open the gates!"

The wooden doors swung wide, and the king spurred his horse forward, lowering his lance as he passed through the guardhouse before raising it again when he was clear. Ahead a cart had been abandoned on the road, one end of its front axle resting on the flagstones beside a broken wheel. Ebon rode past it, then steered his destrier west in the direction of the camp. The clip-clatter of the horse's hooves turned to muffled thuds as the animal left the road.

As the light from the guardhouse faded behind, Ebon kicked his mount to a canter. Shadowy figures moved in the darkness ahead, and for an instant he wondered whether he was riding into a trap. Could Garat Hallon have staged the attack on the camp in order to lure him out of the city? Would a stray arrow strike him down, as it had Janir's wife so many years ago, before the attackers melted away into the forest? *No*, Ebon assured himself. The consel would not risk such an act of treachery so deep into Galitian territory.

A third Sartorian tent had now been set on fire, and scores of combatants fought silhouetted against the flames. Ahead three Sartorians emerged from the blackness, their rust-colored skins unmistakable in the light of the torches held by the Guardsmen behind Ebon. Two women were struggling to support a man between them, his bearded chin resting on his chest. They stumbled to a halt as the Galitians bore down on them.

"Let them pass between us!" Ebon shouted, not knowing if the troop would hear him over the thunder of hooves.

As he drew level with the women, he saw a bare-chested Sartorian horseman in front, hacking down with an ax at three assailants on foot. The enemy wore coats of chain mail to their knees, and wielded curved swords. Ebon blinked. Not Janir's men, but not Kinevar either. Yet they came from the forest . . . *We have our answer to the Kinevar exodus, I think*. Ebon recognized the attackers, he realized suddenly, but from where?

With a growing sense of apprehension, he lowered his lance.

Abruptly, the voices in his mind rose in an angry crescendo, and he found himself battling an impulse to pull the weapon away. *What in the Nine Hells?* The tip veered to Ebon's right, and his arm shook as he fought to bring the lance back into position. He selected his target and aimed for the enemy's chest. The point of the weapon took the man just above the heart, and he was lifted from his feet and thrown several armspans through the dust.

Ebon felt a surge of rage from the spirits, and a stabbing pain shot through his head. Stifling a groan, he dropped his splintered lance and raised his hands to his head. Images flashed before his eyes: a forest ablaze; trees burning to ash in white heat; scarlet flames leaping into a night sky filled with screams. Then the spirits came shrieking up from the dark recesses of his mind, snarling and snapping and grasping as they tried to drag him down into blackness. But this was no dream like the one Ebon had endured at Lamella's home earlier. Here, in the waking world, he was in control, and he emptied his mind, seeking the same focus that had enabled him to resist the spirits' previous attempts at possession. Slowly their screams receded, their grip on him weakening. The images of fire faded.

When his vision finally cleared, he found his destrier had halted fifty paces from the consel's encampment. His troop's charge had driven the attackers back to the camp's perimeter, but now faltered. Ebon could make out knots of Sartorians among the combatants, some still in their night attire, but there was no sign of Garat Hallon. The consel's four armored warriors fought together in the thick of the battle, dealing out carnage with their axes. But they were being forced back a step at a time by sheer weight of numbers, and yet more of the enemy were pouring out of the darkness in a silent tide.

Silent . . . It struck Ebon then that the attackers fought and fell without a sound. No cries of pain or fear, no pleas for help or mercy.

A crash of sorcery to Ebon's left set his ears ringing, momentarily drowning out the murmur of the spirits. He drew his saber. The spirits clearly didn't want him joining this fight, but that only steeled his resolve to do so. To his right, Vale was hacking and slashing at a cluster of assailants surrounding him, and Ebon urged his horse to advance. A woman moved to block his path, her sword stabbing for his stomach. He turned the thrust aside with his saber, then hauled on his reins. His horse reared. One of its flailing hooves dealt the woman a crack to the side of the head that spun her from her feet. As she fell, Ebon caught a glimpse of her face: high forehead, deep-set eyes, bloodless skin.

His mouth was dry as he remembered where he had seen the enemy before. *The spirits of my dreams* . . .

No, it cannot be.

Two more swordsmen rushed from the darkness to his left. The first man was missing half his face; the second had the stub of a broken lance protruding from his chest. There was no pain in their expressions, no hesitation in their movements. *And no blood.* No time to make sense of it now. Ebon blocked a sword thrust from the first assailant and twisted his weapon to hack down at the man's neck. As his blade buried into flesh he felt a stab through his head from the spirits that tore a gasp from his lips. He didn't see the weapon that grazed the armor at his right side, nor the hands that reached up to try to pull him from the saddle. "To the king! Protect the king!" someone was shouting, but Ebon wasn't going to wait for help to come. Using his knees, he set his destrier spinning in a circle. The animal cannoned into an unseen attacker, and the grasping hands fell away.

Ebon looked round and saw a Pantheon Guardsman take a sword in the gut and topple backward out of his saddle. There was no sign of Vale. Then, from the corner of his eye, he noticed one of his attackers—the man missing half his face—rise to his feet again.

Time to get out of here. "To the city!" Ebon yelled, whirling his saber in the air. "The city!"

The cry was taken up by other voices.

Ebon steered his horse toward a Sartorian woman fighting a one-eyed swordsman. The destrier smashed into him, and Ebon offered his free hand to the Sartorian. Seizing it, she swung up behind him, arms locking round his chest. He spurred his mount for the guardhouse.

Ahead dozens of Sartorians were fleeing for the city on foot flanked by riders from Grimes's troop. Ebon could not see Vale among them, but the consel was there, riding back and forth through his kinsmen and calling out something Ebon could not hear. He switched his gaze to the city. A beacon had been lit in the highest turret of the guardhouse, bathing the walls in light. As the king drew closer he saw the battlements to either side were lined with archers fitting arrows to bows.

Moments later he reined up his slavering horse beside the abandoned cart in front of the gates. Two red-cloaked Guardsmen rushed to catch the Sartorian woman as she slid from the horse's rump. Another soldier reached for the destrier's reins, but Ebon waved him away and spun his mount to face the consel's camp.

Grimes rode by, calling for Ebon to follow him into the city. The sergeant had lost his helmet and his left ear was streaming blood. Still there was no sign of Vale. A group of Sartorians stumbled past, followed by a scattering of Pantheon Guardsmen. Next came more Sartorians, then the consel's sorceress, Ambolina, and the giant armored warriors, all seemingly unharmed. As they trotted by, Ebon's destrier shied away.

Garat Hallon emerged from the gloom, still mounted on his horse and looking back all the while. A lone Sartorian man was limping behind him, no more than half a score of paces ahead of a ragged line of the enemy.

"Archers!" Ebon shouted.

A volley of arrows whipped through the air and found their targets.

The lead ranks of attackers, studded now like pincushions, barely broke stride. In front of them, the hobbling Sartorian lost his footing, and the enemy swept over him.

Watcher's tears.

Garat drew his horse up beside Ebon's, staring grimly at the camp. His cloak and doublet were torn at the left shoulder, the blue silk marred by a black stain. His sword was covered with tangled hair and fragments of bone.

Another volley of arrows thudded uselessly into the approaching host. The forerunners were now less than sixty paces away. Ebon's gaze was drawn to a woman at the front. Her robes and hair were aflame, yet still she managed to keep pace with her companions.

"Consel," the king said, slamming his saber into its scabbard. "It is time."

Garat did not answer. He glared at the enemy with an expression of such venom that Ebon thought he intended to charge them. His eyes were darting all the time, first along the line of approaching swordsmen, then to the darkness beyond them, then to the city gates, and finally back to the enemy.

Fifty paces.

Still, he made no move to retreat.

Forty paces.

"Consel," Ebon snapped. "We are within spear range."

Only then did Garat yank on his horse's reins and steer the animal through the gates. Ebon followed him inside.

The wooden gates creaked as they shut behind him.

The marketplace was lit by dozens of torches, and the streets leading off it had been sealed off by cordons of Pantheon Guardsmen. The air was filled with the cries of the wounded, the bawling of officers, the stamping of horses. A short distance away the soldiers of Grimes's troop were dismounting, calling out responses to their sergeant's bellowed questions. Among the Guardsmen a destrier was down on its knees, coughing blood to the cobbles. One of the soldiers drew his sword and knelt beside it.

Ebon looked away.

The surviving Sartorians had gathered to his left, and a blue-robed Royal Physician was moving among them. The consel's first adviser, Pellar Hargin, sat with his back to a wall, his eyes glazed, flinching as the enemy began pounding on the city gates. The consel's four armored warriors were there too, along with Garat's sorceress. She must have sensed Ebon's attention because she turned to stare at him. He inclined his head in greeting, but she did not return the gesture.

Swinging down from his saddle, he passed the destrier's reins to a waiting Guardsman.

"Here," a voice called.

The king turned to see Vale leaning against the guardhouse wall, honing the edge of his longsword with a whetstone. He sheathed his blade as Ebon approached. "You left it late," the Endorian said.

"I lost you out there."

"I didn't lose you."

The king watched as six men struggled to lower a crossbeam into position across the gates. "Casualties?"

"Four we know about. Few more unaccounted for."

"And the Sartorians?"

Vale snorted. "It's a miracle any of them survived. Half the consel's company are servants and diplomats. Why in Shroud's name did he keep them out there so long?"

"Have you forgotten what he said in the throne room? 'I think we can take care of ourselves,' wasn't it?"

The Endorian's expression had a haunted cast to it. "Aye, but against an enemy like that . . ."

He did not need to finish the thought. In Ebon's mind's eye he saw again the faces of the foes he had struck down. So like the Vamilians in his dream, both in dress and countenance. Impossible, of course . . . yet it would explain why the spirits had reacted as they had when he attacked the strangers. *Like they were protecting their own.* If Mottle was to be believed, though, the Vamilians had died out millennia ago. Something these assailants had shown no sign of doing.

Vale caught Ebon's eye and nodded at something over his shoulder. The king followed his gaze to see Garat prowling among his kinsmen shouting questions. Questions that seemed to be going unanswered. With a command for Ambolina to accompany him, he strode toward the guardroom.

"I want to see this," Ebon said. With Vale a step behind, he followed the Sartorians inside and up the stairwell.

By the time he reached the battlements, Garat was already squinting over the parapet. A great host of the enemy had gathered at the base of the wall. A score of them were beating at the gates with their fists, while yet more attackers were scrambling at the wall in a futile effort to climb. At any other time Ebon might have found the sight amusing.

Reynes stood where the king had left him. Mottle was with the general, together with Sergeant Ketes and another officer Ebon did not recognize. There was a stunned note to the silence of the assembled Pantheon Guardsmen. Like the silence that followed a defeat in battle, yet the sortie had gone as well as Ebon could have hoped. The archers had stopped firing and were now staring down at the enemy, their faces pale in the light from the flaming beacon.

"Reynes," Ebon said, joining the general. "What news from the other walls?"

Reynes spat over the battlements. "Same story to the north and south, your Majesty, though it seems there's more of the bastards here than at the other gates. They've started circling east. Another quarter-bell and we'll be surrounded."

"You have sent out messengers, I trust?"

"Aye, to Culin and Kolamin. The garrison at Jagel should also see our beacons."

Unless the village has already fallen. "Mottle, what can you sense on the Currents? Is ours the only city under attack?"

The mage gave no indication he had heard. He was gazing out over the hordes with a look of childlike wonder.

"Mottle!"

"Majestic, is it not!" the old man breathed. "Such power, my boy! A shroud of sorcery envelops this dread host."

"What kind of sorcery?"

"Why, death-magic, of course. An army of the undead, yes?" The old man drew himself up. "It is as Mottle predicted. A storm, he said. A convergence of fell powers. This land is stained in the blood of countless generations. Ancient peoples, civilizations long fallen and now risen again."

"Ancient civilizations," Reynes said, "would be naught but bones by now."

"Reanimated, the Vamilians have been. Clothed in flesh, if not in life—"

Reynes's snort cut him off. "Save your stories for the campfire, old man."

Mottle cocked his head. "Does the general mistrust the evidence of his own eyes? Perhaps he has another explanation for what besets us."

Vale spoke. "I speared one of them, Reynes." He tapped his chest over the heart. "Left a hole in him as big as my fist. The bastard just got up again."

Mottle nodded. "What is dead already cannot die."

The general made to speak, but Ebon raised a hand to silence him. He looked down on the undead army. The glow from the tower's beacon extended a stone's throw from the guardhouse. Within the light were scores of Vamilians along with two dozen Sartorians and even three red-cloaked Pantheon Guardsmen—members of Grimes's troop, no doubt, who had fallen in the ride to the camp. In the darkness beyond, however, Ebon could make out only shadows. "Mottle," he said. "How many are we dealing with here?"

"A good question, my boy. Alas, Mottle's arts cannot—"

"You are an air-mage, are you not? Part these clouds and let us see what the moon shows us."

The old man blinked. "Mottle was just about to suggest—"

He was interrupted by a shout from the consel. "Sorceress!" Garat called to Ambolina. "I see him! There, among the rabble." He was pointing into the ranks of the enemy.

When the dark woman replied, her voice was as deep as Garat's. "He was struck down, Consel. I saw his head caved in."

"Then where is the wound? I see none upon him."

"He is dead. Most likely he has been raised by the same power that animates these others. Why else do the undead not attack him?"

"Maybe I should send you down there to ask them."

Mottle cleared his throat. "Perhaps Mottle may assist in resolving this unsightly altercation. If the consel would indicate the man in question . . ."

Garat stared at him for a few heartbeats before turning back to the plains. "There," he said, pointing. "The boy in Sartorian colors."

Boy? Ebon could see him now—a spotty youth with brown hair, several ranks back from the walls. *Ah yes, Falin, the consel's brother. I had forgotten.*

"Simply done," Mottle said. He gestured with one hand, and the boy was plucked from the ground and lifted to the battlements. Ebon retreated to make space.

Falin's skin was a ghastly gray hue but for patches of dried blood across his forehead and cheeks. As soon as his feet touched down on the fortifications he sprang at the nearest figure—the consel—his fingers curled into claws. Garat's backhand blow caught him on the chin and sent him sprawling. Falin was back on his feet in an instant. Ambolina stepped in and seized his wrists. The boy thrashed in her grip, but the sorceress simply lifted him into the air and held him a handspan above the ground. Ebon wondered at her strength to keep him dangling there.

"Rope, damn you!" Reynes said to the soldiers round him. His cinderhound barked excitedly.

An archer came forward with an arrow string that he used to tie the boy's wrists together. Ambolina then lowered him to the battlements again. Falin struggled against his bindings, the cord quickly

cutting through his flesh to the bone. The youth's arrival was drawing a crowd of Pantheon Guardsmen, but Reynes's order sent them
scurrying back to their stations.

"Falin," Garat said. "Can you hear me?" There was no grief in his
tone, only anger. When Falin did not respond, the consel struck him
across the face. "Answer me!"

"I hear you," the youth replied, his voice barely a whisper.

"Why, Falin? Why would you attack me? Why would you join our
enemies?"

"I'm sorry, I can't . . . I tried to resist . . ."

"Resist? Resist what? What are you talking about?"

It was Ambolina who answered. "All life has left him, Consel, yet
his soul remains chained to his flesh by a power the like of which I
have never seen before."

Mottle clapped his hands together. "A thread of death-magic, yes?
Connecting the boy to whatever power has resurrected—"

"Someone is controlling him?" Garat cut in.

"Like a puppet's strings, yes?"

The consel swung back to the boy. "Who? Who is behind this?"

"I—I do not know."

"Lies!" Garat struck him again.

"Please—"

"Silence!"

Ebon stepped forward. He had been intending to offer the consel
his condolences, but it seemed that was not necessary. "What happened to you, Falin? At the camp."

The boy fixed him with his corpse-empty gaze. "I remember a
spear . . . ," he said, raising his bound hands to his forehead. There
was no mark on his skin where he indicated. "I felt blood in my eyes.
Falling . . . There were shadows round me. A gateway of bones. Then
something seized me like when I was lifted onto this wall."

A heavy silence followed his words. Ebon caught Mottle's eye.
"Snatched from the threshold to Shroud's realm? What power could
do this, mage?"

The old man's eyes glittered. "To keep from death's Lord what is
rightfully his? Only a power to rival the gods."

"But the force that holds him—a thread, you called it . . ."

"Precisely. A most remarkable construction. Magical energies are
by their nature resistant to the imposition of order, yet the sorcery that
holds the boy is breathtaking in its mastery, brilliant in its—"

"Where does it lead?" Ebon said.

"Why, to the forest, of course."

"Can it be broken?"

Ambolina spoke. "That would serve only to release his soul." She turned to Garat. "Shroud would then claim him. The boy cannot be brought back."

"Do it," Garat responded without hesitation.

"As you wish."

"Not here." The consel was already spinning away. "Bring him."

Ebon held up a hand. "Wait. Mottle, go with them."

Garat said, "That will not be necessary."

"Nevertheless, we should work together in this . . ."

The consel paid him no mind. Guardsmen sprang from his path as he strode to the steps to the guardroom. Behind him, Ambolina hoisted the boy over her shoulder and made to follow. As she entered the stairwell, Falin's head struck the stone lintel.

Ebon stared after them. He had known better than to expect thanks from the consel for his rescue at the camp, but still he'd hoped having a shared enemy might have given them common cause on which a partnership could be founded. Not so, it seemed.

To the east a beacon was being lit in one of the towers on the opposite side of the city. The wind tugged so hard at the flames Ebon thought for a moment they would be extinguished. Then the fire took hold and the beacon blazed into life. In the distance a handful of tents in the consel's camp continued to burn.

Reynes spoke suddenly, his voice urgent. "Your Majesty. Seems to me whoever brought the boy back could do the same to ours. We'd best keep an eye on our wounded."

CHAPTER 10

SOMEWHERE THE Spider would be laughing.

On arriving in the Forest of Sighs, Romany soon found that the goddess had deposited her even farther from Estapharriol than last time, and as a result she'd spent half a day wading through muck and leaves piled ankle-high on the forest floor. It seemed as if winter had come to the forest while she had been away, for the branches of the trees were bare. The threads of death-magic were everywhere, drawing the life force from every trunk, every knot of nettleclaw, every blade of grass. Did Mayot even know the effect the Book of Lost Souls was having on the forest? *Such indiscipline!* Power unleashed without thought as to the consequences, but what else had she expected from the old man?

Ahead a bough of one of the ketar trees fell, sending leaves swirling into the air. It was only as the echoes of that noise faded that the priestess became aware of the eerie silence hanging over the forest. She paused to listen. *Nothing.* No birdsong, no chittering from those loathsome ruskits, not even the whine of a needlefly—Romany had never imagined she would come to miss *that* sound. And the air! It made her eyes water and left a bitter taste at the back of her throat as if she were inhaling the foul haze of the leper pits in Mercerie. Worse still, it had spoiled her wine! Having waited a full sixth of a bell to quench her thirst, she had removed the cork to discover the acrid tang of vinegar. Such a deplorable waste! It took her most of the evening to walk off her outrage.

As the time passed, Romany thought back on the moments before she had parted from the Spider in the forest earlier. Her head had been filled with questions about Mayot and the Book, but the goddess, of course, had left before she could put them to her. The Spider did find time, however, to propose a wager as to how many of Shroud's disciples Romany could bring down before Mayot fell. The priestess had scoffed at the idea, for what counted in this game was quality not quantity. She would leave Mayot to deal with the lambs in Shroud's flock while she hunted down the big game. In the end the Spider had been forced to acknowledge the strength of Romany's logic, but had nevertheless made it clear she expected an acceptable return on the time she'd invested in this enterprise. But as to how many of Shroud's disciples constituted "acceptable" . . . The Spider had remained tight-lipped, naturally.

Dusk was falling as Estapharriol came into view, and it was fully dark by the time Romany arrived at the dome. The arched entranceway oozed corruption like an open wound. She paused on the threshold and peered into the passage, but could not pierce the gloom to see what awaited her in the dome. The wind was picking up, and the whisper of lapping waves emanating from the holes in the walls of the passage resembled the hiss of ghostly voices. Romany shivered. Shroud's Gate itself could not be more sinister than this macabre portal, yet it would not do for her to linger. When she confronted Mayot she couldn't afford to show any hint of weakness.

She plunged into the shadows.

Inside, the dome was lit by moonlight filtering through the star-shaped openings in the roof. The light did not, though, penetrate the thickest wisps of death-magic that curled across the floor, leaving scattered pockets of darkness where the sorcery was strongest . . .

The priestess drew up. *Spider's mercy.* A sea of bloodless faces stared back at her from the murk, their owners standing in evenly spaced ranks round the dais.

A trap!

And yet, how could that be? In the temple, the Spider had told her that the first of Shroud's servants were only just drawing near to the forest. How had they made it here ahead of Romany? Had the goddess been deceived? The priestess squinted at the dais. Veiled in shadow, a gaunt figure sat hunched on the chair atop it. *Mayot Mencada?* She would swear to it. But that made no sense. If these people *were*

Shroud's minions, how had the old man kept his throne? And if not, who in the Spider's name were they? The thought of the mage finding allies was just too implausible to contemplate.

Romany looked at the figure closest to her: a man of middling years with a high forehead and prominent jaw. His long, braided hair was swept back at the temples and held in place with silver pins. A handspan shorter than the priestess, he wore an ivory-colored robe buttoned up to the neck and decorated with intricate silver stitching. To Romany's spirit-sight his outline blurred suddenly, and she started as his face was overlapped by a second countenance, its features contorted and stretched, its mouth gaping wide in a silent scream. *As if a soul were struggling to free itself.* Was the man possessed? Had some Krakal shade imprisoned him in his own flesh?

As quickly as the image had come, the second face vanished to leave behind only the stranger's cold stare.

It was then that Romany detected the thread of sorcery burrowing into his chest. The tendril was not unlike the strands of her own web in its fineness, yet this thread channeled death-magic to the man in a sickly stream. She followed its path back to the dais . . . *The Book of Lost Souls.*

The pieces fell into place. *Undead.* The Spider had warned her that Mayot had been busy. *He's resurrected some of the Vamilians. Oh, my Lady . . .*

On the bright side, at least she would not want for servants now.

Romany made for the dais. The undead parted to let her pass, then— she noted with a flutter of alarm—closed ranks behind her. She halted at the foot of the stairs. To her right were the steps that had been melted in Mayot's clash with Lorigan Teele. Immediately below them, the molten stone had collected and cooled to form a misshapen lump of rock.

On the dais itself, Mayot had company. Flanking his throne were four Vamilians, two men and two women, wearing coats of golden chain mail. Behind them, seven young women were drawn up in a line. Unlike their kinsmen, they wore thin white mexin shifts that revealed too much of their faultless figures for Romany's liking.

The sight of Mayot Mencada came as just one more shock. The old man looked to have aged a dozen years in the time Romany had been away. And it wasn't as if he'd been a stripling before. He sat hunched over the Book, strands of lank white hair hanging across his face. His eyes were so dark and sunken they might have been holes in his head. *The death-magic is consuming him.* Would he even survive long enough to do battle with Shroud's minions? Or would his enemies have nothing more arduous to do than pry the Book from his dead fingers when they arrived?

The air stank of urine.

Romany inclined her head. "My Lord."

There was a pause before Mayot answered. "I thought you were gone for good."

"A most distressing prospect, I'm sure. But you need agonize no longer. I have, as you can see, returned."

"Why?"

"To assist you, of course, in your struggles to come. Were you aware that Shroud's servants are even now approaching the forest?"

"And you think I need your help to destroy them?" Mayot's sweeping arm took in the ranks of undead. "In case you hadn't noticed, I've found some new friends while you were away. It appears you have outlived your usefulness."

Your gratitude overwhelms me. Romany looked round before adding just the right amount of contempt to her voice. "You would defeat Shroud's minions with *these*?"

"Not just these. An entire empire now bends its knee to me."

The priestess stiffened. "The Vamilians? You have raised them *all*?" The old man was exaggerating, surely. Romany had neither seen nor heard anyone during her trek to the dome, but it *had* been dark, and perhaps she had not been paying as much attention to her surroundings as she should have done.

A hacking cough racked Mayot's frame. "All I need is a sliver of bone or a grain of ash on which to work the Book's sorcery. Already my army numbers tens of thousands, and I have started recruiting others to my cause."

Recruiting? An unusual choice of word, but there would be time later for Romany to think on it. "Numbers alone will not save you when Shroud's servants come calling. The Lord of the Dead will have learned from your defeat of his knight. He will send his best."

"And you believe my followers are not equal to the challenge?" Mayot gestured to one of the four warriors in golden chain mail. "You have heard of the Prime? No? They were elite Vamilian fighters.

Centuries could pass without a single warrior rising to the rank, for
the trials undergone to obtain such status were formidable. Already I
have four in my power, and others will be found."

Romany raised a hand to one of the invisible threads of death-
magic. "And you control them through these? So . . . delicate."

"You are welcome to try severing one."

Yes, perhaps it *was* time to puncture the old man's inflated ego.
Only an imbecile went into battle against the Lord of the *Dead* with
an army sustained on *death*-magic. Romany's senses brushed the
thread, seeking a flaw, a point of weakness. The brief contact left her
feeling light-headed, for the Book's sorcery devoured her power as
soon as the two came into contact. And whereas the strands of her
own web were ethereal in their elegance—how else could they go
undetected, after all?—the Book's tendrils had an almost physical
presence, as if Mayot had spun matter from pure energy. Romany
shrank back in wonder. *Such power. Such artistry.*

"As you see," the mage said, "the threads cannot be broken."

"Perhaps not by me," the priestess conceded, "but Shroud's servants . . ."

Mayot continued as if she hadn't spoken. "The Vamilians struggle
against my mastery, but in time they come to understand the futility
of their efforts. And while their souls are cognizant, the flesh in which
they are caged remains inert. Do you now comprehend the power at
my command? An army with unquestioned obedience that does not
tire, does not feel pain." The corners of his mouth turned up. "Physical pain, that is."

Romany gathered the ends of her frayed nerves. "And the forest,
my Lord? The death-magic is destroying it."

"A necessary sacrifice. The Book must feed."

"And when you run out of trees?"

Mayot gave a thin smile. "You were unwise to come back, woman.
I have not forgotten our unfinished business. Power is never given
freely." As he spoke, tendrils of sorcery flowed from the Book toward
Romany. She was suddenly conscious of the press of undead at her
back. "I am not so foolish," he went on, "as to think your earlier interference was intended for my benefit. You are up to something, and
I want to know what it is."

Romany flinched as his sorcery engulfed her. The magic was not
meant to harm, she suspected, merely to explore. Her skin crawled
beneath its caress. Mayot's strength had grown since their last en-

counter, but in matters of stealth and subterfuge the priestess was without equal. Her wards held firm against his inept assault, channeling his power away from her or turning it upon itself until it dispersed like shreds of cloud.

She adopted a haughty tone. "I see your manners have not improved since we last met."

Mayot's errant eyelid flickered. "You know I can break you."

Having felt the touch of his sorcery, Romany recognized the truth of that. She could only hope that, notwithstanding his arrogance, the mage did not. "You saw me unlock the secrets of the Book, something *you* could not do, yet still you doubt my power. Twice now you have sought to test me, and twice I have slapped aside your clumsy questings. How many more times must I repeat the lesson before comprehension dawns?"

Mayot eyelid fluttered fast as a hoverbird's wings. "You think you remain a mystery to me? True, my sorcery cannot pierce your shields, cannot even discern the nature of the magic from which they are woven, but that in itself tells me much. It is a singular skill to conceal yourself as you do."

Romany masked her unease. Ultimately that train of thought would lead the mage back to the Spider, if indeed it had not taken him there already. Perhaps he was not as daft as she had thought, but neither was he half as clever as he believed himself to be. "It tells you that I value my privacy. Nothing more."

At a gesture from Mayot, the four Prime put their hands on the hilts of their swords. The old man's color was high. "I have other ways of making you talk. My undead servants have no secrets from me. Perhaps I will add you to their ranks."

It was time to give the mage a touch of the whip. "And perhaps *I* will take back the power I have bestowed on you. It is not too late, you know."

"I am tempted to put that to the test."

"But you will not. For in spite of your bluster, you know you cannot triumph against Shroud's minions alone. You need the breadth of vision only *I* possess."

"So you say."

"There is also the small matter," Romany pressed on, "of the secrets that remain locked within the Book."

"I can discover those for myself."

"As you did the others?"

"You have opened the door, woman. I can walk through it in my own time."

The priestess crossed her arms. "And if I have taken steps to ensure otherwise?"

Mayot did not respond. The Primes' hands, Romany noticed, did not move from their sword hilts.

The first warning she had of approaching danger was some indeterminate sense of foreboding. It was a wonder she could detect anything through the death-magic that filled the dome, but then Romany herself was a wonder, she reminded herself, and an instant later she heard flapping wings. Not just a few birds from the sound of it, but scores. Hundreds, even. In a forest blighted by death-magic, such a gathering could mean only one thing. *Trouble.* "My Lord," she said. "We have company."

It would not do to be seen with Mayot, no matter who or what was about to descend on them, and she swiftly reshaped her wards of concealment so that she resembled the Vamilians round her.

Just as countless small, dark shapes began pouring through the openings in the roof. The light from the moon was blocked out, plunging the dome into near blackness. Mayot and the dais disappeared in shadow, along with all but the closest of the Vamilians. Romany blinked. Then cracks of moonlight started appearing overhead to reveal a whirlwind of swirling forms. Shrill cries sounded, and the priestess ducked as wings brushed her hair. Those birds that strayed too near to the dais dropped dead, and the steps in front of Romany soon became dotted with feathered bodies.

Mayot spoke over the cacophony. "Today seems to be a day for unwelcome guests."

Romany sniffed. "A sorcerer's familiars."

"Spies, you mean. It is past time I shielded myself from prying eyes."

As Mayot spoke he pressed his palms against the open pages of the Book of Lost Souls. His lips moved silently. Romany could feel power thrumming along the tendrils of death-magic, radiating into the city. Sorcery was building outside. The half-light within the dome faded once more. Then, through the lowest openings in the roof, the priestess saw something taking shape beyond—a darkness deeper than the night sky. Death-magic rose on all sides in gleaming black walls to form . . . *Another dome! Could it be? It must cover the entire city!* Her mouth was hanging open, and she hurriedly shut it.

The birds must have seen the sorcerous construction too, for they fled back toward the roof, squawking. For a few heartbeats the darkness inside the dome was complete again. Then moonlight returned as the birds scattered into the night, their cries dying away. Overhead, all that remained of the starry sky was a small gray circle, shrinking rapidly. The birds sped toward it.

Too late.

The net closed.

"It would appear the birds are snared," Mayot said, looking at Romany pointedly.

She ignored the remark. If he thought to include her in that observation, he had just restored her faith in his idiocy. Far above, flashes of black sorcery showed as some of the birds tried and failed to break through the magical barrier. They fell from the sky. Moments later Romany heard their bodies hit the roof of the dome. The remaining creatures retreated screeching to the transient safety of the ruined city—transient, the priestess knew, because their life forces would soon be drained by the threads of death-magic all about. "It is as I warned," she said to Mayot. "The master of those birds is no disciple of Shroud. The Lord of the Dead is not the only one with an interest in the Book. Others will be drawn to this place."

"Let them come. When I destroy them, they will serve me as the Vamilians do."

"*If* you destroy them. Or have you forgotten about Shroud's minions? You cannot defeat them *all*."

Mayot hesitated before replying. "With each death, I become stronger. Soon I will be invincible."

Romany seized on the opening. "*Soon,* my Lord? Forgive me, but that is not the same as *now*, is it? *Soon* you may indeed be able to withstand all that your enemies throw at you. For *now*, though, you need my help, is that not so?" Mayot made to speak, but she raised a hand to head him off. "No, my Lord, the issue is decided. I will hear no more on the subject!" She quickly moved the conversation on to safer ground. "And since we are on the matter of *subjects*"—she gestured to the silent figures standing round her—"it appears you now have a surfeit. I'm sure you can spare me a helper." Her gaze fell on the women behind the throne. "Perhaps one of those—"

"No!" Mayot snapped, his hands clenching into fists. "They are mine!"

Romany took a step back from the vehemence in his voice. There was a covetous glint in his eyes, and the priestess made no attempt to conceal her disgust. *I hope Shroud has something special planned for you, old man.* "Another, then," she said. "I will let you choose. A woman, though. Not too young . . ."

She was interrupted by a squawk to her left. Mayot's head swung round. The noise came from within the ranks of Vamilians, and he gestured with his right hand as if drawing back a curtain. The lines of undead parted. Walking round in circles in their midst was a bird— a razorback judging by the crest of feathers on its head. It tried to take off, but one of its wings was broken, and it fell back to the ground. Smiling, Mayot extended an arm in the direction of the creature. The razorback was lifted into the air, and it floated toward the dais. As it settled onto Mayot's outstretched palm it tried to peck at the old man's flesh.

A knife appeared in the mage's hand. He looked at Romany. "Like you, woman, the sender of this bird has overextended himself. What agonies will the master experience, I wonder, through the death of his familiar?"

Tutting her disapproval, Romany spun round and headed toward the arched doorway. The Vamilians did not part for her this time, and she suffered in silence the indignity of having to weave her way through the host.

The razorback's screams started before she reached the passage leading out.

Parolla picked up a stick and used it to stir the fire. Her mood was somber. The dwarf had been right to chide her for her show of anger, but it seemed she was as incapable now of keeping her emotions in check as she had been since her mother's death. No matter how she tried to shield herself from the bitterness of the past, the pain remained always just a hairbreadth beneath the surface. The truth was, she had not even begun to come to terms with her mother's loss. In some ways she hadn't even tried to. Was that all this quest for vengeance against Shroud was? A way for her to hide from her grief? *No,* she told herself. *It is justice I seek. Justice for what was taken from me.*

A flicker of movement to her right caught her eye, and she looked across. A wraithlike figure was materializing on the opposite side of the fire, and for an instant Parolla took it for one of the earth-spirits of the steppes. Then, as the image gained clarity, she saw the apparition's four hugely muscled arms, and she remembered the Gorlem who had fallen victim to the dwarf. He stood an armspan taller than Parolla and wore a sleeveless leather jerkin and leggings. His lower arms were crossed, his upper arms held out before him with hands steepled. A frown of concentration creased his forehead.

A voice spoke in Parolla's mind. "I bring thee greetings, my Lady," it said in the common tongue.

She eyed the newcomer warily. "What are you doing here, *sirrah*? Your soul should have passed through Shroud's Gate by now."

The Gorlem spread both pairs of hands. "Thou art correct in that. It would appear that I am trapped in this place at present, though I had hoped . . . My Lady, I am here to request of thee a boon."

"I cannot grant your spirit release, if that is what you want."

"I understand. I have nothing to offer in return."

"That's not what I meant. If I could, I would, but I am not one of Shroud's servants."

The man's frown deepened. "I had not mistaken thee. And if thou would'st forgive my presumption, I believe thou dost indeed have the power to grant my request. Mayhap it is simply the knowledge that thou lack'st."

"Either way, my answer is the same. Now, if you will excuse me."

Parolla stared into the fire. She didn't want company. Dawn could not be far off. The sigh of the wind through the trees was soothing, and her eyelids drooped. Perhaps she could risk a bell of sleep. It seemed, though, that the Gorlem had no intention of respecting her solitude, for when she looked up again he was still watching her.

He took a half step forward. "Allow me to introduce myself. Tumbal, I am called." He bowed low.

"Tumbal?"

"Just so. Tumbal Qerivan." When Parolla made no response, he added, "Might I have the honor of thy name?"

"Parolla." Then, since she was clearly destined not to get any rest this night, she continued, "How is it that your soul remains trapped here? What holds you to this place?"

"Holds? Why, nothing, that I can determine. I suspect the responsibility for my predicament lies with Shroud's servants."

"What do you mean?"

The man looked down at his feet. "I have a confession to make. Curiosity is one of my many failings, and I could not help but overhear thy conversation with the Jekdal. Thou canst imagine the profusion of questions that I would like to put to thee. Might I suggest an exchange of knowledge?"

"I'm afraid I have little knowledge worthy of trade."

"I am humbled by thy confession and therefore shamed to admit the like. If not an exchange of knowledge, mayhap an exchange of educated suppositions?"

Parolla smiled faintly. She poked at the fire again. "After you, then. You mentioned Shroud's disciples."

"Just so." Tumbal glanced at the rent. "Unlike thee, I have had the dubious pleasure of traversing these lands in the orthodox manner. The steppes are littered with lost souls such as mine. A consequence no doubt of the, shall we say, unsavory characters abroad."

Parolla raised an eyebrow. *Littered?* "It is unusual for Shroud's servants to be so lax in their duties." The god was never slow to gather up the souls he considered his.

"Most regrettable, my Lady. Most regrettable. Though it may be—a suspicion only, I must emphasize—that we cannot lay the blame wholly at the door of Shroud's minions. Mayhap they have been—how may I put it?—distracted by the same force that draws us."

Parolla added some sticks to the fire. "We are still far from the source of the death-magic. Its effects are too weak here to interfere—"

"Forgive my interruption, but thou hast misunderstood me. I am suggesting, rather, that Shroud's house is in a state of disarray at the moment. That the god's attention, and that of his disciples, is focused on other matters."

"You think some conflict is under way?"

The Gorlem spread his four hands again. "For the natural order to have been so fundamentally disturbed . . ."

"No mortal, not even an empire, is stupid enough to oppose Shroud. And I think we would know if the gods themselves were at war."

"Thy logic is persuasive, my Lady, but still leaves many questions unanswered. What cause is so dear to Shroud—"

"Shroud cares for nothing but himself," Parolla cut in. "He would not interfere unless his hand was forced."

Tumbal studied her as if he could read her thoughts in the lines of her face. "Thou speak'st true. A threat to the god's authority seems most likely. Or mayhap a prize he was determined to gain."

Parolla's eyes narrowed. "The dwarf spoke of resurrection."

"An intriguing prospect, would'st thou not agree? The power to wrest a soul from Shroud's clutches? Reason enough for the god's intervention, surely."

"Could it be a portal that draws us? A doorway to the realm of the dead?"

"Mayhap," the Gorlem said, his tone skeptical. He sat down beside the fire. In the glow from the flames, his spectral form appeared even more translucent than it had before. Through him Parolla could make out bloodstained patches of earth and the scraps of clothing left by the dwarf's demons—all that remained of the Gorlem's corpse.

When she returned her gaze to Tumbal, she found him staring at her again. He held his hands out to the flames.

She said, "I didn't realize a spirit could feel heat."

Tumbal seemed taken aback, and he peered at his hands. "In truth, I cannot. And yet I sensed . . . something. Intriguing."

"Intriguing?" Parolla's lips quirked. "When I meet my end, I hope I can show such good grace as you." She thought to ask him about his encounter with the dwarf, but decided against it, for while the Gorlem did not appear unduly distressed by his death, Parolla had no wish to test the limits of his mood.

Tumbal drew a breath. "My Lady, since we have now addressed thy query regarding Shroud's followers . . . I was wondering whether, in the interests of reciprocity . . ."

"You wish to ask a question?"

Tumbal beamed. "Just so. Earlier, thou did'st ask me why I remain here. I would know the same of thee. Thou did'st pass through the rent, correct? Why hast thou not fled this place?"

"The Kerralai will not come for me. I made a deal with the lord of their realm, Mezaqin."

"And yet thou told'st the Jekdal . . ." A look of delight lit up the Gorlem's face. "Ah! Now I understand. I applaud thy ingenuity. But, if thou would'st pardon my curiosity, how? *How* wast thou able to negotiate safe passage?"

"Mezaqin knew I was traveling toward the source of the death-magic. Whatever it is, I agreed to put an end to it."

"And the demon lord believed thou capable of this?" The Gorlem's eyes glittered. "Who art thou, my Lady?"

Parolla wagged a finger at him. "Not part of the deal, *sirrah*. My name will have to suffice."

Tumbal wrung both sets of hands. "Such cruel intrigue, yet the hope of enlightenment ever endures. I shall await the dawn with impatience."

The heat from the fire was building, and Parolla shuffled back. She tossed into the flames the stick she'd been using as a poker. Shadows flickered round the grove. "Where will you go now, *sirrah*?"

"Why, onward, of course. Mayhap I will find one of Shroud's servants to grant me deliverance. And if I must remain in this world, I shall continue seeking answers to the questions that plague me."

"If you *must* remain? You sound almost regretful."

"Just so. What greater mystery exists than Shroud's Gate? Long have I yearned to witness that dread portal and the realm that lies beyond."

You and I both. "Then I wish you luck in your search."

Tumbal paused for a moment, deep in thought. He looked from Parolla to his hands, then back again. "My luck shall be thine also," he said at last, "for I have decided that I will journey with thee."

Parolla eyed him suspiciously. "Why?"

"Honor demands it. I cannot abandon thee to walk this perilous path alone."

"I make a poor traveling companion."

"I doubt that, my Lady. I doubt that very much indeed."

A woman's cry pierced the night, far off to the south and west. It went on for a few heartbeats, then faded beneath the crackling of the fire. Parolla half rose and squinted between the boles of the trees, but could make out nothing through the blackness. Her first thought was of the dwarf and his demons. By tricking them into fleeing the grove, had she driven them toward some other unfortunate soul? *No*, she told herself, settling down again, *the source of the death-magic is east of here. The Jekdal was heading that way.*

Parolla met Tumbal's gaze and saw the curiosity written there. "I must rest for a while," she said. "Just a couple of bells."

"Alas, sleep is something forever denied to me now. Mayhap I will scout the area."

"In other words, you mean to investigate the cause of that cry."

Tumbal sighed. "Thou art correct, of course. Curiosity has ever been my curse. And now, it seems, predictability also." He rose. "Rest, my Lady. I will keep watch over thee."

Parolla pursed her lips. She should reject his offer, she knew, for it would take more than polite words to make her lower her guard. Tonight, though, she was too tired to care, too tired to argue. Tomorrow perhaps, when her head was clearer, she would think on all the Gorlem had said. "Be careful out there, *sirrah*. Even the dead are not immune from hurt."

"Just so, my Lady. The soul is, after all, infinitely more fragile than the flesh."

Parolla turned away from his penetrating gaze.

Motes of dust hung in the air, twinkling in the rays of morning sunshine that streamed through the guardroom's lone window. Ebon looked out across the marketplace through the grime-streaked panes of glass. On the opposite side of the square, carts had been tipped onto their sides to form a barrier across West Gate Road. A brown-robed woman with flaming eyes—a priestess of Hamoun—was jabbing a finger at one of the Pantheon Guardsman manning the barricade. The angry exchange was lost beneath the whispering of the spirits in Ebon's head.

A shout came from the makeshift infirmary behind the wall to his left. Half a bell ago he had walked between the pallets of the wounded, offering what words he could to the soldiers from Grimes's troop. With them was the Sartorian woman he'd rescued from the consel's camp, her uniform torn and bloody round a deep cut in her left side. Lost to a fever, she had moaned with each labored breath. Like the others who were critically injured, the woman had been strapped to her pallet. Ebon had stood beside her, watching as her chest fell still and the light faded from her frightened eyes. In the space of a few heartbeats, the skin round her wound had knitted together, and an altogether different light had kindled in her gaze.

He had left her thrashing against her bindings.

Pushing the memory aside, he turned to inspect the guardroom. Round the table in the center was an assortment of battered chairs. Rendale slouched in one of them, flicking a coin from hand to hand. The chain mail beneath his cloak was parade-ground bright. Across from him sat Domen Janir, palms down on the table as if he meant to push himself to his feet. Beside an unlit brazier stood Mottle, his gaze as sharp as a crakehawk's. Flanking him were two bleary-eyed Adepts, both women. Their gowns were spotlessly white next to Mottle's tattered and grubby robe.

A booming sound struck up as the undead host began again their assault on the city gates. There were coins on the guardroom table, and they rattled with each blow from the battering ram. When the door from outside opened, a wall of noise spilled into the guardroom, closely followed by Reynes's cinderhound, the general himself, and a hatchet-faced woman Ebon recognized as Captain Hitch. Chancellor Tamarin brought up the rear. He paused on the threshold and wrinkled his nose before entering. Hitch slammed the door shut.

Collapsing into a chair, Reynes pulled a flask from his shirt pocket and took a swig. For a while no one spoke.

We've all woken up to a different world. At least those of us who got any sleep at all.

"Before we start," Janir said, "I would like to know how a Shroud-cursed *army* managed to creep up on us without so much as a *word* of warning."

Ebon frowned. "We went through this in my father's chambers."

"A meeting to which *I* was not invited." Janir looked from Reynes to Mottle. "Let's hear what these fools have to say for themselves. Hells, I could do with a laugh."

"This council has not been called for your entertainment," Ebon said. He pulled out a chair and sat down. "General, I would hear your thoughts on the disposition of the enemy."

Reynes roused himself. "I'd reckon their numbers at maybe eight thousand, with more arriving from the forest every bell." He took another drink from his flask. "Their ranks are also being swelled from the boneyards round the city."

Ebon grimaced. The awakening of Majack's burial grounds had been just one more harrowing development in the longest of nights, but at least the cemeteries were, for the most part, outside the city walls. More fortunate still, it seemed whatever sorcery animated the dead was unable to breach the wards woven into the walls of the palace's throne room. For now the khalid esgaril remained a skeleton. "Is there any sign of a command structure?"

"Not a sniff. No officers, no command centers, no horns, no signals at all. It's quiet as Jirali's grave out there, but the damned orders are coming from somewhere. At dawn, the attack on the walls broke off in the blink of an eye."

"Your Majesty," Captain Hitch said, "whoever's running the show ain't military. The stiffs just claw at the walls like they mean to scratch their way in. Where's the siege engines? The scaling ladders? The bastards ain't even bothered to strip the branches from that battering ram of theirs."

"Do they have any archers?"

"Not a bow or an arrow between them." Hitch touched her forehead, then added, "Watcher be praised."

"Clearly they did not come equipped for a siege."

"They did not come *equipped* at all," Janir said. "Most of them have no armor, some don't even have weapons."

"And yet if the walls are breached . . ." Ebon left the thought hanging. "The gates have to hold."

Mottle cleared his throat. "Your humble servant has spun wards of air about all four of the entrances to the city. The enemy's battering rams will not so much as mark the wood."

"And if the wards themselves are dispelled?"

"Impossible! Impregnable! Impenetrable!"

Janir banged his hands downs on the table, making the coins jump. "By the Abyss, someone's raised a whole army of Shroud-cursed *corpses*! You think a bit of *air* is going to stop him?"

The old man scratched at an armpit. "What Mottle may cede to the enemy in brute force—and he makes no admission in this regard—he more than makes up for in guile, craft, cunning . . ."

As the mage rambled on, Janir's face turned an ugly shade of red.

"Enough!" Ebon said. "The truth is, we do not know what the enemy is capable of. So, we are back to the gates. If the undead break through, we will have no choice but to retreat to the palace."

Captain Hitch spoke. "The streets leading from the marketplace have been sealed off."

"With carts, yes. Not good enough. I want the windows of the buildings surrounding the square blocked up, walls of stone built across the roads. Let's make the marketplace a killing ground. The same with the other gates."

Hitch shrugged. "As you like."

The murmuring of the spirits in Ebon's mind was getting louder, but he paid it no mind. "What have we missed? The river? Have the Water Gates been lowered?"

Reynes looked up from stroking his cinderhound. "Aye, though the enemy have no boats that we've seen."

"What about the threat from within the city? The Necropolis?"

"Its grounds have been barricaded. A few of the stiffs had already flown the coop, but Vale's tracking them down with the help of Sergeant Ketes. There's still the problem of what we do with the undead once we catch them."

Janir snorted. "Throw them in the river. Raise the Water Gate—"

"I hardly think," the chancellor cut in, "that the Merceriens will thank us when that particular catch washes up on their banks."

Ebon's tone was cool. "More to the point, Domen, undead or not, these are Galitians. We do not just flush our people away like refuse. A way may yet be found to help them." He turned to Mottle. "Mage, what of the earth tremors during the night? Are they the work of the undead?"

The old man cocked his head. "Something stirs, my boy, deep beneath our feet. The city around you is naught but a skin over the shifting bones of innumerable generations. We must hope that the weight of ages suffices to deny the involvement of whatever skulks below."

It was becoming increasingly difficult for Ebon to hear the mage's words above the drone of the spirits. A new note ran through their misery, he realized. *Fear.* Were they afraid, then, of what lurked underground?

Janir was speaking. "What of the granaries, the wells? With the river poisoned—"

"Supplies are not a problem," the chancellor interrupted. "Much of the harvest has been gathered already, and so far the wells show no sign of succumbing to the infection that blights the river."

There was a scrape of wood on stone as Janir rose from his chair. He began pacing. "And the palace? If a retreat proves necessary, how many wells are there *within* the fortress's walls?"

Ebon exchanged a glance with Tamarin. "Two," he said. *Not nearly enough.* "What if we start moving the people out by river? Once through the eastern Water Gate, any boat would be vulnerable to attack for only a few moments before the current took it out of range."

Reynes spoke. "We've barely a handful of boats in the city, and precious little wood to build more."

"Then I suggest we find some. Strip buildings, bridges. Anything that will float."

"We're talking about saving a few hundred at most. Not enough to make a difference."

"What of the royal household, your Majesty?" the chancellor said. "Perhaps it would be prudent to evacuate your family now, along with other dignitaries."

Like yourself, no doubt. Ebon's thoughts strayed to Lamella. If the city walls were breached she would have little chance of escaping the undead. He would have to move her to the palace now, whatever his mother's objections. Even then, though, the safest place for her was outside the city. He paused, then said, "No, the royal household stays."

"I fail to see what contribution they can make to the war effort."

"That is not the issue, Chancellor. What message does it send out if my family is seen to flee? We are trying to allay the people's fears, not fuel them further."

Tamarin held Ebon's gaze for a moment before nodding.

Ebon turned to General Reynes. He had to raise his voice to hear it above the moaning of the spirits in his head. "What about support from outside the city? Who commands at Culin?"

"Arin Forbes," Reynes said. "But the messenger we sent won't have reached him yet."

"Another day at least, then, before Forbes gets here." *Time. Time is what we need.* "Culin's garrison has, what? Six hundred men?"

"Aye, give or take. With any normal siege, Forbes could hit and run—wear them down. But against the stiffs . . ."

Ebon nodded. "We have to find another way. Mottle, we need to know more about what we're facing."

The old man smoothed his crumpled robe. "The bounties of Mottle's ineffable genius are ever at your disposal, my boy. Indeed, your humble servant retired to the palace library this very night."

"What did you find?"

"A veritable trove of treasures! Such wonders of erudite scholarship—"

"The facts, mage. Just the facts."

"If only it were that simple. As you know, the enemy force is comprised predominantly of an ancient people—the Vamilians—whose civilization was destroyed during the Second Age. The exact date is a matter of contention, but scholars so rarely agree—"

"*Who* they are is irrelevant," Janir said. "I think we can assume they have not raised *themselves* from the dead. The question is, who controls them? Why are they here?"

The mage sighed. "Alas, Mottle is not all-knowing, though at times it may appear otherwise . . ."

The voices of the spirits swelled still further in Ebon's mind, but he couldn't afford to show any reaction with Janir in attendance. "On the wall, you mentioned we were dealing with a power to rival the gods. Do you sense some immortal's hand in this?"

"Mottle does not deal in speculation, as you well know. But any god interfering on the mortal plain must expect his or her schemes to be countered."

"The convergence you spoke of."

"Precisely."

"Have you been able to sever the threads controlling the undead?"

Mottle's tongue darted across his lips. "Ah, as to that . . . If truth be told—and Mottle is never less than scrupulous in such matters— the threads have, thus far at least, resisted the totality of his efforts. Yet Mottle remains hopeful. Confident, even."

Janir threw up his hands. "He can't even cut *one* of the bloody threads. What chance does he stand with an entire *army's*?"

Ebon was only half listening. The spirits were now gibbering with fear, and their dread was beginning to grip him as if it were his own. His hands shook, and he hid them beneath the table. Only Rendale appeared to have noticed his discomfort. In response to his brother's look, Ebon shook his head. "What of the consel's sorceress?" he said to Mottle. "Has she fared any better?"

"Mottle does not sense in her the ability to succeed where your humble servant has been . . . temporarily thwarted. In any event, the woman's skills lie elsewhere. Her power is demon-aspected."

Demons. Ebon's eyes widened. *The consel's four armored warriors.*

Janir spoke. "Where is she *now*?" His gaze swept the room. "Has anyone seen the damned consel?"

Blank looks.

The domen's face darkened. "Shroud's mercy, I'm surrounded by idiots! Did no one *think* to have the snake followed? Did no one *consider* he might open a gate and let the enemy in?"

For once Ebon was grateful for his uncle's booming voice, because without it he wouldn't have been able to make out his words. "The consel is trapped here just as we are. To open the gates would be to invite his own death."

Janir loomed over him. "Not if he intended to carve his way *clear*. The whole thing's perfect for him. Let the *undead* raze the city, save himself the trouble come the spring. Does anyone here *doubt* he would do it?"

Ebon hesitated, then nodded. "Mottle, see that he is watched. But be discreet."

"Mottle can be nothing less, though the prospect of spying leaves his conscience sorely tested."

"As is our patience, mage," Janir grated, "by your endless prattle."

"It is difficult for Mottle to keep his silence when he has such wisdom to impart . . ."

The wailing of the spirits escalated again. Mottle's lips were moving, but Ebon could no longer make out what he was saying. The spirits' fear broke over him in waves, and he found himself struggling against the urge to flee the guardroom . . . *Away from the walls.* His chest felt tight. *Something is coming.*

Mottle was watching him now, and Ebon took a steadying breath, then whispered, "Mage, take us to the battlements. I sense . . . something . . ."

The old man raised his hands. "Dearest friends. Pray forgive this unseemly interruption, but Mottle suggests a hasty adjournment to the wall may be in order."

Reynes looked across. "Why? The sentries would have warned us . . ."

The general's voice trailed off.

Still reeling from the spirits' wretchedness, it took Ebon a moment to realize the *thud thud thud* of the battering ram had stopped.

Rising from his chair, he stumbled to the stairwell.

CHAPTER 11

LUKER SCANNED the buildings to either side of the rubble-strewn street. The sun had bleached the walls of the red mud-brick hovels a rusty hue, and tufts of straw had torn loose from the roofs to ripple like prairie grasses. Ahead the road shimmered in the heat, and the wind stirred the dust into eddies that swirled as high as the tops of the buildings before falling back to earth. The sound of stones settling came from his left, but when he looked across he saw only a wither snake slithering through a pile of debris. Still the Guardian's hand hovered over his sword hilt. The place didn't have the smell of a trap, but he wouldn't relax his guard just yet. For while an arrow or crossbow bolt had no chance of piercing his wards, Jenna didn't have the luxury of defenses such as his.

"What is this place?" the assassin said from beside him.

"Ontep," he replied. "Used to be a base for slavers raiding across the Shield."

"And?"

Luker guided his horse round the wreckage of a house. Potsherds cracked beneath the mare's hooves. "Emperor shut it down. Many years back now, before the Arandas campaign."

"Then why are we here?"

Luker gestured along the street. "Temple. Other side of the marketplace."

"A temple?" Jenna's voice carried a note of humor. "Why Luker, I had no idea you were so devout."

The Guardian did not respond.

As a boy of seven he had walked these same streets with his father when the sandclaws' migrations drew them to the western fringes of the Waste. He could still smell the stink of the town's slave pens, hear the roar of the spectators at the blood pits, feel the bristling tension on the air as slavers and townsfolk rubbed shoulders with tribesmen from the plains. It had never taken much of a spark to light the kindling, and sometimes it had been Luker's father who had provided it, doused up on juripa spirits and still stupid with grief at the loss of Luker's mother. The Guardian hawked and spat. Too bad he'd been traveling beyond the White Mountains when the emperor gave the order to bury this place. He'd have liked to have been here to watch the work done, maybe even pick up a spade and help with the digging.

As he neared the center of the settlement he saw signs that people had been here recently: the remains of fires within the doorways of buildings; horse droppings baked dry in the sun; scuffed tracks down sheltered side streets. Tribesmen, most likely, or survivors of the emperor's purge come to take back what was theirs. *So where are they now?* The walls of many of the buildings were covered with cracks, but seemed sound enough. *Someone should have claimed this place.*

He entered a dusty basin surrounded by crumbling buildings and littered with pieces of wood and straw. The air carried a hint of decay, but the gusting winds made it impossible to determine its source. At the top of a flight of steps a hundred paces away stood the temple. Its doorway was a jagged wound in the building's façade, as if something huge had forced its way through an opening too small to accommodate it. Blocks of stone were scattered across the stairs below.

Luker drew up his horse. The ground was pockmarked with indentations, and he dismounted to examine them. The marks had been made by clawed feet, three talons in front, a fourth behind and to the side. Both the breadth and depth of the impressions suggested one big Shroud-cursed bastard of a creature.

And they were fresh.

The jingle of bridles marked the arrival of Merin and Chamery. When the tyrin spoke, his voice sounded as dry as the dust beneath Luker's fingertips. "What is it?"

"Tracks," Luker said. "Not from any plains creature—"

Chamery's lisp interrupted him. "Tracks, Guardian? Are we here to admire the wildlife, then?"

Luker looked at him. Chamery's pupils were dilated, and his hands trembled on his horse's reins. The boy was brimful. *Of course—the smell of rot.* The mage must be drawing in the energies released by whatever had died. "Where's the corpse?" Luker asked. "Where's this stink coming from?"

"The temple."

Of course it is.

Chamery's tone was mocking. "What's the matter? Are you afraid of the dead?" Then, before Luker could respond, he spurred his horse toward the shrine.

Merin set off after him.

The Guardian could sense Jenna's smile at his back. He stood and rolled his shoulders. The time was fast approaching when he would have to put the boy in his place, even if that place was a shovel's height under.

Leading his horse by the reins, he made for the temple. The stone steps at the foot of the building were scratched and cracked. At the top, he wrapped his mare's reins round a fallen block of stone and joined Merin and Chamery at the doorway. Peering into the gloom he saw a chamber with another doorway in the far wall. The central part of the floor had caved in, and there was blood on the tiles round the hole. A stink rose from the shadows below, like a corpse washed up in a sewer. The walls and what remained of the floor were frost-rimed, the air so cold it snatched the warmth from Luker's breath even as it passed his lips. Echoes of alien sorcery left the Guardian's stomach churning.

Merin spoke from beside him. "Looks like we missed a fight."

"I recognize the smell now," Luker said. "A pentarrion. I think we can assume it's dead."

"Perhaps whichever god owns this shrine took objection to the creature setting up home here."

The Guardian shook his head. "The temple isn't sanctified. Hasn't been for years." He tested the air again. "I don't know the sorcery."

"I do," Chamery said. "A titan's."

"Where in Shroud's name have you come up against a titan before?"

The mage smiled, but said nothing.

Merin scowled. "I'd have heard if there was a titan on the loose in these lands. The emperor is meticulous in such matters."

"Maybe the titan's on his way to report in now," Luker said.

Merin ignored the comment. "Can you sense the immortal nearby?"

"No, though he can likely hide from me easy enough."

Chamery laughed. "But not from me. The titan has moved on, I am sure of it." He looked at Luker. "It is safe for you to enter. Unless you'd prefer I went in first."

Jenna spoke from behind. "You're going in there? Why?"

"We need water," Luker said. "There's a well inside."

Merin crossed his arms. "Do we have time for this, Guardian? How far behind is the soulcaster?"

"Maybe three bells. It's either the well or a waterhole farther east."

"Closer to the Waste, then."

"Aye. Might be under sand by now."

The tyrin looked once more through the doorway, then nodded.

Jenna snorted and turned away. "Someone has to stay to watch the horses. Knock yourselves out in there."

Parolla crossed her arms as the riders approached up the slope. Earth-spirits crowded the ground beneath them, their rumble of outrage mixing with the thunder of hooves to make it sound as if a great host were bearing down on Parolla instead of the score or so clansmen.

The slope was covered with boulders, but the horsemen guided their mounts round them with the skill of a people born to ride. They wore leather armor and carried spears and shortbows. Black-fletched arrows protruded from quivers strapped across their chests. At the front of the group was a man—the leader, probably—mounted on a gray horse with a white patch across its chest. The rider's eyes were closed, but a large tattoo of a third eye, its lids partly opened, adorned the center of his forehead. A shaman, then. His face was gaunt to the point of emaciation, and his skin had a feverish cast to it. *He's dying,* Parolla realized, his life force no doubt consumed by the threads of death-magic in the air.

As yet the horsemen had not strung arrows to their bows, but she knew it would take but a heartbeat for them to do so. And there was no reason to think this tribe would be any less hostile to strangers than the ones she'd clashed with previously. Releasing her power, she wove wards of shadow about herself. A few days ago a score of horsemen bearing down on her would have set her heart pounding, but not now. For while the touch of the strands of death-magic seemed to be toxic to the tribesmen, for Parolla they had had the opposite effect. Her power had grown since she left the Shades. Disturbingly so.

At a distance of thirty paces the shaman raised his spear and barked a command. The clansmen split into two parties. One group rode to Parolla's left, the other to her right, and moments later she was surrounded by twin circles of riders, turning in opposite directions. A cloud of dust thrown up by the horses' hooves swept over her, and she blinked grit from her eyes. The tribesmen were blurred shapes in the fog. A single arrow came whistling toward Parolla from ahead and to her right. It burst into fire as it passed through her sorcerous shadows and disintegrated. A crackle behind marked the incineration of another missile, then another, and another, as the horsemen wasted their shafts trying to pierce her wards.

Parolla heard one of the clansmen call out, and a dozen voices responded with an answering cry. The pattern of shouts was repeated, growing louder each time, and in the chanting Parolla heard the beginnings of a ritual. The darkness within her started to build in response. Through the murk she could see the savages holding their spears out before them, the points sketching glittering symbols in the air. The ground beneath her feet shuddered, then her skin tingled as whatever power they were fashioning broke against her defenses. She had tensed herself for its impact, but the clansmen's sorcery was weak, and she shrugged it off with ease.

It was time to send a shot across their bows.

She unleashed her power, and shadows rippled outward to deepen the gloom. As the darkness drew near to the tribesmen it was slowed by a wall of their magic. When Parolla pushed against that barrier, though, it gave way like rotten wood. Her tainted blood wanted her to keep pushing, but she held it back.

Suddenly the riders broke on all sides, wheeling away with ululating cries. Another wave of dust rolled over Parolla. She could no longer see the horsemen through the murk, but she could hear their mounts' hooves as they galloped down the slope. The earth-spirits rumbled their fury as they set off in pursuit. Parolla could detect the derision they directed at the backs of the retreating clansmen, but then it was easy to be brave when you were already dead. As the hoofbeats faded, she reached out with her senses to explore the rise in case one of the savages had remained behind to surprise her. The hilltop, though, was deserted.

Parolla surrendered her power, and the gloom began to melt away, revealing a circle of withered black grasses all about, two score paces across. Beyond the circle lay a bow dropped by one of the riders, the wood warping as the last of her shadows lapped over it. The dust cloud was slower to disperse than the darkness. Her clothes were powder white, and she brushed herself down. In truth, she had not expected the tribesmen to withdraw so quickly, for on her journey from Enikalda to the Shades only blood had sufficed to drive her attackers off. Then she remembered the dwarf and his demons, and heard again Tumbal Qerivan telling her about other powers abroad on the steppes, drawn to the far-off source of death-magic. Evidently the clans had learned the wisdom of caution from those who had gone before her.

A cough sounded behind her, and she turned to see Tumbal standing a short distance away. As he approached he spread his four hands as if to assure her he carried no weapons. "Good day to thee."

"And to you, *sirrah*. Forgive me for leaving without you this morning, but when you did not return from scouting . . ."

Was it possible for a spirit to blush? For a heartbeat Tumbal's ghostly cheeks seemed to darken. "The scream we heard . . . It was not, ah, as we believed, but rather two clanspeople, who did not, ah, welcome the interruption."

Parolla covered a smile. "No wonder you were so keen to investigate."

"My Lady! I would not—"

"Of course not, *sirrah*. Yet I notice you did not return to the grove to watch over me, as you said you would."

The Gorlem bobbed his head. "A thousand apologies. I have been in conversation with the earth-spirits of this land, a more arduous endeavor than thou might'st suppose. They are—how may I put it?— somewhat lacking in education. I had hoped to negotiate safe passage for thee across the plains, but it appears the spirits have not the intelligence to see reason."

Parolla looked down the slope at the fleeing riders. "Perhaps not the spirits, but I think the tribesmen may be more accommodating."

"They fear thee, my Lady?"

She did not respond.

The dust cloud was at last settling, and Parolla stared out over the plains below. The land appeared to be in the grip of a drought, for the ground was blanketed in a sickly haze, and the tall swaying grasses were scorched brown. To the south and east a great host was emerging from the fog. First came a line of perhaps fifty wagons flanked by horsemen. Behind was a herd of lederel patrolled by yet more riders and, in the ground beneath, earth-spirits. Dogs ran yapping up and down the column. *An entire tribe.* Were they fleeing from the source of the death-magic she was traveling toward?

The horsemen who had confronted her were riding to join their kinsmen. Parolla would have welcomed the chance to trade for a horse, but she suspected a clan on the move would have none to spare. *If they even let me come close enough to ask.* In front of the host was a broad pillar of rock supporting a horizontal stone slab. A territorial marker. The fugitives, it seemed, were about to enter another tribe's domain, but Parolla doubted their neighbors would open their arms in welcome. The clansmen of the steppes had a reputation for being more hostile to rival tribes than they were even to strangers. Overhead redbeaks were circling. *Even the carrion birds know it.*

Removing the stopper from her water bottle, she took a swig. Tumbal moved alongside her, his outline a blur at the edge of her vision. When she glanced across, the Gorlem was crouching beside a pile of rocks, one of his spectral hands opening and closing round a stone.

"What are you doing, *sirrah?*"

Tumbal did not look up. "I once met a man who had lost an arm to a sword stroke. He told me that, on occasion, he could still feel the missing limb. It is the same for me. When my fingers close round this rock, some part of me refuses to accept that I cannot grasp it."

"A memory of the flesh. It will fade in time."

Tumbal straightened. "It is the same with victuals. At mealtimes I feel cramps from a stomach I no longer possess. Curious."

The Gorlem's look was one of such solemn deliberation that Parolla could not help but smile, and she felt a pang that she had not arrived at the second demon rent in time to save him from the Jekdal. Then the moment passed, and her face twisted. *Don't be a fool. You wouldn't have lifted a hand to help him.* "It seems you have much to learn about being a spirit."

"Just so," Tumbal said, nodding. "Alas, there is one aspect of my condition to which I believe I will never grow accustomed." He settled the palms of all four hands across his ample girth. "If I'd known that I would spend eternity in such poor trim . . ."

"I think it suits you."

"I had not thought of myself as being so . . . expansive."

"Are you sure of that? Your spirit doesn't have a physical form, after all. The image I see before me is no more, I suspect, than a projection of how you see yourself."

"Thou art suggesting I can make myself appear any way I choose?" Tumbal considered her words. "An intriguing proposition. I must needs think on this further."

Parolla returned the stopper to her flask. Her gaze took in the muscles of the Gorlem's forearms. "Tell me of yourself. You are a warrior?"

"No, my Lady. I am a scholar—an engineer by trade."

"What did you build?"

"Cities. Well, dwellings, if truth be told. And only for a time, at that." Tumbal looked at his feet. "Few of my constructions stood the test of time. When demand for my services diminished, I decided to become an inventor."

"And what did you discover, *sirrah*?"

"Only that I was less than accomplished in that calling also."

Parolla's mouth twitched. "I always thought your people were a myth. I've seen mention of your civilization in only a handful of texts, and even those claim you died out centuries ago."

"My civilization, yes, but some of my kinsmen remain, scattered across the world. I fear, my Lady, that I am . . . was . . . among the last of my kind. It is scores of years since I last saw one of my people."

"You have traveled alone all that time?"

"I have."

A cloud passed in front of the sun, and Parolla shivered. "How do you cope? With the solitude, I mean?"

Tumbal crouched to try his luck with a smaller stone. "My kinsmen are, in many respects, a private people, and over time I have grown used to my own company." He paused. "I have also learned to accept those things in my life I cannot change."

Parolla looked back at the column of clansmen. A handful of lederel had broken away from the main herd and were being rounded up by whooping riders. "I wish it were that easy."

"My Lady?" Then, when she did not reply, he continued, "Thou art not a stranger to solitude thyself?"

Parolla should not speak of this to Tumbal, she knew, but the words were suddenly spilling out. "Can you sense what is happening to the steppes, *sirrah*? The effect of the threads of death-magic? The land is becoming barren, the air poisonous. Soon everything will die. It is the same with me."

"I do not understand."

The lead elements of the migrating tribe had reached the territorial marker, and a group of horsemen was gathering about the stones to spit at them and strike them with their spears.

Parolla said, "No living soul can survive in my presence for long. Over time, they fall ill. The skin swells and blisters, the blood runs black, the limbs turn gangrenous. The process can be a slow one, and it took me years to realize I was responsible for the sickness of those round me."

Tumbal edged closer. "Is there no controlling this taint?"

"Don't you think I've tried? A while ago, I met someone I . . . came to care about. In my selfishness I allowed myself to stay with him for a time. Then one day he was taken ill. I fled. I haven't had the courage to return. To see whether he survived. To explain why I left."

"But thou art a necromancer, art thou not? Life and death are but two sides of the same coin. Can thy power not be used to heal as well as harm?"

At the territorial marker one of the clansmen had looped a coil of rope round the supporting pillar of rock and was now pulling on the rope in an attempt to topple the stones. A dozen of his kinsmen dismounted to join him.

"It can," Parolla said in response to Tumbal's question. "Wounds, diseases, I can cure. I can even regenerate lost flesh and bone. But whether I can undo the . . . corruption . . . that I myself cause . . . I doubt that."

"But thou dost not know for certain."

Parolla met the Gorlem's gaze finally. "You would have me find out? And what if I fail? How many more must die before I discover the answer? No, it is better this way. Alone."

Tumbal's shoulders straightened. "Alone no longer, my Lady. Tumbal will abide."

Parolla studied him for a while, then nodded. "The dead, at least, I cannot harm."

The sound of distant hoofbeats came from the west, and Parolla looked across. Two horsemen emerged from the haze that shrouded the steppes, whipping their mounts with their reins. A heartbeat later scores more riders appeared behind them, less than a quarter of a league away. Earth-spirits thronged the ground beneath them.

They were heading toward Parolla.

Muttering an oath, she gathered her power about her again. For a moment she thought to duck behind a boulder, but the horsemen would already have seen her. Apparently the retreat of the shaman and his

men had not been a retreat in truth. Apparently they'd simply withdrawn to wait for reinforcements. She should have taken the chance
to flee when she had it.

Then she noticed the approaching riders, unlike the fugitive tribesmen, wore metal skullcaps and capes made from lederel hides.

They veered their mounts toward the rival clansmen to the south.

Looking down the slope, Parolla saw the fugitives preparing for
battle. To the sound of shouting and yapping dogs, they began to ma-
neuver their wagons to form a circle into which the lederel were driven.
While some of the clansmen took up positions between the wagons,
others unleashed a volley of arrows at the incoming riders. As the rain
of death fell about the horsemen, a loud rumble signaled the clash of
the two groups of earth-spirits that accompanied the tribes.

Parolla turned away. "Let's get out of here, *sirrah*."

Luker crossed the entrance room of the temple, keeping close to the
wall in spite of the aching cold radiating from the stone. What remained of the floor seemed sturdy in spite of the yawning hole at its
center, but Luker was taking no chances, testing each tile before trust-
ing his weight to it. Ahead was a jagged crack in the ground, more
than a handspan wide. The tiles were crumbling along its edges,
while below . . .

Light blossomed at his back, and he started. When he looked round
he saw Chamery a pace behind, the tip of his staff glowing. Too
damned close by half. A nudge at the wrong time would send Luker
plummeting into darkness.

"You trying to climb into my pocket?"

Chamery gave a mocking salute and shuffled back.

The Guardian risked a look into the fissure. A score of armspans
below lay the corpse of a pentarrion. Its black, chitinous carapace was
encrusted with ice, and rivulets of water trickled down its flanks. Of
the subterranean chamber itself, nothing could be made out except
row upon row of amphorae—some whole, but most shattered—stretching into darkness. The floor round the pentarrion shifted like ripples
on a lake, and Luker heard the hissing of wither snakes.

Another hiss sounded, closer this time, and he looked down to see
a serpent slithering between his feet. Instinctively he drew back only
for his left elbow to brush the wall. A stab of cold passed through his
arm, and he jerked away, leaving shirt and skin behind. Cursing, he

kicked out and sent the snake twitching into the air. It disappeared into the hole in the floor. Chamery chuckled.

Just as well the mage was behind Luker at that moment, else he'd have been getting a shove himself.

Stepping over the fissure, the Guardian advanced to the doorway at the end of the room. Beyond was a colonnade of pillars and a court-yard ending at a towering sandstone wall covered with carvings, and set farther back at the top than at the base. The ground was covered with a layer of frost, and there were footsteps in the glittering white, leading *from* the yard, not into it. Clearly the titan had disturbed the pentarrion on its way out of the temple, but how had it got *into* the building if not through this chamber?

Luker edged between the pillars and paused at the edge of the col-onnade. At the center of the wall opposite was a rectangular open-ing, beyond which a ramp led down into darkness. Farther to the left was a smaller doorway, while in the shadow of the pillars to his right was the well he sought.

"The titan's trail leads this way," Chamery said. Ice cracked beneath his sandals as he strode toward the smaller door.

Luker ignored him and made for the well. A wooden bucket lay to one side, its handle still tied to a length of rope. The stone blocks that made up the well were crusted with ice, and the Guardian grinned as he pictured savoring his first cool drink this side of the Shield. Then he caught the stench of rot, noticed the cloud of flies hovering above the shaft. Snarling his disgust, he spun round and went to join Merin and Chamery in front of the wall.

What Luker had taken to be a small doorway was in fact no more than an irregular hole before which were scattered frost-rimed blocks of sandstone. *The titan . . . It just punched its way through.* In the darkness beyond the wall was a Merigan portal, and Luker gave a low whistle. He had come across such gateways before, of course, but al-ways at a distance, for the empires in which they were located tended to guard them closely for fear of unannounced visitors. Carved into the portal's architrave were hundreds of runes, one of which was glow-ing blue. The blackness within the frame sparkled as if Luker were gazing at a starry night sky.

"Whose temple is this?" Merin asked.

Luker cast an eye over the carvings on the wall. Above him a masked and horned figure was firing an arrow at an unseen assail-ant, while to his right a hooded character, winged this time, sat on a throne before a cowering, animal-headed crowd. He had seen images like these before at a shrine in Balshazar. "The Lord of Hidden Faces."

Chamery spoke. "Hah! A conceit! The god is no more than a veil behind which some other power lurks."

"Unless that's what the Lord wants you to think."

The mage paid him no mind. Raising his glowing staff closer to the portal's architrave he said, "Fascinating, wouldn't you agree? These symbols . . . a variant on Fangalar script, I believe."

Merin squinted. "You can interpret the marks?"

"Ah, yes! The emperor's singular obsession." Chamery's gaze flickered from Merin to Luker, then back again. "But why should Avallon need *my* aid to unlock the mysteries of the gateways when he already has the Guardians to help him."

Luker stared at him. "Meaning?"

"You did not know? While you were sulking on Taradh Dor the emperor's pet mages unearthed a second Merigan portal at Amenor to go with the one at Bastion. In an effort to decipher the code behind the symbols Avallon has been sending Guardians through the gateways."

Luker faced Merin. The tyrin's frown suggested irritation at the boy's revelation. "Who?" Luker said. "Who has been sent?"

"Senar Sol. Jeng Elesar. Others."

Admirers of the emperor, one and all. Small wonder Gill was feeling the pinch. "And how many have made it back?"

"None, as yet."

Chamery laughed. "Nor will they." He gestured with his staff at the solitary glowing symbol on the portal's architrave. "This mark indicates the gateway's destination, not its location. One cannot simply pass through a portal, then step back and expect to return to where one started. Hah! The Guardians could be thousands of leagues away."

Merin's tone was unapologetic. "To be able to travel between the gateways would bring great strategic benefits to the empire."

And in the meantime Avallon gets the chance to pluck a few thorns from his flesh. "How did the emperor smuggle that past the Guardian Council?"

"He didn't have to. Avallon's orders are to be obeyed, not questioned."

Luker slammed his swords back into their scabbards. The tyrin's tune was beginning to grate on him. But then the man's mouth had been fastened to Avallon's ass so long it was no surprise he'd started talking shit.

Merin forestalled his response. "Enough of this! We now know *how* the titan came here. The question remains, why?"

"Convergence," Luker said.

"You think the titan was drawn by the Book of Lost Souls? A necromancer, then?"

"Doesn't need to be. I'm no corpse-hugger, but I can still sense the Book like a needlefly buzzing round in my head." He looked at Chamery. "The sorcery's getting stronger, isn't it? Not just because we're getting closer, either."

The mage nodded.

"I've sensed you questing toward the Book. What have you found out?"

"As yet, nothing," Chamery said. "We're still too far away for me to follow the threads to their source."

"But Mayot's using the Book, right? What's he up to?"

"Hah! You'll have to do better than that if you want to trick me into revealing—"

"Is he under attack?"

The mage's eyes glittered. "Perhaps. There will be some that want the Book's power for themselves."

"And if the titan gets his hands on it? I'd like to see you wrest that thing—"

"'You,' Guardian?" Chamery cut in. "Don't you mean 'we'?"

"You heard me."

Merin spoke. "How much of a lead does this titan have on us?"

Luker considered. "My guess? A few bells, no more."

"Can we overtake it?"

"Sure. Right after we grow ourselves some wings."

The tyrin's gaze strayed once more to the carvings on the wall, a frown forming on his face. "Mage," he said. "Is Mayot capable of defeating a titan?"

"Let's hope not," Chamery muttered.

"Explain."

But the mage turned away without answering.

It had taken Romany the night and most of the morning to construct her web, extending her senses deep into the forest on all sides. As she wove each new strand, another part of Mayot's fledgling empire yielded its secrets to her, yet even as she completed the most distant sections, those closest to Estapharriol began to unravel. The Book's threads were to blame, she knew: they were as poison to anything they touched.

The dome of black magic Mayot had raised was proving a particular nuisance, for the strands of Romany's web withered the moment they came into contact with it. In the end she had made a few unobtrusive holes through which her web could pass, but even then the threads would need constant tending to maintain their integrity. A tedious endeavor for someone of Romany's standing, but a necessary one if she was to keep tabs on Mayot's schemes. The old man was certainly keeping his minions busy. Sections of forest round Estapharriol were being cleared to fuel weaponsmiths' forges that burned day and night, and the debris from ruined buildings was being used to fashion barricades across the major roads leading to the city—a senseless undertaking to Romany's mind, since it would take mere heartbeats for anyone traveling along them to step round.

The priestess allowed her consciousness to drift along her web. There were still great gaps in her awareness, of course, but there would be time enough to fill those during the days to come. From what she had seen up to now, the Vamilian kingdom consisted of six cities and a host of smaller settlements, bounded to the east by the White Road, and to the south by the Gollothir Plains. To the north and west, the Forest of Sighs stretched far beyond the reaches of her web.

As she approached one of the cities, something caught her eye. A group of Vamilians were on their knees in the dirt and appeared to be . . . *Digging?* Drifting closer, she saw scores of threads of death-magic disappearing into the ground. In their midst, the undead diggers clawed at the earth, throwing up handfuls of soil and stones as they sought to uncover whatever lay trapped below. Romany shivered as a Vamilian man was pulled stone-faced from his muddy prison. How many undead were still underground, caged in darkness? How long before Mayot decided the effort of freeing those remaining did not justify the reward?

No doubt the old man was even now extending his search deeper for more formidable servants, for who knew what ancient horrors lay buried beneath the forest floor? Fortunately Romany had, as in all things, anticipated him in this. A few discreet questings of her own had discovered the bones of a tiktar no less, just a short distance from Estapharriol, and the elderling's remains were now hidden behind a veil of impenetrable wards. As yet, she hadn't decided whether she would reveal the creature's presence to Mayot, but if she did so it would be on her terms and at a time of her choosing.

Thus far only two of Shroud's minions had entered the Forest of Sighs, but they were too weak to warrant Romany's interest . . .

A sound broke her concentration—a perception not from her spiritual body, but from her corporeal one in Estapharriol. Curious, she sped along the strands of her web to the ruined house where her body lay. Opening one eye, she squinted into the sun. Before her stood a young Vamilian woman with the empty expression only the undead could adopt—an expression which was, Romany decided, most unsuited to the laugh lines round her eyes. The girl seemed in no hurry to speak, and Romany knew better than to test the patience of a walking corpse. What language, though, to choose? She had come across the Vamilian tongue in old scrolls, but had never before needed to speak it. Then again, did not the language derive from High Celemin? Surely the girl would comprehend that. "And who might you be, my dear?" she said.

"The master sent me," the Vamilian replied in the same tongue. Her tone was as flat as her chest.

"You can understand me? Excellent!" Romany rose and looked the girl up and down. Not a day over eighteen, she would swear, or at least that would have been her age when she died, millennia ago. She might have been pretty were it not for the overlong nose and square jaw. Her cream-colored gown was covered with muddy smudges, and there was soil in her hair and scratches on her arms. "What is your name?"

"Danel."

"Well, Danel, I am pleased to make your acquaintance. You may call me 'my Lady.'"

The girl did not respond.

"Have you ever been a servant before?"

"No."

Romany rolled her eyes. Was it really so difficult for Mayot to find a single maid in a civilization of thousands? "Is there a bathhouse in this city?"

"No."

"Nevertheless, I wish to take a bath."

"There is no bathhouse."

"Then you will just have to use your imagination, my dear! Perhaps one of the richer houses . . ." Romany looked about her. "When you're done, you can start tidying this hovel. Sweep the floor, clear the roots and rubble away, that sort of thing."

Danel stood unmoving.

The priestess waved a hand at her. "Well? Be about it!"

She listened to the girl's retreating footfalls, then sat down with a sigh.

Where was I? Closing her eyes, she relaxed and allowed her mind to wander again along the threads of her web. Every tremor conveyed a message, every jolt a new move in the game. All Romany had to do was allow her subconscious to sift the information and take her where it would.

She found herself floating north.

The undead were gathered in force in this part of the forest, sent by Mayot to attack the few remaining occupied Kinevar settlements within striking distance of Estapharriol. Drawing near to one of them, the priestess saw hundreds of Vamilians swarming over its primitive barricades. Two Kinevar mages unleashed a flood of sorcery against their attackers, but the undead were too many. When the slaughter was done, the dead Kinevar rose to swell the ranks of the Vamilians.

Romany yawned. Surely this insignificant skirmish was not what had drawn her attention. There must be something else . . .

Well, well. What have we here?

Concentrations of power at the farthest reaches of her web. The first, and strongest, lay deep within the woods to the north and west, and Romany flashed across the intervening leagues.

The trees in this section of woods were clustered so densely that no daylight penetrated the canopy of foliage, and the air was thick with earth-magic. As yet, the forest showed no trace of the Book's taint, but it was not this fact alone that had drawn the priestess here. Far ahead death-magic and earth-magic warred with a ferocity that made her wince. A battle was evidently being fought between Mayot's forces and those of some unknown adversary, but who? Shroud, perhaps? No, that would not explain the prevalence of earth-magic. The Kinevar? Surely most of the creatures had already fled north. *Patience,* Romany told herself. The mystery would have to wait for another day.

The second concentration of power lay north and east: a sprawling city at the edge of the forest. Majack, if her memory served her correctly. Drawn up before its walls was an army of several thousand Vamilians, and the priestess shook her head in disbelief. *Spider give*

me strength. What was Mayot thinking? Instead of preparing for
Shroud's onslaught he appeared intent on picking fights with the nations bordering the forest. How long before every kingdom this side
of the Sabian Sea knew about the threat he posed? As if that were
not bad enough, the mage was clearly ignorant of even the basics of
siege warfare. The undead were just standing there, looking up at the
city walls as if they were waiting to be invited inside. Did Mayot think
he could simply . . .

Her thoughts were interrupted by movement among the Vamilian
forces closest to the forest. The undead host parted to make way for
a figure dressed in purple robes.

Romany felt the color drain from her face.

Is that . . .?

No, it could not be.

"Oh my!"

By the time Ebon reached the battlements his legs were trembling so
violently they could barely take his weight. He tottered to the parapet and leaned against one of the merlons. His gaze searched the enemy below. A woman was approaching from the direction of the Forest
of Sighs. *This one is no Vamilian.* Straw-colored hair hung unbound
to her waist, and she wore purple robes that shimmered as she walked.
What caught Ebon's attention most, though, was her bulb-shaped
skull, for it was twice as broad at the cranium as at the jaw.

The spirits' terror was a knot in his stomach. His hands were turning white where they gripped the wall. As the urge to flee intensified
he shut his eyes, only to find he could still *feel* the newcomer somehow, like a bright light through his closed eyelids. But hers was not
the only presence he detected. The alien entity from his nightmare had
returned, lurking at the back of his mind. This time the cold detachment was gone, and in its place was a hatred too vast for Ebon to comprehend. Not directed at him, he sensed, but at the woman below. He
groped toward the presence, seeking something, anything, he could
hold on to. The entity, though, remained beyond his grasp, and it was
fading further with each moment.

Who are you?

Silence.

When he opened his eyes again, the purple-robed woman had
moved level with the guardhouse. At some unspoken command, the

Vamilians ahead of her parted to leave an avenue to the gate a score of paces wide. The battering ram lay forgotten along it; evidently the undead had no further use for it. Ebon's stomach lurched. He took deep, shuddering breaths in an attempt to steady himself, but the spirits would not be calmed so easily, and his snatched breakfast of dried fruit came boiling up. He retched over the battlements. A hand shook his shoulder. Someone was talking to him, but the voice was muted as if the speaker were a great distance away.

Ebon's vision blurred. Just like during the clash last night, a series of images flashed across his mind's eye, each so hazy he could pick out only the most cursory of details: a building of white stone falling to ruin beneath a wave of sorcery, trees burning like pillars of flame, a yellow-robed horsewoman bearing down on him with swords in her hands and death in her eyes—a horsewoman with an oversized skull like the woman outside the city. Tightening his grip on the parapet, Ebon forced the visions down.

When his sight cleared he saw the purple-robed woman raise her arms, her sleeves sliding down to reveal milk-white skin.

The howls of the spirits fell to a whimper.

A blast of wind struck Ebon from behind, pinning him to the battlements. From along the wall came cries of alarm, and to the king's right a Pantheon Guardsman stumbled between the merlons. A despairing cry, and the soldier was falling. The woman next to him thrust out a hand in an effort to grab him.

Missed.

The Guardsman tumbled from view.

Clouds were reversing their course in the sky, gathering to form a thunderhead. The light started to fade, and the air about Ebon grew colder even as a tremor shook the ground. The stranger was drawing in power, he realized. Earth, air, and fire, all at once. *Gods below, is that even possible?* Most mages were able only to soak up the energies of their particular element, and even archmages could only absorb two.

Abruptly the air became still again, and Ebon looked left to see Mottle standing beside him. The mage's gaze was fixed on the sky overhead. *He's battling for control of the air.* The old man was winning the struggle too, for the clouds were already breaking up to let in chinks of light.

But who was going to contest the other elements?

A wall of fire was forming in front of the sorceress. Within the flames, Ebon could make out molten rock and burning roots, all wreathed in smoke. An arrow arced out from the battlements, landing well short of the woman.

Reynes's voice rang out. "Hold your fire!"

Ebon silently swore. The general was right not to waste ammunition, but it still rankled that they could do nothing to disrupt the sorceress's preparations. It was too late to sally forth and attack her even if they'd stood a chance of cutting a path through the undead.

Fissures opened in the earth round the woman like the spokes of a wheel. Most of the rifts were no more than a handspan across, but one, extending west toward the forest, was wide enough to swallow the undead in its path. The battlements beneath Ebon began to shake, and a crack appeared in the merlon by his right hand. All the while, the wall of fire before the sorceress continued to grow. The chill had now gone, and waves of heat washed over Ebon. The armor of the Vamilians closest to the sorcery started to glow red, then their hair and clothing burst into flames. The fires spread along the ranks of besiegers until scores were ablaze. The hapless undead stood silent and unmoving as their skin blackened.

Mottle spoke from beside Ebon. "Flee, my boy. Save yourself."

Before Ebon could reply, Rendale was prying his hands from the wall and dragging him along the battlements.

"Wait," the king gasped, but his brother ignored him. Looking back, he saw Mottle and his two Adepts now standing alone above the gates.

The wall of fire and earth rolled toward the guardhouse, throwing up dirt behind it like a great plough. The undead immediately to either side were engulfed by the fiery darkness, and their bodies seemed to feed the sorcery, for the wall swelled and gained momentum.

A dozen heartbeats later it struck the guardhouse.

Ebon was driven to his knees by the impact. The top of the flaming wall flowed over the battlements, swallowing up Mottle and his Adepts. A shriek sounded as the nearest of the three white-robed figures was enveloped in flames. There was a spitting hiss of conflicting magics as earth and fire collided with Mottle's wards of air over the gates, then a stillness like an indrawn breath.

With an ear-shattering concussion, the guardhouse was ripped apart.

The explosion knocked Ebon onto his back, and for a moment he lay stunned, staring up at the spinning sky as chunks of rock looped into the air. Some fell on the plains, while others landed in the city to the sound of screams and collapsing masonry. A block of stone came crashing down onto the battlements where Ebon had stood just heartbeats before, shattering the parapet.

Then a cloud of dust billowed up around him.

Mottle.

Ebon's ears were ringing, and he could taste powder in his mouth. As he levered himself to his feet, the wall shifted beneath him. The guardhouse, or what remained of it, was invisible in the murk. From beyond the wall came the thump of feet, and when Ebon looked over the battlements he saw the undead army moving toward where the gates had been. No order to the advance, just a formless scrum made spectral by the dust. They swept through the newly created breach.

Rendale was beside him again. He seized Ebon's right arm and threw it across his shoulders. Together they staggered along the wall to the nearest tower where they joined a press of soldiers waiting to descend. Cries sounded all around, a turbulent babble to match the clamor of the spirits in Ebon's head. From somewhere below, Reynes's voice bellowed out, but the words were lost in the tumult. There was no sign of Domen Janir or the chancellor. Had they followed Ebon up onto the wall or remained in the guardroom?

Entering the tower's stairwell, the king took the steps on shaky legs and emerged into chaos. Soldiers and townsfolk dashed every way. A man hurtled round a corner into the path of a woman coming the other way, and they came together in a crack of skulls that Ebon heard even above the hubbub. From his right—the direction of the ruined guardhouse—came the crash of battle. Drawing his saber, he set off toward the noise, half swept along by those round him, half battling the tide coming the other way. When he reached the marketplace, his steps faltered. The guardhouse and a section of wall twoscore paces wide had disappeared to leave only a few broken stones protruding from the ground. The Vamilians were pouring through the breach. Some were still ablaze; all were covered in dust.

Pantheon Guardsmen were arriving in scattered squads along the roads leading off the square.

A voice rang out. "Get them into line! Form ranks, damn you!"

Reynes. The general stood a short distance away beneath the awning of a shop. His cinderhound was gone, but around him was a group of messengers and officers that included Captain Hitch and Sergeant Grimes.

Ebon swung his gaze back to the marketplace. Guardsmen were trying to form a shield wall, but there were too few soldiers to span the width of the square, and the defenders fell back toward West Gate Road before they were outflanked. Among the undead pursuing them was a four-armed warrior wielding a spear in each hand. He stabbed a bearded soldier in the neck, and the man fell clutching at the wound, only to rise moments later and attack the Guardsman at his side.

Watcher's tears. Soon we won't be able to tell friend from foe.

Ebon made for Reynes. "General," he called. "We must fall back."

"We've got men arriving from the other walls. If we can push the stiffs back through the breach—"

"It is too late for that. The city is lost."

"Aye, it is," Reynes grated. "If we yield the walls."

Ebon frowned at his tone. "Do the other gates still hold?"

"For now."

"Then retreat to the river and make your defense there. Fall back street by street—you know the drill. Use the time we have left to tear down as many bridges as you can."

Reynes glanced at the fighting. The four-armed warrior had a broken spear protruding from its chest, but still it came on. The carts across Koron Street had been set alight by one of the flaming undead, and the Guardsmen beyond the barricade were being forced back by the blaze. Vamilians swept over the wagons, heedless of the fire. The general bared his teeth, then turned to Captain Hitch. "You heard the man! Find some Adepts and get started on those bridges. Andresal! I want a shield wall at every junction . . ."

Ebon felt Grimes's gaze on him. The sergeant spoke for the king's ears only. "The river won't hold long, your Majesty. Too many crossing points."

"I know that, Sergeant. So does Reynes. If he can weather the tide for just a bell or two he will give people a chance to get to the palace."

Grimes's frown betrayed his doubt. "Can the fortress hold any better against that witch's fireworks . . ." His voice trailed off. He was staring at something over Ebon's shoulder. "Watcher's beating heart!"

Ebon spun round to see a figure floating down through the clouds of dust above them.

Mottle.

The old man's grubby robe was scorched, and a bruise colored the left side of his face. He touched down a few paces away, scratching at his groin.

Ebon gave a half smile. "For once your arrival is timely, mage. I presume you heard the sergeant's question. Can the sorceries invested in the palace's walls withstand an attack by the sorceress?"

"For a time."

"How long?"

Mottle spread his hands. "So difficult to judge without knowing the full measure of the witch's strength, yes? Mottle's best estimation? A day, perhaps."

"Then we ride out now. Cut her down before she enters the city."

The old man nodded. "Assuredly, my boy. Assuredly. Mottle will join you, of course. The slaying of his Adepts demands a response in kind."

"Can you match her?" Grimes said. "Seems to me she's one up on you."

"The gates? Pah! A lucky strike! A low blow when Mottle's guard was down!"

"Who is she, mage?" Ebon asked. "*What* is she?"

"A Fangalar. One of the elder races, responsible, it is said, for the extermination of the Vamilian civilization. My studies suggest—"

"Is she the power behind the undead?" Ebon interrupted. "Can we end this now if we kill her?"

"Alas, no. Can you not sense the thread of death-magic holding her? The woman is just another pawn in this game. If the puppets' strings cannot be cut, you must instead sever the hand plucking them."

"One thing at a time, mage. First we deal with the sorceress." Ebon turned to Grimes. "How about it, Sergeant?"

Grimes scowled. "You're asking me?"

"Unless you have other plans."

"There is that. Tarqeen barracks, then. I'll muster the troop there."

Ebon nodded. "A quarter-bell, no more." He watched the sergeant dart away.

Rendale spoke at his shoulder. "I'm coming too."

Ebon had forgotten his brother. Rendale's face was smeared with dust, and a trickle of blood ran down from one nostril. Ebon gripped him by the shoulders and pulled him close. "No. I need you to do something for me. Find Lamella. Get her to safety."

Rendale screwed up his face. "You don't have to protect me. Any one of the Guardsmen—"

"Please," Ebon cut in. "I need someone I can trust. She will be alone . . . Her house in the Marobi Quarter—you know it? Get her out by the river if you can. If not, take her to the palace."

Rendale stared at him for a while, his expression appraising. Then a flicker of a smile crossed his face. "Spiriting away the maiden in distress? At last a task suited to my skills."

They shared a quick embrace, then Rendale turned and hurried away along the street, pushing against the flow of soldiers coming the other way. Within moments he was lost from sight.

A strangled cry sounded to Ebon's right, and he spun to see a Pantheon Guardsman impaled by a spear wielded by the four-armed warrior. The soldier was lifted into the air and thrown back into the ranks of his companions. An arrow sprouted between the eyes of the undead fighter, but he did not slow. The enemy had now overrun the marketplace, and red-cloaked Guardsmen were retreating down the streets leading off it. With every heartbeat more Vamilians came streaming through the breach in the city walls.

"Come, Mottle," Ebon said. "We have tarried here too long."

CHAPTER 12

LUKER SAT with his back to a needle of rock, looking down into the depression. At its center was a pool of silty water a score of paces across. Beside it, Merin knelt on the cracked mud and withered mosses, sieving water into his flask through an old shirt that must once have been white but was now the same hue as the muck. As if that was going to make the water any cleaner. Chamery was at the opposite end of the pool, stripped to the waist as he scrubbed his upper body. The pasty skin of his hairless chest contrasted starkly with the flush of his face and neck.

Jenna spoke from behind Luker, startling him. "What a charming sight. I can almost smell the roasting flesh."

The Guardian frowned. The assassin had an unnerving ability to creep up on him unheard. But then that was her thing, wasn't it? As she moved alongside, a gust of wind seized her hood and tugged it back. Luker's gaze lingered on her face. While Chamery's healing had repaired the worst of the damage from the attack at the inn, pale crisscrossing scars remained. Like as not, those scars would never fully fade, and they gave her a look of fragility. Of something broken and inexpertly fixed.

Looking back at Chamery, he said, "Enjoy the show while you can. The boy heals himself every half day or so."

"With sorcery? But won't that draw the soulcaster—"

"Aye. Like a fly to shit."

"Then why haven't you put a stop to it?"

Luker shrugged. "What's the point? With or without the boy's help, the soulcaster can track us the same way I track him."

Jenna fanned herself with one hand. It was early morning, but the temperature had already risen to skin-prickling intensity. "Is there no escape from this damned heat?"

"You could try wearing something other than black."

"Unfortunately my wardrobe is a little limited on that score. One of the hazards of my profession."

"Then be grateful the worst of the summer is behind us. Couple of weeks back this pool would've been nothing more than a puddle."

Jenna's expression was thoughtful. "How far to the next water?"

"Day and a half, maybe."

"So if the Kalanese couldn't drink here . . ."

Luker didn't like the glint in her eye. "What are you thinking?"

Jenna inclined her head in the direction of her pack. "I've brought a few surprises that could slow our pursuers down. Just a couple of drops of something subtle . . . With luck they might all wet their lips before they detect the poison."

Luker hesitated. "I'll think on it."

The assassin smiled her crooked smile. "Worried some innocent might get caught out too? Why Luker, I hope you're not going soft on me."

Muttering, he rose. "Need to stretch my legs. Join me?"

"Why not."

The Guardian led the way up a rocky bank and paused at the top to look out over the plains. Over the Waste to the east another storm was brewing, while to the south the flatlands stretched into the distance, broken only by the huge cairns of dead tribal leaders that rose through the ocher haze. Who knows, maybe Luker had put one or two of them in the ground himself.

Jenna had gone on ahead. At the foot of the slope she crouched to examine something half-buried in the sand, and when Luker joined her he saw bones—the curved ribs of a mule, perhaps, now riddled with teeth marks. Farther on was a human skull, both eye sockets cracked. Beside it lay a coil of tarnished silver inset with yellow jewels. The armlet of a Talenese elder.

Jenna gestured to the skull. "Just a few paces away from the waterhole. Do you think he knew how close he got?"

"Won't have been thirst that did for him. Banewolves, most likely. Knew the pool would draw their prey. Cunning bastards—won't hesitate to attack a tribesman on his own."

"Lucky for you that I came along as escort, then." The assassin picked up the armlet and made to slide it over her wrist.

"Don't!" Luker snapped, seizing her arm. Her eyes flashed, but he did not release his hold. "That thing knows who its master is. Put it on, and the coils will constrict till they touch bone. Tribal magic. Saw it happen to some merchant guard in a trader camp near Karalat. Fool ended up losing the arm."

Scowling, Jenna pulled free of his grasp, then dropped the band and crushed it under a heel. "And for a moment there I thought I couldn't hate this place any more."

"You knew what was coming. Or would you rather have stayed in Arkarbour?"

"I don't like these open spaces. Too exposed. The only shadows out here are ours. And I can hardly hide in those, can I?"

"Get used to it. Three days till we hit the Sun Road. Another three before we reach Arandas. Assuming we don't run into trouble in the meantime." Or should that be more trouble?

"How far behind is the soulcaster?"

"When I last checked, same as before—three bells."

Jenna must have heard the uncertainty in his voice. "Would you rather it was two?"

Luker pursed his lips. "Kalanese horses are more used to this terrain. They should outrun ours easy enough."

A wave of sand swept over them, and the assassin lifted a hand to shield her eyes. "You said their leader sensed you. Maybe he wants to keep his distance. Maybe he doesn't like you any more than the rest of us do."

Luker looked at her askance. What, people didn't like him? And he'd always tried so hard to be nice to everyone. "Then why bother trailing us at all? No, the soulcaster's up to something."

"Is it personal?"

"You mean, does he know me?" Luker shook his head. "Doubt it. But he'll recognize a Guardian when one crosses his path. We've always been at the sharp end of Avallon's dealings with Kal Mecath."

Jenna kicked at the sand round the skull in case it hid any more of the dead man's possessions. "What is he, this soulcaster?"

"Spirit-mage. Like a necromancer, except where a corpse-hugger feeds off death, soulcaster drains the souls of the living. Uses his enemies' life forces against them. Unless they're strong enough to resist, in which case he takes from his own troops."

The assassin's eyebrows lifted. "And they just let him, I suppose?"

"Aye. Fanatics, the lot of them. Soulcaster sucks them dry. Their souls never make it through Shroud's Gate."

Jenna had found a dagger with a broken tip. As she examined its jeweled pommel her look became distant. "I can see why that might have its attractions."

Luker searched her eyes, but did not recognize what he saw in them. "If you wanted oblivion the Breakers would've been happy to give it to you."

"Perhaps I'm just too stubborn to make it easy for them."

"Stubborn, aye, I'll not argue that."

Before Jenna could respond, a noise came to them on the wind. Luker tilted his head. At first all he could hear was the whisper of dust. Then, faintly . . . *Hoofbeats.* He exchanged a look with Jenna, then turned and scrambled back up the slope. Stones skittered under his feet. Reaching the top, he scanned the plains once more. There was a disturbance on the horizon, a blur amid the swirling clouds of sand. *Riders.* Drawn up in an arrowhead formation, too. *More Kalanese?* He was sure of it. *The soulcaster's been driving us toward them all this time.*

With Jenna at his heels, he ran back to the waterhole.

Merin looked up from where he was rooting through his saddlebags.

"Riders," Luker called. "Less than half a league away."

The tyrin's face darkened. "Gods, man, you said three bells."

"Not the soulcaster. Another group, coming from the west."

"Kalanese?"

"You want to hang around to find out?"

Merin packed the last of his water bottles and closed the saddlebag. "How many of them?"

"Enough," Luker said, seizing his horse's bridle.

Chamery pulled on his robes as he stumbled from the pool. "Our horses are spent. We won't get far."

"Aye. We ride east for that sandstorm."

"Into the Waste."

"For now. After we lose them in the storm we can head north, skirting the edge of the plains."

"And if the Kalanese follow us in?"

Luker swung into his saddle. "Pray that they do, mage. Pray that they do."

Ebon slowed as he passed through the gates of the Tarqeen Barracks. The barracks yard was littered with shattered roof tiles, discarded weapons, and riding tack. The mess hall beyond must have been hit by falling masonry, for there was a hole in its roof, and its flagpole, broken halfway up, had toppled into the yard. The crimson Pantheon colors lay stamped into the dirt at Ebon's feet. Piled unceremoniously inside one of the empty horse stalls were a dozen twitching bodies—townsfolk, judging by their lack of uniforms. *And now undead.* The wrists and ankles of each captive had been bound. Smears of blood across the yard indicated where they had been dragged.

To Ebon's left thirty soldiers from Sergeant Grimes's troop were saddling horses. Behind them was another group of riders, and the king blinked when he recognized the consel. With Garat were his sorceress, first adviser, and more than a score of his guard. The four armored demons stood to one side, leaning on their axes. There was no sign of the consel's brother.

Grimes approached Ebon, his helmet tucked under one arm. "Your Majesty."

Ebon glanced at the bodies in the stall. "What happened here, Sergeant?"

"Crowd of civvies stormed the barracks. Must've been after the horses. Wouldn't take no for an answer, neither. We had to bloody a few before the others got the message."

"And the consel?"

"Arrived just before you did and started helping himself. Should I have stopped him?"

Ebon gave a half smile. "Give me a moment," he said, then strode toward the Sartorian company.

Garat scowled when he saw him.

"What's this, Consel?" Ebon said. "You're leaving us already?"

Garat gave a tight smile. "I'm afraid so, your Majesty. I have found the hospitality of your city to be somewhat lacking since my arrival."

"I see your brother is not with you."

A look of disgust crossed the consel's face. "The thread of sorcery holding him is unbreakable, or so my sorceress would have me believe."

"The efforts of my mages have proved similarly unsuccessful."

"Then it seems my brother is beyond saving. Only vengeance is left to me now."

"Perhaps we should combine our efforts. We ride to destroy the Fangalar—"

"The witch is of no interest to me," Garat cut in. "Just one more puppet dancing on another man's strings."

"A man, you say?"

"Or woman. It matters not. The insult to me, to my nation, must be answered."

Ebon eyed him skeptically. The consel appeared less concerned about Falin's death than he did about the loss of face he would suffer if his brother's death went unavenged. "You're going after the puppet master, then? The Forest of Sighs is a big place."

"The threads of sorcery will show us the way. Now, if you don't mind, we have preparations to complete."

Ebon held his gaze for a few heartbeats, wondering what the consel was holding back. "We will escort you to the gates."

"As you will."

Ebon turned away. As he crossed the yard to join Grimes's troop he saw Mottle being helped by a soldier into the saddle of a gray. The mage almost overbalanced, and he threw his arms around the animal's neck to halt his slide. The horse tossed its head, snorting. Ebon's spirits rose to see Vale standing to one side, lifting a saddle onto the back of a chestnut stallion. Approaching him, the king said, "Well met, my friend."

Vale grunted.

"How did you find us?"

"Saw the sorceress's fireworks from across the river. Guessed you'd try and pull a stunt like this." The Endorian's gaze shifted to the Sartorians. "We got ourselves some help?"

"Only as far as the gates. The consel has his sights set on the forest."

"Good," Vale said, but as to why that was so, he did not explain.

A Guardsman approached leading a destrier by the reins. Ebon took them from him and stepped into the saddle. The soldier then passed him a spear, a shield, and a helmet. From the west came far-off shouts, the only noise from a city gone eerily silent beyond the barracks wall. Ebon turned to Mottle. "Mage, can you sense the Fangalar sorceress?"

Mottle's horse was turning in a circle, pitching the old man from side to side. "Of course, my boy. She remains where she was, outside the city."

"Is she guarded?"

"A handful of sentinels only. The witch's sorcerous wards are her most formidable defense, but fear not, Mottle will deal with those." The mage tugged on the reins, pulling his mount's head up. The gray rolled its eyes before turning to snap at the old man.

Ebon strapped his shield to his left arm. "Perhaps a change of horse is in order."

"What?" the mage spluttered, seizing a handful of the animal's mane. "Just as Mottle is bringing the querulous beast to heel?"

A clatter of hooves signaled Garat's approach. "It is past time we were leaving," he said. "Which road do we take?"

"We head for the West Gate," Ebon replied.

The consel barked a laugh. "The ruined guardhouse? You would have us ride into the teeth of the enemy?"

"We have no choice. I will not risk opening another gate."

"The city is already lost."

"And I will do nothing to hasten its fall. My people need time to fall back to the palace."

"Fool!" Garat said. "You won't even make it as far—"

"Nevertheless," Ebon interrupted. "My mind is made up on this."

The consel bit back a retort, then wheeled his horse. "So be it. We will cut a way through the rabble. Follow, if you can."

The four armored demons unlimbered their axes and led the company onto Rook Way. Sartorian horsemen drew up behind them, riding eight abreast. Ebon saw Ambolina watching him dispassionately from the second rank. She sat straight-backed in her saddle, hands folded in her lap as if she were about to take a ride in the country. Ebon led Grimes's troop to join the rear of the group, Vale on his left, Mottle on his right.

The streets were deserted. From along Rook Way came distant muted cries, the tread of feet, the jangle of armor. For the most part, though, the sounds of fighting were from the north. *The river.* Had the retreat become a rout already, then? And what of Rendale? Had Ebon's brother managed to reach the bridges before the undead?

From a side street, a woman carrying a baby ran out in front of the consel's demons. On seeing them she skidded to a halt only to slip and sprawl to the cobbles, turning as she fell to protect the infant in her arms. Within a heartbeat she was up again and hobbling back into the alley. As Ebon watched her disappear, his thoughts strayed to Lamella. Was she listening even now to the conflict surging closer, waiting for him to come for her? *No, she knows where my first responsibility lies.* Duty first, always. *Forgive me.*

The company rode in silence. This district of the city had been hit hard by the Red Tide nine days ago, and the shriveled bodies of scores of scorpions lay amid the dust beside the road. One of the houses to Ebon's left had been reduced to rubble by falling debris from the guardhouse; another had lost half its roof to leave shattered beams sticking out like broken ribs. From a first-floor window, an old man stared at Ebon. He flinched as their gazes met, then reached out to close his shutters.

The king looked at Grimes to find the sergeant watching him in turn. A nod from Ebon, and the soldier began shouting orders. Four Pantheon Guardsmen dropped back from the troop, dismounted, and started pounding on doors. Against any other attacking force, the townsfolk's best chance of survival might have been to lie low and wait for the dust to settle. Against an undead army, though, their only hope was to make it to the palace before the bridges fell.

Ebon lowered his helmet into place, his vision contracting to the rims of the eyepieces. The padding deadened the noise of distant fighting, and the spirits were no more than a murmur in his mind. He wiped his right palm on his shirt, then gripped his spear again. Ahead the way remained empty, but that couldn't last long. Even as the thought came to Ebon, three red-cloaked soldiers appeared round a bend, a handful of paces in front of a disordered mass of undead.

Grimes bellowed, and the Guardsmen veered into a side alley.

The consel's four demons sprang to engage the enemy. A Vamilian man was cut in half by a single ax stroke, the weapon entering below his right shoulder and exiting above his left hip. Another demon's ax struck a building in its follow-through, and a wall crumbled into ruin. Mutilated bodies and severed limbs fell to the ground and were trampled beneath the feet of the armored warriors. But as the demons surged on, a handful of the mangled undead lurched upright again in their wake and turned to hack at the creatures' backs.

At the consel's order, the Sartorian horsemen spurred their mounts forward. The front line lowered their spears in unison, shouting battle cries as they smashed into the undead with a sound like a metallic peal of thunder. A Vamilian woman missing a chunk from her skull took a lance in the back with such force the weapon drove right through her and into the gut of another undead, pinning them together and sending them tumbling. A second woman, her stomach caved in where a demon must have stamped on it, was hit by the chest of a horse and flattened to the cobbles.

Ebon kicked his mount forward, a tickle of fear at the back of his throat. Impossibly, the stricken undead were beginning to rise again in the wake of the Sartorian charge. A horseman was dragged screaming from his saddle by a man he'd carved open moments earlier. Another Sartorian, slowing to help his companion, took a sword thrust in the neck and toppled from his saddle.

"Keep moving, soldiers!" Grimes shouted to his troop. "Any whoreson among you eases up, I'll kill him myself!"

Then the undead were all about Ebon, and his world shrank to the few armspans round his destrier.

A woman with a gaping throat attacked from his left, swinging a rusty sword. He caught the blow on his shield, but before he could counter, his horse took him past. A man in the armor of a Pantheon Guardsman closed from his right, and for a heartbeat the king hesitated, suspecting the soldier was one of the undead, but not knowing for certain. A spear thrust at his head cleared up the confusion. Ebon brought up his shield to block, but Vale's horse was already barreling into the attacker to send him sprawling. Vale shouted something Ebon couldn't hear above the uproar, yet he could guess the message all the same. His next hesitation, the Endorian would be saying, could cost Ebon his life, but that was a risk the king would have to take.

A Vamilian woman ran at him from the left, and he buried his spear in her chest, tensing himself in readiness for some backlash from the spirits.

None came.

The woman twisted as she fell, and Ebon's spear was torn from his hands. He drew his saber.

Vamilians were now pouring from a side street. Ahead one of the demons was battling a four-armed spearman, the undead warrior jabbing out with its spears in search of a weak spot in the demon's armor until an ax stroke broke through his defenses and sheared off his head. To Ebon's right, a Galitian woman holding a cleaver was clambering onto the rump of Garat Hallon's horse. Instinctively Ebon spurred his mount forward, reaching the consel just as the woman raised her weapon. The king's blade took her in the side and knocked her to the ground. As she fell he felt something pierce the armor on his right side. The point of a knife scraped against his ribs, sending a twist of agony through his chest. Gritting his teeth, he hacked down at the arm wielding the dagger. Limb and blade fell away.

What remained of the West Gate was visible now to Ebon's right. As Rook Way opened out onto the marketplace, the cobbles gave way to hard-packed dirt and clouds of dust. The padding of Ebon's helmet was becoming damp, and his sword arm was aching from the ceaseless slashing and hacking. A man rushed at him from the left, sword raised—another Pantheon Guardsman, and this time there was no doubting his intent. His gaze locked with Ebon's. The soldier's expression was blank, but there was something behind his eyes, a recognition . . .

The merest hitch in his stride, then he came on.

Ebon lashed out with his shield, and its rim slammed into the man's forehead, snapping his head back. He crumpled to the ground.

The ruined guardhouse was directly in front now, but still tantalizingly out of reach. The consel's demons had slowed almost to a halt, the advancing host of undead plugging the gap in the battlements like a cork in a bottleneck. Blood pounded at Ebon's temple, and he could feel more blood flowing from the cut in his side, soaking his shirt round the wound. Every movement sent a jolt of pain through his chest as if he were being stabbed anew. To his right Mottle was wrestling with his horse's reins. A spear hurled at the mage hit an invisible barrier and bounced away. Then Mottle's mount seemed to trip, and Ebon lost sight of the old man amid the melee.

An unseen blow glanced off the armor at his back. A Vamilian man with a sword lodged in his neck stumbled into Ebon's destrier, tugging its head round as his hands tangled in the reins. Ebon swayed in the saddle, kicked out, and connected with a boot to the man's chin. Ebon found himself looking back the way he'd come across the marketplace. The remainder of Grimes's troop, less than a dozen red-cloaked riders, were fighting a desperate rearguard action. Vale was there, his sword a blur as he dealt out destruction to the undead round him. But for every undead assailant struck down, two more rose in his place.

We are trapped. Retreat was no more an option now than making the gates seemed to be. The end, Ebon sensed, was but moments away, but at least by fighting the undead here he was keeping them from joining the battle at the bridges. The thought came as scant consolation. If he fell, he promised himself no power would make him turn on his kinsmen. But then doubtless every Galitian who had died this morning had believed the same, and he pictured himself raising a sword against Lamella, the look of betrayal in her eyes . . .

Yanking on his reins, he turned his destrier back toward the ruins of the West Gate.

In time to see Ambolina gesture with one hand. The four armored demons surged left and right to leave her standing alone before the undead spilling through the opening in the city wall. A wave of black fire leapt from her hands. The Vamilians in its path burst into flames and disintegrated, flesh and bone collapsing into steaming piles of detritus. The consel's demons charged into the void, Garat's and Ambolina's mounts at their heels. As Ebon spurred after them, his destrier slipped for an instant on the slick ground before righting itself and springing forward. Bones crunched underfoot.

From outside the city, Vamilians came surging back through the gap like a wave through a fissure in a seawall. The demons hit them in a line, axes swinging tirelessly, and the enemy ranks crumbled. An undead warrior had climbed onto a mound of rubble where the guardhouse had been, and now threw himself at one of the demons as it passed. A metal fist swung to meet him, catching him a blow to the skull and half spinning him round. His momentum still carried him crashing into the demon. He slid to the ground and was trampled into the dirt.

Suddenly Ebon was past the wall. The crush of Vamilians was thickest ahead and to his left, while to his right—the direction of the river—the undead were spread more thinly. At a command from Ambolina the demons turned that way, punching a path through the enemy. Rising in his stirrups, Ebon looked round for the Fangalar sorceress, but he could see nothing through the dust beyond a score of paces.

As the numbers of undead fell away, the demons changed course again, curling round to the west and the Forest of Sighs. Ebon caught sight of the wreckage of the consel's camp, wisps of black smoke spiraling up into the sky. The only enemy in front of him now were scattered Vamilians emerging in a trickle from the woods. He looked over his shoulder expecting to see undead following them, but the foe was apparently happy to let the company go, for there was no sign of any pursuit. Whatever the reason for the attack on the city, it seemed neither Ebon nor the consel was its target.

The Sartorian camp was surrounded by a ditch an armspan deep. Earth had been piled up on the inside, faced with turf, and leveled off to form a low rampart. A road crossed the ditch on this side, and the demons followed this into the center of the encampment before slowing to a halt. Ebon drew up behind them. The place was bigger than some of the military camps he'd visited. Towering over him was the consel's pavilion—a mountain of rippling golden canvas from which the Sartorian flag flew. A handful of the tents had been gutted by fire to leave just scraps of charred cloth and squares of blackened grass. The ground between them was dotted with blocks of stone and splinters of wood. Ebon's eyes widened. *The guardhouse?* Could rubble from the explosion have carried this far?

At Garat's order, Sartorian soldiers dismounted to gather supplies and take down the flag over the pavilion. Ambolina had survived the clash unscathed, but the consel's first adviser, Pellar Hargin, was missing.

Ebon's fingers explored the cut to his side. Through his blood-stained armor he could feel a broken knife point beneath his skin. Every breath sawed in his chest, but he would have to wait a while before removing the shard of metal. Vale, Mottle, and the remnants of Grimes's troop filtered into the camp. Aside from the sergeant, only six red-cloaked soldiers had survived, every one of them battered and bloodied. Grimes had lost his helmet, and four angry red scratches marked the left side of his face.

Garat steered his horse to Ebon. "You saved my life," he spat.

It was a moment before the king could respond. "My apologies. I will try not to make the same mistake again."

"Do you claim blood debt?"

"I am unfamiliar with your customs—"

"Blood of my blood has first calling. Do you deny me this?"

For a heartbeat Ebon was tempted to call in the debt and demand that Garat unleash Ambolina and her demons against the undead sorceress. He knew the consel well enough by now, though, to realize the Sartorian would refuse him if he tried to do so. Men like Garat Hallon honored their obligations only if and when it suited them to do so. "I deny you nothing," he said. "Now, leave us. We have work to do."

Garat's humorless smile told Ebon he'd read the man right. The consel jabbed a finger at him. "Stay alive, your Majesty. The debt survives only as long as you do." He wheeled his horse.

Putting the Sartorian from his mind, Ebon took off his helmet. The wind was hot on his skin as he looked back at the city. Between the remains of two tents he could make out the undead army still streaming through the breach in the city walls. There was no sign of the Fangalar sorceress.

Grimes spoke. "What's the plan?"

Ebon looked at Mottle. "Mage, can the Fangalar sorceress sense us?"

The old man was sitting in front of his horse's saddle, his legs wrapped round the beast's neck. "Mottle suspects so, my boy. The witch observed our departure from the city, but she made no attempt to intervene. Her attitude is, Mottle believes, one of indifference." The mage's tone was indignant.

"It appears she does not consider us worthy of her attention."

"Mottle is ever underestimated."

With a rumble of hooves, the consel's company rode out of the camp toward the forest.

Grimes spat on the ground. "Never thought I'd be sad to see the back of that black-hearted whoreson."

Ebon could only agree. "Mottle, how does one . . . incapacitate . . . an undead sorceress?"

"An interesting question. Mottle has been pondering that very subject since we left the barracks. Sever a warrior's sword arm and you nullify his threat, yes? But a sorceress does not need her hands to shape the energies she wields."

"Then what? Her eyes?"

"Precisely. Without her sight the witch cannot direct her considerable might."

"And in the meantime? Can you extend your wards over the whole squad?"

The mage spread his hands. "Mottle could, my boy, but stretched so thinly . . ."

"They would buckle under the first assault," Ebon finished. Meaning if he ordered a straight attack on the Fangalar his company would likely be slaughtered before they got close enough to bring their swords to bear. He looked round. The camp would offer cover of sorts if he could persuade the sorceress to approach, but why should she take an interest in them *now* when she had ignored them thus far? "Can you lure her here?" he said to Mottle. "Can you bring her to us?"

"But of course. Mottle need only call her over. The poor woman can do naught but heed his summons."

Ebon turned to Sergeant Grimes. "The first attack belongs to the mage. I want a couple of your troop watching his back. The rest of us will split into two groups, wait for the Fangalar to draw near, then attack from the flanks."

Mottle's forehead crinkled. "Mottle is to be used as a diversion?"

"Call it what you will. Do whatever you must to keep her distracted. A moment of vulnerability is all we need."

The sergeant spoke. "And if the old man can't take down the witch's wards?"

"Such impudence!" Mottle said. "Such faithlessness! Such—"

"Enough!" Ebon cut in, suddenly feeling his exhaustion. "The mage knows what is expected of him, as do we all."

Luker rode at a gallop through the storm, a few lengths back from the rest of his party. Above him the sky rained sand down in sheets, while the shadowy forms of stormwraiths spun and flapped and twitched in the grainy light as they waited to feast on the maelstrom's leavings. They'd be getting a bellyful and more before this brute was done, Luker reckoned. Last time he'd seen fury like this, whole villages west of Arap had been snatched up into oblivion. Get too close to the core of the storm, and he might suffer the same fate.

He looked over his shoulder to see the Kalanese less than a stone's throw behind and reeling him in so steadily he could almost feel the hook in his mouth. No mistaking them in their gray robes and headscarves. Drawn up in an arrowhead formation, they numbered maybe two dozen, but at least there was no soulcaster among them else the man would surely have made his presence felt by now. As Luker watched, the lead rider rose in his stirrups and hurled a spear at him. Buffeted by the wind, the weapon shivered in its flight before falling to earth to his left.

The next missile followed moments behind. If it had been aimed at Chamery, Luker might have let it find its mark, but instead it came arcing toward him, and he batted it aside with a flick of his mind. Another nudge of his Will sent the spear-thrower's horse careering into the mount to its right, and they went down squealing in a tangle of legs, taking their riders with them and spoiling the stride of a horse behind. The fallen Kalanese disappeared amid the spinning sands.

Luker returned his gaze to the front. Several hundred paces away was a wall of darkness spewing out cascades of dust. No way the Kalanese would find Luker's party in that. He dug his heels into his mare's flanks, and the animal responded with a fresh burst of speed. In front, the hooves of his companions' horses were throwing up sand, and Luker narrowed his eyes to slits, his face burning-raw. Two huge mounds of white stones reared up from the plains, and as Luker steered his mount between them the wind momentarily lost its bite.

Merin had taken the lead, his gelding flowing over the ground with a grace that suggested the tyrin had drawn the trump card at Arkarbour's stables. The animal's leg muscles bunched, and it soared into the air. Luker saw it then: a gulley two steps across, running left to right a short distance ahead. He had time only to register Chamery's and Jenna's horses clearing the fissure before he was upon it. His mare slowed, gathered itself, leapt. A glance below revealed dust pouring like waterfalls over both ledges of the gulley. Then the mare touched down on the other side, its hooves scrabbling for purchase on the sand and loose stones. Luker was thrown forward in his saddle, his upper teeth tearing into his bottom lip. Cursing, he spat blood.

The war cries of the Kalanese were audible now above the hissing dust. Luker did not look round. In front, Merin had reached the wall of darkness. Slowing to let Chamery draw level, the tyrin seized the mage's reins and wrapped them about his wrist. Together they plunged into the maelstrom, Jenna behind.

Ducking his head, Luker followed them in.

The gale hammered him from all sides, lashing him with sand and grit. His horse whickered. The outlines of the Guardian's companions were fading into the haze. A score more heartbeats and the dust would swallow them beyond any hope of the Kalanese following.

A score more heartbeats, though, was time they did not have.

Luker brought his mare round to face his pursuers. The Kalanese would be fools to trail him into the storm, but with their quarry so close, and with the numbers weighted so heavily in their favor, Luker suspected they would do just that. Sure enough, the first riders now materialized in front of him, faceless shadows in the murk. He drew both swords and took a breath. An attack would be the last thing they were expecting. And that made it the only option in Luker's mind.

Tensing his Will, he unleashed it in the midst of the Kalanese, and the air concussed with a roar that transcended the din of the storm.

Mounts and riders went down, screaming.

Luker kicked his mare into the chaos. A woman with a great slab of a nose raised her wicker shield to block one of his sword strokes, but the Guardian was too fast, his blade cutting into her neck. A spear flashed at him, and he swayed aside, watched it fly harmlessly past. The thrower was reaching for a second spear when Luker's sword ran him through. Ahead a man knocked to the ground by Luker's earlier Will-attack was trying to regain his saddle. With the flat of one blade, the Guardian slapped his enemy's horse on the rump, and the animal bolted into the storm taking its rider with it.

Suddenly there were no more Kalanese in front of him, and he wheeled his mount for another pass.

A horseman closed from his right, shouting as he lowered his spear. Luker used his Will to bat the weapon's tip aside with enough force to spin its wielder off balance. A flick of Luker's left sword and the Kalanese toppled from his saddle, hands clutching his throat as blood seeped between his fingers.

Half a dozen paces away a woman was struggling to her feet, leaning on a spear. Luker's cut sent her head tumbling from her shoulders. Even as her spear slipped from her senseless fingers, the Guardian was sheathing his right blade and using his Will to summon the falling weapon to his hand. Grasping the shaft, he charged another rider. The spear's point deflected off the rim of the man's shield and buried itself in his left eye. Luker released the weapon as his mare took him past.

Then, with only dust before him, he galloped into the raging winds.

A count of fifty and he drew up his slavering horse before turning to look back. His eyes were so gritty it felt like he'd got splinters in them, but he kept his gaze moving over the shifting walls of sand. Nothing was visible beyond twoscore paces in every direction. He could see farther with his Will than with his eyes, though, and he knew none of the Kalanese were following. Wiping clean his sword, he resheathed it.

At the edge of his vision a stormwraith spiraled down out of the maelstrom, a patch of darkness broken only by two red eyes. It circled the Guardian once, forcing him to twist in his saddle to keep it in view. Then, with a lazy flap of its wings, it disappeared in the direction of the Kalanese, no doubt drawn by the scent of blood.

Luker dismounted to hood his horse's head. The mare's flanks heaved as it nosed at his hand. Like Luker, though, it would have to wait a while longer before it could eat and rest.

With a final look west, the Guardian swung into the saddle again.

He sent his senses questing into the storm to locate his companions, then spurred his horse east.

"Here she comes," Vale said.

Ebon steered his horse to the corner of a tent and looked in the direction of Majack. The Fangalar sorceress was at the crest of a low rise, walking toward the camp. Whirling funnels of Mottle's air-magic buzzed and zipped against her invisible wards, bouncing off like spinning tops. The wind did not so much as part her hair. Not a good sign in truth, but with any luck Mottle was holding back part of his power. A moment of vulnerability was all Ebon had asked for, and if the old man was able to deliver as much, he would do so when Ebon was bearing down on the witch, not when he was hiding behind a tent a stone's throw away.

Ebon drew back before the sorceress noticed him.

Only to feel something brush his thoughts. No, not some*thing*, some*one*. He glanced at Vale. *The Fangalar.* The woman must have anticipated a trap and was now using sorcery to scan the camp for Ebon's party. There was no question that she'd sensed him. *So much for the element of surprise.* For a heartbeat he considered calling off the attack, but only for a heartbeat.

He wasn't going to get another shot at this.

The spirits in his head had shrunk back at the Fangalar's touch, and in their place the mysterious presence from his dream stirred to life again. At its coming a chill gripped him as if ice ran through his veins. When he shivered a jab of pain went through his wounded side. He groped toward the entity as he had on the battlements, but it withdrew from him now as it had then.

Ebon looked round the corner of the tent again. No point in trying to hide from the sorceress now. The woman was approaching the ditch that surrounded the camp. As the king watched, one of Mottle's vortices cannoned off her wards into a tent, and the canvas was ripped from its stays and sucked up into the sky. Behind her came three four-armed warriors carrying a spear in each hand. Overhead a vast ring of gray cloud was forming.

"Leave the four-armed freaks to me," Vale said. The Endorian swung down from his saddle and tied his horse's reins to a tent peg. Drawing his sword, he moved off in a blur.

Ebon turned to the two Pantheon Guardsmen behind him. "Wait for my signal, understood?"

The first soldier, Corporal Ellea, inclined her head. Blood from a scalp wound had colored her blond hair crimson on one side. She appeared calm, but Ebon could read her tension in the line of her mouth. The second Guardsman, Bettle, gave no indication he had heard Ebon's words. Dark-haired and red-cheeked, he sat slouched in his high-backed saddle, using the tip of the dagger in his right hand to trace patterns on the scarred palm of his left.

A gust of wind slapped at Ebon and sent his destrier sidestepping. The entrance flaps of one of the tents to his right had torn loose and were now snapping in the breeze. A hissing noise came from the direction of the Fangalar, then the air at the center of the camp flashed black and a *whoosh* sounded as a handful of tents burst into flames. *Sorcery.* Doubtless Mottle had been the target of the woman's attack, but the old man's whooping told Ebon she'd missed her mark.

The king lowered his helmet onto his head. Its padding was clammy against his skin. "Let's go," he said to the Pantheon Guardsmen.

He turned his destrier.

The tents in the encampment had been laid out in even rows to leave narrow avenues between them, and he steered his mount along one, looking right for a glimpse of the sorceress as she moved along the road toward the center of the camp. When the moment came to charge, he would need to time it just right. Reach the road before the witch, and he'd likely be greeted by a volley of her sorcery. Reach it too late, and she would have time to see him coming and prepare a similar welcome.

That was a damned fine line he'd left himself to walk.

The wind began to pick up. Ebon passed a tent with a long slash down the back where its owner must have a cut a way out. Trampled into the mud ahead was a blood-speckled nightshirt, a boot missing its sole, a severed hand still clasping the hilt of a sword. Ebon stood up in his stirrups. Over the top of a sagging tent he caught sight of the sorceress's four-armed bodyguards. Vale was in among them, moving so quickly it appeared the undead were fighting each other. Wounds blossomed over the body of one, then he toppled to the ground, his right leg severed above the knee. A few paces in front, and seemingly oblivious to the plight of her defenders, was the witch, a pale shape in the dust whisked up by Mottle's vortices.

Much closer than Ebon had expected.

He kicked his destrier to a canter. The drum of the horse's hooves kept time to the beating of his heart. Tents whipped past to either side. The road was just ahead now, and riding toward him from beyond it he saw Grimes and the other two Pantheon Guardsmen. Ebon drew his saber, wishing he had the extra range a lance or a spear would give. The absurdity of what he was doing struck him. If the sorceress had considered him a threat she could have razed the camp to the ground when she sensed him earlier. Hells, he wouldn't even know if her wards were down until he swung his saber, and that was assuming he got close enough to try.

Strange how you only saw the flaws in a plan when it was too late to do anything about them.

Grimes must have started his charge before Ebon, for he reached the road now, a score of paces ahead.

Just as the sorceress stepped into view. Without breaking stride, she gestured at the sergeant and his companions. Magic erupted about them, and they shrieked.

Behind the Fangalar, Vale appeared. The Endorian had evidently disposed of her four-armed defenders and now lunged for her unprotected back. Only for his sword to strike an invisible shield. Lightning streaked along the length of his blade, and he fell writhing to the ground.

The witch's wards were still in place.

Ebon's limbs felt leaden. "Mottle," he whispered, "if you've got any more cards up your sleeve, now is a good time to play them."

The Fangalar's dead eyes swung to look at Ebon, and her hands came up.

"Split!" he yelled to Ellea and Bettle, hoping the Guardsmen would be able to ride clear.

A wave of flaming earth and roots came roaring toward him from the witch's fingers, igniting the tents to either side. No chance to throw himself from its path. Instead he brought his shield up in what he knew was a pointless gesture, then flinched as black fire washed over him. The darkness was so complete it was as if someone had put a bag over his head. Sorcery crackled in his ears, and his destrier whinnied. He opened his mouth to scream, drew in a mouthful of air that scorched the back of his throat. And yet as the magic sizzled about him he experienced a sensation not of raging heat but searing cold, sharp enough to set him trembling. He felt the weight of his shield lift from his left arm, knew it had been burned away—just the strap remained, clutched in his hand. He shouldn't have been able to feel even that, though. He should have been hurting too, but all he felt was a tingle.

A heartbeat later he emerged from the blackness into dusty light.

Ebon blinked. His clothes were smoldering, and he smelled like he'd been dragged through a bonfire. All he could think of was that there had to be some mistake. No time to dwell on it, though. His destrier hadn't slowed its pace, and the witch was only a handful of paces away. Her protective wards of fire- and earth-magic were visible as glittering multicolored energies, but they peeled away as Ebon's horse thundered closer to leave her standing defenseless.

Just one more impossibility to add to the others.

He swung his saber, wincing at the stab of pain the movement sparked in his wounded side.

The Fangalar must have been as shocked as Ebon that he'd survived her salvo, for she made no attempt to evade the cut. The weapon took her in the face, just above the bridge of her nose, and Ebon surrendered the blade as his charge carried him past.

Pulling on the reins, he wheeled his mount.

In time to see Vale come staggering up behind the sorceress. His face was flash-burned, and the sword in his hands was fire-blackened. Stepping in close, he delivered a decapitating stroke that sent her head spinning to the dust, Ebon's blade still fixed in it. A kick to the back of her knees drove her to the ground. Then the Endorian raised his sword two-handed and brought the point spearing down into her lower back, pinning her to the earth. The Fangalar struggled feebly, hands reaching behind her in an attempt to grab the weapon.

"Get away from her," Ebon said. "Before she starts firing blind."

Vale grunted and retreated.

Ebon slid from his saddle, his legs almost buckling as he touched down. It hardly seemed possible he was still breathing. Fire flickered along his left sleeve, and he rolled the arm against his body to smother the flames. To his left Ellea and Bettle sat astride their horses, watching him blankly, while to his right Grimes lay unmoving, wrapped in his red cloak . . .

A warning shout brought his head round.

Two Pantheon Guardsmen advanced on him with swords drawn— the two Guardsmen who'd been with Grimes when the sorceress attacked. The cautionary cry had been Mottle's, and the mage now came skipping from behind a tent, flapping his arms as if he were trying to fly. A wave of his hand, and the two undead soldiers were lifted from their feet to float helplessly above the ground. Their legs kept moving nevertheless, treading the air as if it were water, and Mottle giggled.

Ebon silenced him with a look, then swung his gaze back to the prone figure of Grimes.

The right half of the soldier's face had been burned away, and where the eye on that side had been was now only bone protruding from weeping flesh. Curls of energy flickered round his wounds. He should have been dead, yet somehow he managed to push his hands beneath him and made to rise.

Ebon knelt and placed a hand on his chest. "Rest easy."

"Help me up, damn you!" Grimes said. "My horse . . ."

"Where would you go, Sergeant?"

"The river. Got to get away . . . I'll not become one of them . . ."

Ebon rubbed a hand across his eyes, lost for anything to say. There would be no recovering from the sergeant's wounds, and the king would not dishonor him by pretending otherwise. Mottle had moved to stand over them and—as the mage explained—began weaving currents of air across the soldier's blistered skin to ease the discomfort of his burns. When Grimes coughed, blood frothed to his lips.

Vale broke the silence. "You'll have to ride round the city, Grimes. The river on this side will carry you into the Water Gate."

"Then Watcher's tears, help me up, man!" Grimes said, his voice cracking. "I can't hold . . ." His words degenerated into a fit of coughing.

Numbed, Ebon helped Vale haul the soldier to his feet. Grimes cried out as he staggered upright, his head lolling forward. His dead horse lay steaming a handful of paces away, so Ebon led his own destrier to Grimes and boosted him into the saddle.

"Sergeant," he said.

"No time, your Majesty," Grimes replied. Clutching the reins in one hand, he forced a grin. "Damned if I'm going to . . . hang round for one of your . . . pretty speeches anyhow."

A tightness gripped Ebon's chest, and he could only watch in silence as the soldier dug his heels into the destrier's flanks and set off east. As the animal reached a canter Grimes started to sway. For a moment Ebon thought he would fall. Then the sergeant's back straightened. Would his gambit work? If he could get to the river, alive or dead it would carry him away and spare him from having to join the attack on the city. Perhaps that was enough. A muscle flickered in Ebon's cheek. A bitter day indeed, when the best a dying man could hope for was to stay dead.

Slowly, Grimes and his horse dissolved into the heat haze that shrouded the plains until all that remained was a smudge of brown within the murk. Then that too faded.

Long after the soldier had vanished, Ebon continued to stare after him.

Finally he turned to look at Majack. The pain in his side had settled to a dull throb. General Reynes must have been using fire to combat the undead, for tendrils of smoke rose from the southern districts of the city, and a pall of gray hung over the rooftops. Farther north, the sky remained clear. *Meaning Reynes still holds the river?*

Maybe.

The Vamilians that had been guarding the north and south walls were now circling round to join their kinsmen at the ruins of the West Gate. If the enemy had left the other gates undermanned, Reynes might attempt to sally forth, but what would be the point? How far could the townsfolk flee on foot with a tireless undead host in pursuit? Where would they go that might offer better protection than the palace? Ebon ran a hand over his shaved head. Ultimately the defeat of the Fangalar sorceress might count for nothing. All he had done was buy the city some time.

Now he had to figure out what to do with it.

He was brought round by the sound of fighting from the opposite end of the camp. "Mottle," he said. "The Guardsmen I sent to watch your back . . . See what you can do to help them." Gesturing at Ellea and Bettle, he added, "You two, go with him."

Vale waited until they were alone before speaking. "What happened? When you attacked the sorceress, I saw you ride through—"

"Later," Ebon cut in. "When we are out of this." He pointed to the struggling Fangalar. "You will leave your sword?"

"Aye, let it hold her here. You want me to take her legs as well? In case she works herself free?"

Ebon hesitated. A memory came to him of the consel's brother on the battlements, pleading for help even as he thrashed against his bonds. Perhaps the sorceress could feel no physical pain, but that didn't mean she wasn't suffering. "No," he said at last. "Anyone who freed her could just carry her, anyway. Round up the remaining horses, then search the camp for provisions. Let's see what the Sartorians left us."

The Endorian's eyes narrowed. "We ain't going back to the city?"

Ebon shook his head. "There's no way we'd fight our way inside."

"Maybe one of the other gates. Or we wait till nightfall."

"And then what? Even if we could somehow get past the outer wall, what chance would we have of reaching the palace?"

Vale held his gaze for a heartbeat before turning to the Forest of Sighs. "You're going after the consel."

"Yes."

"You trust him?"

"I have no choice. We need him."

"And if he decides he doesn't need us?"

"It's a risk we have to take. The palace will fall in time, Vale, whether we are here to see it or not. Defeating the sorceress has gained us, what, a few days?"

"Assuming they don't have another mage."

Ebon scowled. "What would you have me do?"

"Make for Culin. Gather a force together."

"And in the meantime? Majack would fall."

The Endorian looked at the forest. "Then send me in there. Whoever's behind this, I'll hunt them down quicker on my own."

"While I go and hide behind a wall somewhere? No, Vale . . ."

Ebon's voice trailed off at the sound of hoofbeats approaching through the camp. Corporal Ellea rode up in a lather. "More of the stiffs, your Majesty," she said, reining in. "From the trees, heading this way."

"Did you reach the others in time, Corporal?"

"No, sir," she replied stiffly.

And so we are five. Ebon looked over at Vale, who nodded and said, "I'll see to the horses."

The king stole a last glance at the city. Reynes's columns of smoke seemed to have advanced farther north in the last few moments, away from the river. But then perhaps it was just the breeze, for the clouds of dust from the guardhouse were also drifting in that direction. Overhead in the ash-filled sky, redbeaks were gathering.

Grimacing, Ebon looked away.

With the dead on the march, the birds would find no carrion here.

Part III

Breath of the Dead

CHAPTER 13

ROMANY RUBBED her hands together. After so many days of waiting the game was finally under way! The past few bells had seen a host of strangers entering the forest, and they were now sending ripples along her sorcerous web as they blundered through its strands. Most of the intruders were not Shroud's disciples, and these she would leave to Mayot's unsophisticated charms. That left eight unwitting players to take part in her game. Eight versus Romany's one. Hardly the most sporting of odds, but the priestess was here to win, not play fair.

As yet there had been no sign of any collaboration between Shroud's servants, but then somehow Romany doubted the god's minions were team players. There were always petty rivalries between an immortal's followers—for proof of that she had only to think back on her own dealings with the Spider's high priestesses from other cities. Here, those rivalries would have been fueled by the prestige that was certain to accrue to whichever of Shroud's vermin wrested the Book from Mayot's hands. Perhaps Shroud had even offered a reward to the successful disciple. *Fool.* By encouraging his servants to act alone he would only make it easier for Romany to pick them off one at a time.

And the minion she was now tracking through the southern reaches of the forest was sure to be one of the prize scalps. Wearing a hooded black robe and carrying an ebony staff, the stranger walked with a sway that was unmistakably female. The hands protruding from her sleeves were covered in black scales, and each of her fingers ended in a long, curved talon. Where she trod, her footsteps left black impressions on the grass, and the trees in her wake shed leaves in a gentle

shower. That set off a steepleful of bells in Romany's head. As an initiate in the Spider's temple, she had heard whispers of a creature whose
mere presence could cause decay like this. *The Widowmaker*. One of
Shroud's most trusted followers, as well as his sometime mistress. A
guardian of death's gate who had stood at the god's right hand since
his ascension in the Second Age. An abomination whose touch was
death.

Pure poppycock, Romany had assumed. Now she was not so sure.

Whoever the woman was, the enormity of her power was unques-
tionable. *If I could knock her out of the game . . .*

The priestess had warned Mayot of the Widowmaker's approach,
and he had responded with the exact degree of subtlety she'd come
to expect of him. A horde of Vamilians had been dispatched to throw
themselves at Shroud's disciple. She had destroyed them without having to so much as lift a finger. For as the undead drew near they
simply fell lifeless around her, the threads of death-magic holding
them—the threads Romany had believed unbreakable—shriveling like
the grasses beneath her feet. And the Widowmaker would only get
stronger as she feasted on the energies released by the Book. By the
time she reached Estapharriol she would be unstoppable.

Romany, though, had no intention of letting her get that far. Over
the course of the morning she had been following Shroud's disciple
in spirit-form through the forest. It was not easy leading someone's
footsteps astray without them detecting the hidden hand, but the
priestess was a master of the art. A nudge here. A false shadow there.
The Widowmaker had entered the forest from the southwest, near the
foothills of the White Mountains, and set a northerly course for
Mayot's dome. Only for Romany to guide her in a gentle arc east to
the edge of the plains north and west of Arandas.

The Widowmaker had arrived at the tree line a quarter of a bell ago,
and still she stood there, staring across the Gollothir Plains in what
Romany could only assume was disbelief. A shame the woman's hood
was raised, because the priestess would have enjoyed seeing her
stunned expression. Alas, the deception was unlikely to succeed a second time, for the Widowmaker would be suspicious now. In any event,
Romany's efforts to this point had been time-consuming, and it was
hardly fair that she lavish *all* her attention on just one of Shroud's
disciples. She needed a way to remove the woman from the game per-
manently.

Just then the Widowmaker spun round to face the forest. She raised her ebony staff, and a wave of sorcery erupted from the wood. The trees in front of her were incinerated and fell to earth as clouds of powdery ash. When she finally lowered her staff, a wide straight path several hundred paces long had been cut into the forest. To either side of that path, trees burned fiercely.

Romany sniffed. It seemed the opportunities for further misdirection had just lessened somewhat, but so far as this particular contest of wills was concerned she was just getting warmed up.

She flashed back to her body along the strands of her web and opened her eyes to find her undead servant, Danel, staring back at her across her humble abode. She sat up. A look round revealed the girl had not even started sweeping the floor or clearing away the rubble. What in the Spider's name had she been *doing* all this time?

Then Romany saw the bath against the far wall. Steam rose from a tub made of mottled gray metal—tarnica, she presumed, for what else could have survived the millennia? Clambering upright, she crossed for a closer inspection. The rim of the bath was engraved with an interwoven pattern of leaves, and the insides were discolored from what the priestess suspected had once been silver plating. She dipped a finger into the water. Not bad. A bit tepid perhaps, but she was feeling in a gracious mood today.

"This water," she said to Danel. "You did not take it from the poisoned river, I trust."

"No, from a well."

"Good. Excellent, in fact." Through the front doorway, Romany could make out a fire with a battered pan suspended above it. "You even put the fire downwind, my dear. I commend your resourcefulness." She gestured to the pan. "Is that ready?"

Danel approached the fire and lifted the pot before returning to add the boiling water to the bath.

Romany stripped off her clothes and stepped into the tub. That last pan had brought the temperature up to something nearing respectability, and she lay back with a contented sigh. The tub was a tight fit, alas. *Obviously made for a child.* As was often the case after Romany spirit-traveled, the muscles of her neck and shoulders were tight. "I shall require you to massage my shoulders," she told Danel. Then her gaze settled on the ice-white skin of the girl's fingers. "First, though, be so good as to warm your hands over the fire."

As Danel headed outside, Romany closed her eyes. How wonderful to have found a competent servant. Someone who was prepared to use her initiative and did not feel the need for unnecessary talk. If only Romany's servants—*acolytes,* she corrected herself—at the temple could be as capable. True, the girl was a little reserved, but that would surely change once she came to appreciate Romany's company.

The priestess's breathing slowed. A pity she had not brought some oils from Mercerie, but the Spider's undignified haste had left no time for . . . well, anything actually. A distant tremor shook her web, and the Widowmaker's image appeared in her mind's eye. Shroud's disciple was still more than twenty-five leagues from Estapharriol, giving Romany ample time in which to arrange an appropriate welcome. As to what form that welcome would take, though . . . There was no question of the priestess going toe-to-toe with the Widowmaker in a direct confrontation—not because she would lose the clash, of course, but because she could not afford to step into Shroud's line of sight. But then what did that leave? There was always the tiktar to fall back on, but Romany was loath to play her most powerful game piece so early in the conflict.

When she opened her eyes again, Danel was still crouching with her hands over the fire.

Romany frowned. "The water is getting cold, my dear."

Danel straightened and walked toward her.

Only then did the priestess notice that the girl's hands were blistered and charred. The smell of cooked meat reached her, and her stomach flipped. "Spider's mercy," she breathed. "Why did you not move your hands?"

"You didn't tell me to," Danel said. There was no suggestion of pain in the girl's eyes. No suggestion of anything.

"The Book doesn't permit independent action?"

"Your last command was to warm my hands above the fire."

Smoke curled from Danel's fingers, and Romany looked away. "Will it heal? The power of the Book . . ."

"No. Once resurrected, the subject's body does not regenerate." Danel appeared to hesitate.

"But . . ." Romany prompted.

"I've seen the master repair broken flesh before—one of his favorites. He can be . . . rough."

"Spare me the details. I will raise this with Mayot when we next meet. A crippled servant is of no use to me." Romany settled back in the bath. "Talk to me, girl. Tell me, what was your calling?"

"I was a herbalist."

"An earth-mage?"

"No. The Vamilians had no such affinity with the land. We were a people of the sea."

Of course. Where else would a nation of seafarers dwell but a hundred leagues from the nearest water? "I have read much about your kinsmen," Romany said, "though in truth few writings have survived from the Time of the Ancients. As you can imagine, speculation abounds as to what happened on the day your civilization perished."

"What would you have me tell you? How I watched a Fangalar sword disembowel my child? How it felt when the same blade clove through my heart?"

Romany pursed her lips. The girl seemed determined to spoil her mood. "The scholar Isabeya claims your people knew the Fangalar were coming, yet chose not to flee. Is he correct?"

"Yes."

"Truly? You did not believe, surely, that you could defeat the savages."

Danel's hands dripped slime to the floor. "Our ancestors fled from the Fangalar once—boarded ships and scattered across the world. For a time we kept in touch with our kinsmen in other lands. Then one by one those kinsmen stopped replying to our messages." The girl's voice was so dispassionate she might have been reading from one of Abologog's six Treatises on Reverence. "It took the Fangalar centuries to find us here, but find us they did. All that time we lived in the knowledge that one day we would be discovered. That was not a legacy we wanted to pass on to our children, or our children's children."

"What was the cause of your people's enmity with the Fangalar? The texts suggest you discovered a truth about them. Something they would not tolerate your knowing."

Danel nodded.

Romany sat up with a splash. "What was it?"

"I don't know."

"You don't know?" the priestess repeated incredulously.

"A decision was reached, long before I was born, that those who knew the secret would take it with them to their graves. It was hoped the hatred of the Fangalar would die with them."

"Were you not intrigued to find out?"

"Why would I be? No explanation could suffice for what the Fangalar did to us."

Was that a hint of bitterness in Danel's voice? Romany had thought the girl incapable of emotion. "I am curious, my dear. When I first came to this forest, I witnessed a host of spirits near the White Road. Your kinsmen?"

"Yes."

"And they have haunted the forest all this time? Why? Why did you not pass through Shroud's Gate?"

"It was closed to us."

"Closed?" *What an intriguing image.*

"At the time the Fangalar attacked, the gods were at war. Shroud had just taken his throne. The world of his predecessor was destroyed, a new one still being made."

"Ah, you were trapped," Romany said. A thought struck her. "And so in a bid to escape your suffering you tried to . . . usurp . . . the bodies of those who stumbled into your domain."

"Others of my people did, yes. Not I."

"You would prefer to remain a spirit?"

"I would prefer an end to it all. I have existed as a shade for millennia. Dead, but without release. A pity the Fangalar did not destroy my soul as well as my flesh. It would have been a mercy."

Romany rolled her eyes. *Such joyous company.* Just looking into the girl's eyes was enough to send a shiver through her . . . Though now she thought of it, there *was* a breeze coming from the open doorway. Sinking deeper into the water she said, "I wish to be alone now. Sparkling though your conversation is, I feel the need for silence. You are dismissed."

Danel paused, then said, "You're sending me back to the master?"

There was something different about the girl's voice, but the priestess was no longer paying attention. Far to the south and east she sensed ripples along the strands of her web. No, not so much ripples as . . . shudders. Romany's wondrous creation, she realized, was being ripped apart by the arrival of some new power in the game.

And what a power it was.

Not even the Widowmaker . . .

Ebon sat with his back to a tree, listening to the leaves rustle on the forest floor. Dappled moonlight played across the campsite. A few paces away lay Vale, his head pillowed on his rolled-up cloak, resting. Beyond him were the still forms of Mottle and Corporal Ellea. For the past half-bell Ebon had tried to join them in sleep, but he couldn't get comfortable on the hard ground. Yesterday Vale had removed the broken dagger point from his side and stitched the cut, but the wound still oozed watery blood, and a dark swelling was spreading across his ribs and chest, making it painful to raise his right arm. *My sword arm.* He rubbed his eyes. When the party next crossed blades with the Vamilians, he would be at best a passenger, at worst a liability.

It was two days since they'd entered the forest. Two days following the Amber River south and west with no idea where they were going, or what they would find when they got there. For while the air was saturated with death-magic, enough earth-magic remained to thwart Mottle's efforts to quest ahead. It would be days still, the mage said, before he could locate the consel, or scout the forest to find out what awaited them. As yet they had not encountered a single undead warrior, but their luck surely couldn't hold.

Ebon's sight clouded suddenly, and he closed his eyes. After the defeat of the Fangalar sorceress, the spirits had returned to swarm his mind. At first there had been a triumphant note to their babbling, but it hadn't taken long for that elation to give way to the familiar tormented murmur. Yesterday Ebon had succumbed to a fever, and that fever had fueled a flood of spirit-visions: a Vamilian hunting party battling some forest cat with a green striped coat and paws the size of plates; lines of white-robed figures on either bank of the river, keeping pace with a slow-moving funeral barge bearing a black-shrouded corpse; solemn-faced Vamilian children tying wind chimes to the branches of trees; and always in the distance the sounds of fighting, sorcerous explosions, screams. It was becoming harder for Ebon to distinguish what was real from what was imagined. Twice now he had raised an alarm over shadows seen flitting among the trees, only for Vale to give the all clear moments later.

And when the visions relented, his thoughts were haunted instead by Lamella's face. Ebon could not remember the last words he'd said to her, only that they had been spoken in anger. Had Rendale found her in time to lead her to safety? Had they reached the palace or the river before the undead swept over them? *Please, let it be the river.* For not only would that mean Lamella was beyond the reach of the Vamilians, it would also mean she was spared from the whispers and veiled looks she would doubtless endure at the palace. It was two years since he had brought her to Majack after her injury, yet still she remained a stranger to the court. And why? *Because I let her remain so. Because I did not have the courage to choose.* Most likely it was too late now to make amends—for Ebon, if not for her. He could only hope his failing strength held out until he reached wherever it was they were heading.

He shivered in spite of the heat.

Vale spoke. "Is your fever back?"

Ebon nodded.

The Endorian levered himself into a sitting position and began rooting through his pack. He took out two dried sissa leaves and passed them to Ebon.

The king put them in his mouth and started chewing.

Vale said, "Tomorrow I'll hunt out some more galtane or blackroot for the infection."

He would not find any, Ebon suspected. The forest was dying, the color leaching from it as if it had been washed out in the last rain. The farther from Majack they traveled, the more the trees wilted, the deeper the silence about them became as the insects and birds melted away. Ebon studied Vale's face. The Endorian's sorcerous burns had improved markedly since the attack on the Fangalar witch. During the nights, Ebon knew, his friend was speeding his passage through time in order to accelerate the healing process. Still, though, Vale's transformation took him aback, not least the heavy stubble that sprouted each night across his chin and jaw.

Vale unsheathed the sword he had found in the consel's camp and drew a whetstone along its edge. "What happened back there outside the city? You still haven't told me. I saw the witch's sorcery hit you . . ."

Ebon looked at the sleeping figures of Mottle and Ellea before replying. "I'm not sure. I remember darkness and fire, yet I felt only cold. The Fangalar's defenses just crumbled before me."

Vale waited for him to continue, then scowled. "And the rest of it?"

Ebon gave a half smile. The Endorian knew him well enough to sense when he was holding back. "You remember when we were waiting in the consel's camp? The sorceress's awareness sweeping over us? Well, her touch stirred something to life inside me. Something that until then had been only a fleeting presence."

"And you reckon this . . . presence . . . stepped in against the witch?"

"I can think of no other explanation."

"One of the spirits?"

"I do not know. I cannot remember sensing it before the spirits re-

turned, yet my perception is of"—he struggled to find the words—
"something outside looking in. It is difficult to explain."

"Is it with you now?"

The king shook his head.

Vale grunted. "Well, whatever it is, at least it's on our side."

"I am not so sure," Ebon said. He spat the remains of the sissa leaves
from his mouth. The herb had numbed his lips and tongue, making it
difficult for him to form words. "There is some history, I think, between the Fangalar and this presence. It saw a chance to strike at the
sorceress and took it. Will it be there the next time we run into trouble? Who knows. Is its power something I can use? Not a chance."

Vale gestured to Ebon's wound. "I saw how you got stung in
Majack. Protecting the consel's back."

"You disapprove?"

The whetstone paused in the Endorian's hands. "It changes nothing. If the consel gets through this he'll still have his sights set on us.
Maybe more so now we've taken a beating. You can't win him round."

"He spoke to me of a blood debt. The man has some notion of honor,
however twisted it may be."

"Then use it against him while you still can. Strike before he does."

Ebon took a sip of water from his flask. "You are suggesting he
has some sort of accident when we catch up to him?"

"If the chance comes, aye. Stop the war before it starts."

"And when word gets back to Sartor?"

Vale shrugged. "*If* it does, what have you lost? Most likely the consel's court will be too busy squabbling over the scraps of his kingdom to care. At worst, you'd buy us time to regroup." He resumed
sharpening his sword. "Think about it, at least."

Ebon was too tired to argue. "As you say."

At that moment Vale raised a finger to his lips. A figure had come
into view, weaving between the trees to Ebon's left—Bettle, judging
by his red cloak and crablike gait. The soldier scuttled forward to
crouch between Ebon and Vale. "We got company," he said, pointing
behind him.

Ebon had already seen them: shadowy figures approaching from
the south, avoiding the scattered patches of moonlight on the ground.
The king heaved himself to his feet. More shadows, from farther
west this time, flowing soundlessly between the trees. The newcomers must have seen Ebon's campsite then, for they took cover behind
the trunks. Within a dozen heartbeats the forest became perfectly

still. If Bettle hadn't warned him of the shadows' approach, Ebon might have wondered if they were just another of his spirit-visions.

Whoever the newcomers were, they couldn't be undead, for Ebon doubted the Vamilians would be shy about attacking. Then the breeze picked up and he caught a familiar whiff of decay.

Kinevar.

Bettle had shaken Ellea awake, and the corporal was now crouching beside her pack, hands moving smoothly as she locked the crank of her crossbow and slid a bolt into its slot. Bettle stood over her, unlimbering his mace. Ebon held up a hand to signal them to hold. Vale stood with his back to a tree, gesturing to the river. *Retreat?* To what end? There was no boat to carry them away, no bridge they could cross, and any dash for the horses might spook the Kinevar into attacking. Best to remain still and wait the creatures out.

In any case, with his chest as it was, it wasn't as if he'd get far.

He squinted into the gloom, tilted his head to listen. Guttural voices reached him. Then a creak of wood sounded like someone stepping on a loose floorboard, followed by a whistle of something cutting through the air.

A white-feathered arrow thumped into a tree an armspan away.

The king flinched, but held his ground. Strangely enough, the arrow settled his nerves. The archer could just as easily have put it in Ebon's eye if he'd wanted to.

All at once the shadows began to move, darting between the trees. Not toward Ebon, but to the east, circling round the campsite. Cutting off their escape route? Unlikely, for if the Kinevar had wanted to surround the king's party they would have left numbers on this side too. Ebon turned slowly, keeping the creatures in view. Looking for the next arrow. If he'd closed his eyes he wouldn't have known they were there, so silently did they move. Once the camp was behind them, they dispersed into the shadows, taking the smell of rot with them.

As quickly as they had arrived, they were gone.

Ebon released his breath.

Bettle approached. "What in the Nine Hells just happened?"

Ebon looked at the arrow. The white fletching was spattered with black flecks. Insects were pouring from the trunk of the tree the missile had struck. "I believe we have just been given a warning. In case it crossed our minds to follow."

"But if they knew we was here—"

"We're more dangerous to the Kinevar dead than alive."

Vale sheathed his sword. "How many would you say? Fivescore? More?"

"A whole tribe, I would guess," Ebon said. "Fleeing north."

"For once the creatures have the right of it," Bettle muttered.

The king glanced at him sharply. "Something you want to say, soldier?"

The Pantheon Guardsman held his gaze for a moment before looking away. He reached up to grab the arrow.

"Hold!" Vale snapped.

Bettle froze.

"Those black specks on the feathers . . . that's the blood of a Kinevar mage."

"So?"

"So it means the arrow's pumped full of earth-magic. The smallest splinter and you'll be eaten from the inside out by insects, just like that tree."

The Guardsman snatched his hand back, then let out a string of curses.

Ebon said, "When you are finished, soldier, go and make sure the Kinevar have indeed moved on. And the next time someone creeps on us, perhaps you could warn me they are coming before I can see them myself."

With a last look at the arrow, Bettle started out north in pursuit of the shadows.

As his footfalls faded, another noise came to Ebon. Frowning, he turned back to the campsite. Partly buried beneath fallen leaves was the recumbent form of Mottle, his chest rising and falling, his arms and legs flung out at all angles like a rag doll tossed on the ground. He was snoring.

It was less than a bell after dawn, yet the desert sun was already fierce as a naked flame against Luker's skin. Ahead the raised road vanished north into the Waste, its flagstones half-hidden beneath a swirling carpet of windswept dust. To either side waves of sand rippled in the searing gusts.

Luker licked his cracked lips. Time to find some shelter. If his memory served him right the remains of a Talui watchtower were a league along the road . . . Or was that farther north? It was impossible to say with certainty, because the desert, in its relentless march west, had swallowed many of the landmarks in this wilderness. Old trader tracks, karmight mines, Talui barrows: all had been devoured by the sands. The abandoned village Luker had ridden through a quarter-bell ago had been sinking into the desert, all but a few of the crude wooden shacks collapsed and scattered like driftwood.

Riding at the back of the group, the Guardian spat past his bloated tongue. Shroud-cursed deserts. It seemed he'd spent half his life slogging across them, but that hadn't made his time in this one any prettier. His thirst was a fire at the back of his throat, and a headache throbbed behind his eyes. In front, Chamery rode slumped over his horse's neck like he was whispering in its ear. Surprise, surprise, it had been the mage who'd been broken first by the desert, and before the party set off last night Merin had strapped the boy into his saddle to ensure he didn't fall on the ride. To be fair, the tyrin and Jenna weren't faring much better. It was two days now since they'd found fresh water, and what little they had left to drink would have to be saved for the horses.

Luker's mare stumbled, then righted itself. They were pushing the animals too hard, he knew, but a lengthy rest was a luxury their pursuers would not allow them. Each day, Luker spirit-walked to keep track of their hunters. The remnants of the second group of Kalanese—the one that had attacked them at the edge of the desert—had brought a rare smile to the Guardian's lips when they'd followed them into the Waste. How the fools had thought to track their quarry across the sands, he couldn't imagine, and after three days of wandering lost they were now feeding the sandclaws in a dry streambed.

The first group of Kalanese, though—the soulcaster's—had kept to the plains, skirting the edge of the desert as they took a course roughly parallel to that of Luker's party. An ambush by tribesmen had killed three of their number—not the soulcaster, alas—and lost them time, but after giving the Erin Elalese a head start of almost half a day they were now just a few leagues south and west. If they were able to overtake Luker and block his exit from the desert . . .

Suddenly the Guardian's mare stumbled again, its hooves sliding on the sandy flagstones. He shouted a warning to his companions, then pulled on the reins. The animal came to a stuttering halt. Luker swung down from the saddle. He didn't need to search for the problem. At dusk yesterday a sandclaw had attacked the mare as Luker was mounting up, scoring a hit to the horse's front right leg before the Guardian could drive the sandclaw off. That leg was now bandaged above the knee, and foul-smelling fluids were soaking through the dressings. The mare shied as Luker peeled them away. The flesh round the cut was tinged blue by the poultice he had applied, but judging by the swelling to the knee joint the ointment had failed to slow the spread of the sandclaw's venom.

Chamery was watching him through narrowed eyes.

"Get over here," Luker said to him.

The mage's voice was a croak. "There's nothing I can do."

"Like Shroud there isn't. You're a damned corpse-hugger, aren't you? Or are you telling me your powers don't work on horses?"

"My *powers* flow from the energies released in death. This hell-hole you've led us into is dead already. I have nothing more than a trickle."

"Then use it."

"Better save it for one of us."

For you, more like. "If the horses die, so do we. Now get over here before I decide to swap your ride for mine."

Grumbling, Chamery loosened the ties keeping him in the saddle and slid to the ground. He staggered over to join Luker. "You owe me, Guardian," he said.

Luker snorted.

Falling to his knees, the mage closed his hands round the horse's wounded leg, one above the knee joint, one below. Luker felt the release of his power. *A trickle is right.* Not enough to burn away the sandclaw's venom, so a temporary respite at best. *Unless the mage is holding something back.*

Jenna steered her horse alongside. "What is that?" she said, pointing in the direction of the rising sun.

Luker looked across. A few hundred paces away the desert sands were churning like water on the boil. A black tentacle burst from the dunes, twisting this way and that as if testing the air. "Roths," the Guardian said. "Sharks of the desert, the Taluins call them. Never seen why myself—roths grow much bigger."

The assassin shot him a look, but he returned her gaze evenly, and after a moment she glanced back at the roths. "They're coming this way," she said. More tentacles were rising, and a wave of sand rolled toward Luker's party.

"We're safe for now," the Guardian said. "Roths won't leave the deeper sands." He gestured about him. "Lands round here used to be mexin fields. This road was raised above the level of the drainage ditches."

"For how much farther?"

Luker shrugged. "If my bearings are right, though, we're about to reach the site of the old Drifter's Boneyard. Roths tend to steer clear of the area."

"Because the sands are too shallow?"

"No. Because of all the sandclaws."

Jenna gave him the evil eye again.

"What?"

Merin spoke. "Guardian, that reddish tint on the horizon . . . Are we nearly clear of the desert?"

Luker shook his head. "Another day, I reckon. Maybe more at the pace we're going."

"This road leads to Bethin, correct?"

"Aye."

"Farther north and east than I would have liked."

Luker hawked and spat. "You think I wanted this? Direct route to Arandas will take us right into the spears of the Kalanese. Once we're clear of the Waste we can swing north and west, make for the Sun Road. Another three days from there to Arandas, less if we can trade for fresh horses."

"How far to the next water?"

Luker hesitated. "There's a waterhole to the north, half a day's ride away."

"But?"

"It's not by the road—maybe quarter of a league across open sands." *If it's still there at all.*

Merin looked at the roths. The tentacles had begun to slip back beneath the dunes, and moments later the desert was still again. "Do we have a choice?"

"Aye, there's a spring once we're clear of the desert. Stop for water now, and the soulcaster will likely overtake us before we reach the plains."

Silence greeted his words.

After a dozen heartbeats, Chamery rose and lurched away. When Luker knelt to inspect the mare's wound he saw the swelling had diminished. All that remained of the sandclaw's talon marks were puckered scars.

Merin's voice intruded on his thoughts. "Another storm's brewing," he said, nodding at the southern skyline.

Luker turned and stared, gauging the wind's course. *Isn't it just.*

Romany had never seen a titan before, but there was no mistaking the figure that strode through the forest far to the south of Estapharriol. The immortal stood half again as tall as a man and had skin the color of ivory. His face was framed by tufts of black hair that extended down the back of his neck like a mane. Bloodred, bestial eyes peered out from beneath a heavy brow. Slung about his shoulders was the scaly gray skin of some demon, and a warhammer hung from a strap across his back.

Yesterday when Romany told Mayot about the titan, he hadn't believed her at first. Then, when the truth sank in, his eyelid had begun to flutter so rapidly he'd been forced to close his eyes. The smell of urine about the man was never less than overpowering, but a sudden worsening of the stench made Romany wonder whether her news had unmanned him completely. Strictly speaking there had been no need for her to inform him about the immortal, because there was nothing he could do to help her defeat the brute. The only reason she'd told him was to see his mask of pomposity slip, and—in that respect at least—his reaction had not disappointed her.

Romany returned her attention to the titan. There was an arrogance to the immortal's gait that grated on her. Looking neither left nor right, he strolled between the trees as if he wandered the shady paths of some pleasure garden. True, he had swatted aside with effortless disdain those of Mayot's minions he had encountered thus far, but did he really think the Vamilians were his only opposition in this forest? That he would be able to vanquish all of his foes so easily?

Fortunately Romany was well practiced in using her enemies' arrogance against them. It had proved no harder to lead the titan astray than it had the Widowmaker before him. For a day and a night she had steered him west, across the White Road and away from Estapharriol . . .

Until now, finally, he stepped onto the ruined road the Widowmaker was following through the forest. A score of paces behind, Shroud's disciple drew up.

The titan paused in midstride, his shaggy head swinging round.

For a dozen heartbeats neither figure moved.

Romany rubbed her hands together and retreated along the threads of her web to a safer distance. Time to sit back and enjoy the spectacle. For while it was unlikely any history existed between the titan and the Widowmaker, they would surely both realize that chance alone had not brought the other to the forest. And since there was only one Book of Lost Souls . . . Romany found herself holding her breath. Would the Widowmaker flee this clash? Without doubt she was powerful, but even the Spider would think twice before tangling with a titan. And yet to back down now would most likely just postpone the inevitable confrontation and earn her Shroud's wrath into the bargain.

A midnight flash ignited the air as death-magic shot from the Widowmaker's staff toward the titan. Romany had time only to register the immortal's roar of pain . . . before the power ricocheted off his wards toward her. It took a moment for her mind to click into gear. She made to flee.

The wave rolled over her.

She screamed as the world about her darkened. The touch of the death-magic was like acid on her skin. In corporeal form she might have tried to channel the power away from her, but in spiritual form she had no such defense. Instead, she curled herself tightly round the core of her awareness and allowed herself to be swept along by the wave. Nothing to be gained by attempting to stand against it. She needed to ride the crest and stay ahead of the surge, whatever it cost her, for the death-magic was consuming those parts of her web it came into contact with, and if her soul's link with her body were destroyed she would find herself cast adrift as the Vamilian spirits had been.

Until Mayot resurrected her, that is.

Through watering eyes she saw trees flash past to either side, while ahead the trunks withered and rotted as the sorcery flickered over them. A Vamilian patrol caught in its path collapsed into dust. Magic fizzed and popped in Romany's ears. Her spirit was starting to fray round the edges, but if she could just hold on a little longer . . . Already the swell of power was losing momentum like a wave climbing a beach. A score of heartbeats later it broke against a heavily forested rise, depositing Romany at the top.

She groaned. *Oh, the indignity.* For a time she could do nothing except listen to the sound of her ragged breathing. Her senses were spinning as if she'd just come round from a blow to the skull. The ordeal had also left her with a headache the size of Mayot's ego, but if there was one consolation it was that her spirit remained bound to one of the strands of her web. Even now, though, that thread was unraveling, and the priestess fled along it to a place where her web was more sound.

She drew up, breathless. Sorcery raged in the distance, indicating the battle between the titan and the Widowmaker was still ongoing. The shock waves from the conflict sent ripples of pain thrumming through Romany's head, and she massaged her temples with her fingers. What now? Return to Estapharriol? It was tempting to think her work here was done, but she couldn't deny a certain curiosity as to the outcome of the duel between these two behemoths. In any case, her next move in the game would be determined by which of the combatants emerged triumphant.

Her much-deserved rest would have to wait a while longer.

The sections of Romany's web between her and the fighters had been destroyed by the wave of death-magic, but there were other threads she could use to return by another way. In a matter of moments she arrived at the edge of a clearing—a smoldering wasteland a hundred paces wide, dotted with tree stumps. The ground was covered with frost, and clouds of freezing mist hung in the air making Romany's spiritual teeth chatter. At the center of the clearing the Widowmaker and the titan battled amid a storm of incandescent energies. The titan's hair and clothing were aflame, and his hands were blistered red. He wielded his power like a scythe, but not a single blow seemed to land squarely on the Widowmaker, instead glancing off her wards to wreak yet further devastation on the forest. The woman was drawing in the energies released by the dying trees, and her ebony staff bucked in her hands as she hurled a wave of black sorcery at the titan. The air trembled as her power collided with the immortal's.

The Widowmaker was driven back a step.

A stray bolt of magic came hurtling toward Romany, but this time she was able to move out of the way. The two combatants were more evenly matched than she had expected, though doubtless it was just a matter of time before the titan prevailed. Or, at least, that was what the priestess hoped, for her plans for him didn't stop with the Widowmaker's defeat. Oh no! When the brute was finished here, Romany intended to steer him to the next of Shroud's disciples on her hit list, then the next, and the next. In time, suspicion would worm its way into that thick skull of his, but not, she suspected, before she'd had a chance to exploit his presence to the full.

Unless . . . Unless the priestess simply stood back and let the titan march unopposed to the heart of Mayot's squalid little empire. The old man was no match for the immortal, of course, and with the Book in the brute's grasp Shroud truly would have a fight on his hands to keep his throne.

Romany winced as another thunderous concussion rent the air. Then frowned as a thought came to her. What happened after the Widowmaker fell? Would Mayot be able to resurrect her as he had resurrected the Vamilians? He hadn't managed to bring back Lorigan Teele, but then the knight's body had been burned away completely during their clash in the dome. Romany didn't know how she felt about the prospect of Mayot adding the Widowmaker to his collection of servants, but surely Shroud would not permit one of his servants to be raised and used against him in such a manner.

A burst of sorcery from the titan sent the Widowmaker cartwheeling through the air to land heavily among the trees stumps. The immortal moved in for the kill, unlimbering his warhammer. The Widowmaker wasn't finished yet, though, for she rose to her feet, snarling, and bounded across the frosty ground toward her opponent. The titan swung his warhammer to meet the attack, but the woman was too swift. Ducking beneath the strike, she hurled herself at her foe, her finger-length claws plunging into his torso. Death-magic poured from her hands, and the flesh about the titan's wounds started to suppurate and blister. Bellowing in pain, he dropped his warhammer and closed his hands round his tormentor's neck.

The muscles of his forearms bulged.

For a few heartbeats his exertions had no effect, his fingers held back from the Widowmaker's throat by her wards.

Then the woman's defenses collapsed beneath his inhuman strength, and to the sound of cracking vertebrae, the titan tore off her head. Black blood fountained from her neck. Romany drew in air through her teeth. That had to hurt. Instead of falling to the ground, the Widowmaker's body sagged against her killer, held in place by the claws sunk into his chest. Groaning, he wrenched the talons loose and flung the corpse away. Then his legs buckled and he sat down with a bump. Blood seeped from his chest wounds. The death-magic in the air would soon enter the punctures and putrefy the flesh, Romany knew. Already a black stain was spreading beneath his ivory skin.

She frowned. That made things more complicated. In her mind's eye she pictured the Widowmaker strolling through the forest yesterday, the Vamilians falling dead at her feet when they came close. If the woman had won the duel here, Mayot would have been unable to resurrect the titan because any strand of death-magic would shrivel away the moment he was raised. With the Widowmaker gone, though, the immortal would, if he now perished, fall under the old man's control. And that was something Romany could not allow to happen. Yes, the titan would make a powerful weapon in the struggle against Shroud's servants, but a weapon in *Mayot's* hands, not hers. She would lose control of the game. *The old fool might decide he no longer needs me.*

What to do about it, though? The priestess looked at the Widowmaker's body—or where the body should have been. All that remained of the woman was her black robe, snagged on a tree stump. Romany's heart skipped a beat. Evidently Shroud had moved quickly to claim his disciple's corpse, but then why hadn't the priestess detected his intervention? More importantly, was the god still nearby . . . ?

Movement at the edge of the clearing made her freeze. Then a man stepped into sight and she let out a shuddering breath. *Just a Vamilian.* Mayot's redbeaks were already circling. The titan had seen him too. Heaving himself to his feet, he crossed to retrieve his warhammer. For an instant Romany thought he intended to fight, but instead he swung south and stumbled to the edge of the clearing, leaving a trail of blood behind him. If the immortal was to escape the corrupting effect of the Book's death-magic he would have to flee the forest. His part in the game, Romany suspected, was at an end, for by the time his wounds healed—if indeed they ever did—Mayot's fate would already have been decided.

The priestess's immediate concern, though, was to ensure the brute made it safely to the edge of the forest and out of the mage's clutches. She sighed.

A woman's work is never done.

"The spring should be here," Luker said.

Merin grunted. "Should be."

The Guardian knew what he was thinking. *Aye, can't drink "should be."*

Raising a hand to his sweat-sheened forehead, he squinted down into the depression. Where two years ago there had been a pool of water, now there was only cracked red-brown earth and stunted rodanda trees. Scattered about the basin were the carcasses of alamandra. Bloated redbeaks waddled among them, squabbling over the grisly remains. Was it just a trick of the light, or was the soil at the center of the depression darker than at the sides? Dismounting, Luker led his mare down the slope. The carrion birds took flight as he drew near, screeching their displeasure, and the shadow of their wings briefly shaded him from the scalding glare of the midmorning sun. At the bottom of the basin he released the horse's reins and dropped to his knees. He laid his right palm flat against the earth.

It was damp.

His heart beating rapidly, Luker drew a dagger and used it to break up the mud. A finger's width down the soil became softer. Tossing his dagger aside, the Guardian scooped out the dirt with his hands. When he had dug a small hole he stopped and sat back to wait. Merin barked a question, but Luker ignored him. Muddy liquid was pooling in the hole. He lowered his face to the water and sniffed.

No hint of corruption.

Gods below, we made it.

He set to work increasing the size of the hole. Jenna was suddenly kneeling beside him, adding her efforts to his. Looking across at the assassin, Luker saw hope kindle in her bleary eyes. They paused when the hole was an armspan wide.

"We'll have to strain the water," Luker said. "No more than a few sips at a time."

Jenna nodded.

Rising on trembling legs, the Guardian turned to see Merin release the straps holding Chamery in his saddle and support him to the ground. Chamery's straw-colored hair was plastered to his sunburned forehead, and he was mumbling something unintelligible. Merin took a spare shirt from one of his saddlebags before crossing to the seep and pressing the cloth into the water. He folded the sides in to form a makeshift carrier, then lifted it out and carried it to Chamery. As the tyrin knelt, water trickled through the shirt onto the mage's face. Chamery gulped greedily at the liquid, his swollen tongue seeking the drops that splashed to his lips.

Like nursing a Shroud-cursed baby.

Luker waited until the others had eased their thirst before leading the horses down one at a time to the seep. Only then did he accept a flask from Jenna and take a drink of the warm water—just a sip at first, yet it was enough to make his stomach clench. The liquid had a metallic flavor to it.

The tyrin dragged Chamery into the shade of the rodanda trees, then joined Luker and Jenna at the seep. Pushing his spare shirt back into the water, he uncapped an empty flask and began straining the liquid into it.

"What news of the soulcaster?" he asked.

Luker retrieved his discarded dagger and cleaned the mud from it. "Gone to ground. Sheltering in that abandoned village we passed a bell ago."

"Sheltering?"

"Waiting out the worst of the day's heat, is my bet. Bastard knows we won't get far in this state. Even if he leaves it till dusk before setting out, he'll still catch up to us by nightfall."

"So we take a rest and press on."

"A rest of twenty-four bells, you mean? We can't outrun the Kalanese. My ride is lame, the others are dead on their feet. And with the boy like he is . . ."

"Maybe when he's had some more water—"

"You don't believe that any more than I do."

Merin sealed the first water bottle and picked up another. "Are there any settlements near here? Somewhere we can trade for new horses?"

"Not that we can reach in time," Luker said. "There's another option, though." He nodded at Chamery. "Boy needs a death to get his power back—someone strong. I can give him that."

Merin glanced at the dagger in the Guardian's hand. "What do you mean?"

He thinks I'm going to do for him. Another time Luker might have paused to let the tyrin's doubts fester. Instead he gestured south. "I'm going after them."

The tyrin stared at him. "The Kalanese?"

"Unless you know of someone else out here hunting us."

"You're serious? Shroud's mercy, there are, what, a score of them? To say nothing of the soulcaster."

"I've faced worse odds in my time."

"With the state you're in, I doubt it. You should see yourself from where I'm sitting. You've got one foot through Shroud's Gate already. We all have."

"And now the Kalanese will get to feel what that's like. They made a mistake easing off when they could've ridden us down. Means they're cocky. Means they won't be expecting me when I drop by."

"The soulcaster will see you coming."

"Only if he's looking. If he isn't, he won't sense me till I use the Will." *By which time it'll be too late for him.*

"And if you're wrong?"

Luker shrugged. "His death or mine. Either way Chamery gets the power he needs. You get to live. Be grateful."

Merin considered this as he sealed the second water bottle, then nodded. "When you're finished, make for the town of Hamis, east of Arandas. We'll wait a day for you, no more."

Luker grunted. So that was what gratitude smelled like, was it? Explained the warm glow he was feeling. "I'll take Chamery's horse. The boy can heal mine when he wakes."

Merin reached into his belt pouch and drew out two glass globes. He passed one to Luker. "Take this. You might need it."

The orb felt hot against the Guardian's calloused fingers. Holding it up to the light, he saw that the swirling mist inside was faintly green. *Earth-magic.*

"Store it carefully," Merin added. "When the glass breaks—"

"I know how it works."

Luker rose. Slipping the glass globe into his belt pouch, he walked to Chamery's gelding and unfastened the saddle's girth strap before lifting the saddle clear. As he dropped it in the dirt, his sight blurred for an instant, and he leaned against the gelding until the dizziness passed.

Footfalls sounded behind. "I'm coming with you," Jenna said.

Luker made no response. Crossing to his mare, he lifted his saddle clear and transferred it to the gelding.

"You need me," the assassin went on. "This is what I do."

"I work alone," Luker said.

"So do I. This time we'll just work alone . . . together."

"Alone, together, got it." The Guardian placed his flask in one of the saddlebags. "You ever fought Kalanese before?"

"I don't intend to *fight* them, I intend to *kill* them. There's a difference."

He met her gaze for the first time. The desert sun had brought out freckles on her nose and cheeks, and her patchwork of scars was more evident across her tanned skin. "Why?"

"Why what?"

"If you ride away now you might make it out of here alive."

"I could say the same to you."

"Don't screw with me. This isn't your cause."

Jenna's crooked smile held a hint of ruefulness. "Maybe you're right," she said. "Maybe that's the appeal of it."

Luker studied her. There was something she wasn't telling him, but what was new? Truth was, a second pair of eyes might be useful in the Kalanese camp. And in spite of what he'd said about her making a break for it, the safest place for her to be in this godforsaken wilderness was by his side. "All right."

The assassin's smile broadened. "We go for the soulcaster first, yes?"

"Aye. I've got something special planned for him."

Jenna raised an eyebrow. "The globe Merin gave you?"

"I'll fill you in on the way."

"How do you want to make the approach? The soulcaster will have sent out scouts."

"Not when I last looked, he hadn't. Just a couple of guards outside where they're holed up. We'll have to dispose of them quietly."

"Best you leave that to me, then."

Luker stepped into the saddle. "When the trouble starts, I want you out of the way. Find some place to hide and give me cover."

"You trust me to watch your back?"

"Just as long as you're not shooting at it," Luker muttered.

Chuckling, Jenna crossed to her own horse. She tied her hair back in a ponytail, then took a pair of black leather gloves from her saddlebags and slipped them on. "Feels good, doesn't it?" she said, catching Luker's eye. "To be doing something, I mean."

The Guardian showed his teeth. "Aye. Kalanese have been hunting me long enough. Now it's my turn."

CHAPTER 14

EVEN FROM several hundred paces away Parolla could see the Forest of Sighs was dying. The branches of the trees drooped as if drought stricken, and rust-colored leaves swirled between the boles. As the forest died it released a flood of necromantic energies, and Parolla inhaled them on every breath. The effect was intoxicating, a heady rush that made her heart thunder in her chest, made the darkness within her seethe and bubble. Looking down, she saw she was digging her fingernails into her palms. Blood trickled to her wrists, but there was no pain. The wounds healed immediately, the skin knitting together until not even the faintest scar remained.

The deserted tribal settlement she walked through was a haphazard cluster of huts built from planks overlaid with animal hides. At the center of the village was a stand of trees, all of which were dying. Small wonder the savages who'd once lived here had fled if even their sacred glades were succumbing to the infection. The branches of the trees were adorned with fetishes and strips of cloth similar to those that had decorated the glade where Parolla had met the dwarf. Strangely, however, the ditch surrounding the trees was empty of bones.

Pausing in the shade of a doorway, she unstoppered her flask and drank deeply. Water was no longer a necessity, because the death-magic emanating from the forest was all the nourishment she needed. Parolla, though, was wary about becoming dependent on its . . . sustenance. Already the dark energies were starting to stain her mood. Every time she closed her eyes her blood would rise to immerse her, and the black tide brought with it memories from parts of her mind she had long believed closed off. The recollections fanned to new life the flames of her bitterness, her yearning for vengeance. And as her resentment grew, so the voice of restraint inside her became harder to discern.

She should turn back now, she knew. Doubtless the effects of the death-magic would only become stronger as she traveled toward its source. And while she feared she might be overwhelmed by the darkness, she feared even more losing the will to fight it. There was so little in her past that was not tainted. How simple it would be to surrender to her blood and let it burn away the doubt and self-pity. Parolla laughed. Turn back, would she? What did she have to return to? Where would she go? Shaking her head, she replaced the cap in her water bottle. She had chosen her path a long time ago, and it was too late to stray from it now. Especially since she was so close to what she sought. The source of the strands of death-magic was somewhere within the forest, no more than a handful of days' travel to the south and east.

Near enough for her to risk scouting what lay ahead.

Parolla sat down and closed her eyes, then felt a moment of lightheadedness as her spirit floated free from her body. Reaching out to one of the threads of death-magic, she experienced a tug, like dipping her fingers into fast-moving water. The tendrils were channeling necromantic energies to some far-off place. Parolla had only to merge her spirit with one of the threads and it would take her to its source.

She gave herself to the current.

It was like riding a swollen river, and she allowed the flow to carry her along. The world streaked past in a dizzying blur, the colors of the forest changing from rusty green to brown, to gray, broken by flashes of white Parolla assumed to be ruined buildings. Then she detected activity ahead, and she fought the pull of the death-magic. She slowed.

The landscape came back into focus. If the forest had been dying round its borders, it was all but fully dead here, what little life remaining buried deep underground and fading fast. The branches of the trees were bare, the trunks blistered, the undergrowth withered. There was no sight or sound of either birds or insects. So what had she sensed that had made her stop?

A flicker of movement among the trees in front. Moving nearer,

Parolla saw a dark-skinned, mustachioed man wearing studded leather armor beset by a dozen white-cloaked figures carrying spears. The lone stranger wielded a two-handed sword, and Parolla watched as a single swing of his blade beheaded two assailants. *Impressive.* Ducking under a spear thrust, he then delivered a cut to the midsection of a third opponent that carved open his abdomen and sent his intestines tumbling out round his feet.

Only for the stricken spearman to retaliate with a stab that grazed the swordsman's shoulder.

Parolla's breath hissed out.

It was only then that she detected the tendril of death-magic emerging from his chest. Unlike the thread she'd been traveling along, this tendril was pouring sorcery *into* the man, not drawing energy *away* to some as yet unknown destination. *Undead,* she realized, her pulse quickening. And souls summoned back from Shroud's realm could mean only one thing.

A portal to the underworld. It must be!

The swordsman's resistance was almost at an end. Already he was bleeding from countless wounds, and there was an increasing desperation to his cuts and parries, a weariness in his movements. As the undead pressed in all about he put his back to a tree and swung his sword in a wide arc in an effort to keep his assailants at bay. *A waste of time.* A white-robed woman went down with a shattered knee, but a score more attackers were approaching from behind the mustachioed man. Alerted by the sound of footfalls, he glanced over his shoulder.

A look of resignation entered his eyes.

Parolla hesitated. It would be intriguing to see what happened when he fell—whether he would rise again and join the ranks of the undead who'd just killed him.

Turning away, she resumed her journey along the thread of death-magic.

A while later she sensed a concentration of power ahead, and she slowed her flight again. In front of her rose a vast rippling dome of sorcery, the rays of the sun glinting off it like light off a restless sea. All around, the trees were blackened as if a fire had swept through them. Trunks had been sheared in two and branches sliced clean away where the black wall passed through them. Even now one of the giant boles toppled into the trees beside it, snapping branches as it fell.

Parolla approached the dome and brushed her fingertips across it. Such a casual show of power, no doubt intended more as a display of strength than as a means of keeping intruders out. The dome was no barrier to Parolla, of course, for it was fashioned from death-magic, and in her spiritual form she was able to flow through to the other side without leaving so much as a wrinkle to mark her passage.

She found herself at the edge of a derelict city bathed in shadow. The forest encroached far into the ruins, making it difficult for her to determine the settlement's size, but it must once have been home to thousands. In places the walls of the buildings rose to the level of her waist, in others only to her ankles. To her left was a road along which dozens of white-robed figures were moving, dragging young trees behind them by their upper branches. Dark fire played across the wood as it came into contact with the dome, and the trees were still burning as they were hauled into the remains of a long, rectangular building from which smoke curled into the sky. The clang of metal striking metal struck up.

The tendril of death-magic Parolla was following led deeper into the city, and the farther she traveled along it, the more intact the ruined houses became. Ahead was a huge domed structure, and within it, she sensed, was the source of the threads.

Covering the distance in a heartbeat, she floated through the wall of the building.

Inside was a dais shrouded in darkness and surrounded by scores of white-robed figures. Parolla paid them no mind, for her attention was fixed on a throne atop the stage. Flanking it were four undead warriors armored in golden chain mail. An old man sat hunched in the chair amid a cloud of death-magic. Lank white hair hung down to his shoulders, and his beard was matted and streaked with dirt. His deliberate movements spoke of great frailty, his affliction no doubt caused by the touch of the sorcery about him.

Parolla looked round for a portal, but she could see no sign of one. She clenched her hands into fists. She'd come all this way for nothing? Yet for the undead to have been resurrected, their souls would surely have had to pass through Shroud's Gate. Could a portal have been opened, then closed again? Possibly, but then why was the magic still so strong in this place? Was the old man himself responsible? There was something on his lap, but Parolla could not make it out through the fog of sorcery.

Rising above the crowd of white-robed undead, she drifted closer.

The old man was talking to a figure standing at the foot of the dais: a plump woman wearing a voluminous yellow robe trimmed with golden thread. Her long brown hair was tied up and held in position with jeweled pins, and she was wringing her hands in front of her face. *This one is no undead.* Parolla's vision clouded as she tried to focus on the woman's face. Blue eyes . . . No, green. Jowly, with a double chin and . . .

Parolla blinked. A shake of the woman's head, and flesh began to melt from her face. Abruptly her brow appeared more prominent, and her eyes—brown now—became more deep-set. The hue of her gown faded to match the ivory robes of the undead round her, then darkened to gray, and finally black. There was power here, Parolla realized. A sorceress without question. *And a slippery one at that.*

The woman was speaking to the old man, and Parolla heard her mention the name "Lord Mayot." Then her voice faltered, and she tilted her head toward Parolla—her face gaining ten years as she did so.

Parolla's skin prickled.

The old man looked straight at her.

Luker scampered beside Jenna to the stockade surrounding the village and crouched in its shadow. Since leaving the Waste this morning he'd skirted four such settlements, all abandoned to the desert. This one was smaller than the others, and reminded him too much of his birthplace for comfort with its rutted streets and its houses made of salmon-colored mud bricks. There was no sign of movement in the alleys beyond the fence, but the Guardian hadn't expected there to be—he'd swept the settlement with his Will a short while ago and found the only Kalanese abroad were the two guards patrolling the marketplace. Still, there was no point in hanging round for trouble to come calling. To his right, a section of the stockade sagged to the ground where the supports had come loose from the earth. Luker led the way across, scowling as the boards groaned beneath his feet.

Jenna took the lead as they edged toward the center of the village, a small loaded crossbow in each hand. At the end of the next alley she held up a hand, then pressed her back to the right-hand wall. Beyond, Luker saw more mud-brick buildings surrounding a square. Across and to the left was a squat structure of gray stone, and beside it were two makeshift gallows. Two gallows. As if one wasn't enough in a village little more than a stone's throw across. Jenna laid her crossbows on the floor before lowering herself to her stomach and peering round the corner of the building. Moments later she drew back and rose to whisper in Luker's ear.

"Two sentries," she said. "The first is this side of the square, maybe thirty paces to our right. The other is sitting in the shadow of that stone building. I'm thinking the soulcaster is inside—it'll be cooler in there than in those mud-brick hovels."

The Guardian nodded. "Makes sense."

"The sentries can see each other from where they're stationed, meaning we'll have to take them out at the same time."

"Aye. I'll circle round—"

Jenna shook her head. "Best you stay put, old man. The Kalanese might hear your bones creaking. I'll go."

Luker screwed up his face. "These two sentries . . . What are they doing?"

"The one this side—yours—has snared a scorpion and is pulling it apart. Mine's resting in the shade."

"Figures. Might have known you'd keep the easier target for yourself."

"After what happened in Mercerie I thought you could do with the practice. At least here you won't have to worry about the dark or the wind or the height, but if you don't think you can make the shot . . ."

"Shroud's mercy, how many times . . ." the Guardian began, only to trail off as Jenna, eyes twinkling now, raised a finger to her lips and looked meaningfully in the direction of the square.

"Thirty paces away, remember," she said.

Muttering, Luker snatched up one of her crossbows. The weapon was as small as a child's toy and light as a breath of wind. He studied the trigger mechanism, then glanced at the assassin. "You still here?"

Jenna's lips quirked. "I'll signal you when I'm in position." Scooping up the remaining crossbow, she retreated down the alley.

Luker looked about him. To his left the wall of one of the mud-brick hovels had collapsed, spilling debris into the passage. In the gloomy interior, a wooden table was laid out with plates and goblets as if whoever had once lived here had fled in the middle of a meal. Might have been the home of a sandclaw hunter, judging by the pelt fixed to the far wall. Just like Luker's father. Sand had collected in the corners of the packed-earth floor.

Time to scout the Kalanese.

Luker headed for the end of the alley. Before he'd got halfway there, though, he caught the sound of footfalls coming from the direction of the square. Had the sentry heard him? No, the man would have raised the alarm if so. What to do about him, though? Take him down as he turned into the passage? The second sentry might see him fall. Only other option was to take cover, and Luker hastily picked his way through the mud bricks and into the ruined house. The air was thick with heat. Crouching where the shadows were deepest, the Guardian checked to ensure the crossbow bolt was still in its slot. The tip of the quarrel smelled of rose petals. *Red solent,* he realized with a frown. If he ended up having to fire the weapon, his victim had better hope for a clean kill.

A man entered the alley and halted a few paces away. Gray cloak and headscarf. He faced the opposite wall. A short pause, then Luker heard a grunt followed by the sound of splashing liquid. The man was spraying it up and down the wall like he was drawing a picture.

A gust of wind whistled along the alley. The debris from the collapsed wall shifted in a clatter of stones, and the sentry's head swung round. Not likely he would make Luker out in the shadows, but the Guardian wasn't taking any chances. He raised the crossbow and fired. The bolt took the Kalanese through his left eye, and his head snapped back. Luker was already moving. Hurdling the rubble, he landed beside the falling man and caught him a handspan above the ground. The body was still twitching. Luker felt something splash on his feet and inwardly cursed. All that effort to get piss on his boots?

He dragged the corpse along the alley, then wrenched the crossbow bolt clear from the Kalanese's eye socket. It came out with a sucking sound and a dribble of milky blood. Not a bad shot, all things considered. Okay, so he'd been aiming for the man's forehead, but Jenna didn't have to know that. He wiped the missile on the dead man's clothes before locking the crossbow's crank and settling the bolt into position once more. As yet the other Kalanese sentry hadn't started hollering, but doubtless he'd soon become suspicious when his companion failed to return.

Luker crept back to the end of the passage and lowered himself to his stomach. He squinted at the stone building. The sentry sat slouched against it, eyes closed, head lolling to one side. Some new style of keeping guard Luker hadn't heard about, perhaps. Then the Guardian noticed the pool of blood spreading beneath the man. Movement in an alley to the left. Jenna was there, crouched in the shadows, looking across at him. As their gazes met she drew a finger along her throat.

Sharp work. Luker acknowledged the gesture with a nod before holding up a hand, palm outward, to signal she should wait.

Rising, he circled round to join the assassin.

He found her one road back from the square, sheltering in the shade of a rodanda tree. "Any trouble?" he said.

"I came across another sentry a couple of streets away," Jenna replied. "He was guarding the building where they've stabled the horses."

One I missed when I spirit-walked. "You silenced him?"

"Of course. Spooked the horses a little, but it gave me an idea. What if we take four horses and scatter the rest? It's a long walk out of this place."

Luker hesitated. With fresh mounts they should be able to outrun the soulcaster, but what if one of the Kalanese heard the horses being set loose? And how long would it take the enemy to catch the animals once they were scattered? "No, we finish this."

"I was hoping you'd say that."

Tell me that again when this is over. "Have you scouted the targets?"

"Yes. There are snores coming from the stone building and the brick ones to either side. More from the brick than the stone, though."

"As we thought, then. Soulcaster's probably alone in the stone house—not likely he's going to share with the grunts, is it?" Luker took Merin's glass globe from his belt pouch and passed it to Jenna.

The assassin accepted it like he was passing her one of her poison-tipped bolts. "I just throw it through a window?"

"Aye, hard enough so that it smashes. Don't hang around after. From the strength of the sorcery trapped inside, I reckon that thing packs quite a punch."

"Where will you be?"

Luker nodded toward the end of the alley. "Edge of the square. When the survivors stumble out, I mean to hit them hard."

Jenna raised an eyebrow. "All of them?"

"I counted nineteen in the original group. Soulcaster sucked one dry, tribesmen got three, and we've done for three more. When the soulcaster croaks, that'll leave eleven to take care of."

"Eleven, as in one more than ten?"

Luker gave Jenna back her crossbow. "Count of fifty, right? Then we go."

Parolla bowed to the old man on the throne. "Greetings, *sirrah*. My name is Parolla Morivan. Forgive my intrusion. I had not thought to find this place . . . inhabited."

The silence stretched out so long Parolla was beginning to wonder whether Mayot could hear her. "You bring a message from your master?" he said finally. "Perhaps Shroud has had a change of heart, yes?"

She stiffened. "You mistake me. I am not one of Shroud's followers."

"And I am not the fool your Lord takes me for. I sense your power, woman—the mark of your god on you. Did you think I would not?"

Parolla's lip curled. *You see only what you want to see,* feksha. She looked at the book on the old man's lap. Without doubt this was the source of the threads of death-magic. Pulsing like some diseased heart, it gave off waves of black sorcery that made the darkness round the dais shimmer. The power was weakening the veil that separated this world from Shroud's realm. In time it might fail entirely. Was this the old man's intent? Did he even know what he was fashioning here? "You are making a portal, *sirrah*? I sense—"

"Is that what your master fears?" the *magus* cut in. "Yes, I see it now. A gateway to his realm. The souls gathered there, all under my control."

Parolla felt her blood rise, and a shadow settled on her vision. "Your delusions are becoming tiresome. At the risk of repeating myself, I am not one of Shroud's disciples. I seek only passage through the portal you are creating. And if I am not obstructed, our dealings here can remain civil."

"You wish to enter the underworld? Why?"

"I have my reasons."

The old man gave a dry laugh. "Most people try to delay their appointment with Shroud for as long as possible, yet you would have me believe—"

"I give you my word."

"And on that score alone, I am expected to allow a banewolf into the mitrebird's coop? I think not. Your master must be desperate indeed to attempt such a feeble ruse. He should have dealt when he had the chance."

Parolla paused, thinking. Had the old man tried to bargain with Shroud? If so, he had much to learn about the conceit of immortals. What the gods wanted they took, without thought as to those they trampled over. And yet, the fact Mayot was prepared to oppose Shroud made him, what? A fool? *An ally?* Parolla's gaze settled on the book once more. Even in her spiritual form she could detect the power contained within it. The old man had only just begun to tap into its mysteries, she sensed. And if Shroud wanted the book . . . *Then so do I.*

Mayot must have read her thoughts, for he hugged the book to his chest.

Parolla floated down to stand before him. "I see you understand the precariousness of your position. You have power, yes, but it is power that can be taken from you."

"You would not be the first to try." Mayot gestured at a line of figures at the foot of the dais to his right. Among them Parolla saw a short, blond-haired woman wearing the multicolored robes of a Metiscan *magus*; a huge tribesman, the scalps of dozens of foes hanging from his belt; a gray-haired, grim-faced man with a note of steel behind his quiet gaze. "All of these fools," Mayot went on, "harbored the same simpleminded fantasies of seizing what is rightfully mine. Now they serve me."

"It would seem you are not short of enemies. Unwise, then, to make another."

"Unwise?" Mayot sneered. "Tell me, woman, was it *wise* to reveal yourself to me as you have? To warn me of your coming?" He gave a thin smile. "To extend yourself over such a distance."

Before Parolla could react, the old man's hand shot out, death-magic erupting from it to envelop her. Pain lanced her skull, and she felt herself spinning away.

Romany pursed her lips as Parolla's spirit faded. The woman was something of a mystery. For her to have made it here without disturbing a single strand of Romany's web was nothing short of miraculous— *Impossible!*—meaning her spirit must have passed along the threads of death-magic in the same way Romany traversed her web. A feat that only someone well versed in the dark arts could have accomplished. But one of Shroud's disciples? The priestess was not so sure.

Mayot, as ever, had displayed a breathtaking disregard for the nuances of the exchange. Why, for instance, had Parolla not demanded that he hand over the Book? Why had she made no threats, delivered no ultimatums? The poor woman had clearly been as surprised to see Mayot as he had been to see her. And as for wanting to pass through into the underworld . . . Romany's mouth twitched. The woman's story was altogether too implausible to be anything other than truthful. But then who was she, and what was her interest in Shroud's realm?

Safely concealed behind her wards, the priestess had studied Parolla closely. The woman's most striking feature was her eyes, the orbs entirely black like two windows onto the Abyss. There was an ageless quality to her aquiline features that reminded Romany of the Spider. Was the woman a goddess, then? No, Mayot would not have been able then to drive her away so easily. And for all Parolla's power there had been a circumspection in her parlance, a vulnerability in the lines of remembered pain round her eyes that spoke of a humanity altogether alien to the immortals.

A puzzle for another time.

Romany felt Mayot's gaze on her, and she turned to face him. "Where were we, my Lord?"

There was the customary pause while the old man activated his brain. "You were explaining to me how the titan got away yesterday."

"I was?"

Mayot brought his fist down on the armrest of his throne. "Enough games! The immortal was barely able to stand, let alone defend himself. Yet somehow he contrived to escape my undead."

"Most distressing, I'm sure. So hard to find reliable servants these days."

"You are as much to blame as the Vamilians."

Romany tutted her irritation. Though she had come to expect no less from the mage, his lack of appreciation was still galling. "In case you had forgotten, my Lord, the titan was only at your mercy because *I* made it so."

Mayot's errant eyelid started fluttering. "I had not forgotten. Indeed, I could not help but notice that your . . . dealings . . . with the immortal ended fatally for another of Shroud's servants. The second, I believe—"

"Third!" Romany interrupted. Did the old man think she had just been sitting on her hands since the Widowmaker's defeat?

"Third, then. Forgive me, but I see a pattern emerging in your choice of targets."

How perceptive of you. "You think I am pursuing some form of vendetta against Shroud? What of the titan, then? Or would you number the immortal among the Lord of the Dead's followers?"

"The titan did not die."

"Nevertheless, he was defeated."

"And when his wounds heal?"

Romany sniffed. "I would have thought you had more immediate concerns, my Lord. Three of Shroud's disciples are dead, yes, but many more wander freely through the forest."

"My Vamilians will destroy them."

"Their success thus far has been somewhat limited, even you must agree."

Mayot continued as if he had not heard her. "And if *they* do not, I will unleash my champions." He inclined his head toward the line of undead at the foot of the dais.

The gazes of the foreigners bored into Romany. "It will not be enough."

The old man spoke through gritted teeth. "Oh, but it will. Every day my undead army grows stronger. And you seem to forget, if anyone should somehow reach this place they will still have *me* to deal with."

Romany introduced a note of scorn to her voice. "And when Shroud himself enters the game, as surely he must? Are you ready, my Lord, to withstand the full weight of his fury?"

Mayot's composure cracked for a heartbeat. "If you are so concerned for my well-being, why do you not surrender to me the remaining secrets of the Book?"

Romany smiled sweetly. So good of the old man to remind *himself* of her value to him, thus saving her the need to do so. "Perhaps I will, my Lord. Perhaps I will."

With that, she spun round and started weaving her way through the undead toward the exit. As she walked, her smile faded. Enjoyable though it was to tweak the old man's beard, her thoughts had already turned to masterminding the downfall of her next victim. So many pieces now on the game board, so much careful planning to do. Shroud had evidently banged some heads together, for his disciples were finally banding together in their struggle against the Vamilians. It had been a simple matter, though, for Romany to direct Mayot's servants to any hotspots, thus preventing the enemy from uniting to form a sizable host. Yes, Mayot was losing scores, even hundreds, of Vamilians for every one of the Lord of the Dead's minions that fell, but numbers were hardly a concern to an army that comprised an entire civilization. And thus far no one else in the enemy's ranks had shown the Widowmaker's ability to sever the undead's threads through their presence alone.

Of course, there were still a few of Shroud's disciples either powerful or arrogant enough to plough a lone furrow, and it was on these
unfortunate souls that Romany was concentrating her own efforts.
Whenever she moved to neutralize one opposing player, though, another would come to the fore. For the time being the Lord of the Dead's
threat remained a distant one, but, with the god's followers steadily
converging on the dome, the pressure on Mayot's forces would soon
become overwhelming. It would take keen judgment, Romany knew, to
pinpoint the precise instant when the tide turned irretrievably against
the old man. Quit the game too early and she might squander Shroud's
moment of weakness; too late and she risked sharing Mayot's fate. If all
went as expected—and how could it not?—her plans would reach frui-
tion just as the mage began his inexorable slide into ruin.

When the end came, Mayot would face it alone.

Luker paused at the edge of the square. He drew both swords, transferred them to his left hand, then unsheathed a throwing knife with
his right. Looking back the way he had come, he saw Jenna waiting
beneath one of the stone house's windows. Moments earlier she had
found the place where the soulcaster's snores were loudest and expertly prized the shutters open by sliding a razor-thin metal tool
through the wooden bars to lift the crosspiece inside. Now she stood
watching Luker, a loaded crossbow in one hand, Merin's glass globe
between thumb and forefinger of the other.

The Guardian nodded to signal he was ready. In response, Jenna
grinned. The window above her was set high in the wall, forcing her
to jump in order to throw the glass globe through.

She hit the ground running.

A heartbeat later the other shutters along the wall exploded outward with a roar. The ground bucked, and Luker was thrown across
the alley, smashing into the wall of the mud-brick building opposite.
Even as his world spun he saw the running figure of Jenna lifted from
her feet and hurled through the air, her arms whirling.

Shroud's mercy.

Roof tiles came crashing down into the alley. The wall of the stone
house toppled toward Luker with a groan. He scrambled upright and
launched himself into a roll that carried him into the marketplace.
He came to his feet, ears ringing, amid a cloud of dust. Chunks of rock
and wood rained down, and he fashioned his Will into a shield over

his head as he surveyed the carnage. The roof of the stone house had collapsed inward, the four walls outward, spilling rock and earth into the square and the streets alongside it.

No way the soulcaster was walking away from that.

Movement to his left caught his eye. A woman emerged from the door of one of the mud-brick hovels next to the stone building. Luker's thrown knife took her in the throat, and she stumbled backward into darkness, clutching at the weapon's hilt. Transferring one of his swords to his right hand, the Guardian plunged after her.

Inside, all was confusion. Shadowy figures shouted and reached for weapons. Luker tore through them, his swords flashing, and three Kalanese went down. The final soldier, a potbellied man wearing only a loincloth, jabbed at him with a spear. Luker caught the point on his left sword and ran his assailant through with his right. The spearman fell with a gurgling cry.

Five down, six to go.

The Guardian padded back to the doorway before halting to listen. Silence.

Some silences just don't smell right, though. Luker launched himself into another roll, felt the air part above his head as he cleared the building. He regained his feet and spun to face the house. A Kalanese spearman stood to either side of the doorway, and there were three more gray-robed figures to his left, the rearmost holding a crossbow. Five in all, then, but he'd reckoned on six still alive. That left one enemy unaccounted for.

The Kalanese spread out to form a half circle, looking round all the while as if they expected attack from another quarter. The pause suited Luker just fine. More time for Jenna to get back on her feet, assuming she wasn't buried under a mountain of rubble. The five here weren't all dewy-eyed and half-dressed like the ones he'd cut down in the house. A couple even wore hide armor. Luker rolled his shoulders. The fools actually looked confident. A tough guy was mouthing off at the Guardian, but the effect was somewhat spoiled by the fact Luker didn't know what he was saying.

They came at him in a rush. Luker parried a spear thrust for his chest even as he swayed out of the way of a crossbow bolt. Continuing the motion, he blocked an attack from another assailant, turning as he did so to avoid a jab that passed within inches of his face.

He launched himself at the Kalanese soldier farthest to his left— a heavily muscled woman carrying a spear and a wicker shield. Luker blocked her first stab and counterattacked with a backhand cut. She brought her shield up to block, but he used his Will to add force to his blow. The shield splintered under the impact, and Luker heard the snap of bones, a cry of pain. He was already spinning beyond the wounded soldier, pushing her into the path of a lunge from one of her male companions. The man's spear point sunk into his kinswoman's stomach and she fell, snaring the weapon.

The three remaining Kalanese warriors—two shaven-headed men and a woman whose features were hidden by a headscarf—hesitated, each waiting for the others to make the first move. Not so confident now. Behind them the soldier holding the crossbow was struggling to reload his weapon.

Luker attacked. A flick of his Will sent the man in the center—the now-weaponless spearman—staggering backward. A sidestep took the Guardian out of range of a thrust from the attacker on his left and toward the woman on the right. She raised her shield to intercept a head cut, but it was only a feint, Luker dropping to one knee to swing beneath her block. His sword bit into the woman's hip, snagging there. He stepped past her, surrendering his trapped blade even as his remaining sword sent her head tumbling to the dust.

The weaponless soldier had retrieved his spear from the body of Luker's first victim and now advanced. To the Guardian's right the other Kalanese dropped into a fighting crouch. A burning tree was emblazoned on the man's robe, above the heart. An officer, then. A strangled cry brought both spearmen up short. Behind them, the crossbowman slumped to the ground, a quarrel sprouting from his left temple.

Jenna.

The Guardian launched himself forward. He deflected a spear thrust from one Kalanese, his free hand snapping up to catch the point of the other man's weapon. A tug pulled the soldier off balance, and Luker's sword flashed for his enemy's throat. The Kalanese brought the butt of his spear up in a desperate attempt to block.

Too late.

The man spun in a crimson spray, legs buckling.

The remaining spearman—the officer—lunged again. Give him his due, he wasn't running. Luker caught the blow on his sword, angling the point down into the earth. A kick with his heel snapped the weapon's shaft. Snarling, the Kalanese soldier jabbed the splintered remains at Luker's face, almost catching him by surprise.

Almost.

Swaying aside at the last moment, he ran his opponent through.

All too easy.

The officer slid off the Guardian's blade and crumpled to the ground.

Jenna appeared from one of the alleys beside the collapsed stone building, scrambling over the rubble. She was covered in dust and had a gash across her forehead just below the hairline.

"We're missing one," Luker called.

The assassin shook her head. "Dead. I caught him making a break for the horses." She approached the crossbowman she'd killed, then placed a boot to the side of his face and pulled her quarrel free.

"And the soulcaster? You saw his body?"

Jenna looked at the ruins of the stone building. "You want to dig him out? Be my guest."

She had a point. Luker retrieved his sword from the body of the female Kalanese soldier and cleaned the weapon before resheathing it. A pool of blood was spreading beneath the woman's corpse and just as quickly being soaked up by the dusty ground. Looking up, Luker saw Jenna rifling through the clothing of another Kalanese. "Lost something?"

Ignoring the question, the assassin rose and entered the mud-brick building where Luker had started his slaughter. Gone to admire his handiwork, perhaps. He moved into the shade cast by the eaves of the house and sat with his back to a wall. The mud bricks gave off so much heat they might have just been fired in the kiln. The Guardian braced himself for the headache to come. True, he had only used the Will a couple of times in his clash with the Kalanese, but heat and dehydration always made the pain worse.

Jenna reappeared holding an opened flask.

"If it's water you're after—" Luker began.

"It's not that kind of thirst," Jenna cut in. She took a swig. An instant later her eyes widened, and she flung the gourd away and bent over, coughing.

Luker caught a whiff of liquor. "Ganja fire?"

"If you say so." The assassin rubbed a hand across her watering eyes. "Shroud's mercy, I thought my throat was burning before."

"Fermented lederel's piss. It's an acquired taste, I hear."

Jenna stared at him like she didn't know whether he was joking.

Luker heard flapping wings and looked up to spy redbeaks circling.

The birds were never far off when he went about his business. See-ing all the Kalanese bodies in front of him, maybe he should have felt regret or relief, but the truth was he didn't feel anything, and he sus-pected he was better off that way. A few years as a Guardian tended to weed out the ones who got squeamish at the sight of a little blood. He massaged his scalp. "We'll take whatever food and water they've got. A couple of horses too—we'll move quicker with spares."

"Kalanese mounts will stand out."

"Just till we're within sight of that town Merin mentioned. Then we'll cut them loose." Riding into Hamis on Kalanese mounts as the Kalanese marched on Arandas wasn't going to win them any friends.

Jenna cast a final look at the discarded flask before crossing to join him. She grimaced as she sat down.

Luker glanced at the cut to her forehead. "You hurting anywhere apart from that scratch?"

"Still got a hangover from Arkarbour. That Remnerol witch . . . her sorcery still pains me—like a quart of juripa spirits in my gut."

"Not surprised. Night of the Betrayal, the Black Tower threw the whole spell book at me. Took me years to get over it."

"Is that supposed to make me feel better?"

"You'll have taken a smaller dosing than I did. Effects should wear off soon." He uncapped his water bottle and took a sip. "Anyhow, there's an upside. With each knock, you build up resistance. Next time, the hit shouldn't be as bad."

"Can't wait."

A redbeak had touched down beside one of the Kalanese corpses. The bird stared at Luker for a while, then pecked at a dead woman's face.

Jenna pulled off her gloves and tossed them on the ground. "What will you do now? Once you've spoken to Merin's agent, I mean. If Kanon's followed the Book, will you go on alone?"

"No."

"No? Are you starting to warm to our beloved traveling compan-ions?"

"Just keeping my options open, is all. The tyrin and the boy are both holding stuff back. They may still have their uses."

Jenna picked up a stone and threw it at the feeding redbeak, hit-ting it on the head. The bird took flight, squawking. The assassin reached for another stone. Blood was dripping into her eyes from her head wound.

"That scratch must be deeper than it looks," Luker said. "It'll need stitching."

"Are you offering?"

"Aye. Though it'll have to wait till we get back to the horses—my kit's in the saddlebag. Should be cleaned, though."

Jenna nodded her assent, and Luker struggled to his feet. He collected the discarded flask of ganja fire, then returned to where the assassin sat. Kneeling before her, he brushed a strand of hair from her face. "This is going to sting like Shroud's own breath."

"Get on with it!"

"Just saying." The Guardian pulled a rag from one of the folds in his cloak and poured the remaining spirits onto it. Jenna flinched at the touch of the makeshift swab.

"What about you?" Luker asked. "Where are you heading now?"

The assassin gave a tight smile. "Trying to get rid of me?"

He blinked. "Back in Arkarbour, I thought you said—"

"What's the nearest city to here?"

"Bethin. Maybe a day and a half to the north and east. But I'd look elsewhere if I was you. The place is a pit."

"Then I should fit right in," Jenna snapped.

Luker stared at her. At times the woman's mood swings made his head spin. "What about Mercerie? That business with Peledin Kan should've blown over by now."

"There's nothing there for me to go back to."

The Guardian waited a heartbeat for her to continue. When she did not, he poured some water onto the cloth and cleaned the dried blood from her forehead. "You don't talk much of your past."

"No, I don't. Remind you of anyone?" When Jenna spoke again, her voice had softened. "How do you know about Bethin?"

"I was born a few leagues to the south and east—a village on the edge of the Waste, or it was a score of years back. Probably under sand by now."

"Probably?"

"Aye."

"You haven't been back?"

Luker shook his head. He'd considered it ten years ago after the siege of Cenan, but sense had won through in the end. With both his parents dead, there was less even for him there than there had been at the Sacrosanct.

"Why not?"

"No point raking up cold ashes. Because that's what they are: cold." He finished cleaning Jenna's wound, then washed the blood from the cloth and stuffed it into a pocket before settling back against the mud-brick wall. The silence drew out. And it wasn't the sort he could have stretched out and got all comfortable on, either. The redbeak had returned, alighting next to the corpse farthest from Luker and Jenna. This time Jenna's stone missed its mark, and the bird settled down to feed. When Luker looked again at the assassin she was staring across the marketplace, her expression sober.

"Seems to me," the Guardian said, "you need more time to decide on your next move. Maybe you should hang around a while longer."

Jenna looked at him. "Maybe you're right." Then, "We worked well together today."

"Aye," Luker replied, surprised at himself. "We did."

Parolla opened her eyes, then closed them again as a wave of nausea swept over her. Turning on her side, she spat bile to the dust. The sun was strong on her face, and for a while she lay still, listening to a door squeak back and forth in the breeze. The inside of her skull felt as if a blacksmith were pounding on it with his hammer. Mayot had been right: she'd overextended herself in journeying to the dead city. It was difficult to gauge distances when spirit-traveling, but Parolla judged the dome to be more than fifty leagues to the south and east. Stretched thin as she was, it had been a simple task for the old man to drive her away.

When the sickness passed Parolla opened her eyes to find Tumbal staring down at her. The Gorlem's voice sounded in her mind.

"Welcome back. For a time I thought thou wast lost."

"For a time, I was."

"Where hast thou been?"

"Finding answers," Parolla said. She told him of her encounter with Mayot, watched the fires of curiosity burn in his eyes.

Tumbal sighed as she finished. "Answers, thou say'st? Each one raises only more mysteries to afflict me. Who created this book that thou saw'st? What other secrets does it hold? To what end does Lord Mayot use it now? Where hast—"

"Do you ever run out of questions, *sirrah*?"

The Gorlem's face twisted. "Unfair, my Lady."

"Unfair?"

"To compound my misery by asking of me another question."

Parolla smiled faintly, then levered herself into a sitting position. The light was bright in her eyes. She must have spent over a bell traveling the tendrils of death-magic, for the sun had reached its apex in the sky. The journey back from the dead city had taken longer than the journey out because she'd had to struggle against the flow of sorcery along the threads. "At least we now have an explanation for the abandonment of this village and the plight of the forest."

Tumbal bobbed his head. "I think I would like to meet this Lord Mayot."

"To ask him your questions? What makes you so sure he will answer them?"

"Any man who would pit himself against Shroud—who would unleash power of such magnitude and believe he can control it—must be a man of great arrogance." The Gorlem spread both pairs of hands. "And in my experience, arrogant men enjoy talking as much as I delight in listening."

"Have you forgotten the undead? They must once have been spirits like yourself, now resurrected and bound to the *magus*'s will. You'll be taking a risk if you enter the forest."

"Think'st thou so? Is it not true that the act of resurrection requires some part of the subject's body to summon back the soul? Dost thou not recall the Jekdal? The finger bone he carried?"

"We don't know the limits of the book's power, the laws that govern it."

"Another riddle that surely deserves an answer."

"Even if it means enslavement?"

"I am, alas, already a slave to my curiosity; its power over me cannot be denied." Tumbal's eyes glittered. "But what of thee? Thou faces the same risks as I. Wilt thou continue on?"

Parolla was silent for a long time. She started tracing patterns in the dust with a finger. Her hand brushed a piece of pottery. She picked it up and turned it over. On one side was a picture of the hindquarters of an alamandra. The potsherd smelled of malirange oil. "There is a debt I must repay," she said at last. "A death that must be avenged."

"And Lord Mayot is the killer?"

"No. Shroud."

Tumbal's gaze held hers for a few heartbeats. Then a look of comprehension crossed his face. "I begin to understand. The death thou spoke'st of . . . Thy mother? And Shroud . . . Thy father?"

Parolla closed her eyes. "My mother didn't know how Shroud's eye came to fall on her," she said, "for she'd never met him before, nor did she ever see him again after. I asked her about the . . . circumstances . . . in which I was conceived, but she refused to answer my questions. The god's touch is fatal, *sirrah*. It took many years for my mother to die. Her last years were filled with pain."

"I am saddened by thy—"

"I don't need your pity," Parolla cut in. *Hells, I have enough of my own.*

"Is it wrong to feel sorrow at another's loss?"

She snorted. "I too felt sorrow for a time. Then I decided to do something about it. Shroud *knew* the effect his touch would have on her. He *knew* how she would suffer."

The Gorlem's voice was flat. "And so thou hast chosen to seek vengeance."

Parolla's eyes snapped open. "Do you know what it is like to watch someone close to you die? You try to live each day with them as if it were your last, and yet when the end comes it is still too soon. You try to shield them from your grief, when inside you know a piece of you is dying with them. The selfish part of you wants them to live on, whatever the pain they feel, while the other part wants only an end to their suffering." She bowed her head, her anger spent. "I miss her."

"Tell me about her."

"Why?"

"Because I wish to know."

Parolla shook her head. "She is gone, *sirrah*."

Tumbal opened his mouth to speak, then seemed to change his mind. "How old wast thou when thy mother died?"

"Fifteen."

"And did she feel the same way toward Shroud? Did she share thine anger?"

Parolla looked away. "No. She told me she would not have changed the years we had together."

Tumbal reached for her shoulder, but his spectral hand passed through it. "Then I believe she would have wished thee to find happiness rather than pursue this vendetta."

Parolla tossed the piece of pottery aside. "Perhaps you are right. But then I never had my mother's strength. I am my father's daughter, I think. And blood calls."

The Gorlem had gone still. When Parolla glanced across she saw his gaze dart along the street to her right. He spoke in a whisper, his image already fading. "I thought I heard something. From the east."

Parolla looked in the direction he had indicated. The alley was empty except for pieces of broken furniture, scraps of leather and hide, potsherds and animal bones—all testimony to the settlement's hasty evacuation. Beyond, Parolla could see nothing but huts, and over them the treetops of the Forest of Sighs. Then voices reached her.

Cursing, she pushed herself to her feet. After her clash with Mayot she was in no condition for a fight. Whoever these strangers were, they were coming from the forest. Could they be the old man's servants? Had he ordered his undead from the trees to hunt her? No, she would have sensed the threads of death-magic holding them. But then who? The thought of the tribesmen who'd once lived here coming to reclaim the village was no less improbable.

A hundred heartbeats passed before Tumbal rematerialized.

"Kinevar, my Lady," he said. "They are moving north, skirting the forest. They should not trouble thee."

Parolla released her breath. Either the creatures hadn't heard her speaking to Tumbal or they'd already had lunch—it hardly mattered so long as they kept their distance. She edged back into shadow. From what little she knew of them they did not normally leave the woods, but these were not normal times. Doubtless they had been forced to flee by Mayot's undead army.

The Gorlem must have been thinking the same, for he shook his head and said, "For the Kinevar to have been driven from their sacred glades . . . My Lady, the woods must truly have become a place of horrors."

Parolla shrugged. "We will see for ourselves soon enough."

CHAPTER 15

HIS SENSES dulled by sissa leaf, Ebon rode through a dreamscape of shadows and tortured visions. His fever was driving him ever deeper into spirit-dreams. Earlier this morning his party had passed through a Vamilian settlement, and overlying ruined buildings and dying trees he had seen images of wonder: structures of stone and wood fashioned to resemble multidecked ships, with trees emerging from their roofs like masts; swaths of rippling cloth suspended from the branches like mock sails; wood-slat walkways spanning the ships, or curling round the trunks of the trees. And all about, the air was filled with the sound of crashing water, as if Ebon were riding along the shore of a storm-tossed sea.

Then the horror would begin: waves of sorcery that set the very air alight; Vamilians collapsing by the score into piles of ash; stone buildings burning as if they had been doused in oil. Into the devastation rode horsemen wearing bright robes and mounted on destriers the color of ice. *Fangalar.* Wielding long, curved swords, they dealt death to any Vamilian untouched by the sorceries, while through it all the spirits in Ebon's mind keened in misery until the lurch of his horse or the voice of one of his companions wrenched him back to reality.

A reality no less bleak than his dreams. His chest and right side throbbed with pain, and his right arm hung like dead meat from his shoulder. He was vaguely aware of someone—Vale?—riding alongside him. *To catch me when I fall.* Stubbornness alone was keeping him in the saddle. He had been a fool to think he might reach his destination before his wound took him, but it was too late now to turn back. Soon he would have to send the others on without him, for he would not inflict on them the burden of putting him down once he joined the ranks of the undead.

To his left, there was movement in the shadows, but it was only another vision—a spectral Vamilian girl peering out from behind a tree as a Fangalar horseman bore down on her. The forest round Ebon was starting to blend into his nightmares. Everything was dead. The branches of the trees were bare. A layer of crumbled leaf fragments blanketed the ground, and the hooves of the horses threw up thick powdery clouds that fell about like rotting snow. Ahead Mottle was wrestling with his mount's reins. The mage's indignant voice rang out, scolding his destrier for some unknown misdemeanor. Like Ebon, the old man had retreated into his own world since they entered the forest six days ago. Eyes glazed, he would stare vacantly into the distance for bells at a time, or mutter to himself before tilting his head as if to listen to some unseen speaker. *Perhaps he hears the same voices I do.*

Ebon ran a hand across his stubbled chin. His clothes were soaked in sweat, and the sour taste of the sissa leaf lingered at the back of his mouth. He took out his water bottle from one of his saddlebags, frowning at how light it felt. Removing the cork, he took a swig. From ahead came the murmur of the river. If Mottle was correct the consel's party had halted in the derelict town they now approached, but Ebon suspected he would find more there than just the Sartorians when he arrived. For the last half day he had felt something drawing him to the settlement—an insistent tug, as if he were a silverfin on a fisherman's line. Trying to focus on the sensation, though, was like trying to block out his spirit-dreams, and Ebon put it from his mind. He had no more strength left for curiosity than he had to fight the tug.

Ruined buildings became visible between the trees, little more than wall foundations for the most part. The settlement was much smaller than the one the party had passed through this morning. Trees grew among the remains of the buildings, and Ebon's horse had to pick its way through the roots that twisted across the ground. His vision flickered once more. Ghostly boatlike structures reared up from the ruins, and the sound of booming waves and snapping sailcloth filled his ears.

Mottle was muttering: ". . . still ripples in the Currents. Memories thick as pooled water. Such secrets for discovering! An immortal once strode through this city. A goddess? Yes, Mottle is sure of it. The thunder of her footsteps resonates still . . ."

They followed a street that led to the heart of the settlement. Pieces of pottery, stone, and metal protruded from the leaf fragments. The road passed through a clearing, at the center of which was a series of stone constructions made from huge, rectangular slabs of rock, each twice Ebon's height. His visions ceased for a few blessed heartbeats. *The spirits have no memory of this place.*

Mottle's commentary continued: ". . . bones of another civilization, yes? One nation's detritus piled on top of another's. A house built on shifting sands indeed . . ."

Along the street two of Garat's armored demons stepped into view. Beyond them Ebon saw a flicker of light on water and the remains of a bridge. Abruptly the mysterious tug in his mind became stronger, and his gaze was drawn to a white building by the waterline. He realized with a start that it was the first undamaged structure he had seen since setting foot in the forest. The whispering of the spirits in his mind took on a reverential tone.

Ebon urged his horse forward. Some of the consel's soldiers were visible now, gathered by the road in the shade afforded by a section of wall. Ebon saw his exhaustion reflected in the slump of their shoulders. Garat's sorceress, Ambolina, sat across from them on the plinth of a statue that was now no more than a pair of feet. The remaining two demons loomed behind her. Not a bead of sweat showed on the woman's face. She glanced at Ebon as he drew near before looking away, uninterested.

The two armored warriors barring Ebon's path made no move to step aside as he approached. Irritated, he steered his hesitant horse through the gap between them, conscious of their axes hovering over him. He saw the consel then, standing at the foot of a rough staircase leading down into the earth. The steps ended at a stone door framed by an architrave decorated with faded carvings. Garat was running his fingers over the symbols. His clothes were covered in dust.

Ebon dismounted, gritting his teeth against the pain that flared in his chest. The settlement lurched and swayed.

The consel looked up. "Ah, your Majesty. You've arrived in time to settle an argument. My sorceress and I have been discussing this doorway. The grain of the rock, the markings on the stonework . . . so different from the other ruins in this settlement."

Toppling from his saddle, Mottle shuffled on hands and knees to the top of the steps. "Extraordinary find, Consel! See the fluting to the columns, the projecting cornices . . . Of the Fourth Age, Mottle declares—"

"Ah, then we are in agreement," Garat cut in, flashing a smile at Ambolina. "And yet the Vamilians were of the Second Age, were they not? How could something of the Fourth Age come to be buried under a settlement that preceded it by millennia?" He shrugged aside his own question. "I suspect what we have here is the tomb of some king or other dignitary. Clearly someone excavated this stairwell— we can assume, I think, that they knew what they were looking for— but then chose not to open the door. Curious."

"Perhaps the wards defeated them," Mottle said, his fingers caressing the air as if tracing the shape of some invisible obstruction. "An unfamiliar flavor to the sorcery, yes? Weak, but still efficacious. The question Mottle must ask himself is, were the wards about the tomb intended to keep intruders out, or its occupant in?"

Garat had turned back to the door. "The carvings on the lintel are mostly indecipherable, but this one in particular interests me." He pointed. "A creature of fire—the engravings have retained a trace of their red coloring—slaying a dragon."

"The aggressor, Mottle declares, is a tiktar."

The consel raised an eyebrow. "My scholars assure me that tiktars are a myth."

"Nonsense! Mottle has it on the highest authority."

"Whose?"

"Why, his own of course. The Currents reveal all . . ."

This has gone on long enough. Ebon said, "Evidently whatever lies here, Consel, was not meant to be disturbed."

"No doubt," Garat replied, "but does that not make you want to unearth it all the more?" He cast another glance at Ambolina. "Particularly since it has my sorceress and her pets so . . . unsettled."

The king blinked. *Unsettled?* The woman looked as cool as frostbite.

Ambolina said, "We have no time for this, Consel."

Garat gave Ebon a conspiratorial wink before climbing the stairs toward him. "Perhaps not now," he agreed. "On our way back, however . . ."

Ebon felt another pull from the direction of the white building, but he ignored it. "Consel, do you have water you can spare us?"

The Sartorian waved a languid hand. "My soldiers have found a well near the river. The water seems pure enough."

Vale spoke. "What about herbs? Blackroot? Galtane?"

The consel looked at Ebon through new eyes, then covered a smile. "Sadly not. At least, none we can spare." He scanned the members of Ebon's party. "This is all of you? Just five survived your attack on the Fangalar sorceress? I grieve for your losses, of course."

Ebon took a breath to keep his temper in check. "What more have you learned of the power we are facing?"

"Little, admittedly. Since we entered the forest we have encountered the undead only twice, and on both occasions they were on the opposite side of the river. The enemy, it would seem, has spread his forces thinly."

"Agreed. Though we must assume resistance will increase as we approach wherever it is we are heading."

"Inspired reasoning, your Majesty. Thank the Lady you are here to share your wisdom with us." Garat paused before adding, "Though I must confess I am surprised to see you again. It does seem a remarkable coincidence that we should meet in this place."

"No coincidence. As the earth-magic fades, Mottle is able to extend his senses deeper into the forest."

"Ah, so you came to find me. To beg my protection."

"I came to suggest we join forces."

"We don't need your help. By all means, travel with us if you wish. That is, at least until I have had an opportunity to honor my blood debt."

"Honor, Consel? An interesting choice of word."

Garat laughed. "I see you are going to make an entertaining traveling companion. Though while you are with us, I trust you will be quicker than you were in Majack to heed my . . . advice . . . when it is given. Your decision to use the West Gate . . ."

Ebon did not hear his next words. Another tug came from the white building, strong enough this time to almost wrench him from his feet, and he staggered against his horse. His vision hazed. Vale was beside him, offering his arm for support. The Endorian's voice was low in Ebon's ear. "Perhaps it's time for me to give the consel that demonstration he asked for in the throne room."

Ebon looked back at Garat, but the Sartorian had already moved away. The king shook his head. "Find the well. See to the horses."

"Ellea and Bettle can deal with that. Someone should stay with you."

He thinks I mean to follow Grimes into the river. "No," Ebon said, pushing at him. "I need to be alone. There is something I must do."

Luker looked down on Hamis's slave market from the second-floor window. The courtyard—half in shadow, half in sunshine—was thronged with people facing a wooden stage. In the center of the platform stood a squat, bow-legged man. In one hand he clutched the arm of a young, scantily clad woman, shackled at the wrists and ankles. Blood trickled from a cut to her lip, yet there was still defiance in her eyes as she glared at the assembled masses. An expansive gesture from the slavemaster brought an unheard comment from the woman. He responded with a backhand slap that sent her sprawling. The crowd roared its laughter.

Luker slammed the window shut, and the shouting dropped to a murmur.

What in the Nine Hells was keeping Merin?

The Guardian began pacing. The opulence of the slavemaster's quarters bore testimony to the riches that the emperor lavished on his agents. Patterned rugs adorned the tiled floor, and the walls were covered from floor to ceiling with bookcases. On a desk to Luker's right stood an incense burner that filled the room with the scent of jasmine and dewflowers. Chamery lounged on a divan, idly flicking through a book. His straw-colored hair was freshly washed, and his wispy beard had been combed and oiled. The boy's endearing mix of smugness and arrogance had returned with the trappings of civilization, his ordeal in the Waste apparently forgotten. Predictably, he had not said a word of thanks to Luker for taking down the Kalanese.

From behind a door in the far wall came muffled voices, and Merin entered before crossing to the desk and pouring himself a glass of water from a jug. His face seemed to have gained a crease or two since Luker last saw him.

"I was starting to wonder if you'd show," the Guardian said.

"I've been arranging a spare horse." Merin settled into the chair behind the desk. "We lost precious time in the Waste."

Luker glanced at Chamery. "Aye, maybe the boy can tell us what he did with it."

The mage did not look up from his book.

Merin's gaze held steady on Luker. "I understand Jenna was with you when you arrived. I thought she was going—"

"You thought wrong."

The tyrin scowled. "She's coming with us?"

There was that gratitude again. This time Jenna was the lucky recipient. "With what she knows, I'd have thought you'd want to keep her close."

"The emperor can't afford to have his agent here compromised."

"You can trust her as much as you can me. Now, enough of this. What news?"

Merin's expression was calculating. "Little that we didn't already know. Arandas is under siege. Kalanese forces are massing to the west, but as yet they've launched no attack."

"Then they're idiots. If Tantwin marches from Helin now, Arandas's walls will become the anvil to Tantwin's hammer."

Merin nodded. "Something's going on. The Kalanese have the numbers to surround Arandas, but they haven't. Instead it seems a parley has been arranged with the city's Aldermen."

"And while the talking goes on the Kalanese supply lines stretch back nearly a hundred leagues through hostile territory."

"A bit too convenient, yes. This has the smell of a feint, but to what end?"

"Lure Tantwin out of Helin, maybe?"

"That would leave the Kalanese with Arandas at their back. Risky."

With the window now closed, the heat within the room was building. Luker flung himself into a chair. He couldn't pretend he cared about Arandas or Tantwin. Now he'd got Merin's tongue wagging it was time to move the conversation on to more sensitive matters. "Is the emperor still in contact with the Aldermen?"

"Until a few days ago, yes," the tyrin said.

"Meaning?"

"Meaning some of our agents in Arandas have disappeared. The ones that are left are lying low."

"How low? You said there'd be news about Kanon."

Merin sipped at his water. "Kanon was here," he replied at last. "Or rather, he was in Arandas. He left some time ago."

"Go on," Luker said. Then, "Don't make me drag it out of you."

"Kanon came here on Mayot Mencada's trail. Arrived a score of days after him."

Chamery closed his book with a thud. "Mayot was here too? And the emperor's agents just let him slip—"

"Shut it!" Luker interrupted, gesturing for Merin to continue.

The tyrin steepled his hands. "Our agents think Mayot was gone by the time Kanon got here. Kanon tried to pick up the mage's trail again, but it seems someone interfered with his efforts."

"Who?"

"We don't know."

"You said 'interfered.' How?"

"Kanon said someone was spinning him false trails."

Chamery barked a laugh. "Hah! An excuse, no doubt, to mask his incompetence."

Luker rounded on him. "One more word from you, mage . . ." He swung back to Merin. "'Spinning him false trails'—Kanon's exact words?"

"Is it important?"

Luker silently swore. *The Spider. Where in the Nine Hells does she fit into this?* "What did Mayot do while he was here?"

"We don't know."

"Where did he stay? Was he traveling with anyone?"

"We don't know."

Luker turned to the window. Looking down into the courtyard again he saw a naked boy being paraded up and down the stage. Scars from old lashings covered his back. "Maybe I should have a word with these agents of yours myself."

"There's no reason for them to hold anything back."

"It's not them I'm worried about," Luker said, facing the tyrin again.

Merin's dark eyes betrayed nothing. "Kanon left three weeks ago. By my reckoning, the day after we left Arkarbour."

Chamery spoke. "And the day after I first sensed the Book had been activated."

Aye, a trail even the Spider couldn't hide. "Kanon went north?" Luker asked Merin. "Following the Book?"

"Yes."

"To the White Road, then."

The tyrin leaned forward in his chair. "You've been this way before?"

"Aye." The last time was six years ago, playing nursemaid to one of the emperor's rabble-rousers who had to leave Majack in a hurry. "Not a road to take lightly."

"So our agents say. Yet, the stories they tell me . . ."

"Are likely all true. The forest's brimful with spirits that'll claw their way into your head if you stray from the White Road."

Footfalls sounded in the corridor outside, and Merin waited for them to fade before turning to Chamery. "Mage, you can still sense the Book of Lost Souls, correct? How far away are we?"

Chamery's nose was back in his book. "Close," he replied. "No more than fifty leagues."

"Majack is twice that," Luker said.

Merin rose from his chair. "Meaning Mayot is in the Forest of Sighs. Why? What's out there?"

The Guardian thought for a moment. "Bugger all that I know of. A few ruins from some empire long gone Shroud's way. Farther north there's the Kinevar, but not even Mayot is stupid enough to stumble into that grave." Chamery chuckled, and Luker spun toward him. "Something funny?"

"Your ignorance, Guardian. Mayot did not wander into the forest by chance. He *meant* to come here."

"Why?"

Chamery smiled, then turned back to his book.

Merin came to stand over him. "We'll find out for ourselves soon enough, mage. Why continue with this charade?"

"Because the Book is my concern and mine alone. Whatever twisted schemes Mayot has instigated will be countered by my arts. I am more than his match."

"You've been wrong about Mayot before. You said he didn't have the wit to use the Book."

"And I was right! From what Kanon said, someone has been helping him."

"And that doesn't worry you? Who is this ally? What does it want?"

Luker snorted. "Save your breath," he said to the tyrin. "The boy's as much in the dark as we are. He just doesn't know it yet."

Chamery's smile wavered, but held.

Breathing heavily, Parolla leaned against a tree trunk, only for the bark to crumble as she touched it. To the east plumes of smoke rose to form a thunderhead over the forest, and when she wiped a hand across her brow, her fingers came back streaked gray, her sweat mixing with the ash floating down from the smoldering skies.

Two days had passed since she'd entered the Forest of Sighs. The death-magic saturating the air grew stronger with every bell, seeping into her pores until she trembled with dark energy. Her heart beat painfully in her chest, and her skin tingled as if she had been stung scores of times by needleflies. Sleep, when it finally came each night, did not grant her any respite. Nor, when she woke, was merely walking enough to burn off the power raging through her blood. So instead Parolla ran, moving fast enough to make the air whistle in her ears. The exertion helped to cleanse her mind, as league after effortless league passed beneath her feet. She paused only to replace the fluids she sweated out, and even those short breaks were becoming more infrequent as her water bottle grew lighter.

Yesterday the last signs of life had faded from the forest. The branches of the trees now sagged under their own weight. There were no animals, no insects, not even a coral bird to greet the dawn as it broke hot and humid each morning. Parolla hadn't encountered a single soul, undead or otherwise—except Tumbal, of course, and even her times with him were becoming fewer. Sometimes when she stopped to rest, the Gorlem would materialize to share some observation or discuss whatever riddle was tormenting him at that moment. Each time he left her, Parolla wondered if she'd see him again. Each time he then reappeared, her spirits lifted.

She was making a mistake, she knew, in allowing him to stay. Soon her days with the Gorlem would end, and the years of solitude that followed—if she survived—would be harder to endure for the memory of their time together. She should send him away. Now, before it was too late. But she did not. For not only did Tumbal's talk serve to distract her from the discomfort caused by Mayot's death-magic, his presence also acted as a check on the advance of the darkness within her. She needed his light to sustain her own. *Just one more sign of my weakness*.

Tumbal's voice interrupted her thoughts. "Another mystery, my Lady," he said, his ghostly form coalescing beside her. He gestured at the thunderhead. "A forest fire, thou think'st?"

"Fire would explain the smoke," Parolla said dryly. "Though I suspect that is only part of the story. I sense the clash of sorceries ahead."

"Mayhap we should investigate?"

"To skirt the area completely would take several bells."

Tumbal rubbed both sets of hands together. "Excellent! I will scout ahead for thee."

"For *me, sirrah?*"

The Gorlem, though, had already gone.

Shaking her head, Parolla set off at a run in the direction of the smoke.

Half a bell later she noticed the first smudge of green appear amid the sea of grays and browns. Where before there had been only bare branches, now leaves fell from a threadbare canopy overhead. The trees here were in the last throes of death, but they were alive all the same. The faint scent of honeyheather became perceptible.

In the midst of winter, a pocket of deepest autumn.

Parolla could detect it now: almost wholly obscured by the fog of death that hung about the forest was the faintest spark of earth-magic. For the sorcery to have survived Mayot's onslaught, it must once have been powerful indeed, and it occurred to Parolla that she was standing on sanctified ground. *The Kinevar.* She had heard tales about the creatures' holy sites: midnight glades that had never known the touch of the sun, where the trunks of the trees were so huge that even ten people holding hands could not encircle them; where the earth was stained black by centuries of blood sacrifice; where the Kinevar gods themselves made their home.

Now, it seemed, they were under attack.

Parolla smiled without humor. First Mayot picked a fight with Shroud, then he moved on to the Kinevar gods. The old man chose his enemies well.

She slowed to a walk. Amid the smoke that crowned the forest canopy, flames were now visible. Noises were building: the crackle of fires, the clash of weapons, the concussion of sorcery. And beneath it all . . . something else. A voice of earth and wood and stone. Parolla could hear it in the keening of the wind, the hissing of the leaves, the creaking of the branches overhead. A deep-throated rumble sounded beneath her feet as if the forest were giving vent to its outrage.

The smoke started to sting her eyes, and the rain of ash became heavier. As she blinked away tears, Parolla saw movement ahead. She froze. A score of paces in front of her, and several handspans above the ground, the body of a Kinevar male hung from a tree. A branch was wrapped round his neck. Another had burst through his torso below the heart, and shattered ribs jutted from the wound. Yet still the man fought to free himself, fingers tearing at the bough that throttled him, his body twisting round as his legs kicked out. A bone-wood sword lay on the ground below him.

The Kinevar had seen Parolla, and his black eyes followed her progress as she edged forward. Stretching out with her senses she found the thread of death-magic burrowing like a bloodworm into his chest. The man became still for a heartbeat before thrashing about with renewed frenzy. More hanging figures came into view ahead: Kinevar and Vamilians mostly, but there were also Ken'dah tribesmen, snowy-haired Maru, rusty-skinned Sartorians, and others Parolla did not recognize. Those that still held weapons tried to strike at her as she passed, and she was forced to weave a path through the swinging bodies. One of the Vamilians threw a spear at her, but it missed to her left.

Something brushed her leg. She looked down to see a root coiling round her ankle, and kicked out to free herself. To her right another Kinevar male was ensnared in a tangle of nettleclaw, while ahead a black arm emerged from amid mud and leaves, its fingers clawing the air. Parolla drew up. In front of her rose a virtual wall of corpses, swaying in the wind. Above the treetops, shadows wheeled and dived, wreathed in smoke and fire. Shafts of lightning flashed up from the forest to strike at them, and a dark shape fell shrieking to the ground, its wings ablaze. It seemed the battle between Mayot and the Kinevar gods still raged on, but a long way to the east.

She could go no farther.

I should have left the scouting to Tumbal.

As she turned away, her gaze settled on a young Kinevar female hanging from a tree. The girl held a bonewood knife that she was using to saw at the branch round her throat. In doing so she drove the tip of the dagger over and over into the flesh under her chin, and the bone of her jaw was now visible through shredded skin. Her expression was blank, but there was a weight of sorrow behind her eyes. As her gaze met Parolla's she whimpered. It was, Parolla realized, the first sound she had heard any of the undead make.

She hesitated. Now was not the time to linger. Doubtless some of the undead she'd passed were close to freeing themselves from the trees, and Parolla did not relish the prospect of running into them as she retraced her steps out of this Shroud-cursed place. Now she thought about it, perhaps she should raise her shadow-spell about her.

The scattering of leaves on the branches overhead cast just enough shade . . .

The sound of another moan drew her attention back to the Kinevar girl. The tree garroting her was nearly dead, the last flicker of earth-magic concentrated in the branch curled round the girl's neck. When that faded the Kinevar would wrest herself free. But only to fight once more. Most likely she would stumble toward the distant conflict and become trapped in some other part of the forest where the earth-magic was stronger. Most likely she would fight again and again until either Mayot or the Kinevar gods were defeated.

Parolla set her jaw.

The time had come to test Mayot's hold on his servants.

Ebon's gaze tracked a fissure in the front of the white building. The lintel over the doorway had cracked along the center, and the two halves tilted downward at such an angle it seemed the next gust of wind must bring them crashing down. Talking a half step back, he scanned the fascia. The carvings across it had a strangely skewed cast to them, as if a sculptor had tried to fashion new images from ones that had already existed . . .

He felt another tug, the sharpest yet, and he staggered drunkenly through the doorway into darkness beyond. Black spots danced before his eyes. "Show some patience, damn you," he muttered. "I've come this far, haven't I?"

Inside, he waited for his eyes to adjust to the gloom. He was in a square chamber with walls covered in painted plaster that had crumbled in places to reveal carvings behind. The air was tickling-cold, and Ebon drew his cloak about him. The tug led to a doorway on the left, and he tottered across to it, his feet scuffing on the floor.

Beyond was another dark room, empty but for a woman standing with her back to him. She wore a sleeveless white dress and sandals. Her long blond hair hung down to her waist and was plaited with white flowers. When she turned to him, Ebon struggled against an impulse to prostrate himself at her feet. Her green eyes fixed on him. Meeting her gaze was like trying to stare at the sun, and he looked away.

The murmurings of the spirits in his head were coming together, a score of voices rising and falling as if they were chanting some mantra. A name became recognizable. *Galea.*

When the woman spoke, her tone was as welcoming as the chill gray air. "Welcome to my temple."

"Yours?" Ebon said. "The old or the new?"

"The old, of course. The fools who tried to claim it as their own did not realize the ground was still sanctified."

"Perhaps they thought you died with your people."

The woman's eyes narrowed. "You know who I am?"

"You are the goddess of the Vamilians. The one who saved me from the Fangalar sorceress."

"Saved you, yes," she said, regarding him with her depthless eyes.

"Why have you summoned me here . . . Galea?"

If the goddess was surprised he knew her name she did not show it. "What do you know about my people?"

"Little, my Lady, save what I have seen with my own eyes. The horror of their final days . . ."

Galea's already wintry expression cooled another degree. "The Vamilians were not native to these lands. Their homeland was far to the west of here—its name would mean nothing to you, since it has long ceased to appear on any map. They were a people of enterprise. Explorers. Traders. And at the height of their power, their empire was the largest of any of the elder races."

"Until the Fangalar came."

The goddess took a step toward him. The room felt suddenly small. "Millions of my people were butchered. The rest were scattered across the globe. Those that came to this continent took refuge here in the forest. But the Fangalar found them eventually, and the slaughter began again. For millennia they existed as spirits—"

"The ones that tried to invade my mind."

"Invade, yes. Oh, you were strong enough to prevent them possessing you, but still they left behind shreds of their souls." She gave a thin smile. "The voices are becoming stronger, are they not? Soon they will drag you down. Unless, of course, I choose to help you."

"Now why would you do that?"

"Why indeed." The goddess turned to examine one of the carvings on the wall, but Ebon knew she was not finished, and so he waited for her to continue. "Perhaps there is something you can offer me in exchange," she said at last.

"Clearly you have something in mind."

Galea did not look round. "I am aware of the attack on your city."

"An attack by your people."

"But not by my command!" she said, spinning to face him. "If I
had the power to resurrect my subjects would I have waited all these
millennia to do so? Would I save them from one torment only to deliver them into another?" She stabbed a finger at him. "We share an
enemy, mortal. You wish to save your kinsmen, I wish to free my
people from the power that enslaves them."

"You want to ally with me?" When Ebon laughed it felt like someone was running a saw through his chest. "In case you had not
noticed—"

"I will heal your wounds."

"Even so, a goddess asking for a mortal's assistance? Why?"

"For me to intervene directly in this affair would create . . . complications."

"Meaning you fear to surrender the safety of sanctified ground."

"Meaning I cannot risk drawing the attention of other powers.
Powers that might take an interest in what goes on here were they to
discover my involvement."

Ebon's sight blurred as a spirit-dream tried to claim him. He forced
the vision down. "Who controls the undead, my Lady?"

"A mortal."

"Just a mortal."

"A mage. He possesses an artifact of great power. The Book of Lost
Souls."

"This mage, what is he called?"

"Mayot Mencada."

"I do not know the name."

"I see no reason why you should. He comes from Erin Elal—a kingdom to the south."

Ebon had heard of it. "Then why has he attacked Majack?"

The goddess shrugged. "Because he can. Because he seeks more servants for battles to come. Because your city is located on the borders
of the forest."

Feeling bone weary, Ebon rubbed a hand across his eyes. *Is that
all this is, then? Are we no more than victims of circumstance?* He
was struck by the absurdity of the thought. If the attackers were Sartorians, or the soldiers of some other conquering empire, would the
fate of his kinsmen be easier to bear? Would that have given their
deaths meaning? Why should this Mayot Mencada's motives, or his
lack of them, matter? But somehow it *did* matter. Somehow it made

Ebon feel like he had a score of maggots crawling in his gut. "What do you require of me?"

"Only that you accept my aid when it is offered. As you did against the Fangalar sorceress."

"You want to use me to channel your sorcery?"

"Channel, yes."

Ebon considered this. "When you intervened before, you did so without my agreement. Why do you need it now?"

"Because in the days ahead you will face more formidable challenges. To overcome them you must . . . surrender . . . yourself to me."

"As easy as that?"

Galea pursed her lips. "There are risks, I will not deny it. Your body is not attuned to the ravages of sorcery."

Then why do you not seek out a magicker such as Mottle or Ambolina? Ebon did not voice the thought, however—the answer seemed obvious enough. *Because I am the only one desperate enough to consider striking a deal with an immortal.* "What you're saying is, my mind could be blasted away."

"Does the sacrifice concern you? Would the suffering be any worse than what you are experiencing now?"

"What do you offer in return?"

"I have already told you. I will banish the spirits from your mind, heal your wounds."

"Not good enough."

Galea's eyes flashed. "You are in no position to bargain, mortal. Your life hangs by a thread."

Ebon's laugh turned into a fit of coughing. "Do you think I care about my own life? Do you think that is why I am here? My city—"

"You are not listening," the goddess cut in. "I cannot interfere."

"No, Lady, I *am* listening. You said to do so would create complications. That is your concern, not mine. If you wish to ally with me you must help my people, just as I help yours."

Galea was silent for a time. Ebon looked at the floor. He could feel the weight of her gaze on him. The voices of the spirits had grown louder throughout his exchange with the goddess, their tone indignant. Above them the king could hear Vale calling to him from outside the temple, but he did not respond.

"Very well," Galea said at last. "I will do what I can."

Ebon forced himself to look into her cold green eyes. "Do my people . . . Does the palace in Majack still hold?"

"It does."

Ebon's sense of relief almost made his legs buckle. He was a fool, he knew, to trust the word of an immortal. Most likely there was much she had not told him of the power behind the undead, of the risks he faced, even of her motives in choosing to help him. And, of course, there would be no way for him to know henceforth whether the goddess was keeping her side of the bargain. *If she will not step in directly to aid her own people, why should she do so for mine?*

Ebon pushed his suspicions aside. This was not the time for doubts. Galea was offering him a glimmer of hope where before there had been none.

A fact she knows as well as I.

He paused, then nodded. "We are agreed."

Parolla reached out with her senses toward the tendril of death-magic that held the Kinevar girl. Mayot's sorcery was unlike anything she had encountered before, the thread made up of scores of smaller strands of energy, interwoven like knotted steel. Elegance allied with strength, breathtaking in its mastery. The craftsmanship was far beyond anything Parolla could accomplish, but her task here was not to create, but to destroy. Something she'd had lots of practice at over the years. Releasing her power in a trickle, she fashioned it into a cutting edge and brought it scything down.

The thread did not so much as quiver. Parolla, though, was sent staggering backward by shock waves from the clash of sorceries. She had not thought to raise wards about herself, and ripples of death-magic crackled round her, singeing her skin. As quickly as the burns formed, however, they were healed by the dark energy coursing through her. The strand of sorcery remained undamaged. Parolla probed it once more, searching for a weakness, the slightest flaw she could target for her next strike.

Nothing.

Weaving shields about herself, she gathered her strength and struck out again at the thread. It held firm. But this time when the backlash came she was ready for it, and the wave of magic broke harmlessly against her defenses. The energy surging along the strand had increased at the place where Parolla's attack fell, as if some conscious will were directing power to where it was most needed. Was Mayot aware of her efforts? Was he setting his will in opposition to hers? She shifted the focus of her assault to a point closer to where the strand entered the Kinevar's chest. If she could not sever the tendril she might at least interrupt the flow of sorcery along it long enough to break Mayot's control over the girl.

Still the thread resisted her.

As Parolla poured more and more of herself into the effort, she felt the darkness within her build. Her expression tightened. *The darkness* . . . After all these years, she still clung to the pretense that it was something distinct from her—some malign presence for whose actions she was not accountable. The reality was, the taint was a part of her. The part she had tried to suppress for so long. The part that was growing stronger every day. *The part I will need if I am going to defeat Shroud.*

At the point on the strand where she'd concentrated her power, a cloud of death-magic was forming as the warring sorceries bled into the air. The cloud spread outward to envelop the Kinevar girl and the branch holding her. Parolla could sense the earth-magic in the branch waning. That gave her a problem. If the sorcery failed completely the tree would release the girl. And with the thread of death-magic still intact the Kinevar would surely attack Parolla . . .

She had to stop.

All at once the strand of sorcery controlling the girl started to weaken, its edges becoming frayed.

As if scenting victory, Parolla's tainted blood rose in a torrent, pushing against the barrier she had fashioned to contain it. A shadow settled on her vision. For a heartbeat she battled to hold back the flood. Then she stopped herself. What was she doing? She had Shroud's blood in her veins, and she couldn't even cut one of Mayot's strands? Why was she fighting herself when she should be fighting the old man? Embrace her power, and she could tear up any number of these Shroud-cursed threads like they were blades of grass.

She dug her nails into her palms. *No!* Even if she cut the strands of the undead about her, Mayot still had countless other servants to do his bidding. What was she going to do, sever all their threads? Was that why she had come to the forest—to release his undead army? She shook her head. There was no victory to be won here, so far from the dome. All she stood to achieve was to reveal to Mayot a sense of her power, as she had to the Jekdal before. She could not afford these distractions. It was time to pull back.

When she tried to do so, though, the sorcery roaring from her hands only intensified. She'd left it too late! The darkness was growing as it fed off the necromantic energies in the air. The defenses she'd raised against it stretched, then bulged . . .

Crying out, she dropped to her knees and thrust her fingers into the mud, directing her power into the ground. As the magic spurted from her hands, the earth groaned and bucked and heaved, and the air quavered to the sound of grinding stone, cracking roots. Smoke rose from the ground. The tree that imprisoned the Kinevar girl came crashing down, throwing up clouds of leaves and hot ash, and sending broken branches and slivers of wood flying in all directions. Echoes of power rolled between the remaining trees, the death-magic spreading like fire through the hanging undead. For a few heartbeats it flickered over their bodies, devouring them with a palpable hunger.

Enough!

Parolla's sorcery guttered and died.

A moment to gather her breath, then she scanned the ground, looking for the Kinevar girl. All that remained of her body was a twitching mound of charred meat, pierced by splinters of wood. Sorcery clung to her like burning oil, and within an eyeblink her flesh had melted away to leave nothing but a skeleton. Then the bones crumbled to ash. As the dust blew away on the wind, the thread of death-magic controlling the girl withered. *Well, well,* Parolla thought. Maybe she hadn't succeeded in severing the strand, but she'd found a way to break Mayot's hold on his servants all the same—destroy the flesh and free the spirit to wander as Tumbal's did.

And yet, wouldn't Mayot be able to bring the girl back with just a speck of her remains?

A blizzard of ash and leaves fell about. Parolla tasted dust in her mouth, and she coughed and spat to clear it. Pushing herself to her feet, she brushed down her clothes. The shadows staining her sight began to fade.

Tumbal appeared beside her, one pair of hands on his hips, the other crossed in front of him. "A place of horror, my Lady," he said. "I am sorry thou had'st to witness this."

I have seen far worse, sirrah, *and by my own hand besides.* "I've come as far as I can. What lies ahead?"

"A final stand, methinks."

"The Kinevar?"

"Not just the Kinevar. The forest gods themselves have come to do battle."

Parolla stared at him. "And they are being pushed back?"

Tumbal bobbed his head. "The forces arrayed against them are formidable. I have seen demons and Fangalar, Everlords and frost giants, stormwraiths and alakels, and many others besides."

"Centuries of blood sacrifice have made this a fertile ground for Mayot's sorceries. Those that died here under a Kinevar knife now have the chance for revenge. There is a certain justice in that, wouldn't you say?"

The Gorlem frowned. "The controlling hand is Mayot's."

"Even so."

"And what of the Kinevar themselves? Slaughtered in their thousands, forced to fight their kinsmen, their own gods even."

Parolla shrugged. "Why does Mayot attack here in such strength? What threat do the Kinevar pose him?"

"I suspect the mage is concerned less with the threat they pose than with the opportunity they represent. With the Kinevar gods themselves under his sway—"

"Don't be a fool," Parolla cut in. "The gods will flee long before they are truly threatened."

"They have stayed this long. Mayhap they are unwilling to surrender their ancestral domain, to abandon their people."

"The gods care nothing for the fate of mortals."

Tumbal's frown deepened. "Not all of the immortals are as heartless as thou would'st brand them, my Lady. And if thou wilt not intercede on behalf of the Kinevar gods, what of the Kinevar themselves?"

"This isn't my fight."

"Is it not?" Tumbal's gesture took in the swinging bodies round him. "Think of the multitudes Mayot already has at his command. The forces he will control if the Kinevar gods should fall."

"My business with the *magus* will be finished long before that happens."

"And if thou art wrong?"

A root was snaking across the ground toward Parolla, and she kicked it away. "Even if I chose to intervene, you forget, this is sanctified ground. I am an intruder here as much as the undead. The earth-magic of the forest will not distinguish friend from foe."

"Thou need'st not advance any farther into the heart of the conflict, surely. The threads holding the undead—"

"Cannot be broken."

The Gorlem's spectral face grew paler. "Not even by thee?"

"I have tried to do so once. I dare not risk another attempt."

"I do not understand."

Parolla's voice was toneless. "Before Shroud . . . came to . . . my mother, she was an initiate of the Lord of the Hunt. When she died, the Antlered God's priests sought to take my power for their own. I was forced to fight my way free of the temple where I lived." She saw again the shrine's wards sparkling as she hurled volley after volley of death-magic against them; part of the temple toppling into ruin amid black flames, smoke and screams. *Always screams.* The massacre had marked the start of Parolla's *bakatta* with the Antlered God, and she had been dodging his servants ever since. She closed her eyes. "Once unleashed, my magic is . . . unpredictable. Many died before I escaped. Some of them were friends. Innocents."

Tumbal regarded her gravely. "Thou fear'st that in trying to sever the book's threads thou would'st surrender control?"

"It is Shroud's taint. His blood runs through my veins. Each time I draw on it, there is a price."

"With power, my Lady, there is invariably a price."

Parolla opened her eyes again. The tree that had held the Kinevar girl had now disintegrated as the last echoes of death-magic played over it. Parolla's gaze came to rest on the place where the girl had fallen. "Perhaps so, *sirrah*," she said. "But with me, it is always others who must pay."

CHAPTER 16

EBON STARED at his campsite from a fallen tree a short distance away. The whisperings were gone from his mind, and in their absence he had rediscovered a world of sound: the sigh of the wind, the grunts of the Sartorian soldiers, the metallic tread of the consel's demons as they prowled the perimeter of the camp. In the spirits' place, Galea had become a permanent fixture in his mind. At times he could sense her cool regard; at others, her impatience, her scorn, as well as a host of more subtle emotions. When he tried to focus on her thoughts, though, he found she had shielded herself behind a barrier of sorcery. On several occasions he had tried speaking to her, only to receive no response. Either she was ignoring him or her attention was fixed elsewhere.

True to her word, she had healed his chest wound to leave nothing but a scar where he'd been stabbed. His return to health had not gone unnoticed by his companions. Throughout the day he had caught suspicious glances from Ellea and Bettle, and even from Vale, for Ebon hadn't yet had a chance to tell him of his meeting with Galea. Not from Mottle, though. As ever, it seemed Ebon had no secrets from his mage . . .

His thoughts were interrupted by the sound of a twig snapping behind him, and he turned to see Garat approaching. The consel had evidently not slept yet for his hair was freshly oiled and he was still wearing his armor. He came to sit beside Ebon, a ghost of a smile on his face. "You are looking better, your Majesty," he said. "A miraculous recovery, indeed."

"I am full of surprises."

"Not just to me, it seems, but to your own soldiers too. That is good."

"How so?"

"Because a ruler should always keep his subjects guessing. A moving target invariably makes for a more difficult shot."

"I would trust my companions with my life."

"Then one day they will take it from you."

Ebon ran a hand across his head. "I have heard tales of the machinations at the Sartorian court. I had thought them exaggerated."

"Ah, but unlike you, your Majesty, the ruler of Sartor is not born to his position. He deserves to command only for so long as he does so."

"He is fortunate then, for at least the demands of power—the duties it brings—are his by choice."

Garat's smile was sardonic. "The burdens you talk about are all self-imposed. A ruler answers only to himself. You don't believe me? Perhaps you should ask your father."

Ebon was silent for a few heartbeats, unsure what the consel was hinting at. "My father did not choose to rule."

"You believe that?"

"I have heard it said too many times by too many people to believe otherwise. The uprising against his predecessor, the Rook, was not of my father's making."

"Yet he led it all the same."

"With a friend, Domen Calin Bain. When the war was done, the two of them locked themselves in a room for a day and a night. When they came out again, my father was king."

The consel's sole eyebrow rose. "And not a drop of blood spilt? Did they roll dice, then, for the throne?"

"No one knows. My father never spoke of it. As part of the deal that was struck, though, he agreed to marry Domen Bain's sister—my mother."

"And was she not already pledged to another?"

"She was," Ebon said, surprised at the extent of Garat's knowledge. "It appears that while Domen Bain himself was content to abandon his claim to the throne in favor of my father, his kinsmen took more convincing. The creation of a formal bond between the families was deemed necessary to avert another war."

Garat stretched his legs out before him. "And what became of Domen Bain, I wonder?"

"He died the following year in a hunting accident."

"Ah. It seems our peoples are not so different after all."

"What do you mean?"

"In Sartor rivals for the throne also have a habit of meeting unfortunate ends."

Ebon pursed his lips. "He was my father's friend—"

"Rulers have no friends. A friend's smile can so easily mask an assassin's dagger."

"Then he is no friend, surely."

Garat chuckled. "Unfortunately the revelation comes too late to be of any use."

The sound of footsteps reached Ebon, followed by the clank of metal as one of the consel's armored demons walked across his line of sight, its breath huffing through the grille of its helmet. Moonlight glittered off the blade of its ax. Perhaps Ebon should have found the presence of the creatures reassuring, but they could turn on him in a heartbeat if Garat gave the order. It wasn't as if there'd be witnesses out here to his treachery.

The consel said, "I understand this is not the first time you've ventured into the Forest of Sighs."

Ebon glanced at him from the corner of his eye. "No, it is not. Four years ago, I led a raid against some Kinevar settlements."

"In Sartor we have soldiers for such things."

"Your point is well made. Alas, at the time I was still of an age that my pride could be goaded."

Garat looked at him. "A *dare,* your Majesty? I would never have thought you had it in you."

"Not quite a dare. An . . . acquaintance . . . of mine had the presumption to question a young prince's courage." He was not about to tell the consel that the "acquaintance" had been Domen Janir, and that the accusation had followed Ebon's refusal to take part in the attack on the Sartorian village to which Domena Irrella's killers had fled. "The charge, of course, could not go unanswered, so I decided to prove myself by leading a raid into Kinevar territory. Forty-two Pantheon Guardsmen paid for my pride with their lives. Aside from myself, only three survived."

"A valuable lesson. One can never have too many soldiers."

"And yet here you are with but a handful of men, taking as great a risk as I did."

Garat's look became distant, and the ever-present note of mocking humor left his face. "A Sartorian fears anonymity more than he fears death. Our rulers have but a few short years in which to carve for themselves a place in our people's history."

"And how would you wish to be remembered, Consel?" Ebon asked.

Garat gave a half smile, then pushed himself to his feet. "Good night, your Majesty."

The king watched him disappear into the darkness.

A new voice spoke. "An intriguing man, Mottle declares."

Ebon sighed. "How long have you been listening in?"

The old man materialized from the gloom. "Mottle does not have to listen in, my boy, to hear what is said."

"You find the consel intriguing?" Ebon asked, looking in the direction Garat had taken. "Why?"

"Because like you he shapes the Currents where others are only carried along by them."

"Pebbles again."

Mottle nodded vigorously. "Precisely." He settled on the tree trunk in the place Garat had vacated, then lifted his bare left foot and picked at a splinter in his sole.

"Vale thinks I should kill him," Ebon said.

"Yet you will not."

"What would be the point? Doubtless we will both be dead soon."

Mottle cocked his head. "Think you so? Have you so little faith in your newfound ally, then?"

Ebon stared into the darkness. "Should I regret my choice? The goddess wants the same thing that we do. To bring down the power behind the undead."

"One does not bargain with an immortal and hope to win in the exchange."

"You think the goddess has hidden motives?"

"Mottle would not presume to comprehend the workings of an immortal's mind. To attempt to do so would be foolishness itself. And Mottle is anything but foolish, as you well know. Indeed, only a fool would suggest—"

"Mottle," Ebon warned.

Unabashed, the mage continued, "If your humble servant were compelled to express a view, he would speculate—reluctantly—that the goddess considers you not so much an ally as a tool."

Another of the consel's demons stomped by, or perhaps it was the same one Ebon had seen previously. He could not tell them apart, for all four of the creatures wore identical armor. "What do you know of this Galea?" he asked Mottle.

Mottle looked round as if the trees were crowding in upon them. "Hush! To speak her name is to invite her regard."

Ebon quested inward, but sensed only the wall that the goddess had raised between them. "I would know if she were near."

"Certain, are you? Mottle will do naught to catch her eye. He is the chameleon among the mottled leaves, the bug beneath . . ." The old man's voice trailed off. "What's this, a bug? An outrageous slight! No, that will not do."

"Who are you talking to?"

Mottle stood up and began pacing, his bare feet rustling the fallen leaves. "Currents stir the air all about us, my boy. The deepest tides, the darkest eddies. Centuries old, yet undisturbed—uncontaminated, if you will—by the presence of man. The winds whisper dread secrets in Mottle's ear. The air trembles with the memory of black sorcery."

"I know. The spirits showed me what happened here."

The old man's hands were a whirl of excited motion. "Ah, but beneath the echoes of ancient bloodshed lie yet more arcane mysteries. A truth of such profundity that the fate of civilizations may hinge upon it."

"Concerning the Vamilians?"

"And their enemies, yes, the Fangalar. A hint, perhaps, as to the reason for the two peoples' enmity? It must be! Yet ever the truth lies at the edge of Mottle's hearing, tantalizingly beyond his most probing reach."

"Is this relevant? To the undead. To the plight of our people."

Mottle paused in his pacing. "Relevant? Perhaps not directly, but then relevance is ever a relative concept."

"I will be the judge of that. Now, you never answered my question. The goddess . . ."

The old man spread his hands. "Mottle knows only what the Currents tell him."

"And that is?"

"Unsettling, my boy. Acutely so."

Ebon grunted. *He knows nothing, then.* "What of our people? The goddess said the palace still holds."

"Alas, the Currents speak only of death, but in this place antiquity's tormented voice eclipses all else."

"Then I have no choice but to accept what the goddess tells me."

Mottle spluttered. "Accept? Furies bless me, no! Does the lederel believe the mountain lion when it says it is not hungry?"

The moon passed behind a cloud, momentarily plunging the forest into darkness. Ebon shifted on the tree trunk. It was not the discomfort of his seat that troubled him. The old man was right. It would be easy for Galea to tell him only what he wanted to hear, to twist his hopes against him. The sense of renewed optimism he had experienced following his meeting with the goddess began to fade. "I should never have left Majack."

"Nonsense! Here is where your people are best served."

The image of Lamella's face appeared in Ebon's mind. "My people, yes."

"Your duty weighs heavily on you?"

The king gave a rueful smile. Could the old man hear his thoughts now? "What if it does?"

"Heed Mottle's words: To struggle against duty is to entangle oneself still further in its grasping coils." The mage paused, then went on, "A man cannot, however, pursue just one duty to the exclusion of all others."

With that, he sketched a clumsy bow before turning and wandering deeper into the forest. He must have acquired another splinter as he moved off, for the silence was broken by a whispered oath, and the mage's walk became half limp, half hop.

Frowning, Ebon watched him go.

Standing in the midst of the hanging gallery of undead, Romany tapped a spiritual foot on the ground. Somewhere ahead through the smoke and fire and ash the Kinevar gods and their followers were in retreat from Mayot's forces. How did one defeat an enemy that did not die, did not tire? That turned one's allies into foes when they fell? That numbered among its ranks Fangalar, Gorlems, demons, and innumerable other nightmares she had no name for? The sheer weight of the undead's numbers was proving irresistible, for it seemed not even the Kinevar gods had the power to break the threads of death-magic holding Mayot's servants. But then why had they not fled this place of horror? Pigheaded arrogance, Romany supposed. A common enough trait among immortals. Oh, the Kinevar gods were not *true* gods, of course, merely forest spirits twisted over the centuries by earth-magic and blood sacrifice. Immortal, yes, but still cherubs compared to the Spider and the others members of her degenerate pantheon. Would Mayot be able to enslave them if they fell to his undead hordes? It was a question to which Romany hoped she never discovered the answer.

The old man had taken a gamble in attacking the Kinevar's sacred glades. For days now his Vamilians had been busy grubbing in the dirt for bones, and of the ancient powers they had unearthed, the most formidable had been sent here to battle the Kinevar. And who aside from the Vamilians did that leave to shield Mayot from Shroud's minions? A handful of undead champions. *And me . . .* She frowned. Could it be that her presence in Estapharriol had allowed Mayot to commit more of his forces here? That he was using her as much as she was using him? Perhaps the old man was not the blathering fool she took him for. Romany snorted. *And perhaps one day the Spider will learn the meaning of the words "please" and "thank you."*

The priestess had lured a number of Shroud's minions to this part of the forest, hoping they might slay some of Mayot's undead before themselves being destroyed. A group of lizard-skinned disciples had even come as far as this ghastly hanging gallery. But no farther. Romany's magic, after all, worked through deception, manipulation, misdirection, and no illusion, however masterly, could disguise the hellishness of this place. Trying to goad Shroud's minions into continuing on was like trying to make them walk into fire. And yet, the fact they had come this far meant Shroud would now know the seriousness of the Kinevar gods' plight, and hence the scale of the danger he himself was facing. If the Lord of the Dead had not taken Mayot seriously up until this point he would have to do so now.

The time was fast approaching when Romany would have to retire from the game, but there was still much to do before that happened. One newcomer to the forest in particular would require her most assiduous attention, for the scoundrel's coming here presented an opportunity to right past wrongs she could not pass up. She had already devised the rudiments of a scheme to snare her victim, but the devil, as ever, was in the detail. In order to finalize her plan she needed to know how much longer the Kinevar gods could resist the forces attacking them, and hence how much time she still had to work with before she bid this miserable forest good-bye.

Infuriatingly, though, she could get no closer to the heart of the distant struggle. Twice now she had paced the perimeter of the battlefield—an area covering several square leagues—searching for a navigable route through to the Kinevar sacred glades. No matter which approach she took, however, she was met by a maelstrom of warring sorceries that consumed the strands of her web as quickly as she could weave them. She stamped a foot. *This is intolerable!* There had to be a way of scouting the forest ahead.

A flap of wings sounded above as a huge shape swooped low over the treetops. Instinctively Romany ducked, but it was just another nameless monstrosity resurrected and enslaved by the Book. She shuddered at the touch of its shadow.

Then she noticed the thing was heading in the direction of the battle.

The priestess smiled. *Spider's grace, I'm good.* Extending her senses, she spun a strand of magic round the creature's tail and watched as it was drawn up and over the forest. Then she flashed along it.

Perching on the tip of the beast's tail, she paused to inspect her unwitting mount. Its back was a rippling mass of interlocking gray scales, and its flanks were scarred by sorcery. Plumes of black feathers sprouted from its neck, obscuring Romany's view of its head. A fact for which she was grateful.

The flaw in her plan became apparent when the creature flicked its tail. The motion sent her twisting this way and that, battling to keep her seat. As stomach-churning experiences went, it eclipsed even her ill-fated sea voyage along the coast from Mercerie to Koronos, when the waves of the Sabian Sea had battered her ship to within an inch of Romany's life.

Now she came to think of it, she wasn't overly fond of heights either.

Steeling herself, she risked a glance at the forest below and found herself looking down on a seemingly endless vista of smoke and flames. Through the smoldering canopy she saw snatches of a vast shadowy throng of undead. Half a league ahead was a flash of green—a cluster of trees where the fires had not yet taken hold. In the ash-filled skies above it, undead stormwraiths circled like redbeaks over a corpse. Of the Kinevar gods and their surviving followers, however, Romany could make out nothing.

A burst of earth-magic shattered the air ahead, and her mount pitched to one side before righting itself. Clearly someone had taken objection to the creature's presence, and if the priestess was honest, she couldn't blame them. With a mighty beat of its wings the beast climbed higher. Fighting down nausea, Romany looked back and was relieved to see that the magical thread she had woven about the creature's tail remained intact. Next time, though, she might not be so lucky. If the strand was broken—

A shaft of lightning flashed up from the smoke below, punching a hole through the right wing of the priestess's mount. With a shriek, it started to lose height, spiraling down toward the forest. The treetops came rushing up to meet it.

Romany was already fleeing back to the ground along her thread of sorcery, the strand unraveling even as she raced along it.

When she reached the safety of the hanging gallery of undead she whispered a heartfelt oath never to surrender the safety of land again. Her heart was pounding so quickly she could no longer distinguish individual beats. An ignominious retreat, perhaps, but she had more immediate concerns at hand than a bruised ego. For not only was she no nearer to discovering how far the Kinevar gods were from capitulating, she *still* had no idea how to get close enough to the action to find out.

Romany sniffed and smoothed her gown. No need to panic, the setback was only a temporary one. A solution would come to her in time.

It always did.

Ebon's horse pranced nervously, its hooves sending up puffs of leaf fragments. The distant clang of weapons echoed through the forest—a handful of combatants at most, judging by the number of strikes. The battle was otherwise being fought in silence, which had to mean the undead were hosting the gathering. But then who were they entertaining?

To Ebon's left, the consel and his sorceress were in hushed conversation. Garat signaled to one of his troops, and the soldier swung down from his saddle. He unslung a shortbow and set off at a scamper toward the sounds of fighting.

Ebon steered his horse forward. "Consel, we should keep moving."

Garat did not look round. "Are you not curious to know what is happening? It is safe to assume, I think, that the undead are not fighting each other."

"It is also safe to assume the Vamilians are not going to break off their attack to answer our questions. We should leave now before we are drawn into the conflict."

"What, and leave their victims in the lurch? Before now, you've always seemed so anxious to make new friends."

"I'm learning my lesson on that score."

Garat chuckled.

Corporal Ellea came riding up from the opposite direction to that which the consel's scout had taken. Her face was caked in sweat and dirt. "Stiffs, your Majesty," she said. "Scores of them, all around us."

Ebon faced Garat. "It appears the net is tightening."

"But on us or on the mysterious combatants ahead, I wonder?"

"Does it matter? If the Vamilians catch us here they are unlikely to spare us just because we are not their intended target." Ebon caught Ellea's eye. "Corporal, where are the lines of undead thinnest?"

She pointed west.

Garat smiled. "Excellent! That will take us close to this confrontation. Now, if my scout would just . . . Ah! Such commendable timing."

The man had stumbled into view ahead, pushing his way through a thicket fifty paces away. Another of the Sartorian soldiers rode to meet him, leading his horse by the reins. The scout stepped into his saddle, then rode up to report. "Two score of the stiffs, sir," he said to Garat. "Vamilians mostly, but I saw a Kinevar—"

"Who are they fighting?" the consel cut in.

"Couldn't see. Too many of them—the stiffs, I mean. Moving this way, though."

Garat's expression went cold. "You were spotted?"

"By the Vamilians? Not a chance. Bastards were too busy getting chopped up."

A moment of silence greeted his words.

Garat gathered his reins and nodded at Ambolina. "Sorceress, get your pets moving. Tarda Sulin, have your soldiers take up flanking positions . . ."

Ebon was no longer listening. In front and to his right he could now see flickers of movement between the trees—white-robed figures mostly, but with a splash of black among them. Unstrapping the shield from his back, he settled it on his left arm before drawing his saber. "Galea," he whispered. "Are you with me?"

There was no response. Evidently the goddess had no intention of intervening in the struggle to come.

The consel's demons had moved off, Garat and Ambolina immediately behind, the Sartorian soldiers fanning out to either side. Ebon kicked his horse forward and took up a position behind the consel, Vale and Mottle beside him. The company skirted a thick wall of brambles. Then the demons veered west, and broke into a run.

The ground trembled in their wake.

Heartbeats later Ebon drew abreast of the unknown combatants. A hooded figure—a man, judging by his height—was visible between the trees, black robes billowing as he twisted and turned in the midst of a crowd of undead. The stranger wielded an oversized, golden-bladed sickle in each hand, and Ebon watched as a long, graceful swing cut a Vamilian warrior in half, the sickle passing through armor, flesh and bone without apparent resistance. The wielder was already spinning away, swaying to evade a disemboweling spear thrust. A reverse slash from one of the sickles tore open the throat of another enemy.

Ebon looked round to locate the stranger's companions, but he could see only Vamilians. Were the sickle-wielder's friends hidden by the trees, perhaps? Had they fallen already? Surely the man could not have survived on his own for this long.

It was only then that Ebon registered the motionless bodies of the Vamilians piled round the stranger. His eyes widened. *Motionless? Watcher's tears, can it be?*

His mare took him past and out of sight.

He spurred his mount up an incline after the Sartorians. Above the drumming of hooves came the crackle of sorcery ahead and to his left. Vamilians carrying swords and crude spears of sharpened wood materialized between the trees in front. *Barely a score of them.*

This should be simple enough.

The consel's demons charged into the undead. A cut from one of the monstrous axes carved through the skull of an enemy warrior in a spray of bone fragments. In the creatures' wake a Vamilian woman missing both arms struggled to her knees, only to be caught by a flying hoof. Then Ebon was among the foe. He used his shield to turn aside a thrown spear before parrying a sword thrust with his own blade. No need to strike back, his horse was already taking him out of range. He ducked beneath a branch that would have swept him from his saddle and stayed low for a score of heartbeats in case one of the undead should aim a spear at his back.

As quickly as that he was clear.

The company rode for half a league, the consel finally signaling a halt at the edge of a deep depression scarring the land from northeast to southwest. Ebon resheathed his saber and looked round. The party had emerged unscathed from the clash, although one of the Sartorian soldiers was cradling his left arm. And Bettle was missing, Ebon noticed suddenly. Glancing back in the direction of the fighting, he saw a red-cloaked rider weaving between the trees. The Pantheon Guardsman cantered up.

"No sign of pursuit," he said. "Stiffs are all converging on that sickle-wielder."

Garat scratched his chin. "It would appear we are not worthy of the Vamilians' attention."

Meaning all of us here are minor players on this stage, even Ambolina and her demons. "Consel, did you see as I did? The undead lying motionless round the stranger?"

It was Mottle who answered. "The puppets' strings have been cut, my boy, the frayed threads left—"

"How?" Ebon interrupted. "How were they cut?"

"A necromancer of singular skill, perhaps?"

"Then why was he fighting sickle to sword?" The king spun to face Garat. "We should go back. The stranger may have information of use to us."

"Who was it who said, 'The net is tightening,' your Majesty? The sickle-wielder will be dead by now."

"And if he isn't?"

"Then it will still be too late to pull him out. How many would we lose carving a way through the undead?"

Ebon studied him for a moment. "Your demons—"

"Are mine to command," Garat cut in. "Sacrifice your own soldiers, if you must. It is what you are best at, after all."

Ebon's face twisted, but he said nothing. A few moments ago the consel had been curious to find out who the stranger was, yet now his interest was gone? The very fact an idea was Ebon's, it seemed, was enough to turn Garat against it. In future he would need to use a subtler means of persuasion if he was to influence the consel's decisions.

Garat had moved away and was speaking to Ambolina, their horses drawn up at the edge of the depression. The floor of the valley was hidden by brambles and gnarled branches, though Ebon could see a glitter of light on water below and to his right. In the distance, beyond the opposite side of the depression, came the sound of something smashing its way through the forest, snapping tree trunks as it went. The noises were moving away from them.

Ebon tried to listen in to Garat's conversation with Ambolina, but they were speaking in Sartorian, and he could make out only the occasional word. When they fell silent, he said, "Next move, Consel?"

Garat was a long time in answering. "This valley runs south and west. The undergrowth should hide us for a while."

"It will also lose us the speed of our horses if we are discovered."

"I don't recall asking for your opinion, your Majesty."

"Consel," Ambolina began.

"Nor yours either, sorceress," Garat said.

"Earth-magic is strong in this place," the woman went on. "Much may be concealed beneath . . ."

But Garat had already wheeled his horse away. He shouted orders to his soldiers, pausing to bark a curse at one of the demons when it did not move from his path.

Ebon found himself alone with the sorceress. Ambolina paid him no attention. The sound of crashing trees had faded, yet she remained staring out west over the depression. Her hands were folded in her lap, her forefingers tapping against each other. A flicker of apprehension crossed her face, the slightest tightening round her eyes.

It was, Ebon decided, the most disturbing sight he had seen since entering the forest.

Luker urged his horse along the mud track that curled toward the village through fields of mexin. The crops were more brown than green, their withered heads sagging to the earth. Tools lay scattered about: scythes, hoes, pitchforks, even a plow was going to rust. A dozen dead goats were in an enclosure. There was no sign of their herder. Now Luker thought of it, he hadn't seen anyone in the fields for more than a day, and there was no more evidence of life in the village itself—a cluster of wooden shacks surrounding a watchtower on the western bank of a dry riverbed. The gates in its palisade stood open, and brushwood had been heaped against the fence as if someone had intended to fire the place.

Raising a hand to signal his companions to stop, he reined up a hundred paces away. A gust of wind made his horse skittish. As he shook his reins he felt a pull from behind and turned to see the spare mount, tied to his saddle horn with a rope, take a few steps backward, eyes wide, whickering. Only when the breeze veered again did the animals settle.

Jenna drew alongside. "This place is dead," she said. "The Kalanese, you reckon?"

"We're too far from Arandas for raiding parties." Luker gestured at the dead goats. "Anyhow, they'd have taken the animals, not slaughtered them." He looked at Chamery. "Could the Book have done this? The air feels . . . corrupted."

"Corrupted!" the mage scoffed. "Yes, I imagine it would seem that way to you. The touch of death-magic can be unsettling to the unenlightened."

"It's fatal, then? For us too?"

"For *you*, yes. In time."

The wind had changed again, and the horses were shifting uneasily.

Merin spoke. "Why is Mayot doing this, mage? What does he gain?"

"Power," Chamery said. "Each death releases energy he can draw on."

"So he's blighted this entire land? Why? What does he need such power for?"

Chamery did not respond.

"We should move on," Luker said to Merin. "We'll find nothing here that isn't poisoned."

"But our water—"

"Will have to be rationed now. Happy memories, eh?"

Merin stared back, expressionless. "How far to the White Road?"

"Dusk, maybe, before we reach it." *If you ever stop asking questions, that is.*

They skirted the village to the west, following a winding track flanked by dry-stone walls. Once clear of the fields, Luker led them at a gallop toward the forest.

A bell later he saw the glittering line of light on the ground that marked the White Road. At some time in the past it must have ended at the edge of the trees, but now it protruded several hundred paces across the plain like a jetty into the sea, evidence of the forest's retreat in the face of centuries of ax and flame. Even though Luker had traveled this way before, the sight of the road still made his skin prickle. Glowing faintly, the white paving stones were perfectly clear of dirt and leaves, as if an army of broom-wielding servants had swept them clear just moments earlier. Streams of wind-borne dust blew across the stones but never settled on them.

The hooves of Luker's horse clattered as he steered it onto the road, and a short while later he reined up at the edge of the forest. There was no movement between the trees save for the rippling of the leaves on the ground. Strands of death-magic spanned every tree and bush like some monstrous spider's web. *Too bad for you, Mayot, that I'm no fly.* The air was soaked with power, so highly charged it felt as if a thunderstorm were about to break. Maybe it was, judging by the powers converging on this place. Had they come to claim the Book from Mayot?

Six years ago when Luker had last traveled the White Road with one of the emperor's agents, scores of spirits had converged on him as soon as he entered the forest from the north. Unable to attack the Guardian and his charge for as long as they remained on the road, the phantoms had trailed them day and night, jabbering in mindless misery—the same wretched sound, Luker recalled, as the emperor's agent had been making by the end of their four-day journey. Now, though, the woods were silent. Where were the spirits? Lurking deeper among the trees, perhaps, watching him even now? Or bickering over Mayot's rotting corpse?

Odds were Luker would find out soon enough, for regardless of whether Mayot was alive or dead, the Guardian doubted the mage, or Kanon for that matter, would simply be waiting for him on the road ahead. At some point Luker and his companions would have to surrender the safety of the White Road and strike out into the forest, thus laying themselves open to attack by the spirits. Luker wasn't concerned for himself, of course—the spirits' clumsy efforts at possession posed no threat to someone with a Guardian's training. Jenna and Merin, too, were strong-willed. The problem, as ever, would be Chamery. For all his arrogance the boy was weak-minded, and like as not the spirits would scent his vulnerability like a shark scenting blood. At the first sign of the mage succumbing to their wiles, Luker would not hesitate to do what needed to be done. *Hesitate?* Hells, the boy had had it coming long enough.

Right on cue, Chamery's lisp sounded behind him. "Why have you stopped, Guardian? Are you thinking of turning back?"

"I've never backed down from anything. You'd do well to remember that before you open your mouth again."

Merin spoke. "If you two are finished, we need to press on. Do we risk the road?"

"No choice," Luker said. "It's the only thing that'll keep the spirits off our backs."

"Can you sense anything ahead?"

"No. Death-magic's like a fog. I'll be blind once night falls."

Chamery laughed. "The Guardian's finally realized what the rest of us have known all along."

"You fancy a shot at point?" Luker said, gesturing ahead with a sweep of one arm. "Be my guest. Maybe Mayot will save me the trouble."

"Of killing me, you mean? Hah! You forget, Guardian, we are entering *my* world now. Mayot is not the only one who can draw on the energies released by the dying forest. Here I am invincible!" With that the mage kicked his horse forward and disappeared into the woods, Merin close behind.

As Jenna drew alongside, Luker held out a hand. She gave him a questioning look.

"It's not too late, you know," he said. "You can still go back."

Jenna flashed her crooked smile. "What, just as things are heating up?" She leaned in close. "My money's on the boy, by the way." Then, before Luker could respond, she dug her heels into her horse's flanks and cantered away.

Scowling, he watched her retreating back. The branches of the trees cast long shadows on the forest floor, and the assassin's form was quickly swallowed by the gloom. Behind Luker the spare mount whinnied as if impatient to be off. The Guardian turned to check his back trail, then caught himself. *Waste of time.* No one was stupid enough to follow them into this Shroud-cursed nightmare.

Spurring his horse forward, he plunged into the forest.

Ebon dismounted and led his horse into the valley, its hooves slipping and skating down the muddy bank. By the time he reached the bottom his boots were caked in muck and his arms were scratched bloody by brambles and nettleclaw. The trees were more closely spaced here, and the canopy of branches overhead all but blocked out the fading sunlight. Good place for an ambush, Ebon thought, but it seemed the consel had made up his mind, and that was that. He cleaned the worst of the mud from his boots, then swung into the saddle and watched the last few Sartorian soldiers make the descent.

At a command from Garat the company formed up in a ragged column behind the four demons. There were no trails traversing the undergrowth, so the metal giants simply pushed their way through, using their axes to clear a path where the brush was thickest. The scratch of nettleclaw on their armor set Ebon's teeth on edge. There was no conversation as they traveled. The sound of fighting came from the east. For now the clash of weapons remained distant, but that could not last, for the Vamilians were sure to hear the demons crashing through the undergrowth. And when the undead came pouring into the valley there would be nowhere for the company to run . . .

The consel rode a few paces ahead, surrounded by soldiers. Ebon was beginning to think Vale was right when he said Garat would not be won round by the king's efforts at friendship. If they were to be enemies, though, Ebon intended to learn all he could about him during their time together. In war, a commander's primary target was the mind of his opposite number, and for all Garat's undoubted cunning he had demonstrated himself to be impulsive, headstrong, easily goaded into reckless action. He showed no respect to his opponents, nor did he appear to command any affection or loyalty from his soldiers. And yet, if the reports were to be believed, the consel had ended decades of stalemate by crushing the Almarian League. Either he was a man of singular tactical genius or—Ebon's gaze swung to Ambolina—his sorceress was the real threat to be countered.

The demons inched their way forward. After a bell and a half the trees and brambles grew thicker, and Ebon was forced to dismount and lead his destrier by the reins. To his right he caught sight of the body of a stag in the midst of a knot of nettleclaw, its antlers snared in the undergrowth, its sightless eyes rolled back in its head. There were other shapes too, apparently trapped in the brush, little more than shadows in the deepening gloom.

The ground underfoot became boggy, and gray ooze sucked at Ebon's boots as he trudged through scum-laden water. When he finally reached dry ground again he saw scores of objects sunk into the mud ahead: doll-like figures made of twigs and dried grasses; scraps of colored cloth; feathers and fragments of flint tools. *And bones,* the king noticed with a jolt. Animal? No, the skulls were clearly human-oid. Why, then, had their owners not been resurrected like the Va-milians? Ebon pictured the bones moving across the ground, rattling together to form skeletons, flesh and skin materializing as the un-dead rose . . .

A needlefly buzzed in front of his face, and he raised a hand.

Then stopped. A needlefly? If his memory served him right he had not seen an insect for days. *Watcher's tears, is the power of the Book fading?* Had Mayot Mencada already fallen?

A whisper of derisive humor from Galea gave him his answer.

The carpet of detritus extended for several hundred paces. Ahead the boles of the trees were marked with runes. Ebon passed a fallen trunk with shackles fixed to it. The wood and the ground beneath it were stained black, and he felt a tingle across his skin—a sensation he had felt before, he realized, though he could not recall where. Turn-ing in his saddle, he beckoned to Mottle. The old man guided his horse forward.

"Mage, what is this place?" Ebon said.

Mottle wrinkled his nose. "A Kinevar holy site. The stink of earth-magic is still strong here, yes?"

"Strong enough to hold the death-magic at bay?"

"For a while longer, Mottle laments."

"Laments? You prefer death-magic to this?"

The old man threw up his hands. "Of course Mottle prefers! Earth-magic is the bane of his existence, the very scourge of his wondrous art! Your humble servant is blind, do you hear me? Blind and deaf besides! The Currents dare not stir in this cursed place, yet here is Mottle, most beloved of the Furies, tainted by its filth! Fouled by its . . . foulness! Woe is Mottle!"

Ebon left him to his grumbling. Glancing up, he saw the consel was peering at the ground with his tarda, Gen Sulin. Ebon crossed to join them.

"Tracks," the tarda explained as he approached. "Fresh, too."

"One set," Garat mused. "Heading in the same direction as us. See how small the impressions are? The length of the stride?"

"A child?" Ebon said.

"Incisive as ever, your Majesty. One of the undead, we must hope." The consel looked at Ebon pointedly. "I'll be damned if I'll take on any more baggage . . ." His voice trailed away.

"Consel?"

Garat rose, his gaze fixed on something over Ebon's shoulder.

Turning, the king saw the four demons staring south into the forest. His hackles rose. There was something in their bearing, the way they clutched their axes perhaps, that spoke to him of . . . *readiness*. Ambolina stood behind them, hands hidden in the sleeves of her robe.

Garat said, "Sorceress, what is it?"

For a dozen heartbeats Ambolina paid him no mind. Then she swung to face him. "Wait here."

Without any command from the woman, the demons lurched forward into the gloom. Ambolina followed, a pace behind.

The consel stepped into the saddle, then wheeled his horse round and made to follow. A whisper of steel sounded as the Sartorian soldiers drew their swords. Tarda Gen Sulin had moved ahead of Garat and called orders to his troops in a low voice.

Ebon unsheathed his own blade. *The Vamilians—they've caught up to us at last.* And yet, could the undead enter a place such as this, where earth-magic held back the power of the Book? When they set foot here, would not the threads controlling them wither? Questing inside for Galea, he was confronted by the wall she had put up between them. Through it he detected a sense of . . . expectation . . . from the goddess. Ebon realized he had begun treating her like a weathervane, using her emotions to judge which way the wind of fortune was blowing. *Not good enough.* He closed his eyes. "Galea, attend me, please," he silently said.

There was no response.

"Goddess," he said, more insistent this time.

Nothing.

"We had a deal, my Lady. Will you dishonor—"

The force of Galea's outrage struck him like a blast of arctic air, strong enough to drive him to his knees. For several heartbeats her anger crushed him. His chest felt tight, and he struggled to draw in a breath.

Abruptly the goddess was gone from his mind.

For a while Ebon could do nothing but wait for his breathing to settle. The cold of Galea's touch lingered, yet his cheeks burned hot with indignity. It seemed his pride could still be goaded after all. He opened his eyes to see Vale in front of him, a sober expression on his face.

"You still with us?" the Endorian said.

The king nodded stiffly. Ignoring the hand Vale extended to him, he rose and stumbled to his horse. The Sartorians had gone, but Ebon could see the direction they had taken from the trail left by the demons.

Remounting, he set off in pursuit.

CHAPTER 17

THEY CAME in a silent rush from the shadows. Riding at the rear of his party, Luker had time only for a half shout to his companions before the white-robed attackers, twoscore in all, were on them. Drawing his swords, he struck out with his Will at the figures approaching from the left. The lead runners were hurled backward, bringing down those behind, and the charge on that side faltered. From the right, a wave of warriors rushed in.

The first attacker, a dark-haired man with sunken eyes, came within range. The Guardian parried his sword thrust and kicked him in the face, knocking him down. Two women took his place. A swing from Luker's right blade sent the first woman's sword arm tumbling away, then a reverse cut connected with the other assailant's temple, shearing away the top of her head. Expecting the woman to fall, Luker was almost taken by surprise by her counterattack, and he raised his second sword just in time to turn aside a cut to his abdomen.

Shroud's mercy, what is this?

Just then Luker's horse pitched into the woman and sent her stumbling into one of her fellows. The Guardian felt something rub against his side, and his gaze fell on the rope tied round his saddle horn. It was drawn taut, and he suddenly remembered the spare horse. For a heartbeat the line went slack before stretching tight again and jerking Luker's mount about so it faced back along the White Road. A score of paces away the spare horse—a gray—was tossing its head as it tried to pull free of the rope holding it.

A sword glanced off one of the scabbards at Luker's waist, then another skittered across the leather armor at his back. All around him was a shifting sea of bloodless faces, grasping hands, thrusting swords. Cursing all the while, he struggled to keep his seat as blows rained down on him.

A blinding black flash, then a wave of sorcery cut a swath through the attackers to his left. It seemed Chamery had woken up at last. Moments later there was a groan of wood followed by a crack as a tree crashed down across the road behind Luker. Close enough for him to feel the wind of it as it fell, but then no doubt Chamery would have counted it as good luck if it had hit him. Leaves were thrown into the air before falling back down to settle not on the White Road but on the mud to either side.

Another tug from the spare horse.

Luker tried to gather his thoughts. If he cut the gray loose, it would take most of their supplies with it. *No choice.* Before he could deal with the animal, though, he needed to buy himself some breathing space, and so he tugged on his reins and brought his mare sidestepping to the right. The rope, now drawn tight between his mount and the spare horse, struck the white-robed figures on that side with enough force to sweep three of them from their feet. Even as they fell Luker lashed out with his Will at the enemies to his left. The weight of attacks eased for a heartbeat, and he switched his focus to the rope.

He swung his right sword to sever it.

Just as it went slack. His blade cut a shallow nick along his mare's neck, before tangling in the animal's mane. The rope itself was unmarked. His horse whickered.

Luker let off a stream of curses. A white-robed swordsman sprang at him, and he raised his blade to defend, only for a jerk from the gray to pull his sword round. His enemy's weapon missed Luker's own to flash a finger's width from his knee cap. Struggling to control his temper, the Guardian leaned forward and aimed a backhand cut at his assailant's head, adding a touch of the Will to strengthen the attack. When the swordsman parried, his weapon was torn from his hand. Luker's follow-up caught him a blow to the chin, spinning him from his feet.

Now was his chance.

Shifting his attention to the spare horse, Luker unleashed his Will again, this time at the gray itself. The animal's head snapped back, and its legs gave way—back legs first, then front. When Luker tugged on his reins to make his mare retreat, the rope came taut and stayed taut. He swung the sword in his right hand.

The rope parted at the second cut.

Using his calves to exert pressure, Luker turned his horse in a circle, hacking down at the white-robed figures encircling him. Grisly work this, but work that needed doing. His assailants fought in unnatural silence, not a cry escaping their lips as the Guardian took pieces out of any who came within reach. Up and down his swords went until his muscles began to burn. He recognized a face among the press: one of the women he'd struck earlier, now missing half her head. Shards of bone clung to her scalp, but there was no hint of pain on what remained of her features.

Luker risked a look at his companions on the other side of the downed tree. Merin and Jenna had steered their mounts to take up positions flanking Chamery, and as a knot of white-robed figures bore down on them, the mage raised his hands and released a wave of black sorcery. The enemy went up in flames. More fighters were gathering in the trees behind, though, and they now came pouring onto the White Road.

Luker served up another mouthful of steel to one of his attackers. He didn't like running, but these bastards weren't playing fair. You took a sword in the face, you went down and stayed down. Seemed like there should be a rule about that somewhere.

"Break!" he shouted to his companions before digging his heels into his horse's flanks. The mare bolted forward, barreling through the ring of Luker's assailants. He used his left blade to block a swing from a foe on that side, then found himself with a few paces of clear ground. Ahead two white-robed figures were trapped beneath the fallen tree, struggling to free themselves. A woman lay on the ground beside it, the bones of her lower legs protruding from her flesh at impossible angles, but still she tried to rise before falling back again.

As Luker reached the tree his horse leapt, its hooves clipping wood as it sailed over.

His companions were already on the move, and he spurred to join them as they galloped deeper into the forest along the White Road.

After half a league Merin reined in at the head of the group. The tyrin was bleeding from a cut to his temple. Jenna, too, had been injured, and blood seeped from gashes to her shoulder and thigh. For once Chamery did not need prompting. Sliding from his saddle, he approached the assassin to heal her wounds.

Jenna's face was pale. "Who in the Nine Hells were they?" she gasped. "The bastards just kept coming."

Luker's gaze swung to Chamery.

"Undead," the mage said. "Spirits of the Vamilians, raised by Mayot." He looked at Luker. "Did you not wonder why we hadn't encountered any spirits since we entered the forest?"

Merin's voice was cold. "You knew they'd be here? And you didn't think to warn us?"

"I thought I'd be able to break the threads, damn you!"

"Threads, what threads? What are you talking about?"

"The threads from the Book of Lost Souls, of course! With the Book, Mayot can regenerate dead flesh, bind the soul to it—even if it has already passed through Shroud's Gate. You wanted to know what Mayot was doing with all that power, here's your answer. Legions of undead! Every Shroud-cursed soul that ever died in this godforsaken forest! The Book's magic sustains them. Not just sustains them, controls them too."

"And if the threads are severed?" Merin asked.

"Shroud take you, I've tried!"

"Then how do we defeat them?"

"We don't!" Chamery shrieked. He spun away from Jenna and staggered to his horse. "I need time to think! Mayot should never have been able to . . . So soon . . ."

The tyrin turned to Luker. "The boy can't break these threads. Can you?"

Luker had already reached out with his Will toward the undead trailing them along the White Road. Honing in on the lead man, he located the thread of death-magic emerging from his chest. There was no time to study the sorcery or probe it for weaknesses. The strand was no wider than a piece of string, though, so how difficult could it be to cut the thing?

Tensing his Will, Luker hammered a blow to the thread of death-magic.

Nothing. Not even a twitch.

Three more times he struck at the strand. On each occasion it resisted him, its sorcery burgeoning even as Luker's own power increased. Frowning, the Guardian withdrew.

In answer to Merin's inquiring look he said, "Not easily."

"What in the Abyss does that mean?"

"It means those walking corpses are closing fast. It means I'm not going to waste my strength trying to cut a single thread when there are scores of the stiffs out there."

Merin's scowl deepened as he faced Chamery. "What else haven't you told us, mage? What other surprises—"

"Later," Luker cut in. He switched his gaze to Chamery. "And as for you, you were supposed to be our eyes and ears. Riding point means you don't fall asleep in your Shroud-cursed saddle."

"I could not—"

"Spare me the excuses. Just keep your senses sharp. Next time we might not be so lucky."

"Lucky!" Chamery snorted.

"Aye, lucky. Whoever organized that ambush doesn't know one end of a sword from the other. Thought he could get by on numbers alone. Why didn't the undead strike at the horses? Where were the arrows, the spears, the crossbows? Why did the attacks come in two waves instead of one?"

Merin spoke. "Because they've got a mage calling the shots, that's why."

Luker scratched his scar. "Aye. And right now, that's the only damned thing we've got going for us."

Ebon caught up to the Sartorians at the edge of a clearing ringed by standing stones, each carved from a different type of rock. In spite of the waning light, the obelisks cast distinct shadows on the ground, all pointing at the center of the glade. The Sartorian soldiers, silent but for the rustle of armor, had spread out left and right to half encircle the clearing. The consel's demons waited in a line beyond, Ambolina between them, Garat immediately behind.

Standing by a fallen tree in the middle of the clearing was a figure no taller than Ebon's waist. The child whose tracks they had seen earlier? No, not a child, he realized suddenly. A halfling. And since the Book's magic could not penetrate this place . . . *Alive, too.* The man wore only a loincloth. His body was covered in thick white hair, and his face was daubed with black paint. He was speaking to Ambolina as Ebon arrived.

". . . fortunate indeed, *paramir*," he said. "I did not think to find fresh meat in this forest."

Garat said, "We have no provisions to spare you, little man. Now, step aside."

The dwarf's smile revealed filed teeth.

Ebon swallowed. *Somehow I do not think that is what he meant, Consel.*

Garat turned to Ambolina. "You know this man?"

"No. But I recognize the mark of his power. He is a patron of De-ran Gelir."

Deran Gelir. Fourth of the Nine Hells. *Watcher's tears, more de-mons.* And if the dwarf's conjurings were not from the same world as Ambolina's . . . Ebon shifted his grip on his saber. His gaze raked the trees round the clearing, but he could make out nothing through the pools of shadow between the trunks.

"What is your interest here, Jekdal?" Ambolina said.

The dwarf sat down on the fallen tree and fingered a bone tied to a string round his neck. "Is it not obvious? I am waiting for the earth-magic to pass."

Garat laughed. "The bone? You fool! The death-magic will not re-turn its owner to life."

The halfling ignored the comment, his gaze still on Ambolina. "You serve this man?"

"There is no victory to be gained here," the sorceress said. "The death-magic cannot penetrate this place now, but the resistance of the earth-magic is fading. Whichever of us should fall would only rise again."

The dwarf laughed. " 'Whichever of us,' *paramir*? Spare me your dissembling! I can smell your fear."

"The threads of death-magic cannot be broken. Even by such as you."

"What makes you think I will have to? Your soul will be taken far beyond the influence of the powers here." A flick of the halfling's hand, and the forest behind him blurred, an alien landscape overlapping the trees as if Ebon were witnessing another of his spirit-dreams. A bar-ren, rocky plain stretched for leagues into the distance, and the far-off horizon was shot through with crimson streaks like a promise of approaching flames. "In any case," the dwarf went on, "my pets are hungry, and that hunger cannot be denied."

" 'Cannot,' Jekdal?" Ambolina said. "Who is master here, you or them?"

The halfling's smile faded. "They serve me, as soon shall you."

"I've heard enough," Garat grated. "Sorceress, you will have to continue flirting with this freak some other time. If he will not stand aside—"

"Consel," Ambolina cut in, "you must leave."

A muscle in Garat's cheek twitched. "You do not command *me*. Tarda Sulin, have your men—"

"No," the sorceress interrupted again. "This is personal."

"And since when have your personal concerns taken precedence over my orders?"

Ambolina studied him for a while, then said, "I will hold him as long as I can."

Ebon's eyes widened. Even with her demons flanking her the sorceress knew she was outmatched. And with Mottle hamstrung by the earth-magic, and Galea unwilling to assist . . . Ebon hesitated. If he were to step into the dwarf's path, perhaps the goddess would be forced to intervene.

And then again, perhaps not.

In response to the woman's words, Garat's eyes blazed in anger.

The king caught a flicker of movement in the forest behind the consel. Darkness swirled between the trees.

"Look to the shadows!" he shouted.

The Sartorian soldiers were already turning.

The gloom erupted.

Screams rang out as a pool of blackness flowed over three Sartorian horsemen before closing on one of Ambolina's demons. Its armor screeched and buckled, huge gashes appearing across the chest. The hapless creature was lifted squealing from its feet, its ax falling from its gauntleted hands.

That was the last Ebon saw of the clash, for his destrier turned and bolted from the clearing, whinnying in terror. The air flashed red, and a wall of heat struck his back. A shriek sounded, so close behind it seemed the screamer must be sitting on the destrier with Ebon. His throat closed up tight. He didn't know whether to kick his mount on or try to turn it to help those left in the clearing. He was dragged through a patch of brambles. Branches scratched him, thorns plucked at his sleeves.

The red glow faded, and darkness returned.

There were more screams now, all around him. Horses pressed in tight to either side like he was on a battlefield, and he was jostled as he fought to bring his mount under control. He looked for Vale and the others. They'd been behind him as he approached the clearing, so they should be in front of him now, but he couldn't make out faces in the gloom. Ahead a horse with its mane alight went down, throwing its rider. Ebon hauled on his reins, tried to slow his mount's rush, but he might as well have been trying to hold back a landslide. To the sound of crunching bones his destrier half leapt, half scrambled over the thrashing forms before veering right to avoid a tree. Ebon swayed and clung to his saddle horn.

Suddenly he was on the path the demons had cleared through the brush. There were horses in front and behind. The forest bounced and crashed round him, shadows rearing all about. He glanced back, saw nothing but more shadows and a skyline edged crimson as if the sun were setting in the south. A blubbering shriek sounded, followed by a chorus of squeals like someone had set loose a banewolf in a pigpen.

Ebon gave his destrier its head, and it fled into the darkness, following the tail of the horse in front.

It drew up finally in a pool of water, one hoof pawing the ground, its trembling flanks bleeding from nettleclaw scratches. Looking round, Ebon saw Vale farther along the trail. The Endorian kicked his mount forward, mouthing something that was lost beneath a sorcerous explosion. Fires now raged through the trees to the south.

Garat's horse came stumbling through the gloom, and Ebon seized the consel by the arm. He had to shout to make himself heard above distant bestial roars.

"Consel—"

"Get your hand off me!" Garat snarled, pulling away and wheeling his horse. "Sulin! Sulin, where are you, by the Abyss!"

Vale drew alongside Ebon. "Let him go."

Before Ebon could respond a shadow came crashing through the undergrowth. The king raised his saber, but it was only a riderless horse, stumbling as it splashed through the muck. Another scream sounded, a stone's throw away at most. "Where's Mottle?" Ebon called to Vale. "Ellea? Bettle?"

The Endorian shook his head. "No time."

"We can't just leave—"

"Think! We'll not find them in this light, and Watcher only knows what we'll run into instead."

"And Ambolina?"

"Not our problem." Vale's tone suggested he was glad to be rid of her.

The consel had gathered half a dozen Sartorian soldiers to him and was now striking west on a course at right angles to the path to the clearing.

Vale grunted. "Sense at last. We've got to get out of this valley. We can regroup in the morning."

Ebon made a sour face. *If we live that long.* The Vamilians could not have failed to notice the sorcerous exchange between Ambolina and the dwarf, and were doubtless converging even now on the depression. The earth-magic would keep them away for a time, but it would still be folly to wait here.

The consel's voice bellowed out, calling on more of his soldiers to rally to him. Behind Vale's horse Ebon saw a woman in Sartorian colors lying facedown in standing water, her back torn to bloody shreds. He stared at her corpse for a few heartbeats, then sheathed his saber. Perhaps Mottle, Ellea, and Bettle had stayed together, he told himself. Perhaps Mottle would be able to track him down once they moved beyond the range of the earth-magic's influence.

"Seek me out, mage," Ebon said. "When these words reach you, get your head out of the clouds and find me."

The consel and his soldiers were nearly out of sight, carving a path through the undergrowth with their swords. Ebon dug his heels into his horse's flanks and set off after them.

There was rain on the close, early morning air, and the dawn mist had given way to unbroken cloud, turning the sky the color of clay. A storm was coming from the west, Parolla knew, but the rain would not be enough to breathe new life into the dying forest round her.

Since leaving the battlefield of the Kinevar gods she had run without resting for three days and four nights. With every step the death-magic in the air had grown stronger. Running now only granted her limited respite from the dark energy building inside, and her skin burned as if a fire raged within. As the discomfort increased, she ran harder and faster, pushing herself to the limits of her endurance in an effort to suppress the urge to lash out at someone, something. The muscles of her thighs and calves now throbbed, and her every breath was a rasp.

Thus far it had been easy to evade the undead legions, bypassing any concentrations of death-magic she detected ahead. Soon, though, there would be no avoiding the Vamilians. Mayot's city was but a few bells away, and the forest in front was swarming with the *magus*'s servants, the book's threads knotted among the trees like the tangled strands of a ball of wool.

No more so than in the settlement before her.

Standing beside the buckled flagstones of some ancient highway, Parolla peered through the trees toward ruined buildings a stone's throw away. A few tendrils of mist persisted, curling round the stones and the trunks. The ground between the boles was scarred with trenches, over a dozen in all, each five paces wide and fifty long. Mounds of freshly churned earth were piled up beside them, and covering everything was a layer of leaf fragments. A handful of ghostly white threads disappeared into the trenches, meaning some of the undead were still buried underground, trapped in darkness and unable to move, without even the promise of death to offer them release. The sight should have touched Parolla, yet when she searched inside she found nothing.

Tumbal Qerivan materialized beside her. He took in the scene, then said, "Among my people there are legends of a half-life, a world of shadow that existed before Shroud's realm—before any realm of the dead—was forged. The Rivenghast, we call it. A place of purgatory, of lost and tormented souls . . ."

He did not need to finish the thought. "What happened here, *sirrah*?"

"The Fangalar, my Lady."

"They destroyed the settlement?"

"They destroyed *every* Vamilian settlement. Butchered every man, woman, and child. These are their graves."

"Why?"

Tumbal spread his hands. "Would that I knew. It is one of the great mysteries of the Second Age. The Vamilians were explorers and seafarers, and for centuries the Fangalar tolerated their empire building. A fragile peace existed, though there was little in the way of trust or friendship on either side. Then toward the end of that Age . . ."

"War."

"Genocide, my Lady. The Vamilians had no answer to the sorceries unleashed on them, yet the Fangalar showed them no quarter. They hounded their prey even unto the ends of the earth. Millions perished. Entire continents were laid to waste."

Parolla's lips quirked. "Perhaps it is as well, then, that you have not discovered this secret, *sirrah*—the reason behind their enmity."

The Gorlem frowned. "How so?"

"The Fangalar might not take kindly to your knowing."

Tumbal sighed. "Thou may'st have the right of it. At times, the search for knowledge is a hollow pursuit, my Lady. What truth could possibly explain what the Fangalar did here? What justification could suffice?" He shook his head. "I fear the solution to this riddle, were I ever to find it, would bring only disappointment."

Parolla looked down into one of the graves. Two threads of death-magic burrowed into the earth. She thought she saw the soil around them move, but maybe it was just the wind. "Your people's civilization dates back to the time of the conflict, does it not? Why did you not try to help the Vamilians?"

"We did, my Lady. Missives were sent to the Fangalar. Delegations. Endless requests for audiences. Some of my kinsmen chose to stand with the Vamilians, in the hope it might stay the Fangalars' hand. Others, like myself, came after"—he gestured to the graves—"to bury the fallen. To honor them in death as we could not in life."

Parolla blinked. "You, *sirrah?*" *That must have been twoscore thousand years ago.*

"We are a long-lived people, my Lady. Or rather we were. In a way, the death of the Vamilians also marked the beginning of the end of our civilization. The question of whether to aid them split our nation."

"Would it have made any difference to the outcome if you had entered the war?"

The Gorlem rubbed a hand across his eyes. "No, it would not. A simple enough answer to thy question, yet many thought it the wrong question to ask. Ultimately the rifts that developed among my people proved irreconcilable."

"Civil war?"

"No, never that, Ral be praised. Many of my kinsmen fled across the seas, fearing the Fangalar would retaliate for the actions of those who died alongside the Vamilians. Others turned their backs forever on their people, appalled that they had done so little in the face of such slaughter."

"And you were among them?"

There was a weariness in Tumbal's eyes. "I stood aside once at the Vamilians' time of need. It pains me that I can do nothing to aid them now."

"Yet you think I can, is that it? I've told you already, this isn't my fight."

Tumbal tried to mask his disappointment, but there was no mistaking the slump of his shoulders. Parolla found herself wondering whether she would have felt differently about the Vamilians' plight if the Gorlem had told her his tale before she'd entered the forest. Dark energy had raged through her veins for the past six days. So much of herself had already been burned away in the blackness. Now she was finding it increasingly difficult to see beyond the shadows that stained her vision.

An image came to her, then, of the dead Fangalar she had seen at the Merigan portal a dozen days ago. "*Sirrah,*" she said, "would the Fangalar be able to detect what is happening here? The rebirth of the Vamilians?"

"I do not know, my Lady. Why dost thou ask?"

"I saw a Fangalar at the gateway to the Shades—not the rent where we met, but another entrance, farther west toward Enikalda. He had passed through a Merigan portal inside the demon world and died for his transgression."

"Thou think'st he was a scout?"

Parolla shrugged. "The resurrection of the Vamilians is not a rebirth in truth. Perhaps the Fangalar were unsure of what they sensed. Perhaps they sent someone to investigate."

Tumbal's ghostly face seemed to become paler still. "If thou art correct others will follow."

"The demon that killed the scout said it might destroy the portal."

"The Fangalar will find another way, my Lady. No doubt there are other gateways of which we know'st nothing." The Gorlem looked round at the forest with new eyes. "Perhaps they are here already."

"To finish what they started all those centuries ago? Or to punish the one who brought the Vamilians back?"

"Perhaps both."

Parolla chuckled. "I wonder if Mayot appreciates the danger."

Tumbal opened his mouth to speak, then froze.

Faint sounds reached Parolla: the tread of feet, the clink of metal on metal. The noises came from the south and east. She squinted between the trees, but could make out nothing through the undergrowth. Parolla did not need to see the Vamilians, though, to know they were there. Judging by the distant concentration of threads of death-magic, a large group of undead was but a quarter of a league away and approaching rapidly. Had she been spotted? She'd already sensed scores of Vamilians in the settlement now behind and to her right. Was this new group driving her toward them?

Parolla hesitated. Her best chance of evading the undead was to take cover in the ruins at the edge of the town, but if the Vamilians already knew she was here, there would be no hiding from them. Instead she would be walking into an ambush. Anything, though, beat standing here waiting for the newcomers to arrive, and she strode toward the settlement along the road that led between the graves.

It was only as she reached the first of the buildings that she heard a crackle of sorcery from the center of the town. Black smoke rose over the ruins.

Death-magic.

Then, as the echoes of power washed over Parolla, her eyes widened.

For the signature of the sorcery was one she recognized.

Dozens of corpses lay scattered across the White Road, and Luker raised a hand to signal a halt. The fallen were Vamilians, yet he could not detect any threads of death-magic coming from their chests, nor was there any sign of the enemy they had been fighting. Another surprise attack gone wrong? He scanned the ground between the trees on either side. Or a trap?

The Guardian dismounted to examine the body of a man wearing an ivory-colored gown over a hauberk that extended to his knees. The Vamilian's hair and beard were plaited with silver thread, and a spear lay alongside his body. The eyes staring back at Luker were dead, yet the Guardian still half expected the corpse to twitch back to life. His gaze was drawn to a hole through the warrior's armor over his heart. *The killing blow.* It had been delivered with near-surgical precision by some thin-bladed weapon. The edges of the bloodless wound were stained black, and the Vamilian's skin had peeled back to reveal a breastbone covered with hairline cracks.

Jenna spoke from behind Luker. "At last, a corpse that stays dead."

And all the more interesting for that. "There's some sort of residue round the wound. Sorcery, I reckon."

"An invested weapon?"

"Maybe." Luker turned to Chamery. "What do you make of this?"

The mage stared at him blankly before sliding from his saddle and approaching. Kneeling beside the body, he closed his eyes. "The tremors are faint. Death-magic."

"No shit."

"Not from the severed thread," Chamery snapped. "From whatever weapon caused these wounds."

"You reckon the stiffs have started fighting each other?"

The mage seized the spear lying beside the Vamilian's body. "Do you sense any sorcery in this?" he said, sneering.

"Then who?"

Chamery's gaze returned to the wound over the dead man's heart. "One of Shroud's inner circle," he said. "I can think of no one else with the power to cut the Book's threads."

A moment of silence passed. Luker shook himself. *Things just got a whole lot more complicated.* "Seems Mayot has been stepping on a few toes."

"It's taken you this long to work it out? Hah! Mayot's dragged countless souls back from the underworld—"

"The Vamilians never passed through Shroud's Gate."

"But others did. Others that died in this forest. Then there are the souls of the recently departed—souls Mayot has stopped from passing over. Souls that belong to Shroud. Of course the god wants the Book!"

"You knew this all along, yet still you came here? Why? You going to risk butting heads with Shroud himself?"

"The Lord of the Dead won't intervene personally. He wouldn't dare set foot in the mortal realm."

"Whether it's him or his lackeys, he won't take kindly to you sticking your staff in. You're playing with fire."

"For power to rival the gods? The rewards are worth the risks."

Luker laughed. "And here I was thinking you meant to take the Book back to the Black Tower."

"I was speaking of Mayot," Chamery muttered, rising to his feet. He flung the broken spear shaft into the trees and walked back to his horse.

Luker looked at Merin. "What about you? You going to spit in Shroud's eye as well?"

The tyrin's expression was grim. "The emperor's orders haven't changed."

"The *emperor* can't have known how things would turn out here, else he wouldn't have sent just the three of us along. Would he want you to go on, knowing what you do now?"

"All the more, I expect."

"Shroud can make eternity damned uncomfortable for you."

Merin held his gaze for an instant, then looked away. "I gave an oath."

"Right. Just don't forget to tell Shroud that when the time comes. I'm sure he won't hold it against you."

Romany stood before the dome of death-magic that spanned Estapharriol, her arms crossed in front of her chest. The surface of the sorcerous construction shimmered like rippling water, making the trees beyond appear blurred. With the approach of the storm, the air inside the dome had turned stifling. Looking over her shoulder the priestess saw Danel, the wounds to her hands now healed by Mayot, dutifully fanning her with a branch of dead honeyheather. The servant's efforts, though, served only to wash yet more of the fetid warmth over Romany, and she signaled the girl to stop.

Sounds of fighting were audible in the distance, but the priestess had a little time yet before the combatants drew near. She transferred her gaze to the burial pits beyond the sorcerous dome. Dozens of Vamilians were crouched on all fours in the trenches, displaying typical indefatigable zeal as they tore at the earth with their hands. Their efforts caused a young tree to be uprooted, and work halted briefly as it was dragged away. Standing at an angle amid the freshly disturbed dirt to the diggers' left was a pillar of gray rock. Some monument to the fallen, perhaps? There were carvings on it.

"Girl," Romany said, gesturing. "What does the inscription say?"

"I have no idea. I died before the stone was raised."

"Truly? How intriguing! History records that barely a handful of your people survived the massacre by the Fangalar, and yet clearly the burial pits did not dig themselves. So who tidied up after your conquerors? Not the Fangalar themselves, surely."

"I have no idea," the servant said again.

Romany scowled. The girl was obviously in another of her moods. Perhaps a few words of admonishment were in order . . .

"What are they digging for?" Danel asked.

The priestess raised an eyebrow. Was that the first question the girl had asked in all their time together? *Maybe her reserve is finally start-ing to thaw.* "Some ancient monstrosity that ought never to see the light of day again. Fortunately Mayot still has to unearth the thing."

"Will he succeed?"

"This time? I think not. Too far underground."

"But there are others?"

Romany smiled. "One or two, yes." Among them, of course, was the tiktar she had hidden from Mayot, still safely shielded behind her wards. That particular game piece would have to wait a while longer, though, before she played it.

Danel turned back to the diggers. "I had hoped . . ."

"Yes?"

"There are still some of my people trapped underground."

"Somehow I doubt Mayot has any real interest in freeing them."

The branch of dead honeyheather slipped from Danel's hands. "My mother and daughter both died with me here. I have not seen them since my . . . rebirth. Perhaps they have been sent elsewhere."

Romany pursed her lips, but did not respond.

"Why have you allied yourself with the master?" Danel said sud-denly.

"We are not allies. We simply share a common enemy."

"Is it the Vamilians?"

"I'm sorry?"

"The enemy you speak of, is it the Vamilians?"

Romany was left speechless for an instant. "My dear, why ever would you think that?"

"Have my people not suffered enough already? Slaughtered by the Fangalar, cast adrift as spirits for generations, now resurrected and enslaved. You see dead flesh, yes? Did you think the same was true of our spirits?"

The priestess sniffed. "Your kinsmen are not the targets in this."

"So we are merely pawns in a greater game. And I am supposed to take comfort in that?"

"Perhaps you should ask Mayot. He is the one pulling your strings."

"I was not talking about the master. I was talking about you."

Recovering some of her poise, Romany drew herself up to her full height. "My reasons for being here are my own—"

"No doubt," Danel cut in. "I trust the cause for which we are sac-rificed is a noble one."

The priestess had no response to that. On reflection she preferred

Danel's silence to this uncharacteristic loquaciousness, particularly if the girl insisted on speaking of matters beyond her understanding. Imagine suggesting Romany would willingly associate herself with Mayot! Did the girl think her devoid of both scruples and discernment? For a time Romany watched the diggers scrabbling about in the burial pits, scooping out handfuls of soil and stones, or hacking at roots with their swords. The walls to one of the trenches collapsed, burying the workers in soil.

Romany looked across at her servant. "When Mayot falls, you will be freed from his grasp."

"*If* he falls."

"No, my dear," the priestess said softly, holding the girl's gaze. "When."

There was a flicker of emotion behind Danel's eyes, and Romany blinked. *Spider's blessing, is that sadness I see?* Had the girl mistaken her meaning, then?

The moment was broken by the distant crash of steel on steel.

Romany looked back at the burial ground. She could see movement between the trees beyond the dome of death-magic. *Ah, my next victim has arrived.* A black-bearded man came into view in the midst of a knot of Vamilians. Over banded armor he wore a surcoat adorned with the image of a rearing black bear. In one gauntleted hand he held a bronze-faced shield bearing the same emblem; in the other, a butterfly-shaped ax that he wielded with breathtaking grace. Each blow when it landed was accompanied by a flash and a dizzying release of death-magic.

Among the undead surrounding him was a four-armed Gorlem clutching a spear in each hand. As Romany watched, the axman's weapon crashed through the spearman's defenses, splintering his ribs before exiting above the left hip. The Gorlem toppled to the ground, the thread of death-magic holding him snapping free and dwindling to nothing. The ranks of undead were quickly receding, each elegant swing of the disciple's ax sending two, three, sometimes four attackers spinning away. More Vamilians—children among them, Romany noticed with distaste—were rushing from the city to intercept him.

"We had best find cover," she said to Danel.

The girl nodded.

Romany led the way into a ruined house. Crossing to the far corner, she sat with her back to a wall.

To business.

This wasn't the first time Romany had encountered this particular disciple of Shroud. Yesterday she'd watched him approach from the east mounted on a bone-colored palimar. A handful of the Vamilians that Mayot tossed into his path had fallen to his ghastly ax, but most had simply been outdistanced by the prodigious strides of his horse. The priestess had brought the palimar's running days to an end by using sorcery to conceal a pothole in the road Shroud's disciple was galloping along. She had then withdrawn, thinking Mayot's servants would complete the formality of dispatching the axman himself.

She should have known better.

The warrior was not the first of Shroud's disciples to reach the dome of death-magic, but he was certainly the most capable. Romany had a plan to knock him out of the game, yet it would require her to approach to within a few paces of him—far closer than she could risk in the flesh—and so she relaxed her mind and allowed her spirit to float free from her body, then followed the strands of her web out of the building and toward the battle. The numbers of undead surrounding the axman had risen to threescore, yet he seemed untroubled by their attacks, surging forward with no hint of tiredness in his strokes, no hesitation in his steps. He reached the dome of black sorcery and pushed through without pause. A net of crackling energy engulfed him, obscuring his frame in scintillating blackness. Then the mesh of death-magic dissipated to leave the bearded warrior unharmed. He continued on, leaving a tear in the dome behind.

As she drifted closer Romany rubbed her spiritual hands together. The art of illusion lay in conforming to her victim's expectations. If she had wanted to, she could have conjured up any number of formidable foes to throw themselves at the axman, but why bother painting an entire canvas when a single brushstroke would suffice? Real mastery required subtlety, guile, a delicacy of touch. A woman's touch, in fact. Releasing her sorcery, she began spinning threads about the warrior. As ever, timing would be critical. Shroud's disciple moved with inhuman speed, his ax chopping and cutting. He used his shield not only to intercept attacks, but also as a weapon, slamming its rim into the faces of the undead to cave skulls or crush eyes. The Vamilians had no answer to the ferocity of his assault. His ax moved faster than the weapons that tried to parry it, or simply smashed through the undead's spears as if they were made of kindling.

The bearded warrior was now level with Romany's hiding place.

Without the dome of death-magic to blur the scene, the priestess was forced to witness the true gruesomeness of the destruction wrought on the man's assailants: the smashed faces, the crushed rib cages, the severed limbs. She could not avert her gaze, however, for she was looking for the smallest mistake, the slightest opening in the warrior's defenses. Few of the Vamilians came close enough to strike at him, and still fewer had the opportunity to deliver a killing blow. Romany, though, was nothing if not patient.

Then she saw her chance. As a Vamilian woman pressed forward on the axman's right, he turned to meet the attack of two undead spearmen on his left. Dropping to one knee, he raised his shield at an angle so his enemies' spear points deflected over his head, then swung his ax in a murderous arc below his shield, cutting through the legs of his assailants. As they fell he was already rising to his feet, lashing out with his shield to hurl their bodies into the ranks of undead behind them.

The maneuver had taken only a heartbeat, and the bearded warrior now spun to face the Vamilian woman attacking from his other flank.

A heartbeat, though, was all Romany needed to spin her deception.

The axman's weapon swung low to intercept the woman's sword . . .

Only to find himself parrying air. The Vamilian's blade, disguised by Romany's sorcery, passed over the ax and bit into the warrior's neck in a spray of blood. A look of bewilderment momentarily clouded his eyes. Then he toppled to the ground.

So simple.

The undead rushed in to hack him to pieces.

Returning to her body, Romany opened her eyes. A stone in the wall behind her was digging into her back, and she sighed as she shifted position. The warrior's death brought her tally of victims to fourteen, and many more of Shroud's disciples had fallen to Mayot's undead servants. The Lord of the Dead would feel their loss keenly, she knew. And yet her defeat of the axman had left her feeling somehow . . . empty. Where was the thrill she usually felt at having outwitted another opponent? Had she expected more of a challenge, perhaps? A suitably dramatic climax to the encounter, more in keeping with the warrior's explosive entrance?

No, there was more to it than that.

The game, Romany realized with a start, had begun to lose its appeal.

Ebon leaned back against a tree and listened to its branches creak and crack in the wind. Vale sat across from him, hood drawn up against the leaves that swirled round the camp. The Endorian was running a whetstone back and forth along the edge of his sword.

Ebon rubbed a hand across his eyes. He had spent the best part of the night floundering through muck and brambles, searching for a way out of the valley where they had encountered the dwarf. When he finally found a clear section of bank to climb, it had taken a quarter of a bell to coax his destrier up the steep slope, its hooves quickly churning up the mud. Then, having linked up with the consel again, he had helped set up camp a short distance from the depression and waited for stragglers to arrive. By morning just two Sartorian soldiers had stumbled upon the encampment, bringing the number in Garat's troop to eight. But there was no sign of Mottle, Ellea, or Bettle. Unable to call out or light a fire for fear of attracting the wrong kind of attention, Ebon had sat staring into the blackness for his companions. *Assuming they are still alive.* Hells, he did not even know whether they had survived the attack by the dwarf's demons. Yet again he had been powerless to keep his people from harm.

Ebon's thoughts turned to Lamella, as they had so often of late. He would have liked to see her one last time; to hold her and breathe in the scent of her hair; to share with her the truths he had come to realize too late. Hard words, perhaps, but ones that needed saying. Mottle had been right when he'd talked of the futility of trying to evade duty, and Ebon had been neglecting his for too long. His expression tightened. It was easy to say this now, though, so many leagues from Majack, with Lamella's fate unknown and his own life hanging in the balance. Would his courage hold if they were ever reunited?

Ebon accepted a strip of dried meat from Vale and chewed on it. The camp was almost silent, the only sounds the snorting of the horses and the consel's voice as he spoke to his new tarda—a mustachioed man whose name Ebon could not remember. Was Garat thinking of turning back? He had to feel vulnerable now Ambolina and her demons were gone, but doubtless his pride would not countenance a retreat. And yet, the loss of the sorceress was as much a blow to Ebon as it was to the consel. For while Vale would argue the sorceress's death—

if indeed she was dead—meant the threat of invasion had been lifted from Galitia, that would count for nothing if Ebon could not defeat this Mayot Mencada. And his chances of doing that had just taken a hit with Ambolina's disappearance.

Closing his eyes, Ebon quested inward for Galea. Seeking her out was like groping for a faded memory. Somehow, though, he was able to fashion a hold on her presence and pull himself toward it. After a moment of disorientation he found his spirit back in the goddess's temple. Galea stood facing away from him, but she swung round at his arrival.

Ebon forced himself to meet her gaze. "My Lady, we have to talk. I needed your help yesterday."

"You forget yourself, mortal," Galea said. "I am not some dog that you may summon to heel. It is *you* who are indebted to *me*."

"And I will stand a better chance of honoring that debt if my companions remain alive."

"You are referring to the demon witch and her spawn?"

"They were powerful allies."

"Until such time as they chose to betray you."

"You know for a fact they would have done so?"

Galea's only response was a chill smile.

Ebon paused, considering. He thought to ask her what had happened to Mottle and the others but knew his kinsmen's fate would be beneath her notice. "How far are we from Mayot Mencada and this Book of Lost Souls?"

"If you ride swiftly you will arrive at the mage's stronghold as the sun reaches its apex."

"And when I face him, is that to be the first time I draw on your power? Would it not be prudent—"

"To test yourself beforehand?" Galea cut in, her voice mocking. "Careful, mortal. You may get what you wish for sooner than you think."

"Meaning?"

But the goddess was already waving a dismissive hand, and Ebon found the temple fading to black around him.

Damn you, woman.

A moment of blurred light, then his vision cleared and he found himself back in the camp.

To see the consel bearing down on him. The Sartorian had shaved his face and oiled his hair, but his shirt remained creased and spattered with dried mud. Ebon pushed himself to his feet, Vale rising beside him.

Garat halted before them. "We have waited long enough, your Majesty."

"My companions are still missing, Consel. My mage—"

"Is probably dead, else he would have found us by now. The next person to stumble on our camp is as likely to be an enemy as a friend."

"I am aware of that. We will be taking as much of a risk, though, if we go on without Mottle's ability to scout the forest ahead. Another quarter-bell—"

Garat turned away. "Stay if you wish. My men and I are leaving."

As the consel retreated, Vale leaned in close. "Let him go."

Ebon shook his head. "He is right. Mottle can catch up to us if he still lives."

"That's not what I meant." The Endorian gestured at Garat's retreating back. "Let him go. Without the witch and her demons . . . We don't need his help anymore."

Ebon frowned. "Maybe not. But he needs ours."

Parolla moved from one low wall to the next as she made her way through the ruined settlement. The clamor of battle was drawing rapidly nearer, as if the combatants were moving toward her even as *she* approached *them*. A flash of sorcery blackened the air, and she shivered as the shadows washed over her, felt an answering surge of darkness within.

She entered a square at the center of which were the remains of a huge sculpture of a ship riding a turbulent sea of stone. Chunks of rock littered the ground. To Parolla's left was what looked like a section of the mast, while beneath the ship's bow lay a broken statue of a woman clutching a shaft of lightning in her right fist. For a few heartbeats Parolla stared at the detail of the carvings on the ship's prow: the rivets in the planks, the barnacles along the hull . . .

Then a sorcerous thunderclap sounded, making the rubble on the ground shudder.

She set off across the square. On the opposite side was a stone stairway leading upward to nothing, and she climbed to the top. Within the settlement to the south she saw light glinting off the armor of scores of Vamilians. At first all she could make out of their opponent was a shadowy glow partly hidden by a cluster of ruined buildings.

Then, from behind a wall, a figure came into view: a dark-skinned man dressed in black leathers. He was taller than Parolla remembered, and he wielded a sword that left tendrils of shadow behind where it cut through the air. Sorcerous wards glittered about him. There was a casual arrogance to his movements, an almost lazy elegance to his attacks as he blazed a path through his assailants.

As each Vamilian warrior fell, the strand of death-magic holding him shriveled and vanished.

The undead were converging on the man from all sides. Those that came within range of his wards burst into flames, but they pressed ahead regardless, burning like torches until the swordsman's blade cut them down. From behind a protective cordon of spearmen, a Vamilian *magus* unleashed a volley of sorcery at the man. He countered with sorcery of his own, and the magics collided with a hiss and a thump that set the ground trembling. Parolla threw out her arms to steady herself. When the shadows lifted there was no sign of the undead *magus* or his protectors. The nearby ruins had been razed to their foundations, throwing dust into the air.

Tumbal's spectral form materialized beside Parolla. "My Lady, dost thou see? Where the stranger's blade falls, the Vamilians lie still."

"The book's threads have been cut, *sirrah*."

"Hallowed weapons," the Gorlem breathed. "We knew Mayot had thrown down his gauntlet at Shroud's feet. Now we see the god's response."

"And also, I think, a measure of how seriously he takes Mayot's threat."

Tumbal looked over. "Thou dost recognize this stranger?"

Parolla nodded. She'd only met him once, but the encounter was hardly one she was likely to forget. "His name is Andara Kell. One of Shroud's elite."

"A friend?"

"Hardly. Years ago, while I traveled in the west, I made it my business to . . . be present at . . . the deaths of certain powerful individuals. My hope was that Shroud would appear in person to lead their souls through his Gate. He never did, of course. Instead I met the disciples he sent in his place. On one occasion—the death of Muthin Qumari, the Sun Blade and First Protector of the Qaluit Empire—it was Andara Kell who came."

"He wanted to honor this warrior?"

"No, to challenge him. To test this champion's skill for himself."

The Gorlem cocked his head. "But would not Qumari's defeat have meant—"

"The destruction of his soul, yes. My presence put an end to Andara Kell's plans."

"A turn of events for which he did not thank thee, I presume?"

That was one way of putting it. Parolla saw Andara's head turn in her direction, and she ducked down. "Most of Shroud's servants ignored me when I met them," she said to Tumbal. "Some were civil enough. Andara was different. He took a keen interest in me. I suspect he would have killed me if my replies to his questions had not been to his liking."

"He would dare to slay one of his own master's progeny?"

"Oh, come, you should know by now that my blood grants me no paternal privileges. A fact that Andara was at pains to point out. All that saved me, I believe, was his contempt. I was newly come into my power, then. No threat to him." Now, though . . .

Shroud's disciple continued his advance. Black lightning streaked from his blade as he carved a path through the spearmen defending a Vamilian sorceress.

"Dost thou intend to intervene?" Tumbal said.

"On whose side?"

The Gorlem raised an eyebrow. "My Lady? Will not Andara Kell also have come here to bring about Mayot's downfall? Dost thou not share with him that goal?"

Parolla did not reply. Andara had fought his way to the Vamilian sorceress. The remaining warriors guarding her burst into flames at his approach, then melted away beneath his flashing sword. A backhand swing cut the sorceress in half even as her white cloak caught fire. Andara stepped over her body and turned left at the next intersection. Parolla said, "The fight is coming this way, *sirrah*. Perhaps we should leave now, while we still can."

"I fear it may already be too late for that."

Parolla glanced sharply at the Gorlem. He was not looking at her, though, but to the south and east. Following his gaze, Parolla saw dozens of Vamilians streaming through the ruins toward her. Cursing, she retreated down the steps. Tumbal had vanished, and not for the first time she found herself envying his ability to disappear whenever danger loomed. Her mind raced. She did not know whether she or Andara Kell was the newcomers' target, but it hardly mattered now— the Vamilians were a mere stone's throw away, meaning they couldn't have failed to see her. Judging by the state of the ruined buildings nearby, there was nowhere for her to hide. She could conceal herself in shadows, of course, but her sorcery would doubtless draw an undead *magus* to her.

Then her gaze fell on the statue of the ship in the middle of the square. Could she take cover within what remained of its hold? There were no openings in its hull on this side, but perhaps on the other . . .

Even as she strode toward it, the first of the Vamilians poured into the square.

CHAPTER 18

LUKER WATCHED leaves blow across the deserted settlement. A rumble shook the air. For an instant he thought
the storm was breaking. Then a flash of red lit up the skyline, and he realized it was just magic he was hearing. The rumble
sounded again, louder this time. It came from the direction they were
heading in. Since leaving the White Road in the early hours this morning the Guardian had witnessed dozens of distant sorcerous clashes,
and he wondered whether someone had got to Mayot already. Maybe
even Kanon. His master had lost days in Arandas chasing after the
Spider's false trails. If he'd picked his way through the forest with his
usual care then perhaps he was just catching up to Mayot now.

Footfalls sounded behind Luker. He looked over his shoulder to see
Jenna picking her way toward him through the ruined buildings. Her
hair was tied back in a ponytail, and she had strapped a baldric of
throwing knives across her chest. There were black bags beneath her
eyes, and her movements betrayed a weariness that had nothing to
do with the pace Luker had been setting. It was the Book's threads,
he knew, drawing out her life force like a spider leech sucking on
her blood. Luker himself had started to feel a lethargy settle on him
over the past few bells, but it had lifted once he fashioned his Will
into a shield against the death-magic.

Not for the first time, he was struck by how young Jenna was. The
scars she'd earned in Arkarbour had aged her, yet she still looked more
than a dozen years his junior. He felt those years. Jenna had never told
him how old she was, but then she'd never told him anything about
her life before they ran into each other on that rooftop in Mercerie.

Three years ago now. Three years since she had made a shot few professionals could match. How long had she been an assassin before he met her? What had forced her into the game so young? He suspected he would never find out.

She halted in front of him. "Is this your idea of keeping watch? Sitting on a wall?"

"Ruins here means less trees, means less death-magic," Luker said. "I'd sense the stiffs coming before I saw them."

The assassin sat beside him. "Where are they, then, these Vamilians? After that first attack the only ones we've seen have been dead."

"Maybe Shroud's lackeys are hurting them."

"You reckon this'll all be over by the time we get wherever we're going?"

"Hope not."

Jenna laughed. "After what happened on the White Road—"

"I've a thought about that," Luker cut in.

"About how to deal with the undead?"

"Aye."

"Well?"

"You'll see."

The silence drew out. Luker cast a look over the settlement. The ruined building where Merin and Chamery were resting was visible through the branches of a wolsatta tree. Hobbled beneath the tree, the horses stood with heads bowed. Yesterday Luker had pressed on through the night, ignoring Merin's request for a halt until they reached this settlement a couple of bells ago. Luker had been standing guard the whole time since then. Maybe he should have woken one of the others and snatched some sleep, but he had too much on his mind to rest.

Jenna made to rise. "I'll leave you to your thoughts."

Luker laid a hand on her arm. "No. Stay a while."

The assassin searched his gaze for a moment, then nodded.

Feeling restless, Luker stepped down from the wall. The building of which it formed part must once have belonged to someone wealthy, for the black and white tiles of a mosaic floor were visible beneath the dirt and leaves. Beside Luker's foot was the head of a statue, its features erased by the centuries. "I've been thinking," he said at last. "About what I'm going to do when this is over."

"You really think you'll live through this?"

He shrugged. "Just because Merin and Chamery are going to step into Shroud's path doesn't mean I have to. I'm not here for the Book."

"But Kanon is. You didn't come all this way just to let him stand alone."

"Kanon can't speak my lines forever. He's always been tight with the Guardian Council. Not me, though. I could never make Kanon's cause my own, however much I might've wanted to." It had to mean something, right? And if it didn't, he had to find something that did, no matter how long the search took. "Aye, I'll not walk out on him now, but when we're done here . . ."

"What will you do?"

Luker picked up one of the black mosaic tiles only for it to crumble in his fingers. "Wish I knew. Since we left Arkarbour, first time in a while I've felt . . . steady. Not plagued by the same old doubts."

Jenna's expression was unreadable. "Why?"

"Maybe because I'm where I want to be. Maybe because I've not had to worry about why I'm doing what I'm doing. After I find Kanon, though . . ."

"You think the doubts will come back." The assassin forced a smile. "You could always ask Kanon to run off again. After you've tracked him down, I mean."

"Funny," Luker said. "What about you? You thought any more about where you'll go? What you'll do?"

Jenna's smile faded. "I'm not going to get out of this alive."

"Sure you will. Just stay close to me. I'll see you through."

The assassin said nothing.

Luker held her gaze for a few heartbeats before looking away. "It's time we were moving. We'd best wake the others."

Romany peered into the clouds of smoke that shrouded the domain of the Kinevar gods. The trees around her burned with a sorcerous heat she could feel even in her spiritual form. The threads of Romany's web were withering in the glow, and she retreated to the hanging gallery of undead, tutting all the while.

Still she could find no way of approaching the battle between the Kinevar gods and Mayot's forces, which meant she *still* had no clear idea of how long the conflict had left to run. The sands of time were running out quickly, though, for the battlefield was now a league across at most, a fraction of the size it had been when she had last come this way three days ago. On all sides legions of undead were clawing free of their arboreal prisons as the last vestiges of earth-magic faded from the trees holding them. The tipping point in the conflict was close, Romany sensed. She had just a few bells left in which to engineer the death of her final victim before retiring from the game and leaving Mayot to the tender care of Shroud's disciples.

The clang of steel on steel interrupted her thoughts—a perception not from her spiritual body, but from her corporeal one back in Estapharriol. She paid it no mind.

Scores of Shroud's minions were now converging on Mayot's stronghold, cutting a swath through the undead hordes with their weapons of oblivion. Up until now the Vamilians, under Romany's direction, had prevented the foe from banding together in great numbers, but Shroud had responded by assembling squads of his disciples beyond the borders of the forest. Now they were on the march. The largest, a group of Black Priests under the command of an Everlord, was just thirty-five leagues west of Estapharriol, and Mayot had sent a veritable army of undead to intercept them. As a result, dozens of Shroud's other followers wandered unopposed through the more distant parts of the forest. Romany had given up trying to track them all, confining her attention to Estapharriol and the woods round it. It was a move she had been loath to make, since it meant new pieces might appear on the game board without warning, leaving her insufficient time to orchestrate a countermove. Just a handful of days ago, for instance, she had seen a small party of Fangalar enter the forest to the west and start butchering the Vamilians with reprehensible fervor. Where were they now? And why had—

The crash of weapons sounded again in the ears of her corporeal body. What *was* that racket? More to the point, why was it getting louder with each moment? Hastening back along her web to her house in Estapharriol, Romany opened her eyes. Danel sat by the far wall of the room, watching her with her unblinking gaze. The priestess rose and crossed to look out of the doorway along the west-facing wall.

In the street outside, four strangers were engaged in a frenzied clash. One of the combatants, a giant of a woman clad in blackened chain mail, was a disciple of Shroud. Shaven-headed, she had a nose that had evidently been broken so many times she'd given up trying to reset it. She carried a longsword and a shield that had been mangled into something barely recognizable. Facing her were three brownrobed figures carrying maces and figure-eight shields. Each wore his hair in a topknot and had a long plaited beard. Their flaming eyes marked them as warrior-priests of the fire god, Hamoun.

The combatants were only a dozen paces from Romany's vantage point, but she was not concerned. Thanks to the sorcerous wards she'd spun about her abode, there was no risk of the strangers seeing her, let alone stumbling inside. That being the case, and since Romany was in no hurry to return to the hanging gallery of Kinevar, perhaps she could spare a few moments to watch this drama unfold.

The swordswoman had shoulders wider than any of her three male opponents and wielded her sword with a speed that belied her bulk. This particular disciple of Shroud had proved to be something of a nuisance to Romany, having survived the three previous encounters with the undead the priestess had arranged for her. On one occasion she'd even contrived to blunder into an ambush intended for another of Shroud's minions, thereby saving the fortunate man's life, albeit temporarily. This time, to put the matter of her fate beyond doubt, Romany had enlisted the unwitting help of Hamoun's monks, all of whom remained, for now at least, among the living.

It was of course absurd that these enemies of Mayot Mencada should be fighting each other so close to where Mayot himself was holed up. Or rather it would have been were it not for the illusory threads of death-magic emerging from the chests of all four strangers—threads that Romany herself had spun just a quarter of a bell ago. She smiled. Such a simple ruse, yet the fools were clearly so accustomed to tripping over Mayot's servants that, on encountering each other earlier, they had not hesitated to attack.

Ah, and here come the Vamilians to join the fun.

The street was suddenly swarming with undead, surging from the ruins on all sides. If the swordswoman and the monks had stopped to think about it they might have wondered why the Vamilians were attacking not just them but also their erstwhile opponents. *Then again, they probably have other things on their minds just now.* The undead had driven a wedge between the four strangers, and the swordswoman retreated down a side street, leaving a trail of motionless corpses in her wake. The monks, meanwhile, were fighting with their backs to each other, wielding their maces against . . .

Romany blinked.

The Vamilians had thrown down their spears and were now hurling themselves at the warrior-priests with only their bare hands as weapons, seeking to seize the monks' maces or shields.

Curious.

She must have spoken the thought aloud because a moment later Danel said, "The master wants them taken alive."

Romany looked at the girl. "What's that, my dear?"

"He bleeds them dry. The weaker ones—those not fit to be his champions. Their life force gives him back the years the Book takes from him."

"You have seen him do this?"

"I have seen what he leaves behind. Empty husks, their owners' souls consumed."

Romany suppressed a shudder. Yet another of the Book's powers that the Spider, in her wisdom, had not seen fit to warn her about. It seemed the old man had found a way to negate the harmful effects of the Book's death-magic on his health. His strength was growing.

The monks' maces were inflicting terrible damage on the unarmed Vamilians. A mound of twitching bodies now surrounded the warrior-priests, and it swelled as more undead fell broken beneath their attacks. Romany saw a female Vamilian clamber over her fallen kinsmen and succeed in wresting a shield from the grasp of one of the monks before a blow from his mace smashed her knees to shards. To the woman's left, a white-robed man took a mace full in the face. His skull crumpled with a wet, crunching sound, gray matter spurting between cracked bone. Somehow, though, he managed to stay on his feet, and he continued groping toward the warrior-priests, his fingers hooked into claws.

Romany tore her gaze away.

The expression of the Sartorian scout was hidden by the mud plastered across her face. Shifting her weight from one foot to the other, she kept her gaze on the ground between the hooves of Garat Hallon's horse. *But is she more concerned,* Ebon wondered, *about the news she brings, or the consel's reaction to it?*

Garat took a drink from his flask. "Report!" he said at last.

"Sir, the river curls away north and south—"

"What you're telling me, soldier, is that we're trapped in a bend."

The scout nodded. "The stiffs have already moved to cut off our retreat."

"How many?"

She shrugged.

"Any gaps in the line? Any places we could attempt a breakout?"

Another shrug.

From beside Ebon, Vale said, "They've been herding us like lederel for the last bell."

"I'm aware of that," Garat said, still looking at the scout. "What I'm less clear on is how this was allowed to happen . . ."

Ebon did not hear his next words. A flash of light, then Galea stood before him in his mind's eye. The sleeveless white dress she'd worn previously had been replaced by a long, almost translucent gown dyed green to match the color of her eyes. She gave no greeting, but then Ebon doubted she was here to exchange pleasantries. "We're in trouble, aren't we?" he said.

"You've walked into a trap, mortal. A *geralid* mage is at your back—one of my elite from the days of empire."

"A pity you did not think to warn us earlier."

"Be grateful that I'm warning you at all. Were it not for me, you would soon be joining the ranks of Mayot Mencada's servants."

Ebon struggled to hold her piercing gaze. "Are we to fight them?"

"No. I will not aid you in attacking my people."

"Can you break the threads holding them?"

"I could. The power required to do so, however, would burn you to a crisp."

"Then why are you here?" Ebon grated, his temper rising. "We do not have time for this."

Galea was a long time in answering. "There is a bridge to the south and west."

"Is it guarded?"

"No."

"But . . . you said this was a trap. Why would the undead go to the effort of driving us here, only to leave us an easy way out?"

"You will see for yourself soon enough."

Ebon mastered his irritation. "What lies beyond the bridge?"

"The city of Estapharriol, once the capital of this forest kingdom." The goddess's mouth twitched. "And for you, the end of the journey."

With that, she was gone.

Another burst of white and the forest came into focus once more. Garat was still ranting at his scout.

"There is a bridge, Consel," Ebon cut in. "South and west of here."

Garat rounded on him. "My patrol would have seen . . ." His expression grew wary. "How? How do you know this?"

Ebon ignored the question. He could now hear the jangle of armor to his left, see flickers of movement between the trees—white-robed figures for the most part, but there were larger, darker shapes among their ranks. Two four-armed warriors strode ahead of the throng, stripped to the waist. In each hand they carried a spear. The nearest of the two pulled back an arm and hurled a spear at Ebon, only for the weapon to tangle in the low branches of a tree.

Ebon wasn't waiting for the next. He turned his horse. South and west the goddess had said, but with the sun hidden behind storm clouds one direction looked much the same as the next. The river lay ahead of him, though, a faint rustle of water above the wind, and he urged his destrier toward it.

Within moments he came upon the remains of a road, its flagstones half-buried beneath dead leaves. It made sense it should lead to the bridge, so he swung his mount onto it. To either side, the trees leaned over the road to form a brown latticed tunnel, and one trunk had fallen across the way. As Ebon's horse hurdled it he heard a cry from behind, but he dared not take his gaze from the road to look round. Already the murmur of water had risen to a hiss in his ears, and as the trees thinned, the muddy banks of the river came into view, covered in froth and scum. Ebon saw the bridge . . .

Or where it must once have been.

Now all that remained were stubs of broken rock protruding an armspan over the swift, gray sweep of the river. Chunks of stone were scattered along its banks and in the shallows at the water's edge, and patches of white foam in the center of the channel hinted at more blocks beneath the surface. Ebon drew up his destrier next to the ruined crossing.

Garat sawed on his horse's reins as he came alongside. He laughed. "Is this your bridge? Would you have us walk on water, then?"

Ebon glanced up- and downriver. The watercourse curled away for fifty paces in each direction before disappearing from view behind the trees and nettleclaw growing thick along its banks. No bridge in sight. Downriver a ketar tree had fallen partway across the flow, but Ebon doubted that was what Galea had been referring to. Could there be a second crossing farther along one of the banks? If so, it was useless to him now, for the undead horde would descend on him before he hacked his way through to it. The Sartorian horses were stamping and milling about. Someone shouted a warning, and Garat ordered the soldiers to turn and face the enemy.

Ebon sent a thought questing inward. *Well, my Lady, what now?*

Even before he had finished framing the question, Galea swirled into his mind like a breath of glacial air. He felt her release her power through him and gasped as his blood ran cold. A chill started at the tips of his fingers and toes before spreading along his arms and legs. His palms itched, and he rubbed them along his saddle.

From the corner of his eye he saw Garat drag his sword from its scabbard, raise his blade to signal the charge.

The chunks of rock along the banks began to rise, making sucking sounds as they pulled free from the mud. There was movement within the river too, water frothing as more stones broke the surface, streaming foam. The rocks spun slowly round as they lifted and converged on the place where the bridge had once been. They came together with a grinding noise to form a new crossing, wide enough for half a dozen horsemen to ride abreast.

The Sartorians had fallen silent, and Ebon could now hear the stamp of feet from the east as the undead host approached. They were closing quickly, no time to hesitate. Stepping down from his saddle, he led his destrier to the crossing. The centuries had smoothed the edges of the stones, and through the gaps between them he could see the river rushing below, misty gray air between. A handful of dead birds swept past on the current.

He shuffled closer to the bridge, then paused.

"If you're gonna do it, do it now," someone behind him said.

Whispering a silent prayer to the Watcher, Ebon tested his weight on the first suspended block.

It held.

He took another step, then another. Many of the stones were caked in mud and slick with water, and the largest of the cracks between them were wide enough to snag a boot or a hoof. Ebon moved from one rock to the next as if they were stepping-stones, stopping each time to allow his destrier to find footings. The stones were set firmly, thank the Watcher. At the center of the bridge he looked back and gestured for his companions to dismount and follow.

Vale came first, his horse's reins held lightly in one hand in case the animal slipped or bolted. Behind him was the consel, his expression calculating. The Sartorian soldiers brought up the rear, and Ebon counted them as they filed past. *Seven.* Meaning one had fallen during their flight to the river—the cry he had heard earlier? He did not trust the goddess to hold the crossing in place any longer than she had to, so he waited until the last of the soldiers passed before turning to follow. Ahead one of the Sartorian horses took fright and dragged its rider to within a handspan of the edge before it was brought under control.

Hurry, Ebon silently urged.

The tramp of enemy feet from the east became louder. On the far bank one of Garat's men unslung his bow and fired an arrow at something behind Ebon. When the king looked back he saw the two four-armed warriors emerge from the trees, each now carrying but a single spear. They stepped onto the bridge and set out across it.

Just as the last of the Sartorians reached the other side. Ebon was a pace behind.

Abruptly Galea's power faded in him, and the crossing collapsed, pitching the undead into the river and sending up fountains of spray.

The first Vamilian spearman ran across the square toward Parolla, and she released her power. A stream of coruscating blackness hit the man. Blisters formed on his face. Then his hair, his robes, and finally his armor burst into flames. Parolla didn't ease up on her attack, though—the Vamilian wasn't going to let a small thing such as being set on fire slow him. Sure enough, he tried to advance against her sorcerous onslaught, only for his boots to slide on the chips of stone on the ground. He went down. As wave after wave of Parolla's magic battered him, his flesh turned black and sloughed from his bones. Moments later his skeleton crumbled to ash.

A group of Vamilians had entered the square behind, and Parolla's power cut through them like a scythe through a field of mexin. A shadow fell across her vision, making it seem as if dusk had fallen. Among the undead was a black-robed *magus,* bald and stooped with age. He sent a shaft of fire roaring at her, and it thundered into her wards with a concussion that hurled the nearby Vamilians from their feet. Parolla's counterattack shredded his defenses like they were wisps of cloud, and he was ripped apart by the dark swell of her sorcery.

Parolla's lip curled. Were these the best Mayot had to send against her? He might as well have left them buried in the ground for all the threat they posed.

Time became a blur. More Vamilians rushed at Parolla, only to be cut down by her power. A wall to her left came crashing to the ground.

She was vaguely aware of something thrown at her—a spear?—and watched with detached interest as it struck her wards and disintegrated. The rubble on the ground, the buildings round the square, even the remains of the statue of the ship: all were crushed to dust by the storm of sorcery. Clouds of powdered stone now hung in the air, tugged this way and that by the wind.

Slowly Parolla became aware that there was no one left to face her. *More!* She looked round for the next enemy, but the square was empty. All about, the ruined buildings had been reduced to banks of ash. Nothing remained of the Vamilians except for the occasional helmet or piece of armor, warped and smoldering. Reluctantly Parolla gave up her power, and the shadows across her vision paled, but did not fade entirely. How long had the skirmish lasted? How many of the undead had she killed? *No, not killed,* she told herself. *Released.* The Vamilians were dead already, after all. Their souls were free now, weren't they? Liberated from Mayot's enslavement. What she had done to them was a blessing.

There was movement at the corner of her eye, and she turned to see Andara Kell approaching. His eyes shone in the gloom, yet in spite of their glow they remained somehow lifeless, as if they were windows on a soul as dark and foreboding as the sorcerous shadows that enveloped him. He was breathing heavily. Earlier when Parolla had watched him fight it had seemed as if not a single opponent had got close enough to lay a glove on him, but closer now she saw his shirt had been cut to ribbons and was soaked through with blood. Had her presence here saved his life by drawing some of the undead away? She doubted it, for there was still a disturbing poise to the swordsman, an avidness to his gaze.

And he had not sheathed his blade.

Parolla drew in a whisper of power again, felt it tingle in her fingertips.

Andara stopped a few paces away. "Well, well," he said. "This is indeed a pleasant surprise."

"The pleasure is all yours, *sirrah*. For me, one meeting was enough."

The swordsman smiled. "I have been looking for you everywhere, *jezaba*. So many questions left unanswered after our first meeting. So many doubts unresolved. Countless empires I have traveled, seeking word of you. And yet after all my searching, it is *you* who come to *me*."

Parolla held his gaze. If he expected her to back down as meekly as she had the last time, he was mistaken. "I didn't come here to find you."

"Indeed. Why *are* you here, then?"

"I could ask the same of you."

Andara lifted his sword and inspected it for nicks. "I do so dislike having to repeat myself. Please don't make me ask again."

Parolla considered. Her safest option was to feign ignorance concerning Mayot and the source of his power, and so she shrugged and said, "The forest is brimming with death-magic. It draws power like a lodestone. Where else would I be?"

"I really don't care, so long as it is somewhere else."

"Can you blame my curiosity? Here is a power that can call souls back through Shroud's Gate, can animate an army of undead, all to the considerable irritation of my beloved father, no doubt. And now here you are, one of his most trusted servants"—Andara scowled at her use of the word—"come to this place in order to, what? Challenge whoever wields that power? Take it for yourself, perhaps?"

"This does not concern you, *jezaba.*"

"*What* does not concern me?"

"Any of it. The pretender's claim—"

"'Pretender'?" Parolla cut in. "Does your master consider this rival a threat, then?"

"A nuisance, no more than that. Even now the mage's defenses are being torn asunder, assailed from all sides."

Parolla stiffened. *All sides?* Had Shroud sent other disciples to the forest, then? If his servants were here in numbers she might be forced to reconsider her plans. She forced a light tone. "All sides, *sirrah?* Does your master not trust you to complete the job alone?"

Andara's eyes flashed. "It is *because* he trusts me that I am here now. To finish this before there are further losses."

"Who? Who has been lost?"

"The Widowmaker, Bar Kentar, Jelan Gelan, others. A much-needed whittling down of the weaker elements of my Lord's forces."

Parolla covered her surprise. She had heard those names before. *Weaker elements?* "Have they been resurrected like the Vamilians? Do they now fight for the pretender?"

"Of course not. Shroud would never permit his disciples to be used against him like that." Andara's smile returned. "Doubtless the fools cower before him even now, begging forgiveness for their incompetence."

A gust of wind blew Parolla's hair across her face, and she reached up a hand to push it aside. "It would appear your Lord underestimated the scale of the opposition he faced."

"No longer."

"You are sure of that?" An image came to Parolla's mind of the undead forces battling the Kinevar gods. "Perhaps the pretender has held back the greater part of his strength."

The swordsman took a step toward her. "And perhaps you know more of this than you are letting on."

Parolla kept her expression even. "I was simply observing that there seem to be more of these undead as we approach the pretender's stronghold."

Andara sneered. "The Vamilians are weak."

"And if the Vamilians are not the only opponents you have to contend with? There may be others drawn to this place as I have been."

"Then they will meet the same fate as the pretender." He looked at her pointedly. "If they are foolish enough to step into my path, that is."

"Perhaps I can be of assistance."

The swordsman went still, the aura of darkness around him deepening. "Now why would you make such an offer, my dear?"

Parolla's pulse quickened. Had she made a misjudgment? Not a genuine offer of help, of course, but Andara could not have known that. "Such suspicion, *sirrah*. Do you count me as an enemy, then?"

His gaze bored into her, but she did not look away. A moment's inattention was all he needed to launch an attack. "Stay out of this," he said at last. "Shroud is in no mood to tread softly. Your presence here will only muddy the waters."

"You're saying he does not trust me?" she said with exaggerated hurt. "His own flesh and blood."

Snorting, Andara sheathed his blade. "I have wasted enough time on you. Leave this place. Run while you still can. Because when this is over I will come looking for you again. And the next time we meet will be the last, I promise you that."

As he strode past, his shoulder brushed Parolla's, and her skin tingled at the touch of his wards. She turned to watch him walk away.

Tumbal's ghostly form appeared at her shoulder. "What now, my Lady?"

"We follow."

The Gorlem's brows lifted. "Thou wilt risk Andara Kell's wrath?"

"Will he risk mine? He fears me. There is no other explanation for what just happened here. For all his talk of hunting me down, he would never have left a loose end at his back unless he had to."

"And is he right to fear thee?"

Andara had reached the edge of the settlement and now vanished into the forest beyond. He must have had a horse, for Parolla heard it whinny. "For years now, *sirrah*," she said to Tumbal, "I have sought Shroud out, and always he has ignored me. Soon, though, he will have to break his silence. Soon . . . when I have what he wants."

"Then I hope he is able to give thee the answers thou seek'st."

Parolla frowned at the note of regret in his voice. "You do not need to go on. If Shroud has other servants nearby they may be able to grant you release."

"No, my Lady."

"No?"

"I will see this through. Having come this far, I cannot abandon thee now."

Parolla gave a faint smile. "A noble gesture. Though no doubt you are also curious to see how this sorry tale ends, am I right?"

The Gorlem sighed. "There is that."

Hovering in spirit-form at the foot of Mayot's dais, Romany stared up at the old man on his throne. Danel had warned her of Mayot's newfound ability to steal the life force of others, yet still the mage's transformation shocked her. His hunch was less pronounced, and there were flecks of gray in his white hair and beard. He sat poring over his wretched Book, not yet deigning to acknowledge her presence. On the floor in front of him was the body of a naked man, sprawled in death. His hands were bound behind him, and his skin was wrinkled as if he had just been fished from the river. Romany grimaced. It was only a small mercy his face was turned away from her, for she could read the suffering of his final moments in the contortions of his limbs.

Romany looked round the dome. The ranks of Mayot's champions had swelled, as had the crowd of Vamilians drawn up behind them. A sure sign, the priestess told herself, of the mage's growing fear, for it was a characteristic male failing to equate numbers with strength, brute force with power. The old man had good reason to fidget in his chair. It turned out the incursion by the Everlord and his Black Priests had been no more than a feint, for they had retreated west as Mayot's army of undead drew near. Meanwhile, another group of Shroud's followers, perhaps thirty in all, had gathered to the north and was now advancing on Estapharriol. Recognizing the danger, Mayot had redirected some of his forces from the attack on the Kinevar gods in an attempt to head off this new threat, and along the threads of her web Romany sensed a fierce battle taking place fifteen leagues from the city. A smaller band of disciples was approaching on boats along the Sametta River from the south, and while the Vamilians had begun felling trees in order to fashion crude obstructions across the waterway, Romany doubted they would delay Shroud's minions for long.

She brought her attention back to her immediate surroundings. Among the undead in the dome were scores of wraithlike figures. When the priestess had first arrived she'd assumed they were merely shadows. Now that her eyes had grown accustomed to the gloom, though, she could see them for what they really were. *Spirits.* Shades from beyond Shroud's Gate. The barrier that separated the mortal realm from the underworld was being dissolved by the Book's magic. For now the spirits were little more than faceless black blurs, but their forms would coalesce as the veil weakened further.

Romany cleared her throat.

When Mayot's gaze fixed on her, his eyes held their usual bloodshot malice. "Ah, it's you, woman. But in spirit-form only, I see. Do you no longer dare to face me in the flesh?"

"You mistake fear for distaste. In any event, it is becoming a little crowded in here."

"What do you want? My time is precious."

"I can imagine. You are keen, no doubt, to savor your last few bells among the living."

The old man's errant eyelid began to flutter. "You have taunted me for the last time."

"I fear that may be wishful thinking—"

"Silence!" Mayot roared. The golden-armored Vamilians flanking the throne had put their hands on their sword hilts, though what damage they thought they could do to Romany's spirit she could not guess. "Do you think," the mage went on, "you are safe from me just because you are here in spirit-form? I shall send your soul shrieking to the Abyss."

"You are not interested, then, in the gift I bring you?" Romany said mildly.

Mayot sat forward in his chair. "Gift?" he whispered. "You will surrender the remaining secrets of the Book to me?"

"I had in mind knowledge of a different kind. The final resting place of—"

The mage's snort cut her off. "You're wasting my time. I have already resurrected every creature my servants can dig up."

"Every creature you could *find*, yes."

His eyes narrowed. "You have hidden something from me?"

More than you could possibly imagine. "Not so much hidden as held back until the appropriate moment. A tiktar, my Lord. I see you are familiar with the name. A worthy addition to your forces, yes?"

Mayot's eyes shone greedily. "Where is it?"

Romany wagged a finger at him. Did he really think she would yield the knowledge to him here, with his knife pressed to her throat? "When I am ready. After all, I have in mind a very particular target for the elderling."

The old man wriggled on her hook. "Who?"

Luker squinted through the trees but could make out nothing through the clouds of leaves whipped up on the wind. There could be a whole Shroud-cursed army just a stone's throw in front and he wouldn't know it. Nor was there any point trying to use the Will to scout ahead, so thickly were the strands of death-magic clustered.

Each time he rode through one of the threads he felt a whisper of cold, chilling the sweat on his skin. Of his companions only Chamery seemed unaffected by the Book's sorcery. The mage had been soaking up dark energy all morning. Now he was filled to bursting, his face flushed as if with excitement, his outline blurred amid a fog of death-magic. Even to look at the boy made Luker's vision swim. Whenever their gazes met Chamery would give him a challenging smile, and it occurred to the Guardian he'd missed a trick by not putting the mage in his place before they'd entered the forest. Chamery's indiscipline would likely cost them all before this was over. Already his horse was suffering from his excesses. The animal, partially obscured by the shadows that swirled about its rider, stumbled onward with head bowed and eyes glazed as if it were walking in its sleep.

Distant sorcerous explosions split the air on all sides. Thus far Luker had been able to steer a rough course between them, but it would not be long before trouble found them. Even as the thought came to him, a dozen Vamilians appeared to his left. Like their kinsmen who'd attacked on the White Road, they were on foot, suggesting either the Vamilian civilization had never used horses or Mayot hadn't thought to resurrect them. Luker didn't much care which was the case so long as it meant the undead could be easily outrun. *Looks like our luck still holds.*

Digging his heels into his horse's flanks, the Guardian led his companions north. The undead changed course in an effort to head them off, but Luker's party was already more than a score of paces in front and pulling farther away with each heartbeat. In this part of the forest the trees were spaced widely apart and the ground was free of nettle-claw, allowing the horses to lengthen their stride. When Luker next checked over his shoulder his pursuers had vanished. Still, he kept the pace steady, knowing the Vamilians would not tire in their chase.

His mare crested a rise.

And ran headlong into another group of undead, twice as large as the last one. Luker swore. Had that first group intended to drive them into a trap? He doubted it, for this new enemy was scattered in ones and twos, not set to receive a charge. The Guardian drew his swords and spurred his mount toward a helmeted man holding a spear. The Vamilian brought his weapon up, but Luker batted the point aside with his Will, then used his left blade to parry a blow from a second attacker. No need to counter with a strike of his own, it wasn't as if he was keeping a score. His horse smashed into the undead warriors and sent them reeling.

As easy as that he was through . . .

Another two score Vamilians appeared between the trees ahead, and Luker tugged on the reins to slow his mount. Looking right and left he saw yet more undead. *Surrounded.*

They had to keep moving, but which way?

A woman brandishing a sword stepped from behind a tree in front of him. Luker parried a cut, turning his wrist at the last moment to send his assailant's blade spinning from her hand. Then he leaned forward and struck her in the face with the hilt of his sword. She sprawled to the ground. A wave of heat broke against Luker's face, and he heard a crackle followed by the sound of splintering wood as a tree came crashing down behind. Chamery laughed.

Missed me again.

Merin was ahead of Luker now, Jenna to the tyrin's right. The assassin had acquired a spear from one of the undead and was twirling it with easy swings to crack the skull of any Vamilian who came within range. Then behind her . . .

Luker's eyes widened as a four-armed man, bare-chested and carrying a sword in each hand, pushed his way through a knot of undergrowth. Like a monster had stepped off the page of a Shroud-cursed picture book. The Guardian spurred his horse to intercept him, and the undead warrior swung round. He darted out of the mare's path before spinning to meet Luker's assault. He wielded his four blades in staggered attacks, each contact sending a jolt down Luker's arm as he parried. For a while the Guardian could do nothing but defend the torrent of blows. Then a feint with his left blade earned him a moment's respite. He lashed out with his Will, sending his opponent toppling to the ground.

Luker yanked on his horse's reins, and the mare reared. To the sound of crunching bone, its hooves came hammering down on the undead warrior once, twice, three times. The man struggled to rise, fell back on shattered legs.

Luker wheeled his mount. A look round revealed the noose of undead tightening about them. "Merin!" he yelled. "Time to leave!"

The tyrin, hacking down at two Vamilian spearmen, growled wordlessly in response.

A cry brought Luker's head round.

Chamery.

The mage had fallen behind and was now surrounded by white-robed figures. His horse had taken a spear in its chest and was coughing red froth. Its front legs buckled. Chamery tumbled from his saddle into a Vamilian spearwoman, and the two of them went down. Luker didn't know whether he was pleased or pissed to see the mage rise again. Chamery's staff stabbed out, striking the woman on the chin. Her outline flashed black, and she crumbled to ash. Chamery's laughter rang out once more.

Luker hesitated before spurring his horse toward him.

Parolla followed the hoofprints of Andara Kell's horse in the powdery leaf fragments on the road. A growl of thunder sounded overhead, and as it faded she heard the distant clamor of battle. The forest round her, though, remained oddly silent, and she could detect no threads of death-magic ahead. Perhaps the presence of Shroud's disciples meant the undead were stretched thin, but so thin not even a single Vamilian patrolled the forest this close to Mayot's stronghold? Parolla frowned. After the power she'd unleashed in the settlement, the old man was unlikely to let her walk up to his front door unchallenged. When her next encounter with his servants came, it would doubtless be more of a test.

The ground sloped downward. Ahead the road split left and right. Beyond the junction was a vast lake—man-made, judging by the stone walls that marked the opposite shore. Washed up on a bank of cracked mud in front of Parolla were the bodies of dozens of animals and birds: wildcats and black boars, ruskits and dusken deer, coral birds and firedrifters. Yet more dead creatures bobbed in the shallows.

Parolla looked along both forks of the road. No sign of Andara, but that wasn't surprising considering how thickly the trees were clustered to either side. The wind was strong in her face, rippling the surface of the lake and forming waves that lapped at the bank. Along the waterfront to Parolla's right was a small harbor, empty of boats, while to her left the road hugged the lake as it curled to the east. Beyond the far shore, a quarter of a league away, the land rose to a line of mounds covered with trees—mounds formed, most likely, from the soil excavated when the lake was created. What had Tumbal called the Vamilians? *Seafarers.* Parolla saw again the statue of the ship in the settlement behind her. Forced to hide from the Fangalar in a place far from the oceans, the Vamilians had apparently tried to bring the sea to them in order to keep alive the memory of their ancestry.

Another rumble of thunder sounded. No, not thunder, the ground was shaking. An earthquake? As the tremors grew in intensity, the waves breaking on the shore started to swell. A hundred paces ahead light blossomed in the depths of the lake, first white, then yellow, then deepening through orange to red. Flames? In the middle of a lake? No, that couldn't be right. And yet suddenly the water was boiling and bulging like a hot spring as something ascended from the depths. Vapor rose in hissing clouds as a fiery shape broke the surface, and within the flames Parolla saw twin pits of blackness that might have been eyes, long arms ending in blazing swords, wings tucked tight to narrow shoulders.

A flicker of fear tugged at her guts. A wave an armspan high came rolling toward her as if the water itself were fleeing the arrival of the creature. Parolla took several quick steps back from the edge of the lake, but the wave still caught her, climbing the shore and spilling onto the road to swirl round her legs. Water poured into her boots. It was several heartbeats before the wave started to recede, pulling at her legs as it retreated.

Tumbal Qerivan materialized beside her. When she glanced across she found him staring at the creature with a look of awe.

"*Sirrah,* what is that thing?"

"A tiktar, my Lady. An elderling from before the dawn of the First Age. I had thought them all dead."

"No doubt they are," Parolla snapped. "Can you not sense the thread of death-magic holding it?"

Tumbal inclined his head. "Of course. In my excitement, I was not thinking. Never did I imagine I would behold such a wonder in the flesh."

"I expect you'll be seeing it at much closer quarters soon."

"Thou must flee, my Lady. The elderling's strength is formidable."

Parolla did not need to be told. She had felt the unveiling of the tiktar's power like a slap in the face. It seemed she'd been too quick to dismiss the threat offered by Mayot's undead servants. It seemed the old man might even have fed her some easy meat in the settlement to make her lower her guard. "Flee, *sirrah*?" she said, her gaze settling on the elderling's wings. "What is the point? It would chase me down easily enough."

The tiktar unfurled its wings and lifted itself clear of the lake with a single flap. Even from this distance Parolla could feel the resulting disturbance in the air. Did the elderling's presence here explain the dearth of Vamilians in this part of the forest? Had the creature been lying in wait for her?

"What do you know about these tiktars?" she asked Tumbal.

The Gorlem blew out his cheeks. "Little, sadly. One of the elder races, without question. Sired, so the ancient writings claim, in the fiery tears of the god Hamoun. Legend has it they were hunted to extinction by the Antlered God himself . . ."

Parolla was no longer listening. The tiktar had risen to the height of the treetops, its head turning from side to side as it searched for something.

"Move away from me," she said to Tumbal.

The Gorlem did as he was bid.

Parolla gathered her power and wove wards about herself. A shadow settled on her vision, dampening the glow of the tiktar's aura. The elderling's head snapped round, and as its gaze locked to

Parolla's she felt the strength of its will, the depths of its cunning. Within her the darkness simmered, and she found her fear draining away. She gave a slow smile. In the settlement she'd wondered if there were any among Mayot's servants who could challenge her. Now she was about to find out. *Come on, then. What are you waiting for?*

As if in answer, the tiktar gave a triumphant shriek. Casting its power out before it like a battering ram, it angled its wings and dived.

But not at Parolla.

It was only then that she saw Andara Kell, mounted on his horse halfway round the lake to her left. His outline was small at such a distance, and Parolla might easily have missed him were it not for the glittering wards of death-magic that suddenly flared about him. Wrestling with his horse's reins, he drew his sword. A wave of black sorcery flashed from it to meet the tiktar's dive. As it hit home the elderling gave another shriek, of rage this time, but it did not slow its descent. It streaked toward its target, trailing flames like a comet.

Andara's retreating horse took him behind a cluster of trees and out of Parolla's sight. She did not therefore see the instant when the tiktar struck, simply heard it as a *whoosh* as of a barrel of blay-fire oil catching light. Picking her way through the dead animals on the bank, she moved forward for a better look. When the combatants came into view again she saw Andara's horse go up in flames. Its cries sounded across the lake until a single swing of one of the tiktar's swords cut it in half.

Andara had already thrown himself clear, and he came to his feet in time to parry a cut from the tiktar's other blade. A flurry of blows from the elderling drove him back into the trees, and his attacker followed, setting fire to the trunks nearby. The combatants disappeared from sight once more.

Parolla chuckled. *And to think I believed the ambush was meant for me.* Such conceit. And yet, something told her she had not seen the last of the tiktar. For in the heartbeat their gazes had met, Parolla had felt an unmistakable sense of threat in the elderling's look, like a warning of intent. If it succeeded in defeating Andara, she suspected it would come for her next.

She looked at Tumbal. "Can Andara win? Can he defeat that thing?"

The Gorlem shrugged helplessly. "How can I say? I know even less of Shroud's disciple than I do of the elderling." His expression brightened. "Perhaps we should stay to—"

"No," Parolla cut in. "Whoever should win here, I would be foolish indeed to pass up this chance to slip away. With luck the two of them may keep each other busy long enough for me to finish my business with Mayot."

Tumbal's face fell, but he bobbed his head. "As thou say'st, my Lady. Thou art correct, of course."

Returning to the road, Parolla pulled off her boots and emptied them of water. A final look at the burning trees along the road to her left, then she turned to the Gorlem.

"I think we'll take the right fork, *sirrah*."

A group of undead spearmen stood between Luker and Chamery, and the Guardian detonated his Will in their midst, hurling them from his path. Chamery was whirling his staff in a circle, spraying sorcery in every direction and laughing all the while. One of the waves of power flashed toward Luker, and he threw up a Will-shield, ground his teeth as the death-magic slammed into it. An accident, that attack? This once, Luker would give the boy the benefit of the doubt.

As his horse butted another undead from its path, the Guardian sheathed his left sword and reached out to Chamery. Grasping the mage's outstretched hand, he hauled him onto the mare behind. The contact left Luker's fingers numb, and he shook out his hand, already regretting his decision to come to the boy's help. If Chamery turned on him now, unleashed everything he had at close quarters . . .

Luker swung his horse round.

Merin and Jenna were no more than a flicker of movement between the trees to the north, and Luker spurred his mount toward them. Half a dozen Vamilians blocked his way. As he gathered his Will to scatter them, Chamery's left hand appeared in his peripheral vision. A crackle of sorcery briefly drowned out the mage's laughter, and a burst of death-magic flashed from his fingertips toward the Vamilians, burning them to ash before rolling on to shear through the base of a tree. As the trunk toppled, another volley of sorcery tore into it, and Luker rode through a rain of glowing cinders and splinters of wood.

"Watch it!" he shouted over his shoulder. "One stray burst and you'll hit the others."

Chamery's only response was another laugh. Luker wished someone would let him in on the joke; he was struggling to see anything funny about their predicament.

He could make out Merin and Jenna more clearly now, fighting back-to-back against a constricting ring of attackers, and the Guardian wondered if the tyrin still objected to her coming along. Jenna thrust the point of her spear into the throat of one of her assailants. It lodged there, and the weapon was torn from her hands as the Vamilian fell to the ground. She pulled a dagger from the baldric across her chest and sent it spinning into the eye of another spearman. The Vamilian did not so much as break stride.

"Keep moving!" Luker called, not knowing if the assassin could hear him.

From the north a group of undead was closing on his companions, two four-armed spearmen at the front. The Guardian urged his horse to greater speed. A Vamilian warrior jumped into his path, and Luker's right sword flashed out to sever the man's sword arm. Another undead reared up, ahead and to his left, but when Luker tried to unsheathe his blade on that side, he found his fingers—still numb from the contact with Chamery's hand—could not clutch the weapon's hilt tightly. The half-drawn sword slipped back into its scabbard.

The mare veered into the Vamilian, trampling him underfoot.

At that moment Merin reached into his belt pouch. There was a glimmer of white as he pulled out a glass globe.

"Shroud's pity, man, wait!" Luker yelled.

But either the tyrin did not hear his words or chose to ignore them, for his arm snapped out and the globe went sailing through the air at the approaching four-armed warriors.

Odds were, Merin had never witnessed the power of the globes first-hand, but Luker had, and the experience with the Kalanese soulcaster had taught him that if you wanted to avoid getting caught in the sorcerous backlash, you'd better throw the damned thing as far as your arm would take it. And how far was the globe going to fly with trees on every side?

He reached out with his Will to catch it.

A spear came hurtling toward him from between the trees. No time to sway out of the way. As he batted it aside with a flick of his mind, his concentration on the globe faltered.

It smashed against the bole of a tree, barely two dozen paces ahead of Merin and Jenna.

Not far enough.

There was a rip of air, then the roar of a storm-tossed sea. A huge wall of gray water, taller than the tops of the trees, appeared at the point where the globe landed and went thundering away in the direction of Merin's throw. The trunks in its path snapped like twigs, and the approaching group of undead vanished beneath the towering swell just as Luker drew level with Merin and Jenna. He halted. The ground was shaking as if a troop of cavalry were bearing down on them. A smaller wave came foaming and crashing through the trees—smaller, but still big enough to loom over Luker in the saddle. To make him wonder why he was sitting here when he could have been fleeing the other way. What was the point in trying to run, though? Better chance of outrunning old age.

Gathering his Will, he fashioned it into a barrier in front of the party. Merin and Jenna, unaware of the invisible wall now shielding them, turned in their saddles and braced themselves for the water's impact.

The wave hit Luker's Will-barrier with a force that made him wince, throwing jets of spray into the air that came splattering down on the Guardian moments later. He blinked water from his eyes. To either side of his shield the wave swept past in a white-flecked tide, plucking Vamilians from their feet. One man was lifted high and folded round a branch. Another was driven into a trunk with bone-breaking force. He tried to grip the wood as the water churned about him, but he was dragged free and sent rolling and spinning to thump into another tree.

Suddenly Luker realized he hadn't extended his Will-barrier behind the party, too. Water now came sloshing round the legs of the horses, and Merin's mount tottered sideways into the invisible shield. Luker's mare whickered and reared. He felt a weight slide from the animal's rump, heard a curse and a splash as Chamery landed in water. The Guardian grunted. *Well enough*. The boy could do with cooling down.

As quickly as the wave had come, it began to subside, leaving the ground submersed like the party had stumbled into a bog. Luker spat out a mouthful of water. It tasted of salt. He was as wet as if someone had emptied a barrel over his head. Still, things could have been a lot worse. As he recalled, Merin hadn't even looked at the globe when he took it from his belt pouch. Might have picked fire instead of water.

Letting his Will-barrier fall, the Guardian turned to survey the devastation. The closest Vamilians were fifty paces behind, bedraggled but mostly unharmed. Even now they were clambering to their feet and reaching for weapons. The section of forest ahead had borne the brunt of the water-magic. The first wave—the bigger one—had created a rough clearing a stone's throw across, littered with branches and the stumps of shattered trees. Fish twitched on patches of clear ground. Fish trapped inside the globe when the wave was caged?

Luker had seen stranger things in his time, he supposed.

Movement to the north snared his attention, and he saw a hooded swordsman splashing toward him. The stranger's cowl concealed the upper part of his face, but a neatly trimmed beard was visible on his chin. One of the undead, Luker realized, for he could sense a thread from the Book emerging from the man's chest. The figure wore black leggings and boots, and an unadorned leather breastplate beneath a cloak of gray wool.

Something familiar about him.

With a growing sense of unease, Luker noticed the swordsman's clothes were dry. The stranger could only have been a short distance from the globe when it smashed, so how in Shroud's name was he still standing when everyone else had been carried away? And why wasn't he wearing the same robes and antique armor as the other Vamilians?

The man raised his hands and pulled back his hood.

The air crawled in Luker's throat.

It was Kanon.

PART IV

RIVER OF LOST SOULS

CHAPTER 19

EBON STARED at his reflection in the dome of death-magic. A shadow of a beard covered his cheeks and jaw, and dark hairs had sprouted across his shaven head. His eyes had lost their mark of spirit-possession, yet they still retained a haunted cast, for while the Vamilians were gone from his mind, when he now closed his eyes he saw the faces of those he had left behind in Majack. Were they ghosts now that they should appear to him like this? Or were they no more than his fears made manifest, a reminder of what he stood to lose if he failed? *If they are not lost to me already.*

The trees closest to the dome had been cut to pieces by the magical construction to leave broken branches scattered across the ground. Any wind-borne leaves that came into contact with the dome burst into flames. Beyond, Ebon could make out the shapes of ruined buildings among the trees. All else was a blur.

Vale moved to stand alongside him. There were dark bags beneath the Endorian's eyes and an uncharacteristic slump to his shoulders. "Looks like someone doesn't want us here."

"Too bad."

"You going to cut a way through? Won't that draw the stiffs to us?"

"Perhaps. Though I suspect this will not be the first time the dome has been breached."

"Any of those other breaches nearby? Can we follow the wall round?"

"We do not have time. I sense . . . urgency . . . from the goddess."

"And?"

"And that's all. I have found her to be more possessive of her se-crets than even Mottle was."

Vale studied him for a moment. "You know what you're doing?"

Ebon read the unasked question in his eyes. "You are wondering if it's still me in here?"

"Is it?"

"For now. If the goddess were to possess me, her fate would be tied to mine."

Vale snorted. "Meaning you're in the firing line while the bitch hides in your shadow."

"It is a risk worth taking, Vale. Even you would not deny that. What chance do we have without her help now that Mottle and Ambolina are gone?"

The Endorian grunted, but did not argue the point. "Just keep your eyes open," he said. "When the time comes, cut her loose before she does it to you."

Ebon ran a hand across his head. He had been thinking the same, but how did he outwit a goddess? A goddess to whom he was oath-bound. A goddess who could read his mind. He felt a whisper of amuse-ment from Galea. "You do not," came her reply. "Now, enough of this foolishness. We are running out of time."

"Time? Time for what?"

But the goddess had already withdrawn.

Shaking his head, Ebon raised his hands with palms facing the dome. As at the bridge he felt ice run along his veins as Galea's sor-cery flowed through him. A cut formed in the black wall, the edges peeling back to leave a gash several paces across, sorcery crackling about its sides. Ebon looked through. In the distance, a vast domed structure rose above the treetops. Closer, he saw the ruins of scores of buildings, little more than crumbling walls and piles of rubble. An image came to him of the gatehouse destroyed by the Fangalar. Was Majack a city of the dead, too, now that the Vamilians had swept through it? Was this all he had left to go back to? "How long has it been since we entered the forest?" he asked Vale. "Nine days?"

"Ten."

"The goddess said the palace still stood. That was four days ago. Could Reynes have held out all this time?"

Vale gave no response, but then Ebon had not expected him to. There were too many unknowns for the Endorian to form an opin-ion. Did the undead have another sorceress like the Fangalar, and if so was she stronger than those of Mottle's Adepts who still lived? How many of Reynes's troops had been able to retreat to the safety of the palace? And most important of all, what, if anything, had Galea done to aid the defense?

Footfalls sounded behind Ebon.

Garat Hallon spoke. "I see you've managed to cut a way through. Impressive. A pity you did not see fit to use your . . . abilities . . . when Ambolina faced the dwarf. A failure of courage, perhaps?"

"If I could have intervened," Ebon said, "I would have."

"Of course. How silly of me to have doubted you. Though I cannot help wondering whether you would find yourself similarly constrained if it were my life that hung in the balance."

Vale barked a laugh. "How many times has he got to save your skin? Seems to me you're still in his debt from Majack."

Garat's expression darkened. "Your dog needs a muzzle," he said to Ebon.

Vale reached for his sword, but the king seized his arm. The Endorian stared at him for a few heartbeats, then shot a glance at the Sartorian. "That's two you now owe him."

Garat ignored the remark, his gaze still on Ebon. "It appears your dog wants me dead. Now why, I ask myself? Surely not because he perceives me as a threat to your kingdom. Doubtless that will have fallen already."

Ebon looked back through the rent in the dome. Magic flickered through the murk ahead, and a distant scream rang out. "Are you sure of that, Consel?" he said. "Have you not wondered at the source of my . . . abilities? The powers I can now call on?" He faced Garat. "The alliances I have forged?"

The Sartorian's attempt at a smile came out more as a grimace.

Then he turned at the sound of weapons being drawn. His soldiers were on their feet, peering between the trees to the north. His new tarda gestured for him to take cover.

Ebon cursed. Had the undead found another way across the river? Or had a second Vamilian force been lying in wait on this bank? If the enemy knew they were here, they might still slip away if the goddess could close the breach in the dome behind them after they passed through it.

Just then one of the consel's soldiers emerged from the trees. The man made a chopping motion with his right hand before pointing back the way he had come and holding up a single finger.

Ebon blinked. *Just one?*

A voice became audible.

"Brute! Foul-tempered beast! Forward! Forward, Mottle commands! No, not that way . . ."

For the first time in days Ebon smiled.

Luker reached out with his senses to examine the thread of death-magic entering Kanon's chest, hoping he had imagined it, knowing he had not. When his gaze finally locked to his master's, he saw his fears confirmed in Kanon's bloodless skin and blue-tinged lips. Luker searched his eyes for some hint of recognition, of friendship even. There was none.

Kanon raised a hand, and the Vamilians closing in halted at the edge of the clearing.

A laugh sounded, and Luker turned to see Chamery advancing. Water dripped from the mage's hair and robes. Did he know who he was facing? If so, he clearly hadn't learned anything from the Black Tower's mauling on the night of the Betrayal. His power roared to life, black waves pouring from his hands to strike a Will-barrier in front of Kanon. The Guardian almost disappeared within a haze of shadow, his shield a pale outline in front of him. The tree stumps about him burst into flames and disintegrated.

Kanon stood unmoving, his gaze still on Luker. If Luker had thrown his weight behind Chamery at that moment, their combined powers might have cracked Kanon's defenses. Instead Luker just watched as his master gestured at Chamery and released his Will. The attack lifted the mage from his feet and hurled him across the glade. The mage hit a tree stump and flopped down into ankle-deep water, his sorcery winking out.

Luker heard Merin speak his name, but none of the words that came after. "Stay out of this," he told the tyrin, dismounting with a splash.

As he approached Kanon, his slow steps were in marked contrast to the whir of his thoughts. He should not have been surprised, he knew, to find his master among the undead. Kanon had lost time in Arandas, yes, but he'd still left the city weeks before Luker left Hamis, and he would have had to crawl here for Luker to stand any chance of overtaking him. The whole thing seemed so obvious now. Kanon would never have left the forest empty-handed, and since Mayot remained in control of the undead and thus in possession of the Book . . .

Luker took a breath. It was, he realized, a truth he'd been hiding from for some time.

A part of his mind, though, still refused to believe. He could feel the force of Kanon's Will in the strength of his gaze. Among the surviving Guardians perhaps only Gill was more powerful, and a mere handful of others could claim parity. Senar Sol, maybe. Sekel Endrada. If Luker hadn't walked out on the Guardians—if he and Kanon had faced Mayot together—this would likely be over by now. No force on earth could stand against the two of them. No force ever had. His eyes narrowed. *Maybe there's still a way.*

He inclined his head. "Master."

"Luker," Kanon said. The lines round his eyes had deepened since Luker last saw him.

"You don't look surprised to see me."

"Mayot sensed your approach. He thought it would be amusing if he sent me to intercept you. A mistake he will come to regret."

"Why?"

"Because you are going to beat me."

"Glad one of us is sure of that."

A hint of a smile crossed Kanon's face. "A crisis of confidence, my friend? Clearly a first time for everything."

"Aye, maybe." Luker nodded at Kanon's drawn sword. "But then, this'll be the first time we've played for keeps. What makes you so certain you know which side the coin will come down on?"

"Against you, my Will is at its weakest."

"You reckon it's any easier for me?"

"Why not? You at least still have something to fight for. The Book of Lost Souls—"

"I'm not here for the Shroud-cursed Book. I came to find you."

Kanon frowned. "It's too late for me, Luker. You must see that."

"The thread holding you—"

"Cannot be broken."

"Maybe together—"

"You don't understand," Kanon cut in again. "Mayot has ordered me to kill you. The Book holds me in an iron fist. I don't have the strength to oppose it directly—it has taken all my Will just to give us this time to talk. Even now my resistance falters. Can you not feel it?"

Luker could. Kanon's power was closing round him like the coils of a boa snake. He focused his own Will, and the pressure eased a fraction. "If you can't help me cut the thread, I'll do it myself."

"If you try, I will kill you." Kanon raised his blade a handspan, then halted the movement with an effort that showed as a tremble in his sword arm. "Even if you succeed, you cannot bring me back. If my soul is freed, it will pass through Shroud's Gate. There's nothing you can do to stop that."

Luker was finding it difficult to breathe. He needed space to think. "What happened to you?"

"We do not have time."

"Tell me!"

Kanon shrugged. "I failed. Mayot is guarded by four undead Vamilian champions. Alone, I was no match for them."

Alone. "I should've been with you."

The shake in Kanon's sword arm was becoming stronger. "But you were not. Do not follow that line of thought, Luker. It will only weaken your resolve. To defeat me, you must control your doubt, your remorse. Clear your mind."

His words stirred in Luker a memory of his first days studying under Kanon on the Sun Road west of Bethin. His concentration slipped, and his master's Will tightened about him. A gasp escaped his lips. His ribs felt as if they would crack.

"You must fight me," Kanon said.

"Fight? I can . . . hardly breathe."

"Focus your Will."

"I'm trying, damn you!"

"Anger will serve you no better than guilt." Kanon paused, then said again, "You must fight me."

Luker's face twisted. *As easy as that?* The thought of finding Kanon had been the one thing driving him since he had left Arkarbour. Now he was supposed to cross swords with him? True, he could not kill his master—Kanon was dead already—but to . . . incapacitate . . . him would just inflict suffering of a different kind. The invisible coils about him tightened again. "There must be . . . another way . . ."

"To save me? No, my friend." Kanon looked over Luker's left shoulder. "But you can still save your companions."

Luker had forgotten the others. He could hear Merin's and Jenna's horses snorting, but their riders remained as silent as if they were spellbound. *Jenna.* The pressure about Luker eased slightly, and he gulped in a lungful of air.

"Better," Kanon said.

"There must be another way," Luker repeated. "Of breaking Mayot's grip on you. If the threads can't be destroyed, what about the Book?"

His master smiled faintly. "To destroy the Book you must first kill Mayot."

And to kill Mayot, I've first got to beat you, aye. So his master had been trying to tell him, but Luker was not of a mind to listen. When he reached out again with his senses toward Kanon's thread of death-magic, though, his master shook his head and raised his sword. Luker swore. He should have found time before now to test the undead's threads more fully, for he still did not know whether it was possible to break the things. But then even if it could be done it would likely take all his concentration. And since Kanon had made it clear he would attack if Luker tried . . .

Luker bowed his head. He understood then what he had to do. Perhaps he could not restore Kanon to life, but there was at least a form of release he could grant him. Luker had always believed his quest would end when he found his master. Now it seemed that was not to be.

The crushing weight around him diminished further, and he drew in a heaving breath.

"About time, my friend," Kanon said. "I had begun to wonder if I'd overestimated you."

Luker unsheathed his swords. "This may hurt some."

His master attacked.

The way ahead was blocked by a throng of undead standing two or three ranks deep. They were turned away from Parolla, facing a clearing barely visible through the trees. A rapid series of clangs sounded.

She should give this place a wide berth, she knew. There was little cover afforded by the trees, and the undergrowth had been trampled into the mud by scores of feet. If she tried to approach any closer she risked being seen, and there was no guarantee that whatever was distracting the Vamilians would continue to claim their attention. And yet, what was it that could hold the undead in such thrall? A duel, judging by the clash of swords, but that did not explain why the Vamilians were standing round watching.

Parolla crept forward. It was slow going, moving from tree to tree, checking all the time for twigs that might snap underfoot. The ground was becoming heavier. Mud sucked at her boots, and her footprints left impressions that quickly filled with water. She frowned. *Water?* As yet the storm clouds had failed to deliver their promised deluge, and even then only the fiercest of downpours could have created such a quagmire. Was there another lake ahead, perhaps? A river that had burst its banks?

Parolla had come as close as she dared. The Vamilians, no more than a score of paces away now, partly obstructed her view, but she could still see enough to recognize that what she had taken for a clearing was in fact . . . something else. Dozens of tree stumps rose like broken columns from the boggy ground. The devastation was worse to her left, where splintered trunks lay partly hidden beneath standing water and tangles of branches.

Near the edge of the clearing to her right, a young man dressed in black robes lay facedown in the mud. Beside him were two riders, one of whom—a grim-faced, middle-aged man with gray hair—was even now swinging down from his mount and hoisting his stricken companion across his saddle. The attention of the other rider, a woman, appeared fixed on two swordsmen battling among the tree stumps.

Parolla shifted her gaze to the combatants. The older of the two seemed familiar—one of the undead she had seen in Mayot's dome when she surprised the *magus* six days ago? It was difficult to know for sure in the half-light. The warrior fought with a breathtaking economy of movement, seemingly always unhurried despite the speed of his opponent: a younger, taller man who wielded two blades as if they were extensions of his arms.

Together the strangers spun a dazzling web of steel in the air. There was a hidden battle taking place as well, Parolla sensed. The clearing thrummed with the clash of invisible energies, a whirlwind of conflicting wills with as many strikes and parries as the swords. There was a bond between these two warriors, she realized—so closely matched in skill, so similar in style and movement that it was like watching a single swordsman duel his own shadow.

What have I stumbled onto here?

Both fighters appeared to be waging some inner conflict too. The soul of the undead warrior thrashed in the grip of Mayot's spiritual chains. Though his efforts did nothing to weaken the book's hold on him, they did have the effect of creating occasional gaps in his defenses. Yet in spite of the younger man's speed, he seemed unable or unwilling to take advantage of the openings when they came. Did he believe his opponent's moments of vulnerability to be no more than shams?

A truly mesmerizing spectacle all in all, though in witnessing it Parolla felt as if she were intruding on something personal.

Whatever the outcome of the duel, there would be no victor here, she knew.

A final look at the combatants, then Parolla began retreating the way she had come.

When Romany had first seen Andara Kell enter the Forest of Sighs she'd immediately recognized him as the man who had attacked her temple all those months ago. Unable to match his power, she had been forced to watch helplessly as he ransacked the shrine. She might have forgiven him for the slaying of her servants—any acolyte careless enough to get caught in his sights was hardly destined for great things, after all—but the blow to her dignity, not to mention the damage to her quarters, was another matter entirely. Had the fool thought he would get away with such an outrage? *Preposterous!* Her only regret was that she could not reveal herself to him now and let him know who had engineered his downfall. Over the past few days she'd worked tirelessly to lead him to the lake beneath which the tiktar was buried. The rest had been easy: simply release her spells of concealment from around the elderling's bones and inform Mayot of their whereabouts.

She watched the tiktar drive Andara backward through the trees with a flurry of attacks too fast for her eyes to follow. The elderling's strength was formidable, and if what she'd read about the creatures was true Shroud's disciple had a few more unpleasant surprises awaiting him. The tiktar had set ablaze the trees round it, and was now drawing on the flames to fuel its power in the same way Andara drew on the death-magic in the air. A burst of fire streaked toward Shroud's disciple from the end of one of the tiktar's blades, causing cracks to appear in the man's sorcerous shields.

With characteristic deftness, Romany started weaving strands of magic about Andara as he fought. Nothing that would arouse his suspicion, of course. Just a touch here to slow his sword arm, a nudge there to hinder his footwork. As ever, it was the little things that made a difference. No doubt the tiktar didn't need any help in dispatching its opponent, but the priestess was not about to take any chances. Truth be told, she'd had doubts about this part of her master plan. By awakening the tiktar she was delivering into Mayot's hands a weapon that could win him the war. For the opportunity to eradicate this particular disciple of Shroud, though, she was prepared to take that risk.

She had watched with interest as Parolla took the right fork round the lake and continued alone toward Estapharriol. Clearly the woman knew Andara, for Romany had seen them talking together after their massacre of the Vamilians in the settlement to the west. But then why had they not traveled together to the lake? And why had Parolla made no move to intervene in Andara's clash with the tiktar? The priestess stroked her chin. Come to think of it, how in the Spider's name had the woman managed to cross half the Forest of Sighs in only six days? A journey of more than fifty leagues? On foot? *Impossible!*

Her thoughts were interrupted by a disturbance in what remained of her web. Another player had entered the game, a short distance to the north. Looking back at Andara and the tiktar, Romany saw Shroud's disciple momentarily seize the initiative, his blades flickering with black flames as he forced the elderling onto the defensive. She hesitated for a heartbeat before flashing toward the new arrival across the intervening stretch of forest.

Well, well.

Not one arrival, as it turned out, but a dozen. Huntsmen, to be precise, riding along a road leading to Estapharriol. Each horseman wore an antlered helm, the front piece of which was shaped to resemble a snarling mountain cat. The lead rider was a huge man garbed from head to toe in plate-mail armor. In one hand he held a half-moon ax; in the other, a battered shield. The antlers on his helm were tipped with silver. Antlers also sprouted, Romany noted with distaste, from the head of the horse he was riding.

A disordered group of Vamilians blocked the road ahead, but the Huntsmen did not check their advance. To the sound of clanging metal and breaking bones, they smashed through the undead.

Frowning, Romany watched the riders thunder into the distance. What interest did the Lord of the Hunt have here? Had the god sent his followers to claim the Book? If so, did he really think he could defeat Shroud's legions of disciples with but a handful of Huntsmen? Then Romany saw the nets hanging from the saddles of the rearmost riders. Magic was woven into the fibers—magic intended to drain the power of anything that became entangled in the nets' links. And since it was safe to assume the Huntsmen weren't here on a fishing trip, they had to be stalking someone. Someone their Lord must want badly indeed to have sent his minions into this godforsaken place. But who? Mayot, perhaps? One of his undead servants?

It mattered not. Whoever the Huntsmen's intended target, their presence here would inevitably bring them, and consequently their Lord, into conflict with Mayot.

And that, Romany decided, could only be a good thing.

Rain had started to fall, and Parolla raised the hood of her cloak. The world all about her was gray, from the cloud-filled skies, to the charcoal husks of trees, to the leaf fragments and ash that had mixed with the rain and mud to turn the ground into a morass the color of steel.

The Vamilians were becoming more numerous, and Parolla had abandoned the main road for a game trail. As she followed it east she had to battle against the urge to run. During the clash at the settlement she had burned off much of the dark energy inside her that had built up since entering the forest, but her power was swelling again.

Tumbal appeared beside her, walking with both sets of arms folded across his chest. "Thou took'st a grave risk at the clearing, my Lady. If but a single Vamilian had observed thee . . ."

"Perhaps your curiosity is catching, *sirrah*."

"Then why did'st thou withdraw? Dost thou not wish to know the outcome of the duel?"

"No, I don't think I do."

Tumbal nodded. "I fear for thee. So many fell powers are converging on this place. I am grateful thou had'st no argument with either of those two dread swordsmen."

"Not *yet,* perhaps," Parolla said. "You forget, one of them is already under Mayot's control. As for his opponent, he will be here for the book, just as I am."

"Thou dost not—"

Parolla raised a hand to cut him off. Ahead there was movement beyond a tangle of undergrowth, and she stepped behind a tree and shot a warning look at the Gorlem. Tumbal's image, though, had already faded to the point that he was almost invisible against the drizzle. The rustle of armor became audible above the patter of rain. Parolla extended her senses. Threads of death-magic, a dozen Vamilians at most. Not a threat, of course, but perhaps she should silence them anyway in case they spotted her and raised the alarm. Power bled from her fingers.

Abruptly she heard hoofbeats, yet she could see no horses between the trees.

Then she realized the noises came not from in front, but behind. And she remembered the Vamilians didn't have horses.

She turned into a wave of light and screamed as sorcery flickered over her. Instinctively she let slip the chains holding back her tainted blood, and the darkness came surging up inside. Power erupted from her, blackness warring with the light in a detonation that ripped apart the trees on all sides and drove Parolla to her knees. For a handful of heartbeats she could see nothing but a fierce white glow. Then, as her vision started to clear, she became aware of blurs of color sweeping past. A trunk groaned and creaked as it fell, hit the ground in a splash of leaves. The ground trembled, and Parolla lowered a hand to the mud to steady herself—a hand raw and blackened from the touch of magic, she noticed. The stench of scorched flesh filled her nostrils, and she tasted blood in her mouth, felt it running down her forehead into her eyes. The pain finally registered, and she stifled a scream. Already, though, her wounds were closing, her burns fading, her charred skin flaking away and pinching tight as scars formed.

The hiss of a drawn sword sounded. As the last of the glare fell away from Parolla's eyes she saw four riders—three men and one woman—mounted bareback on white horses a score of paces away. *Fangalar.* Their garishly colored robes contrasted starkly with their ice-white skin and cold blue eyes. Behind them, all that remained of the Vamilians Parolla had sensed earlier were smoking stumps of mangled flesh, oozing black slime. Strangely, the threads of death-magic holding them remained intact, but the souls of the Vamilians were gone, annihilated by the Fangalar's sorcery.

Parolla stared at the riders. *I wasn't even your target, was I?* She dug her nails into her palms. *Just in the wrong place at the wrong time. The wrong Shroud-cursed time!*

One of the Fangalar, a man in orange robes, edged his horse forward. His hair had been shaved at the temples, emphasizing the contours of his outsized cranium. For a while he looked at Parolla as if weighing her soul in his hands. Then his lips curled upward at the corners. He held his hands out, palms toward her, in a gesture that might have signified apology were it not for his sardonic smile. Moments later he wheeled his horse and led his companions east.

Parolla watched them until they disappeared from sight.

"My Lady." Tumbal's voice was a rasp in her mind.

Tumbal. She spun to find the Gorlem floating an arm's length away, his image fading in and out of focus. There was a gray cast to his face, and his brow was lined with pain. The black tide within Parolla receded. "*Sirrah,*" she said. "You're hurt."

"The Fangalar's sorcery . . . intended to destroy the Vamilians . . . the spirit, not just the body . . ."

Parolla's glanced at the undead, uncomprehending. Then understanding came to her. The Fangalar, after their massacre of the Vamilian centuries ago, must have thought whatever secret their enemy possessed was safe. Having arrived here and seen the Vamilians restored to the flesh, though, they had obviously resolved to destroy their souls in order to ensure their silence.

"I am . . . grateful, my Lady," Tumbal said.

"Grateful? For what?"

"For saving me . . . Thy magic . . ."

A coldness touched Parolla. "What I did, I did for me. I never stopped to think—"

"Thou could'st not have known."

"I should have realized."

"Thou had'st no warning."

Parolla rounded on him. "I should have realized!" The darkness came bubbling back, and she took a shuddering breath to calm herself. "I cannot heal wounds of the spirit, but perhaps one of Shroud's servants . . . Can you hold on?"

Tumbal forced a smile. "I have little choice . . . but to try . . ."

Parolla stared in the direction the Fangalar had taken. "Wait for me here."

"Do not . . . pursue them, my Lady."

"Did I say that I would?"

"Please. I would not be . . . the cause of more pain to thee . . ."

Parolla could feel the Gorlem's gaze on her, but she did not turn to meet it. Steeling herself, she set off at a run.

Romany rubbed her hands together. The end for Mayot was close, for the powers drawing near to his stronghold were too great to be held back by his feeble collection of undead servants. Yes, the largest bands of Shroud's followers were still some distance from Estapharriol, but over a score of his disciples had now pierced the dome of death-magic, to say nothing of the various strangers drawn here by the Book's power.

Sensing the Fangalar's burst of sorcery, Romany had flashed along her web to investigate the ruckus. She had arrived too late to witness the newcomers' confrontation with Parolla, but the fact that both sides remained standing indicated they had exercised restraint, evidently recognizing that Mayot was their real enemy here. Was it too much to hope that they might work together to bring about the mage's downfall?

Romany's gaze moved to the steaming remains of the Vamilians. The Fangalar had not, alas, shown the same forbearance in relation to their ancient enemy. Thus far the priestess hadn't sensed any other groups of Fangalar along the strands of her web, and since four riders could not possibly expect to hunt down every Vamilian in the forest, their goal would be the elimination of the power animating the undead. And that meant exterminating Mayot. In other circumstances Romany might have found it amusing that, in destroying the Book, the Fangalar would free the Vamilians from the misery of their enslavement . . .

Unless, of course, they intended to use the Book's mastery of the undead for some altogether darker purpose.

Frowning, Romany went in pursuit.

Luker had ceased to be aware of anything beyond his master's sword. He needed every last scrap of concentration just to stay alive, thrusting and parrying with the Will even as his blades danced to keep Kanon's sword at bay.

Luker had long considered himself a match to his master's skill. During their final days traveling together he had held his own when they sparred, getting past Kanon's guard as often as his own defenses were breached. If they had been dueling now with swords alone, perhaps the scales might have been weighted more evenly. When it came to the Will, though, his master was stronger—even struggling in the grip of that Shroud-cursed Book he was stronger. If Kanon had wanted him dead, the fight would have been over by now. Indeed, Luker suspected it was only his familiarity with his master's technique that had kept him alive this long.

He had not been helped by the lingering numbness in his left hand caused by Chamery's death-magic. Early in the duel a Will-strengthened cut from Kanon had almost wrenched Luker's sword on that side from his deadened fingers, and full feeling was only now beginning to return. Luker already had a new problem to contend with, though. An attack from Kanon, only partly blocked, had opened a gash along his left wrist, and blood ran in a steady trickle to his palm, making his grip slick.

As he was forced back by a flurry of strikes, he slipped on the boggy ground. He turned the stumble into a dive that took him out of reach of Kanon's blade, rolling behind a tree stump. Now covered in mud, he regained his feet in time to meet a blow from his master's Will that sent him reeling back a step. Sparks flew as he parried another lightning-quick thrust from Kanon's blade.

Defending, always bloody defending. True, his master's struggles against the Book had presented a handful of openings, but the wounds Luker had been able to deliver as a result were inconsequential to an undead opponent. To end this fight he would have to deliver a more telling strike. But how? For just as Luker knew Kanon's technique, so his master knew his. How could he not—Kanon had taught him everything he knew. *Well, not everything.* Could Luker gain some advantage from that? Did Kanon know his moves *too* well? *Maybe it's time I showed him some of the tricks I've learned in the years we've been apart.*

A clash of their Wills rumbled across the clearing. Luker swayed back from a cut, then winced as his opponent's sword nicked his left shoulder.

Now seemed as good a time as any to try.

Attacks rained down on Luker once again, but instead of retreating he turned on his heel, his left blade flashing for his master's head. Kanon blocked the move, of course—it was one of Luker's favorites— then countered. Luker caught the thrust, rolled his wrist, and stabbed for the chest, his master parrying.

All as it should be.

But as he stepped in to follow up his momentary advantage, Kanon's sword was already sweeping down to intercept the next move in the sequence: a cut to the right hip.

Which never came.

A feint. The slightest pause, then Luker's left blade clanged against his master's weapon, pinning it for an instant as Kanon tried to disengage.

Enough time for Luker's right sword to flash in a horizontal arc, aiming a cut to his master's neck.

Surprised though he must have been, Kanon had time to see the blade coming, to sway back or turn the attack aside with his Will. Instead his master stood unflinching, a shadow of a smile crossing his face.

Luker's sword carved through flesh and bone, and Kanon's head went tumbling to land with a splash in a pool of water.

Vamilian warriors swarmed toward Ebon from the side streets, only to strike Galea's invisible sorcerous barrier and be thrown back. The numbers of undead about him seemed to swell with each moment, yet he'd seen dozens more lying motionless among the ruins, and his thoughts turned to the sickle-wielding stranger he'd glimpsed in the forest yesterday. Could a single warrior, however skilled, be responsible for killing so many? Ebon doubted it. During his ride here he'd seen numerous pockets of fighting in other parts of the city. Plainly *someone* was taking the battle to the undead, but were all of those mysterious warriors able to sever the threads holding the Vamilians, as the sickle-wielder had been? If so, who in the Watcher's name were they and why hadn't they joined forces in one coordinated assault?

Just as there was little sign of collaboration between the attackers, nor was there any evidence of organization among Mayot's defenders. For while many of the city's streets were blocked by fallen trees or mounds of rubble, there were no barricades, no shield walls or lines of archers, no dead-ends into which riders could be channeled. Unsurprisingly, Mayot was showing the same lack of tactical acumen in his defense of the city as he'd displayed during his attack on Majack.

The dome was directly ahead of Ebon now at the center of a district of buildings that remained mostly intact. He had assumed that would be his destination, but as he skirted the debris of a collapsed house he sensed a surge of anger from the goddess, and she ordered him to make for a hill to the east. Ebon swung his destrier right, onto a tree-lined avenue. Half a dozen Vamilian spearmen blocked his path, but a nudge from Galea, channeled through Ebon, bowled them from their feet, and he thundered past.

Ahead the avenue divided. Ebon took the right fork leading to the hill, the dome now on his left. As the ground began to climb he sensed the goddess's anger rise with it. A short distance away the ruins ended. The slope of the hill beyond was covered with trees. There were no buildings, not even a single undead warrior to contest his passage.

Frowning, Ebon sent a thought questing inward. "Galea, where are you taking us?"

Predictably the goddess did not answer.

After a few hundred heartbeats Ebon reached the summit. He drew up beside a fallen tree trunk and glanced back to locate his companions. They emerged from the rain in ones and twos, Vale and Garat at the front followed by the consel's soldiers, with Mottle bringing up the rear. A quick head count revealed the company had made it here without losses. Wherever "here" was.

Ebon wiped water from his eyes and turned to look down on the city. Through a gap in the trees he could see the domed building, shrouded in shadow and towering over the ruins round it. Wisps of black mist curled upward from holes in its roof into a sky already darkened by the sorcerous dome, and becoming gloomier all the while as the storm approached.

"Impressive view," Garat said. "Have we come, then, for a tour of the sights?"

Before Ebon could respond he felt a hand on his arm and looked round to see Vale gesturing to the far side of the hill. From the shadows between the trees four riders emerged along a track. They were

dressed in brightly colored robes, and their skin was so pale it seemed
to glow in the darkness. Ebon felt Galea's rage burgeon inside him,
so all-consuming that for an instant he thought it his own.

Fangalar. Now he understood.

The newcomers saw him and halted.

One of the Sartorian soldiers spoke. "A trap, Consel! We have been
lured—"

"Silence!" Garat snapped.

The consel said something to Ebon, but the king was not listening.
He summoned the goddess. "Galea, attend me."

Nothing.

Ebon hurled his thoughts at the wall the goddess had raised between them. "Do you think I don't know why you led me here? I did
not come all this way to settle old scores between you and the Fangalar."

Galea was with him suddenly, cold and indignant. "You will do as
I tell you, mortal. Were it not for me, you would have died countless
times already. Your life is mine!"

"This was not part of our arrangement. We agreed—"

"I know what we agreed. I am changing the bargain. You had better hope I don't change it any further."

Ebon scowled. He'd been expecting Galea's knife in his back for a
while, but that didn't make it cut any less. "Why are you doing this?
If I die here, you lose your chance to bring down Mayot. And I lose
my chance to save my people."

"I am willing to take that risk."

"And if I am not?"

There was a note of humor in the goddess's voice. "It is too late for
that. The Fangalar sense my presence in you."

Ebon felt his blood rising. "Then their quarrel is with me, and
me alone," he said. "I will not sacrifice my companions in your
cause."

"You cannot win without them. Two of the Fangalar are mages—"

Ebon broke off the contact. He'd have liked to have severed for
good the ties between them, but he needed her power now more
than ever.

Across the hilltop one of the riders—a man dressed in orange
robes—was shouting something lost to the wind.

Garat maneuvered his mount across Ebon's line of sight.

"Shroud take you, your Majesty!" the Sartorian said. "I will not be ignored. Why have you brought us here? Are these the ones controlling the undead?"

Ebon shook his head. "There is no time to explain, Consel."

"The Abyss there isn't! I want answers!"

"Then head for the dome," Ebon said, pointing through the trees. "The threads of death-magic lead there, to a mage named Mayot Mencada. He is the power behind this."

"You expect me to—"

"Please, Consel. This is not your fight."

"But it is yours? Why? Who are these Fangalar? How did you know they would be here?"

Ebon did not respond. He doubted the Fangalar would sit idly by while he enlightened the consel, or that the Sartorian would believe him if he did.

Garat studied him for a heartbeat, then spun his horse round, his face twisted with fury. "Very well," he said. "As of this moment, consider my blood debt repaid. If we meet again I will cut you down where you stand." With that he whipped his mount with his reins and galloped back down the hill. His troops spurred their horses after him.

Ebon turned to Vale and Mottle. "You too," he said. "Go."

Vale shook his head.

"Listen to me. There is no need for us all to die here."

"Save your breath. I ain't going nowhere."

"This is not a request, Vale. We came here to cut the undead's strings—"

"No, *you* came to cut the undead's strings. I came to watch your back." He nodded at the Fangalar. "Once we're finished with this lot we can deal with the stiffs."

Ebon smiled faintly. *Finished?* They had barely managed to defeat one Fangalar at Majack. What chance did they have against four, even if, as the goddess claimed, only two of them were sorcerers?

Only.

Ebon looked at Mottle. The old man's eyes were closed, his head cocked to one side, a frown creasing his brow.

"Mage, are you with us?"

Mottle's eyes remained shut. "Can you sense them, my boy? The Currents are strong in this place. Innumerable secrets swept up by the storm and borne across empires and oceans. A cacophony of voices all clamoring for Mottle's scholarly attention—"

"Later, mage," Ebon cut in, eyeing the orange-robed Fangalar. "Just now I fear you have more immediate concerns at hand."

Mottle opened a single beady eye and looked at the riders.

Then he closed it again.

CHAPTER 20

LUKER HEARD voices calling to him, but he could not make out any words above the roaring in his ears. Kanon's head lay facedown in a pool of water. For an improbable heartbeat his decapitated body stayed upright. Then his legs gave way, and he collapsed. The thread of death-magic holding him remained intact, though, meaning his spirit was still trapped inside his body. Luker stood frozen. He couldn't leave Kanon here any more than he could take him with him, but suddenly the Vamilians were lurching forward to spare him the choice. A blessing, really—no time to dwell on what had happened.

Reins were thrust into his hands, and he looked up to see Merin mounted on his horse, the motionless form of Chamery slung in front of him across the animal's shoulders. Luker stepped into his own saddle. He glanced round the clearing, hoping he would be able to find his way back here when the time came. Then he dug his heels into his horse's flanks and set off after Merin and Jenna, already carving a path through the undead at the end of the clearing.

Time passed in a blur. Luker was vaguely aware of leading his companions along a game trail, Vamilians closing from the sides. He reached for his Will, fumbled it, realized his flesh was hot and his hands were shaking. He needed to clear his head. Just cut away from it, concentrate on the business at hand. There'd be time for all the other stuff later. Too much time. But he kept seeing again the last moments of the duel, his master's head lying in water. Kanon had let him win, he knew. Helped him, even. For as Luker's blade was flashing for his master's neck he had sensed Kanon throw his Will against the Book's mastery in a final attempt to break free. He had failed, of course, but the effort had bought Luker the instant he needed to land the decisive blow.

His stomach heaved, and his rage came boiling up his throat. So Mayot had thought it would be amusing to reunite the two of them, had he? *Are you laughing now, mage? Can you see your death coming for you?* Not even Shroud would stand between him and Mayot now. Then Kanon's words from the clearing came back to him. Four Vamilian champions, his master had said. What chance did Luker have of defeating Mayot's bodyguards where Kanon had failed? He pushed the thought aside. He would succeed because he had to.

He also had one distinct advantage over his master: the presence of Shroud's disciples in the forest. *All I have to do now is find one of the bastards.*

After a while he came to a muddy road leading north toward the source of the threads of death-magic. Steering his horse onto it, he saw something that shook him from his reverie. A wall of black sorcery. No, a dome curving up to brush the storm clouds. As rain fell on it, its surface twinkled with a thousand sparks of dark fire. There was a gash where the road passed through it, and scattered across the ground were the motionless bodies of scores of Vamilians.

Luker drew up his horse at the opening, Merin alongside. The tyrin half stretched out a hand to the dome before letting it fall. When he looked at Luker, there were flames reflected in his eyes. "What is this thing?"

Ignoring the question, the Guardian rode through. From half-light into gloom in a heartbeat. Ahead the road was flanked by huge pillars and lined with Vamilian corpses. Nothing but darkness beyond until a flicker of light from some distant sorcerous confrontation revealed ruined buildings and dead trees as far as the eye could see.

Luker pressed on, conscious that the undead from the clearing would be following behind. After a few hundred paces he turned into a rubble-strewn alley, looking for a building with four walls intact. In the end he had to settle for a house that was sound on three sides with its remaining aspect partly screened by the drooping branches of a ketar tree. Swinging down from his saddle, he picked his way through a tangle of roots and led his mare inside. The floor of the building was covered in stones, potsherds, and a covering of dirt and leaves. The branches of the ketar tree acted as a shield against the worst of the rain.

Merin and Jenna followed him in.

"Why have we stopped?" the tyrin said.

Luker did not respond. He took a length of rope from one of his saddlebags and crossed to Merin's horse. Seizing a handful of Chamery's robes, he dragged the mage to the floor. The boy's robes were soaked with blood. Luker checked him over for wounds, slapped him hard in the face. Nothing. Flipping him onto his front, he began tying his wrists behind him with the rope.

"What are you doing?" Merin said.

"Practicing my reef knots. What does it bloody look like I'm doing?"

"The mage needs healing."

"And who's going to give it to him? You? The boy's got a chest full of broken ribs. Chances are, he's bleeding out inside."

"You're just going to leave him here?"

"You got a better idea?" Luker pulled a knot tight and started working on Chamery's ankles. "If he comes round, he can heal himself. If not, at least when Mayot brings him back he can't come after us."

Merin was silent, considering. "We need him."

"The Abyss we do! The boy's a liability."

"In case you hadn't noticed, we're somewhat thin on allies at present."

"Is that what he is? And when we take the Book from Mayot, what then? You want to fight Chamery for it as well?"

There was a pause. "Since when have you cared what happens to the Book?"

Luker met the tyrin's gaze. "The Book must be destroyed."

"Our orders—"

"To the Nine Hells with our orders! Shroud's mercy, man, get your head out of the emperor's ass for a moment and think! Have you stopped to ask yourself why Avallon wants the Book?"

"I don't question—"

"He wants it because he means to use it," Luker cut in. "That's why he got Mayot to steal it in the first place."

It was no more than a hunch, but Merin was not bothering to deny it. "You don't know what Avallon is up against. The scale of the threat the empire is facing."

"The Kalanese—"

"The Kalanese are the least of our worries."

"Then who?"

Merin did not answer.

With a snort, Luker finished tying the rope. Not that he gave a shit anyhow. He'd been born in Talen, not Erin Elal, and aside from Kanon there were precious few in Arkarbour who'd shown an interest in helping him forget it. And most of those were dead. He rose. "Even if I believed you, not even Avallon is stupid enough to think the Book will help him." He pointed outside as another burst of sorcery lit up the room. "He'll be too busy fighting this lot off to use it."

"What the emperor does with the Book is not our concern. All that matters is that he has ordered us to bring it to him."

"And how are you going to do that, for Shroud's sake? Even if you get your hands on the thing, what chance have you got of getting home with it alive?"

"Whoever holds the Book controls the undead."

"If he's a corpse-hugger, maybe. Are you?" Luker squinted at him. "Unless, of course, you're planning on cutting a deal with Mayot."

The tyrin gave no reply.

"What can the emperor offer Mayot that he can't take for himself?"

"I'm done answering your questions, Guardian. It's time you decided where your loyalties lie. I won't face Mayot with an unknown at my back."

Luker laughed. "You know where the door is."

Merin stared at him for a while, rubbing a hand across his neck as if remembering their clash at the inn in Arkarbour. Then he swung his mount round and left the building.

Jenna had dismounted and now stood to one side, her arms folded across her chest. Steel glinted in one of her hands. She cast him a querying look.

The Guardian shook his head. "Let him go."

The orange-robed Fangalar leader was shouting again, but when Ebon tried calling back in the common tongue the man's expression only darkened. Galea had said the riders could sense her. If that was true, they did not appear overawed by her presence. Were the leader's attempts at communication directed at the goddess? Was he expecting a reply from her?

Ebon looked at Mottle. Strands of the old man's hair were plastered across his forehead, and his grubby white robe hung sodden from his shoulders. "Do you understand their language, mage?"

"One does not need to comprehend the words, my boy, to deduce their meaning."

"I have only the goddess's word that their intent is hostile. Perhaps they seek to parley."

Mottle raised an eyebrow. "The Fangalar are not renowned for their love of diplomacy." His sweeping arm took in the ruined buildings visible between the trees. "Observe, if you will, the destruction wrought on this once fair city."

"If conflict were inevitable the Fangalar would have attacked by now. What is their leader saying? Why is he seeking to talk at all?"

"Perhaps you should direct your questions at the goddess."

"Would you trust the answers she gave? She *wants* this confrontation."

There was a rasp of steel as one of the Fangalar drew his sword. Another of the riders, a yellow-robed woman, was speaking to her leader in an urgent voice. Without breaking Ebon's gaze, the orange-robed man raised a hand to silence her.

The king looked at Vale. "Options?"

"If we back off now," the Endorian said, "we surrender the initiative. I say strike first."

"To what end? We cannot win here. Even if we defeat the Fangalar they will just be raised . . ." His words trailed off. The wind had died abruptly, the branches of the trees round them falling still as the driving rain gave way to drizzle. Ebon turned to Mottle. "What's happening?"

The old man was shaking his head in disbelief. "The Fangalar are drawing on the power of the storm! Furies bless me, such witlessness! Do they not realize Mottle is the master here?" His eyes glittered. "With your leave, my boy."

"Wait—"

Before Ebon could finish, the wind rose with a whistle to hammer into the Fangalar. One of the riders, the man who had drawn his sword just moments ago, dropped his weapon. Another of them, the yellow-robed woman, sawed on her mount's reins as the animal reared. The leader, though, remained sitting unmoving astride his horse, his hair and robes unruffled by the gale. His stony gaze remained fixed on Ebon for a few heartbeats. Then he smiled.

In answer to the unspoken challenge, Galea's anger grew within Ebon. Her power flooded his veins, and a chill gripped him as if he had been plunged into a pool of ice-cold water. He ground his teeth together.

The clouds overhead were spinning to form a huge vortex centered on the hilltop. A gust of wind battered Ebon, and his destrier side-stepped, snorting. He shouted to Mottle, but the mage did not respond. Instead the old man raised his arms and was snatched into the air with a squeal of delight, his arms windmilling. He disappeared amid the swirling gray clouds.

Watcher's tears.

Suddenly the Fangalar leader gestured, and the air round Ebon ignited. Galea's wards shielded him from the brunt of the sorcery, yet still he was sent toppling backward over his destrier's rump. As he landed on his back the air was driven from his lungs. His head struck the ground.

The world spun.

Luker watched the fight from the shadows of a doorway.

Through the hordes of Vamilians he caught only glimpses of the shaven-headed swordswoman they were attacking. More than a head taller than her assailants, she wielded a longsword in one hand as if it weighed no more than a dueling rapier. In her other hand she clutched a battered shield adorned with the image of a crakehawk. Her features were hidden behind a mask of blood, and her right ear had been cut clean away.

The most striking feature about her, though, was the strand of death-magic emerging from her chest. The swordswoman wasn't one of the undead. One only had to look at the trail of motionless corpses in her wake to figure that. But then what else could explain that thread? An illusion? If so, it was a good one, for Luker could detect no differences between the strand coming from the swordswoman and those holding the Vamilians. Then Merin's words from the slavemaster's house in Hamis came back to him—about someone spinning Kanon false trails. *The Spider.* If anyone had the skill to weave this deception—not to mention the will to bring about the fall of one of Shroud's disciples—it was that slippery goddess or one of her minions.

The shaven-headed swordswoman retreated down the alley past Luker's hiding place, only to find her way blocked by the ruins of a collapsed house. There was a doorway to her left leading into one of the houses, but the Vamilians must already have found another way into the building because a white-robed man appeared at the opening. The swordswoman carved him open from shoulder to crotch, then grabbed him by the throat and tossed him into his kinsmen following along the alley. Her sword was a blur as she rained destruction down on her tormentors.

Like spitting into the wind.

The Vamilians appeared numberless. Wave upon wave poured into the passage, scrambling over the corpses of their kin to get at the foe.

Jenna's voice was a whisper in Luker's ear. "Are we just going to watch?"

"Damned right," he said. "The bitch is more useful to us dead than alive."

"Until Mayot raises her."

"Shroud won't let that happen to one of his own."

"You're sure of that?"

"Watch."

A sword finally pierced the swordswoman's defenses, stabbing her in the left shoulder. It might have been a scratch for all it slowed her, though, for her blade was already flashing down to sever her attacker's arm. She had retreated as far as the rubble blocking the street, and now she attempted to clamber backward over the stones, only for the debris to settle underfoot. As she threw out her arms for balance, a Vamilian spear slammed into her midriff, half spinning her round. Then a sword thrust from a second attacker caught her leg a blow above the knee.

With a roar of frustration she went down.

The Vamilians swarmed over her, hacking and slashing.

A score of heartbeats later it was over.

As the undead returned down the alley, Luker drew back into the shadows and listened to their footfalls die away until only the drumming of the rain could be heard.

When he risked another look outside, the street was still.

"Wait here," he whispered to Jenna, then crept into the gloom.

The Vamilian bodies were piled knee-high in the alley, and it took him an age to scramble over the shifting mound of flesh, looking round at every sound to check the undead hadn't been alerted to his presence. Shroud's disciple lay half-hidden beneath a decapitated white-robed spearman. Luker seized the Vamilian and heaved him off. Then almost wished he hadn't since it gave him a clear look at the swordswoman's head. She must have taken a blade in the face, and it hadn't done much for her looks if he was honest. Her left cheekbone and lower jaw had been sheared away, and the bone round the wound was smashed to shards. Everything else was blood.

Luker located her right arm and followed it down to her hand. Even in death Shroud's disciple clung to the hilt of her sword, and he had to pry apart—

The woman's eyes snapped open, the fingers of her left hand curling round Luker's wrist. Blood frothed at her lips as she tried to speak. The Guardian growled wordlessly. Didn't anything die in this Shroud-cursed place? Curling his free hand into a fist, he struck her on the bridge of her nose. Her whole face shifted, and blood spattered his shirt. With a groan, the swordswoman slumped back.

Luker waited a handful of heartbeats to see if she would stir again before resuming his search for weapons. Sheathed in a scabbard at the woman's waist was a longknife, and strapped to her wrist, a dagger. The Guardian removed these, then wiped his now bloody hands on the woman's cloak. A breath rattled in her throat . . .

And her body began to fade.

Stiffening, Luker took a half step back and almost lost his footing as his heel came down on something soft. By the time he recovered, the swordswoman's corpse was pale as mist, the flagstones of the alley visible below. Moments later she was gone. Luker grunted—evidently Shroud was wasting no time in claiming his disciple's body. The Guardian had been fortunate to reach the woman when he had, he realized, for if she'd succumbed to her wounds any sooner she would have disappeared taking her weapons with her.

A last look round to ensure nothing moved in the passage, then Luker hurried back to the building where Jenna waited. The assassin's eyes widened when she caught sight of the swordswoman's weapons. "Of course," she said. "The corpses that stay dead."

"Time to find out whether it's the weapon or the hand that wields it that's responsible." He ran a finger along the flat of the longsword, tracing a line of blackened symbols etched into the metal. The contact numbed his skin. He smiled. "Seems the odds just evened out in our favor."

"Sorcery?"

"Aye. Damned thing reeks of death-magic."

He took a few practice swings with the sword. The blade was longer than his own weapons, but lighter and equally well balanced. He offered the longknife to Jenna, but she shook her head and took the dagger instead. It vanished up one of her sleeves.

"Follow me," she said. "You're going to want to see this." She led him to the opposite side of the building. In the far wall was a window, and Jenna gestured beyond.

Luker peered into the gloom. At first his gaze was drawn to a hill ahead and to his left. A fight seemed to be taking place on its summit, for a burst of sorcery momentarily lit up the sky. Then he saw a domed structure near the foot of the slope, rising above the ruins in its shadow. The threads of death-magic converged on the building like arteries leading into some diseased heart, and the air round it shimmered with black sorcery.

"Let's go," Luker said.

Jenna shook her head. "You should know by now I never use the front door."

"You want to split up?"

"I'll be more use to you in the shadows."

He searched her eyes. Was she making a break for it? No, she'd had plenty of chances before now to walk away if that's what she'd intended.

When Jenna spoke again, her voice sounded hollow. "You think I'm going to run." Her expression was hidden by the darkness.

"Never said—"

"You didn't have to."

"Jenna—"

"I don't blame you for doubting me, Guardian. I doubt myself. Perhaps we both have good reason to."

Before Luker could respond, she crossed to the doorway and slipped out into the shadows.

Running as fast as she could, Parolla followed the trail of Vamilian corpses left in the Fangalar's wake. In a short time she reached a well-trodden road and tracked the riders' hoofprints east. A few hundred paces brought her to the dome of death-magic she had encountered on her first visit to the city, now hissing and sparkling where the rain struck it. The Fangalar had made a breach in the black wall, and curls of death-magic crackled round the opening. Parolla passed through without slowing.

Inside the dome there was a chill in the air. From the right came the sound of running water, and she looked across to see a stone watercourse. The river flowing along it foamed as it divided into three smaller channels that snaked their way between the ruined buildings before cutting across the road ahead of her. Each channel was narrow enough for Parolla to jump over, and she continued on.

A scattering of undead moved to block her path, and she swept them aside with her sorcery. In the distance she heard the din of a score of minor battles, but the gloom about the city was such she couldn't see the combatants. She should be taking more care herself to avoid detection, she knew. Andara had warned her of other disciples abroad, and at the pace she was traveling she risked running headlong into the arms of one. Thoughts of the Fangalar, though, spurred her on. If the four riders reached Mayot before her, would they destroy the book? It was not a chance she was prepared to take.

A forested hill materialized in the murk ahead, and visible beyond it—though almost entirely obscured by the hill's southern slope—was Mayot's dome. Parolla slowed. Swirling round the summit of the hill was a vast spiral of gray cloud that had ripped a hole in the dome of death-magic. From within the vortex a shaft of lightning flashed down toward the hilltop where it was met by a burst of white light. The lightning ricocheted away to hit a tree, and the trunk exploded.

Parolla smiled without humor. She recognized the signature of that defensive sorcery, for its caustic residue still prickled across her skin. *The Fangalar.* And it seemed from the clash of powers that they had come up against an opponent worthy of their enmity. So much for them reaching the dome ahead of her. Who had they picked a fight with this time, though? A disciple of Shroud? One of Mayot's undead champions? Curious, Parolla began the ascent.

She followed a muddy track that led up the heavily wooded, southwestern slope of the hill. The path had been churned up by the footsteps of those who had gone before her, and she slipped and slithered through the muck. The wind strengthened. The branches of the trees round her thrashed in its grip. A few Vamilians struggled up the trail ahead, bent almost double against the gale. Parolla's sorcery cut them down, left them twitching and smoldering behind her. It had to be done, she told herself, but in truth was she was getting tired of this need to justify everything she did. As she approached the crest of the rise another flash of lightning illuminated the sky.

She halted.

There was something moving in the storm. No, not some*thing,* some*one*. An old man dressed in a white robe, cackling as he spiraled round on the vortex. An air-*magus* without question—and judging by the lack of any thread of death-magic holding him, not one of the un-dead. On the hilltop beneath him were two Fangalar sitting astride their snow-white horses. *Only two?* Parolla's gaze searched the trees to either side for their missing companions, but she could make out nothing through the shadows between the boles. One of the mounted Fangalar—a woman—sent a shaft of sorcery streaking up toward the circling air-*magus,* and the magic detonated within the tattered clouds, briefly setting them alight. The old man, though, had already disappeared deeper into the maelstrom.

Beside the sorceress, and facing away from Parolla, was the orange-robed leader. His attention was fixed on a figure half-hidden among the trees in front of him, and Parolla moved to get a clearer view. A shaven-headed man was on his knees in the mud, writhing in the grip of a fist of light. All about him the ground was crusted with ice, and his body convulsed as waves of sorcery blazed from his hands. Like the air-*magus,* he was no undead. *Meaning he is here for the book.* Once more her rivals for the prize were contriving to remove them-selves from her path.

Parolla's body started to tremble in response to the power raging on the hilltop. She looked at the two Fangalar, felt her blood rise. In her mind's eye she saw again the lines of pain across Tumbal's earnest face, the disconsolate look in his eyes . . .

She shook her head. *No!* This was not her fight. The Gorlem him-self had told her not to avenge him, and even if he hadn't, the Fanga-lar were not her enemy. Yes, they had hurt her in their attack on the Vamilians, but that attack had not been directed at her. She should leave them and their opponents to tear each other apart. She was not here for Tumbal or the Vamilians, any more than she was here for the Fangalar or the unfortunate souls they were battling. She owed them nothing. Nothing!

I came for Mayot. For the book.

For Shroud.

Taking a breath, she turned to leave.

Sorcery roared about Ebon. A blinding white light, bright as sunshine on snow, burned his eyes through their closed lids. The goddess's magic coursed through him, scalding his blood with freezing fire even as it shielded him from the Fangalar's attack. He shivered uncontrollably, teeth chattering so hard he thought they might crack. Still Galea poured more and more power into him. It was not enough for the goddess merely to hold the Fangalar at bay, yet when Ebon attempted to push back against his opponent's sorcery the pressure bearing down on him only seemed to increase.

He could sense Galea raging at his weakness. Doubtless she was more than a match for the Fangalar leader, but Ebon was not. The goddess's power was flooding into him faster than he could channel it. He was losing feeling in his hands and feet, and the chill was creeping along his limbs, first to his wrists and ankles, then to his elbows and knees. If it reached his chest he would die, he knew. He was caught between the breaker and the cliff. The wards around him were failing beneath his enemy's assault, yet if Ebon tried to strengthen them by taking in more of the goddess's magic it would kill him as surely as the Fangalar's. Black spots flashed before his closed eyes. The darkness started to build as unconsciousness reached for him.

It took Ebon a while to register that the Fangalar's attack had broken off. The crackle of magic in his ears gave way to the rush of the wind. Galea continued to deluge him with sorcery, but he wrenched himself free from her grip. Perhaps he should have been curious as to why the enemy had halted their attack, yet he could not think past his next tortured breath. Sensation gradually returned to his limbs, and he felt the rain on his face, the cold muddy ground beneath his knees. He opened his eyes a crack. Through a film of tears he could make out two of the Fangalar, the leader and the sorceress, still mounted on their ghostly white horses. There was no sign of their companions.

Twin forks of lightning flashed down toward the two riders, only to deflect off invisible wards. One bolt struck the ground a handful of paces from Ebon, throwing up a spray of earth that was caught by the storm and whisked away. The smell of rancid eggs filled his nostrils. The female Fangalar sent a shaft of sorcery lancing up into the gloom. Amid the clouds Mottle rode the maelstrom with arms outstretched, whooping like a child. The mage's robe had ridden up above his waist, and Ebon was suddenly grateful for the darkness that cloaked the hilltop.

The king's gaze shifted to the orange-robed Fangalar. The man was no longer looking at Ebon. Instead he had half turned to glance back along the trail he had followed here. There was a figure among the trees. *Vale*. It had to be. The Endorian must have circled round, hoping to catch the Fangalar unawares with an attack from the rear. Now that Vale had lost the element of surprise, though, he would have no defense to a sorcerous strike.

Grimacing, Ebon pushed himself to his feet.

As Parolla began to turn away, the Fangalar leader's head came round, his blond hair fluttering behind him. His expression showed uncertainty, then a look of recognition crossed his features. His scowl set Parolla's heart drumming in her chest.

She was not going to let him catch her unawares as he had in the forest, and she spun wards of shadow about herself.

The Fangalar flinched, then gestured at her.

A flash of sorcery exploded round Parolla, and her blood roared up in answer.

That, she thought grimly, *was a mistake.*

Romany stamped a spiritual foot. This was not supposed to happen!

She had watched events unfold on the hilltop with increasing bewilderment. The actions of the shaven-headed man on his knees—Ebon, she had heard him called—had come as the greatest surprise. Romany had observed his party when it first entered the forest many days ago, but she'd paid no notice to Ebon, believing any threat would come from his companions: the black sorceress with her lumbering mountains of scrap metal, or the ridiculous old man now cavorting among the clouds. Yet here Ebon was, holding back a torrent of magic so powerful even Romany herself would have been hard pressed to withstand it. There was a strange flavor to his sorcery, she decided, reminiscent of the elite mages among the Vamilian undead. A curious detail, but not one of any significance, for whatever the source of his magic he was no match for the Fangalar leader. It had taken a while for the orange-robed rider's superior might to tell, but Ebon's wards had eventually begun to collapse in the face of his opponent's offensive.

Then Parolla had appeared, and the balance of power had shifted. She'd done no more than raise defensive wards about herself, but the Fangalar had obviously interpreted her actions as a precursor to a strike for he had responded by attacking. The woman's strength was prodigious, fueled as it was by the threads of death-magic in the air, and if she were to combine forces with Ebon the two of them might well overwhelm the Fangalar. Ebon, though, had apparently been driven from the game by the orange-robed rider's earlier assault. Clambering upright, he had managed only a half step forward before being bludgeoned to his knees by the storm. He did not rise again. His capitulation had left Parolla to face the Fangalar alone, and she was now being forced back by the man's sorcery.

Romany cast her eye over the combatants once more, then threw up her hands in disgust. How by the Spider's grace did these fools expect to bring down Mayot Mencada if they spent all their time squabbling among themselves? Didn't they realize Mayot was likely rubbing his hands together as he watched the battle? The old man would be the only winner here, for whichever faction emerged triumphant would probably be so weakened by the conflict that they'd make easy pickings for the undead now converging on the hilltop. And if Mayot was to resurrect the losers, their conquerors' triumph would be short-lived indeed . . .

A flicker of movement caught Romany's eye. A third Fangalar rider had appeared among the trees behind Ebon. Bending low over his horse's neck, he thundered toward the shaven-headed man's unprotected back, brandishing a sword in one hand.

A shadowy figure sped to intercept him, and suddenly the Fangalar and his mount were tumbling to the ground. The rider turned his fall into a dive, twisting in the air before rolling on one shoulder and coming to his feet in a crouch. A blur of motion before him, and the Fangalar's eyes started streaming crimson tears. He lifted his hands to his face, screaming. A gray-haired, grizzled man wearing chainmail armor appeared beside him for a moment, a bloody dagger in his right hand.

Romany blinked and he was gone.

Oh my! An Endorian!

Clever of the timeshifter to incapacitate his victim rather than kill him, thereby ensuring he could not be resurrected by Mayot. Clever, if a little . . . clinical. In any event, with the Vamilians closing in on the hilltop, the stricken man's stay of execution would not last long.

As Romany looked away, she sensed another tremor along the strands of her web. Ordinarily she would have ignored it—the whole city was going to the Abyss, after all—but this disturbance came from one of the entranceways to Mayot's dome. It seemed someone had managed to fight their way through the hordes of undead and was now knocking on the old man's door.

Taking one final look at the combatants, Romany sighed. There was nothing she could do to untangle this particular knot, even if she had known which faction to side with.

Perhaps at the dome she could be more of a thorn in Mayot's side.

Looking round the corner of an alley, Luker studied the dome. The building was no more than two hundred paces away at the end of a street choked with bodies. From an arched entranceway, curls of black sorcery snaked like tendrils of smoke. The air was flush with power. It just needed a spark and the whole damned place would go up.

A spark Luker intended to provide.

First, though, he had to get to the archway, and while nothing stirred in the blackness ahead, he could sense dozens of threads of death-magic converging in the shadows between the buildings. No doubt there were other entrances to the dome, and other roads leading to those entrances, but he suspected they would offer no better prospect of safe passage.

One road to the Abyss was as good as another.

The rain was sheeting down now, and Luker edged closer to the wall on his right. After separating from Jenna he had spent a quarter-bell weaving through the city's streets. Only once had he met trouble, and that was of his own making. He had been seeking a victim on which to try out his newly acquired weapons, and a one-legged Vamilian man crawling along an alley had proved too tempting a target to pass up. The encounter had brought both good news and bad, for while the Vamilian had ultimately died beneath Luker's sorcerous blades, it appeared that simply bringing the weapons into contact with the undead did not sever the threads of death-magic holding them. For that, a mortal wound was required.

A noise sounded in the alley across from Luker, and he shrank back into deeper shadow. There was movement in the darkness opposite— a lone figure picking its way through rubble and corpses. Not one of the Vamilians, since there was no thread of death-magic emanating from the stranger's chest. Jenna, maybe? He couldn't decide how he felt about that, because if the assassin had walked out on him then at least she'd be out of harm's way.

The newcomer halted at the mouth of the alley facing Luker. A man, judging by his height. His features were hidden by a cowl, but his eyes were still visible, shining with yellow light. He was clothed all in black, and in his gloved hands he held oversized, golden-bladed sickles. Death-magic swirled about the weapons.

When the stranger spoke, his voice was soft and sibilant. "Greetings, Luker. My name is Kestor ben Kayma. I've been expecting you."

Luker said nothing.

Sickle Man looked at the sword in Luker's hand. From the shadows of his cowl came a flash of white teeth. "I see you've met the lovely Lady Carlem. Such a tragic loss."

The Guardian shifted his grip on the sword's hilt. "I'm not the one with her blood on my hands."

"If you were, we wouldn't be having this conversation. Shroud sends his greetings and bids me convey to you an offer."

Luker hawked and spat. "Things going that bad for him, eh?"

"There have been setbacks, yes. Temporary only."

"So he's decided he wants to add me to the ranks of his lapdogs. How flattering."

Kestor did not react to his sarcasm. "He'll be pleased you see it that way. My master is aware that you've distanced yourself from the Sacrosanct. That you are now, shall we say, a free agent."

"The answer is no."

"You haven't heard my offer yet."

"I don't like the strings attached, whatever they are."

Sickle Man examined the blade of one of his weapons. "What if I were to tell you my Lord has information that may be of interest to you? That Mayot Mencada is no more than a pawn in someone else's game, and that the responsibility for Kanon's death ultimately lies with another?"

"The Spider, you mean."

Kestor's lengthy silence confirmed Luker's shot had hit the mark.

A man's strangled cry ripped through the air from somewhere behind and to Luker's right. It rose in pitch to an agonized shriek, then was cut off.

The Guardian raised an eyebrow. "Friend of yours?"

Sickle Man's eyes flashed a deeper yellow. "Shroud is a generous master—"

Luker's snort interrupted him. Was this joker for real? A leash round his neck was still a leash, irrespective of the hand holding it.

And when you signed up with a Lord such as Shroud, you wrote your name in blood. "I am no one's servant. Not now. Not again."

Kestor's voice held a note of warning. "The friendship of Shroud is not lightly spurned, friend."

"Your master wants Mayot dead, right?"

"Correct."

"So do I. Means we're on the same side."

"Allegiances can change."

"Aye," the Guardian said, "and if that's your intent, you're going the right way about it, *friend.*"

There was a long pause. Carried on the wind came the sound of running feet from a few streets away. Sickle Man's gaze, though, held steady on Luker. "As you will," he said finally. "I assume I don't need to warn you about the perils of treachery."

"I reckon you just did."

Kestor showed his teeth again, then looked at the dome. "Mayot resides within. He has assembled a formidable host of guardians."

"So what are we still doing out here?"

Sickle Man swept out an arm. "After you."

One of Shroud's lackeys at my back? Does he take me for a fool? Luker shook his head and returned the gesture. "No, please. I insist."

Kestor hesitated before stepping out into the street, Luker a pace behind.

Ahead the shadows came to life and rushed toward them.

Floating high above the dais, Romany felt giddy as she looked down on the inside of the dome. In the shadows between the ranks of Vamilian undead she could see scores of spirits, their blurred forms making it appear as if she were seeing double. That double vision, together with her light-headedness, stirred a recollection of an unfortunate night many years ago in Koronos when, posing as a pearl trader at a banquet held by the city's satrap, she'd had her first and only experience of fermented mexin husks . . .

Feeling nauseated, she pushed the memory away.

The veil separating the world from Shroud's realm had weakened markedly in the time since she'd last spoken to Mayot. Now only the thinnest of barriers remained, and Romany could feel it eroding further with every pulse of dark energy from the Book. How long before

it failed completely? A day, maybe? Two at most. And when it was finally gone . . .

Countless more souls for Mayot to enslave.

She could hear rain hammering on the roof of the dome. In spite
of the star-shaped openings overhead, the inside of the building remained dry thanks to whatever sorcery had preserved the structure
through the ages. Romany cast an eye over the assembled undead. If
anything she had carried out her mission *too* well, for her efforts in
thwarting Shroud's minions had allowed Mayot to amass an impressive array of champions. Drawn up like an honor guard round the dais
was a cordon of twoscore foreigners, lured here by the power of the
Book. Among them Romany saw a woman dressed in the multicolored
robes of a Metiscan sorceress. To her left was an enormous four-armed
Gorlem spearman, and farther along were the three monks of Hamoun the priestess had encountered previously, their fiery eyes blazing
in the gloom. Evidently the Vamilians had failed in their efforts to
take the warrior-priests alive.

She felt a flicker of doubt. For all that Mayot's undead army round
Estapharriol was on the retreat, the old man had yet to unleash his
most powerful servants. And with Romany's web warning her that
the fall of the Kinevar gods was imminent, she was starting to suspect
there was no one in this wretched city who could take the wind out
of the old man's sails.

From one of the passages leading out of the dome, four men and
two women strode into view. Their rust-colored skins marked them
as Sartorians. The lead figure, a young man with oiled hair, managed
to effect a swagger in spite of the multitude of undead facing him.
Pausing at the edge of the host, he swung his gaze to Mayot. "I am
Garat Hallon," he shouted, "consel of Sartor, and I claim blood debt!"

The echoes of his voice were quickly drowned by the storm outside. Mayot gave no reply.

A gust of wind set the leaves on the floor swirling round the consel. "Do you hear me, old man? I claim blood debt! You are the leader of
this worthless rabble, are you not?" Then, "Answer me, damn you!"

Mayot's eyelid fluttered. Turning to one of the Prime standing
beside his throne he said, "Bring them to me. The consel especially—
I want him alive."

Romany glanced at a withered corpse on the floor behind Mayot's
throne, then suppressed a shudder.

As the four Prime descended the steps from the dais, the Vamil-

ians between them and the consel parted. Romany's gaze lingered on
the coats of golden chain mail worn by the undead champions. Such
an uncivilized use of gold, particularly since, as even the priestess
knew, the metal was soft and therefore entirely unsuited for use as
armor. Such wanton profligacy! Such vulgar exhibitionism! Perhaps
when this was over she would find a better use for that gold.

Garat Hallon barked an order, and his soldiers spread out to form
a rough semicircle, the consel at its center.

The Prime covered the last steps in a rush.

It was, Romany decided, a somewhat uneven contest. She had never
seen the Vamilian champions fight before, and she had to admit
they brought a certain grace to the savagery of combat. They seemed
to flow over the ground, their blades flashing out, fast as striking
snakes. In spite of the advantage of numbers, the Sartorians were
hopelessly outclassed. Only the consel himself possessed the skill to
match the Prime, and even he could do no more than defend his opponents' attacks.

Within moments the Sartorians had retreated into a tight ring and
were battling for their lives. Romany was tempted to intervene, but
what was the point? Even *her* skills would be insufficient to turn the
tide of this conflict, and besides, if Mayot were to detect her interference it might jeopardize the success of her final move in the game.

A move she would now initiate.

Closing her spirit-eyes, she silently called to the Spider.

Nothing.

Romany paused before trying again, more insistent this time.

Still no answer.

She rolled her eyes. Typical. The goddess seemed to delight in dropping by unannounced, yet when her presence was actually needed . . .

A scream interrupted her thoughts, and Romany opened her eyes
again. The skirmish was nearing its end. The consel was now fighting
alone against the four undead warriors, retreating all the while toward the archway through which he had entered. He didn't get far,
though. One of the female Prime stepped in and used the flat of her
blade to deal him a blow to the back of his skull. He crumpled to the
floor.

Most of the Sartorians were merely wounded or unconscious, but
one soldier had been killed in the clash. Romany watched with sick
fascination as the dead man's wounds closed, and he rose soundlessly
to join the ranks of Mayot's undead. Garat Hallon, meanwhile, was

being hauled to his feet by the Prime who had struck him. The consel's eyes were bleary, yet still they blazed with defiance.

"Such poor entertainment, Consel," Mayot said. "I expected better of you."

"You think this is over?" Garat hissed. "It is just beginning. I'll be waiting for you on the other side of Shroud's Gate."

The corners of Mayot's mouth turned up. "Somehow I doubt your soul will make it that far. You were a fool to venture here in such feeble company. A hundred of your pathetic soldiers would not have been a match for my Prime . . ."

The old man's voice trailed off, and he turned toward one of the dome's archways.

Startled, Romany looked across to see two more strangers enter the building. She recognized the first as one of Shroud's disciples. Dressed in voluminous black robes, his face was hidden by a cowl and he clutched a golden-bladed sickle in each hand. His companion was a giant of a man with a scar running down the right side of his face. His mud-spattered clothes were devoid of adornment, and he was armed with a sword and a longknife. The weapons were invested with death-magic—a surprising detail since their owner was clearly no servant of the Lord of the Dead.

It was this second stranger who spoke in response to Mayot's words.

"Try me instead."

CHAPTER 21

LUKER WATCHED the shrunken, white-haired old man—Mayot Mencada, he presumed—lean forward in his throne. The mage's matted beard grew wild to his waist. He clutched a leather-bound book to his chest with skeletal hands. His gaze when it settled on Luker was dismissive.

Surrounding the dais was a throng of undead, perhaps twentyscore in all, though it was difficult to judge numbers with so many face-less black spirits drifting through the gloom. Luker could sense the veil to the underworld dissolving before the waves of death-magic emanating from the Book. Soon the dome would become as much a part of Shroud's domain as it was the mortal realm. Luker scratched his scar. Did Mayot even realize what was happening here? Was he stupid enough to think he could control the power he had unleashed?

When the mage finally spoke his voice was barely audible above the rumble of the storm and, bizarrely, the crashing of waves. "Well, well. It seems the day's entertainment is not yet done."

Sickle Man stepped forward. "I am Kestor ben Kayma, emissary of Shroud. You should have groveled before my Lord when you had the chance. An eternity of torment—"

"Yes, yes," Mayot cut in. "I've heard the empty threats before. Tell me, does your master now regret not striking a bargain when it was offered?"

"Shroud does not deal with mortals."

"Even now, with the powers at my command?"

Kestor's voice purred. "I hear the yearning in your voice. You seek an escape from the grave you have dug for yourself, yes? Would you surrender the Book to me now? Would you throw yourself on my Lord's *mercy*?"

Mayot scowled. "You misunderstand. I have no intention—"

"It matters not," Sickle Man interrupted. "The truth is, you were lost the moment you set foot on this road. There is no going back."

The silence stretched so long that Luker wondered if Mayot had dozed off. Finally the old man said, "You think I fear Shroud? Why? What has he done since I destroyed the first fool he sent here? Nothing, save send more fools for my servants to blunt their swords on. And now"—he gestured to the undead surrounding the dais—"I have an empire to protect me."

"Yet here I am," Kestor said.

Mayot stroked the Book of Lost Souls. "You think the hard work is done now that you've reached this place? My strength has grown tenfold since I first opened the Book. Each day more of its secrets fall into my hands. Soon I will have the power to overthrow your Lord."

"You would challenge him in his own realm?"

"Would he challenge me in mine? No. Instead he sends his pitiful minions against me. Why? Because he dares not set foot in the mortal world. He is afraid—"

Luker snorted his contempt.

Mayot's cold gaze fixed on him. "Ah, the Guardian. Luker Essendar, I believe. I remember you from the night of the Betrayal—our attack on the Black Tower."

"I don't remember you."

The old man's left eyelid started fluttering. "You seem to have misplaced your companions. I was so looking forward to renewing my acquaintance with that arrogant pup, Chamery."

For once Luker agreed with him. He'd have liked to see the two corpse-huggers square off too, though he doubted there was room enough in the dome for both their egos. "Shame he won't be joining us, then. Like all mages, he got ahead of himself. A little power and suddenly he thought he shit gold. He was put in his place, just like you will be."

There was another pause. One of the unconscious Sartorian soldiers had come to and was retching noisily.

"You are unwise to mock me," Mayot said. "No doubt you bring some feeble offer from Avallon. A pity your journey was wasted."

"I'm not here for the emperor."

The old man's lips quirked. "Of course. Your master, Kanon. I confess I am surprised you managed to defeat him."

"I had help—from Kanon himself. Maybe your grip on your servants isn't as strong as you think."

"Impossible!" Mayot snapped.

Luker said nothing.

The mage leaned back in his chair. "I will have the truth soon enough, Guardian. You do know that whatever . . . damage . . . you inflicted on your master can be repaired? In time you will both serve me."

"I'm done talking."

"As am I." Mayot waved a hand at the four golden-armored Vamilians. The woman holding the dazed consel released him, and he fell to the ground. The warriors then advanced, their footsteps rustling the leaves on the floor. "Let's see if you fare any better against my Prime than Kanon did."

Luker's eyes narrowed. *So these are the ones*. He had seen the final moments of their fight with the Sartorians. The bastards were quick, sure . . . but there were only four of them. *Four against two. I like those odds.*

Rolling his shoulders, he moved to his left to put some distance between himself and Sickle Man.

On his knees, Ebon watched as the female stranger was forced back a step by the waves of white light surging from the Fangalar leader's hands. The woman's form was cloaked in shadow, a darkness so deep even the sorcery assailing her could not pierce it. Ebon sensed her drawing energy from the death-magic in the air. A necromancer, then. Was she one of the undead? He could detect no thread protruding from her chest, but then there was little he *could* make out through the storm of powers.

The king switched his gaze to the two Fangalar. The yellow-robed sorceress had steered her horse between Ebon and her leader. Bathed in the light of the man's magic, she sat watching Ebon, her expression disdainful. But she didn't attack.

Galea was a swirl of ice in his mind. "What are you waiting for? The stranger is being driven back."

"Who is she?"

"Would I call her a stranger if I knew?"

"Then why has she intervened?"

The lines around the goddess's eyes tightened. "Why don't you ask her?"

A sorcerous concussion shook the hilltop, and Ebon swayed on his knees. In the air between the female stranger and the Fangalar leader, light warred with shadow in a shower of sparks. The brightness had advanced an armspan toward the woman, creating fissures in the wall of blackness surrounding her. Ebon raised a hand to shield his eyes.

"Is she the one controlling the undead?" he asked the goddess.

"No."

"But she is a necromancer."

Galea hissed with frustration. "The Book draws on the power of Shroud's realm, you fool! Of course it has drawn necromancers here."

"Meaning she wants the Book for herself."

"Then kill her next, mortal, when you are done with the Fangalar. Cut her down for sparing your miserable life."

Ebon frowned. Did Galea expect him to believe she cared anything for the stranger's fate? Once again the goddess was trying to manipulate him. And yet, she was right about the woman saving him. To stand aside and simply watch her die after she had come to his aid . . .

He hesitated an instant longer, then nodded.

Galea's power flooded into his veins, and he winced. "You must strike now," she said, "while the leader is distracted. The Fangalar sorceress would have attacked you if she dared. She is no match for you."

Ebon was not so sure. He still had no feeling in his hands and feet, and he twitched in the grip of the goddess's magic like a puppet on a madman's strings. "When I'm ready."

"When you're ready?" Galea sneered. "Tell me, is it my sorcery that makes you tremble so, or your fear?"

This from a goddess who cowers behind a human shield. Ebon sensed Galea stiffen at that, but he did not give her a chance to respond. "When I'm ready," he said again, breaking the contact.

The shadows round the female stranger were burning away under the Fangalar leader's onslaught. The trees to either side of her had warped and withered, and one toppled over, crumbling to dust as it fell into the path of the sorceries.

Overhead the whirlwind had ripped apart the dome of death-magic, the edges of the breach flapping like rent sails. Gray clouds poured through the opening, making it appear as if the sky were caving in.

Dark forms moved in the murk, and Ebon heard a stormwraith screech. There was no sign of Mottle, but the old man would be up there somewhere.

He pushed himself upright. A gust of wind hit him, and he lurched to his left. The clash of powers had thrown up earth and leaves that swirled about the hilltop in dense, speckled waves. He fixed his gaze on the yellow-robed Fangalar sorceress. She had steered her horse away from her leader and now tensed as a burst of magic shattered the air above her.

"In your own time, Mottle," Ebon whispered.

Right on cue a shaft of lightning lit up the gloom, spearing down from the clouds to strike the Fangalar sorceress's wards. Blue fire crackled across them. She flinched, but did not counter.

Ebon raised his hands to add his own power to Mottle's. Waves of energy burst from his fingertips to leave ripples of frozen air in their wake. They hit the sorceress's defenses with a sound like splintering ice, and spidery cracks spread across her shields.

"Again, Mottle!" Ebon called, and the mage responded. Thus far the old man's attacks had been intermittent, but now the spears of lightning came down one after another, four, five, six bolts striking the Fangalar's wards in as many heartbeats. Her shields disintegrated in a flash of searing blue. The woman screamed.

Sorcery rushed over her, drowning her cry.

Ebon shifted his attack to the orange-robed Fangalar. As his power struck the man's defenses, the leader's head turned toward him. The sorcerer's look was one of irritation not fear, and Ebon sensed Galea's hatred burn with renewed ardor. The king's arms were now heavy with cold, and his body felt so brittle he thought it might shatter if he fell. Perhaps he was becoming more accustomed to the demands of the goddess's sorcery, though, for when she channeled more power into him he found himself able to withstand it. The Fangalar's wards retreated a handspan, and the light flowing from the man's fingers dimmed. Scowling, he threw out a hand toward Ebon, stopped the king's attack dead in his tracks.

In doing so, though, he had weakened his defense against the female stranger's assault, and the black tide of her death-magic surged to join with Ebon's sorcery. The Fangalar's wards started dissolving like walls of sand before the incoming tide.

Just as another shaft of Mottle's lightning flashed down from the storm and slammed into them.

They buckled, then collapsed.

The three powers—Ebon's, Mottle's, and the dark-haired woman's—hit the orange-robed figure together, colliding with a blast that sent magic roaring into the sky like a geyser. Within the conflagration Ebon saw the Fangalar raise his hands to his face. The man was chanting, but his voice faltered as the sorcery continued to rage about him. For a dozen heartbeats he and his horse burned with black flames.

Then their forms dissipated like smoke to leave nothing behind but a patch of blasted mud.

Darkness swept in from all sides.

Parolla's hood had come down during her sorcerous duel, and she raised it once more against the rain. Her hands shook in the wake of the magic she had unleashed. She'd almost lost control against the Fangalar, fighting to hold back part of herself even as she struggled to resist the sorcery thrown at her. If the shaven-headed *magus* hadn't come to her aid when he had . . .

She watched the man rise and walk toward her. The vortex above the hilltop was dispersing, yet the *magus* still staggered as if the wind might knock him from his feet at any moment. His gaze when it fixed on hers had an unsettling, almost ascetic, intensity. He wore richly tailored clothes and a mud-spattered cloak that must once have been fit for a king. There was a blue tint to his lips, and his eyebrows were crusted with ice—ice that was now melting as the rain fell about him. Each step brought a grimace to his face, but there was no sign of any injury upon his body. This man's wounds, Parolla suspected, were all on the inside.

The *magus* had lowered his magical wards, a gesture no doubt intended to reassure her that he meant no harm. Parolla, though, felt a growing sense of unease. The stranger's sorcery had the same signature as that of the Vamilian *magi,* yet he was not one of the undead. She pursed her lips. It appeared there was more to this man than met the eye.

He halted in front of her. "My Lady, are you hurt?" he asked in the common tongue.

Parolla looked at her hands and saw they were crusted with dried blood. *Of course—the attack in the forest.* She raised tentative fingers to her face. While the burns inflicted earlier by the Fangalar's sorcery had mostly healed, a few blisters remained. In response to the man's question she said, "The blood is not mine, *sirrah*." A lie, yes, but fewer questions that way.

The *magus* considered this, then bowed. "Allow me to introduce myself. My name is Ebon Calidar." He looked round. "The old man touching down to your right is Mottle, and my other companion, wherever he is, is Vale Gorven." He paused, apparently expecting her to say something in reply. When she did not, he added, "I am grateful that you came to our aid."

Then why did you take so long to come to mine? Parolla wanted nothing more than to leave this place, but she felt obliged to say something. "You were attacked by the Fangalar?"

"In a manner, yes. You did not tell me your name."

She could think of no reason to withhold it. "Parolla."

"Well, Parolla, forgive me for speaking bluntly, but are our paths likely to cross again when we leave this place?"

"You mean, are we enemies?"

"If you prefer."

Parolla glanced at the dome on her right, partly visible through a break in the trees. She saw Ebon's companion, Mottle, eyeing her with a troubled expression as if he were trying to place her face, yet she could not recall ever meeting him before. She turned to Ebon. "That depends. I seek the death of the man controlling the undead."

"To what end?"

Parolla shook her head. "You first, *sirrah*."

"My city is besieged by an undead army," he said. "The attackers' strings must be cut. So, I ask you again: Are we enemies?"

"No, we are not."

"And the Book of Lost Souls?"

That last was said casually, yet Ebon was watching her intently. *The Book of Lost Souls?* So that's what it was called. She'd heard the name before, she felt sure, but where? It came to her suddenly. *My conversation with Olakim in Shroud's temple in Xavel.*

She was spared having to respond by the arrival of a gray-haired man—Vale, she presumed—who came splashing through puddles between the trees. He carried a sword in one hand, a bloody dagger in the other, and he wore a coat of chain mail that rustled as he walked. He gave Parolla a cursory look, then spoke to Ebon. "No sign of the horses. And that fourth Fangalar has disappeared. Must have done a runner."

"Let him go," the *magus* said. "We don't have time to hunt him down."

"And if he's gone to find help?"

Ebon's face twisted.

Parolla's mouth twitched. *Yes, he sees it now. He's let slip through his fingers a witness to all that has taken place here.* And if the missing Fangalar were to return to his kin . . . Well, Ebon need only look round him at the Vamilian city to see what the enmity of the Fangalar would bring.

"It changes nothing," Ebon said. "The man was not a sorcerer. What chance does he have of escaping here—"

"Watcher's tears," Vale cut in. "What is *that*?"

Parolla turned to look where the gray-haired man was pointing and saw a ball of fire rolling through the streets near the outskirts of the city. The trees and the Vamilians that it passed burst into flames, leaving a blazing trail behind. It was heading this way, and Parolla found herself struggling against the urge to laugh. How long had it been since she'd left Andara Kell battling the tiktar by the lake? Less than a bell, she judged. *Oh, Andara, was that the best you could do?* In answer to Vale's question she said, "One of the undead, *sirrah*. A tiktar."

Ebon frowned at the smile in her voice. "You have encountered it before?"

Parolla nodded, remembering the look the elderling had given her before attacking Andara. "It is coming for me."

"Then we will stand beside you."

"Why?"

The question seemed to puzzle him. "You helped us, my Lady. It is only proper—"

"Had the choice been mine," Parolla interrupted, "I would have left you to your fate. The Fangalar attacked me, just as they did you."

"Even so, we share a common goal. One we'll stand a better chance of achieving if we work together."

Parolla studied him. Was he really such a fool as to think they could trust each other? True, she had no interest in the enslavement of his city, but she suspected Ebon would never allow the Book to fall into her hands. *He wants it for himself. They all do.* Ebon's eyes lost focus suddenly, and he cocked his head as if trying to catch a sound. He stared straight through her. There was something there . . . A whisper in Parolla's mind. Voices? When she tried to concentrate on them, the noises died away.

The *magus*'s face darkened as the aura of power around him faded. Parolla's eyebrows lifted. It seemed Ebon had a hidden benefactor. One that had just withdrawn its support. *Clearly his offer of assistance was not his to make.*

Ebon came to with a start, his gaze fixing on her once more. His hands were clenched into fists, but his anger did not appear to be directed at Parolla. She looked across and saw that the tiktar was now approaching the foot of the hill. There was little chance, she knew, of her reaching the dome before it caught up to her. She had no choice but to stand here and fight. Mayot would have to wait.

"We don't have time for this," Vale said. "That thing will be on us long before you two have finished staring into each other's eyes."

Mottle cleared his throat. "Mottle, as ever, has a suggestion. A most elegant solution to the troublesome problem that presents itself. A perfect expression of his creative genius, inspired in its—"

"We're listening," Vale growled.

The old man spread his hands. "Mottle's idea is simply this: Your humble servant will stay here to assist the mysterious lady in her travails. Our destination is the dome, yes? Mottle's punch is far more potent on this hilltop, where he can draw on the storm's power unfettered by walls of stone."

Vale looked at Ebon. "I don't like it. We may need him."

Ebon was looking down the hill. The tiktar had begun climbing the slope. "He can join us when he is finished here."

"Shroud's mercy. Did I just dream that stuff you said about sticking together?"

Ebon turned on him. "Enough! My mind is made up. Mottle, you know where to find us." He gave Parolla a stiff bow. "Until we next meet, my Lady." Then, with a gesture to Vale, he spun on his heel.

The gray-haired warrior gave Parolla a long look before turning to follow. Together the two men moved off in the direction of the dome, leaving Parolla alone on the hilltop with Mottle.

When she glanced at her new ally she found him scratching furiously at an armpit.

Luker had to admit they were good.

By separating from Sickle Man he had forced Mayot's bodyguards to split into two pairs, a man and a woman in each. The man facing Luker had a boxer's nose and a harelip. Broad-shouldered and thick-necked, he wielded a sword that made a high-pitched whine as it cut through the air. A bit like Chamery's voice had sounded. The woman fought with two longknives, blackened on one side. Half a head shorter than her companion, she might have been attractive were it not for the pox scars that covered her cheeks.

It had taken Luker only moments to size up their strengths and weaknesses. Poxface was the more accomplished fighter, but while her reactions were lightning-fast, her reach was poor and she parried with both blades when she defended. Harelip had more weight behind his blows, but his low guard was suspect and he had a tendency to over-balance on the backhand cut. More interestingly, both Vamilians seemed intent on blocking Luker's route to Mayot at all times. Not once had they divided in an effort to attack from opposite flanks.

Now all the Guardian had to do was think of a way to exploit their vulnerabilities.

Against either of the Prime singly he would have wrapped this up long ago. Together, though, the Vamilians fought seamlessly—Poxface on Luker's right, Harelip on his left—alternating their strikes when they attacked, moving to the other's defense on the rare occasions Luker managed to work an opening. Thus far he had scored a few cuts to Harelip's body, but nothing significant.

The dome was quiet. Eerily so, considering the atmosphere in which most of Luker's duels were fought in. Ten years ago, in the early days of the Confederacy, he had battled in the gladiatorial pits in Bethin when his opponent, the then champion, made the mistake of speaking out against Erin Elal. The chants, the roars of bloodlust, the screams of the crowd had been an almost physical force. Until Luker had carved their favorite into slices. Here in the dome the only sounds were the clang of blade on blade, the rustle of leaves underfoot, the scuff of boots on stone.

Then a grunt and a whispered curse from Luker's right.

He risked a look at Sickle Man. Shroud's disciple was on the re-treat, twisting and turning in a whirlwind of motion, his sickles two smudges of golden light. He ducked under a decapitating cut from one of his opponents, then spun away to resume the dance. Luker frowned. He was going to have to think of something quickly, since he had no intention of waiting on the outcome of Kestor's contest. If Sickle Man were to fall, dealing with four Prime alone could be . . . tricky.

An idea occurred to him, but for it to work he would need to ma-neuver his opponents around. A head-high cut from Harelip gave him his chance. A nudge of the Will to obstruct the man's sword arm, then Luker dived under his blade and rolled to the undead warrior's right before rising to his feet again. Poxface rushed round to block off his route to Mayot, but Luker's move had nothing to do with opening a path to the mage. When the Prime attacked again, Poxface was now on his left, Harelip on his right.

Another exchange of blows, feint, parry, disengage. Block Poxface's thrust, sway aside from Harelip's slash. Now when Harelip's backhand cut slid off Luker's sword and the warrior overbalanced, his momentum carried him toward Poxface.

The Guardian stepped to his right to take him beyond the range of Poxface's flashing longknives. An overhand strike forced Harelip to block high, leaving his body exposed as Luker dropped to one knee and lunged with his other blade.

The exchange had taken no more than a few heartbeats.

It might even have worked, had Poxface—unable to reach Luker—not acted quickly to defend her companion. Luker's thrust slid off one of her knives and delivered no more than a glancing blow to Harelip's hip.

Now the Guardian was the one exposed. He parried Harelip's counterattack, then lashed out with his Will to knock Poxface back a step. Another roll and he was back on his feet in time to block a flurry of attacks from Harelip.

Luker kicked up some leaves to distract his assailants. Like that was going to hold them up for long.

He would have to try something else.

Romany watched the duels drag on. The scarred stranger—Luker Essendar—fought with stunning skill, his swords a blur. He was using some form of sorcery, parrying the Prime's attacks or supplementing his own with a deftness of touch that the priestess could not help but admire. His companion, Shroud's disciple, fought with no less ability, catching an assailant's sword on one of his sickles before turning his wrist to trap the blade and countering with his other weapon. It had taken some time for the two Vamilians facing him to adjust to his style of fighting, but adjust they had, and they were now forcing him back. And while the Prime had yet to score a decisive strike, there could be no question that Shroud's disciple—like Luker—was the one doing most of the defending.

The end, Romany decided, was near. In any event Mayot was simply toying with the two strangers. With rank upon rank of undead waiting on his order, the mage could end this spectacle whenever he wanted, and doubtless he would do just that if either of his enemies were to gain the upper hand against the Prime. Romany studied the old man. He sat slouched in his throne, watching the contests with a smile. As ever the mage's pride was his greatest weakness, for he was risking his champions for nothing. He was too blinkered in his arrogance, too comfortable in his perceived invincibility.

Then again, was there anyone in this godforsaken place who could take advantage? Which of his hapless enemies had both the wit and the power to exploit his failings?

Spider's blessing, must I do everything myself?

Questing inward, Romany called once again to the goddess. Still there was no reply. Could the death-magic that filled the dome be preventing her message from getting through? She doubted it, for the Spider often boasted that the strands of her web could infiltrate the Abyss itself. Most likely the goddess was simply ignoring her, maybe even reveling in her discomfort. A picture came to Romany of the Spider making herself comfortable in Romany's quarters at the temple, her feet up on the desk, a bottle of Koronos white wine open before her . . .

Tutting her disgust, the priestess returned her attention to the floor of the dome. Consel Garat Hallon had roused himself sufficiently to crawl a short distance away from the steps to the dais. Reaching the nearest of his unconscious soldiers, a woman with a bruise across her left temple, he shook her insistently.

A score of paces away Shroud's sickle-wielding disciple was fighting with increasing desperation to stay out of range of his assailants' attacks. From the sluggishness of his parries Romany judged he was tiring quickly. Yet on the few occasions the Prime were able to pierce his guard, their blades seemed to meet no resistance when they passed through his robes, as if he were no more than a wraith. There was some trickery at play here, but one learned to expect as much from Shroud's followers. Romany felt an itch in her fingers, an almost instinctive urge to begin weaving her threads about the man.

That game, though, was already won. Dozens of Shroud's minions had been slaughtered, and yet more would likely fall before this business was done. It would not take the Lord of the Dead long, Romany suspected, to enlist new servants, but she had at least bought the Spider valuable space in which to make her next move in the greater game. A game of which Romany knew nothing, she realized. *In a way, I am no less a pawn in this than the Vamilians.*

A most unedifying thought.

"Isn't this entertaining?" a voice said.

Romany sighed as the Spider's image appeared in her mind's eye. Would the goddess never tire of these melodramatic entrances? For once, however, the priestess's exasperation was tempered by relief—though she was not about to let the Spider know that, of course. "If you say so, my Lady."

The goddess's expression was one of wry amusement, and Romany remembered with consternation that the Spider could read her thoughts. "I've been following your progress with interest," the goddess said. "You have done well. Verrry well, in fact. What is your personal tally now? Seventeen?"

"Eighteen."

The Spider eyed her skeptically. "I hope you are not counting that Demonstalker from the Broken Lands."

"I most certainly am!"

"As I recall, he contrived to impale himself on his own sword."

"True. A most unfortunate tumble from his horse. But then the tumble would not have happened had the animal not been panicked."

"By a falling tree, I believe."

Romany sniffed. "Trees do not fall by themselves."

"No, a stray burst of sorcery from a Vamilian mage, wasn't it?"

"And who do you imagine led the mage to the Demonstalker? If you mean to—"

"Peace," the Spider interrupted, holding up her hands. "If it means that much to you, I will give you the Demonstalker. With or without him, your haul is impressive." The goddess paused before gesturing at the sickle-wielding fighter. "Although I couldn't help but notice you appear to have missed one."

Romany scowled. With the Spider there was always a "but." "We need to talk."

"I guessed as much from your . . . summons. I presume you wish to withdraw from the game?"

Romany shook her head. "This isn't over yet."

The goddess looked down at the combatants. "Perhaps not, but soon now."

"That's not what I meant. My Lady, I have an idea."

The tiktar hurtled up the hill. Alone, Parolla knew, she was no match
for it—at least not without drawing more deeply on her power than
she had ever dared before. All the same she had yet to decide whether
her newfound ally, Mottle, was more likely to prove a help or a hin-
drance. She looked at the old man just as the wind lifted his robe above
his waist, and she hurriedly averted her gaze. "Do you know anything
about tiktars, *sirrah*?"

"What doesn't Mottle know! Born in the darkness that preceded
the First Age—"

"I mean, do you know anything that may be of use to us in fighting it? What are its weaknesses?"

The *magus* cocked his head. "Weaknesses?"

"How can we destroy it?"

"How can we not? Granted, the elderling's strength is formidable,
but Mottle is peerless in guile, matchless in cunning . . ."

Parolla had stopped listening. The tiktar had passed momentarily
from sight behind a cluster of trees. "Your element is air, is it not?"

"It is."

"Neutral against fire, then."

The old man puffed out his chest. "In the fullest of his power Mottle has been known to bend air's servant, water, to his will."

Parolla raised an eyebrow. "You are an *archmagus*?"

"Mottle is ever underestimated, my girl."

The tiktar came into view again, no more than a hundred paces
away. Parolla had not appreciated at the lake just how tall the elderling was. Twice the height of a man, it flashed between the trees. She
could now make out the blazing swords in its hands, the black pits
that were its eyes.

Fifty paces.

A blast of wind struck the tiktar, but did not slow it.

Parolla took several steps to her left.

Thirty paces.

She released her power, glorying in the darkness coursing through
her. This once she didn't have to second-guess the need to draw on her
blood. As the shadows across her vision deepened, death-magic erupted
from her hands, hammering into the approaching elderling.

The tiktar cut through her sorcery like the keel of a boat through
water.

Parolla blinked.

Ten paces.

Hells. She tensed to throw herself to one side.

Too late.

Suddenly she was lifted into the air, the tiktar passing beneath with a roar of flames, its swords cutting the air a hairbreadth from her feet. For a heartbeat Parolla hung helpless above the ground, legs kicking, before she began to descend. Touching down, she looked at Mottle and gave a brusque nod in thanks. The old man winked at her.

The tiktar had shuddered to a halt, colliding with a tree and setting it on fire. A single slash with one of its swords sent the trunk toppling to the ground. Then the elderling turned to face them.

When it charged again Parolla was ready for it.

Sensation was finally returning to Ebon's hands and feet, the icy tingle giving way to a burning itch. He still couldn't draw his sword, but the numbness in his legs was the greater concern, for his right foot dragged across the ground when he walked, and if he stumbled on any undead he wouldn't be outrunning them. As luck would have it, this part of the ruined city was still, the sounds of distant combat muffled by rain. Down a side street he saw the corpse of a horse, blood leaking from a wound in its chest. One of the Sartorians' mounts, maybe? Had Garat succeeded in fighting his way through to the dome? Or did the consel and his soldiers now number among the ranks of undead, perhaps lying in ambush ahead?

Ebon glanced at Vale. The Endorian would like that, he suspected.

A score of paces away the road was half-blocked by the debris of a collapsed building. The king slowed and squinted into the gloom, waiting for the blacks to melt into grays. Amid the rubble . . .

He shrank back.

Protruding from the stones was an arm half as long as Ebon was tall. Its four fingers ended in claws, two of which were broken. The arm itself was crisscrossed with bloodless cuts and covered in scales. Whatever body it was attached to remained immersed in shadow.

"You think it's just playing dead?" Vale whispered.

"No," Ebon replied. "But I *do* think it's time we found out what killed it." He sent a thought questing inward. "Goddess, attend me, please."

For once Galea did not keep him waiting. "What it is?" she said as she swirled into his mind.

"The creature ahead . . . You said the Book's threads cannot be cut."

"What I said was, they cannot be cut by *you*."

"Then who? Who has the power to do this?"

Galea's lip curled. "Are we talking hypothetically?"

"Enough of your games. First that sickle-wielder we saw in the forest, now this creature. The cuts across its arm are bloodless, meaning it was undead before it was slain."

"As I have already told you, the Book will have drawn to it a host of powers. As to which particular individual slaughtered this creature, I cannot say. Nor do I think it relevant who else might have an interest in acquiring the Book. All that matters is that you are first to the prize."

Ebon's eyes narrowed. A certain softening of the goddess's eyes suggested she was being less than fully honest with him, but that wasn't what concerned him most. "Prize, my Lady? I thought the Book was to be destroyed."

"Not necessarily."

"I thought you wanted freedom for your people. I *know* you promised freedom for mine."

"I honor my bargains, mortal."

After you've rewritten them, perhaps. "You pledged to help my city."

"And I have done what I can for now. Its fate still hangs in the balance, a fact you would do well to remember . . ."

Her voice trailed off, and through the link between them Ebon sensed a bloom of power far to the north and west that was followed by an explosion like a thousand peals of thunder. The aftershock of the blast swept through the ground moments later, and the road bucked beneath him.

"My Lady? What just happened? My Lady!"

Galea's voice held a note of apprehension. "The first of the Kinevar gods has fallen. The rest will soon follow."

Ebon's blood ran cold. "Gods? What do you mean, gods?"

"There is no time to explain! Mayot will summon the immortal here. You must hurry! To the dome!"

The Spider's expression held a mixture of curiosity and suspicion. "An idea, High Priestess?"

"A way to burst Mayot's bubble," Romany said.

The goddess shook her head. "The game is over for us. We have achieved what we set out to do."

"But the old man—"

"Will fall with or without our help . . ." The Spider paused as a ripple of power shook the dome. A distant shriek sounded, raw and primal, then a grinding noise came from the roof. Powdered dust fell about Romany's spectral form. Below, Mayot gave an exultant cry.

"My Lady," Romany breathed.

"Yes. The first Kinevar god has fallen."

"Has Mayot been able to enslave it with the Book?"

"He has. Even now it approaches."

"How long?" Romany said.

"A few bells."

"Then there is little time left for us to act. Will you now intervene to end this?"

"Why would I?"

"Because with the subjugation of the Kinevar gods we will lose control of the game. In time Mayot may become a threat even to you."

"Then I will deal with him when he does," the Spider said mildly. "For now, he remains a thorn in Shroud's side, and a useful thorn at that."

Romany tried a different tack. "Did you foresee this? The power Mayot would come to wield?"

The goddess shrugged. "I knew what the Book could do. In truth Mayot has been surprisingly creative in exploiting its powers. His preemptive attack on the Kinevar gods has proved to be a masterstroke. More unexpected still, though, was your victory over Shroud's minions—"

"A moment, my Lady. *Unexpected?*"

"The extent of it, yes. High Priestess, you have excelled yourself."

Romany frowned. When had she ever done less? "Then you will not object to granting me a boon."

The Spider's expression was calculating. "You seem rrremarkably anxious to engineer Mayot's downfall. I trust you haven't let this become personal."

The priestess looked at Mayot on his throne. The old man was hugging the Book to his chest, his eyes shining with exhilaration.

Romany's gaze shifted to take in the ranks of undead round the dais, the line of Vamilian girls behind the throne, the naked withered corpse on the floor beside them. "We have created a monster, my Lady."

The goddess covered a smile. "But of course we have. How else could the game have been won? Mayot is precisely what we needed him to be. What other man would have dared to take on Shroud?"

"And yet the suffering he has caused . . ."

The Spider laughed. "Oh, Romany," she said, not unkindly. "Your nose has been buried in scrolls for too long. I blame myself for that. In the games we play there are always winners and losers. Enjoy your victory while you can. Or have you already forgotten the attack on your temple?"

Romany saw again the face of her servant, Danel. "When I spoke of suffering, I was not referring to Shroud's disciples."

The Spider's smile only broadened. She remained silent for a time, her fingers stroking their invisible strings.

A grunt sounded below, and Romany looked down to see Shroud's sickle-wielding disciple take a sword cut to his leg. His riposte opened a gash along the cheek of the female Prime fighting him, but the woman did not so much as flinch.

"What did you have in mind?" the Spider asked finally.

Romany clasped her hands together. "I will go to Mayot and offer to deliver to him the Book's final secrets."

"And when he lowers his defenses you wish me to seal off the sections already accessible to him?"

"Can it be done?"

"In theory. But then Mayot already believes himself to be invincible, and soon he will have the Kinevar gods on his side. Why would he risk dropping his shields?"

Romany snorted. "*Because* he thinks himself invincible. And because a man such as he can never have too much power."

The Spider studied her. "You are taking a great gamble. For me to act through you, you will need to attend the mage in person. I will not be able to intervene if things go wrong."

"The risk is to me alone."

"And is it a risk worth taking?"

Wetting her lips with her tongue, Romany looked away.

———

The tiktar sped toward Parolla, trailing flames that set alight the trees to either side. She drew in as much power as she dared, then released it in a roar that eclipsed the growl of the storm. A wave of death-magic struck the elderling, stopping it no more than ten paces away. It stood writhing in the grip of her sorcery, hissing and spitting and stabbing its swords at her. Parolla could now see a naked humanoid form within the fire, but already that form was melting away. Soon nothing remained of the elderling except the flames that had once clothed it, and those flames now flashed to merge with the fire consuming one of the trees to her right.

Parolla scowled. Nice trick, but the tiktar couldn't escape her that easily. She sent a volley of sorcery smashing into the trunk, and it toppled to the ground, throwing up sprays of muddy water. The flames, though, continued to lick greedily at the blackened wood, seemingly unaffected by Parolla's magic.

She hesitated. What now?

Twin pillars of fire erupted from the burning tree, streaking toward her. As they struck her wards she felt a burst of heat and was hurled backward. She hit the ground and slid through greasy puddles, took in a mouthful of muck, spat it out again. Through the water in her eyes she saw a blur of orange as the elderling took physical form again. It came rushing at her, and Parolla struggled to one knee, tried to raise her hands . . .

Mottle stepped in front of her.

A funnel of air closed around the tiktar, lifting it high and flinging it aside. The elderling twisted in the air, landed nimbly between two trees a short distance away. It raised one of its swords. Flames lanced from its end toward Mottle, only to be caught by the wind and directed harmlessly away. Parolla rose, caked in muck, and let loose another barrage of sorcery. The tiktar screamed as it struck, holding its shape for a moment before dissolving to blend with the flames devouring one of the trees beside it. Parolla blasted the trunk to ash, only for the fire to leap to the next tree. She destroyed that too, then the next and the next until the air was heavy with ash.

Mottle said, "The trees have done something to offend you, my girl?"

She let her breath out slowly, then lowered her arms. The tiktar had transferred to a fallen tree several score paces away. Within the fire that consumed the trunk Parolla could make out black spots that might have been the elderling's eyes. Other trees on the hilltop were ablaze, and the crackle of flames was loud all about. "The creature is restoring itself," she said to Mottle. "Any damage we inflict to its physical form is burned away in the fire."

"Fire feeds off earth," the old man replied simply.

"Then what do you suggest? We can't kill it—the thing is dead already. How do we destroy something that can make itself anew in the flames?"

The *archmagus* grinned. "As ever the answer lies with Mottle." His eyes were wide, his voice breathless. "Your humble servant has been making good use of the time afforded him to draw on the storm's energy. Observe, if you will."

All at once the air was filled with water as if Parolla had stepped beneath a waterfall, and the hilltop disappeared beyond a few fuzzy armspans in each direction. She flinched, hunched her shoulders. Her clothes were plastered to her skin, her hair to her face, yet still she managed a half smile. Of course. You fought fire with water, and no flame could withstand such an onslaught. Parolla wondered why she hadn't thought of it before. Even if the tiktar's flames were extinguished, though, that didn't necessarily mean it would be left completely powerless . . .

A score of heartbeats passed, the rain roaring and hissing in her ears. Then the deluge abruptly petered out as if the clouds had been wrung dry. She blinked wet from her eyes and looked round. The ground was covered in water, and a fine mist hung in the air, a mist that was already being shredded by the wind. The black trunks about her were smoking . . .

Except one, which continued to burn—the fallen tree where the tiktar sheltered. The breeze felt suddenly cold against Parolla's skin.

An image came to her, then, of her first encounter with the elderling, its flaming form rising from the lake. *The lake* . . . Her stomach felt sour. Hells, how could she have thought water alone would be enough to destroy it? How could she have forgotten? And yet the rain must surely have sapped the tiktar's strength. Sodden wood would burn less easily, slowing the elderling's recovery. She should strike now while it was weakened. But how did one *destroy* fire?

The thread of death-magic holding it. It's the only way.

Mottle giggled and gestured with one hand. Lightning arced down from the storm clouds and struck the blazing tree, sending splinters of wood spinning into the air.

"What are you doing, *sirrah*?" Parolla snapped. "The lightning will feed the flames."

Mottle's only response was another giggle. A gust of wind set his robe billowing, and he flapped his arms as if he were trying to fly. Parolla snorted her disgust. The old man was intoxicated on power. He'd drawn in too much of it when he called down the storm, and now it was oozing from every pore.

A new sound reached her suddenly: a faint drumming. It came from the north, and when she looked across she saw shapes taking form in the gloom beyond the tree where the tiktar waited. Parolla started. Riders, a dozen in all. More Fangalar? No, these horsemen wore not garishly colored robes but plate armor and full-face helms with antlers protruding from them . . .

Antlers.

She began laughing then, conscious of the hint of madness in the sound. She laughed until her chest ached and her eyes streamed and even Mottle had stopped his arm-flapping to stare at her.

The Hunt had found her.

The wound to Luker's wrist that he'd suffered in his duel with Kanon had opened again. Blood ran down his palm in a steady trickle, making his grip slick on the hilt of his longknife. He had scored a number of similar cuts to the arms and bodies of his opponents, but to no effect—the bastards didn't bleed, after all, and moral victories counted for little in a fight against undead adversaries. Luker searched his opponents' eyes for any sign they were battling against Mayot's hold in the same way Kanon had. There was nothing. But then neither of the Prime possessed his master's strength of will, nor would they have any interest in seeing Luker survive this encounter.

A strike from the Guardian's Will rocked Harelip's head back, but the undead warrior rolled with the blow. Meanwhile Poxface launched a blistering series of cuts and lunges at Luker's head and chest. He parried her first few efforts, then counterattacked with a Will-reinforced slash to her midsection. When she defended the blow with both of her weapons, Luker's second blade was already sweeping down with a cut to her right leg.

Harelip's sword flashed to block.

The Guardian disengaged, parrying Harelip's backswing before turning to meet Poxface's next attack. Close again, but still no breakthrough. Truth was, this tag-team thing was beginning to piss him off. The outcome of the clash would depend on who made the first mistake, and it was looking more and more like that would be Luker. He could not sustain this level of concentration for much longer, for he could feel the first tendrils of a headache taking root in his brain. Time to take a few more risks if he wanted to force an opening . . .

The thock of a crossbow sounded an instant before a quarrel buried itself in Poxface's right knee. The woman staggered.

Luker gave a dark smile. If the bolt had hit where Jenna intended, it was an inspired shot.

Mayot must have taken objection to the assassin crashing his party, for the dome lit up with flashes of sorcery. With luck the mage was shooting blind, but there was no time to worry about that now. Luker needed to press home his advantage before Mayot weighted the odds against him once more.

Poxface was hobbling, and Luker retreated, forcing her to come to him. As she shuffled forward, the Guardian lashed out with his Will, striking at the woman's knee just as her weight came down. A crack of bone, and she stumbled and fell.

Luker's gaze swung to Harelip. *You are mine.* A flurry of blows forced the undead warrior backward, then a strike with Luker's Will knocked him off balance. The Guardian followed up with a disguised attack, feinting with the longknife in his left hand before slashing with the sword in his right. The Prime read his intent late but still brought his weapon up to block. *Not this time.* Another flick of Luker's Will batted aside the parrying stroke, leaving his blade unimpeded as it swept down to sever his opponent's sword arm at the elbow. A backhand cut came next, aimed at Harelip's neck. As the undead warrior attempted to sway out of the way, he lost his footing and ducked into the blow. Luker's sword took him full in the face and caught there, just below the nose. The undead warrior went down, poleaxed, wrenching Luker's blade from his hand.

The Guardian looked at Poxface to see her struggling to regain her feet. No danger there.

He transferred his longknife to his right hand, then spun and threw in one motion. The blade flashed end-over-end through the gloom.

To impale one of Sickle Man's opponents through the neck.

A roar of sound was Luker's only warning. He raised a Will-barrier just before a wave of sorcery struck him, and it pitched him onto his back in a pile of leaves. Shaking his head, he rose to one knee. Another burst of power slammed into his defenses. He gritted his teeth as death-magic raged about him. A dozen figures were making their way round the dais toward him, and the stranger in the lead, a woman dressed in multicolored robes, raised her hands to send another wave of blackness thundering against his defenses. A second undead sorcerer added his strength to hers, then a third and a fourth. What, four on one now, was it? Seemed Mayot had had enough of sporting chances.

As each assault struck, the Guardian felt an answering flash of agony in his skull. Poxface was caught in the path of the attack, and her body disintegrated to ash.

Then a flicker of light caught Luker's eye—an arc of movement through the darkness. A glittering object—no, two—sailed through the air toward the undead sorceress and her coterie. Through his pain, it took Luker a heartbeat to recognize what the things were.

Merin's globes.

He recalled the two globes that had already been used: earth against the soulcaster, water in the forest. Assuming the tyrin had one of each element, that left . . .

Shroud's mercy!

Luker flung himself to the ground.

CHAPTER 22

VALE SWEPT through the undead, leaving a dozen broken bodies twitching in his wake. Ebon followed behind, his gaze searching the shadowy doorways to either side. A single Vamilian swordswoman had escaped Vale's initial pass, emerging from the darkness to his right. She sprang at the Endorian, her ivory-colored robes flapping about her.

There was no time for Ebon to shout a warning. Instinctively he struck out at the woman, and an invisible force hit her, sent her crashing into the wall of the house on her left. The wall groaned and collapsed, then the entire building folded in upon itself. Vale spun round, his eyes darting. Three quick steps brought him to the mound of debris that was all that remained of the house. His sword swung down, and the Vamilian woman, already making to rise, toppled back into blackness, her right leg severed.

Ebon lifted his hands and stared at them. Had that burst of sorcery been his? If so, why had there been no icy prickle when he'd lashed out? And why had Galea intervened to help one of his companions when thus far she'd been at best indifferent to their fate? *Unless* . . . He quested for the goddess, found her a distant presence at the back of his mind. Could he now draw on her magic without her agreement? Had he inherited some of her power through the link between them?

His questions would have to wait. From a street or two away came a clatter of stones and the sound of running feet. Gesturing for Vale to join him, Ebon ducked into shadow mere heartbeats before more

Vamilians dashed past. As their footfalls faded, he slipped into their wake. Mayot's dome was just a stone's throw away, and he led Vale at a jog toward an arched entranceway.

They drew up in darkness beyond the threshold. A hissing noise filled the air like waves breaking against a shore. Within the gloom ahead he could make out nothing except shadows, but the clash of metal striking metal was unmistakable.

Looking back at the hill where he had left Mottle and Parolla, he saw a ring of trees ablaze. Galea had refused to let her power be used in the battle against the tiktar, insisting that Ebon make his way to Mayot's dome. At the time he'd been incensed, but now, following the death of one of the Kinevar gods, he understood the reason for her urgency. *A god* . . . He had felt its power through his link with Galea. There would be no defeating the immortal, the goddess had told him, if it reached this place, and this once Ebon had had no trouble believing her. His only hope was to cut its strings—to cut all the undead's strings—before it arrived.

Vale's face was pale. Blood leaked from a cut at the top of his left arm, and his shirt round the wound was torn and drenched crimson.

"How bad is it?" Ebon said.

"A scratch."

"We should find somewhere quiet so I can stitch it."

"Yeah right. And maybe one of the stiffs will lend you a needle and thread."

Ebon hesitated, then took the Endorian's arm in his hands. Without the goddess to guide him he had no idea how this worked. To swat the Vamilian swordswoman aside he'd done no more than will it to happen. Was it the same with healing? Peeling back the blood-soaked cloth, he focused on the wound. Vale flinched as the flesh knitted together. An instant later, all that remained was a jagged scar.

"Not a work of art," the Endorian said.

"Neither are you."

"Have I got the goddess to thank for that?"

"No."

Vale frowned, but said nothing more.

Another crash of blades sounded from inside the dome. Ebon shot a look at the Endorian. "The consel, do you think?"

"Maybe we should give it a while longer before going in."

Ebon gave a half smile.

Suddenly a gust of wind hammered into him from behind, propelling him down the corridor. A deep-throated rumble sounded from within the dome, followed by an explosion that shook the walls of the passage. The ground beneath Ebon's feet heaved, and he stumbled into Vale.

A blast of cold signaled Galea's arrival in his mind. The goddess shouted a warning.

Then a wall of fire came rushing at him from inside.

Luker watched the glass globes smash at the feet of the undead sorceress in the multicolored robes.

The floor kicked like a horse. A flash of orange lit up the dome, then the firestorm rolled over Luker's Will-shield. He closed his eyes. Above the roar of the flames he could hear the shriek of the wind, feel it tugging at his limbs even as it crushed the breath from his lungs. Gasping, he drew in a mouthful of fiery air, then clamped his teeth shut as flames seared his throat. The hairs on the back of his hands began to curl and crisp. Biting down on the pain, he honed his concentration in an effort to strengthen his shields. Just stick it out a bit longer, the sorcery had to fade soon.

Another score of agonized heartbeats passed before the wind started to die down. The heat eased as well, leaving Luker's skin feeling tight as if he had spent too long in the sun. When he opened his eyes it seemed as if the whole dome was on fire. One of the trees at the corners of the dais had been incinerated; the others were pillars of flame. The leaves blanketing the floor had also been set alight and now rippled like the surface of a lake of fire. All about, the Vamilians blazed like human torches. Of Mayot's undead sorceress and her coterie, nothing remained except oily black fumes. A section of the dome's roof on the opposite side of the dais collapsed. Chunks of stone came thumping down onto the motionless ranks of undead. Not one of the Vamilians tried to evade the falling masonry, and dozens were crushed or crippled. Rain swept down through the hole in the roof.

Even Mayot himself had not escaped the inferno unscathed. His throne had been toppled, and the mage was on his hands and knees beside it. The Book of Lost Souls lay on the floor, smoldering. For an instant Luker wondered if the fire would take hold, but the old man used his robes to beat at the Book's cover, and the smoky flames faded.

The Guardian clambered to his feet and looked about him. No sign of Jenna. He hadn't seen where she'd fired her crossbow from, but she must have been close to make that shot. Had she had time to retreat before Merin's globes smashed? Hells, had she even survived Mayot's sorcerous tantrum earlier? He thought to shout her name, then decided against it, for if she still lived he would do her no favors by calling her out of the shadows.

To Luker's right, Kestor ben Kayma lay curled in a pool of blood, his black robes slashed in scores of places. *Looks like he'll be sitting the rest of this one out.* The man's cowl had slipped down to reveal blue-black skin that was scaled like a snake's. His sickles jutted from the corpse of one of the Prime, and Luker considered taking the weapons but rejected the idea. If Shroud's disciple had been dead, his body would have vanished. Perhaps he might still recover enough to take part in the struggle to come.

Merin stood beside Sickle Man, his beard and eyebrows singed, his face a lurid red. Beyond him Consel Garat Hallon stooped to retrieve the sword he had lost in his fight with the Prime. Two of his soldiers crouched beside a fallen comrade, shaking the woman.

The Guardian's longsword lay among the calcined remains of Harelip's skeleton, and he used the Will to summon it to his hand. Next he retrieved his longknife from the body of one of the Prime that had been fighting Sickle Man.

The nearest Vamilians lurched into life and shambled toward him, their ivory robes ablaze.

Merin approached.

"What in Shroud's name are you playing at?" Luker said to him. "If you'd landed those globes in Mayot's lap this would all be over now."

The tyrin gave him a dark look. "I will not risk damaging the Book."

Luker's laugh was little more than a croak. "You still think Mayot will deal? Gods, man, you just tossed away your last bargaining chips."

"As ever, you underestimate the emperor."

"You've got more of those things?"

"No."

"Then what?"

Merin rubbed a hand across his jaw. "Mayot will bargain when he hears what I've got to say."

"Assuming he even lets you get the words out. The bastard said—"

"I heard what he said! He'll change his mind before this is done."

The undead were almost on them. Luker's gaze fixed on a charred figure in the front rank, its flesh so badly burned it was impossible to tell if it was a man or a woman. The warrior's left eye had melted and was running down its cheek. Its chain-mail armor glowed red beneath scorched robes.

Luker handed Merin his longknife. "You know how to use this, right?"

The tyrin accepted the weapon with a frown.

A new voice spoke. "Gentlemen, I am Garat Hallon, consel of Sartor. While you've been wasting time arguing, the undead have moved to block our path to the archway. When I give the order—"

"Save your breath," Luker cut in. "Last time I looked, I wasn't wearing one of your soldiers' pretty uniforms."

"That can easily be arranged." Garat glanced at Merin. "Much as the notion offends me, a temporary withdrawal would seem—"

"Run if you want," Luker said. "We're staying."

"You think you can put out all of these human torches? Just the two of you?"

Luker looked at Mayot. "Won't have to. Just enough of them to carve us a path through to that bag of bones on the dais."

Romany's spirit returned to her body, and she opened her eyes. She started. Danel stared back at her from where she sat a few paces away. The girl's eyes glittered as if with some inner light, but the rest of her features were hidden by shadows. She looked small and alone in the dark, knees drawn up to her chest, arms wrapped round her knees.

Romany propped herself up on one elbow, then sank back as hot needles of pain stabbed her head. How long had she been spirit-traveling? Three bells? Four? Her body could not match the fortitude of her mind, alas, but then again, what could?

She had fashioned invisible magical barriers over the windows and roof of her house to shield it from the rain, yet still she could hear a steady drip, drip of water nearby. Then she realized her right sleeve was wet. Tutting with disgust, she lifted it out of a puddle and wrung it dry. For a time she lay looking up at Mayot's dome of death-magic. Over the past bell the storm had swelled, and she could hear the wind prowling outside, gusting strong enough to shake the walls of the house. The air inside, however, remained hot and humid and thick as butter.

I could be back at the temple by now. A bottle of Koronos white . . .

Pushing the thought away, she rose to her feet. In order to carry out her plan she would have to confront Mayot in person, and that meant braving the storm. True, the old man's dome was not far from here, but the wind and rain were hardly conducive to a dignified entrance. Romany felt her pulse quicken. There was a certain thrill to being part of the game once more. It was not for her, this standing in the wings, watching the other players stumble over their lines. Admittedly the Spider had seemed less than enamored with her plan, but then the goddess probably resented the fact that the idea had not been hers.

Lifting the hem of her robe so it did not drag in the puddles, Romany made for the door.

Danel spoke from the darkness. "You are leaving?"

"Yes, my dear."

"For the dome?"

"Indeed."

The girl rose, her hands clenched at her sides. "Perhaps you should remain here. There are fell powers converging on the city."

"Such nonsense!" Romany scoffed. "Formidable these strangers may be, but they are none of them immune to a woman's wiles. The fools will not even see me."

"And if the strike aimed at you is also unseen?"

The priestess halted. There was something odd in Danel's voice. *It's nervousness,* she decided. *The poor thing fears for my safety.* Did Danel really think, though, that any of Romany's enemies could hide from her? An absurd suggestion, for her web would long since have alerted her if someone had come close enough to be a threat.

Still, it would not hurt to check, if only to assuage Danel's concerns. Tentatively Romany probed the threads of magic woven round the building. If anyone waited in the shadows outside, she would sense them.

Nothing.

How could she ever have doubted herself? She would have to be wary, of course, as she made her way to the dome. A confrontation with one of Shroud's vermin would be most regrettable, but it should be a simple matter to slip past anyone who crossed her path. She looked at Danel. "Do you wish to accompany me?"

"No."

Romany pursed her lips. "Yes, perhaps it is best that you stay. The city *is* dangerous, after all."

"I have my orders."

Romany stared at her. A strange thing to say, but there was no time to think on it now. She crossed to the door, then paused. If her plan worked—*If? When!*—the souls of the Vamilians would be freed and she would not get another chance to say good-bye to Danel. A word of farewell was only proper, yet if she observed the correct social niceties she risked alerting Mayot to her intent if he were somehow listening in on the conversation. Unlikely, considering his current predicament, but Romany had ever been one for details.

A footfall sounded behind her.

Then the priestess felt a lancing pain as something cold and hard entered her back, scraping against one of her ribs. A moment later the dagger—for that was what it surely was—was twisted and withdrawn.

She collapsed.

Parolla wiped tears of laughter from her eyes.

These would not be the same Huntsmen from Xavel, she knew, for there was no way they could have tracked her through Mezaqin's demon world. But then where had the riders come from? She had passed through no settlements on her journey across the Ken'dah Steppes, and besides, these riders did not have the look of tribesmen. Perhaps the high priest had sent word ahead to a temple in one of the nearby cities, but then how had he known she would come this way?

The lead Huntsman was a huge man wearing dented plate-mail armor. The antlers on his full-face helm were tipped in silver, and he wielded a half-moon ax. When he saw her he bellowed a challenge and dug his heels into his horse's flanks. Its hooves threw up spray as it splashed through the puddles.

"Huntsmen," Mottle said. "Servants of—"

"I know who they are," Parolla cut in.

"Just as *they* appear to know *you*. Mottle presumes their intentions are not friendly."

The leader approached the fallen tree where the tiktar sheltered. As his horse gathered itself to leap, the flames flickering over the trunk roared to new life. The elderling was suddenly among the startled Huntsmen, its blazing swords leaving glowing trails in the gloom.

Parolla smiled. "It seems the tiktar is as not perceptive as you, *sirrah,* when it comes to distinguishing friend from foe."

"There are few that are, it is true."

A lone rider had broken free from the melee and was galloping toward Parolla. He lowered a lance.

"Allow me," Mottle said.

A fist of air punched the man from his saddle, and his legs wheeled over his head as he tumbled backward. He landed in the mud with a crash of armor and lay still. His now riderless mount continued toward them.

"Take the horse," Parolla said to Mottle. "Get out of here."

"What, and entrust my life again to one of those brutes?"

"This isn't your fight. It never was."

The old man appeared not to have heard her. He gestured at the Huntsmen. The tiktar was cutting a swath through the riders. "Ought we not to intercede? With the elderling distracted . . ."

Parolla saw the corpse of one of the horsemen rise to its feet. "If we drive the tiktar off, the Huntsmen would only attack us. We should use this time to think of a way to destroy the creature."

"Alas, it appears we may have other demands on our time. Uninvited guests, yes? There, among the trees."

"I see them." A dozen Vamilians were approaching along a track to Parolla's left. A look round revealed yet more undead drawing in from all directions. "You have an idea, *sirrah*?"

There was a gleam in the *archmagus*'s eyes. "Mottle is ever brimming with invention, overflowing with—"

"We don't have time for this."

"Of course." Mottle looked up at the sky. The wind had faded since the torrential downpour earlier, but now it picked up again as the old man drew on the energy of the storm. Not a good idea, to Parolla's mind, with the *archmagus* still drunk on power, but it seemed he wasn't waiting for her blessing because a vortex of gray cloud was already re-forming above the hill. "The storm holds the answers," he cried. "The storm holds *all* the answers. Mottle will call in the storm!"

The sky overhead darkened as the clouds began to thicken. Barbs of lightning speared the gloom. The vortex spun faster and faster, the gale tearing at Parolla's hair and clothing, lashing rain into her face. She lifted her hood and held it in place with both hands. Mottle raised his arms to the storm. She half expected him to be hoisted into the air so he could ride the wind as he had against the Fangalar, but instead the whirlwind descended on the hill, Mottle and Parolla at its center. The city at the foot of the slope disappeared behind dark, whirling walls. At first the storm's eye was more than tenscore paces across. Then it contracted.

To Parolla's left a Vamilian boy was plucked from the hilltop, limbs flailing, and sucked up into the murk. Another of the undead followed, then another, and another. One woman had the presence of mind to seize a branch of one of the trees. A heartbeat later her legs were pulled out from under her, and she pivoted round the branch, her feet in the air as if she were doing a handstand. Then a wall of cloud engulfed her.

Parolla looked across to where the battle between the tiktar and the Huntsmen still raged, saw the combatants were far enough from the vortex to resist its tug. Only four of the riders remained in their saddles, among them the leader. Even now, though, he was being dragged to the ground by two of his erstwhile companions. His ax caught one of them a blow to the helmet, shattering its antlers. Then one of the tiktar's flaming swords punched through his jaw, dislodging his helmet.

As the elderling turned in search of another opponent, Parolla sent a wave of sorcery crackling toward it. Caught unawares, the creature shrieked as the death-magic struck. It swung to face her and tried to take a step forward, but was prevented from doing so by her sorcery.

Got you.

"Closer, *sirrah*!" Parolla cried to Mottle. "Bring the storm closer! The tiktar!"

Giggling, the old man nodded.

The whirlwind came roaring in. A bank of cloud rolled first over the Huntsmen, then over the tiktar itself, and the elderling was lifted from the ground. It unfurled its wings with a crack and began beating them swiftly in an attempt to control its ascent.

In vain.

Parolla saw flames amid the gray as the creature spiraled upward into the belly of the storm. Mottle whooped his delight, spinning round and round as he tried to follow its path.

In the blink of an eye the tiktar disappeared.

Romany felt herself supported to the ground. A dagger slipped from Danel's hand and clattered to the floor. The blade was covered with blood.

Her head cradled on Danel's lap, the priestess looked into her servant's eyes. *No, not my servant. Mayot's all along.* Somehow over the course of the past few days Romany had managed to lose sight of the thread of death-magic jutting from the girl's chest. Enslaved by the Book, Danel was no less a creature of Mayot's will than the hundreds of hapless souls who threw themselves beneath the blades of Shroud's disciples.

When Danel spoke, the hollowness of her voice was in marked contrast to the sorrow in her eyes. "I tried. I tried to warn you."

Yes, you did, Romany realized, thinking back on their conversation. "And if the strike aimed at you is also unseen?" the girl had said. "I have my orders." Romany, though, had long ago stopped seeing Danel as one of the undead. Instead the Vamilian had become, what? A confidante? A companion? Romany's soft laugh brought blood frothing to her lips. How the Spider would scold her now if she were here.

"Mayot's first command," Danel went on, "was that I should kill you if you attempted to leave. His second, to say nothing of the first. The Book . . . I tried to resist . . ."

Romany patted the girl's hand. "Hush, my dear."

Her sleeve was lying in water again, but she did not have the strength to move it. It seemed Mayot had not, after all, been ignorant of the threat she posed. It was quite flattering, really, for even with so many powerful enemies closing in the old man had kept her at the forefront of his mind. Had he feared she might ally with Shroud's minions to bring him down? Perhaps try to take the Book for herself?

A memory came to her then of a discussion she'd had with Danel by the burial ground at the edge of the city. The girl had been unusually loquacious that day, and the priestess now wondered whether her questions had in fact been Mayot's. Something Romany had said came back to her: "When Mayot falls you will be freed from his grasp." "*If* he falls," Danel had replied. "No," Romany said. "When." She'd spoken the words to give the girl hope. Instead perhaps all she had done was reveal her hand to Mayot, and in hindsight Danel's answering look of sadness had borne testimony to Romany's mistake. What other unguarded comments had she made during her time with the girl? What other clues had she given as to her plans?

"The dome . . ." she whispered. "I was going . . . to free you . . ."

Danel looked away. "I know."

Romany coughed. "I . . . did not mean . . ." *To make you feel worse than you already do,* was what she had intended to say, but the words would not come. Every breath now gurgled in her chest and sent a stab of fire through her back. A sob escaped her lips.

"The pain will not last long," Danel said, raising a hand to her chest. "I still carry the memory."

The Fangalar blade that killed you, yes. I had not forgotten. Romany shifted uncomfortably, expecting another throb of pain. Instead she found Danel was right—the agony was already fading to be replaced by numbness. She felt cold, too. Heartbeats ago the room had seemed stiflingly hot, but now Romany's teeth were chattering, and Danel shrugged out of her cloak and laid it across her.

The Spider would not step in to save her, Romany knew. The goddess's power had to be channeled through the priestess herself, and she was in no condition to work sorcery. Nor would the Spider risk setting foot on the mortal realm. *My risk, I said.* Romany looked past Danel at the dark, stormy skies. Was the goddess watching her even now? Was she aware of Romany's ignominious fall from grace, or had she already moved on to the next game?

Danel stroked her hair. "I'm sorry."

"Nonsense," the priestess said. "Not your fault . . . Just a pawn . . ." *A pawn in a game initiated by my own hand.* Strangely, the thought lifted her spirits—to think that in some way she, and not Mayot, had ultimately been the architect of her own downfall. *Perhaps in the end I outwitted even myself.*

Danel was speaking again, but Romany could not focus on the

words. Darkness hovered at the edges of her vision, and each of her breaths was shallower than the last. There remained one move left to her in the game, and that was to take her spirit beyond Mayot's reach. True, it would mean oblivion, but the magic of that cursed Book could not work on her if there was no soul to call back to her body. It would be a small victory over Mayot, all things considered, but Romany hoped the old man lived long enough to know of it nonetheless.

It was hard to concentrate through her discomfort, but eventually she succeeded in freeing her spirit from her body. Rising into the air, she paused to look down on herself. Her face was now as pale as Danel's, and her lips were tinged blue, yet even in death there was a striking dignity to her expression, a nobility to her features.

The world, Romany decided, would be a poorer place without her.

With a sigh she fled along the threads of her web until she came to the end of the longest remaining strand.

There, to her surprise, she found the Spider waiting for her, smiling wryly as she opened her arms to welcome Romany into her embrace.

As it turned out, Luker did not have to carve a way through the undead to Mayot—the mage did that for him. Mayot had shuffled to the edge of the dais, his face twisted with fury at the loss of his undead champions. With one arm he clutched the Book to his chest; with the other he pointed at Luker. The aura of darkness about him expanded, swallowing the line of Vamilian girls behind the throne. The Guardian watched as they burst into flames, feeling glad he wasn't on Mayot's side—right now the old man was doing more damage to his own servants than he was to the enemy.

Then, from the mage's fingers, a wave of blackness came speeding toward Luker, incinerating the undead between them.

Gathering his Will, the Guardian hit back.

Their powers clashed with a thunderclap that shook the dome. Death-magic sprayed in all directions, tearing into the Vamilians round the dais and shearing through the trunk of one of the flaming trees.

It toppled.

The slightest pressure from Luker's Will changed the course of its descent, and it plummeted toward Mayot.

The old man gestured. A burst of sorcery smashed the tree to splinters before continuing upward to strike the roof of the dome. Luker heard a crack, felt thuds through his boots as masonry came crashing down to his right. A pity none of those stones had come down near Mayot else the Guardian could have tried to land them on the mage's head as he had with the tree. Rain fell about him, driven on the wind that still whistled through the building.

The tree had distracted Mayot long enough for Luker to launch a counterattack. Cleaving a path through the waves of the old man's death-magic, he drove against the wards surrounding him.

He might as well have been slapping his hand against a cliff face for all the effect he had.

Laughing, Mayot increased the ferocity of his assault. The air trembled again as his power collided with Luker's, but this time the Guardian's defenses withered before the onslaught. If he could shunt the attacks to one side he might ease the pressure that was building, but if he did so he risked deflecting the sorcery into the path of Merin or one of the Sartorians. From the sounds of fighting behind, the consel and his soldiers had given up on trying to escape and were now battling for their lives. Whether they survived or not mattered nothing to Luker, but as of this moment they were the only ones guarding his back.

The wall of darkness loomed closer.

Did Shroud's sword hold the answer? If Luker hurled it at Mayot would the sorcery invested in the weapon protect it from the Book's death-magic? He adjusted his grip on the hilt. It would be a difficult throw. Mayot's outline was little more than a shadow through the waves of blackness, but then Luker was fast running out of options, his defenses unraveling before him with alarming swiftness.

He drew back his sword arm.

Galea's intervention had sealed the passage against the wall of flames, shielding Ebon and—inadvertently, he suspected—Vale as well. Now Ebon stood at the end of the walkway, the sound of crashing waves in his ears. The inside of the dome was lit by a number of roving fires, and it took him a moment to recognize them as blazing undead. The flames guttered as rain swept down from two holes in the roof.

Ebon took in the piles of corpses scattered across the floor, the ranks of faceless spirits standing motionless like discarded shadows, the exchange of sorcery between an old man on a dais and a younger man below him—one of a small knot of fighters surrounded by Vamilians.

Then he saw the consel.

"Vale," he said, but the Endorian was already moving. He crossed the dome in a ripple of motion, cutting into the ranks of undead.

Drawing his saber, Ebon ran to keep up. The goddess's power flowed cold in his veins, and he knocked from his path an undead warrior that tried to intercept him. A spear flashed for his head, and he raised his saber to parry, but the impact never came, the weapon glancing off his wards. The Sartorians were fivescore paces away. The consel was fighting between two of his soldiers, an expression of controlled rage on his face. To his left, a grim-faced stranger with the look of a veteran about him wielded a sword and longknife with cool efficiency. A pile of motionless corpses was forming in front of the man, yet still more of the Vamilians were scrambling over their fallen kin to attack him. Ebon picked up his speed.

Fifty paces.

Vale was a blur at the edge of his vision. The king saw him decapitate a brown-robed monk with flaming eyes before passing from sight again. Ahead the consel's sword had snagged in the chest of an undead spearman. Abandoning the weapon, Garat kicked his assailant away and reached behind him. "Sword!" he shouted. His companions, though, were too hard-pressed to obey. Cursing, the consel seized an undead warrior's wrist and pulled him into a head-butt, then wrestled his sword from his grasp and spun him into the path of a woman behind.

Suddenly Ebon was directly in front of him. Garat's blade flashed for his neck, only to strike his defenses and bounce off. The consel's look of recognition was followed by a frown. Ebon nodded to him. No doubt that attack had been an accident, yet still he felt a prickle between his shoulders as he stepped past and drew level with the man battling Mayot.

Flames from those of the Vamilians still ablaze threw a flickering light on the stranger's scarred face. His features were a mask of concentration. In one hand he held a sword that throbbed with power.

"Fool!" the goddess hissed in Ebon's mind. "An attack from the flank would have caught Mayot off guard."

Sheathing his saber, Ebon gestured at the man on his left. "How long can he hold?"

"What does it matter? We must use this diversion—"

"You have a short memory, my Lady," Ebon cut in. "Or have you forgotten the Fangalar already? Mayot is more powerful than their leader, is he not? I cannot bring him down on my own."

"You, mortal? You are nothing! Without my help—"

"Enough! How do we defeat the old man?"

"The Book gives Mayot power, but he wields it indiscriminately, without craft or refinement."

"Meaning he is vulnerable to a focused attack."

"Focused, yes."

The scarred stranger's defenses were buckling beneath Mayot's assault. A few more heartbeats and they would fail completely. "Let's finish this," Ebon said.

At that moment the stranger drew back his sword arm.

The force of the sorcery battering Luker diminished abruptly, and he let out a groan. A new power had joined its will to his, driving Mayot back. He became aware of a figure beside him, and he looked right to see a shaven-headed man. He was shorter and more slightly built than Luker, and the lines about his eyes gave him the look of someone older than he no doubt was. Waves of magic poured from his hands with a chill that steamed the air. Luker had never seen him before.

"You took your bloody time," he said.

A tight smile was Baldy's only response.

Luker lowered his sword arm. Risking a look behind, he saw that Baldy had come alone. No, not alone, there was a second stranger fighting the undead, moving so fast that eyes other than Luker's might not have seen him. The Vamilians were being hacked to pieces by his whirling blade.

A timeshifter.

Luker's gaze swung to the sword he'd been about to throw at Mayot. He grinned. "Endorian!" he bellowed, flinging the blade high into the air behind him.

Knowing that by the time it came down again, the man would be there to catch it. With the invested sword in the timeshifter's hands, the tables would turn on the undead host.

Leaving just Mayot himself to deal with.

Luker bared his teeth.

Time to see what Baldy here is made of.

Having spun himself dizzy trying to follow the tiktar's ascent into the vortex, Mottle sat down heavily in the mud. Parolla strode to join him, her gaze moving constantly over the surging walls of cloud. The elderling would still be out there somewhere, she knew, for if a storm's worth of rain couldn't destroy the thing, it seemed unlikely a bit of wind would do the job. All Mottle had done was to buy them some time.

"*Sirrah!*" she shouted. "The storm! Push it back! We need to see . . ."

The old man ignored her. Giggling, he struggled to his feet and stretched out his arms. A lazy flap lifted him into the air. Then, when he began to sink, another flap kept him hovering above the ground. Parolla seized his sleeve and tugged him back down.

"*Sirrah!*"

The gale had caught one of the trees felled in the battle with the tiktar. First its upper branches and then its trunk were hauled from the ground as the tree was snatched up into the gloom. Mottle whooped as it disappeared from view.

A flash of light to Parolla's right.

Releasing the old man's sleeve, she had time only to half turn before the fireball was upon them. With a cry she raised her wards, braced herself for the tiktar's impact . . .

But this time she was not the elderling's target.

From the corner of her eye she saw Mottle flap his arms again, frantic this time as he sought to lift himself out of the tiktar's reach.

Too late.

As the elderling struck, Mottle was knocked backward to within a few armspans of the swirling vortex. He beat helplessly at the flames that engulfed him, his screams terrible to hear.

No!

Driven back by the heat, Parolla could only watch as the tiktar wrapped its arms round the struggling old man. She started to gather her power, but a volley of death-magic would simply hasten Mottle's passing. "To me!" she screamed at the elderling, but it paid her no mind. Lowering its head, it sank its teeth into the *archmagus*'s neck.

Mottle's screams continued as he clawed at the creature's face.

Then he gestured.

And the whirlwind came roaring in.

Ebon shivered at the touch of Galea's sorcery. He had lost sensation in his arms and feet again, and the numbness was beginning to travel along his limbs. The goddess's pinpoint strike cleaved through Mayot's power like the tip of a spear through flesh, dissolving the shadows about the dais until the blackness contracted to a dark core round Mayot. Her assault faltered, though, as it reached the old man's innermost shields, the Book's death-magic devouring the sorcery that assailed it, stealing its momentum.

The tide started to turn.

Then the scarred stranger standing next to Ebon reentered the fray. His attack on Mayot landed like a drum beat, throwing the old man from his feet and sending him skidding across the dais toward his toppled throne. His head cracked against an armrest, and he grunted. Somehow, though, he managed to retain his grip on the Book. And while the combined powers of Ebon and the stranger continued to rage about him, his defenses held.

Mayot pushed himself to his feet.

Ebon could now see the old man clearly through the shadows that surrounded him. His wispy white hair and unkempt beard were flecked with blood, and more blood trickled from one side of his mouth. Tilting his head, he spat red phlegm onto the floor. When he counterattacked, the warring sorceries of the two sides momentarily canceled each other out.

Then Ebon felt the mage draw further on his reserves. The flesh of Mayot's hand where it clutched the Book started to blister, and sores formed on his skin, darkening through purple to black. The old man's agonized shriek rode the burgeoning waves of death-magic.

As the balance of power tipped in the mage's favor, Galea tried to increase the sorcery flowing through Ebon, but he had nothing more to give. She shifted her attack, searching for some point of weakness in Mayot's onslaught.

Without success.

For while there was no more focus to the old man's assault now than there had been before, the sheer weight of his magic was irresistible.

Ebon was driven back a step.

Luker muttered an oath. He'd nearly had the bastard!

Baldy's power had driven a fissure through Mayot's wall of death-magic, and Luker had released his Will all at once against the old man's inner defenses, expecting to see them come crashing down. Instead Mayot's wards had held, and the chance had passed. To make matters worse the mage evidently possessed powers he hadn't yet called on, for the waves of death-magic surging from him had increased in intensity, annihilating the sorcery that opposed them.

Mayot's rally, though, came at a price. The mage was aging before Luker's eyes, the flesh of his face becoming sallow, the gray in his beard fading to white. The blackness claiming his left hand had reached his wrist and was now spreading up his arm where it disappeared beneath the cuff of his robe. Another quarter-bell, Luker judged, and the mage would likely be on the other end of one of those threads of death-magic.

A quarter of a bell, though, was time the Guardian did not have. Handspan by handspan Mayot's sorcery drew closer. The magic was weakening still further the barrier separating the world from Shroud's realm, for the shadowy spirits residing there now burst into flames where they came into contact with the old man's power. The stone floor in front of Luker had melted, and a section of the steps leading up to the dais had become a stream of molten rock. He blinked sweat from his eyes. The effort of keeping Mayot at bay was taking its toll. His head felt as if a score of demons were trying to claw their way out, and his concentration was slipping away. In an effort to rediscover his focus he tried recalling the moments leading up to Kanon's death, but the pain was beginning to eclipse all else.

It was clear to Luker that, even with Baldy's help, he could not match Mayot. Nor could he hope to retreat with so many undead assembled behind him—the frenzied clash of swords still rang loud in his ears. And with Shroud's blade now in the Endorian's hands, that just left . . .

His eyes widened.

Luker turned to Baldy. The stranger's eyebrows were crusted with ice, and his labored breaths misted the air in front of him. Luker leaned close. "Hold him," he shouted. "I've got an idea."

Without waiting for a response, he withdrew his power from the sorcerous shield holding back Mayot's assault. Baldy stood firm for an instant, then sank to his knees.

A few moments. Just give me a few Shroud-cursed moments.
Luker prepared to hurl his Will at an altogether different target.

Hold him.

Ebon barely had time to register the scarred stranger's words, never mind protest, before the full crushing force of Mayot's sorcery settled on him.

Galea's response was to channel yet more power into him, until Ebon thought his blood would freeze. He struggled against the flood for a heartbeat, then stopped himself. What was the point in resisting? What was he saving himself for? The goddess's words from their first meeting came back to him. "You must surrender yourself to me," she had said. Was that the answer? Let go, and allow Galea to use him as she would?

Ebon felt his heart lurch. The numbness was spreading beyond his arms and legs, and he was battling against a rising tide of blackness. His awareness of the goddess's contest with Mayot receded. Instead his thoughts turned inward, and he saw again Lamella's face in the moments before they had parted for the final time; the hordes of Vamilians sweeping through the breach in Majack's walls; Grimes's swaying back as he rode into the haze that shrouded the plains outside the city. As Ebon's breathing became more ragged, he clung to the memories, painful though they were. *All the better for that.* Because the pain meant he was still alive, still fighting.

Then, as waves of darkness started to break over him, he ground his teeth together and struggled to hold on for a few moments more. One faltering breath at a time. Not because he expected it to make a difference, but because there was nothing else he could do.

His chin struck his chest.

Oblivion reached for him.

Parolla stood alone at the eye of the storm, staring up into the gloom. There was no sign of the tiktar or the *archmagus*. Could the old man still be alive? It was no accident, surely, that the vortex had come rolling in moments earlier. Mottle had *wanted* the whirlwind to claim him, and the gale would have carried him up into the center of the maelstrom, the very heart of his power. Could the storm sustain him? Restore him, even?

Parolla snorted. Who was she kidding? Another companion lost to her. And, as with Tumbal, she had done nothing to help. When the tiktar had sped toward them she'd thought only of protecting herself. It was no excuse that the elderling had ignored the *archmagus* until that point. Twice already Mottle's interventions had saved Parolla, so of course the tiktar was going to turn on him eventually. Why did enlightenment always come to her too late? Why was Parolla always the one to survive while those around her fell? *Because my blood is cursed. Because death is drawn to me like a lodestone.*

The wind was dying away now, the walls of cloud thinning until Parolla could once again see the shadows of trees beyond. Mottle's power was fading, she realized—a clear sign the old man was dead. Dark shapes fell from the sky as if spat out by the storm. With a crunch the body of a horse hit the ground. Beside it, a Vamilian woman was using a spear as a crutch as she struggled to rise on broken legs. She managed a single step before collapsing again. Not all of the undead were similarly incapacitated, though. Parolla could see ghostly figures gathering beyond the vortex. When the breeze dropped further, they would come for her.

As for the tiktar . . .

Parolla turned slowly round, wondering from which direction the elderling would attack. Last time she had not seen it until it was almost upon her. Would she have a chance to react before it struck? Parolla barked a laugh. What did it matter? Even with Mottle beside her she had been no match for the elderling. Now she would have the Vamilians to contend with, too. There would be no holding back their combined threat.

It ends here.

Parolla felt a surge of bitterness, and the darkness in her blood came boiling up in response. She had the strength to defeat the tiktar if she would just embrace it. What did it matter if she had to draw on powers she'd never dared to wield before? Both Tumbal and Mottle would be safe now if she'd had the courage to take the charge upon herself sooner.

But at what cost?

A memory came to Parolla of the time she had fled the Lord of the Hunt's temple after her mother passed away. Dozens of innocents had died in her confrontation with the temple's keepers, for even after the priests were dead she'd gone on killing anyone unfortunate enough to step into her path. When the slaughter was done it had taken her weeks to . . . rediscover . . . herself. And she was more powerful now than she had been then. What if this time there was no coming back?

Parolla's fingernails bit into her palms. *What choice do I have?* The chance she had been seeking for years was within her grasp. With the Book of Lost Souls in her hands she could strike at Shroud himself. Make him pay for the pain he had caused her. Had she come all this way for no reason? Would she simply surrender herself to Mayot and the Book's control?

Would she do nothing?

A burst of flames from the corner of her eye. She spun to her left, death-magic erupting from her hands.

A wave of blackness hit the tiktar as it flashed across the hilltop. The elderling held its form for several heartbeats before melting away, flames leaping to the trunk of a fallen tree.

Parolla crossed to stand over it, sorcery pouring from her fingers. Death-magic incinerated the trunk to ash that was then seized by the wind and carried away. The tiktar, though, remained caught in the grip of Parolla's power, thrashing helplessly as the sorcery devoured it. Parolla laughed. Blood pounded in her temples, filling her ears with its roar. As the elderling howled its torment, a part of her looked on in horror at what she had unleashed.

Then that horror, too, was burned away by the darkness.

Luker had no real understanding of what made up the veil that separated this world from Shroud's realm, nor why Mayot's death-magic was eating away at it. Was the Book's sorcery somehow weakening the reality of this world or strengthening that of the next? Did the distinction matter, and if so, how did that help him? In order to concentrate his Will, after all, he needed to know what he was trying to accomplish.

Whatever he was going to do, he would have to do it quickly, for he could hear the clash of blades close behind, see the raging storm of Mayot's sorcery creeping ever nearer. Reaching out with his senses, he focused on the maelstrom of death-magic pounding against Baldy's defenses. The power at the heart of the conflagration was too intense for Luker to make out what effect the sorceries were having, but around the edges . . .

His eyes narrowed. *Aye, I see it now.* The energies feeding the Book came from the dying forest, but the act of shaping those energies drew on the forces of Shroud's realm. It appeared the sorcery required to animate Mayot's undead army had forged an enduring link between the two worlds, bringing them closer together. To weaken the barrier still further would, the Guardian suspected, increase the power of the Book. Much good that would do Mayot, though. The old man wouldn't be getting a chance to use it.

Assuming Luker's hunch was correct, of course.

He rolled his shoulders. With or without his aid, the veil would come down soon. Might as well be around to see it when it did.

It was time for the final roll of the dice.

In order to bring the full weight of his Will to bear, Luker needed to block out the world round him using an exercise he had learned many years ago as Kanon's apprentice. First, he shut his eyes. Next, he started to screen off the perceptions of his other senses: the crackle of Mayot's sorcery, the heat of the air on his face, the shouts of the fighters behind—even now a man's death cry sounded above the tumult. *Not my problem.* The tightness of Luker's burned skin, the ache at the back of his throat, the throb of his headache: all began to fade away as if his mind had fled the ravages of his body. Then, as his focus sharpened, awareness of his thoughts diminished too: his doubts concerning his future, his grief and guilt at Kanon's loss, his worries over Jenna's fate. One by one they left him, until all that remained was his Will.

He felt a moment of euphoria, of intoxicating power, as if all things were now possible if he had but the breadth of vision to imagine them. He had experienced the sensation often enough, though, to recognize it for the dangerous illusion it was. While the likes of Chamery and Mayot might succumb to their delusions of omnipotence, Luker had eyes only for the task at hand.

Steeling himself, he hurled his power against the veil.

It happened gradually at first—layers of existence peeling back, a skewing of reality, one world melting away as another took shape. The barrier was already so gossamer-thin that it seemed a mere breath of wind would rip it apart, and once again the Guardian found himself wondering whether Mayot had deliberately tried to tear down the mantle. For if the mage, like Luker now, had *wanted* to fashion a way through to Shroud's realm it meant one of them had made a big misjudgment. Then again, perhaps Mayot had intended to repair the damage at a later time. Perhaps the Book gave him the power to do so.

Pushing such thoughts aside, Luker hammered over and over at the barrier. It started to weaken, but slowly, slowly. Even through his sensory detachment, the Guardian could feel Mayot's wall of death-magic edging closer. It appeared Baldy's resistance was fading, but then if Luker was right the power of the Book, and hence the forces assailing the shaven-headed stranger, would be increasing as the veil weakened.

He readied himself for one final assault.

Even as he did so there was a ripping sound, and the barrier's dissolution took on a momentum of its own. Flinching, Luker pulled back lest he be drawn fully into the realm that was taking shape beyond the rent he had created.

A new wind blew through the dome, cold like the breath of the dead. He heard whispering voices all about, hushed at first, then growing louder. When he opened his eyes he saw the spirits of the underworld were no longer black blurs, but rather people with features as clear and empty as those of the Vamilians among whom they stood. Mayot was still visible at the top of the steps. Beyond him, though, other images were forming: a range of hills silhouetted against a cloudless gray sky; a circle of standing stones ahead and to Luker's left; shadows moving across the landscape, silent and swift.

He had done it. The dome was now as much a part of the underworld as it was the mortal realm.

Luker released his hold on his Will.

Pain lanced his skull, hot and white, and he groaned. Never before had he drawn so intensely on his power. A wave of dizziness swept over him. His stomach spasmed, and acid burned the back of his throat. Raising his hands to his temples, he sank to his knees and retched. When he took a breath, he found the air tasted of ash and smoke, and he vomited again.

He did not know how much time passed before he was able to look up. At some point Mayot's attack had stopped, and the old man now stood at the edge of the dais, clutching the Book to his chest as he gazed about in wonder. The corruption to his left hand must have spread along the full length of his arm, for the skin round the neckline of his robe was black and withered too. He turned to Luker and gave a dry laugh.

"You fool!" he crowed. "Do you know what you've done? An entire world delivered into my hands! Countless more souls to serve me!"

Luker scanned the barren landscape. Nothing stirred, and for a moment he thought he had made a mistake. Then, from the direction of the hills, a darkness came rushing toward the dais.

The Guardian smiled. "You forget, old man. These souls already have a master. And you're now standing on his patch."

What little color remained in Mayot's cheeks drained away. He made to turn to face the oncoming blackness, but before he could do so a huge claw punched through his chest, emerging in a spray of gore. Wide-eyed, the mage looked down at the claw, disbelieving. Then his back arched and he screamed. Blood fountained from his mouth as he was lifted into the air.

The dais was enveloped by swirling shadows, a great wall of them so dense the light from the fires in the dome could not penetrate them. Black tendrils snaked from the darkness toward Mayot, wrapping themselves round his thrashing body. Where they came to settle, the mage's skin blistered and split with a hissing noise like water tossed in boiling oil. He screamed again. Shadows poured into his mouth, smothering the sound.

A good thing, too. All that screeching wasn't doing anything for Luker's headache.

Mayot hung above the dais, tearing at the claw as if he thought he might pull himself free. Then he was drawn back. As he reached the wall of shadows, the Book of Lost Souls slipped from his fingers. A taloned hand shot out from the gloom, snatched for it, but succeeded only in knocking it farther away.

A growl of frustration set the air quivering. The hand withdrew.

The Book skidded across the dais and slid partway down the steps to the right of the molten river of rock. It came to rest a dozen paces from Luker, its pages open, facing down.

Stillness descended on the dome. Even the wind seemed to have died. Mayot had disappeared into the blackness on the dais, but another figure was beginning to take shape there. Luker's headache burgeoned as the newcomer's power washed over him.

Shroud, for it had to be the god, stepped into view. Standing half again as tall as Luker, his form was as smoky and insubstantial as the darkness that cloaked him. Black tendrils clung to his form as if unwilling to release him to the light. The impression of a face was visible within the gloom, but the shifting shadows made it impossible to discern any features save for the eyes that glittered like twin chips of obsidian.

Wincing, Luker forced himself to his feet. *Wouldn't want the bastard thinking I'm kneeling on his account.*

The Lord of the Dead turned his head from side to side, taking in the dome.

Then his gaze settled on the Book.

Luker scowled.

Oh no you don't.

Even after the tiktar had stopped fighting back it was some time before Parolla broke off her attack. The elderling had shrunken to a single flickering flame, tugged this way and that by the wind. Parolla gathered it in her hand. The fire licked at her skin, but she felt no pain. Had this creature really threatened her? It seemed difficult to believe, a lifetime ago. It would be so simple for her to close her fingers and snuff out the flame forever.

She cast the tiktar to the storm.

Looking round, Parolla saw the hilltop had been devastated by her sorcery. Nothing remained standing for a hundred paces on every side. Blackened tree stumps protruded from the ground, none of them more than an armspan tall, while beyond, scores of Vamilians stood statue-still in the rain. Parolla sensed the threads holding the undead were still in place, but the flow of energy along them had ceased. That could mean only one thing: the hand controlling the Vamilians was gone. She frowned. Mayot fallen? *The death stroke should have been mine!*

She took a shuddering breath and attempted to let go of her anger, found she could not.

Wiping rain from her eyes, she scanned the undead. They stood in ranks three deep, their gazes staring through her. Those with shattered limbs had stopped trying to rise and now lay unmoving in the mud and standing water. Parolla was not deceived by their sudden lifelessness, though. They were still a threat to her, for doubtless a new hand would take up the Book and assume Mayot's place as puppet master. She should strike now while the undead were defenseless. The darkness flooding her veins demanded release.

Parolla dug her nails once more into her palms, shivering at the pain it brought. Looking down, she saw the blood flowing to her wrists was black.

She could sense the rent within the dome now. So this was it. The way was finally open to her—a gateway to Shroud's realm. The years of searching were over. How had the path been opened? Mayot, perhaps? Had he spent his life in its creation? Parolla shook her head. It mattered not. The Book would soon be hers, and with it the power to bring about her vengeance.

But there was something else, she realized. A new presence was entering the dome through the rent. Parolla's heartbeat quickened as she felt the stranger's power bloom outward—a power that surpassed even her own.

Then her lips curled in a smile.

Better and better.

There was no longer any need for her to run. Her strength was such that she could now ride the strands of death-magic in body as well as in spirit. Gathering her power around her, she closed her eyes.

CHAPTER 23

EBON'S FIRST thought was that he must have died and passed through Shroud's Gate, for when the blackness finally cleared from his vision he found himself staring not at Mayot Mencada but at a dread apparition wreathed in shadow. Galea had fled from his mind at its approach, leaving Ebon in no doubt as to the newcomer's identity.

Shroud.

Through his struggles to stave off unconsciousness he had sensed nothing of Mayot's fate, nor of the creation of the rent. He recalled the scarred stranger saying he had an idea. Had he summoned Shroud to this place? Was he one of the god's disciples that he could call on the Lord of the Dead? Or had Shroud intervened of his own accord to crush the pretender to his throne?

The floor round Ebon was blanketed with frost that was beginning to melt in the rain. The Book of Lost Souls lay on the steps to his right, no more than a dozen paces away. Was this victory, then? It did not feel so to Ebon. True, the undead now lacked a master. The attack on Majack—if his city still held—would have halted, but those of his people who had already fallen would remain enslaved by the threads of death-magic. And if a new hand were to take up the Book . . .

To his left, the scarred stranger rose to his feet. Vale stood a few paces away, dozens of Vamilian bodies piled round him. The Endorian's shoulders were slumped, and his left arm hung limp. In his right hand he clutched a sword dripping blood to the ground. *Blood.* Ebon drew a breath.

The undead did not bleed.

Consel Garat Hallon lay unconscious or dead beneath a Vamilian spearman. The only surviving Sartorian soldier, a woman, was kneeling beside him, her right ear pressed to his chest, listening for a pulse. Evidently the consel was alive, because the soldier tore a sleeve from her shirt and started fashioning a sling. The only other survivor, the veteran who Ebon assumed was a friend of the scarred stranger, was sheathing his sword and tucking his longknife into his belt. When his gaze met Ebon's his expression was appraising, but doubtless the king's own look was no more welcoming. Moments before, the powers assembled here had been allies in their struggle against Mayot, but what were they now with the old man gone? Ebon glanced at the Book of Lost Souls. If the only way to stop someone taking Mayot's place was to claim the Book himself, would he do so?

Still kneeling, he shifted his gaze back to Shroud. The room spun suddenly. He threw out a hand to steady himself, and sparks flickered as his fingers touched the frosty ground. Galea's sorcery still raged through his blood. His arms and legs were numb, and he staggered as he pushed himself upright. He could not feel the floor beneath his feet, nor the stubble on his chin as he passed a hand across it. Was this how it felt to be one of the undead? Trapped in a prison of senseless flesh?

There was a pause. Who would break the silence? Who would make the opening move?

He didn't have to wait long to find out. The black tendrils twisting round Shroud started to snake their way across the dais toward the Book.

Then they shrank back.

Ebon sensed a new presence at his side, and he looked right to see a woman standing there. It took him a heartbeat to recognize the necromancer from the hill. Something about Parolla had changed. Her midnight eyes burned, and her blood-streaked features were darkened by a shadow that had nothing to do with the gloom within the dome. Her gaze was fixed on Shroud.

There was no sign of Mottle.

When Parolla spoke, Ebon assumed he must have misheard.

For what she said to Shroud was, "Hello, Father."

Parolla watched Shroud retreat a half pace toward the wall of darkness. The shadows about him were too deep for her to make out his face. Shades of black hinted at features, but his expression was shielded from her. *He hides from me now as he always has.* She risked a look round the dome. There was no sign of Mayot Mencada, but the blood dripping from Shroud's fingers told her all she needed to know of the old man's fate. The Book lay a score of paces away on the stairs. All she had to do was take a few steps and reach out her hand . . .

No.

First she wanted answers.

She looked back at Shroud. The weight of his gaze was crushing, but Parolla forced herself to meet it. "What, nothing to say to me?" she said. "Is the emotion of the moment too much for you?"

When the god spoke his words made the air tremble. "Why are you here?"

She nodded at the Book. "Perhaps for the same reason you are." Her lips quirked. "Or should that be for the same reason Mayot Mencada was?"

The tendrils of darkness round Shroud reared and darted forward.

"I spoke to the *magus* several days ago," Parolla went on. "He believed the Book would give him the power to defeat you."

"He was wrong. And for his impertinence he now faces an eternity of suffering. As will all those who stand in my way." Shroud had raised his voice to speak these last words, no doubt intending them as a threat to the others assembled in the dome.

Parolla did not look round to see how his warning was greeted. Glancing again at the Book, she adopted a light tone. "Careless of you, Father, to let the Book fall into the hands of another. But then it was never yours to begin with, was it? It belonged to your predecessor. You remember him, don't you? The god you betrayed."

Shroud did not reply.

"I have seen the place of lost souls," she continued. "The world you destroyed in claiming your throne."

"Indeed. I trust you enjoyed your stay."

"Don't play games with me! Or would you have me believe your power is any more permanent than that of the god you usurped? For all your arrogance, you are vulnerable."

Shroud's laugh shook the dais. "Of course I am vulnerable! Every immortal is. There will always be those whose ambition drives them to challenge us. Like Mayot Mencada." He paused. "And like you, my dear."

"You're wrong. I don't want to take your place."

"Then why are you here? Why have you embraced the dark?"

Had she? *No! The tiktar . . . I had no choice.* Shroud was trying to confuse her, to distract her from the real reason she had come.

"My Lord Shroud," one of the men to her left began.

The god's raised hand commanded him to silence.

"I searched for you," Parolla said. "For a portal that would lead me to the underworld. I even tried to contact you—left messages with your disciples. You ignored me."

"Perhaps I had nothing to say to you."

"Or perhaps you didn't have the stomach to hear what I would say to you."

"Oh?"

"You know what I'm talking about," Parolla said. Her mother's face appeared in her mind's eye. "You will pay, Father, for what you did to her. You . . . forced yourself on her."

The god was silent for a moment, his gaze steady on Parolla. She needed to see his face to know what he was thinking. His expression, though, remained veiled in shadow. "Aliana told you that?"

"She didn't have to! You took what you wanted, and you left her." *Left us.*

"You think I should have dropped in on the two of you from time to time? Perhaps let you ride on my shoulders?"

"Your touch killed her!"

"*My* touch? Aren't you forgetting your own part in her death?"

"A part I knew nothing about until it was too late. I didn't have the power to heal the damage you caused. But you . . . You could have saved her."

"And if she did not want to be saved?"

Parolla was stung silent for a heartbeat. "What do you mean?"

A note of amusement entered Shroud's voice. "If Aliana didn't tell you, I don't see why I—"

"Lies! You pretend a higher motive where there was none."

"And you will hear only the truth as you would have it. Is that not so, my dear?"

Parolla hesitated, then shook her head. Even after all Shroud had done she still wanted to believe him. The reality, though, was that he was trying to twist the truth to his own ends, to poison Parolla's memories against her. "Aliana told me . . . At the end . . ." An image came to her then: sitting beside her mother's bed in the inner sanctum of the Antlered God's temple, holding Aliana's left hand while trying not to notice the gangrenous stump where her right should have been. The skin of her mother's balding scalp was crisscrossed with black veins, and the stench of rot hung in the air. Aliana's voice had been no more than a whisper, but she'd said . . . She'd said . . .

Shroud's tone was mocking. "What? What did she say?"

The memory, though, was fading. Aliana's face, the white walls of the inner sanctum, the candles scented with malirange and dewflowers: all were dissolving into shadow. Parolla struggled to hold on to the scene, but the dark tide within her rose to engulf it. She rubbed a hand across her eyes. Had Shroud cast some enchantment to steal the memory from her? No, she would have sensed him drawing on his power. *What's happening to me?*

The god must have guessed her thoughts, for he said, "It is the blood, Parolla. *My* blood. You never learned to control its power, did you? No doubt you believed you could master the darkness, but instead it is claiming you. You should not have come."

A shadow fell across Parolla's vision. "Perhaps not. But I am here nonetheless."

Shroud took a step forward, and Parolla tensed. If he made any move for the Book, she would be ready. Instead the god said, "You think you would fare any better than Mayot with the Book in your hands?"

"You know I would."

"And if you fail? Are you prepared for the consequences?"

The shadows behind him began to swirl. Shapes took form, pushing against the darkness as if it were a black curtain. A face appeared. A young man . . . someone Parolla knew. Yes, she recalled now—from the temple where she'd been raised. An acolyte—one of those she had killed while escaping from the Antlered God's priests. Parolla hadn't meant to harm him—the power had slipped her control. She felt a stab of guilt, but it was quickly swept away by her blood.

The shadows rippled again. One after another, a host of faces appeared, all victims that Parolla had sent through Shroud's Gate. She recognized one of the guardians of the Thousand Barrows who had died screaming when he tried to deny her access; a man from an inn in Calad whose hands had wandered presumptuously; the slave girl she had silenced in Xavel during her flight to the river.

Had there really been so many?

Could they all have been mistakes?

And now, finally, the image of Aliana materialized. Parolla remembered the kind sad eyes, the gentle smile, the lines of pain that had been a feature of her mother's final days. Aliana had tried to hide that pain from Parolla, but her face had betrayed her at the end, as had the force with which she had gripped Parolla's hand. Parolla blinked back tears.

Shroud's cold voice cut through her thoughts. "All of these and more, their souls are now mine. Gifted to me by you, no less. If you challenge me and fail, they will share your torment. Is that what you want? Have they not suffered enough already?"

At his words something shattered inside Parolla. The waves of darkness came surging up again, immersing her. Drawing her lips back in a snarl, she took a step toward the Book.

Which suddenly rose into the air as if lifted by invisible hands.

Pages flapping, it flew across the dome.

Luker rolled his shoulders. Touching though this family get-together was, it was time to start winding things up.

Carried by his Will, the Book of Lost Souls settled into his hands, its cover slick with blood, its pages lying open. The paper was the color of bone and soft as cloth. Staring at the spidery script inside, he felt a disorientation as if he were falling into the Book. From the corner of his eye came a ripple of movement, and when he looked across he saw the heads of the undead turning toward him, their hollow gazes fixing on his.

Luker slammed the cover shut.

He could sense the threads of death-magic emanating from the Book, and for a moment he wondered whether it was possible to locate the strand that held Kanon. He shook his head. One among thousands? And even if he somehow found it, how was he supposed to sever it? Any attempt to use the Book, after all, would likely bring a swift response from the other players assembled here.

So now what?

Luker looked at Parolla. The woman had begun to gather her power, only to hesitate. If she attacked him she would leave herself open to a broadside from Shroud, and without the Book's power to call on that was surely not a fight she could win. But the Lord of the Dead was vulnerable too, Luker reminded himself. For while the dome was now part of the underworld, it remained no less a part of the mortal realm. *Meaning Daddy here is ripe for the picking.* Would Shroud risk a move against Parolla before the fate of the Book was decided? Luker doubted it.

Stalemate, then.

A stalemate the Guardian could use to his advantage.

"Well, well, Luker," Shroud said. "Wisdom returns quickly, I see. After you turned down my offer of service—"

"My answer stands," Luker cut in. "The Book must be destroyed."

From behind him Merin spoke in a low voice. "We can salvage this, Guardian. For the empire. There is still some benefit we—"

"There is no 'we.'"

The tyrin raised his voice. "Lord Shroud, I speak for Emperor Avallon Delamar of Erin Elal. I trust there is some arrangement—"

"Shut it!" Luker snapped. "The Book isn't yours to bargain with!" To the god, he said, "You deal with me, Shroud."

The Lord of the Dead's shadowy form swelled, and behind him the tendrils of darkness curled and hissed. "Was Mayot's example lost on you? I do not bargain with mortals!"

Luker hawked and spat. Were the histrionics supposed to impress him? "Then it's time you started. You're only here because *I* opened the way, remember?" He cast a meaningful glance at Parolla, then looked back at Shroud. "If you had the balls to step out of your box, you'd have done so by now. So we deal."

The god studied him. "Kanon's soul will soon be mine, Guardian. As one day will yours."

Luker turned away. "Maybe your beloved daughter—"

"Wait! The Book does not have to be destroyed for Kanon to go free."

The Guardian snorted.

"You don't trust me to make good on my word?"

"The Book's destruction serves your purpose as well as mine. What difference . . ."

Luker broke off at a sound from behind—the scrape of a sword being drawn from its scabbard. He swung round, recalling as he did so that he had given the invested weapons to Merin and the Endorian. His own blades were still sheathed at his waist, but in the time it took him to draw them . . .

A sword flashed toward him.

Luker gathered his Will, knowing already that it was too late.

———

Ebon's gaze lingered on Parolla. The woman looked . . . lost. Hurt shone from her eyes, and her voice was all rough edges. Ebon was not fooled by her talk of revenge. She had come here seeking, what? Understanding? Acceptance? But when she'd reached out to Shroud, he'd slapped her hand aside. The Lord of the Dead would come to regret trying to intimidate his daughter, Ebon suspected, for instead of being cowed she had made a move for the Book. If the scarred stranger—Luker—hadn't snatched the thing away, all Nine Hells would have broken loose by now.

But then perhaps that was what Shroud intended all along. Perhaps he *wanted* to set his opponents at each other's throats. Perhaps he had foreseen that Luker would intervene as he had. If so, the god had nevertheless misjudged the man, for the scarred stranger had shown he was not simply going to toe the god's line.

Ebon heard only the opening exchange between Luker and Shroud before Galea entered his mind. The goddess had been quick to abandon him when Shroud arrived, but now it seemed she was not yet done with him. When he spoke his coolness was a match to her own. "What do you want?"

Galea ignored his tone. "The Book must be preserved, mortal."

"Why?"

"Why?" she repeated scornfully. "Have you any sense of its power? No, of course you don't. The things you have witnessed thus far are but a fraction of what the Book can do. It can restore life. *Real* life, not this tortured existence that has been forced upon my people." She left the thought hanging for a moment, then added, "And yours."

"Why have you not told me this before?"

"Because you didn't need to know. You *need* the Book, mortal. Your people need it."

Ebon's mouth was dry. "My people? You said you would help them."

"And I have done so. But did you think there would be no further casualties? That *all* of those close to you would survive?"

"Who? Who has died?"

"We don't have time for this. If the Book is destroyed, the opportunity is lost. With its power in your hands you can repair the damage Mayot has done."

Ebon struggled to marshal his thoughts. Every time the goddess opened her mouth her credibility shrank, and to discover she'd been withholding information from him just made him wonder what else she was keeping back. Even if she spoke the truth about the Book, she would doubtless have plans for it herself—the restoration of her empire, perhaps; vengeance against the Fangalar. And yet, if there was even the smallest chance Ebon's people could be saved . . . He needed time to think.

"If you would earn my trust, Lady, lower the wards you have raised between us. Show me what is in your mind. Show me what you have done to aid my kinsmen."

"There is no time! My presence will be detected."

Ebon looked at Luker. The scarred man was speaking to Shroud, but their words had faded to a whisper. "What would you have me do?" he said to the goddess. "He will not give up the Book."

"Then take it from him."

Ebon did not respond.

"Have I offended your sense of honor, mortal? Does your duty to your people count so little that a mere stranger—"

"Don't speak to me of duty."

"Is he your ally, then, that you value his life above theirs? You know nothing of his true purpose here!"

"I might, if you were quiet long enough for me to hear him speak."

"He wants to destroy the Book. What more do you need to know?"

Ebon looked at Shroud to find the god watching him in turn. He swallowed. To take the Book would be to earn the enmity of the Lord of the Dead.

"And what of me?" Galea said. "Would you wish *me* for an enemy?"

"He senses you. He knows."

"Then strike! Now, before the moment is lost!"

Ebon's sword was suddenly in his hand. The hilt slipped for an instant in his numb fingers, then he grasped it tight.

He lunged forward.

Luker could only watch as Baldy's sword stabbed out.

To block a cut from Merin that had been aimed at Luker's chest. The impact jarred the weapon from Baldy's hand, but he had done enough to parry the tyrin's blow. Merin, though, had a second blade— the longknife Luker had given him—and it now flashed for Luker's neck.

At that moment a crossbow bolt sprouted from the tyrin's arm, just below the wrist. His longknife flew from his hand and went skittering across the floor. He jerked his injured arm to his chest, his face screwed up in pain.

Luker's Will crashed into him, catapulting him through the air. He sailed fully two dozen paces before landing somewhere out of sight behind the nearest ranks of undead.

Looking across, Luker saw Jenna's familiar outline among the undead to his left, her arm outstretched, a crossbow in her hand. The Guardian nodded to her, then turned to Baldy and repeated the gesture. The man looked more dead than alive, his gaze bleary, his forehead beaded with sweat. A trail of blood ran down from one nostril.

An unexpected source of help that, but welcome all the same.

Luker faced Shroud again.

"Where were we?"

Parolla remembered the scarred man, Luker, from his duel with the undead warrior in the forest. The intervening bells had not been kind to him, for his hair was singed at the temples, and he was bleeding from cuts on his face and arms. Since seizing the Book he had raised wards about himself, but Parolla could see what it cost him to maintain them. His left eye was half-closed, and every turn of his head was accompanied by a wince. There was no give in him, though, for he hadn't backed down in the face of Shroud's threats, not a single step. Parolla wished she had his strength.

A shame, then, that he had to die. When she tore down his shields, Shroud would retaliate against her, and without the Book she was in no doubt as to how that battle of wills would end. But what choice did she have? After years spent seeking out the god, he had given her nothing . . . except perhaps an end to the childish hopes she had clung to since Aliana's death. There was a gift in that, she supposed. It made it easier for her to do now what had to be done, for she could not just stand back and allow the Book to be destroyed.

One way or another, it had to end here.

When the attack on Luker came, Parolla knew this was her moment. There had been no need for Ebon to parry Merin's first sword thrust, for Luker's defenses were strong enough to withstand the blow. Merin's second lunge, though, was with an invested weapon—death-magic, no less—and would have pierced Luker's wards like a needle through cloth. The crossbow bolt fired by the unknown woman had disarmed Merin before he could bring that blade to bear, but his attack had already broken Luker's concentration. His shields wavered.

There was a risk, of course, that the Book would be damaged when Parolla struck, but that could not be helped. There was no time for second thoughts.

She raised her hands.

And froze.

A sword had been leveled across her throat. Looking over her shoulder, Parolla saw a man wearing chain mail behind her and recognized him as Ebon's companion from the hilltop. A heartbeat ago he had been standing a score of paces away. How in the hells had he moved so quickly? Parolla struggled to remember his name, then stopped herself. What did it matter? What did anything matter?

The man's free hand settled on her left arm. There was a flash of black fire as death-magic sparked across the contact, and the stranger flinched. The sword in his other hand, though, remained steady. He said nothing to Parolla, just scowled and shook his head.

Fool! He should have killed her while he had the chance. The darkness inside Parolla would not be denied. So easy for her to snuff out the man's life force. Fast though he was, he would have no time to use his sword before she reached out and seized his wrist. He would be dead before he hit the ground.

Parolla tensed to strike.

Ebon saw death in Parolla's eyes.

"Vale!" he shouted. "Back off!"

But it was too late. If anything, his words just distracted the Endorian, allowing Parolla to grab his arm. Vale's sword slipped from his twitching fingers to clatter on the floor, and his back arched. Then shadows swept up all about him. He remained on his feet, though—alive, for now at least.

Ebon sought out Parolla's gaze and held it.

Watcher's tears, Lady, wait!

But wait for what? What could he offer her that might stay her hand? Not the Book of Lost Souls, plainly, for neither Luker nor Shroud would let her have it. And even if there were some other prize she might accept, what chance did he have of delivering it? For when he had stepped in to save Luker, Galea had disappeared from his mind again, and this time, he suspected, she would not come back. He was on his own now. And as his brother Rendale was wont to say, that left him haggling for a maiden's virtue with a handful of coppers.

Not that Shroud needed to know that.

Ebon took a breath and let it out slowly. If Parolla went down in flames she would take the rest of them with her, starting with Vale. *Leaving Shroud to pick up the pieces.* Was that so terrible a prospect, though? Surely the god would want the souls of the dead, including those of Ebon's kinsmen, to be freed from the Book's chains so they could pass through to the underworld. *But is that even true?* The spirits of the Vamilians, after all, had been abandoned in the mortal world for millennia.

An idea took shape in Ebon's mind. He looked at Luker. The scarred stranger had broken off his conversation with Shroud and was now staring back at the king, his expression unreadable. Would he hold off long enough to allow Ebon to play this out?

I've earned that much, surely.

Ebon stepped forward. "Greetings, Lord Shroud," he said, bowing to the god. "I am Ebon Calidar, king of Galitia. And I have a proposal for you."

The rumble of Shroud's voice made his ears hum. "Of course you do. Is there no end to the insolence of mortals?"

Ebon wet his lips with his tongue. The Lord of the Dead had sensed the presence of Galea earlier. For Ebon's ruse to work he would need to convince the god that she remained with him, and so he said, "Mortals, my Lord?"

Shroud watched him for a moment before turning to Mayot's fallen throne and righting it. There was a groan of metal as the god settled himself on the seat. The blood on the armrests bubbled and hissed. "Your . . . patron . . . is taking a grave risk by interfering in matters that do not concern her."

"Not concern her, Lord? The Vamilians—"

"Oh, come now," Shroud cut in. "Do you take me for a fool? If she cared anything for the fate of her people she would have sought me out long before now. She wants the Book for herself."

Ebon added a note of steel to his tone. "And perhaps she will yet have it. The question of her support has still to be decided."

"You speak for her in this?"

"I do."

"Strange. I do not sense her presence in you now."

Ebon's voice held steady. "With respect, Lord, you sense only what I—we—wish you to."

Another lengthy silence followed, but Ebon was not about to break it—let the god's imagination fill in the gaps the king left. The tendrils of darkness behind the throne were swaying hypnotically. Finally Shroud said, "You are unwise to place your trust in her, mortal."

Ebon held back a smile. "We have reached an understanding, my Lord."

"Indeed," the god replied, steepling his hands. "What is it that you offer me, then?"

"My—our—noninterference in this matter. Simply that."

"And I am supposed to believe that has value?"

"Can you afford to assume otherwise?"

"That rather depends," Shroud said, "on what you expect in return."

"The Book must be destroyed. The spirits of my people and the Vamilians shall be allowed to pass through to your realm."

"That is all?"

"Not quite." Ebon felt sweat trickle down his back. "I require the release of a soul."

Another pause. "One in my keeping?"

"Yes."

The Lord of the Dead leaned forward. "Who?"

Luker saw where this was heading a heartbeat before Shroud's breath hissed out.

"Out of the question," the god said.

Baldy—Ebon, he had called himself—crossed his arms. "Why?"

Shroud did not respond. Instead he turned to Luker, and the meaning in his look was clear. *He wants me to choose sides.* More precisely, he wanted Luker to choose *his* side—to bring this wrangling to an end by delivering the Book of Lost Souls into his hands.

The problem was, Shroud hadn't agreed to any of Luker's demands yet: not the destruction of the Book, not even the release of Kanon's spirit. With the Book in the god's possession, the balance of power would shift irreversibly, and the Guardian wasn't such an idiot as to think Shroud would play fair when it did. The bastard was probably still sulking about Luker refusing to bend the knee. Most likely any deal would include a demand that the Guardian pledge his allegiance to the god.

He tightened his grip on the Book. His head hurt like someone had it in a vice, and as he glanced up at the dais a fresh burst of agony made his vision swim. Shroud was looking too damned comfortable for Luker's liking, perched on the throne like a king holding court. The Lord of the Dead might not yet have the Book in his grasp, but it still felt to the Guardian as if everyone was marching to the god's beat. Perhaps Shroud had been working from the start to engineer a stand-off among those facing him. All he needed to do was sow the seeds of discord and wait for the fragile alliances to tear themselves apart.

Luker looked at Parolla. *And his little princess is playing right into his hands.* He had sensed the woman gathering her power to attack before the timeshifter stepped in. Now, once again, she seemed ready to cut loose, for evidently Shroud's threat of eternal damnation wasn't enough to stop her doing something stupid. He understood what Ebon was trying to do: keep the woman sweet by prying her mother's soul from Shroud's grip. Would it work?

It had to.

For Luker was under no illusions. If he was going to destroy the Book and keep his life his own, he needed Parolla in his corner. *Okay, Shroud, I'll choose a side if that's what you want. But it won't be the one you're expecting.* He exchanged a look with Ebon. Then, to the expectant god, he said, "The man asked you a question."

The black tendrils behind Shroud flared up, writhing and hissing. When the god spoke there was fury in his voice. "I *gather* souls, I do not *release* those that are mine."

"So you make an exception this time."

"Indeed?" Shroud jabbed a finger at Ebon. "The one he is referring to . . . she is not like those here." A shadowy arm swept out to encompass the ranks of Vamilians. "Her soul has already passed through the Gate. There is no coming back."

"You expect us to believe it's not in your power? Is there some other Lord of the Dead we should be speaking to?"

Shroud's hands clenched into fists. "Do you have any idea what you're asking me to do? A soul needs a home. Would you clothe it in dead flesh, as the Vamilians here? Or are you intending to steal an-other's body to house it?"

Luker mastered his irritation with an effort. "You're a bloody god, aren't you? Think of something."

"You would have me father another child, perhaps?"

"Cut the bullshit! If there isn't a spare body going, make one."

"You believe me capable of that? As you were so keen to remind me, I am Lord of the *Dead*."

Luker shrugged. "If you can't do it, find someone who can. Must be one of your cronies who owes you a favor. The White Lady, perhaps. If not, you'll have to accept a debt."

Shroud said nothing for a time, drumming his fingers on the armrests of the throne. Through the holes in the roof, a flash of lightning lit up the dome, but it did not penetrate the shadows that clung to the god. "If I agree to this," he said finally, "her memories would have to be taken from her. There are secrets of my realm that must remain hidden."

Ebon cleared his throat. "I agree, my Lord." He turned to Parolla as he spoke, and Luker realized he was directing his words as much to her as to the god. "This will be a new beginning—a chance to start over. To right the wrong that was done to her."

Parolla had remained quiet throughout the exchange. Now Luker studied her for any reaction to what they were proposing. Her face seemed expressionless, though it was difficult to know for certain with so many false shadows and overlapping images inside the dome. All he could see clearly were those dead black eyes staring back at him.

The silence dragged out.

A gust of wind brushed Luker's fire-touched skin. He shivered, then scowled as the movement sent another sharp pain through his skull. *We're wasting our time here.* Hells, how did they know all that mummy talk wasn't just a smoke screen? Maybe Shroud was right. Maybe all the woman wanted was to try out his throne for size.

It was time for plan B.

Luker looked at Jenna. The assassin always had a surprise in her bag of tricks. The rain had put out most of the fires in the dome, but if she could conjure up a flame he might be able to send the Book up in smoke before it all kicked off. And if Shroud and Parolla kept each other entertained for a while there could yet be a way to get out of this alive.

Jenna stood motionless behind the front rank of undead to Luker's left. Her figure was swathed in shadow, but he could still make out a flash of teeth as she grinned at him. Had she read his intent? Was her smile a signal for him to stir things up?

At that moment her crossbow slipped from her fingers.

Then her legs buckled, and she collapsed.

They were waiting for an answer.

Parolla looked at Ebon. The man was swaying on his feet, yet there was still an intensity in his eyes, a fierce determination, as if he could influence Parolla's decision through sheer will alone. His gaze moved to her hand, and she was aware suddenly of her grip on the arm of his companion—Vale, Ebon had called him. The man was now leaning heavily against her, and Parolla could feel his life force bleeding away as her death-magic flickered about him.

Luker's expression, meanwhile, was more guarded. His look seemed to say to Parolla, "Take it or leave it, just get on with it." In spite of herself she almost smiled. *A man of few graces, this.* He clutched the Book to his chest in a manner strangely reminiscent of Mayot Mencada. As yet he hadn't tried to use it, but then the Book's power was doubtless not a power he could wield even if he had been minded to do so. Abruptly he broke her gaze and turned to stare at something to Parolla's left. It was several heartbeats before he faced her again, and when he did she saw that cracks had appeared in his mask of indifference.

They were trying to help her, she knew. Of course, their motives for doing so were far from altruistic—they understood that their lives rested in her hands, just as hers rested in theirs. And yet neither of the strangers wanted the Book for themselves. Neither was here seeking personal gain. Could the same be said of her? Shroud's words came back to Parolla: "Why have you embraced the dark?" She'd never intended to. Since entering the Forest of Sighs she had fought to resist the call of her blood. She'd come seeking a portal to the underworld, a means to strike at Shroud, to hurt him as he had hurt her.

And yet she had always known, hadn't she, that the only way she could overthrow the god was to unleash the darkness within.

Parolla scanned the dome. Her gaze came to rest on a Vamilian woman. The left half of her face had been burned away, and her scalp was a mass of raw, blistered flesh. She clutched a broken spear in her right hand. Her left arm hung from the shoulder by threads of tendon. If Parolla claimed the Book for herself, could she use the undead

as Mayot had done? Did her cause justify the suffering they would experience? Did any cause?

Yes! She could bring an end to Shroud's rule—save others from
going through what her mother had endured.

But at what cost? Through the portal beneath Shroud's temple at
Xavel, Parolla had seen the shattered world of his predecessor. Even
if the Book *did* give her the power to overthrow him, what destruction would be wrought in their clash? How many would die? Parolla's
shoulders slumped. She could not win here. Ebon and Luker were offering her another way, if she could just step back from the edge.

But did she even want to?

Aliana's face remained frozen in the black wall behind Shroud.
Could her mother see out from her shadowy prison? Had she heard
the words spoken here? Or was her image just another of Shroud's de-
ceits? Parolla was not such a fool as to think she and Aliana could re-
capture the life they had once shared. No memories, Shroud had said.
A new start . . . *But a start without me.* There could never be any place
for Parolla in Aliana's life, for her presence would poison her mother
now just as it had before. Did Ebon and Luker understand this? That
ultimately what they were offering her was just one more twist of the
knife?

Yet for Aliana, a new beginning. A life for the one that had been
taken from her.

And for Parolla, perhaps, an easing of the guilt that had haunted
her since her mother's death.

Luker's voice broke the silence. "That's far enough."

Startled, Parolla looked round. There was movement from one of
the archways leading out of the dome. Two hooded, gray-robed figures emerged from the shadows. One was as short as the Jekdal she
had encountered on the Ken'dah Steppes; the other was twice its
height. Both shuffled closer as if their bones were brittle as tinder
wood. The taller stranger rested a clawed hand on the shoulder of its
companion.

From a second archway appeared a woman wearing dark leathers
crisscrossed with sword slashes. Her face was tattooed with black and
gray stripes to make her resemble a flintcat. Then Parolla noticed a
tail swinging between the woman's legs as she walked.

"Enough, I said," Luker growled. "Shroud, call off your freaks."

The god waved a hand, and the newcomers halted.

Parolla took a breath and turned to Ebon. Gesturing at Shroud, she said, "Can he be trusted, *sirrah*? If I go along with this . . . When the Book is destroyed, what guarantee do we have that he will honor his promises?"

"You dare question my word?" the god said.

Ebon kept his gaze on Parolla. "What we say, my Lady—all that takes place here—is being witnessed by another. Shroud's bargain is with her too. He might be willing to betray *us*, yes, but not my . . . patron."

Parolla's eyes narrowed. Was this the same benefactor who had pulled the rug from under Ebon's feet on the hilltop? Was he truly expecting her to put her trust in this mysterious entity? "Forgive me, but I must hear it from Shroud himself." To the god, she said, "Well, Father, what do you say? Will you seal the vow in blood? There is power in that even you cannot deny."

Shroud stretched out a wrist. "You wish to make the cut yourself?"

"Are you offering?"

The god snorted, then took out a knife from a fold in his robe and drew it across his palm. A single drop of blood splashed to the dais with a noise like a peal of thunder. The black tendrils behind Shroud darted toward the point where the droplet landed before recoiling. "Satisfied?" the god said.

"Not yet," Parolla replied. "I want your word that you will keep to the spirit of the agreement as well as the letter. I would not have Aliana born into suffering."

"Suffering is all you mortals know."

"And have you ever wondered why? Look in a mirror, see for yourself."

There was a sneer in Shroud's voice. "You would have her born to a king or an emperor, perhaps? A palace in the clouds in a land where the sun never sets? No doubt you wish to choose the color of the brat's eyes as well."

Before Parolla could respond, Ebon spoke. "My Lord, which immortal will you treat with in this matter? The White Lady?"

Shroud inclined his head. "Why do you ask?"

Ebon looked at Parolla. "I suggest we leave the circumstances of the child's birth to the goddess. Her judgment, at least, I think we can trust."

Parolla considered this, her gaze still on Shroud. "Agreed."

Ebon turned back to the god. "And after the child is born? Will you—"

"No!" Parolla snapped. She pointed at Shroud. "You will stay out of her life, do you hear me? You and your damned servants."

"What, not even a gift on her naming day?"

Parolla swung toward Ebon. "*Sirrah,* I have no right to ask, but it would . . . comfort me . . . to know that someone was watching over the child. From time to time, at least."

"My Lady? I had assumed you—"

"I cannot," Parolla cut in. "My presence would kill her, as it did when we were last together."

The shaven-headed man cast a questioning glance at Luker, who shrugged. Ebon faced Parolla again. "We will do what we can."

Parolla's voice hardened. "Only the three of us must ever know who Aliana is. I would not want anyone using her against me."

"As you wish."

Luker nodded, his look distracted.

Slowly Parolla released her grip on Vale's arm. "So be it."

It was done.

Ebon turned back to Shroud. "My Lord, you will tell us when and where the babe is born?"

"When I know myself."

"And the rent here? It will be closed after the souls have passed through?"

The god flashed a look at Parolla. "Of course. I cannot very well leave it open for just anyone to wander through to my realm."

"How long—"

"Long enough," Shroud interrupted. "When the Book is destroyed, the spirits will begin to feel the underworld's pull."

Luker grunted. "Enough talk. Let's get on with this."

The time that followed passed in a blur to Parolla. Luker declined Shroud's offer to create a fire, perhaps fearing some final act of treachery on the god's part. Instead Ebon and Vale cleared the bodies from a dry section of the dome's floor and gathered a pile of leaves. Vale kindled a flame with flint and steel before feeding the blaze with spears taken from the Vamilian undead.

Without ceremony, Luker tossed the Book onto the fire and stepped back.

Parolla watched sparks swirl up into the air. It took a while for the Book to catch light, and Parolla briefly wondered whether some protective sorcery had been woven into its cover. Then the flames took hold and the Book started to burn with a heat so intense Parolla was forced back.

Shroud had stayed to ensure this part of the agreement was fulfilled, but now Parolla saw him retreat into the shadows about the dais. She replayed their conversation earlier, studying the god's words for every hint of meaning, every hidden nuance. Shroud had been prepared for her coming, of that she felt sure. Unsurprisingly, he had shown no remorse for what he'd done to Aliana. Instead he had spun Parolla a web of lies and tried to provoke her into attacking him. *He wants me dead.* By goading her into making the first move—into attempting to take the Book for herself—he had hoped to bring her into conflict with the others assembled in the dome. It was only the intervention of Ebon and Luker that had prevented the confrontation from ending in bloodshed.

If Shroud thought, though, that the deal they had struck meant an end to Parolla's enmity, he was mistaken. And yet, the god would know from the start where Aliana lived. Wouldn't he always be able to use the threat of retaliation against her to keep Parolla in line?

A problem for another day.

After what seemed like an age, the flames about the Book swelled with a flash of black light that seared Parolla's eyes. She heard a high-pitched keening, followed by a sharp cracking sound as of a thousand bones breaking. All at once the undead in the dome began toppling to the ground, the threads holding them withering to nothing.

Only then did Parolla release her power—a little at a time, like a long-held breath. As the darkness within her leeched away, so too did some of the pain she had been holding on to for so long.

Her shoulders shook silently as she hugged her arms about herself.

Luker found Jenna among a tangle of corpses. A Vamilian spearman had fallen across her, his head against her left hip, one arm flung across her midriff. When Luker seized him by the wrist and ankle he discovered the man's flesh was still warm from the touch of Merin's firestorm. The Guardian dragged him off.

Jenna lay on her side, curled up as if in sleep. The scars across her cheeks and forehead had split again, and her face was covered with blood. Beneath the blood her skin was ghostly white in the firelight. The left sleeve of her shirt ended just below the elbow . . . Luker's heart

skipped a beat. The lower part of her arm had been sheared off—by
sorcery, he assumed—to leave a stump of black suppurating flesh.

Luker sank to his knees. The fabric of his trousers quickly became
soaked through, and it was only then that he noticed the pool of blood
beneath the assassin. And since the stump of Jenna's arm wasn't bleeding, that could only mean she had other wounds. His fingers moved
under her shirt, exploring her side. As he reached her chest, she stirred
and gave a murmur of protest. Her ribs were a sticky mass of shattered bone, and when Luker withdrew his hand it was smeared crimson.

Jenna's eyes opened a crack. "Did we win?"

Luker's breath was tight in his chest. He could feel the heat of the
fire on his back, hear the crack and pop of the flames as the Book of
Lost Souls burned.

No. No, we didn't win.

Chamery's face appeared in his mind's eye. If the mage were still
alive, and if Luker could somehow find him among the countless ruined buildings . . . Cursing, he shook his head. Even if the boy had recovered enough from Kanon's mauling, Jenna would likely be dead
before Luker could bring him here.

The assassin spoke again, her voice so faint the Guardian had to
lower his head to catch her words. "The bastard got me—Mayot, I
mean. Just a glancing blow. I don't think he even knew where I was."
She flashed him a rueful look. "After the soulcaster . . . you said I'd
be more resistant to sorcery." There was fear in her eyes, but her pained
smile took the edge off her words.

Luker could think of nothing to say. Slipping out of his cloak, he
folded it into a bundle and placed in under the assassin's head. Then
he reached for her remaining hand. The flesh was clammy.

"That swordswoman you were fighting," Jenna said. "She was fast.
I had to . . . read her attacks, then . . . hit the one part of her body that
would . . . slow her down. Not a bad shot, eh?"

"I couldn't have matched it."

"Ah!" the assassin said. "Three years it's taken . . . Three years for
you to admit I'm the better shot . . . Now I can die happy." Her breathing was coming quicker now, every inhalation causing a grimace.

"I never doubted you," Luker said.

"I did."

"You came."

It was a while before Jenna responded. "No regrets. Not this time."

"About leaving Arkarbour?"

"About any of it."

"No," he agreed, tightening his grip on her hand. "We . . . we made a good team."

Jenna's mouth twitched. "Ah, Luker. You say the nicest things."

He bowed his head, and they sat in silence for a time. To Luker's left one of Shroud's disciples—the cat woman—was helping Sickle Man to his feet. Together they hobbled toward the rent, Kestor ben Kayma's left arm draped round his companion's shoulders, his right foot dragging across the floor. Eventually the cat woman lost patience, lifting Kestor into her arms before carrying him up the steps of the dais. They vanished through the portal.

Jenna said, "Makes a change . . . me saving you." Her gaze was suddenly intent. "Why did you, Luker? Save me, I mean . . . That first time."

"The road to Koronos?"

"I wasn't exactly . . . friendly to you before."

The Guardian shrugged. "If I'd taken the shot at Keebar Lana instead of you, it would've been me the demons were hunting."

"That's not an answer."

He stared at her.

"Why?" the assassin asked.

Luker struggled to find the words, but they would not come. The breeze blew strands of hair across Jenna's eyes, and he reached down to brush them aside. After a while her grip on his hand began to weaken, and perhaps it was this that made him take a breath and say, "Maybe it was because I saw something of myself in you on that rooftop in Mercerie. Maybe I thought you needed saving like I did." He hesitated, then added, "And maybe because even then I knew you were special."

Jenna did not reply.

Luker gave the assassin's shoulder a shake. "Jenna? You still with me?"

"Where would I go?" she whispered.

No, the Guardian thought. *It was me who left you.* Two years ago he had left them both, Kanon and Jenna, when he'd gone to Taradh Dor. *Gone looking for something that was there right in front of me all along.* Now they were leaving him in turn.

A shadow fell across him, and he looked up. Ebon stood a few paces away, his expression masked. "Excuse my interruption. While I would not wish to raise your hopes needlessly, I have some limited healing abilities. Your friend . . ."

Luker's face twisted. *Not raise my damned hopes? How could you do otherwise?* He nodded.

Ebon moved to Jenna's side and crouched across from Luker. He paled when he saw the assassin's ruined arm.

"Sorcery?" he asked Luker.

"Aye."

Closing his eyes, Ebon placed a hand on the assassin's forehead. The Guardian felt him reach out with his senses, but it was a tentative questing only. "Death-magic," Ebon said. "It is eating away at her. The initial blast of sorcery cauterized the stump when it took the arm. The biggest concern is her ribs. Death-magic has infected the wound."

Luker could hear the defeat in his voice, and he swung his gaze back to Jenna. A peaceful look had stolen across her face. Perhaps the pain was easing. Luker felt at her neck for a pulse. *Just a flicker.*

Ebon drew his hand back, then opened his eyes and looked at Luker. "I am sorry, there is nothing I can do. I do not have the skill to regenerate flesh and bone, nor replace the blood she has lost. I could try to close her wounds, but my touch will not be gentle. I fear she would die in the attempt . . ."

Luker was no longer listening. Ebon had given him an idea—one he should have thought of sooner. *Stay with me, Jenna. This isn't over yet.* Maybe Ebon didn't have the power to heal the assassin, but there was one here who did. Perhaps it was not too late to accept the Lord of the Dead's offer of service. Perhaps the god would be prepared to make one final deal.

"Where's Shroud?" Luker asked Ebon. "Is the bastard still here?" Without waiting for a response, he rose. *He'd better be. If I have to drag him kicking and screaming . . .*

His thoughts were interrupted by a footfall behind.

When he turned he came face-to-face with Parolla, her cold black eyes watching him dispassionately.

Sitting on the steps leading up to the dais, Parolla watched through the holes in the roof as Mayot's dome of death-magic slowly dissolved into gray clouds. In the half-bell since the Book's destruction, the worst of the storm had passed over to leave a chill in the air, and Parolla pulled her cloak about her shoulders. She could hear the hiss of foaming waves above the wind.

A watery light illuminated the burned and twisted bodies scattered across the dome. The last of the fires had gone out, but the smell of roasted meat still filled the building. Who would bury the Vamilians this time, Parolla wondered, now that Tumbal's people were gone from the world? *No one.* The corpses would stay here as Mayot Mencada's legacy, and a fitting one it would be, for the old man had forged his empire in the image of the underworld—a place of death and bones. How long before the earth-magic buried deep underground rose to rejuvenate the forest? Years? Decades, even? For while the Book of Lost Souls was gone, the air remained saturated with necromantic energies. Parolla could feel them seeping into her skin, and she shifted uncomfortably on the steps.

Shroud had stayed good to his word and left open the portal to his realm. The souls of the Vamilian dead were pouring into the dome in four ghostly white streams, one from each of the arched gateways. Strange, Parolla thought, that the spirits should still use the doors to enter when they could just as easily float through the walls, but then habit, she imagined, was just one more memory of the flesh. The four tributaries converged on the dais in a pale river that faded to black as it snaked into the underworld. Was Tumbal within one of those streams? It was several bells since they had parted company in the forest. If the Gorlem had succeeded in resisting the dissolution of his spirit he would now be feeling the tug of Shroud's realm.

Raised voices sounded to her left, and she looked across to see Ebon in conversation with one of the Sartorians—Consel Garat Hallon, she had heard him called. Garat's right arm was bound in a sling, and he was using his sword as a crutch. He also appeared to be doing most of the talking, addressing Ebon in a voice first beseeching, then insistent. Throughout, the shaven-headed *magus* listened with a guarded expression. When he finally spoke, his response brought a mocking smile from the Sartorian.

Parolla turned away. In truth, she had no interest in what they were discussing. She wanted only to be rid of this place—to put the Forest of Sighs far behind her, along with the memory of all that had happened here.

Soon.

Her gaze swept the dome. Ebon's companion, Vale, was offering

Luker a sword, which the scarred man accepted. Luker stood over the sleeping form of Jenna. He had not thanked Parolla after she'd healed the woman's wounds, but he hadn't needed to. The spark of relief and gratitude in his eyes had spoken for him.

Ebon approached her and halted at the bottom of the steps. Parolla waited a few heartbeats to make it clear his presence was unwelcome before turning to look at him. There was still a blue hue to the man's lips, and the skin at the tips of his fingers was a darker color than the rest of his hands. *Frostbite.* In this instance, though, Parolla knew her healing powers were not required. Ebon was now more than capable of taking care of himself.

It had been easy enough to deduce from his earlier conversation with Shroud that his mysterious benefactor was the patron goddess of the Vamilians. Odds were, the shaven-headed man wasn't a sorcerer at all—or rather, he hadn't been before meeting Galea. Now, though? Parolla blew out her cheeks. Ebon's power had grown since their meeting on the hilltop, suggesting he had been forced to call on unexpected reserves in his struggle with Mayot. What had the touch of the goddess's magic done to him? What was he destined to become?

Ebon bowed. "Forgive my intrusion, my Lady. I was wondering what became of Mottle. Did he not accompany you—"

"He is dead," Parolla cut in, then watched as yet another weight settled on the man's already hunched shoulders.

"Tell me."

She spoke to him of the clash with the tiktar, ending with Mottle being carried away by the vortex. "The elderling . . . engulfed . . . him, *sirrah.* No one could have survived the injuries he sustained. And yet . . ."

"Yes?"

"The hill is only a short distance from here. If he were dead, would not his spirit have passed through the rent by now?"

Ebon turned toward the river of souls. "You have been watching for him?"

"No, *sirrah*, but surely *he* would see *us.*"

The *magus* considered this, then gave a half smile. "You are correct, of course. Mottle would never go quietly. He could not pass us by without stopping to regale us of his exploits."

Parolla gave her voice a note of hope she did not feel. "He *wanted* the storm to take him. Perhaps it sustained him."

Ebon's gaze was knowing. "Perhaps you are right." He ran a hand over his head. "From which direction did you approach the Forest of Sighs, my Lady?"

"From the north and west. Why?"

"I was hoping for news of my city, Majack."

Parolla had no words of comfort to give him. "There is nothing I can tell you. If you stay here, though, the spirits of your dead kinsmen will reach this place in time. Perhaps then you will find out—"

"Forgive me," Ebon interrupted. "But I cannot just wait. I must go and see for myself. Farewell." He turned to leave.

"A moment," Parolla said. The *magus* looked back over his shoulder. "I'm sorry," she added. "For your friend, Vale. When I held his arm . . . I cannot give back the years I took from him."

Ebon nodded. "If Aliana should require help at any time," he said at last, "may I call on you?"

"I won't be staying in these parts. How would you get a message to me?"

The corners of Ebon's mouth turned up. "I will find a way."

Parolla watched him retreat. The king of Galitia, no less, or so he had introduced himself to Shroud. The man was so assured in some ways, so hesitant in others. *A king without a kingdom.* Majack was, what, ten days on foot from here? *Ten days under siege by an undead army.* And the man wanted news? Parolla shook her head. Ebon would be returning to nothing more than cold ashes, and from the bleakness she'd seen in his eyes he knew it too.

A cough sounded to Parolla's right, and she looked round to see the spectral figure of Tumbal Qerivan. The Gorlem stood watching her with his head cocked, lower arms folded, upper arms held out in front of him with hands clasped as if in prayer. Floating closer he said, "It warms my heart to see thee again, my Lady."

Parolla rose. "I feared you would not make it, *sirrah*. You are still in pain?"

"A little," Tumbal conceded. "I am hoping the underworld will bring some surcease."

A flicker of movement to the Gorlem's left caught Parolla's attention. Threescore paces away, two of Shroud's disciples stood staring at her—the hooded halfling and its companion. No doubt there were others too, watching from the shadows beyond the rent. In future, Parolla suspected she would have not just the Antlered God's servants to look over her shoulder for. Turning back to Tumbal, she said, "I avenged you. Against the Fangalar."

"I am sorry to hear that," the Gorlem replied. His gaze slid away to take in the dome, and his grave expression gave way to a look of enchantment. "I remember this place from when I came to bury the Vamilians. Never did I imagine it would still be standing."

"Soon it will fall. The sorcery that preserves it is almost gone now, destroyed by the Book's death-magic."

"And yet the sounds of the sea remain." The Gorlem's look became wistful. "A pity thou could'st not have seen the Vamilians as they once were. A people of beauty and invention. In order to escape the Fanga-lar they were forced to flee far from their homeland, yet their affin-ity with the sea remained. This building was once filled with fountains. The Vamilians discovered some means of pumping water to the top of the dome so that it ran down the outer walls. How was that done, dost thou suppose?"

"Why not ask them yourself? There must be someone in the river of souls who can tell you."

Tumbal eyed her thoughtfully. "The river carries much informa-tion, it is true. I have heard tell of what took place here from one of the Vamilians who witnessed Mayot's untimely demise."

"Untimely?"

The Gorlem spread his four hands. "But of course. Where now will I obtain solutions to the riddles that have vexed me so?" His look brightened. "Perhaps I will meet the mage in the underworld."

"I doubt that, *sirrah*."

"Why, my Lady?"

"Somehow I think Shroud has other plans for him."

Tumbal bobbed his head. "What of thee? Did'st thou find answers to thine own questions?"

"From Shroud, I heard only lies and half-truths. Yet I learned much all the same."

"How so?"

"I discovered that my father fears to face me beyond the confines of his own realm. And that he has powerful enemies in whom I might find allies."

Tumbal's form was starting to distort, stretching toward the rent. "Thy quest continues, then?"

"What else is there for me?"

"But with the rebirth of thy mother, have not some of the wrongs been righted? A new beginning—"

"Not for me. I will never be able to see her. Even if there comes a time when I can control the call of my blood, Aliana will have her own life. Better for her if she knows nothing about me, or the history we share."

"Perhaps so in her tender years, but later . . ." The Gorlem studied her closely, then sighed. "What wilt thou do next? Where wilt thou go?"

"I have not decided."

Tumbal's form was becoming more misshapen with each moment. He took a breath as if summoning up his courage. "A word of advice, my Lady, if thou would'st forgive me the presumption. Before we met I spent many years traveling these lands. I was ever an explorer at heart, and I have witnessed such wonders as made my spirit sing. I have walked the streets of Dian and watched the Dragon Gate rise and fall over the Sabian Sea. I have seen the Tears of Heaven rain down on parts of the Broken Lands and breathe new life into a realm laid waste by the death throes of a god. I have climbed to the summit of the Thorn and observed khalid esgaril weave their dance of death over clouds tipped with fire." Parolla could tell from Tumbal's distant look that he was seeing these sights again in his mind. Then his gaze focused on her. "But always, my delight was tempered by the sense that something was missing. Too long, I now believe, I lived with only my poor self for company. It was thy friendship that shone a light on the emptiness within me. I do not know where thou wilt find a worthy companion, but make finding that person thy goal. Thou dost deserve—"

"You are wrong, *sirrah*," Parolla cut in. "I deserve nothing more than what fate has granted me. Your faith in me is unwarranted. It always was."

"No, my Lady, it is thy lack of faith in thyself that is misguided. I have heard the role thou did'st play in dethroning Mayot."

"It was not I who secured passage to the underworld for the undead. It was not even my idea to seek release for my mother."

"And the woman that thou did'st heal? Jenna?"

"Her companion was about to pledge himself to Shroud. I sought only to spite my father."

"I do not believe that."

"Believe what you will."

Tumbal appeared about to speak again, then changed his mind. A frown creased his forehead, and Parolla wondered what the Gorlem saw in her that always drove him to melancholy. Finally he said,

"It pains me to leave thee, but I feel the draw of Shroud's Gate. Somewhere on the other side, my people await."

Parolla had known the time was upon them, and she forced a smile. "Go then. I pray the underworld is all you hope it will be."

Tumbal returned the smile. "I doubt that is possible, but then I was never able to master the art of keeping my expectations in check. Farewell."

He descended the steps without a backward glance and moved to join the river of souls. The Gorlem was taller than the Vamilians round him, and Parolla was able to follow his progress as he was swept into the gloom beyond the rent. For a few heartbeats his image flickered amid the swirling shadows.

Then he was gone.

As she watched the darkness claim him, Parolla had never felt so alone.

To reach Vale and Luker, Ebon had to cross the river of souls, and he hesitated at the edge of the flow before plunging in. The touch of the spirits made him shiver, and their restless whispering stirred uncomfortable memories of his days of spirit-possession. Who was to say that the Vamilians who'd once tried to invade his mind were not the same as those flowing round him now? And while most of the spirits were doubtless content to pass through to the underworld, might not some be tempted to try to possess him in a final effort to avoid Shroud's embrace?

Grimacing, he quickened his pace.

Vale was waiting for him on the other side. The Endorian's gray hair had thinned, and the crow's-feet round his eyes had deepened. How many years had his companion now lost in service to the Galitian throne? A decade ago, when he had first pledged himself to Isanovir, he had looked no more than a dozen years Ebon's senior; now he appeared old enough to be his father. The time was fast approaching when Ebon would have to release him from his oath, however much the Endorian protested.

But not yet.

Drawing level with his friend, the king put a hand on his shoulder. "Give me a moment," he said, then crossed to speak to Luker.

The scarred man was crouching beside Jenna, but he rose as Ebon approached. His look seemed friendly enough, yet there was something in his bearing that put Ebon in mind of a lioness standing watch over her sleeping cub.

"How is she doing?" he asked.

"Steady," Luker said. "Forced healing will have been hard on her. She's resting now."

Ebon stared down at the sleeping woman, taking in her healed left arm protruding from its scorched half sleeve. "Not even a scar to show where the arm was severed. I suppose we should not be surprised considering who Parolla is. And yet . . ."

"Aye."

"You will stay here until she recovers?"

Luker shook his head. "Another bell, maybe. Shroud may have crawled back under his rock, but this place still stinks of death. Sooner we're off, the better."

Ebon shared his sentiments. "Would you mind looking in on Aliana first when she is born? There are a few things I must attend to."

"Aye." Then, "Vale told me about your city. Don't give it up just yet. That fortress will stand up to sorcery better than your gates did."

"You have been to Majack?" Ebon said, covering his surprise.

Luker returned his gaze evenly. "Many years ago now. Just passing through."

Ebon decided he didn't want to know the details. "And the fortress?"

"Seen a few of them around—Andros, Karalat, couple of others. Made by the titans, it's said. If that's true, means they were built to last."

"You've witnessed them under attack by sorcery?"

"At Karalat, aye."

"And?"

"The walls held."

Something about the scarred man's expression told Ebon the story did not end there. "But the citadel fell nevertheless?"

Luker gave a dark smile. "Relax, man. Mayot Mencada didn't have half a dozen Guardians to send over the walls."

Ebon wasn't sure what comfort he was supposed to take from that. Bowing, he turned to leave.

Luker's voice drew him up. "Meant to thank you before. For stepping in against Merin Gray."

Merin Gray? Ah, yes. "Just as I am grateful," Ebon said, "that we were fighting on the same side. You are not the only one whose allies have proved unreliable of late."

Luker squinted at him. "Your hidden benefactor—"

"What hidden benefactor?"

A slow smile spread across Luker's face. He offered his hand, and Ebon shook it.

The king returned to Vale, then led the way to the arch through which they had first entered the dome. The sound of waves was loud in his ears as he walked along the passage through the river of souls. Vale glanced back.

"Consel not joining us?"

"No. He is going to search for Ambolina."

"Too bad."

Outside, all was deathly still. It was early afternoon, Ebon judged. The dome of death-magic had gone. Drizzle fell from the clouds, and the king raised his hood. Everywhere he looked there were Vamilian corpses piled high, along with severed body parts and shattered armor and weapons.

From a ruined house a short distance away came the sound of a horse whinnying, and Ebon crossed to the building to find the Sartorian mounts hobbled inside. There were six in all, one less than had set out from the hilltop. Ebon exchanged a look with Vale. "Are you thinking what I'm thinking?"

The Endorian shrugged. "Not as if their dead will need them now." He paused to scan the animals. "Which one is the consel's, do you reckon?"

Ebon chose a chestnut gelding and began adjusting its stirrups. Its previous owner must have taken a wound, for there were splashes of blood on the saddle. Ebon used the hem of his cloak to wipe it clean.

"I saw you jawing with the consel earlier," Vale said. "What was that about?"

"Garat has offered me his sister's hand in marriage. To seal an understanding between our two peoples."

"And?"

"Her name is Belena—"

"That's not what I meant and you know it."

Ebon sighed. "I said no."

Vale was silent for a moment as he rooted through his saddlebags. When he spoke again there was a smile in his voice. "Good for you."

"It is not what you think. When we return to Majack, I intend to abdicate the kingship."

The Endorian took a sharp breath. "Why?"

"Because of the Fangalar. The one that got away."

"You don't know he survived. Hells, you said yourself on the hill—"

"The odds of him living through this are slim, I know. But if he did, the Fangalar will come for me. I will not put the kingdom at risk."

"Then let me go after him. I might still be able to find his tracks."

"No."

"He can't have got far—"

"Enough, Vale. My mind is made up."

The Endorian muttered something, then swung up into the saddle. "How did the consel take the news?"

"With a healthy measure of skepticism. The idea of anyone renouncing power is unthinkable to him."

"It means war, then?"

Ebon placed a foot in the stirrup and mounted. "I think not. The loss of Ambolina will have weakened him. The very fact he made the offer suggests he is feeling vulnerable. When he returns to Sartor I suspect he will have too many other things on his mind to think about an invasion."

"You suspect."

The king gave a half smile. "While I was speaking to Shroud, it seems the consel spent most of his time drifting in and out of consciousness. When I told him what he had missed, he was most aggrieved. He feels the Lord of the Dead cheated him of his blood debt."

Vale snorted. "Shame he didn't get a chance to share his thinking with the god. Shroud might've done us all a favor."

"Perhaps. The point is, the consel felt *Shroud* owed *him* a favor."

The Endorian's brows knitted. "What did he want?"

"I asked him the same thing. He even started to tell me before he realized how much he was revealing." Ebon gathered the reins. "He wanted to know where Ambolina is. He needs her, Vale. Her and her demons."

Vale's expression was skeptical. "Even if you're right, after the beating we've taken there'll be other redbeaks circling. Mercerie won't pass up the chance to rub salt in the wound." He turned his horse. "Someone's going to have to pick up the pieces Mayot left behind. If not you, who?"

"I've a thought to that," Ebon replied. *If he still lives.*

Then, with Vale still waiting for an explanation, he dug his heels into his horse's flanks and steered the animal out of the building.

They rode in silence, Ebon leading the way toward the hill where they had fought the Fangalar. In the ruins to either side he sensed hidden eyes—more of Shroud's servants perhaps, or other strangers drawn by the Book who had arrived too late to take part in the fight with Mayot. None of the watchers approached.

When Ebon reached the hill he saw the slope facing him was covered with the bodies of scores of Vamilians. A handful of trees had been uprooted by the storm, and his eyes widened when he noticed a trunk suspended dozens of armspans overhead in the upper branches of two trees. On the hilltop itself, a circle of corpses surrounded a sea of churned mud perhaps two hundred paces across. Tree stumps jutted from the ground, and on one was impaled the body of a Vamilian woman. Death-magic hung so thickly in the air that every breath scratched the back of Ebon's throat.

For a time he sat staring at the devastation, his horse prancing beneath him as the wind buffeted them. To the east a flicker of lightning lit up the sky, and a score of heartbeats passed before a rumble of thunder sounded.

There was no sign of Mottle.

Ebon glanced back over the city. The damage caused to the dome by Mayot's sorcery looked worse from up here than it had inside. There were two holes on opposite sides of the roof, each a dozen armspans across, and cracks had begun to snake their way across the intervening stonework.

Ebon told Vale of his conversation with Galea in the dome. "Was I right, Vale? To refuse her?"

"You did what you had to."

"She all but admitted she had done nothing to help Majack. And yet . . ."

"You still think she might have come good after all this time? Let it go. Even if the Book could do what she said, the bitch wouldn't have shared."

"And if you are wrong?" Ebon asked. "What have we really accomplished here, Vale? For my kinsmen, I mean. Release for those enslaved by the Book? Dead is still dead. What if I just threw away their last chance of redemption? That is something I suspect I will always carry with me—the not knowing."

Vale frowned, but said nothing.

As the silence drew out, Ebon shifted in his saddle. Now that the time had come to leave, his stomach had turned sour. For a few more days only he could hope. For a few more days he could dare to believe that Lamella and the others had survived the attack on Majack. He took a final look round, then gazed up at the sky and said, "Mottle, if you should hear this . . . You know where to find me, friend."

Wheeling his horse, he set off down the hill.

A chill wind blew across the clearing. Luker rose from beside a mound of packed earth, his knees leaving deep impressions in the ground. It had taken him a bell to scrape out a shallow grave using only his hands and a spear he had found half-hidden beneath mud and roots. Water had seeped into the pit faster than he could bail it out, so in the end he'd had to tip Kanon in and cover his floating head and body as best he could.

Brushing dirt from his hands, Luker retrieved his master's sword from a puddle. He looked round the clearing. After his duel with Kanon, the undead had moved on to leave nothing but a sodden patch of torn and trampled earth. The Guardian scratched his scar. His master deserved better than an unmarked grave in this Shroud-cursed backwater. Perhaps one day Luker would return here to collect his bones and take them to their proper resting place in the grounds of the Sacrosanct.

He heard a rustle of leaves behind.

"I didn't get an opportunity before," Jenna said. "To say I was sorry for your loss."

Luker did not turn round. He plunged Kanon's sword into the ground at the head of the grave and leaned on the pommel until only the hilt and a handspan of the blade were visible. Then he stepped back. It seemed he should say something in Kanon's memory, but he'd never been good with words, and his master had always preferred silence in any case.

"Pity you never got to meet him," he said to Jenna. "I reckon I knew Kanon as well as anyone, but still not as well as I would have liked. We spent years traveling together, first when I was his apprentice, then later when I came back from beyond the White Mountains. Even then, he kept to himself. Must have said more before our fight than he'd said in years." He heard Jenna take a step forward, felt her hand rest briefly on his shoulder.

"Does he have family?" she said.

"Not that he ever spoke of. Guardians were probably the closest thing he had." Luker's expression tightened. "Kanon spent his life serving an ideal his commanders couldn't live up to. I think he came to see that before the end, but his honor kept him from walking out."

"How did you meet him?"

Luker watched the wind ripple the surface of a puddle. A part of him was surprised he'd never told Jenna the story before, but more of Kanon had rubbed off on him than just the Will, he supposed. "He saved my life. Edge of the Waste, not far from Ontep—that abandoned slaver town we passed through. I was seven. My father had been drinking. Don't think he even saw the sandclaw till it was on him. Kanon arrived to spit the creature before it could turn on me. Reckon he felt guilty for not getting there in time to save us both. Maybe that's why he made me his apprentice." Or maybe, as Luker liked to think, it was because Kanon had seen something in him that he approved of, for after Luker's father had fallen Luker hadn't simply waited to die, but instead snatched up a spear and advanced on the sandclaw.

"He never told you why he took you on?"

"I never asked." Luker saw again the closing moments of their duel. "He let me kill him, you know. At the end. Even smiled as the blow landed."

"He was already dead. You didn't kill him."

"Maybe not. Feels like it, though."

"He knew you came after him. You got a chance to tell him that, at least."

Luker nodded. "Aye, there's some blessing in that, I suppose." He turned to face Jenna. The assassin glowed with health. Her hair shone, her freckled cheeks were blushed with color, and even the crisscrossing scars from the attack in Arkarbour had disappeared. "How are you feeling?"

"Strange. My mind hasn't caught up to the fact my body has been healed." Jenna held up her left hand and studied it. "I keep looking at my arm expecting to see a stump."

"Give it time."

The assassin smiled her crooked smile. "I'm not complaining."

Water was pooling round Luker's boots, and he retreated to drier ground, Jenna following him. His horse was nosing through the muck, searching in vain for some grass to crop. He caught Jenna's eye. "Did you find the others? Merin? The boy?"

"Chamery was where we left him—dead. His wrists were chafed, but whether his struggles came before or after he died, I couldn't tell. As for Merin, I didn't find his body." The assassin watched Luker for a reaction before adding, "You don't seem surprised."

The Guardian shook his head. "Tough old bastard."

"Will you go after him?"

"Maybe."

"He betrayed you."

"Did he? Can't betray someone who's not on your side. We both knew the way it was."

Jenna frowned. "If he lives to tell the story of what happened here . . ."

She had a point. Luker had no intention of going back to Erin Elal, but there was something to be said for not giving the Breakers another reason to come looking for him. "I'll think about it."

Jenna stared at him for a few heartbeats before reaching into a pocket in her cloak and withdrawing a hip flask. In response to Luker's questioning look she said, "From one of the Sartorian soldiers—the one who survived. Want some?"

"What is it?"

The assassin unscrewed the cap and took a swallow. "Not bad. Like juripa spirits, but stronger." She offered the flask to Luker, and he accepted it. "So if we're not following Merin, where are we heading?"

The Guardian grunted. *We?* "Not sure. Said I'd take first watch on Aliana."

Jenna's eyes twinkled. "Never had you down as a nursemaid."

"I said I'd look in on her. Nothing more."

"And that's all you feel you owe her? Parolla, I mean."

Luker studied the assassin, then looked away. "Shroud said he'd get word to us when the kid's born. Until then, I've got a few ideas of how we could pass the time."

"Care to share them with me?"

Luker's lips quirked. "Maybe Mercerie. Maybe we'll go find that rooftop for some shooting practice. It's been three years, right? Peledin Kan must've forgotten about you by now."

"Well I haven't. Forgotten, that is. In the dome, you admitted I'm the better shot."

"Must've taken a blow to the head. Amazing the stuff people come out with when the world's spinning."

Jenna searched his eyes. "You'd take it all back, then? The things you said?"

Luker kept her waiting while he took a sip from the flask. "No," he replied at last, holding her gaze. "No, I wouldn't."